BY ROBERT LITTELL

THE REVO

ROBERT LITTELL
LUTIONIST

BANTAM BOOKS
NEW YORK · TORONTO · LONDON · SYDNEY · AUCKLAND

For Victoria

THE REVOLUTIONIST

A Bantam Book
Bantam hardcover edition / May 1988
Bantam paperback edition / October 1989

Grateful acknowledgment is made for permission to reprint the following: Excerpt from "THE TIME OF STALIN" Portrait of a Tyranny by Anton Antonov Ovseyenko. English translation copyright © 1981 by Harper & Row, Publishers, Inc. Reprinted by permission of the publisher. Excerpt from GUT YUNIF GUT YOHR by Marie B. Jaffe, 1965. Courtesy of the Citadel Press. Excerpt from ANNA AKHMATOVA: A Poetic Pilgrimage by Amanda Haight copyright © 1976. Courtesy of the Oxford University Press. "Mandelstam's Poem on Stalin (November 1933)" from HOPE AGAINST HOPE by Nedezhda Mandelstam. Translated from the Russian by Max Hayward. Copyright © 1970 Atheneum Publishers. English translation copyright © 1970 Atheneum Publishers. Reprinted with the permission of Atheneum Publishers, a division of Macmillan, Inc. Excerpts from I LOVE: THE STORY OF VLADIMIR MAYAKOVSKY AND LILI BRIK by Ann and Samuel Charters. Copyright © 1979 by Ann and Samuel Charters. Reprinted by permission of Farrar, Straus and Giroux, Inc. Excerpt from SELECTED POEMS by Osip Mandelstam. English translation copyright © 1973, 1975 by Rivers Press Ltd. Reprinted by permission of Farrar, Straus and Giroux, Inc.

For information address: Bantam Books

Library of Congress Cataloging-in-Publication Data

Littell, Robert, 1935–
    The revolutionist / Robert Littell.
        p. cm.
    ISBN 0-553-27792-8
    1. Soviet Union—History—Revolution, 1917–1921—Fiction.
I. Title
PS3562.I7827R48   1988
813'.54—dc19
                                        87-27072
                                          CIP

Published simultaneously in the United States and Canada

Bantam Books are published by Bantam Books, a division of Bantam Doubleday Dell Publishing Group, Inc. Its trademark, consisting of the words "Bantam Books" and the portrayal of a rooster, is Registered in U.S. Patent and Trademark Office and in other countries. Marca Registrada. Bantam Books, 666 Fifth Avenue, New York, New York 10103.

PRINTED IN THE UNITED STATES OF AMERICA

OPM   0 9 8 7 6 5 4 3 2 1

BOOK 1

Deserves death, but, thank God, we have no capital punishment, and it is not for me to introduce it. Make him run the gauntlet of a thousand men twelve times.

> —Tsar Nicholas I ordering the punishment of a student who attacked his professor, in Nicholas Tolstoy's story, *Hadji Murad*

Let not God see the Russian rebellion—the rebellion without mind and without mercy.

> —Alexander Pushkin, writing one hundred years before the Bolshevik Revolution

TO PUT IT INTO TIME . . .

One Saturday in March, 1911, a boy came hurtling down down the narrow staircase of the Asch Building in Manhattan screaming incoherently. Alexander Til, working in an airless loft off the stairwell, looked up from his sewing machine. "What's going on?" he called.

"There's a fire," a girl shouted from the door. "Upstairs. In the Triangle loft."

Alexander, who was one week short of his seventeenth birthday, bolted for the stairs. "My father works for the Triangle Company," he cried. "My brother too."

Hundreds of girls were stampeding for the street. Struggling against the current, Alexander tried to fight his way up the stairs but he was carried back on the tide. At the ground floor the mass of bodies piling up made it impossible to force the door, which opened inward. Smoke began drifting down from the upper floors. The screams grew louder. Alexander tripped and scrambled to get up and couldn't. Covering his head with his arms, gasping to keep from suffocating, he heard, over the screams, the firemen outside smashing the hinges with their axes. The door was pushed in over the heads of the workers and a spotlight stabbed through the smoke. Alexander caught a glimpse of light and clawed his way to his feet and stumbled out, his eyes stinging, into the street, into the air.

Alexander's stepbrother, Leon, who worked in a loft on the next block, had come running over when he heard the sirens. He grabbed Alexander. "Where's your father? Where's Abner?" Leon shouted.

Alexander looked up. The three top floors of the building were an inferno. Water from the pumpers couldn't reach the flames. Dozens of hysterical girls had climbed onto a fire escape. The firemen were shrieking for them to go back, that it couldn't support their weight, but the girls didn't hear—they were screaming too—and then the fire escape collapsed and they plummeted through the air like shot birds.

3

At every window girls were crawling onto ledges to escape the heat and the flames, and pitching themselves into space. The firemen, their faces streaked with tears, spread safety nets, but the girls were leaping from too high and crashing through them to the sidewalk.

Alexander spotted his brother, Abner, crouching in an open window on the ninth floor. He helped a girl crawl from the sill onto the ledge, then held her away from the building and let her drop. He did the same for a second girl. And a third. Later, the newspapers would describe what Abner had done as a "terrible chivalry." He guided a fourth girl onto the ledge. It must have been his steady girl, Nora, because she put her arms around his neck and kissed him.

In the street, people became silent. With incredible gentleness Abner held Nora into space and dropped her to her death. And then he jumped too.

They found the broken body of Alexander's father at the bottom of the elevator shaft the next day. He still had his portable sewing machine strapped to his back.

Inside Alexander something stopped dead, like an overwound clock—he stopped talking, he stopped thinking, he stopped feeling. For weeks Leon never left his side. When they went anywhere, he kept one arm clasped tightly over Alexander's shoulder. Watching his stepbrother's lifeless eyes drift aimlessly over the peeling walls of their apartment, Leon wondered if he would ever be the same again.

Then one morning toward the end of April, a spark of life appeared in Alexander's eyes. His lips worked. A word emerged. "Justice," he whispered hoarsely.

Leon leaned toward him. "What about justice?"

"Justice," Alexander said, "is what's missing."

With that, Alexander started ticking again, slowly at first, then with a panicky feeling that time would run out on him if he didn't hurry. He began to talk about what had robbed Abner and his father and a hundred and forty-four others of their lives. They were the victims, he said, reasoning it out carefully, measuring his words, of a system that operated by a single standard: profit. That was why the staircases in the Asch Building were only thirty-three inches wide and the door on the ground floor opened inward, and the single elevator could hold only twelve at a time, and his father had been forced to jump down the shaft to escape the flames. That was why the building had ten floors, but the firemen's ladders reached only to the sixth. That was why the insurance companies had offered twenty-three families seventy-five dollars each in full payment for their losses.

The following Sunday Alexander and Leon and several union people went to talk to the owner of the Triangle Shirtwaist Company, who lived on Long Island in a country home that the workers called Tsarskoye Selo, after the tsar's country estate near St. Petersburg. At first the owner refused to see the delegation, but he reconsidered when Alexander tossed a brick through some French windows.

His shirt open at the neck, his hands thrust into his trouser pockets, Alexander stepped forward. "Do you consider the seventy-five dollars the insurance companies are offering the families adequate?" He took another step toward the owner. "Do you feel any moral responsibility for the deaths of your employees? Are you going to offer additional compensation? Are you going to improve working conditions for the survivors?"

At the sight of the delegation, the owner had sent his butler to fetch the local police. Two of them came roaring up the driveway in a brand new Ford motorcar to arrest Alexander and the others for trespassing, for damaging private property, for menacing the life of one of their leading citizens. When one of the policemen tried to snap a pair of hand irons on Alexander's wrists, he punched him in the jaw. He and Leon and the others scattered across the fields.

It was at this point in his life that Alexander Til began to think of himself as a revolutionist.

1

New York, 1917

The moment the Jew saw the gold and silver badge he tried to push the door shut, but the federal agent was too fast for him. He had already wedged a sturdy oxford against the jamb.

"He is certainly not what you would call hospitable," the visitor complained to his colleague.

"You'd think he didn't want to let us in," the second agent agreed.

The Jew sized up the two men as they filed in. They had thin-lipped, midwestern faces and wore identical soft-brimmed Lansdowne hats and Ennyweather Shine-or-Sprinkle belted topcoats. One allowed as how his name was Hoover. The other didn't say. They slipped their badges into their pockets and methodically wiped the imagined traces of the Lower East Side off the soles of their shoes on the scrap of rug that served as a doormat. Then they trailed after the Jew through the narrow hallway lined with hip-high stacks of books to the small room off the central air shaft. There the one named Hoover, a young man in his early twenties, produced a fist-sized spiral notebook, moistened his thumb, and leafed through it until he came to the appropriate page.

"His real name is Alexander Til," he said to the Jew. His voice, hoarse, strained, seemed to originate in his barrel chest. "He is a white male. Twenty-three years of age. Naturalized American citizen of Jewish-Russian origin. Five feet ten and one half inches in height. Lean frame. Receding hairline. Green eyes. The subject wears eyeglasses, and has a three-inch scar behind his left ear, the result of a wound inflicted when he resisted arrest for illegal picketing during the 1912 garment workers strike. The blow to his head impaired the hearing in his left ear. He has a way of cocking his right ear toward people when he talks to them. He is known to have disguised himself by growing a mustache and a beard."

The Jew, who rented the three rooms on Hester Street and sublet the smallest one off the central air shaft to make ends meet, fixed his eyes on Hoover. "The name Til I never up to now heard," he replied cautiously. "The tenant I rented to, he told me his name was Rosenstein."

The other agent wandered around the room, absently running the tips of his fingers over a tabletop and the windowsill and the spines of books the way a woman does when she suspects the presence of dust. "Did your

Rosenstein have a beard?" he asked the Jew without looking at him.

The Jew shrugged. "Beards many people around here have."

"Was he hard of hearing in one ear?"

"I never talked to him enough to notice."

The agent turned to stare directly at the Jew. "How long ago did he clear out?"

"Four, maybe five days."

"Why'd he leave?"

"He left is all I know."

"He didn't say where he was going?"

"No."

"And you naturally wouldn't know where we could find him?"

"That is correct. I would not know."

"You're an alien too, aren't you? Lying to authorized agents of the Bureau of Investigation could get you into hot water."

"I do not know where he is," the Jew insisted stubbornly.

The Jew's twelve-year-old son came into the room. The boy, like most tenement children, reeked of kerosene; it was spread daily on his neck and wrists and ankles to ward off lice. He planted himself timidly behind his father's legs, hooked his hands through his suspenders, and stared at the intruders with enormous black eyes.

Hoover wrinkled up his nose in disgust and began jotting in his notebook a list of the few objects in the room. There was a low steel bed with a straw mattress, and two sentences chalked on the wall over it: "Capitalism creates producers and consumers. Communism creates beings who also happen to be producers and consumers." Next to the bed stood an upside-down wooden crate that served as a night table, with a kerosene lamp and half a dozen back issues of a radical magazine called *The Masses* on it. One of the magazines was open to an article by John Reed, written from Mexico, about Francisco Pancho Villa, a fact duly noted by Hoover, who recalled reading extremely uncompli-

mentary things about the notorious Villa in an inter-
departmental circular. There were several tin plates
and cups and a grimy teakettle on an old table, along
with a copy of Emma Goldman's anarchist journal called
Mother Earth, an edition of *Das Kapital* in German,
Chernyshevsky's novel *Chto Delat* in Russian, and a
book entitled *A Portrait of the Artist as a Young Man.*
Chalked on the wall under the tiny window that opened
onto the air shaft was a single line: "Property is theft—
Proudhon." The word "is" was underlined, as if the
person who wrote it had heard the phrase many times
but only recently become convinced it was really true.
Tacked to the back of the door was an article torn from
the *New York Tribune* about the townspeople of Erwin,
Tennessee, lynching a circus elephant from a handy
railroad derrick for trampling a man to death, an adver-
tisement for a Caruso concert at Carnegie Hall, and an
hectographed leaflet announcing that the famous Russian revolutionist Leon Trotsky would speak at a Socialist Circle on Bedloe's Island the following Sunday, March
18, 1917. "Come one, Come all," it read, "bring your
own picnic." Across the bottom, in bold letters, it warned:
"Positively no alcohol."

Hoover glanced up from his spiral notebook. "These
books on the table, are they his or yours?"

"His."

"He coming back for them, you suppose?"

The Jew shook his head. "He told me to sell them for
the week he owed me."

The other agent turned a glass paperweight upside
down, and held it at eye level to watch the snow settle
in it. "What with this business in Russia," he said, "we
have got to be more vigilant than ever. One revolutionist like Til can infect thousands.

"From our point of view," Hoover said, "this Til is a
dangerous idealist." Flashing a smile as thin as a pencil
line, he baited the Jew. "You do see our point of view?"

The Jew pulled thoughtfully at an earlobe that looked
as if it had been pulled at before. "I see your point of
view," he finally said. "And you are clearly right from
your point of view. But your point of view is wrong. In

the United States of America, idealism has not yet been declared a crime."

"It is not a question of idealism," Hoover said impatiently. "It is a question of property."

"Property," the Jew pointed out, "is theft."

"Scratch a Jew," sneered the other agent.

Zander—as Alexander's friends had taken to calling him—stood at the fringe of the crowd watching the men from the slaughterhouse, in blood-stained aprons, struggling to cut away a horse that had collapsed in its tracks while pulling a wagonload of coal down Third Avenue. Several passengers were hanging out of the windows of a passing trolley offering advice. The horse, which had blinders on its head and ribs bulging out of its hide, whinnied and lashed out feebly with a hind leg, catching one of the workmen on a shin. Cursing, he hobbled off. A young fresh-faced policeman bent over the horse and pressed the tip of his revolver to its ear. Most of those watching looked away. The passengers pulled their heads back into the trolley. A boy in corduroy knickerbockers giggled nervously. The young policeman squeezed the trigger. The pistol jerked in his hand. Blood and foam gushed from the horse's mouth. The animal heaved once and lay still.

Zander edged away from the crowd. Being in one made him uncomfortable; he was always afraid he would be trampled to death. Looking back, he caught a glimpse of the dead horse, a hind leg sticking up grotesquely like a finger pointed accusingly at the sky. It occurred to Zander that in capitalist countries it wasn't only the animals that died in their traces. Human beings were also worked to death, and then disposed of while those more fortunate looked away in embarrassment. Well, Zander had never averted his eyes; he had stared at every living death until he had memorized it. He had seen factory hands collapse just as the horse had collapsed; seen people incapable of lifting another sack, of taking another step. The bosses had not put pistols to their ears; they had simply cut off their paychecks and discarded the workers, like used shoes, in the street.

But what was that if not another form of execution?

"Nothing intimidates you," Zander's stepbrother, Leon, had exploded during one of their regular battle royals over the best way to set the world straight, "not the possibility of death, not the possibility of failure, nothing!" Leon had been dead wrong, of course. Zander *knew* how things were, and *dreamed* of how they could be—and he squirmed. What if it weren't in his power to put them right? What if nobody could put them right? What if Marx was mistaken and the revolution was not inevitable and the great massses of people out there were meant to be exploited to death like the horse pulling the coal wagon down Third Avenue? What if the factories and the mines and the ghettos and a permanent pecking order were the things that were inevitable? No! Zander would never accept that. And he would never abandon the struggle. He would man the barricades whenever and wherever the workers threw them up.

Since the death of his father and brother in the Triangle fire, he had been doing just that. New York, Connecticut, New Jersey, Michigan, Ohio, Colorado all had warrants out on him for illegal picketing, illegal assembly, inciting to riot. Inciting to riot! He had been inciting to more than riot, something the federal government understood when it issued a warrant for his arrest under a 1903 law calling for the deportation of alien anarchists. The Justice Department's Bureau of Investigation had been tracking Zander for the better part of a year for "preaching sedition, armed uprising, and other Communistical theories aimed at overthrowing the existing order." At least that's what the caption under the fairly accurate drawing of his face on the wanted poster had said.

Zander continued on toward the pawnshop one block up Third. He wore a wide-collared shirt of unbleached linen and a suit that had been "turned" by a Greek tailor on East Broadway; in its new incarnation it buttoned right to left. He had a thick tangled beard, soft skin that he vaguely thought of as unmanly, and eyes that a Yiddish actress, in a flash of insight, had once described as "bruised."

The bell screwed to the inside of the door tinkled as Zander entered the pawnshop. The pawnbroker appeared from the back room. He had a skull so narrow it looked as if it might have been deformed in a birth accident, and enormous red ears that flapped out at right angles to his face. "Are you a buyer or are you a seller?" he demanded in a whiny nasal voice.

From the back room came the staccato sound of a typewriter. The typing stopped abruptly. A woman's voice muttered, "Oh, shit!" Then the typing started again.

"If the price is right, I am a seller," Zander said.

The pawnbroker laughed under his breath. "For a seller, when is the price ever right? So show me what you got." He pushed aside harmonicas and pocket watches and cuff links and compacts to clear a space on the counter.

Zander pulled a folded handkerchief from his jacket pocket and carefully placed it on the thick glass. He peeled back the folds of the handkerchief to reveal a silver cameo brooch, with a small red stone in the center. His mother, Rivka, had given it to him in 1908, on the pier in Rotterdam as he and his father and brother were about to board the ship for America. Alexander's father had turned back at the foot of the gangway. "I have changed my mind," he had said miserably. "We will all wait in Rotterdam with you."

"We settled that last night," Rivka had insisted. "When I am well enough to travel, rest assured I will cross the ocean to this America of yours." She had tried to smile encouragingly. "Tuberculosis is after all not the end of the world."

"Mama," Alexander remembered crying out, "I am sorry I made us leave Russia."

"You didn't make us leave Russia," Rivka had rebuked him. "God did."

She had blessed Alexander, and Abner, and her husband, in Yiddish, and had kissed each of them on the forehead, and Jack on the lips in full view of the boys, something she had never done before. Then she had pressed the cameo brooch into Alexander's hand. "You are the most fragile," she had whispered. "I want you to have something of mine."

As the *Darmstadt* was pulled clear by two steam tugs, Alexander remembered seeing his mother standing with several other women near an enormous crane. Although she had never uttered a word of reproach to him, he had been struck by the fact that she hadn't waved. Nor had he; his arms had been leaden with guilt. Across the widening gulf they had stared numbly at each other.

It was the last time he ever saw her.

The pawnbroker fitted a jeweler's glass to his right eye and picked up the brooch. Zander noticed a copy of *The New York Times* on the counter. It was dated Friday, March 16, 1917. The banner headline splashed across the front page read, "REVOLUTION IN RUSSIA: TSAR ABDICATES." The pawnbroker turned the brooch to examine its back. Zander glanced around the pawnshop. Posted on a wall was a printed notice saying that as typewriters were now in general use, and as they were exclusively operated by ladies, gentlemen were kindly requested to abstain from smoking or spitting on the premises.

"How much you want?"

"How much are you offering?"

"If I seen one like this, I seen ten thousand. Name your price. I will give you a yes or I will give you a no."

Zander hesitated. "The ruby alone ought to be worth thirty-five dollars," he said.

A laugh was coughed up from the back of the pawnbroker's throat. He dropped the brooch back onto the handkerchief and covered it with the corners almost as if he didn't want to look at it any longer than he had to.

"Make me an offer," Zander said in a tight voice.

The pawnbroker inserted a thick finger into a narrow nostril and picked at it. He shrugged. "The cameo is nothing special. What you call a ruby is cut glass. Only the silver in the setting has any value. I can maybe pay two dollars and fifty cents. Not a penny more. You can take it or you can leave it."

"Two fifty!" Zander's heart sank. He pocketed the brooch and produced the Seth Thomas railroad watch that Maud had given him on his twenty-third birthday. "What about this?"

The pawnbroker snorted through his nostrils. "Wrist-watches is the wave of the future."

Walking back downtown past a line of grim, gray tenements, Zander decided he would not let the pawn-broker depress him. There had to be a way to get enough money to buy the steamship ticket. It was only a matter of figuring out how.

He was still racking his brain for a solution when he noticed McSorley's up ahead on Seventh Street. He pushed through the swinging door and made his way to the bar.

"What'll it be?"

Zander ordered a pint of ale, and helped himself to a penny hardboiled egg from the basket. He rolled it between his palm and the bar to crack the shell and began peeling it. The bartender filled a mug, scraped off the foam with a wooden tongue depressor, and set it down in front of Zander.

Farther along the bar someone spilled a glass of beer. There was a scuffle and good-natured cries of "Break it up, boys." Zander strained to see what was going on. A very large man was allowing himself to be coaxed back to his drink. Zander recognized him instantly. He collected his mug of ale and his hardboiled egg and shouldered his way through the crowd.

"Atticus?"

A. (for Atticus) O. (for Orson) Tuohy—six foot two and sporting a rust-colored walrus mustache—spun around. "Jesus, I almost didn't recognize you," he said, pumping Zander's hand. "With that beard of yours, you're the spitting image of one of those old daguerreo-types of your grandfather." Tuohy pulled over the man he had been drinking with. "Say hello to Emilio Ortona," he told Zander. Tuohy lowered his voice. "Emilio here's an anarchist from New Jersey. Emilio, meet an old movement buddy of mine named Zander Til."

Ortona nodded without offering to shake hands. Zander nodded back politely. Their paths had crossed before, once at a meat-packers' strike in New Jersey, once at a mass meeting of the Ludlow miners in Colorado. Whenever he saw Ortona, Zander wondered if he was really the anarchist he claimed to be or the hoodlum he looked like.

"Where you hanging your hat these days?" Tuohy asked.

"I got a room on Essex, off Hester, over a delicatessen," Zander said.

"Every Italian knows that delicatessen," Ortona said. "It's the only place in Manhattan you can find *baccala mante.*"

Tuohy launched into a description of his most recent girlfriend, a hot little number from Hunter College who moonlighted in Margaret Sanger's Brooklyn birth control clinic; she had been arrested twice for violating the Comstock Act, which classified birth control information as obscene. "There's only one thing wrong with her," quipped Tuohy, whose red hair was parted in the middle and slicked back and whose nose was permanently atwitch for the female of the species. "She's so short, every time I look at her I think she's half a block away."

"What have you been up to?" Zander asked Tuohy.

"What have I been up to?" Tuohy repeated the question. He smiled at Ortona. "Show him the artillery, Emilio."

Ortona offered Zander a peek into the canvas satchel he was holding. There were two pistols in it. Zander recognized one as a Nagant, a Russian Army revolver manufactured before the turn of the century, and the other as an American Smith and Wesson. "The Nagant is my personal property," Ortona said with pride. "The other is borrowed."

"We were over in Brooklyn this afternoon," Tuohy said with a twinkle in his eye.

"At the Mechanics and Metals National Bank on Schenectady Avenue," Ortona put in.

Tuohy turned on him. "Who's telling this story?"

"I beg your fucking pardon," Ortona said stiffly. He worked a finger under his starched collar to relieve the itching on his neck.

"Anyhow," Tuohy continued, "we waited until they were closing for the day. Then we made our play. Emilio here cut the telephone line with his pocket knife. I gave them a gander at my lovely Smith and Wesson and ordered the teller to open the door of the walk-in Mosler. You will never guess what the son of a bitch said."

Zander sipped his ale.

"He said he couldn't!" Tuohy exclaimed.

"He couldn't open the fucking safe," Ortona said, "because it had been fitted with a newfangled invention."

"A sort of timing device," Tuohy said. "The damned door automatically locks itself on the stroke of four, and nothing short of dynamite can open it before nine Monday morning." Touhy tossed down the rest of his tequila, something he had developed a taste for during the Mexican civil war, and signaled for the bartender to bring him a refill. "Here lies Atticus Tuohy," Tuohy said, composing one of the epitaphs for which he was famous, "a revolutionist who couldn't rob a capitalist bank if his life depended on it."

"I didn't know you were into expropriations," Zander commented.

"Expropriations!" Ortona snickered. "You"—he almost said "Jews" but he caught himself in time—"Marxists make everything sound so fucking serious." Muttering about how this was the last time he was going to get involved with half-assed Bolshevist bank robbers, Ortona headed for the door.

Tuohy tapped his empty glass on the bar impatiently; the bartender had forgotten about his refill. "Are you going to catch Debs tomorrow night? Ought to be interesting to see what he has to say about this revolution in Russia."

"Remember Trotsky's description of Debs and his

Socialists?" Zander asked. "It's the ideal party for successful dentists."

"Debs is different—he has fire in his belly."

"Look," argued Zander, "the only thing these Socialists and Wobblies and garment union people are interested in is thicker pay envelopes and shorter hours and
paid vacations and one wet dream more a week."

"The Socialists may be halfhearted, but that doesn't
mean there's anything wrong with socialism. Any serious study of economics leads to socialism—"

"Any serious study of the factory," Zander whispered
fiercely, "leads to communism. Read the terrible chap-
ter in *Das Kapital* on the working day and see if you're
ever the same again."

Tuohy cocked his head and studied Zander. He had
known him longer than most. He had taken Zander to
meet Trotsky and his wife in their apartment in the
Bronx soon after they arrived from Europe— Trotsky,
the legendary Russian revolutionist who could complain
bitterly about having to pay eighteen dollars a month in
rent, casually furnish his apartment on the installment
plan, marvel at the existence of a chute for garbage, and
talk passionately and endlessly about that "old *canaille*
Europe" and the permanent revolution that he was
convinced would sweep across it like a wind-driven
brush fire, though unfortunately not in his lifetime. Yet
now it had come, a full-blown spontaneous rising up of
the people, and in the place they had all least expected:
Russia. "I can read the handwriting on the wall as well
as the next man," Tuohy said suddenly. "There's no
revolution brewing here, so you're going back."

Zander's fingers closed over the brooch in his jacket
pocket. "When the workers throw up a barricade," he
said, "it's the obligation of someone who thinks of himself as a revolutionist to man it."

"You're in love with revolution," Tuohy decided. He
waved his hand to catch the barman's eye. "What does
a man have to do to get a drink around here?" He
turned back to Zander. "Well, why not? A good revolution is a lot sexier than some girls I know. The trouble
is, by the time you get to Russia it'll probably be over."

"Or the second revolution, the one that puts Lenin and the Bolsheviks in power, will be beginning."

"You Russians are all dreamers. Do you remember Russia?"

Zander remembered it all right: the wild whinnying of horses and the rhythmic hammering of hooves as the Cossacks galloped into his village, the geese scattering in panic, the axes splintering doors, the human screams so full of terror that they reverberated in his head long after he had ceased to hear them. He remembered the desperate rush to descend into the tunnel that his father and his brother had dug out under the floorboards, carting away the dirt in straw baskets and throwing it into the river at night so that nobody, not even the Jews, would guess what they were up to. He remembered being caught in the open during the last pogrom, remembered the sound of horses pounding up the hill on the other side of the rise and the pitiful cries of the man they were chasing, remembered burrowing like a mole into a mound of manure and watching from his hiding place as two giant fur-hatted Cossacks spurring stunted horses ran Adler, the fat kerosene hawker, into the ground. One of the Cossacks had leapt from his horse, had pulled the bottle of kerosene from the wooden harness on Adler's back, and had splashed it over the clothing of the fallen man. Then the Cossack had lighted a match. Alder had pleaded with God to save his servant. Adler had sobbed. Adler had struck his forehead against the ground. Adler had gone up in flames. Howling like a wounded animal, he had plunged down the hill, his limbs askew, into the almost frozen river, piercing the paper-thin ice with the hiss of a red-hot iron going into a pail of rainwater. Zander remembered his parents, afterward, agonizing over whether they should all emigrate to America. "To tell you the truth," he had told them, "I am not absolutely sure where America is. But I will go there, with or without you, and with or without your blessing." Rivka, her eyes burning, had hugged the trembling boy to her. "Then . . . we will all go," she had said quietly.

"Russia," Zander told Tuohy, "is not something you forget."

"How old were you when you left?"

"I suppose I must have been a hundred."

Humming an Italian melody under his breath, Emilio Ortona made his way through the bar, which was filled with longshoremen from the Jersey docks, and down the long dark corridor to the office in the back. Light seeped under the door. Ortona entered without knocking. Silvio, fitting pieces into a jigsaw puzzle at his rolltop desk, appeared startled.

"It is only me, huh?" Ortona reassured him.

"I wasn't expecting you so soon," Silvio remarked, sinking back into his swivel chair. He refilled a tumbler with whiskey and took several quick sips. Ortona could see his Adam's apple bobbing. "How'd it go off?" Silvio inquired nervously, waving Ortona to a seat, studiously avoiding his eye.

"The fucking Bolshevists have as usual fucked up," Ortona said. He shifted the satchel with the two revolvers to his left hand and took a more careful look around. The thick velvet drapes in front of the back door were drawn, and the electric desk lamp was already lighted. Silvio seemed extremely ill at ease. "What is eating you, Silvio?" Ortona demanded. He backed toward the door. "I did not lose your artillery, huh?"

Two men stepped from behind the drawn curtain. They both held Browning automatic pistols in their hands. One of them said his name was Hoover and that they were agents of the Justice Department's Bureau of Investigation. The other didn't give his name. "We'll take those," Hoover told Ortona. "They must be heavy."

"I didn't have no choice," Silvio apologized to Ortona. "They knowed you was coming. They knowed about the bank in Brooklyn."

"Clear out," the second agent ordered. Silvio rolled down the top of his desk to protect the jigsaw puzzle, locked it with a small key attached to a solid gold chain across his vest front, and disappeared out the door like a spider ducking into a crack in the wall.

"So I borrowed some revolvers for target practice," Ortona appealed to the agents, his hands spread wide, palms up, to convey absolute innocence. "So where is the crime?"

The second agent shifted his Browning to his left hand, stepped up to Ortona, and punched him sharply in the stomach. Sucking in air, Ortona doubled over. The two agents lifted him under the armpits and settled him into Silvio's swivel chair.

"How well do you know a bearded man called Zander?" demanded Hoover.

"So what makes you think I know a Zander—"

Hoover spun the chair so that Ortona faced the other agent, who slapped him hard across the face several times. Then Hoover swiveled him back again.

"About this Zander—how well do you know him?"

"Why are you protecting him?" the second agent demanded from behind Ortona. "He's a Yid."

"Zander is short for Alexander, isn't it?" Hoover asked. Ortona nodded.

"Now we are getting somewhere," said the other agent enthusiastically.

"And Alexander is the first name of Alexander Til?"

"I do not know his last name," Ortona insisted. Hoover reached down to give the chair a spin, but Ortona put a hand on his forearm. "Til sounds familiar," he admitted.

Hoover rearranged his lips in a thin smile. "What we want to know is where we can find this Alexander Til."

"We are hungry," said the second agent.

"What's in it for me?" asked Ortona.

2

Making his way down Houston Street, Zander glanced up at the maze of fire escapes. Very little had changed on the Lower East Side since a police reporter for the *New York Evening Sun* named

Jacob Riis had published his exposé on tenement life, entitled *How the Other Half Lives*, before the turn of the century. A great many wooden buildings had been torn down, but larger brick tenements had been constructed in their place. The cockroach population had increased. Fire hydrants had been installed on the streets. A city ordinance had obliged landlords to put in fire escapes, and the Jews had promptly turned them into spare rooms, airing bedding on them during the day, sleeping on them during the stifling summer nights.

Most people had been in favor of fire escapes. But Zander's brother, Abner, had been against them from the start, had argued that what modern buildings needed were well-lighted interior staircases with heavy fireproof doors and fire hoses on every floor. But then Abner had always been ahead of his time. He had argued for a forty-five-hour work week and paid vacations, and even compensation for employees who fell sick or were laid off because a factory had fewer orders. Toward the end he had obviously moved closer to Zander's notion that the root cause of the inequities around him was the system itself; it would have to be changed, he would say, though he had not yet come to grips with the idea that it could be changed only through violent revolution. Poor Abner . . . Zander still missed him enormously. He mourned his father, but he *missed* his older brother. Sometimes he felt as if he were looking out at the world through Abner's eyes. He irrationally considered himself to be Abner's physical double and imagined they had the same facial expression, the same way of half-closing their eyes when they listened to things they disagreed with, the same sudden squalls of fury when others didn't respond to their logic or their passion. And most of all, the same moral center.

Like Abner, Zander was a creature of the Jewish ghetto on Manhattan's Lower East Side. There was the motion picture house on Canal Street where he and Abner had smuggled in a bottle of moths and released them in the dark to seek the only source of light—the projector; the giant shadows cast on the screen had sent the lady piano player scurrying from the theater in hysterics. There was the "Pig Market," as the Jews called it, on Hester Street, where everything under the sun *except* pigs could be bought; it was here that Alexander got his first job in America, selling spools of thread and wool by the pound from a dilapidated pushcart pulled by a horse so thin its rib cage stood out like scaffolding. There was East Broadway, which Jewish intellectuals referred to as *ulitza*, the Russian word for street, in the belief that it was more cultivated to speak Russian than Yiddish; it was on *ulitza* that Jack Til installed his second wife and her young son, Leon, who was the same age as Alexander, along with his own two boys, in the winter of 1909. There was P.S. 160 on Suffolk and Rivington, where Alexander and Leon, during their single year of formal schooling, leapt in panic from a ground floor window when the newly created Board of Health sent around a doctor to examine tonsils with tongue depressors; Leon had convinced Alexander that the doctor was surgically removing tonsils through the neck.

Zander's thoughts drifted to Leon. The last time he had seen him, which was months ago, the conversation had been strained. Leon was being drawn deeper and deeper into the Zionist movement; he had even talked about emigrating to Palestine in the hope of creating a Jewish homeland. When Zander had asked sarcastically what the Zionists planned to do with the Arabs already living there, Leon had exploded. "The land was ours two thousand years ago. It will be ours again. The Arabs who want to stay will live alongside us in peace and prosperity, which is more than the rest of the world does for us."

Leon, Zander thought as he turned down Essex Street toward the delicatessen and his room over it, was putting his eggs in the wrong basket The Jews had as much chance of . . . Zander suddenly felt someone tugging at his sleeve. "Mister! Mister!" A small boy wearing suspenders and smelling of kerosene was peering up at him. "These books belong to you."

He handed Zander the books he had left behind in the room off the air shaft on Hester Street.

"You came all the way for this?"

"My father sent me to warn you. Two men with badges came around looking for you."

"Did your father tell them where they could find me?"

"They asked, but he said he didn't know."

Zander smiled. "Your father is a good man." He dug into his pocket for a nickel. "This is for you."

The boy shook his head. "It is the Sabbath," he said with a seriousness beyond his years. "I am not permitted to touch money."

"I'd like to give you something for your trouble," Zander insisted.

"You can tell me something," the boy suggested.

"Tell you what?"

"The men who were looking for you called you a revolutionist. What does that mean, a revolutionist?"

"I had a grandfather who was a famous revolutionist," Zander said. "It was in Russia, many years ago. He belonged to a movement called Narodnaya Volya—the Will of the People. He wanted to change the lives of the masses who lived in poverty and ignorance. He believed in this so strongly that he abandoned his wife and son and moved to a small village. He organized classes. He tried to teach the peasants to read."

"And what happened to your grandfather?"

"The peasants, who were very suspicious of strangers, treated him like dirt. One by one he and his comrades gave up and left the villages. The lesson my grandfather learned from his experience was this: that history moves slowly, that you have to give it a push."

"So a revolutionist is someone who gives history a push."

"That's a good working definition," Zander agreed.

"Did your grandfather give history a push?"

"He tried to. He and several others attempted to assassinate the tsar. Do you understand the word 'assassinate'?"

The boy's eyes widened. "Kill!" he breathed in disbelief.

"They were betrayed and arrested before they could succeed," Zander continued.

"What happened to them?"

Zander recounted the story the way it had been told to him by his father, who was the son who had been abandoned. "Their ankles were fettered," he said, "their heads were shaved, and they were put on trial. When my grandfather's turn came to speak, he told the judges his blood would serve as fertilizer from which the seed of socialism would sprout."

"And then?"

"And then they convicted him and sentenced him and the others to death, and executed them. The hangman put a rope around my grandfather's neck and a black hood over his head and dropped him through a trap door in the scaffold, and an assistant hung on his ankles until he strangled to death."

The boy swallowed. "And did socialism sprout as he said it would?"

Zander thought of the headlines in the *Times*. "It is sprouting," he assured the boy.

Still under the spell of the story, the boy backed slowly away down Essex Street. Zander let himself into the entrance of number twenty-seven, next to the delicatessen, and started up the stairs toward his room on the fifth floor. At one landing he was almost overcome by the odor of urine. On the fifth floor he felt along the wall until he came to the second door on the right. He inserted his skeleton key in the lock and heard it click open. He pushed the door and entered the room.

In the fading light that filtered through the single, grimy window that looked out onto Essex Street five floors below, Zander could make out two shadowy figures standing near the bed. As his eyes became accustomed to the dimness, he saw that the two men were wearing identical hats and belted topcoats and pointing revolvers at him.

"Like I was saying," one of the figures remarked to the other, "all good things come to those who wait."

"Patience," the second figure said, "is what is next to cleanliness."

"Alexander Til," the first figure intoned, "I have a legal warrant for your arrest duly signed and attested to by officers of the Justice Department in Washington."

"You're making a mistake," Zander told them. "My name is Rosenstein."

"That's not what your friend Ortona told us," the first voice said. "Now be a good boy, walk over to the table and light the lamp so we can have us a look at the scar over your left ear. And keep your hands where we can see them. We get mighty nervous if we do not see your hands, isn't that correct, Henry?"

"We certainly do," agreed the other figure.

"I have papers to prove who I am," Zander insisted.

"Well, light up that there lamp and let's take a look at them."

Zander moved to the table, set down his books, and felt around for the box of wooden matches he always left next to the lamp. He found it and struck a match and touched it to the wick. Then he fitted the glass chimney over the wick and picked up the lamp to adjust the flame.

Zander imagined, more than he saw, the two pistol barrels boring in on his chest and he remembered Abner commenting, as the police were forming up to charge the picketers during the 1912 garment strike, "One man dies of fear, another is brought to life by it." With a snap of his wrist he threw the lamp at the feet of the two figures. It shattered, splashing kerosene onto the shoes of one of them. In a flash flames skidded along the spilled kerosene.

"Son of a—" cried the other agent, ducking to one side, flexing his knees and snapping off two quick shots through the flames. Zander, leaping for the door, felt a burning sensation on the skin of his left forearm, as if he had been stung by a wasp. Behind him the agent with his shoes on fire beat furiously at the flames with his soft-brimmed hat. "For Christ's sake, help—" he screamed at his companion. The other agent didn't know whether to attack the flames or to pursue Zander, who was disappearing through the door. His hesitation gave Zander the seconds he needed.

Zander had scouted the escape route when he first moved in—up two flights, through the unlocked door, across the roof to the next tenement, down a fire escape to a lower roof, across four roofs to an unlocked door, then down six flights to Hester and the safety of the streets.

"Well, I'll be damned," the agent who had raced up the steps after Zander exclaimed in frustration. Darkness was settling over the Lower East Side like a cushion of soot. Breathing heavily, his revolver cocked, he peered across the rooftops looking for the slightest movement at which to shoot.

Below, on Hester Street, Zander stuffed a handkerchief up his jacket sleeve to staunch the flow of blood and, counting his blessings, started east in the direction of the Brooklyn Bridge—and Maud's.

3

Except for the gentleman walking his bulldog, Pierrepont Street was deserted. Zander waited until he had disappeared around the corner before he mounted the steps of the brownstone and pulled on the bell. After a moment he pulled it a second time. An electric light came on upstairs. A moment later the downstairs lights flashed on and Maud, wrapped in a man's bathrobe, appeared in the vestibule. She parted the curtain on the narrow window next to the door and looked out. She obviously didn't recognize the bearded figure on her doorstep. "Go away or I'll scream for the police," she cried in a frightened voice.

"It's me," Zander said.

"Zander!" she exclaimed. She struggled with the lock and flung open the door. Then she remembered she was angry at him. "You think you can walk out of my life for a year and then turn up on my doorstep as if nothing had—" She noticed the dried blood on his forearm. "Oh, my God!" she gasped. "You and those childish picket lines of yours." She pulled him inside.

To Maud fell the distinction of being the first woman Zander had ever slept with who didn't wear dirty underwear. He had once been wildly, albeit briefly, in love with a nearsighted actress in Maurice Schwartz's Yiddish Art Theatre, but she didn't count because, being something of a bohemian, she didn't wear underwear. Before her there had been a series of girls, all of them anarchists or Wobblies or garment union organizers or Marxists of one stripe or another, all of them dirt poor, all of them in the habit of undressing hurriedly in the dark to hide their underwear.

Maud was another story. Zander had first met her on Christmas Day, 1915, at one of Professor Baldwin's legendary Wednesday organ concerts in the Great Hall at City College. Sitting in a back row, his good ear cocked toward the Bach arpeggios echoing from the rafters, Zander had been introduced to an older woman with bobbed hair, a blue band across her forehead, and noticeably tired eyes that conveyed the impression that they had seen more of life than they could cope with. "Mr. Til, Mrs. Pruett," a friend had whispered. They had nodded at each other without smiling. Later, in a Greenwich Village bar, Zander had gotten his first good look at her. In her mid-thirties, she had a quick laugh and a nervous habit of dispatching her bony fingers over her tight skirt in search of offending pleats.

It turned out that Maud was a divorcee; a lapsed Catholic who would have abandoned the church even without the divorce (she could live with the crucifixion, but she couldn't swallow the resurrection); the mother of a brilliant fifteen-year-old named Kermit who had a deformed arm; independently wealthy; the owner of a town house on Pierrepont Street in Brooklyn Heights just across the Brooklyn Bridge from Manhattan; and an eager lover who believed that an unimaginative bed partner opened a man to fantasy rather than limiting him to fantasies about her. Her principal advantages from Zander's point of view were that she had incredibly smooth skin and a soft womanly body and was willing to share both with him; that she was not known in leftist circles and thus could offer him a house that he could retreat to when the streets became too dangerous for him. Her principal drawbacks, on the other hand, were, first, that she lived in Brooklyn, which was difficult to get to, and second, that she was hopelessly immature when it came to politics. She considered, to give only one example, that the biggest disadvantage to industrialization was the fact that it had brought with it noise.

Zander, by then a professional revolutionist working for the tiny Bolshevik Party, had devoted long, tedious hours to Maud's education. Stifling yawns, her eyes glazing over in boredom, she had pretended to pay attention. But one night, while he was reading aloud a section from *Das Kapital,* he had caught her humming a popular jazz song called "You Can Always Come Down My Rain Barrel." "If all this bores you silly," he had blurted out, "say so and I'll shut up."

Maud had plucked up her courage. "It does bore me silly," she had admitted, elevating her chin in defiance. "If you want my opinion, sexual centers are every bit as important as moral centers. Oh, Zander, come on, loosen up. Why don't we catch a trolley up to the Hippodrome and listen to Sousa and his band? Or go see Florence Reed in *The Eternal Sin* on Broadway? Talking about sexual centers, I hear she's a knockout."

Maud's callousness toward things he cared passionately about had been too much for Zander. They had argued: over Maud's desire for a more permanent arrangement between them; over Zander's involvement in various labor conflicts in New Jersey and Connecticut ("Every time you hear the word 'strike' you race off like a chicken without a head," she had complained); over food, which Maud considered, after sex, one of the main reasons for living, whereas Zander treated it merely as fuel; over his table manners (he used a fork as if he had come to it late in life); and finally over her underwear, which he had come to think of as symbolic of her unrelenting, indestructible bourgeoisie-ness.

When Zander had left that morning almost a year before, he had taken his copy of *Das Kapital* with him. Maud had noticed it under his arm. "So you are not coming back," she had observed coldly from the door. She had cocked her head to one side and had smiled bitterly. "I suppose it's better this way. I mean, you can't really live with a man who doesn't understand that my underwear is *my* underwear, can you?"

Now, mesmerized by the dried blood on Zander's arm, Maud forgot about her underwear and his table manners. She raced down to the basement and threw several shovels full of coal into the furnace. When the water had heated, she ran Zander a hot bath. As he soaked in it, she cleaned his wound with cotton and alcohol. "I'm sorry," she said when she noticed him wincing. "God, it's ugly. What caused this?"

"I caught my arm on some barbed wire climbing over a fence," Zander explained tiredly.

From the hallway Maud's son, Kermit, called, "What's going on? Who's here?"

"It's only Zander."

"Zander's back!"

"You'll see him in the morning." To Zander she whispered, "If you were climbing over a fence, it was probably because they were after you again for picketing."

"They were trying to arrest me, and I was trying not to be arrested," Zander admitted.

"One of these days they're going to do more than chase you. They're going to actually shoot at you." Maud eyed Zander's beard. "God knows what vermin live in there," she groaned. Wielding a sewing scissors with unexpected dexterity, she trimmed his mustache and beard, then pressed a hot towel to his face to soften the hair. She lathered his face with the delicate brush and the shaving soap she used for her legs, supplied Zander with one of those new Gillette safety razors, and sitting on the edge of the tub, held a mirror for him while he shaved. When he finished, Zander rinsed his face with cold water from the tap and took a good long look at himself in the mirror. He had nearly forgotten what his face looked like.

He had started growing the beard and mustache as a result of a talk with Trotsky late one night about the practical side of being a revolutionist. The conversation had taken place in the kitchen of Trotsky's apartment on 164th Street in the Bronx. Trotsky had been oiling the Browning automatic he always carried in his pocket. The scratchy sound of a Puccini opera could be heard coming from the living room; Trotsky's wife would rewind the gramophone and replace the disc with the next one in the series. "You have to hone your revolutionary instinct," Trotsky had advised Zander. "If you are following someone, for instance, walk with a limp; people never suspect someone who limps of following them. If the authorities become too interested in you, grow a beard. For one thing, it makes court identification difficult; a good lawyer can make a case that a witness is identifying the beard and not the man behind it." Trotsky had smiled at a particularly beautiful aria. "Ah, that Galli-Curci is a witch," he had said, shaking his head in admiration. "It is hard to believe she is not actually in the next room." A faraway look had come into Trotsky's eyes. "Where were we?"

"You were talking about the advantage of beards," Zander had reminded him.

"Just so. The other advantage it offers is the possibility of making yourself instantly unrecognizable by the simple expedient of shaving it off. People will have become accustomed to you with your mask and won't recognize you without it."

Emerging from Maud's bathtub, Zander realized Trotsky had been right; if he barely recognized his own face, others certainly wouldn't recognize it. The thought lifted his spirits enormously. All that remained was to find the money to pay for his voyage to the revolution.

Tucked into Maud's clean sheets, Zander slept fitfully. He dreamed about a man aflame plunging with a sinister hiss into a frozen river. He began sweating profusely and moaned in pain when he turned onto his wounded arm. Maud bathed his brow and his limbs with a damp towel. The fever abated and he settled into a profound sleep. When he finally woke up, Maud was

sitting on the edge of the bed observing him with her
tired eyes. She had opened the shutters, and the daylight streaming through the windows behind her seemed
to bathe her body in an almost surgical light, which
turned her silk nightdress transparent. He could see, as
he was meant to, the outlines of her heavy breasts
against the fabric. When she saw that he was awake she
slid a cool hand under the blanket. Zander worked her
nightdress so that it rode up over her hips. Kicking off
the blanket, he guided her down on top of him.

"Where's Kermit?" he asked into the hair that fell
across his face.

"I sent him off to play on the docks," Maud murmured.

She lifted herself and lowered herself in measured
movements, riding the troughs and crests like a buoy.
"Not yet," she warned, whispering her instructions with
the part of her head that navigated. "Wait," she ordered him a few moments later—and then she moaned
"Now," and sank onto him from a great height.

"Ah, I did that nicely," she laughed, collapsing across
his body, shivering with pleasure, and Zander reinforced the self-compliment with one of his own. "You
choreograph the best lays in Brooklyn," he told her.

She served him breakfast in the top-floor room crowded
with straw furniture and plants in wicker stands. Filling
an empty milk bottle from the tap, she watered her
white geraniums as he took his tea, Russian style, from
a glass, stirring in a spoonful of jam as he sipped.
Without turning her head, keeping her voice casual,
she asked him how long he thought he would be staying
with her. When he didn't immediately respond, she
said she was inquiring only out of curiosity. As far as
she was concerned, he could come and go as he pleased.
She had no intention of trying to pin him down to
something permanent. Zander thanked her, and asked
if she had seen Friday's *Times* and the stories about the
revolution in Russia. She elevated her chin in defiance
again. "Revolutions don't fascinate me the way they
fascinate you," she said. Then, as if her words had
suddenly planted a terrible idea in her head, she burst
out, "You're not thinking of . . . oh, Zander, you are,

aren't you? You've just come back and you're going off again. Only this time it's to Russia."

Zander cleared his throat. "As a matter of fact, I was going to ask you if you could see your way clear to lending me money for passage." He lowered his voice. "I need to go back, Maud."

The skin on her face appeared to tighten over her bones. "It always ends the same way, doesn't it? The biggest thing a woman has going for her is mystery. When you sleep with a man you lose your mystery. He knows how you put yourself together. And knowing, he will leave for a new mystery—another woman, a revolution." She shook her head in disgust. "You have a hell of a nerve. It's one thing to come and go as you like. It's another to ask me to pay for the trip. I have my pride, you know."

A long stone's throw down from the ferry slip, a dozen Chinese laborers wearing baggy pants and skullcaps were passing heavy timbers up from the rocky beach and loading them on an enormous open wagon drawn by six shaggy work horses. A wooden whaler had broken up the week before in heavy winds, and parts of it had washed up at South Ferry in Manhattan. The Chinese, employed for $3.50 a week by a coal and firewood company in the Bronx, were retrieving the wood to cut up and sell to homeowners the following winter.

Oblivious to the frantic lapping of the tide against the pilings and the maniacal screams of the gulls circling overhead, Zander watched several Chinese stagger up the incline with part of the whaler's mainmast on their shoulders.

"What are you smiling at?" asked Maud. She and Kermit were waiting with Zander for the ferry to arrive.

"I'm not smiling. I'm grimacing in empathy."

"Here it comes," Kermit cried, pointing excitedly at the ferry slipping in between the wooden pilings draped with used automobile tires, ricocheting gently from one side to the other until its bow kissed the jetty. A small bell rang and the seventy or so people who had been waiting for the late morning ferry to the Statue of

Liberty began lining up in front of the ticket seller's wooden booth. "Let's go," Kermit begged, tugging at Zander's sleeve with his good hand.

"Wait a minute more," Zander said. "I don't like crowds."

Leaning casually against the whitewashed wall of the equipment shed, Zander studied the two men in soft-brimmed Lansdowne hats and Ennyweather Shine-or-Sprinkle belted topcoats who stood on either side of the booth surveying the people as they passed. One of them seemed familiar—or was his imagination working overtime? If they were federal agents, as Zander suspected, were they merely watching to see who would turn up to hear Trotsky speak at the Socialist gathering? Or were they looking for him? He had never mentioned Bedloe's Island to Ortona, as far as he remembered. He hadn't even told Maud until after breakfast that morning, and he had been with her and Kermit since. And then Zander remembered the hectographed leaflet he had tacked to the back of the door. What an idiot! The agents searching his room on Hester Street had spotted the leaflet. They were here for him. But would they recognize him with his freshly shaven pink face, without eyeglasses, a straw boater belonging to Maud's ex-husband planted at a rakish angle on his head, Kermit's woolen scarf wrapped around his neck, the costume completed by an old pair of white flannel trousers and a thick knitted green sweater that Maud had found in an attic trunk?

"Please, Zander, there won't be any places left if we don't get in line," Kermit pleaded.

"Pull up your socks," Maud called after the boy as he dragged Zander off.

Waiting their turn, drawing nearer to the ticket window, Zander held the picnic hamper with one hand and kept his other arm tightly linked through Maud's—the perfect family man on a Sunday outing. Behind them a four-cylinder Mercer taxi pulled up and Trotsky, along with his nine-year-old son Seryozha and three other men, got out. Two of the men kept their right hands buried in their overcoat pockets. Zander was not surprised to see that one of them was Tuohy; he had heard that he took on occasional stints as a bodyguard.

"How many?" the ticket seller demanded from behind his grille.

Zander glanced at the prices printed on a wooden board. "Two adults, one child," he said, putting a dime and two pennies on the counter.

On the ferry Kermit scampered off to the upper deck. Maud and Zander settled onto a wooden bench on the port side. Nearby, a heavy woman complained to a nun sitting next to her, "I want to tell her 'don't,' but the truth of the matter is I don't know what she shouldn't!"

Maud squeezed Zander's arm conspiratorially. Above their heads a thread of black smoke corkscrewed up from the ferry's thin stack. Under their feet the deck vibrated. Slowly the ferry pulled away from the slip and angled out into the choppy waters of the bay. Behind, on the jetty, the two men Zander had taken for federal agents were staring after the departing ferry in bewilderment, almost as if they had heard a joke but did not quite understand the punch line.

As soon as the wind picked up, Maud announced she was going inside. Zander climbed the ladder to the top deck. Kermit, Trotsky's son Seryozha, and two other boys were at the railing gazing back wordlessly at the Manhattan skyline. Off to the right Zander could see the Brooklyn Bridge and the Brooklyn docks; a once-graceful clipper ship was rotting away at a dilapidated pier. The ferry passed Governor's Island and came abreast of Ellis Island. Its long, low red brick registry hall with paned windows, the four Turkish-looking minarets, the manicured lawns, were all familiar sights to Zander, though he had set eyes on them only once before in his life.

He had a sudden vision of himself and his father and his brother waiting on the Ellis Island dock for the ferry that would take them to the Battery. He remembered hearing someone weeping hysterically behind him. At the door of the registry hall, a child was being pried free of his mother's legs, to which he clung like a

tangled vine. Zander never discovered whether it was
the mother or the child who had been refused entry
into America and was being sent back to Europe, but
he knew from personal experience that it didn't really
matter. For both the pain was the same.

To this day Zander bitterly regretted that he hadn't
clung like a vine to his own mother on the pier in
Rotterdam.

He watched Ellis Island glide past before shifting his
gaze to Trotsky, who was sitting on a bench built around
the base of the ferry's smokestack. Splinters of silver
light flashed from his pince-nez when it caught the sun.
He was scribbling notes in the margin of a manuscript
and carrying on a conversation with the man next to
him at the same time. Zander headed in their direction.

Tuohy drifted over from his post at the after ladder to
shake hands.

"Come to hear our friend convert the dentists' wives,"
he commented. "You saw the feds at the ticket booth, I
take it?"

"I had to find out sooner or later if they'd recognize
me without a beard," explained Zander. He nodded
toward Tuohy's left hand, which was in his overcoat
pocket. "You really have a pistol in there?"

"You have got to be making a joke, don't you? Where
would I get the money to buy a pistol? All I have in my
pocket is myself to play with. Even erect it's not lethal." Tuohy obviously enjoyed his little joke. "Mind, I
wouldn't turn down Ortona's Nagant if out of the kind-
ness of his black anarchist's heart he suddenly offered it
to me."

"Ortona's poison. He fingered me for the feds—they
were waiting in my room the other day."

"It figures. Out of the blue he came sucking up to
Trotsky yesterday. Trotsky's got a nose for informers—he
wouldn't give him the time of day. Someone ought to
take care of Ortona."

"You think so?" Zander squinted at Tuohy. "Are you
volunteering to put the matter right?"

"I'd be willing. Unless, of course, you have your
heart set on it."

"What does Trotsky think?" Zander asked.

"I haven't taken the matter up with the man. But I will."

"Do that." Zander walked over to where Trotsky sat and said in Russian, "Comrade Trotsky, do you remember me? I'm Alexander Til."

Trotsky stared at Zander through his pince-nez. His eyes widened in recognition. "Of course, of course," he said jovially. "Come meet Nikolai Bukharin. Nikolai, here is Alexander Til, the grandson of Til."

"*The* Til?" Bukharin asked.

"*The* Til," Trotsky confirmed.

Zander and Bukharin shook hands. Trotsky motioned Zander to sit on the bench next to him. "Here we are, sandwiched between the so-called Statue of Liberty and the famous Wall Street, concocting a second revolution in Russia. Delicious, no? What do you think, Alexander?" —Trotsky pointed to a passage in the typed text—"I am for saying, straight out, that the provisional government of Prince Lvov is doomed to disappoint the working classes that ousted the tsar in the first revolution. Nikolai here thinks it will make us out to be opportunists, that we should play along with the provisional government until its shortcomings become self-evident, and then join with the other Socialist parties—"

"Even with the Mensheviks," Bukharin cried exuberantly. He was almost thirty years old, but he could still muster a boyish enthusiasm for any idea that appealed to him.

"With all respect," Zander offered, "Lenin will never agree to a coalition with the Mensheviks."

"Just so," agreed Trotsky with a wry smile; he himself had identified with the Mensheviks for many years and had been on the receiving end of Lenin's acid tonguelashings more than once. "Lenin should take up a clearly defined position to the left of the Mensheviks, so that when the working classes eventually turn from the provisional government he will be the only possible alternative."

Seryozha came over and pulled at Trotsky's hand. "Papa, I say that Petrograd is bigger than New York and a boy there says it isn't, that New York is bigger. So which is it?"

"He is right and you are wrong," Trotsky told his son. "But there are other things to see in New York beside its bigness."

"Like?"

"Yesterday I saw an old man fish out a crust of bread from a garbage can." Trotsky told the story intently, carefully observing the boy to see what his reaction would be. "He tried the crust with his hands, and then he touched the thing with his teeth, and finally he struck it against the can. But the bread did not yield. In the end he thrust his find under his faded coat and shambled off down St. Mark's Place. This little episode did not in any way interfere with the plans of the ruling class."

The boy nodded solemnly. "The only thing that will interfere with the plans of the ruling class is you."

"Nicely put," Bukharin commented. Trotsky beamed with pleasure.

Tuohy called over, "We're almost there."

Ahead, the tarnished green Statue of Liberty was clearly visible astride its eleven-point base that had once been part of the old Fort Wood. "There are two things of significance to remember about this statue," Trotsky instructed his son. He winked at Zander. "First, she is standing with her back to America. This is an important symbol." Bukharin chuckled. "Secondly, you can clearly see that she has a torch in her right hand. But what is that in her left hand?"

"A book," the boy said brightly.

"Just so. A book. But what book?"

The boy pulled a face and turned up his palms.

"The book," Trotsky announced dramatically, "is Marx's *Das Kapital!*"

"Ahh," said Seryozha, impressed once again with the fact that his father seemed to know everything.

As the ferry maneuvered alongside the wooden pier, Trotsky, leaning over the railing next to Zander, commented that it was nice of him to come all this way to hear him speak.

"I didn't come to hear you speak," Zander confessed.

Trotsky removed his pince-nez and began polishing the lenses with the tip of his tie. "What is it you think I can do for you?" he asked directly.

Zander said simply, "I want to go back."

Trotsky fitted his pince-nez onto his nose and studied Zander. "How long have you been in this country, Alexander?"

"Ten years."

"You are an American then. Stay and make a revolution here."

"If I stick around much longer," Zander retorted, "the feds are going to catch up with me. They're going to lock me in a penitentiary and lose the key."

"Why come to me?" Trotsky asked. "I will have enough trouble getting myself back."

"I need money to buy my passage. I need false papers. I need a letter of introduction to the comrades in Petrograd."

On the main deck people were already filing off the ferry onto the pier. Maud looked up and saw Zander and waved to him. Clinging to the ladder with his good hand, Kermit called, "Come on, Zander."

Trotsky was clearly annoyed. "What am I, a capitalist, that everyone comes to me with a hand out for money?" Shaking his head in frustration, he stalked off to join Bukharin and his two bodyguards.

The municipal authorities had recently started posting signs in public parks around the city ordering people to keep off the grass, but they hadn't gotten around to Bedloe's Island yet. So Maud, normally a stickler for written injunctions, had no compunction about depositing her hamper and spreading her chintz tablecloth on the grass near the base of the statue. Trotsky, surrounded by four dozen or so ardent Socialists, most of them ladies, held court on the shady side. Waving a chicken bone like a baton, breaking into German or Russian when he couldn't come up with the word he wanted in English, he gave a short course on the events that had led to the overthrow of the tsar. He described the soaring inflation, the severe rationing, the harsh food and fuel shortages, the bread queues forming in the icy hours before dawn, with some of the women hugging babies to their breasts to keep them from freezing to death. The average factory worker put in ten and a half hours a day and took home thirty-five rubles a month; an ordinary pair of leather shoes, Trotsky said, bending to slap the side of his own, cost more than one hundred rubles.

And then there was the Great War against Germany. The tsar had plunged his country into it on the side of the Allies. Fifteen million men had been mobilized, including hundreds of thousands of children; when they didn't obey orders, their officers either spanked them or shot them, depending on their moods. "Do you understand?" Trotsky cried. "Are my words penetrating your brain? *Spanked* them or *shot* them!" Millions of soldiers had been dispatched to the trenches without winter clothing or boots, and some without rifles; they were expected to scavenge for them on the battlefield. The Russian dead, estimated in the millions, were never properly counted. The Germans often had to bulldoze mounds of Russian corpses piled up before their trenches to clear a field of fire for the next attack. While back in Petrograd (the name of the Russian capital had been changed from St. Petersburg at the start of the war), the bourgeoisie took tea with one another in the afternoons, plucking sugar from little silver boxes in their purses, wagging their heads at the deterioration of the social order and the inconveniences caused by the war.

Nicholas II, tsar of all the Russias by the Grace of God and force of habit, was, Trotsky plunged on, a total incompetent, ignorant of elementary economics and indifferent to the seething social problems that threatened his empire. His wife, the German-born Empress Alexandra, a granddaughter of Queen Victoria of England, was even less intelligent and more narrow-minded than he was.

"On the eighth of March," intoned Trotsky, his head tilted to the sky, his goatee parallel to the ground, "twenty thousand women chanting 'khle-e-eba . . . khle-e-eba . . . bread . . . bread' marched through Petrograd to celebrate Women's Day. The next day two hundred thousand workers joined the women in the streets. The army, which has always stood between the ruling class and the workers, ignored their officers and swarmed into the streets. Massing in the great boulevards of Petrograd, the soldiers raided an arsenal on Liteiny Prospekt and distributed rifles and machine guns to the workers.

"The mutinies spread like wildfire. Nicholas, away at the front, had no choice but to abdicate. And now, gentlemen and ladies, begins the struggle to see what institutions, what political philosophies, will take the place of the Romanov dynasty."

"This is what you came for," Maud told Zander.

"Russia," continued Trotsky, "has opened a new epoch of blood and iron. The powerful avalanche of the revolution is in full swing and no human force will stem it. All those who have been oppressed, disinherited, deceived, will rise up. All efforts to put an end to class warfare will lead to nothing. The philistine thinks that it is the revolutionist who makes a revolution, and can call it off at any point he wishes." Trotsky talked as if his audience had ceased to exist; he seemed to be flinging a challenge at the horizon. "Not so! The people make a revolution."

There was a commotion in the back of the group. Heads turned. Two young ladies were trying to calm a young man. He leapt to his feet. "He's full of shit," he exploded. "For years he's been criticizing Lenin and siding with the Mensheviks. Now suddenly he sees the light and reverses himself. Which Trotsky are we to believe?" The young man spun toward Trotsky. "You talk a great deal—"

"Revolutions," Trotsky observed laconically, "are verbose."

"But you don't really understand the dialectic. Everyone knows that before you can make a Socialist revolution, you have to have an industrial base and proletariat. Russia has neither."

"What do you propose?" Trotsky demanded with a passion so controlled his jaw trembled. "That the workers get rid of the tsar and then calmly hand over the reins of power to the bankers and professors, who will set up parliaments and other edifices of rotten liberalism? I say no! Why come this far and stop? This is not the time to lose one's nerve."

The young man advanced on Trotsky. Tuohy and the other bodyguard rose to their feet. Trotsky fingered the pistol in his pocket. "Russia is a land of peasants," cried the young man, "not proletarians. So there is a revolution in Petrograd. What about the rest of the country? What about the dark masses out there in the villages who never heard of Marx, of socialism, or Leon Trotsky?"

"The dark masses have heard about land," Trotsky declared in a ringing voice. "We will give them land! They have heard about bread. We will give them bread!" He seemed to choke with emotion now. "They have heard about peace. We will give them peace!" He turned to the rest of the group and raised his arms theatrically over his head. "We are witnessing the beginning of the second Russian revolution. Let us hope that many of us"—he glanced quickly in Zander's direction—"will be its participants."

The ladies in the audience burst into applause; many of them wore lace gloves which muted the sound of their clapping.

The young man who had challenged Trotsky, and the two young women with him, stalked off arguing fiercely among themselves. Tuohy looked over at Zander and shrugged. The other bodyguard took off his hat and waded into the Socialists muttering, "For the glorious Russian revolution—give what you can." The ladies dipped into their pocketbooks to fill the hat with bills. When the bodyguard confronted Maud with the hat full of money, she told him, "I'm against all revolutions," but the bodyguard only smiled and moved on.

Maud began packing the picnic dishes in the hamper. Kermit, who had climbed up to the statue's torch with Seryozha and several other children, came trotting back excitedly. "What a view!" he exclaimed to his mother. "You can see way up the shore in Brooklyn." He took a piece of paper from his jacket pocket and offered it to

Zander. "The man over there, the one with the funny beard, he said to give this to you."

Zander grabbed the paper. On it was written in a thick authoritative hand "*Novyi Mir* office, Tuesday at 11." The note was signed "T."

4

Bleak, vaguely menacing clouds were drifting in from the Narrows. At the Battery, storm warnings snapped from government flagpoles. Out in the roadstead, freighters were dropping second anchors in case the wind picked up during the day.

The weather matched Tuohy's mood. Striding down the street with his long knitted scarf wrapped around his neck and an end trailing over his shoulder like exhaust from one of Mr. Wright's flying machines, his hands thrust deep into his trouser pockets, he was in a dark mood, a state of affairs he attributed to basic boredom: with the weather; with Trotsky; with Socialist circles and their droning dialectic; with bank vaults that closed automatically at the stroke of four; with life in general and his sex life in particular. And the note Trotsky had slipped into Tuohy's pocket when he deposited him at his Bronx apartment late Sunday night after speaking to a group of Lower East Side Bundists— "*Novyi Mir*" office, Tuesday at 11"—didn't look as if it would change his life one way or the other. Probably another Socialist circle; another batch of dentists' wives, as Til called them, dipping manicured fingers into silk purses to finance world revolution.

Tuohy groaned out loud. World revolution was about as likely, his instinct told him, as sending a man to Mars. He, Tuohy, would settle for any revolution, it didn't matter much where, something to stir his blood and give to his fucking an urgency which came only

when he was confronted with the possibility that he was
indulging his carnal appetite for the last time. Maybe
Til was on to something after all. Russia was where the
action was. Tuohy spoke the language, albeit with lapses
in grammar, thanks to his mother, may she rest in
peace; he had even been there in the summer of 1911,
installing Otis elevators in the tsar's Winter Palace.

The mere thought of a revolution reminded Tuohy,
with considerable nostalgia, of the heady days scarcely
two years before in Mexico, with Emiliano Zapata on
his farting white horse leading his peasant army against
the *huertistas*. Tuohy had smuggled four spanking new
water-cooled U.S. Army machine guns and twenty thousand rounds of ammunition across the border in crates
that were supposed to contain plungers for Otis elevators. Zapata, reeking of sweat and garlic, had flung his
arms around Tuohy and had called him brother, and
had supplied him with a steady stream of señoritas
eager to singe their pubic hair on a gringo's revolutionary flame.

Tuohy was so engrossed in his memories that he
walked past Frank Shay's radical bookshop before
he looked up and realized where he was. Annoyed, he
retraced his steps. He was on his way to a rendezvous
with the Hunter College girl who moonlighted in Margaret Sanger's Brooklyn Clinic weekends. She was five
foot one, with enormous brown eyes and narrow hips
and big breasts, and considered herself a Bolshevik and
a revolutionist—though the revolution she had in mind
had little in common with Tuohy's.

"We women," Marlene would argue passionately with
him, "have to fling off the yoke of male oppression that
has kept us sexually docile and orgasmless for centuries.
My God, the male conspiracy against the female body,
against the clitoris, against our potential for an endless
number of consecutive orgasms, is as plain as the bulge
in your pants when you're face-to-face with a woman
talking openly about sex. Oh, no, it's not the vote we
need. It's not the right to work at the same jobs men
work at, and, incidentally, hate. It's the right to make
love when we want and where we want and with whom

we want and how we want. And it all boils down to birth control—"

Tuohy put up with these endless tirades because Marlene was a hot number in bed. She considered any sexual act that departed from what was commonly referred to as the norm a salvo fired in the cause of the forthcoming inevitable and glorious women's revolution. Here lies Atticus Tuohy, Tuohy thought, who made hay while Marlene made war.

The hinges on the door of Frank Shay's bookshop squealed as Tuohy opened it. Marlene stood at the checkout desk trying to interest Shay in Margaret Sanger's latest tract on birth control. The article concentrated on technique and was accompanied by line drawings. Shay shook his head reluctantly. He had nothing against Margaret Sanger or birth control, or explicit line drawings, but the municipal authorities, spurred on by the offended wives of some of Tammany Hall's Catholic politicians, would leap at the opportunity to close down his store for selling smut. "Thanks," Shay told Marlene, "but no thanks."

"I struck out," Marlene complained as she and Tuohy headed uptown in one of the new motorized buses the city of New York had recently purchased from the Ford Motor Company. The party in a West Side tenement was going full blast by the time they arrived. About two dozen people, most of them associated with Tin Pan Alley, were scattered around the three rooms and the tiny kitchen. They were drinking straight gin served from water pitchers, or sniffing, through rolled-up dollar bills, cocaine supplied by a young East Side hoodlum named Charlie Luciano.

"Marlene," the hostess shrieked, and a barefoot girl with short curly hair and one breast slipping out of her unbuttoned shirt sprang from a low couch to kiss Marlene on the lips. She took in Tuohy as he took in her visible breast. "Who's your friend?" asked the hostess, whose name was Connie. She reached up to flick playfully at Tuohy's walrus mustache with her bright red fingernails, then laughed and put her arm around Marlene's waist to lead her into a room where a black man with his head shaven down to his shiny, oiled scalp was playing the xylophone. A short, half-naked, completely drugged bearded man with one thin, stunted leg limped into the middle of the room and began swaying to the music. Several people applauded. Someone whistled.

"Move your Jewish ass," called Connie.

"It's the other side you tell the Jews by," said Tuohy.

"Don't I know it," laughed Marlene.

"You have something against Jews?" Connie asked Tuohy.

"Some of my best friends are unfortunately Jews," said Tuohy. "It's not their fault."

Marlene said, "Some of my best lovers are circumcised."

Connie laughed wildly. "I have a thing for circumcised cocks. Oh, don't get me wrong, I don't turn away the ones that aren't."

About three A.M. the last of the guests vanished into the night. The musician packed his xylophone in a wooden case, planted a wet kiss on Connie's breast, and departed. Tuohy kicked off his shoes, stretched out on a double mattress in the bedroom, and called to Marlene, who was helping Connie pile dirty glasses in the kitchen sink. "Say, who gets to do what to whom?"

"You're obsessed with sex," Marlene called back.

"Everyone is obsessed with sex," Tuohy retorted. "The world is divided into those who admit it and those who don't."

When the two girls finally showed up in the bedroom they were both wearing their shirts—and nothing else. "We're going to revolutionize fucking," Marlene announced. Connie giggled.

Tuohy sat upright, staring at the two patches of pubic hair. "Here lies Atticus Tuohy," he remarked enthusiastically, "who discovered, to the everlasting benefit of mankind, that three is not a crowd after all."

Tuohy had been born in 1891, the year work began on Count Witte's Trans-Siberian Railroad, the accidental and only son of Eamon Tuohy, an adventurous Irish tunnel engineer employed on the single-track, 5,500-mile line, and Nadezhda Beliankova, the rebellious daughter of a provincial tsarist official posted, to his frustration, to the backwater Ural town of Chelyabinsk. Nadezhda turned up for the marriage ceremony seven months pregnant. Two months later the child was brought into the world by a gypsy midwife who, following an old Russian custom, placed him next to a bowl of perfect fruit so that he, too, would grow up to be a perfect specimen. When Eamon's contract expired four years and three months later, he hustled his wife and baby son off to New York, where he eventually got a job working for William Barclay Parsons, the chief engineer of the newly formed Rapid Transit Commission, which was planning to build a subway system under the city's streets.

Except for an occasional visit to one of the early tunnel heads near City Hall, Atticus saw precious little of his father. He went to a West Side public school, where the children made fun of his English, and spent most of his free time with his mother and her Russian friends, who made fun of his Russian. When word was brought, by a special motorcycle messenger with knee-high leather boots, that Eamon had been killed by an earth slide in a stretch of tunnel going from City Hall to Grand Central Station, both mother and son thought the world had ended. Nadezhda was obliged to quit her Russian sewing circle and take on work as a saleswoman in a midtown corset emporium. Atticus eventually followed in his father's footsteps, winning a scholarship at seventeen to Columbia University's School of Mines. He attended classes weekdays and worked the night shift and Saturdays on one of Parsons's tunnel heads creeping up Broadway. As he grew in size and matured, the Irish in Atticus gradually overpowered the Russian. Invited one Sunday to a reception at the spacious West Side apartment of the dean of the School of Mines, he cornered a wide-eyed blonde and wowed her with stories of the Trans-Siberian, mostly invented, and accounts of fatal accidents under the city's streets, mostly true. The girl instantly fell in love with the giant, irreverent Irishman who talked about tunneling as if it were a sexual activity. Before the evening was out she had seduced him into seducing her, a conquest that the young Tuohy lived to regret when he discovered, at roughly the same time as the dean, that his latest mistress was the dean's youngest daughter. Which is how Tuohy, despite his passing grades, came to be expelled from the Columbia University School of Mines.

Wanderlust took him out west and he worked in a series of mine and tunneling jobs until he wound up in a construction gang on a Chicago building of nine stories, at which point Tuohy fell promptly and profoundly in love with elevators, which he described, in all simplicity, as "tunneling up."

Elevators had come into their own at the Crystal Palace Exposition in New York City in 1853 when Elisha Graves Otis rode one over the heads of the spectators and then had the cable cut. The elevators didn't fall thanks to a spring cable device that Otis had invented.

Tuohy took a six-week crash course from the Otis company and set off to fill the world's buildings with Otis elevators. He joined the team that installed the first elevator in Kansas City. His crusade took him to Texas and California and back to New York City, and then across the Atlantic to London, Amsterdam, Stockholm, Berlin, Vienna, Warsaw, and, in 1911, St. Petersburg and the tsar's Winter Palace. At each stop Tuohy left his mark—a plunger-driven Otis elevator.

Back in Paris in the fall of 1911, looking considerably more mature than his twenty years, the lighthearted bubble of a life Tuohy was leading burst. A letter from his mother finally caught up with him. "People who speak with authority," she wrote, "say I am to die very soon. There is a certain satisfaction to be had from the slowness of the postal system, for when you receive this you will be able to take comfort from the fact that at least it is over with."

Curiously, the very day Tuohy got the letter he attended the funeral of two people he had never heard of, Paul and Laura Lafargue.

In Paris Tuohy had taken up with a Russian girl who had been forced into exile because of her political activities on behalf of a little-known splinter group of revolutionists who called themselves Bolsheviks. The girl, whose name was Nyura, appeared at Tuohy's door on the morning of November twentieth. Her eyes were red-rimmed. "The Lafargues are dead," she sobbed. "They committed suicide."

The Lafargues, as everyone but Tuohy seemed to know, were famous French Socialists. Paul had been a member of the legendary Paris Commune uprisings of 1870. Laura was the daughter of Karl Marx. At the age of seventy they had concluded that their social usefulness was finished and had decided to put an end to their lives.

The funeral at the Perè Lachaise Cemetery in Paris attracted everybody who was anybody in the European Socialist movement. The main speaker was the French Socialist Jean Jaurès. He was followed by a strongly built Russian of medium height with a pointed reddish beard. Except for a ring of red hair he was almost bald, which made him look a good deal older than his forty-one years. People referred to him as "Starik"—Russian for "the old man"; the name had been given to him by an old peasant he boarded with when he was exiled to Siberia. His real name, Tuohy discovered, was Vladimir Ilich Ulyanov, but he was better known by his party nom de guerre, Lenin. He was the leader of the Bolshevik Party. "If you cannot work for the party any longer," Lenin told the crowd of mourners—he spoke in Russian and a young woman named Inessa Armand translated his remarks into French—"one must be able to look the truth in the face and die like the Lafargues."

After the funeral Nyura took Tuohy back with her to Lenin's apartment at number 24 Rue Béaunier, near the Avenue d'Orléans and the Parc Montsouris. Over tea, served in kitchen tumblers, Lenin held court. When he discovered that the young elevator engineer had recently returned from St. Petersburg, he questioned him closely on conditions in the Russian capital. Were there bread lines? What did the working people talk about aside from the weather? What, in Tuohy's opinion, was the relationship between the factory workers and the army conscripts in the streets?

Responding to the questions, Tuohy found himself strangely drawn to the eyes that narrowed thoughtfully, taking on a distinctly Mongolian look as they drilled into him. When Lenin spoke, his manner was direct and his language simple. Still, he managed to convey the impression of someone in a hurry; of a man who had only a limited amount of time. He appeared to be physically uncomfortable, fidgeting in his chair, shifting position, then suddenly bursting out of it to pace back and forth, his face turned away, contorted—in thought? in pain?

"You have read *Das Kapital*?" Lenin asked Tuohy, and when Tuohy admitted he hadn't, Lenin advised him to acquire the book. "Marx is like a musician with perfect pitch," he said. "He has absolute revolutionary sense."

The hour and a half Tuohy spent with Lenin gave him a new outlook on life. It was the first time he had been in the presence of people who were wholeheartedly engaged in something other than making money or having fun. The Russian in Tuohy readily accepted the notion that the best of the best dedicated their lives to ideas. The Irish in him responded to the romanticism of revolution—of living and working clandestinely to overthrow an existing order.

"Revolutions," Lenin had said, quoting Marx, "are the locomotives of history."

"Here lies Atticus Tuohy," Tuohy told himself as he left Lenin's apartment that fateful day, "who could never resist a train whistle."

5

An impeccably dressed wino, gulping from the throat of a bottle wrapped in a brown paper bag, almost staggered into Zander as he crossed Tompkins Square going toward St. Mark's Place. "Free your mind and move your ass," the wino sputtered in indignation. He stopped in his tracks and, swaying slightly, blinked rapidly as if he were trying to bring Zander into focus. Then he belched, and executing an elegant pirouette continued on his way, tossing over his shoulder, "Move your ass, yeah, but don't get caught."

Move your ass but don't get caught. What better credo for a modern revolutionist, Zander thought. He was about to enter number 77 on St. Mark's Place when he spotted Tuohy coming toward him, accompanied by a girl a good head shorter than he was; Zander suspected that she was the one who moonlighted at the Margaret Sanger clinic.

"What's up?" Zander said. He noticed that Tuohy had distinct bags under his eyes.

"Search me." Tuohy made no effort to introduce his friend. "We both got notes telling us to show up here at eleven."

"Maybe they're going to run off a special edition on the Russian revolution and need people to deliver it," the girl suggested.

Tuohy's walrus mustache bobbed in indignation. "Do I look like a delivery boy?"

The three of them entered the basement of number 77 and made their way down the corridor to the rear room that served as the editorial office of *Novyi Mir*. Since his arrival in New York, Trotsky had been churning out a stream of articles for the émigré publication inviting workers to turn on their exploiters and transform the capitalist war into a civil war. In America, at least, there had been very few converts.

Trotsky appeared in an agitated mood. "You're late," he snapped, barely glancing at the new arrivals. Three young men, two of whom had been on picket lines with Zander at one time or another, lounged against the far wall under the barred window that looked out onto a dingy rear alleyway. A young woman who worked as Trotsky's unpaid secretary was wading through a packing case full of letters. "Be sure to set aside all the ones from Lenin," Trotsky instructed her. "I want to take them with me."

Trotsky finished sorting a stack of telegrams. "So," he began, pushing aside the papers and hefting himself onto the edge of an enormous oak table, "you are all no doubt wondering why you are here." He felt in his jacket for an article he had torn from the Sunday *Times*, and holding it in front of his nose read out the headline. " 'BERLIN SEES NEW REVOLT IN RUSSIA.' " Trotsky crumpled the article and tossed it into a wastepaper basket. "By a curious coincidence this is my analysis precisely," he said. "There will be a new revolution, gentlemen and ladies. It may be the good fortune of some of us in this room to take part in the creation of the first Communist state on the face of the planet. I myself hope to return to Russia on a Norwegian ship, the *Christianiafjord*, which leaves New York in a week's time. I can also tell you that we have been in touch, by cable, with Lenin in Zurich. He and the comrades there are trying to arrange with the Germans for passage by train to Finland, from whence they will proceed to Petrograd. The six of you here today have proven over a long period of time your devotion to the cause of the proletariat. Also, you all speak Russian. Unfortunately, we don't have the resources to finance the return of all of you—"

"How many can go?" Zander demanded.

Trotsky regarded Zander with an amused expression. "One."

The five men and one woman exchanged looks.

"How will you decide who is to go?" Tuohy inquired.

"It was my thought," Trotsky said, "that you would draw lots."

"I'll never win," lamented Marlene. "I have no luck when it comes to games of chance."

Zander announced, "I'm ready to try." He felt an irrational surge of confidence; he was absolutely sure he would win. It was a matter of wanting it so badly that he *had* to win. His entire adult life—the endless days and weeks and months on picket lines, the stints in jail, the monklike devotion to socialism and revolution that had obliged him to spend years hiding out in miserable furnished rooms—had been a preparation for his return to Russia and the ramparts the workers had thrown up.

How else could he explain all the suffering, all the loneliness, all the longing? He was meant to go back! He had to go back! He would go back!

Trotsky took six scraps of paper, marked an "X" in ink on one, folded each several times, and put all of them into his cap. "Who will begin?"

"In America, ladies usually go first," Tuohy offered gallantly.

Trotsky held out the cap to Tuohy's lady friend. She plucked a piece of paper and opened it. "I told you I'd never win," she groaned.

One by one the three young men against the wall helped themselves to slips of paper from Trotsky's cap, opened them, and held them aloft to show they had drawn blanks. Two of the three appeared to be more relieved than disappointed.

Now Zander was positive the "X" was meant for him. Trotsky extended the cap to Tuohy, who casually selected the slip nearest him. He held it between his fingers and teasingly offered it to Zander.

"I'll pick for myself," Zander said softly.

Tuohy accepted this with a nod. He slowly opened the folds of his piece of paper and looked up. It was impossible to tell from his expression whether he had drawn the "X" or a blank.

"Well?" Marlene demanded in irritation.

"You should have taken it," Tuohy told Zander. He held the slip aloft. The "X" in the middle was clearly visible. "Looks as if it's old Tuohy who's Russia bound."

The other young men crowded around Tuohy to congratulate him. His girlfriend kissed him vigorously on the lips. Everyone laughed. Trotsky's secretary produced a bottle of vodka and began passing out glasses. Zander, shattered that fate had deprived him of something that was by right his, started down the corridor. His head was swimming with dizziness, his eyes unable to focus. Outside, it was beginning to drizzle. Zander tilted his face up at the gray sky. The raindrops fell into his eyes and coursed down his cheeks. To have come so close . . .

Trotsky emerged from the basement behind Zander.

He had a curious half smile on his lips. Wordlessly, he took a sealed envelope from a breast pocket and offered it to Zander. When he didn't immediately accept, Trotsky reached over and stuffed it into Zander's jacket pocket. The two men looked at each other. Trotsky nodded to indicate that nothing needed to be put into words, and headed back to his office. Zander took the envelope out and studied one side and then the other. He tore off a strip at the edge of the envelope and extracted the contents. There was 112 dollars in American currency, seventy-five Russian rubles, a note identifying the purser on the *Christianiafjord* as someone named Kaare Ingvaldsen, the name and address of a print shop on Second Avenue with the word "passport" after it in parenthesis, and another letter on a separate sheet of paper, handwritten in Russian, that read:

> Comrades—A revolutionary movement to be effective must be made up of gifted writers, able organizers, and a few imaginative scoundrels. I recommend the bearer, Alexander Til, whose family name will be familiar to you, as an imaginative scoundrel.

The letter was signed "Trotsky."

A sensation of ecstasy spread through Zander's nervous system; his fingertips gripping the letters and the money tingled. Two women holding umbrellas over their heads made a detour around him. Thinking he was drunk, they carefully avoided his eyes as they passed. "It's not even noon," one of the women said, clucking her tongue.

"Move your ass," Zander called ecstatically after the two women, "but don't get caught!"

The printer, an old German Jew who looked like a bantam rooster, scrubbed the ink off his fingertips with a bar of Marseilles soap and a stiff brush. "Ah, if I had your age," he told Zander, shaking his head nostalgically, "I'd be making up one of these things for myself." The printer dried his hands on a towel, pulled a single sheet of paper from a file folder, and gave it to Zander. "What do you think?"

"It's beautiful," Zander said, studying the paper. The photograph, taken the previous day by the printer's son-in-law in the small room behind the press, had been glued onto the upper left-hand corner, and the Department of State stamp appeared across Zander's face.

"It was easier when they didn't use these newfangled photographs," the printer explained. "Next year it will be even harder. They're going to make passports with protective covers, something like a booklet."

"How did you get the stamp right?" Zander asked.

"Professional secret," the printer replied proudly. "But I will tell you anyhow. You slice a potato in half. You use the flat part to lift the inked impression off a genuine passport. You press the potato down on the photograph. The impression comes out lighter, but readable."

Zander checked the description down the left side of the paper—age, height, hair, eyes. "What made you choose the name Litzky?" he asked curiously.

"I knew a Litzky once," the printer replied. "It was the spring of 1906. I was just off the boat. Litzky gave me a job in his grocery store on Attorney Street and a cot in the back until I could fend for myself. It was a very big favor and I never forgot it."

The printer watched Zander carefully fold the single-page passport in half, and then in half again. "Don't take such good care of it," he told him. "Finger it, crease it, put it in and out of your pocket a hundred times. It is better if it looks old and used."

"How much do I owe you?" Zander asked.

The bantam rooster's eyebrows shot up. "There is no question of money changing hands," he said with dignity. "I do this for Mr. Trotsky and for the common cause. I envy you, young man, going to the revolution. If I can give you a word of advice? You don't mind? It's only this: Once you have made the revolution, you must every morning, without fail, stand quietly for a moment and remember *why* you made it. People who make revolutions have a tendency to forget the *why*."

"I'll remember the why," Zander vowed. "You can count on it."

Maud raised no objection when Zander asked if he could stay until the following Tuesday, when the *Christianiafjord* was due to sail on the evening tide. She even offered him an old duffel bag and whatever clothes he could find in the trunk her former husband had left in the attic. Zander and Maud went on sleeping in the same bed and made love several times, but it was more a question of servicing each other than anything else. Maud's heart was no longer in it. To protect herself, she was falling out of love with Zander. Which is why she didn't mind his hanging around until the boat sailed. In her experience it was easier to fall out of love with men while they were still physically there.

One night Zander found Maud brooding in the dark next to the living room fireplace, an almost empty cognac bottle on the coffee table in front of her, a cigarette dangling from her lips, which was curious because he had never seen her smoke before. Her eyes, barely visible in the moonlight that filtered through the window, looked swollen. "Remember the first New Year's Eve we spent together?" she asked. "We wrote out wishes on scraps of paper and burned them in an ashtray and ate the ashes. You said it was an old Russian custom. What did you put on your paper, Zander?"

Zander had to think a moment. " *Etsi omnes ego non.*' That's Latin for 'Even if everyone else, me no.' "

Maud smiled in the darkness. "I wrote 'Please God, hurry.' "

After a moment Zander quietly asked if she would prefer him to leave the house right away.

"I'd prefer you never to have come," she burst out. But when he started to pack his belongings in the duffel bag, she turned up at the door of the room to say in a wooden voice, "Stay, stay, it's all the same to me."

The next afternoon, the Sunday before the Tuesday, Kermit came racing up the stairs and knocked at Zander's door. "There's a man downstairs asking for you," he whispered excitedly.

"For me?" Zander eyed the window, trying to remember if there was cement or grass underneath in case he had to jump. Then he forced himself to think logically. If the police were at the door, they wouldn't have sent Kermit up to "ask" for him; they would do the asking themselves. And the police usually came in twos. "Describe the man," Zander ordered the boy.

"He's shorter than you. Big shoulders. Looks like a prizefighter. Bald here—" Kermit patted the top of his scalp with his palm—"and wears thick eyeglasses."

"Leon!" Zander cried. "What's he doing here?"

In the vestibule the two men embraced, to the astonishment of Kermit, who had never seen grown men hug each other. "You weren't followed?" Zander asked in Russian, slipping immediately into the familiar "thou" form of address. Because they were speaking Russian, with its lack of articles, the conversation took on a cryptic quality, as if they were exchanging telegrams.

"No, no, not to worry, I was careful," Leon assured him. "They came looking for you early in the week. Two feds. One named Hoover. Know them?"

"I met them briefly." Zander laughed. "How did you find me, Leon?"

"Wasn't easy," he admitted. "I wanted to warn you—the feds really seem to mean business this time—but you had changed rooms again. So I tracked down Tuohy's girlfriend, the one who works weekends at the Sanger clinic in Brooklyn, and through her I found Tuohy. And Tuohy told me you were with a woman who lived in Brooklyn Heights who had a boy with a deformed arm. The kid doesn't speak Russian, does he? I spent four days hanging around the candy store on Henry Street until I spotted him. All I had to do was follow him home." Leon threw his arm over Zander's shoulder. "Tuohy tells me you're going back to Russia."

Zander nodded. "I'm going *home*, Leon. On the *Christianiafjord*, which sails on the tide Tuesday."

Leon shook his head vigorously. "We need to have a long, serious heart-to-heart, Zander."

Leon took Zander to a tiny Rumanian restaurant on Second Avenue, where the specialty of the house was stuffed delicacies, which you ate until you were "stuffed." The bill for all this, for two, came to seventy-nine cents.

Leon, who was flush that week, ordered a bottle of Polish vodka. "To your father and to my mother, may they rest in peace," he said, and solemnly clicking their glasses he and Zander drained their vodka *do dna*—to the bottom. "It seems like yesterday that Jack married my mother and set up housekeeping in that tenement on *ulitza*," Leon reminisced.

"The first thing you did when we met was ask me my age," Zander reminded him. "When you found out you were four months older, you were very pleased with yourself."

"Remember how we used to tell the teacher in P.S. 160 we were twins? When she said we didn't look alike, we said maybe not, but we thought alike."

"Remember how we used to swipe books off the pushcart and then fight over who got to read them first?"

"Could I ever forget?" Leon said.

"You're losing your hair, Leon," Zander teased him. "Every time I see you you have a fistful less than before."

"Woman troubles," explained Leon. "I'm nuts about a lady pharmacist in the Bronx." He filled the vodka glasses to the brim. Zander bent his lips to the glass and sipped off enough so he could lift it without spilling any. "She says she loves me," Leon continued, "but she categorically refuses to live in Palestine."

"You know what Tolstoy said," Zander remarked. "He said he'd tell the truth about women when he had one foot in the grave. He'd tell it and jump into the coffin and pull the lid closed over his head."

"Women are dangerous," Leon agreed with a chuckle, "but not *that* dangerous."

"About Palestine," Zander said.

"About Russia," Leon said. They both smiled.

"Listen, Zander, I can understand that Russia has

captured your imagination, what with the revolution and the abdication of the tsar. But you're making a big mistake. Russia will break your heart."

"You're a Zionist, Leon. I'm not. For me, Palestine is not the promised land, but Russia could be."

"You're a Jew," declared Leon.

"I'm a revolutionist before I'm a Jew," insisted Zander.

"So you dash off to the first revolution available—"

"The good thing about having a revolution available, Leon, is you get to see who is a revolutionist and who isn't."

"What's that supposed to mean?"

At the next table customers glanced curiously at Zander and Leon. Zander shrugged. "We've been over this before," he said more calmly. "What it means, Leon, is that I think the best way to help the Jews is to help everybody." Zander spoke with quiet intensity. "If we succeed in making a Communist revolution in Russia, it will spread across Europe. We'll put an end to the economic iniquities that breed antisemitism. We'll create a new race of people—Communist men and Communist women—who won't be anti anything. Going to Palestine is not a solution, Leon. Even if you manage to carve out a Jewish state, which is a one-in-a-million shot to begin with, all you're going to do is displace a lot of Arabs and humiliate the others. You'll wind up creating a whole new area of antisemitism where there is none today."

"I respect your idealism," Leon said in a troubled voice, "but not your ideas." He massaged his high forehead with his fingertips. "This revolution is a terrible dream. The theory sounds reasonable enough, I grant you that, but the people who will put it into practice—your Lenins, your Trotskys—are human like everyone else. Can't you see the handwriting on the wall, Zander? The first order of business for those who take power is to *keep* power. So they resort to what men who have power always resort to—lies, exaggerations, repression, propaganda, wars. Revolutions don't change things, they just rearrange them. Come with me to Palestine, Zander—not to make a revolution, but to till the soil."

Leon filled the vodka glasses again. The waiter noticed that the serving bowls on the tables were untouched. "So what's the matter with the stuffed?" he asked, obviously insulted.

"Eat, if only to please him," Leon ordered.

They both nibbled thoughtfully at some green peppers stuffed with chicken liver. Zander broke the silence. "Tell me something, Leon. I know you don't believe in God. So in what sense are you Jewish?"

Leon shook his head as if to say that the answer was self-evident. "In the sense that every twenty-five or fifty years the world reminds me by trying to murder me." He started to elaborate, but then shrugged. "Listen, Zander, you wouldn't by any chance know who Chaim Weizmann is?"

"What do I get if I answer correctly?"

"A story."

"Maybe I should answer wrong. He's the leader of your Zionist movement."

"Well," said Leon, "Weizmann has a brother whose name is Shemuel. And Shemuel is something like you, which is to say he's an idealist and a revolutionist and a raving idiot—don't interrupt, Zander, I'm older than you are. Anyway, Weizmann's mother once said, 'If Shemuel wins, we will live in Russia in peace and security. And if Chaim wins, we'll go to Palestine and live in peace and security there.'" Leon raised his vodka glass. "Here's to Chaim!" He tilted his head back and drained off the vodka in one long gulp, then shivered from its effect and flung his glass against the wall, where it shattered into a hundred pieces.

Alarmed, the other diners turned to see what was happening. "Russians," one of them muttered as if it explained everything.

Now it was Zander's turn to raise his glass. "To Shemuel," he said. And he, too, drank and threw his glass against the wall—but it bounced off without breaking and rolled noisily under a chair.

Leon and Zander exchanged solemn looks. Then Zander laughed uneasily. "You're not superstitious, are you?" he asked.

"The question is, are you?" Leon said gravely.

They both knew that according to the Russian ritual, if the glass didn't break, the wish wouldn't come true.

Later Leon walked Zander partway across the Brooklyn Bridge. Underneath their feet a gray four-stacker destroyer was steaming out on the evening tide from the Brooklyn Navy Yard toward the Narrows and the Atlantic. "America will be in the war soon," Leon commented.

"If we get our way, Russia will be *out* of the war soon," Zander said.

From somewhere on the Brooklyn side came the distinct peal of church bells marking midnight. "They're ringing for me," Zander said. "They're calling me back to Russia."

The two men stopped in the middle of the bridge. Leon shifted his weight from one foot to the other. "You don't hold it against me, my having tried?"

Zander looked at his shoes and then up again at Leon. "I take it as a sign of affection. I owe you a lot, Leon. After the Triangle fire, I never would have survived without you."

Leon waved Zander's thanks away with his hand. "God bless you, Zander. I love you dearly, but when it comes to Russia and revolution, you're full of shit."

"I love you too, Leon, but in the end we aren't twins—we don't think alike."

"It may be a long time before we meet again," Leon said.

Zander nodded grimly.

Leon studied the wooden planks of the walkway; he had run out of words. The two of them embraced and then kissed, Russian style, on the lips. Leon turned quickly and hurried toward the Manhattan side without looking back. Zander watched him go, then headed toward Brooklyn Heights. He walked slowly, wondering if he would ever see Leon again, and wishing he had thrown the vodka glass against the wall with more force.

* * *

For Zander it came under the heading of unfinished business. For Tuohy it seemed more like sheer sport.

If Ortona was surprised to see them, he didn't show it. "Hey, Zander, Tuohy, what you guys got, a United States of America government passport to come over here to New Jersey? You need one, you know—a passport, roadmaps, a dictionary to speak with us natives, huh? What you want to drink? I got a fresh block of ice in the icebox, I can chip you off some, no trouble."

Zander accepted a glass of seltzer and crushed ice and Tuohy agreed to a vodka that Ortona swore was home-brewed by a Serbian lady in Newark. "So we really fucked up the other day," Ortona told Tuohy conversationally.

Tuohy looked around. "You have a very nice place here."

"I do, don't I?" agreed Ortona. He felt more relaxed. It seemed evident Zander didn't have the vaguest idea who betrayed him to the federal agents.

"Is the furniture yours or do you rent it with the apartment?" Tuohy asked.

"Some is mine, some is not. The table with the glass top, the rugs, the chair you are sitting on, I buy the stuff off the boats cheap."

"You know your way around," Zander commented.

Ortona shrugged modestly. "Where is the crime in that?" He smiled at Zander and then at Tuohy. "So what do I owe the pleasure to?"

"Here's the thing," Tuohy said. "The Smith and Wesson—we need it again. We're organizing another expropriation."

Ortona absently picked at the inside of an ear with a fingernail. "You Bolshevists tickle me, you got such fancy words for things. Expropriation." He snorted. "When you need it for?"

"Today. Now," said Zander.

"Today, now! Maybe you need a machine gun today now also. I got to ask the man that owns it. I got to convince him to make it available to me." He looked at Tuohy. "Last time you gave me forty-eight hours and even that was rushing the normal nature of the transaction."

Zander said nervously, "We need to have the gun today. It's very important."

"How about the Russian Nagant of yours?" Tuohy asked.

"It is so old I am not sure it can shoot straight."

"I'd take it as a favor, Emilio," Zander insisted.

It suddenly occurred to Ortona that he was being tested. Maybe Zander suspected him after all, and if he didn't lend him the pistol, it would confirm his suspicions. "Sure, when you put it like that—" Ortona went into the other room, pulled a package wrapped in cloth from under the mattress, came back, and put it on the table.

Tuohy looked at Zander, daring him. Zander undid the flaps of cloth and picked up the weapon. It was old but in mint condition, well oiled, heavy in the palm of his hand. Four bullets lay in the folds of the cloth. Zander picked up one and fitted it into the chamber and clicked the chamber into firing position.

"Hey, watch that—"

Zander stretched out his arm until the barrel touched Ortona's chest.

Ortona's eyes bulged. "You are trying to scare me is what you are doing," he said in an unrecognizable voice.

"Get it over with," Tuohy said.

"For the love of Christ," Ortona cried, "I had to do it, huh? They grabbed me by the balls. They squeezed." He looked around wildly. "Oh, sweet Jesus. How does it help your fucking revolution if you shoot me?"

"Do it," Tuohy snapped impatiently.

Zander bit his lip. The hand holding the pistol trembled.

"If you kill me, they will only go out and get themselves another pigeon." Ortona was having trouble breathing. "Leave me live, this way you know who they got, huh?"

Shaking his head in disgust, Tuohy grabbed the pistol from Zander, wedged the barrel deep into the stomach

of the cringing man, and pulled the trigger. The bullet
flung Ortona halfway across the room and left a gaping
hole in his shirt front. Tuohy knelt beside the body and
felt for a pulse. There was none. He fitted Ortona's
fingers over the butt of the Nagant and glanced up at
Zander. "Here lies Atticus Tuohy," he said with a grim
smile, "who knew how to even the score."

Zander went into the bathroom, vomited into the
toilet bowl, flushed it, and when the overhead tank had
filled, flushed it a second time. Then he and Tuohy let
themselves out the back door, descended the creaky
wooden staircase to the alley, and started to walk back
through the night to the ferry landing.

Departures of any kind are a tearing away, which is
why travelers invariably linger until the last possible
moment. The passengers of the *Christianiafjord* were
true to form. Tuohy showed up in a yellow taxi escorted
by three girls, and took his sweet time about kissing
them good-bye. Trotsky didn't arrive until the steam
was up, and even then he sent his two young sons and
his wife aboard while he huddled in the dispatcher's
dockside shack dashing off last-minute notes to American friends. Zander, standing on the wing of the bridge,
felt a stab of pain as he recalled looking down at his
mother on the pier in Rotterdam and not waving. He
had asked Maud if she wanted to see him off, but she
had coolly declined the invitation, saying she knew how
to conduct herself like a lady only at arrivals.

The captain of the *Christianiafjord*, an incredibly
thin man with tufts of blond hair protruding from the
middle of his cheeks, darted impatient glances at the
ship's clock inside the pilot house and at the tide tables
posted in chalk on a small blackboard hanging from the
bulkhead. Finally he barked an order in Norwegian to a
sailor, who leaned over the railing and shouted down
through a megaphone to the main deck. Immediately
half a dozen hands grabbed the lines securing the gangplank and threw them ashore. Trotsky jumped for the
gangplank.

Tuohy ambled up beside Zander and together they

watched Trotsky scramble onto the main deck. "See the brunette with the frizzed hair over there?" Tuohy said. He waved and the brunette waved back. "I almost didn't leave because of her. What a body. Someone hired her to pose naked on a pedestal at a cocktail party. That's where I met her." Tuohy waved again at the three girls who had accompanied him to the pier. "I can't wait to get my hands on the females of the species in Mother Russia."

"Are you going for the girls or the revolution?"

Tuohy leaned his back against the railing and helped himself to a cigarette from a silver case. He cupped his hands around the flame to light it and inhaled deeply. "Of course I believe in the dialectic and the historic inevitability of class warfare and all that sort of thing, but I am a revolutionist because of the bonus—it results in bigger and better erections."

Below, the dock workers removed the last lines from the bollards and the sailors on the ship pulled them in hand over hand. A tug with a line to the *Christianiafjord*'s bow started easing her out into the Hudson River. For an instant Zander imagined that the ship was standing perfectly still and the pier was backing away from him. Then he felt the deck tremble under his feet as the giant screw slowly bit into the water. With a shriek of its whistle, the tug cast loose its bow line and the *Christiania-fjord* came around into the wind. Pennants strained on the halyards. Engine bells rang in the pilot house.

His hair flying in every direction, Trotsky climbed up the outboard ladder onto the bridge for a better view of the city. "I want to get a last look at this monster," he told Zander and Tuohy.

The ship passed close to the end of a dock on Forti-eth Street that jutted into the Hudson. Zander could make out the lone figure of a man standing on a crate next to the last piling. He was waving his hat wildly at the ship. "Leon," Zander breathed. He leapt onto the lookout's perch so that Leon could make him out.

"Leon!" he shouted, but his voice was carried away in the wind.

This time Zander waved.

BOOK 2

Living in Petrograd is the same as lying in a coffin.

—Osip Mandelstam

In April, drifts of clouds straying in from the Gulf of Finland began pelting Petrograd. Ribbons of rain, curtains of it, chipped away at the wooden blocks with which many of the streets were paved. People muttered nervously about a "second flood," and several Orthodox priests wondered aloud from their pulpits which of the political factions vying for power would organize the construction of an ark.

On the Neva quays, Cossacks in glistening black ponchos spurred their stunted horses up to heaps of thawing garbage and rummaged through them with their long needlelike lances. Occasionally one of the Cossacks would spear a rat and hold it aloft, still squirming, to auction the meat. Off Nevsky Prospekt, which cut through Petrograd like a spine, hundreds of army deserters, many of them drunk, some of them insane, roamed the side streets breaking windows, looting shops, and beating to a pulp anyone who tried to stop them. Near the Tuchkov Bridge the ice cracked one morning at mid-month and a drowned woman surfaced. A patrol of Pharaohs (as everyone called the Mounted Police) reined in their horses and regarded the body, which was floating facedown, legs spread, arms laced back at a grotesque angle. The Pharaohs concluded that it was just another suicide—there had been so many recently, newspapers had given up listing them individually—and trotted off.

Halfway between the Finland Railroad Station and the bridge over the Bolshaya Nevka, an open army lorry pulled up in front of a government bread shop. Deserters with their legs in irons, guarded by two bearded corporals, began unloading gunnysacks full of freshly baked black bread. Within minutes word flashed through the surrounding streets and a line formed, snaking down the sidewalk and disappearing around the corner. The wife of the man who ran the shop made her way down the queue, writing numbers on the palms of hands to avoid disputes over the order in which customers would be served.

Cackling with pleasure, a toothless old woman using a folded English umbrella as a cane limped out of the store with a loaf under her arm. A bare-headed soldier with civilian trousers tucked into his army boots snatched the loaf away from her and sprinted off. In a voice that was almost animallike, the old woman howled in despair. The people queuing for bread took up the cry. "Thief! Thief!"

Some passing bicycle troops gave chase. They caught up with the thief at the bridge, twisted both his arms until the bones snapped, then walked him back to the bread shop.

"What do you want to do with him?" one of the bicycle soldiers asked.

"Call the police," someone suggested.

A Bolshevik leader with the nom de guerre of Stalin was on the breadline. "We don't need capitalist police," he called. "We need revolutionary justice!"

Everyone agreed enthusiastically. The bicycle soldiers presided over a brief court-martial on the sidewalk. The thief, his limp arms dangling at his sides, passed out and had to be slapped back to consciousness. He pleaded for leniency. He had a common law wife and a child, he moaned; the bread had been for them.

"If he wanted bread," shouted a young man on handmade crutches, "he ought to have queued like everyone else." He looked around. Heads nodded in agreement.

"Killing is too good for the likes of him," shrieked the toothless old woman who had lost her loaf.

"Comrades," the wife of the man who ran the shop called out, "the thief's arms have been broken. He has already been punished."

"His bones will knit," Stalin remarked, "and he will steal again."

"We can't stand around arguing all day," said another of the bicycle soldiers. "All those who judge him guilty and vote for revolutionary justice, lift a hand."

Dozens of hands shot into the air.

"All those who vote innocent?"

The wife of the man who ran the shop started to raise her hand, then with a shrug turned away.

"The guilties win," shouted the bicycle soldier who had taken the vote.

With a whine of excitement the crowd surged in on the condemned man and kicked him to death.

1

Petrograd, 1917

Heading from the Finland station toward the bridge over the Bolshaya Nevka, Zander felt dizzy from the pull of Russia on his feet. The duffel bag slung over his shoulder had no weight, no existence. He bent to touch the ground with his knuckles, and laughed. "I can't believe I'm here," he called to Tuohy. "I can't believe I'm home again."

Tuohy, ten paces ahead, called back, "Welcome to Mother Russia," in a peculiar voice, and then pointed at the body of the soldier crumpled on the sidewalk in front of the deserted bread shop. A toothless old woman crouched over the corpse, beating feebly on his broken limbs with a splintered English umbrella. "They caught the thief," she wailed bitterly, "but in all the excitement someone made off with my loaf."

Zander reached into the pocket of the ankle-length overcoat that he had taken from Maud's attic. "Here, little mother," he offered, holding out what was left of the loaf they had bought during their brief stopover in Helsinki.

"Hey, that's the last of our bread," Tuohy protested.

The old woman seized it and brought it directly to her nose. "What are you, a messiah, that you give away bread as if it had less value than gold?" She deftly tucked it out of sight inside the folds of her shawl and made the sign of the cross over Zander with the tip of her umbrella. "Go with God," she muttered, disoriented by the act of generosity, "only watch out for the Bolsheviks."

"Did you hear what the old bag said?" Tuohy roared

as they crossed the Bolshaya Nevka. "Watch out for the Bolsheviks! Ha! We're the Bolsheviks!"

On the Old Petersburg side of the Bolshaya Nevka, Zander, more subdued now, asked a sailor pushing a wheelbarrow full of leaflets for directions to the Kshesinskaya Mansion. A double file of conscripts, peasants from the ragged look of their clothing, shuffled past on their way to an army depot and, eventually, the western front. An Orthodox priest with a stovepipe hat and a thick metal-tipped staff stopped to regard the conscripts, and made the sign of the cross over those who nodded in his direction.

"God's chosen," the priest called to Zander when he saw him staring after the conscripts, "off to battle the German Satan."

"Cannon fodder," Zander shouted back, "off to make the capitalists richer."

The priest's face turned beet red and he pounded the wooden paving blocks with his staff three times, then spat in Zander's direction. "Bolsheviki," he sputtered. He started off, turned back, and cried, "Christ killers," then started off again only to turn once more and shout, "Yids!"

They found the Kshesinskaya Mansion without much difficulty. Several dozen Bolshevik Red Guards, wearing belted jackets and peaked workers' caps and red armbands, were drilling in an empty lot next to it. And a huge red streamer across the mansion's white brick front bore in giant gold letters the Bolshevik slogan, "Bread! Land! Peace!"

The mansion, with its palatial façade and crystal chandeliers and mahogany banisters and marble floors, had once been the city residence of the famous prima ballerina *assoluta*, Mathilde Kshesinskaya. Traditionally it was the young ladies of the world of ballet who initiated Russian royalty into the mysteries of physical love. Kshesinskaya, a small woman who always dressed in coal black, had performed this delicate service for Nicholas when he was a fledgling grand duke. After Nicholas's sudden abdication the previous month, the Bolsheviks in Petrograd, in desperate need of a suitable headquarters, had simply confiscated her house "in the name of the people."

Now, under a mirrored ceiling in the mansion's spacious entranceway, Zander and Tuohy came upon a studious young woman sitting behind a plain kitchen table. She had a Cossack's cape draped over her shoulders and a net sack filled with onions between her feet. A handwritten card propped up against a pewter inkwell announced her name: Arishka. Tuohy cleared his throat. "We have only this instant arrived from America, from New York, with important letters for the boss from Comrade Trotsky," he said in Russian.

"You are Americans?" the woman asked; she had never come face-to-face with one before.

"Actually, I'm half Irish and half Russian," Tuohy told her. He settled onto the edge of her table and toyed with the lid on her inkwell. "But I was raised in America. Maybe we could take a stroll after you get off and I'll tell you all about it. What do you say?"

"What I say is"—the young woman gestured saucily with her chin toward the wide staircase—"the boss is on the second floor, first door on your left." And she added sweetly, "Maybe he'd like to go for a stroll with you and hear about America."

Tuohy flashed what he thought of as his most ingratiating smile. "You don't know what you're missing."

"Come on," Zander called impatiently from the stairs.

"A little respect, please, for the chemistry of the situation," Tuohy called in English. "Revolutions produce sex the way trees produce sap," he added. Smiling at Arishka over his shoulder, he followed Zander up the stairs.

They skirted half a dozen soldiers curled up on the corridor floor, fast asleep, and came to the door the young woman had indicated. Zander knocked. When nobody answered, he opened it a crack. The room buzzed with activity. Two women—Lenin's sisters—were sorting through cartons of leaflets and dividing them into three piles. Two teenage girls were snipping tiny red ribbons from a bolt of cloth and inserting pins in them so they could be worn in lapels. Several men in sailor uniforms were stamping and signing laissez-passer cards. From the corners of the room four men were yelling into different telephone receivers. "Petrograd needs one hundred and twenty railroad wagons of flour a day," a young man with almost jaundiced skin shouted angrily into one phone. "Yesterday we received only thirty-nine." He hammered the table with a fist. "We demand an explanation." The young man, whose real name was Vyacheslav Skryabin but who was called Molotov—*molot* means "hammer" in Russian—covered the mouthpiece with his hand. "He's stammering, that's how nervous he is," he announced with a wink. "What?" he yelled into the phone. He listened for a moment. "And you expect us to swallow that bullshit?"

Across the room a stocky man hunched in a wooden swivel chair behind a table stared out of the French window while he absently picked *semitchki*, dried sun-flower seeds, out of a twist of paper, cracking the shells with his teeth and spitting the husks onto the floor. Judging from the pile of husks at his feet, he had been at it for some time. He swiveled around, caught a glimpse of Zander at the door, and gestured vaguely with his right hand for him to come in.

Zander and Tuohy deposited their duffels in a corner and walked over to the man's table.

"On another matter," Molotov yelled into the phone, "we must at all costs put on a good show when Lenin arrives at the Finland station. How many people can you send us?" He listened for a moment. "What do you mean, whoever wants to go will go? What kind of an answer is that?"

The stocky man in the swivel chair nodded as if he had confirmed something. Looking up, he noticed the expression on Tuohy's face. "You think you have stum-bled into a madhouse," he said. He spoke Russian with a heavy Georgian accent, and Tuohy had to strain to understand him. "Admit it, you think so." He spat a husk onto the floor. "Tolstoy used to tell a story. He saw at a distance a man whose motions suggested he was a maniac. Coming closer, he realized that the man was sharpening a knife." The stocky man slapped the edge of the table with his fingertips, content with his own story. "It may not look like it, but that's what we're doing—we're sharpening knives."

"Two hundred," Molotov thundered into the phone, "is not acceptable. You will have to come up with twice that many."

"What is it you think we can do for you?" inquired the man from his wooden swivel chair.

"We have letters of introduction from Trotsky," explained Zander. "We want to see the boss."

"It's me, the boss," the stocky man said simply. He permitted the vaguest of smiles on to his face and uttered his name matter-of-factly: "Stalin."

Zander had heard of this man who had been in the day-to-day business of overthrowing the tsar since his expulsion from a seminary at the age of nineteen. His real name was Josef Dzhugashvili, Soso (short for Josef) to his Georgian cronies. It was he who, under his party name of Koba, had organized the famous Tiflis bank "expropriation," which ended in a shootout in the town's main square and brought a much-needed infusion of five hundred ruble notes into the party's coffers.

Stalin—the name means "steel" in Russian—scraped back his chair and came around the table. "Where are these letters you have come all this way to show us?" he demanded. His eyes narrowed into what had become a permanent squint of suspicion. Zander could see that his face above the thick mustache was scarred with pockmarks. His left arm was shorter than his right and seemed to hang from his shoulder. A short man, he wore a khaki military tunic buttoned up to the neck and thick civilian trousers tucked into the tops of scuffed leather boots with especially thick soles, designed—so Zander assumed—to make him appear taller.

Zander and Tuohy handed over the letters. Stalin scratched at a nostril with the joint of a finger as he read them one after the other. When he finished he tossed them onto the table. "Which one of you is Alexander Til?" he asked with the slightest lift of one eyebrow.

"I'm Til."

"Any relation to *our* Til?"

Zander nodded. "He was the father of my father."

"Your name is a better recommendation than a dozen letters from Trotsky," declared Stalin. "I don't beat around the bush. I never had much use for him. I first met Trotsky at a congress in London, in 1907, at a reception given by some English friends. I was obliged to use party funds to rent a tuxedo—to get decked out like a corpse in one of those capitalist monkey suits. Trotsky was also wearing a tuxedo, but he looked comfortable in his. He was very elegant, very . . . intellectual, if you get my thrust. Shit, I wipe my ass with articles written by coffeehouse revolutionaries like Trotsky. Half the time I never understand what he says anyhow." Stalin self-consciously covered the back of his left hand with the palm of his right hand to hide a patch of warts. "Well, what use shall we make of you? What did you do for the party in New York?"

Tuohy answered before Zander could get a word in. "Sometimes we served as bodyguards for Trotsky."

Stalin nodded thoughtfully. "We are organizing a pool of bodyguards to protect our people who go out to the factories and barracks to propagandize the masses." He fetched a carton from a closet, took out two brand new German Mauser Parabellums fitted to wooden shoulder holsters, and handed them to Zander and Tuohy. Then he scribbled an address on the back of an envelope, scrawled his initials under it, and gave the paper to Zander. "It is a house run by comrades," Stalin told him. "You will find beds and board there. Report back here tomorrow morning." He fixed his narrow Georgian eyes on Zander. "We will see how much of an imaginative scoundrel you really are."

The house, planted like the prow of an icebreaker on the corner of Shirokaya and Gazovaya, turned out to be one of the architectural curiosities of Old Petrograd. People in the neighborhood, dreaming of voyages they took only in their imagination, had dubbed it "the Steamboat." It had been built the previous century by the outrageously wealthy owner of the Volga Steamship Company. The sliding paneled doors of the drawing rooms had been imported from England, the fountain inside the main entrance from France, the stained glass windows in the chapel and the marble for the fireplaces from Italy, the teak for the staircase from East India, the tapestries in the ballroom from Central Asia, the chandeliers from Venice. On the death of the shipping magnate, the house had passed into the hands of his oldest son, a syphilitic who eventually lost it at cards to one of his cronies, the young Prince Felix Yusupov, who at the time was in drag and accompanied by four ramrod-straight Guards officers who took him for a woman. The prince subsequently made a name for himself by shooting Rasputin, the illiterate "holy wanderer" who was both spiritual confessor and political advisor to the royal family, while a record of "Yankee Doodle Dandy" turned on the gramophone to drown out the sound of the pistol. Forced into discreet exile as a result of the episode, the prince signed over the house to his twin sister, for whom he harbored a secret passion. Her name was Lili, but she came to be known in Bolshevik circles as the Red Princess, both because of her political leanings—since red flags were flown during the French Revolution of 1789, the color has been associated with radicalism—and the fact that in Russian red also means beautiful.

Tuohy danced a little jig when he caught sight of the Steamboat. "If I had known this is how revolutionists live, I would have become one sooner."

Zander unhooked the latch on the large wrought-iron gate and pulled the bell on the massive oak door. Almost instantly it flew open to reveal a muscular woman with her sleeves rolled up and her hands covered in soapsuds. Behind her Zander caught a glimpse of laundry hanging on cords stretched across the entrance hall over the fountain. Half a dozen cats were visible, some curled up asleep on piles of laundry, others scampering around playing with a cork from a wine bottle. "Well?" the woman demanded, drying her hands on her apron, sizing up the two men on the steps.

"We were sent to this address by—"

A stifled scream interrupted Zander. Then a second.

Both came from behind closed double-doors off the entranceway.

"Who's the lucky victim?" Tuohy asked.

A third scream, shriller than the previous ones, pierced the double-doors.

"By Comrade Stalin," Zander continued uncertainly. "He told us we would find beds and board here."

"That being the case," snapped the woman impatiently, "why are you standing there like statues? Come in and close the door behind you. And wipe your boots on the army blanket there. You might as well learn right off, that's one of our house rules, and we're strict about house rules. Violators are brought before the house committee and dealt with harshly."

"Here lies Atticus Tuohy, summarily hanged by the neck until dead for failing to wipe his shoes," Tuohy mocked her in English. "If I had known this is how revolutionists die, I would never have become one."

"So you're a foreigner," observed the woman suspiciously. "We have a German here already. He's a dentist. That's what the screams are about. What are you then? English? Italian?"

"We are Chinese," Tuohy said with a straight face.

"We're from America," Zander told her.

"I'm glad one of you keeps a civil tongue in his head. What you need to do is speak to the princess—she's in charge of logistics. She'll figure out where you can lay your heads."

Tuohy perked up. "A princess lives here?"

"A *Russian* princess," observed the woman haughtily, "not a Chinese princess." To Zander she explained, "They're coming from her, the screams—she's having a hole in a tooth plugged."

The double-door slid open and the German dentist poked his head out. "You two, yes, you, come please, yes?" He beckoned Zander and Tuohy. "I am at the crucial part and need some strong hands to restrain the patient."

Zander and Tuohy leaned their duffels against a wall, and ducking under the drying clothes followed the dentist into the room. A padded leather barber's chair was bolted to the floor in the center of what had once been an elegant drawing room. The dentist's drill hung from a slinglike contraption screwed into the ceiling. The drill was connected to a gear box, which in turn was connected, through a series of lathe belts, to the rear axle of a bicycle that had been fitted onto a wooden stand. A husky young teenager, the son of the woman washing clothes in the fountain outside, sat astride the bicycle, waiting for the dentist's signal to pedal and turn the drill.

Sitting in the dentist's chair, breathing through her open mouth, one cheek swollen from a wad of cotton stuffed in it, was Princess Lili Mikhailovna. In her late twenties, she had short dark hair that she flicked behind her ear with a finger, dark eyes that were the color of a rain cloud, and a chipped front tooth that failed to mar an extraordinarily beautiful face with a hint of Tartar blood in it—slightly high cheekbones, a hint of flatness to her nose, the faintest suggestion of a slant to her eyes. She wore brightly colored loose-fitting trousers, and a skin-tight high-necked black sailor's sweater that buttoned across one shoulder. Her body was long and thin and flat and hard. Her skin seemed particularly white against the black sweater. "Fuck," she said, and she pried the wad of cotton from her cheek and spat some blood into a tin dish.

"Perhaps that is enough for one day, yes?" suggested the dentist, Otto Eppler.

The princess shook her head curtly. "I would prefer to get it over with. What's left to do?"

"I must pack the cavity with a mixture of zinc oxide and ground cloves to desensitize the root, yes? Then I will heat up a number four lead shotgun pellet to sterilize it and soften it. After that it is only a matter of tapping it into the cavity."

"I promise to give up masturbation if it doesn't hurt too much," the princess announced gravely.

Tuohy said, "That's a high price to pay."

Eppler nodded toward Zander and Tuohy. "You comrades will hold her down, yes? If she moves, I will not be able to get the pellet in and we must do the entire operation over again."

Tuohy, by far the stronger of the two, took Lili's forehead in an iron grip and pinned her against the back of the barber chair. Zander pushed against her shoulders. Lili closed her eyes and opened her mouth.

The dentist changed eyeglasses and, straining for a better view, started to coat the interior of the cavity with a small artist's brush that he dipped from time to time into a mixture in a kitchen tumbler. Lili moaned softly. The dentist lighted a candle on his table and held a teaspoon containing a lead shotgun pellet over the flame. When he judged it hot enough, he picked up the pellet with the working end of a warped tweezers and deftly plugged the pellet into the hole he had drilled in her tooth. The boy on the bicycle put a finger in each of his ears and screwed up his face. A long throaty sigh of pain emerged from Lili. Her forehead, damp with perspiration, strained against Tuohy's grip. Her small breasts rose and fell near Zander's hands.

"I am nearly finished, yes?" Eppler whispered. Moving with precise gestures, he placed the tip of a pointed chisellike instrument against the pellet, now nestled in the cavity, and tapped sharply against the other end of the instrument with a small hammer. A hoarse scream came from Lili's throat, shattering the silence. The dentist tapped again and Lili screamed a second time. Crystals in the wall-mounted chandeliers tinkled.

"She can't take much more," Zander said.

"Pay no attention to him," Lili contradicted him, panting through her open mouth.

"One last time, yes?" Eppler said. He positioned his chisel and cocked the hammer. Tears appeared in Lili's eyes. The dentist tapped against the chisel. Lili howled in pain. Eppler peered into her mouth and nodded happily. "It is in place. I must tell you, in all modesty, it is a very beautiful job."

The princess seemed to melt into the barber chair. When she had regained her composure, she mustered a weak smile. "At least now I won't have to give up masturbation."

*   *   *

That evening Lili, presiding from the head of the table, told Hippolyte Evgenevich Evremov, "You are the oldest present. It is for you to make the toast."

"If I could remember their names," the old man called across the table—he was hard of hearing and wasn't aware that he talked in a loud voice—"I would gladly propose the toast."

"Never mind their names, Granddad," shouted the woman who had been washing clothes in the entranceway. Her name was Serafima Fedorovna, and she was the common law wife of Sergeant Kirpichnikov, who sat across from her.

The boy who had been pedaling the bicycle for the dentist tugged at Serafima's sleeve. "More salt, Mama."

Serafima turned to Zander, who was sitting on her other side. "We call the boy Melor," she explained with obvious pride. "It stands for 'Marx-Engels-Lenin-Organizers-Revolution.' He was born in Siberia, which is where the little father, God damn his putrid soul, sent us after the uprising of oh five."

"Melor," Zander said, "is a very original name."

"His real father was a revolutionist," Serafima continued. "He never survived Siberia." She pointed her fork at Sergeant Kirpichnikov across the table. "He's the stepfather. His name is Pasha. He was a sergeant before he deserted. Now he is a Bolshevik."

The sergeant, the Cross of St. George conspicuous on his unbuttoned Red Guard tunic, proudly held up his left hand. The name Pasha was tattooed on the back of it, one letter to each finger.

"The salt," whined Melor.

"Speaking of salt," said Appolinaria Antonova, the tall, graceful wife of Ronzha, the poet. She darted to the sideboard and removed a small plate on which she had put some black bread and salt, and set it before Zander and Tuohy. "For our new arrivals," she said timidly. "It is an old Russian tradition."

Lili said coldly, "Here we pride ourselves on breaking traditions."

"Dear Lili Mikhailovna," the poet called from the other end of the table. He had a lean, pale face, a long hawk's nose, a high forehead, and deep, dark eyes, and was nicknamed Ronzha, after the large blue-gray bird native, as he was, to the Ural Mountains. "If you break all traditions simply because they are traditions, there will be no glue to hold together this new society of yours."

"Maybe I can make the toast without knowing their names," yelled Hippolyte.

"Yes, yes, by all means make the toast," agreed Otto Eppler, the German dentist.

The old man scraped back his chair and swayed uncertainly to his feet. Vasia Timofeyevich Maslov, the lanky photographer, went around the table filling everyone's glass but Melor's to the brim with vodka.

Hippolyte, who was ninety-two years old, tapped a knife against the side of a glass for silence, then cleared his throat. "It falls to me as the oldest revolutionist at the table to raise my glass in welcome to the two comrades who have come to us, come to join the revolution, from across the seas, from—"

"From America, Granddad," prompted Serafima.

"From America," continued Hippolyte.

"Bravo, Granddad," cried Melor.

Tears formed in the old man's eyes. "I had two sons once," he said in his loud voice, "but I lost them to Siberia, one to typhus, one to frostbite." Around the table people began to look at one another in embarrassment. "Vladimir Ilich once warned me that sentimentality is a crime. Maybe, maybe not. Fancy frames," concluded the old man abruptly, "are what we put on pictures of people who die."

The old man sank back into his chair and stared off into space. There was a moment of uncertainty. Then Sergeant Kirpichnikov pounded the table with his fist. "Drink!" he shouted, and he threw back his head and downed his glass in one deft swallow. The others touched glasses and followed his lead

Zander got to his feet. "To be back in Russia, to be

breaking bread with fellow revolutionists—for us it is a dream come to life."

"Enough talk," cried Melor. "Let's eat."

With a laugh Otto Eppler lifted the lid of the stew, which was made of cabbage, potatoes, and some horse-meat bones that Serafima had scrounged from a garbage can outside an officer's mess, and began to serve. Holding the loaf against her chest, Serafima sliced the black bread. Everyone ate in silence, concentrating on the stew. At the far end of the table Ronzha and Appolinaria spoke to each other in undertones. Suddenly Appolinaria pushed away her plate in annoyance. "That's not it at all," she told her husband. "What I say is that everything contains within itself an essence that defies description."

"And what I say," Ronzha argued, "is that the role of the poet is to describe the essence that defies description."

"If something defies description," Zander inquired politely from his end of the table, "how is it possible to find words that will describe it?"

Ronzha elevated his chin slightly and took his first good look at Zander. "The poet is someone who can describe the essence of things in the spaces between the words."

"More stew," called Melor.

"Fancy frames," muttered Hippolyte, "are what they'll put around my picture soon."

Otto Eppler nodded in Ronzha's direction. "He's a poet," he informed Zander as if it explained everything.

"You look like a poet," Tuohy commented good-naturedly.

"And what are you?" Appolinaria challenged Tuohy.

"Why, what I am is a revolutionist," he said.

"You must be familiar with guns, then," Sergeant Kirpichnikov said.

"I have a working knowledge of both ends of them," Tuohy admitted. "My friend too."

"Both ends?" Melor whispered to his mother.

"He means he's been shot at," Serafima explained.

"Everyone in Russia's been shot *at*," Pasha said. "The trick is to be the *shooter*."

"That's what I mean to be," Tuohy said.

Lili looked directly at Tuohy. "You call yourself a revolutionist. But what permits you to do so? Do you look at art differently? Do you listen to music differently? Do you make love differently? Have you freed yourself from the conventional male approach to sex—seduction, erection, emission, sleep? Do you love men? Do you make love to men you love? Do you masturbate without feeling guilty?"

"Do you?" demanded Tuohy.

The princess smiled innocently. "You don't expect me to answer, but I will. I masturbate whenever I feel like it and without a trace of guilt. I have even made love to my machine gun. Literally. I have taken the barrel in my mouth and caressed it with the tip of my tongue—"

"Bravo, Lili," cried Ronzha, the poet. "You have been suitably outrageous."

"Melor, it's past your bedtime," Serafima snapped.

"Since when does a Communist have a bedtime?" whined the boy.

"But you still haven't answered the question," Lili reminded Tuohy. "What permits you to call yourself a revolutionist?"

"What permits anyone around this table to call themselves revolutionists?" Tuohy responded vaguely.

"Appolinaria and I are not revolutionists," Ronzha declared. "Revolutions kill people. We are against the killing of people."

Appolinaria inched closer to Ronzha without touching him. "What comes after violence is not justice," she added, "but more violence."

"And the future?" demanded Sergeant Kirpichnikov. "What about the future?"

"The future," the poet said, "will inspire propaganda where the past inspired—inspires—poetry."

"You and your poetry," grunted Sergeant Kirpichnikov.

"There is nothing evil about someone dominating language," the poet observed evenly.

Hippolyte leaned toward Lili. "What are they talking about?"

"They are discussing what permits someone to call himself a revolutionist," she shouted into his ear.

"As for me," the old man boomed, "it is in my blood. It is in my testicles. In my heart I have been a revolutionist since I slipped handfuls of bread to the tsar's convicts going off to Siberia. I was never anything else."

"How about you, Alexander?" The princess fixed her eyes on Zander.

"I am a revolutionist," he began—he noticed that everyone around the table, including Ronzha and his wife, was hanging on his words— "because of my conviction that we must respect those"—Zander looked directly at the poet—"who have *not* dominated language, who can't express themselves precisely either with words or in the spaces between words; who in their frustration shake their fists at the sky or nervously finger the triggers of stolen rifles. It seems to me that they are trying to tell us something. It is our sacred obligation, before history, before the past *and* the future, to listen."

Ronzha said quietly, "So a revolutionist is someone who listens?"

Zander nodded. "Listens"—he thought of his grandfather—"and when the right moment comes, gives history a push."

"That's as good an answer as any," commented Otto Eppler.

"It is well said, if you ask me," agreed Vasia, the photographer.

"It is one way of looking at things," Lili said grudgingly.

Dear Leon,

Greetings from proletarian Petrograd!

Here is a quick note to let you know I have made it to *my* promised land. You will be hard put to believe this, but coming out of the train station this morning I felt the gravitational pull of Russia through the soles of my shoes. The Russia I knew as a child is not the Russia I have come back to. Too much time has gone

by. Too much of America has seeped into my blood. I
will admit it to you, at moments I am uneasy. I feel
like a stranger in my own home.

But at least I am home!

As for Petrograd, there is a distinct whiff of chaos in
the air. (I saw the body of a thief who had been kicked
to death in the street this morning.) I get the queasy
feeling that the chaos could be clamped over my
mouth like a wad of ether-soaked cotton, and I would
go under. The ground, which gave me such a tug of
welcome when I got here, could open under my feet.

What morbid thoughts. It's late and I am exhausted.
We will resist the chaos-soaked cotton, Leon. Great
things are going to happen here, I feel it in my bones.

I have come to the right place!

> From your brother,
> With love,
> Zander

In the corner of the attic that Lili had assigned to
them, Tuohy sat on his cot, pulling off his boots and
thick socks. Zander, exhausted from his first day in
Petrograd, crawled fully dressed under several army
blankets and rested his head on his folded overcoat.
The voices of Sergeant Kirpichnikov and Serafima drifted
up through the floorboards; they were in a room directly beneath the part of the attic where Zander lay.

"Poems or no poems, there's no place for them under
this roof if they're afraid of violence," shouted Pasha.

"Lili says his poetry is revolutionist," Serafima shouted
back, "and it's her house."

"Her house," mocked the sergeant. "That's a bourgeois way of looking at things if ever I heard one. It's
everybody's house."

"If it's everybody's house," declared Serafima triumphantly, "then it's also the poet's house, whether or not
he is for violence."

"You are full of shit," shouted Sergeant Kirpichnikov.

Serafima burst into a torrent of tears. "When all is
said and done," she managed to say, "you don't need
me."

"I need you."

"I wish to God you did. I wish to God you were crippled and needed me to do up your buttons."

"Bite your tongue, woman!"

Tuohy stamped his bare foot several times on the floorboards.

"Quiet overhead!" shouted the sergeant. "We're trying to sleep down here."

"Say," Tuohy said suddenly. "I wouldn't mind getting my hands on that princess downstairs."

"I can't stop thinking about that old lady beating on the body of the thief," Zander admitted.

Tuohy plucked his cigarette from the holder and stubbed it out on the floorboards. "Revolutions," he said, repeating a line he had heard Trotsky use more than once, "are not to be confused with tea parties." He lay down on the mattress and pulled the blanket up to his chin. "The trouble with you," he remarked, "is that you're ready to die for the revolution, but you're not ready to kill for it."

Zander thought, the trouble with you is that you're ready to kill for it, but you're not ready to die for it. But he didn't say anything.

"Look at it this way," Tuohy said, turning on his side so that his face was only inches from the wall, "the thief got what was coming to him. And his death will serve as an example to others."

After what seemed like an eternity, Zander fell into a twilight state, sure he was awake but actually dreaming. He could make out the sound of hooves of several horses beating on the wooden pavement of the streets. I have to hide from the Cossacks, he thought, tossing in his blanket. He became aware of voices. Two people were yelling at each other. It must be my parents, he figured out, arguing about whether to go on to America without my mother. "Never!" he heard his mother cry— only the voice was not his mother's. It was probably Serafima, arguing with Sergeant Kirpichnikov under the floorboards. Zander opened an eye. Thick gray light indistinguishable from mist filtered through the window in the sloping roof over his head. Tuohy was snoring away on his mattress in the corner. Wide awake now, Zander could still hear the voices arguing. They didn't come from under the floor, but from farther away. A man's voice, pitched high. A woman's voice, frustrated, furious. "Over my dead body!" she shouted. Zander recognized the woman's voice now. It belonged to the princess. "Never!" A door slammed. Boots tramped down the staircase. The front door flew back against its hinges. A whip cracked. And then the sound of horses' hooves again.

2

Sucking nervously on a hand-rolled cigarette, Stalin paced back and forth along the platform under the red and gold triumphal arches. Looking up, he spotted the single headlight of an engine in the distance. He flicked his cigarette onto the tracks. "Here it comes," he shouted.

"Sailors," bellowed a bearded giant petty officer, "stand to attention. Present rifles."

Alexandra Kollontai, a Bolshevik close to Lenin, readied her roses. Molotov pulled a whistle from his pocket and blew three long blasts on it. Outside, a giant mobile spotlight atop an armored car stabbed out into the night overhead.

The train, with red bunting draped across the front of the engine, pulled slowly into the station. There were three passenger cars, and the worried faces of men and women and one child could be seen peering from the windows of the middle car.

"I see him, boys," Stalin yelled, and he headed on the run toward the far doorway of the middle carriage. Kollontai hiked up her skirt and sprinted alongside Stalin; for a moment they seemed to be racing to see who would get there first. Lenin stepped down onto the platform with a bewildered look on his face. Kollontai thrust the bouquet of roses into his hands. Stalin came up and pumped Lenin's hand. The flying squad of bodyguards, led by Sergeant Kirpichnikov and with Zander and Tuohy in their midst, closed in around the group.

In the imperial waiting room, the band struck up "The Marseillaise." The sailors on the platform pounded their rifle butts to the pavement and snapped them smartly up to eye level.

"So I'm not to be arrested after all," Lenin noted dryly. His face was drawn, his eyes tired, his nerves frayed.

Several other leading Bolsheviks, including an eager Molotov, shouldered their way past the bodyguards and pumped their leader's hand. Lenin smiled weakly and raised his peaked worker's cap over his head to salute those who couldn't get close to him. He became aware of the band playing "The Marseillaise." "I thought for a moment I had arrived in Paris," he quipped. Stalin explained that very few of the comrades in Petrograd, and certainly none of the members of the regimental band mustered for the occasion, had even heard of "The Internationale." Frowning, Lenin said, "There are quite a few things we will have to set straight here."

Sergeant Kirpichnikov signaled with a finger, and the bodyguards closed in around Lenin as he stalked off, the balls of his feet slapping against the pavement, to review the sailors. From outside the Finland station came a thundering chorus of hurrahs. To Zander it sounded like waves pounding a shore.

The sailors abandoned discipline and, cheering wildly, flung their caps into the air. Brandishing Kollontai's roses over his head, Lenin—surrounded by the bodyguards—made his way down the platform into the imperial waiting room, which was packed with party members. "I salute you as the vanguard of the worldwide proletarian army," Lenin shouted in a high-pitched voice. Suddenly he spotted Hippolyte, and lunging past his bodyguards he caught the old man in an awkward bear hug. "So you are still alive!" he said.

"I'm hanging on with my fingernails for the revolution you promised," Hippolyte replied.

"It won't be long now," Lenin told the old man.

From a corner of the waiting room Lili yelled, "Long live our Lenin." Vasia Maslov took up the cry, "Long live our Lenin, long live our Lenin." Outside the waiting room hundreds of people, responding to the chant, surged forward and began hammering on the windows.

"Is this part of the program?" Lenin blurted out.

A pane shattered, and another. The noise from the crowd grew louder. "You must speak to them," Stalin told Lenin.

Sergeant Kirpichnikov called, "A flying wedge!" The bodyguards linked arms and led Lenin outside. He stepped through the door of the imperial waiting room into the sickly yellowish glare of the headlights. The roar of the crowd filled the night. Arms reached out of the rim of darkness to touch the Bolshevik leader, to shake his hand. Someone plucked Lenin's cap from his head. The flying wedge fought its way to an armored car parked ten yards away. They reached it and hoisted Lenin up onto it. His head and shoulders jutting from the turret, he made a quick speech. "Comrades . . . worldwide Socialist revolution . . . salute you . . . long live . . ."

Tuohy, sitting on one fender, pounded on the driver's hatch. The armored car's engine revved up. Zander, on the other fender, frantically waved the mob aside. He caught a flash of Lili in one of the headlights, her arm linked through Kollontai's, her face phosphorescent with excitement. "Alexander!" she yelled, but the rest of what she said was lost when the armored car lunged forward.

The crowd scattered, broke up into islands, then individuals. Workers carrying flaming torches raced alongside. A searchlight stabbed out from Peter and Paul Fortress, filling the teeming streets with long, slanting shadows. The armored car crawled along Simbirsk Street, past the Villy Clinic, then crossed the Sampsoniyevsky Bridge to the Old Petrograd side of the city. At every intersection it jerked to a stop and Lenin's torso popped up in the turret. Instantly a crowd gathered and Lenin, his voice strained from yelling, launched into another of his stock speeches.

"Dear comrades, soldiers, sailors, workers . . . greet you as the vanguard . . . Russian revolution has paved the way . . . long live . . ."

"Pssst."

Otto Eppler's head bobbed at the partly open double-door, along with a bottle and two kitchen tumblers. "I offer you a nightcap, yes?" the dentist said formally, bowing Zander into his office. "I forbid you to refuse me. While you were off welcoming the king of Communists, I was pulling a tooth for a Polish diplomat who paid me with this." He thrust an open bottle into Zander's face so that he could read the label. It was in French. Zander could make out the word "cognac." "There is more where this came from," Eppler said. "I am commissioned to make him a false tooth of ivory set into a gold plaque." Eppler hiccuped. "For the comrades I produce teeth in rubberized vulcanite. But for someone who can pay with French cognac I dip—yes?—into my supply of ivory and gold. Why not?"

"Why not?" Zander agreed. They clicked glasses.

Eppler waved Zander to the barber's chair in the middle of the room and settled onto a stool near him. "So. What impression did he make on you?"

Zander sipped his drink. It was every bit as good as the cognac he had tasted at Maud's. "Things will not be the same in Petrograd now that he is here," he told Eppler.

"Exactly what I think. Things will not be the same. That much is evident. But will they get better, yes—or worse?"

"From what point of view?" Zander asked. It was late; he longed for his mattress in the attic.

"From the point of view of us Communists, what else?" Eppler ran his forefinger around the edge of his tumbler thoughtfully. "You are a Leninist, yes?"

"I am a Bolshevik. Given the hierarchical nature of the party, that makes me a Leninist."

"Exactly," cried Eppler triumphantly. "We are Leninists by default. Did you ever stop to consider, young man, young comrade, what our king of Communists has done to this party of ours?"

"I'm not sure I follow you, Otto."

Eppler drew his stool closer and lowered his voice. "Lenin has molded the Bolshevik Party into a *vanguard party*, yes?"

"We are the advance guard—the vanguard—of the entire proletariat," Zander agreed. "What's wrong with that?"

Eppler pressed a forefinger to his lips. "What I say will go no farther than these doors?"

Zander assured him it wouldn't.

Eppler collected his thoughts. "A self-appointed vanguard has come to think of itself as the working class in whose name it speaks. So, first the vanguard party substitutes itself for the entire working class, yes? Then the party organization substitutes itself for the entire party, yes? Then the Central Committee substitutes itself for the party organization, yes? You see where it leads? It is inevitable! One day a single dictator will substitute himself for the Central Committee, yes?" Suddenly Eppler's forefinger flew to his lips again. "This is what our critics say about us. It goes without saying, I personally do not believe a word of it, yes?"

3

Melor carefully wound the length of cord around the homemade wooden top and snapped his wrist. The top went twirling across the floor of the entranceway and bounced, still spinning, off Zander's boot.

"Where's everybody?" Zander asked.

"Comrade dentist's been called to the hospital for an emergency—someone's teeth came to a sudden stop against a pair of brass knuckles," the boy said. He seemed moody, preoccupied; it was evident to Zander that Melor had a chip on his shoulder. He retrieved the top and wound the cord around it again. "Everybody else, including his highness Ronzha"—Melor's way of pronouncing the poet's name indicated there was no love lost between them—"is off one place or another, except me and Granddad Hippolyte, who's got the runs and's afraid to be far from the toilet." The boy jerked at the cord and the top spun off in a long, graceful arc. "You want maybe to see pictures of the princess without no clothes on? It's Vasia who took them. And I know where he keeps them."

"I need a needle and thread and some buttons," Zander told the boy.

Melor persisted. "She got no hair on her cunt."

"How old did you say you were?"

"Twelve, almost, but I seen a lot for my age."

"I guess you have," Zander agreed. "Which is Hippolyte's room?"

The boy gestured with a toss of his head toward the second floor.

Halfway up the stairs Zander turned and called down, "What is it you want to be when you grow up?"

Melor screwed his face as he considered the question. "What I want," he said sullenly, "is to be taken seriously."

Hippolyte was shuffling back to his room from the toilet. "Fifth time today," he said in his loud voice. "What I need is a plug."

"You wouldn't have a needle and thread and some buttons?" Zander asked.

"You'll have to speak up," Hippolyte called.

Zander shouted into his ear, "I need a needle and thread and some buttons."

"Shouting like that makes you feel as if you're far away from me, don't it? Well, you are—about seventy years away, I figure." He cackled like a witch. "How the hell did I get so old so fast? That's what I want to know. Needle and thread I have," said Hippolyte. "Buttons we can get from an old suit which is too big for me."

He shooed Zander into his room, rummaged in a worn leather valise for the old suit, and began cutting away the buttons with a pearl-handled strop razor. "Used to fit me, this suit," he called. "Funny thing how you grow smaller as you grow older."

Looking around, Zander was struck by the number of calendars on the wall. The old man had obviously put up every calendar he could get his hands on. There was a Bolshevik calendar with the cartoon of a fat capitalist smoking a worker squeezed into the form of a cigar. There was a calendar from the local fire brigade with a drawing of the latest motorized fire engines on it. There was one printed up by a boarding stable with water-color paintings of horses. The central bank had distributed a calendar bearing illustrations of the various ruble notes. There was even an English calendar, issued by a steamship company, which was thirteen days ahead of the Russian calendars that were based on the old Russian system. In his mind's eye Zander could imagine Hippolyte making the rounds at the end of every month, tearing off the top page from each of his calendars. Somewhere along the way he had skipped one; a calendar from Central Asia with a picture of pretty peasant women picking cotton was still set to February.

"This one's still on February," Zander said.

"I like the picture, not the month," Hippolyte called. He detached the last button and deposited a handful of them on the table, then produced a small sewing kit with several needles and spools of thread.

Zander threaded a needle and set to work to repair his overcoat. Hippolyte lowered himself into an easy chair that had once been elegant. "Death's not something you think about at your age," he said. "Here I am, ninety-two years old, and not a day goes by, not an hour, not a breath goes down my throat, not a fart comes out of my ass but I think it could be my last—my last day, my last hour, my last breath, my last fart. Not that I hang on to life for life's sake, far from it. Old age is a shipwreck is what the peasants say, and I'm the living proof. No sir, what I breathe for, what I fart for, is to live long enough to see the Socialist revolution sweep across Europe the way Vladimir Ilich promised me it would."

Zander had noticed, when Lenin arrived at the Finland station, that he knew Hippolyte personally. "When did he promise you that?" he asked, intrigued.

"It was in Siberia, in my village of Shushenskoye," Hippolyte recounted. "The new century was a stone's throw away. I was working as a dam builder, and when the bosses discovered it had been built in the wrong bend of the wrong river, a dam breaker. A political exile, one of those slick city lawyers from St. Petersburg, turned up on my doorstep wanting to know if I could rent him a room. That was Vladimir Ilich, of course. He was serving a three-and-a-half-year stint for illegal political activity. I took him in, naturally; I never in my life refused somebody who needed a favor. He was only about twenty-five, but I took to calling him Starik, the old man, because his hair was already getting pretty thin. He spent the entire winter in front of my fireplace reading and copying out passages into a lined notebook. Jesus, he was a methodical son of a bitch, Vladimir Ilich was. I remember he kept the needles in that sewing kit of his threaded with different color thread so one would always be ready when he needed it.

"It all seems like yesterday. Come the first thaw, I'd hitch up my plow horse and we'd set out for Minusinsk, me to trade the pelts I'd trapped during the winter for seed, him to the tavern and the redheaded girl that we later found out was sick—"

"What was wrong with her?" Zander asked, but Hippolyte was off on another tack.

Gazing at the photographs in cheap frames on a table with only three legs, his eyes watered. "Sometimes, I admit it, I get confused. I think this is 1905 and the workers are marching on the Winter Palace carrying icons and images of the tsar. I know it is going to end badly and I try to head them off before the Cossacks open fire, before the blood stains the snow, but nobody listens to an old man who has to go to the toilet a dozen

times the day—" Hippolyte Evgenevich Evremov shook
his head in despair.

"It is not 1905," Zander said softly. "It is 1917. This
time things will turn out differently."

"Speak up," snapped the old man irritably. Suddenly
a desperate look flashed across his face and he heaved
himself out of the chair and tottered off through the
door toward the toilet.

"Mind if we join you?" Tuohy said as he slid onto the
canteen bench next to Arishka. Zander climbed in after
him and nodded to Lili across the table.

"What have you two been up to?" Arishka asked.

"I was baby-sitting for Trotsky's brother-in-law,
Kamenev, when he went over to the Lessner factory
this morning," Tuohy said.

"How'd things go?" Lili asked.

"They listened politely, and gave him a decent hand
when he finished," Tuohy recounted. "Then Kerensky
showed up and denounced Lenin for traveling across
Germany to get to Russia. He even implied that Lenin
was on the kaiser's payroll."

"How did the workers react?" Arishka wanted to
know.

"They gave him an even bigger hand than they gave
Kamenev. Seems to me like they fall for the last line
they hear."

"Which is why we have to get our people out into the
factories more," Arishka said.

"I think we have to come up with a message that is
simpler than the opposition's message," Lili said.

"If there's one thing you can't accuse Lenin of,"
Zander said, "it's lack of an easily understood message."
He was referring, as everyone at the table understood,
to what had become known as Lenin's "April Theses,"
which bluntly called for the overthrow of the provisional government, the destruction of the bourgeois
state, and an end to Russian participation in the Great
War.

"If you want my opinion," Arishka said, "I think
there's something wrong with him."

"What's wrong with lighting a fire under Stalin and the others?" Lili insisted.

"That's not what I meant," Arishka said. "I meant there's something wrong with Lenin physically. I spent two years working as a nurse's aide. And I tell you he has the look of a sick man."

"He does walk a bit funny," Tuohy said in English, "but that doesn't mean he's sick. You saw him yesterday morning, Zander, what do you think?"

Zander had been summoned from the bodyguard pool at midmorning. "I want you to go over to Lenin's apartment and show him one of the posters," Stalin had instructed him. "Maybe he'll realize those of us who stayed in Russia over the years know a thing or two after all."

Lenin had moved into the sixth-floor apartment of his sister, Anna, at Number 52 Shirokaya Street; he slept in the room his mother had used until her death the previous year.

Lenin's wife, Krupskaya, kept Zander waiting in the small entranceway. He could hear Lenin, beyond the door that led to the bedroom, pacing up and down as he dictated. "Revolutions arouse great expectations . . . great expectations . . . you have that? The masses will inevitably . . . inevitably turn to the party they think is best able to meet these great expectations." Another voice, a man's, said, "Whenever you're ready." A moment later Lenin cried out in pain, then cursed. Soon after, a short, well-dressed older man wearing a starched collar and carrying a small leather satchel emerged from the room. He spoke briefly with Krupskaya in an undertone at the front door. Zander thought he overheard the man say something about "arsenic" and "injections." Krupskaya closed the door behind him, a grim look on her face. From beyond the door of his bedroom Lenin had resumed dictating. "In the present situation there is no single party with a majority. The only question, then, is which minority . . . which minority will wind up on top of the heap . . . of the heap."

Krupskaya asked Zander why he wanted to see Lenin.

"Stalin instructed me to show him this," Zander said,

and he flattened the poster on a table so Krupskaya could read it. It had been circulated by the members of the guard of honor that had greeted Lenin at the Finland station. "Having learned that Mr. Lenin came to us by permission of His Majesty the German emperor," it said, "we express deep regret that we participated in his solemn welcome to Petrograd."

"*Mister* Lenin indeed," snorted Krupskaya. "They didn't even have the courtesy to call him *Citizen* Lenin." She rolled up the poster and ushered Zander to the door. "Tell Comrade Stalin there is no purpose in showing him this kind of thing. It will only send him into one of his rages."

"She actually used the word 'rages'?" Lili asked when Zander recounted the story of his errand to Lenin.

"Rages, yes," Zander said.

"That's a curious choice of words," Lili ventured. "Makes you think of a dog with rabies."

The nightspot had reopened after the abdication of the tsar under new management and a new name, The Comedians' Shelter, but the regulars who showed up still referred to it by its original name, The Stray Dog. Because of wartime prohibition, only ersatz coffee or apple juice was served in the café's chipped teacups. Clients paid a twenty-five-ruble entrance fee, and provided their own entertainment when the spirit moved them.

Under a niche in the wall that contained a carved wooden phallus illuminated by a single church candle, Yitzhak Feldstein, a thin, frail Yiddish poet with sunken eyes, pulled a scrap of paper from the breast pocket of his threadbare jacket. "I translated some lines of the American poet Emily Dickinson into Yiddish," he said, and he began to recite them in a singsong voice:

> *Oib ich ken machen eyn hartz gringer,*
> *Dan leb ich nit umzist . . .**

---

*"If I can stop one heart from breaking,
  I shall not live in vain . . .

Vladimir Mayakovsky, his overcoat draped over his shoulders, made a splashy entrance on the arm of Lili Brik, with whom he was having a longstanding affair. Her husband, Osip, trailed after them. Gazing into his mistress's eyes, Mayakovsky intoned one of his love poems.

> If you wish—I'll be irreproachably tender:
> not a man, but—a cloud in trousers.

At midnight Ronzha, who had been polishing a new poem at a corner table, stood up. A hush settled over The Stray Dog. Around the basement, people swiveled to look at him as he began to recite.

> An inexpressible sadness
> opened two enormous eyes
> the vase of flowers woke up
> and splashed its crystal out.
>
> The whole room is invaded
> By languor—sweet medicine!
> Such a tiny kingdom
> has swallowed so much sleep.
>
> Fragments of red wine
> and sunny May weather—
> and, breaking a thin biscuit,
> the whiteness of the slenderest fingers.

A cigarette bobbed excitedly on the lips of a gaunt young lyric poet named Boris Pasternak. "The red wine and the thin biscuit make me think of a church service."

"Why 'tiny kingdom'?" asked Lili Brik thoughtfully. "And how could it 'swallow sleep'?"

"It 'swallows sleep' when its petals close," suggested Ilya Ehrenburg, a young, balding, almost toothless poet sitting at a large table near the lavatory.

"Kingdoms are for tsars," mumbled the theatrical director Vsevolod Meyerhold.

"I like the poem very much," said Pasternak seriously. "I like its mood. I like the mixing of solids and liquids—"

"Ah," said Mayakovsky, discovering something. "Not 'drops' of red wine, but 'fragments' of red wine. Now I see."

Pasternak leaned forward. "What do *you* think of it, Ronzha?"

"I don't know yet," he replied. He seemed drained. "It's for you, my first listeners, to interpret the poem into existence, and then judge it. I am capable of judging only my old poems."

Across the table from Ronzha, Tuohy suppressed a yawn. "Let's get out of here," he whispered to Zander.

"Go if you want to," Zander whispered back. "I'm staying."

Near the lavatory door Ilya Ehrenburg spiked his cup of apple juice from a hip flask and began pontificating about the role of the artist in a violently changing society. Mayakovsky waved his arms theatrically. "In any case," he cried, "revolutions are supposed to destroy the past and give everyone a chance to start over again fresh."

Pasternak shook his head. "For myself, I find it ominous when poetry puts itself at the service of politics. What's to prevent the state from suddenly deciding that society no longer benefits from what a particular poet has to say?"

Appolinaria, sitting on the other side of Tuohy, sighed. "I knew we shouldn't have come," she said. She tugged at Ronzha's elbow and whispered something into his ear, but he could not restrain himself. "Who here can guarantee that these Bolsheviks will manage things more justly?" he asked in a loud voice.

"If we Bolsheviks get our way," Meyerhold blurted out, "it's the people who will manage their own affairs—"

"And I suppose your Lenins and your Trotskys and your Stalins will simply retire to the shores of the Black Sea," Ronzha sneered, and he spat out a line from one of Pushkin's poems.

In the night, beyond the Volga
The robber gang flocked 'round their fires . . .

Meyerhold leapt out of his chair, spilling a glass of apple juice. "If you are insinuating that the Bolsheviks are robber gangs—"

"Robber gangs," shouted the Yiddish poet Feldstein, "is exactly what they are!"

Pasternak pleaded, "Calm yourselves, gentlemen, I beg you . . ."

"I'm not at all excited," Ronzha said excitedly.

"Failure to commit yourself during a time of violent transition should be interpreted as a lack of nerve," flared Meyerhold.

"We shall see who lacks nerve," Ronzha said, trembling with anger. "We shall see who compromises his integrity when the managers of the economy begin to manage art."

The arrival of the prima ballerina Tamara Karsavina, who was starring in Tchaikovsky's *Swan Lake* at the Mariinsky Theater, interrupted the argument. Trailing a black silk cape with a border of white ostrich feathers, she drifted down the stairs to the landing. Several waiters hurriedly cleared an open space in the center of the cellar and placed a large gilt-edged mirror flat on the floor. Karsavina shrugged off her cape, kicked off her slippers, and hiking her skirt above her bare knees began to dance on the mirror.

Tuohy nudged Zander. "Maybe I'll hang around after all," he said.

Appolinaria caught the look on Tuohy's face. "Is it the dancer you are looking at, or the reflection of her body in the mirror?" she asked sarcastically.

Tuohy, who had had several spiked glasses of apple juice too many, smiled at her slyly. "It is in the nature of things for the male of the species to lust after the sight of, a whiff of that holy of holies between the legs of the female of the species," he said, and so saying dispatched a playful hand up her skirt. She drew back with a shriek. Ronzha, who had seen what had happened, leaned over the small table and slapped Tuohy across the face so hard that his chair tipped backward and his head banged against the wall.

Distracted by the scuffle, Karsavina landed on the

mirror with such force that it splintered under her naked feet. "I'm bleeding!" she screamed in French.

Mayakovsky sank to his knees, brought the ball of her foot to his lips, and began sucking the blood from it. In a jealous rage Lili Brik dashed up the stairs from the cellar. The waiters began sweeping up the shards of broken mirror.

"I suppose," Feldstein announced in his singsong voice, "this means we are in for seven years of bad luck."

"If it brings only seven," Ronzha said grimly, "we shall all be very lucky."

4

The princess, normally as passive and pale as death, vibrated with emotion and color. "Get it very straight in your half-Russian, half-Irish skull," she told Tuohy, whose head still ached from the night before. "Not only are they both guests in my house, but he is probably the poetic genius of our age—the kind that comes along once in a hundred years."

"He's antibolshevik," Tuohy insisted sullenly. "He's a prisoner of the past."

Lili stabbed a strand of hair away from her eyes. "He is nourished by the past. He is afraid of change. Who in his right mind isn't? He'll come around when he sees how the new order treats its artists."

"The past is something one escapes with difficulty," Zander commented pointedly.

Lili bridled. "What do you mean by that?"

"I think that in profound ways we are all prisoners of our pasts," Zander explained thoughtfully.

"You think because I was born a princess I can't become an honest revolutionist?"

"What if your poet friend doesn't come around when

he sees how our new order treats its poets?" Tuohy asked.

The princess's tongue flicked at her lips. "In Uzbekistan," she said, "they tell the story of a peasant who took his revenge on someone after a hundred years—because he was in a hurry and couldn't wait longer. If you make another pass at Appolinaria, I'll kill you." Lili produced a tiny nickel-plated pistol from under her skirt and brandished it before Tuohy's nose. "I know very well how to use this."

"I don't doubt it," Tuohy assured her in a respectful voice.

Zander said, "Could you please not wave it around like that?"

"We understand each other, then?" Lili asked Tuohy.

"Any lady armed with a pistol can assume she is understood," acknowledged Tuohy.

They had been summoned to Lili's cubbyhole on the top floor of the Kshesinskaya Mansion when they arrived that morning. The small office was four flights up under a slanting roof with an oval window from which, weather permitting, you could see the skyline of Petrograd. The room reeked of Uzbek incense and exuded an air of elegant disorder. Crude hand-painted Bolshevik posters hung on the walls side by side with icons that Lili had salvaged from a bonfire outside a church. Piled on the floor in no apparent order were dozens of cardboard file boxes with letters and telegrams spilling out of them. A solid silver samovar and a half-dozen crystal glasses stood on a table. Under the oval window was a small love seat that had been stolen from the lounging room of the English Overseas Officers' Club near the Winter Palace. An out-of-focus photograph of a round-faced young girl with wide, frightened eyes and short curly hair was tacked to one wall. Stacked haphazardly on the floor and on the ledge that ran along one wall were several dozen leatherbound books by Pushkin, Chekhov, Tolstoy, Gogol, and Dostoevsky.

Years before, Lili had attended a revolutionist workshop in Bologne organized by Leon Trotsky. She had come away from the three-week course with a basic

knowledge of coding and decoding, and had been ap-
plying this expertise in Bolshevik communication centers ever since. The ciphers Lili worked with were
simple. Each book in her office had been assigned a
code word. The person enciphering a message signaled
which book he was using by starting the text with the
code word. The message itself consisted of numbers
substituted for letters. Each letter in the plain text was
transformed into three numbers separated by dashes.
The first number represented a page in the book, the
second a line on the page, the third a letter on the line.
Enciphering and deciphering was a tedious business,
but unless someone knew which edition of which novel
was being used, the cipher could not be broken.

"I had another reason for getting you both up here,"
Lili admitted. "Stalin suggested I speak to you."

Tuohy was only too happy to change the subject.
"Dear lady, the Irish in me is at your beck and call," he
assured her.

"It is this way," Lili began, clearly troubled. "As
much as I hate to admit it, there appears to be a traitor
living at the Steamboat."

Tuohy glanced at Zander. "You've come to the right
place. Traitors are a specialty of ours."

"Someone stole a letter Lenin sent to the comrades
here before he came back," Lili went on. "It turned up
in a right-wing newspaper, word for word, this morning. Of course we are claiming it is a total fabrication,
but the fact of the matter is that Lenin did write the
letter. Krupskaya enciphered it using Gogol's *Dead Souls*.
The letter arrived late in the day and I took it back to
the Steamboat with me because I had an appointment
with our dentist. I arrived just as everyone was sitting
down to supper. I ate quickly, went upstairs to decipher the letter, and then foolishly left it on a table in
my room when I went downstairs to have my tooth
drilled."

"How can you be sure the traitor saw that particular
copy of the letter?" Zander asked. "Or that someone
didn't get his hands on it here in the mansion the next
day?"

"It was that copy all right. When I transcribed the letter from the cipher, I misspelled the name of the German diplomat who arranged Lenin's passage through Germany. The text printed in today's papers has the same spelling error, proving that someone got his hands on my copy. As for it happening anywhere else, that can also be ruled out. I showed the letter to Stalin the next morning. He read it and then burned it in an ashtray."

"Which narrows it down to the Steamboat," Tuohy said.

"Since the theft of the letter took place before you two arrived in Russia, we know it wasn't one of you," explained Lili.

"I hate to be the one to bring this up," Tuohy started to say, but the princess cut him off. "If you are going to accuse Ronzha or Appolinaria, it is out of the question. I will personally vouch for both of them."

"And who will vouch for you?" Zander asked boldly.

Lili flashed one of her icy smiles. "You have my permission to treat me like the others—as a potential suspect."

"What does Stalin expect us to do?" Tuohy asked.

"He thought you might start by searching all the rooms."

"Was there any discussion about what we do to the traitor when we find him?" Tuohy asked.

"Or her?" Zander added.

"Such a discussion," Lili said pointedly, "is not necessary."

On their way down from the attic, Tuohy asked Zander, "Hey, what is it between you two?"

"Once a princess, always a princess," Zander said.

Tuohy asked, "Do you think she's in love with that poet friend of hers?"

Zander shrugged. "She certainly goes out of her way to protect him."

"We'll start the search with the poet's room," Tuohy announced dryly.

On top of their regular bodyguard assignments, Zander and Tuohy managed over the next several days to search all the Steamboat's rooms. Tuohy was visibly disappointed when the only thing out of the ordinary he found in the room occupied by Ronzha and Appolinaria was an English book reproducing Indian temple friezes. Zander came across a cardboard box hidden under the mattress in Vasia Maslov's room, but it turned out to be filled with dozens of photographs of Lili's naked body. Old Hippolyte had nothing more incriminating in his possession than several tins of pickles with German labels and a translation of the American Declaration of Independence on which someone had scribbled in the margin "High sounding enough, but all men created equal meant all white men." Lili had stashed an ivory dildo in a hamper under her underwear, all of which, Tuohy was intrigued to notice, was pure silk. Sergeant Kirpichnikov had managed to hide a carton of Bulgarian cigarettes behind a loose stone in his chimney. Serafima had hidden several pairs of silk stockings in an old corset. Under Melor's cot was a wedge of American chewing tobacco, an Austrian bayonet, a half-full bottle of Italian hair lotion, and a photograph of the princess that the boy had obviously swiped from Vasia Maslov's collection. Remembering Otto Eppler's late-night criticism of Lenin, Zander made an especially thorough search of the dentist's rooms, but all he turned up was a supply of ivory and gold for making false teeth and, curiously, a packet labeled cyanide.

When Zander and Tuohy reported back to Stalin, he took their failure to link anyone to the stolen letter badly. "It is essential in this kind of affair," he lectured them, "to make an example of the traitor in order to discourage others who might be tempted to follow in his footsteps. For this purpose you don't necessarily have to find the guilty party; anyone will do."

The air was thick with incense. Thin tapers flickered in golden wall brackets. A young priest with a curly beard and black robes arced his brass censer at an old woman. With her fingers curled as if she were plucking feathers from a goose, she crossed herself urgently, then sank to her knees and prostrated herself on the floor, her fore-

head pressed to the cold stones in a sign of total sub-
mission to the church. From behind a lattice in one of
the alcoves, the thin sound of a boys' chorus spiraled up
like smoke to the golden cupolas. The priest challenged
Zander and Tuohy with his censer, swinging it in their
direction as he made the sign of the cross with his free
hand, but they stared back belligerently and he moved
on to older worshippers who were more likely to respond in the prescribed fashion.

They had followed Vasia Maslov, the photographer,
into the church on a hunch. Tuohy's hunch, actually.
"Whoever sneaked into Lili's room when she left Lenin's letter lying around must have been in a hurry to
get out again," he theorized. "What better way to copy
it quickly than by photographing it?"

"Stalin or no Stalin, I absolutely refuse to pin it on
Vasia if he's not guilty," Zander said.

"I'm not suggesting we pin anything on anybody. I'm
only saying being a photographer makes him a prime
suspect."

Standing on tiptoe, peering over the heads of the
worshippers, they could see Vasia now; he was looking
through his viewfinder at a painted life-sized statue of
Christ on the cross illuminated by a single beam of
sunlight angling down from a slit high in a wall.

Vasia quit the church and Zander and Tuohy followed
at a discreet distance as he made his way across the
Nikolaevsky Bridge to the university grounds on
Vasielevsky Island. He stopped to chat with two boys in
high school uniforms, then waved to another in a window. "I'll be right up," he yelled, and entered the
building on the run. In the distance the chimes atop
the slender spires of the Peter and Paul Fortress struck
up "Bozhe Tsaria Khrani"—God Save the Tsar; the
people had dethroned the tsar but they hadn't gotten
around to changing the tune yet.

"Wait here," Tuohy said. He glanced at the window
from which the student had waved down to Vasia. It
was four flights up and directly over the entrance. He
made his way up the stairs into the building. Groups of
boys in student uniforms stood around the lobby en-

grossed in discussions; Tuohy heard someone describe "April" as "ridiculous," though he wasn't sure if he was referring to the month or to Lenin's thesis. On the fourth floor Tuohy found a door with a brass plaque that read STILL LIFE PAINTING, and a card tucked under it containing the word "photography." He opened the door. The room was deserted. A dozen easels faced a small platform draped in red velvet. Light poured through oversized windows. Tuohy began to think that he had miscounted the floors when he heard a muffled moan coming from behind a closed door with a red bulb glowing over it. Another moan emerged from the interior. Tuohy, who considered himself something of an expert on such things, identified it as a definitely sexual sound. Smiling smugly, curious as to what state of undress he would find the girl in, he gripped the knob and yanked the door open.

Vasia was passionately kissing a teenage cadet as he caressed the back of his neck with one hand and the bulge in his tight breeches with the other. He jerked his head around in alarm, recognized Tuohy, and stared at him with pure hate in his eyes.

They disposed of the less serious transgressions first. Serafima accused Hippolyte Evremov of clogging the flush toilet with newsprint, which was cut into strips and kept handy for hygienic purposes.

"How do you know it was me?" yelled the old man.

"You use the toilet more than any three people combined," Serafima yelled back.

"That's not proof," sneered Hippolyte.

"He's right," said the Steamboat's newest boarder, a demolition expert named Alyosha Zhitkin. "It could have been any one of us."

"Accusation dismissed for lack of evidence," said the princess from the head of the table. "What's next?"

Next was the case of the missing cat.

"It's the gray one with the white spot on the tip of its right ear," Lili said. "I'm not accusing anyone—I'd just like to know what became of her."

Old Hippolyte maliciously suggested that Serafima's

son, Melor, had probably sold it to the local butcher who, according to rumor, passed off cat meat as rabbit delicacies imported from France; as few Russians had ever tasted either, they could not tell them apart.

Sergeant Kirpichnikov, responding to Serafima's kick under the table, leapt to Melor's defense. "Accusing someone without evidence," Pasha said, "is the mark of a wrecker of the new order, as opposed to a builder."

"Me a wrecker!" Hippolyte exclaimed, his eyes bulging innocently. "After all that I've done for the party?"

"I agree with Pasha," Alyosha Zhitkin said calmly. The demolition expert, a thin man with a neatly trimmed black goatee, chain-smoked cigars hand-rolled in a twist of newspaper and packed with strong Bulgarian tobacco. When he talked, the ever-present cigar bobbed comically on his lower lip. "It will be a tragic day for our party and for our country," he continued, "when someone can denounce another person without providing the slightest proof."

"There is proof," Hippolyte cried indignantly.

"Then name it," Appolinaria demanded.

"Why, the cat's missing!" cried the old man.

"And you call that proof," sputtered Serafima.

"Accusation dismissed for lack of evidence," the princess said. "What else do we have?"

"What we have," announced Otto Eppler, his German accent more guttural than usual, "is Comrade Tuohy's accusation against Comrade Maslov."

"I won't have any part of this," announced Ronzha, getting up and heading for the door.

"Nor will I," said Appolinaria. "It's disgraceful to drag a man through the mud because of his sexual preferences." She followed Ronzha out, slamming the dining room door behind her.

"Are you sure you want to go through with this?" Lili asked Tuohy.

Vasia Maslov, his face contorted, stared at the ceiling without saying a word. Zander said to Tuohy in a low voice, "It's *privatsache*, Atticus. It's no one's business. Nobody calls you to account for how you make love, or with whom you make it."

"Homosexuality isn't compatible with socialism, or with being a Bolshevik," Tuohy said sternly. "I don't like this any more than you do, but you're all being sentimental. You know what Lenin said about sentimentality—he said it is no less a crime than cowardice in war."

"As long as you're quoting Lenin," Lili said, "I want to remind you of something else he said. Love, by which he clearly meant sex, has been ennobled by socialism and made as free as a glass of water."

"Still," muttered Otto Eppler, "nobody wants to drink from the gutter."

"If it is true about Vasia," Hippolyte said in his booming voice, "it is unmanly and unbolshevik, and our house committee should deal with it before the higher organs of the party have a chance to."

"Why let others wash our dirty linen in public?" Sergeant Kirpichnikov agreed.

"It is also a question of security," Tuohy argued. "If I caught Vasia in a homosexual act, someone else could catch him at it also, and that someone might use the information to blackmail him—to turn him into a spy for our enemies."

"I'd kill anyone who tried to blackmail me," Vasia declared.

"It seems to me," said Alyosha Zhitkin, his cigar glued to his lower lip, "that the question before us is not without interest. Is there a place in our scheme of things, in this socialism we are constructing, for homosexual love?"

"You all know how I feel about women making love to women and men making love to men," Lili remarked. "I am a follower of Lenin because he proposes to set us free—from economic straitjackets, from sexual straitjackets too."

"Still," cried old Hippolyte, "a pederast is a pederast . . ."

"If every Socialist was a homosexual," Serafima put in, "there would be no baby Socialists. Then what would become of socialism?"

"I believe in free love as much as the next man,"

Pasha maintained, "but there's the matter of what's normal."

"And who decides what's normal?" Zander asked quietly.

Vasia sneered. "Tuohy here decides, that's who."

"Someone has to decide," Tuohy said, unperturbed. "Otherwise the matter doesn't get decided."

"We decide," Alyosha Zhitkin said firmly, "right here, right now, at this meeting of our house committee."

"Normal is . . . normal!" insisted Sergeant Kirpichnikov. He looked toward Serafima for support, but she seemed confused.

"Back in New York," Zander said, "back in the sweatshops of the Jewish ghetto, a *normal* workday is twelve hours. And a *normal* salary for that day is three or four dollars. And a *normal* vacation doesn't exist. It's *normal* for a worker who is injured on the job to be laid off without salary until he is well enough to work again."

"Zander's making a good point," Alyosha Zhitkin said. "What's normal to some isn't necessarily normal to others."

"Look," Zander continued, "the aim of Socialists is to create a society, an atmosphere, in which men and women can express their innermost selves freely. If a man feels he needs to make love to another man in order to express himself sexually, where is the harm as long as nobody is forced to go along with him?"

Serafima said, "It's true he didn't hurt anyone . . ."

Sergeant Kirpichnikov shrugged. "In Siberia some youngsters begin by, excuse the expression, fucking chickens because there aren't enough women to go around. Everybody knows about it, but nobody ever says anything about it being antisocialist."

"Can you speak louder?" shouted Hippolyte.

Tuohy said, "There's still the matter of security. What if somebody tries to blackmail him?"

"Who can blackmail him," Alyosha Zhitkin asked, "if we all know he makes love to men and don't give a damn?"

"I vote we put it to a vote," announced Lili. "All

those who think that there is a place in a Socialist society for homosexual love raise their hands."

Zander, Alyosha Zhitkin, and Lili immediately raised their hands. Otto Eppler hurriedly followed suit. Serafima glanced at Sergeant Kirpichnikov, and they both raised their hands at once. Hippolyte shouted, "Since I can't hear, I vote with the majority," and he raised his hand too. Everyone looked at Tuohy.

"I'm against," he said. "I think you're making a mistake."

"Well, that's over with," Alyosha Zhitkin said with relief.

Outside, Tuohy muttered to Vasia, "You haven't heard the end of this."

"Fuck you too," Vasia retorted.

5

The Mercedes, drawn from the Bolshevik automobile pool, had seen better days. It originally belonged to a wealthy Swedish businessman who had crammed his wife and children and their trunks onto a horse-drawn sleigh and dashed off across the snow for Vyborg as soon as he got wind of the tsar's abdication. The car, abandoned on the edge of a frozen-over canal, had fallen into ruin. A Bolshevik mechanic, a deserter from the ambulance corps, had jury-rigged a carburetor swiped from a carelessly parked Pierce Arrow, and had replaced the rusting exhaust system with one from a wrecked American Lincoln that had skidded into a horse-drawn artillery piece. As a result, the Mercedes ran, but jerkily and with periodic backfires.

"I missed what you said," Zander told Lili after one particularly loud backfire.

She kept her eyes glued to the road ahead. "I started to ask you what it was about me that rubs you the wrong way. Everyone at the Kshesinskaya Mansion, everyone at the Steamboat, accepts me as a comrade. The fact that I was born into an aristocratic family is as unimportant as the fact that Pasha Kirpichnikov was born into a peasant family or Otto Eppler into a German family. Only you seem to hold my birth against me."

"I suppose," Zander heard himself say, "it is difficult for me to believe that someone who never experienced poverty can be a serious revolutionist."

The Mercedes backfired again.

Lili caught up with an open army truck crammed with recruits who, spotting a woman at the wheel of the automobile behind them, began to make suggestive gestures. "Here are your peasants," she told Zander, "straight off the farms. Do you really think they know more about being a revolutionist than I do?"

"Any one of them knows more than you do. Any one of them knows what hunger is, what cold is, what humiliation is, what condescension is, what dirt is, what it means to break your back getting in the harvest before the weather turns only to have most of it confiscated by the aristocrats who own the land." He couldn't restrain himself now. "You play with revolution the way a child plays with a new toy—only waiting for something better, something newer, something more stimulating, to come along."

Lili honked her horn irritably and swerved past the truck. "You are an incredible snob," she told Zander. After a while she added, "You are angry with me because you are afraid to admit you want to go to bed with me."

Boom! The Mercedes backfired again; some peasant women herding emaciated cows along the side of the road with long birch branches leapt away in fear. "I have my obsessions," Zander admitted tiredly, "but your body is not one of them."

"Name your obsessions—name one."

Zander regarded her profile; he couldn't deny that she was extraordinarily beautiful. "I am obsessed with the central question every revolutionist must deal with—

how much suffering you have the right to inflict on the present generation in order that future generations may lead freer lives."

"It is a question that interests me too," Lili said defensively.

"It only *interests* you. It doesn't *haunt* you. It doesn't *consume* you. Millions will die painful deaths, or live painful lives—and you are only *interested*."

"People like you are dangerous."

"People like me are dangerous to people like you."

Vasia, sound asleep in the backseat, his fur hat pulled tightly over his ears, stirred. "Are we almost there?"

"Go back to sleep," Lili said curtly. "I'll let you know when we arrive."

On the outskirts of Tsarkoe Selo, some twenty miles from Petrograd, Lili got fed up with the backfiring. "We'll go on foot from here," she informed her passengers. They left the car in the shade of a fir tree and entered the town under the triumphal arch. They walked past the small wooden house in which Pushkin had lived after his marriage, skirted the long, low rococo palace built by the Empress Elizabeth to eclipse Versailles, and eventually came to the Alexander Palace, the tsar's summer residence and current prison.

An army checkpoint stood about a hundred yards from the entrance. The princess presented her pass to the soldier on duty outside the low wooden guard hut.

The soldier turned Lili's pass in his hand. It was obvious that he couldn't read. "It is signed by Comrade Stalin," Lili said helpfully.

"The Stalin who is a Bolshevik?" the guard asked.

"That Stalin."

"Ha! You are all Bolsheviks, then. I, too, am a Bolshevik—I think."

Zander asked, "What do you mean 'think'?"

The young soldier smiled broadly, revealing a row of decaying teeth. "When the Bolshevik recruiter passed by here, I made my mark in his notebook. He talked about ending the war and giving the land to the peasants, and I am all for that."

The guard rang the bell summoning the duty officer.

A colonel came strutting from an outbuilding, impatiently tapping a riding crop against his canvas breeches.

"We have come," Lili explained to him, "on the authority of the Bolshevik representatives in the Soviet, to verify that the Citizen Romanov, formerly known as Tsar Nicholas, along with the various members of his family, are in fact here, and to confirm under what conditions, and, most important, under what security arrangements, they live."

The colonel, who had a livid hairline scar over his right eye, tightened his jaw muscles at the mention of the word "Bolshevik," but otherwise never uttered a sound. He adjusted a pince-nez and read the pass that Stalin had signed as a member of the Executive Committee of the Soviet. Then he turned on his heel and retraced his steps, disappearing into the outbuilding.

"What are we supposed to do now?" demanded Vasia, polishing the lens of his Krugeñers "quarter-plate" Delta Patronen with a piece of silk.

"He is goddamn fucking rude, if you want my opinion," Lili said.

"You have to excuse him, your excellencies and madam," the soldier said. His open, honest peasant face stared at Lili in curiosity; he had never before been in the presence of a lady who cursed like a man. "The colonel comes from a line regiment where the senior officers were murdered by Bolsheviki during the uprising against the one we now call Citizen Romanov."

A young subaltern wearing a spotless white belted blouse emerged from the outbuilding and beckoned to Lili and the others.

"Does *he* at least talk to Bolsheviks?" Lili muttered under her breath.

"This one's so wet behind the ears he thinks horse sense is something only horses have," sneered the guard.

Inside the palace, Lili, Zander, and Vasia found themselves in a "mud room" for the guard contingent; the walls were lined with sabers and scarlet cloaks hanging from hooks. "Citizen Romanov has been invited to meet you in the music room," the young officer said. He spoke with a slight lisp that revealed, if his demeanor left any doubt, his upper class origins; his lieutenant's commission had been purchased, not earned.

"Invited?" Lili flicked a wisp of hair behind her ear in irritation. "Is his status here such that he is *invited* to attend meetings with representatives of the Petrograd Soviet?"

The young officer realized his mistake. "*Invited* in a manner of speaking. His royal . . . what I mean to say is that Citizen Romanov understands perfectly well that invitations are extended as long as they are not declined."

They followed the young officer through a series of carpeted corridors. At one point they passed a large bay window that looked out onto an enclosed garden in which a giant sailor was pushing a young boy around in a wheelbarrow. They could hear the boy squealing in delight as the sailor made as if to spill him to the ground. "That is Crown Prince Alexei," Lili told Zander. To one side of the garden, three teenage girls wearing white lace dresses and white smocks and short fur-lined capes were playing croquet. "The one swinging the mallet is Anastasia. To her left is her sister, Marie. Behind her is the third sister, Tatiana." A fourth girl leading a dog on a leash came in through a small door in the garden wall. "And that one is Olga."

The young officer's eyebrows lifted in surprise. "You know the members of the royal family on sight?"

"That is why I was selected for this assignment," Lili said. And looking directly at Zander she said, "When I was very young I traveled in aristocratic circles. Anastasia was a childhood acquaintance of mine. She once spent two weeks vacationing on my grandfather's estate. We slept in the same room. Another time I took tea with her and her family in the Winter Palace."

The man known as Citizen Romanov appeared punctually. As the clock in the music room chimed the quarter hour, a gentleman in waiting flung open the double-doors to the room and the former tsar stepped through. With a wave of his hand he dismissed the attendant, who stepped back through the doors and closed them soundlessly after himself.

Citizen Romanov had aged considerably in the last

few months and barely resembled the photographs of him that Zander had seen. His face was thin, his cheeks sunken, his shoulders stooped. His eyes appeared to struggle to bring things into focus. He blinked a great deal, as if from a nervous tic. He wore ordinary army trousers tucked into elegant felt boots, and a white belted officer's tunic with stains on the sleeves; he spent a good deal of his waking hours sawing firewood for exercise. When he saw Vasia setting up his camera on a tripod, he turned to the lieutenant and said reproachfully, "If you had informed me they intended to take photographs I would have changed my clothes."

"The photographs, Citizen Romanov," Lili explained, "are not for publication, but only for members of the Soviet who are eager to see evidence that you are still here."

"And where would I be?" Nicholas asked haughtily. He sat down abruptly on a stool in front of the grand piano, swiveled a half turn, and came to a stop facing his visitors, who were ranged before him on an upholstered couch in the middle of the room. He crossed his long legs, removed a cigarette from a silver case, tapped it several times to pack the tobacco, and lighted up.

"There have been rumors," Lili said vaguely. She was referring to a story that the British ambassador in Petrograd had offered Nicholas asylum in England. Plans had been made to send the members of the royal family by train to Murmansk, where they would embark on a British man-of-war. At the last moment the Soviet got wind of it, raised a storm of protest—and sent Lili to Tsarkoe Selo to confirm that Citizen Romanov was still there.

The former tsar laughed self-consciously. "I have heard those rumors—that I have flown off on my magic carpet to one of my cousin's castles in England." Nicholas shook his head at the absurdity of the idea. "If I am to go anywhere, I would much prefer my estate in the Crimea. But it is not clear that I am to be given a choice in the matter." Nicholas sucked on his cigarette and exhaled through his nostrils. "I want to ask you what is being done about the complaint I lodged with the colonel of the guard contingent the day before yesterday."

Lili said, "We have not come here to discuss—"

"I am told that a gang of soldiers was responsible," Nicholas plunged on. For the first time he appeared to be fully interested in the conversation. "They pried Rasputin's coffin out of the niche in the chapel, removed the body, soaked it in petrol, and burned it on a pyre of logs. I have so far managed to keep the news from my wife and the children, but they will learn of it eventually. Ah, my poor Rasputin. Murdering him wasn't sufficient—they had to desecrate his body. I absolutely insist that those responsible be identified and severely punished."

"Citizen Romanov, look this way," Vasia instructed Nicholas. The former tsar swiveled a quarter turn toward the camera, his eyes heavy-lidded and almost closed, and Vasia pushed the plunger exploding the phosphate. The flash of light made Nicholas wince.

He swiveled back to face Lili. "About my complaint."

"It will be taken up by the appropriate organs of the Soviet," she assured him. "Do you have any comments to offer on the way you or your family are being treated?"

"Comments? No, no comments. Everyone is very courteous, very correct. I would like access to more books . . ."

"Are you and the members of your family in good health?"

"I suppose you can say we are in good health, yes."

"How do you spend your time here?"

Zander noticed Nicholas squinting in Lili's direction as if she had stirred a memory. "I cut firewood," Citizen Romanov said. His eyes opened wider. "I teach geography and history to young Alexei. I read a great many . . . Am I mistaken in thinking that you are somehow familiar to me? Have we met before?"

Vasia's flash of phosphate exploded as he took a photograph of the profile of the former tsar. Startled, Nicholas turned to Vasia and coldly asked, "Are you finished?"

Vasia began dismounting the camera from the wooden tripod. "I have what I came for," he told Lili.

Citizen Romanov, distracted by the last photograph, forgot his question to Lili. "Where was I?" he asked.

"I think we also have what we came for," Lili told the young officer. She rose and started toward the door; her abrupt departure was meant to bring home to Nicholas that he was there at *her* pleasure. Zander got up to follow her.

Nicholas, left sitting on the piano stool, called after them, "How long am I to be kept prisoner here, can you at least tell me that much?" The question opened the flood gates. "I don't mean to offend the new authorities in Petrograd, far from it. But what purpose does it serve . . . I have legally and formally abdicated . . . I have even abdicated my son's claim to the throne . . . the boy is not well, you know . . . hemophilia . . . he will have enough trouble leading a normal life without taking on the responsibilities of tsar . . . it is not that we are not well treated . . . it is the uncertainty . . . yes, the uncertainty . . . we are not unmoved by the hostility to our person evident in certain circles . . . I am not making accusations . . . not complaining . . . merely stating facts . . ."

Back in the mud room, they were surprised to see sandwiches and cider set out on a table. Several officers, all wearing belted white tunics, all young, lounged against the walls. "The sandwiches are for you," one of them said. Zander whispered to Lili that they should leave right away in order to cover some of the route before darkness fell. But she said they couldn't very well refuse this show of hospitality.

When they finally returned to the Mercedes, they discovered that one of its tires was flat and the tools necessary to put on the spare were missing. Vasia eventually managed to borrow tools from the driver of an army truck delivering firewood to the guard barracks, but by the time they had changed the tire and returned the tools, the sun was sinking out of sight behind the forest of white birches surrounding Tsarkoe Selo. They discussed whether to stay the night and start back the next morning; driving at night with the road in the state it was could easily result in a broken axle. Vasia was all for staying over, but Lili and Zander had had enough of each other's company and outvoted him. Lili switched on the headlights and, maneuvering the automobile around the potholes she could see, headed back toward Petrograd.

They had been on the road for ten minutes when two armored automobiles, their sirens screaming, exhaust streaming from their tail pipes, raced past the Mercedes. Moments later a Rolls-Royce and a Pierce Arrow, both running with dimmed headlights, overtook them. Lili slowed down to escape the dust kicked up by the speeding cars.

"There's quite a lot of traffic for the hour," Vasia commented uneasily. "What do you think it means?"

"Maybe something's up in Petrograd," Lili said casually, but she gripped the steering wheel tensely and peered into the dust swirling up in their path.

And then suddenly, at a bend in the road, the headlights of the Mercedes, penetrating the dust, settled on something solid. The armored cars had pulled up in the middle of the road, blocking it. Their headlights flicked on now, blinding everyone in the Mercedes. Lili gasped, braked the automobile, and threw the stick shift into reverse—but two other cars, roaring out of a forestry road, jammed up behind the Mercedes. Zander grabbed his pistol from its wooden holster; he caught a glimpse of Lili clawing desperately at the pocket of her overcoat for hers.

Outside, someone leaned on a horn. There were cries and oaths as a half-dozen men in white-belted tunics slid down the embankment on either side. In an instant the Mercedes, pinned in the high beams of eight headlights, was surrounded by men pointing pistols through the windows. One heavyset officer leveled a machine gun that he braced on his hip; Zander caught the glint of light bouncing off the bullets in the ammunition belt that trailed to the ground.

In the glare of the headlights the attackers were only silhouettes. "Don't shoot, for God's sake," Vasia cried from the back seat.

"Roll down the windows and throw out your weapons," a voice ordered.

Lili fingered her nickel-plated pistol. "They're going to kill us anyway—we might as well not die like lambs." But her tone was uncertain; she looked to Zander for confirmation.

"If they were going to kill us, they would have started shooting from the woods when we stopped," he said.

"You have ten seconds to do as we say," the voice called from the darkness.

"The food they put out for us. The flat tire." Lili shook her head in frustration. "If we had started back when you wanted to—"

"You couldn't have known," Zander said.

Vasia yelled, "I'm surrendering." He clawed at the handle and rolled down the window. A gust of icy air filled the Mercedes as he tossed the pistol he kept in his camera bag to the ground. Lili shrugged in resignation and followed Vasia's lead. Zander reached across Lili and threw his pistol out her window. The doors jerked open. Rough hands pulled the three of them from the Mercedes. Someone laughed viciously. Motors coughed, then started up. The officer holding the machine gun wedged the tip of the barrel into Lili's chest and spit in her face. Someone brought a thick woolen stocking stuffed with pebbles down on Zander's skull.

Zander woke up on the floor of an armored car, face-down, his hands bound behind his back with wire at both the wrists and elbows. The car sped along the road; with each pothole Zander's face banged against the metal floorboards. He thought he felt blood trickling down the side of his cheek. A searing point of pain stabbed through his head—and he passed out again.

The next time he regained consciousness, several officers were half-pushing, half-pulling him down a flight of stone steps. He thought he heard Lili's voice somewhere ahead of him saying "Fuck you, you son of a —" but the world began spinning like Melor's top and he pitched forward into the darkness and fainted.

When he regained consciousness again he found himself in a twilight world, neither completely awake nor completely asleep. He was bound to a wooden beam in a room so devoid of light that he had the impression he was adrift in space. His head throbbed with the regularity of a pulse. From time to time he heard scurrying sounds, as if several rats were darting between holes. Eventually he heard a faint sob, and he whispered into the darkness, "Lili? Vasia?"

"Alexander?"

Lili's voice. But he was so disoriented he wasn't sure if he had heard it or imagined it.

The next time he awoke it was to find someone sponging his face with icy water. "Drink," a voice whispered. The sponge was squeezed against his bone-dry lips and water trickled down his throat. The man with the sponge murmured under his breath: "Yea, though I walk through the valley . . ."

"Priest, go peddle your prayers elsewhere." Lili's voice again. This time Zander was sure of it. "Here, we are all dead people," she said bitterly.

"No, no, they don't mean to kill you," the priest whispered. As Zander's eyes became accustomed to the darkness, he began to make out the short, cowled figure. "They mean to . . . hurt you . . . to hurt two of you and let the third drive the others back to Petrograd . . . they want to terrorize the Bolsheviks," the priest said.

"Hurt? How hurt?" Vasia asked, but if the priest answered him, Zander never heard it. Sagging into his bindings, he felt consciousness slipping away.

"Alexander," Lili called. "Alexand . . . Al—"

He awoke to a half-dozen kerosene lamps casting a yellow light across a room filled with officer cadets in white-belted tunics. Zander realized he was in a basement coal storage room; on one side were partitioned bins filled with coal, and above each a wooden chute that led to a small shuttered window. The walls crept with shadows. Vasia was tied to one beam, Lili to a second, and Zander to a third, facing them.

The colonel, brandishing a curved cavalry saber in his gloved hand, turned toward Vasia. "Have pity, have pity," Vasia sobbed as the colonel cut away his suspender buttons. Vasia's trousers sagged to his ankles.

One of the young officers holding a kerosene lamp caught sight of Zander's open eyes. "This one's conscious, my colonel," he reported.

"Let him watch then," sneered the colonel.

"You are pigs," cried Lili, straining against the ropes that held her to the beam, "to kill a man in cold blood."

The colonel's saber nicked away the buttons holding up Vasia's underpants. "Who would take notice of another dead Bolshevik?" he asked rhetorically. Several of the young officers snickered. The point of the colonel's saber circled Vasia's limp penis. He wielded the weapon with the precision of a razor blade. "But a wounded Bolshevik . . ."

Vasia gaped in terror at the silver saber. "You wouldn't do that? Oh, God, you wouldn't—"

"A mutilated Bolshevik . . ." The scar above the colonel's eye burned bright red.

"You are a beast," blurted Lili.

The colonel lifted the tip of Vasia's penis with his gloved fingers and brought the saber down.

"*Aiiiiiiiiiiiiiiiii!*"

The colonel turned to the officers, some of whom had paled; one particularly young officer vomited into a coal bin. "This is our answer to those who want to take Mother Russia out of the war," declared the colonel. "They are cowards—they have no need of their manhood. In any case, I have only circumcised him, in a manner of speaking."

With the blade of his saber he cut through the rope binding Vasia's hands. Vasia, whimpering like a wounded animal, collapsed onto his knees and brought the tails of his shirt to the raw wound to staunch the flow of blood.

The colonel turned to the princess. The tip of his saber plucked away the top three buttons of her shirt, then pulled it open to expose one white breast. The cold steel caressed her nipple. Inhuman sounds emerged from the back of Lili's throat.

Zander, straining against his bindings, tried to remember what the priest had said . . . something about hurting two and letting the third take the others back to Petrograd. Pain filled his skull. He felt as if it were cracked and his brains were seeping out with his thoughts. Then the fog lifted and what he had to do became perfectly clear to him.

"Your colonel is insane," Zander announced in a weak voice. The young officers looked at him, surprised to hear him speak. "He is also a coward," Zander taunted. "He is comfortable attacking a woman who is tied and helpless. He doesn't have the courage to face a man."

Lili stared at Zander. "You have no right to take on yourself what is meant for me—"

The colonel, his features lost in the shadows, only the gleam in his eyes visible, turned slowly away from Lili.

Zander started to go under again. "You are—a sadist—a coward," he mocked as the colonel advanced on him.

Lili cried, "Pig, come back," but she saw that the colonel had his eyes fixed on Zander. "*I detest you!*" she cried—not at the colonel, but at Zander.

"More light here," the colonel ordered curtly. One of the officers approached with a kerosene lamp. The colonel's saber cut away Zander's suspender buttons, then his fly buttons. His trousers dropped to the ground. Across the room Vasia sobbed softly.

"If you are one of those Bolshevik Yids, already circumcised," hissed the colonel, "I will cut the whole thing off."

Trembling, the young officer held the lamp closer to Zander's crotch. "He's a Yid all right."

The colonel grabbed the lamp and placed it at Zander's feet. Then he reached down and took hold of Zander's penis. "Tell your friends in Petrograd," he snarled, "that before we are through we are going to whittle off every Bolshevik cock in the country."

Zander opened his mouth and screamed, but the

sound was drowned out by the explosion, though he couldn't tell if it originated inside or outside his head. Then there was a ripple of echoes that faded away, leaving nothing but the blackness and the emptiness of his broken imagination.

6

"**Y**ou've got to speak up, sonny, if you expect me to hear you," Hippolyte Evgenevich shouted.

Melor was afraid to yell because he didn't want anyone else to overhear the conversation. He cupped his hands around his mouth and funneled the words into the old man's ear. "You maybe want to buy a picture without no clothes on of the Princess Lili?"

Hippolyte's eyes narrowed in suspicion. "And where would you get your dirty little hands on such a thing?"

"Where I got it," Melor informed him haughtily, "is my secret. You want to buy or you don't want to buy, which one is it?"

"I'll have to see the merchandise before I can make a decision."

Melor screwed up his face as he gave the matter some thought, then reluctantly reached under his shirt and handed over the photograph to Hippolyte. A lascivious smile competed with the wrinkles on the old man's features. "I will give you a ruble in exchange," he finally announced, and he began to fumble in his purse for a coin.

"One *stinking* ruble!" Melor's fledgling business instinct was in full flight. "That's exploit . . . exploit . . ." Melor had trouble remembering the word. "That's exploit*eration*, is what it is. One ruble! Why, she even got no pubic hair on her cunt."

"Two rubles then," snapped the old man irritably. "I

am buying this only because it should not be in the hands of a minor."

"Sure, Granddad," laughed Melor, pocketing the money and skipping toward the door. "You're doing it to give the proletariat a hard-on, don't I know it."

Hippolyte threw the bolt on the door as soon as the boy was out of it, and settled into the seat near the window to study the photograph. He held it at arm's length, straining to bring it into focus. Lili was a looker, there was no doubt about it. Her eyes, with their slight Asian cast, stared directly at the camera, as if challenging it to a contest of wills. Her breasts were flat, with large nipples, and another man might hold that against her, but Hippolyte had always been partial to small-breasted women. As for the lack of pubic hair, it brought back, in a flash flood of memories, the time he had lost his virginity. He had been a tall, lean, laconic twenty-year-old prospecting for gold in the Siberian wilderness when he seduced the illegitimate daughter of the expedition's cook, a scrawny girl who claimed to be fourteen, though everyone suspected her of adding a year or two to her age. Staring now at the photograph of Lili, Hippolyte tried to summon the memory of *that* erection, but even so simple an act seemed beyond his capacity. Not that he regretted the failure. It seemed to him to be the single advantage to old age. When he had been young, so many things—everything!—had been imbued with its sexual side. With old age this utter dependency on sex as stimulant faded away. Everyday events, not to mention people, appeared in a quieter, saner light. He liked women for their comradely qualities rather than for their profiles, or their availability. No longer obsessed with undressing in his imagination every woman he came across, he could actually pay attention to what they said. Always assuming he could hear it. Ah, if only he had enough money to afford the solid brass ear trumpet he had seen for sale in the old marketplace behind the Kazan Cathedral, he wouldn't have to keep asking people to speak up. To hear an entire conversation instead of an occasional phrase, to know what he was voting for and not just raise his hand with the majority—this would be better than all the erections he had ever had put together.

He glanced again at the photograph of Princess Lili. It gave him an idea! Why hadn't it occurred to him sooner? The photograph of the sister of Prince Yusupov, the man who shot Rasputin, naked as the day she came into the world, might have a value to someone. Lili herself would never find out about it. Even if she did she would probably not mind as long as the cause was a good one.

Hippolyte carefully slipped the photograph into the inside breast pocket of his suit jacket and began to lace up his high shoes. If he believed in God, which he didn't, he would have said that the photograph of the naked princess was heaven sent.

Except for some old people scavenging rotten fish from the garbage bins, the marketplace behind the Kazan Cathedral was almost deserted; the vegetables and live chickens and fresh fish that had trickled in from the countryside surrounding Petrograd had long since been sold, and the only stalls that remained were those offering used household articles, and bridles and saddles and medals pawned by hungry soldiers. Hippolyte sidled up to the stand with the solid brass ear trumpet, picked up some cylinders from a player piano, and absently began to turn them in his hand.

"Don't finger the merchandise unless you are a buyer," rasped the merchant behind the counter, a very fat Uzbek in a tattered business suit and a squarish embroidered skull cap.

"Speak louder," Hippolyte called, cupping his own hand around his ear.

"I said, don't finger the merchandise," yelled the Uzbek, "unless you are a buyer."

"What if I'm a trader?" inquired Hippolyte hopefully.

The fat man bared his teeth like an animal anticipating a kill. "Everything depends on what you have to trade, doesn't it?"

Hippolyte beckoned the Uzbek into the corner and drew the photograph of Lili out of his breast pocket.

The Uzbek slipped a pair of gold-rimmed spectacles over his nose and studied it. A slow, slurred hiss seeped from between his front teeth.

"This is a photograph of the princess—" Hippolyte began, but the Uzbek cut him short with a wave of his hand.

"It has no value, but I will give you one roll from the player piano for it anyway."

Hippolyte shook his head vigorously. "No, no—"

"Two rolls then," shouted the Uzbek, "but that's my final offer."

"How would I hear a player piano?" demanded Hippolyte in frustration.

It dawned on the Uzbek what the old man really wanted. "The ear trumpet is worth much more than a photograph."

Hippolyte's face fell. He started to slip the photograph back into his jacket pocket.

"Let me see it again," called the Uzbek. He held the photograph up to the light and regarded it with bulging eyes. His fat nostrils flared, as if he had gotten a whiff of the perfume of a woman. "Out of deference to your age and physical condition," shouted the Uzbek, "I agree to the trade."

Hippolyte snatched up the ear trumpet, polished the brass on his sleeve, and gingerly held it up to his ear.

"Live to a hundred, old man, if you have the nerve," called the Uzbek gleefully, tucking the photograph away between the folds of a leather wallet.

The creases of a benign smile took up position, like an occupying army, on Hippolyte's face. "You don't have to shout," he informed the Uzbek with great dignity. "I can hear you perfectly well."

Light streaming through cracks in the shutter illuminated slowly rising dust particles. A woman's hand bathed his forehead with a damp piece of cloth.

"Opened his eyes . . ."

"Feverish . . ."

"Concussion . . ."

"Must hope for the . . ."

"If only he gets well, I will give up sex . . ."

"Alexander, can you hear . . ."

Zander pressed his eyes shut. Behind his lids he could see Abner reaching out and gently dropping the girl he loved to her death.

Flickering light now. A wall alive with shadows.

His head felt heavy. He reached up with a hand and felt . . . bandages. He might still be alive, he thought. It was a possibility to be considered. He shifted his head on the pillow. The flame of a candle came into his field of vision. For someone who never expected to see anything again, it was excruciatingly beautiful. Next to the candle stood a woman, her naked back toward him. It dawned on him that it might be his mother. When she turned around he would ask her why she hadn't waved. Dipping a sponge in a basin, the woman washed under her arms. She moved like the flame. Like the flame, she was excruciatingly beautiful.

The flame on the candle went out. Or his eyes closed. He figured out he could light the candle by opening his eyes. He struggled to open them, to see the flame, the woman. But his lids seemed too heavy . . . he had to settle for the memory of the flame, the memory of the woman.

Perhaps this was what death consisted of, he thought: always, only, remembering . . .

7

Arishka pulled her Cossack's cape up over her breasts until her toes protruded from it at the foot of the bed. She wiggled them playfully against Tuohy's thigh as she studied him. "*Nevozmozhno,*" she said.

"That means *impossible,*" Tuohy told her.

"Im-puss-ee-bull," Arishka repeated with a giggle.

Tuohy asked, "What else?"

"Doloi voinu," she offered.

"In English, down with the war."

"Down wit de wor."

Tuohy tugged at the hem of the Cossack cape until her breasts again became visible. "Let it alone, *drouzhok,* I like to look at your nipples," he said.

"Tell me something, Americanitz. When did you first get it into your head that you wanted to sleep with me?"

"Why, when I first saw you sitting behind the table at the entrance of the Kshesinskaya Mansion," declared Tuohy with a disarming grin. "I saw the sack of onions at your feet and my heart skipped a beat. I can't resist the odor of onions on a woman's breath."

"You are an impossible young man," the young woman concluded. "You are never serious." Arishka cocked her head saucily. "You are very different from my husband."

"And where is he now, this husband of yours?"

"At the front," she said, suddenly moody. "He is a Bolshevik agitator with the Four forty-third Regiment of the One hundred tenth Division." Her eyes appeared to focus on a thought. "If you ever visit that regiment, you won't miss him. He has long hair that he ties into a knot at the nape of his neck. He made a vow not to cut his hair while Russian soldiers were dying in a capitalist war."

"You love him, don't you?"

"Of course I love him!"

"And you sleep with other men?"

The young woman stared back at Tuohy boldly. "Of course I sleep with other men. I am twenty-three years old. My husband has been away for twenty-eight months."

Reporting for work at the Bolshevik headquarters the next morning, Tuohy was summoned to Stalin's office.

"While some others were roughing it in the cafés of Europe," he was lecturing to everyone within earshot when Tuohy opened the door of the room, "I was sweating out four years in Turokhan of Northern Siberia. In the winter the temperature dropped to minus forty centigrade. At minus forty your fingernails stop growing. Your shit freezes before it hits the ground. We used to chip off slivers of frozen milk and suck on them until they melted in our mouths. The arrival of the annual vodka shipment was the most important event of the year. A procession led by a priest carrying a cross met the wagon bringing it. Can you see me marching behind a priest with a cross? Well, I did. Shit, I would have crawled to get my ration of vodka. And now we take tea like ladies and gentlemen and discuss verbs as if they could spur the masses to revolution and all we had to do was hang on to their coattails." Stalin spotted Tuohy leaning against the wall. Grabbing him roughly by the elbow, he steered him out of the room toward the window at the far end of the corridor.

Speaking Russian with his usual Georgian accent, Stalin said, "I am told you once eliminated a traitor in New York."

Tuohy didn't bat an eye. "Where did you pick up that bit of information?"

"I hear things. This is the story: We have accounts in several banks in Petrograd through which our German friends filter money to us from Stockholm. They are in the name of a Bolshevik named Alexinsky. Gregory Alexinsky. We have reason to believe that Alexinsky is on the verge of going over to Kerensky. If the provisional government gets its hands on this information, we'll be finished." Stalin came to the point. "Alexinsky is arriving from Moscow by train this afternoon. He'll be carrying some family jewels in a briefcase. You must be sure to take them—"

"I don't understand—do you want me to rob him or kill him?"

"Both. That way he won't complain about the robbery. The peasants have a saying: a man who has lost his head doesn't cry over his hair." Stalin emitted a guttural laugh; it sounded as if he were clearing his throat. "Be sure you dump the jewels into the river. With the briefcase gone, robbery will appear to be the motive, but we don't want to take the chance that the death can be traced back to us through the jewels. As soon as you have accomplished this, you must drop out of sight until the affair has died down. Trotsky's going off tonight to make a tour of the front. I've arranged for you to join him as a bodyguard." Stalin tilted his head and added, "Take care of this job correctly and I will not forget it."

Stalin had given him a perfect description of Alexinsky, and so Tuohy had no trouble picking him out when the afternoon train from Moscow pulled into the station. The platform teemed with soldiers and sailors returning for leave, along with peasant women lugging large burlap sacks, and a file of silent nuns, their faces lost in the shadows of their peaked hats, on a pilgrimage to Petersburg's holy places. Alexinsky, tall, thin, wearing an overcoat with a mink collar and pointed Italian patent leather shoes, hugged a briefcase to his body and struggled with a heavy leather valise.

Tuohy blocked his path. "Comrade Alexinsky," he said in a respectful voice, "I greet you in the name of the Minister of Justice of the provisional government, Alexander Kerensky. Here, let me help you with the valise—"

A trace of doubt flickered across Alexinsky's face, and instantly disappeared in the folds of an ingratiating smile. "How extremely thoughtful of Kerensky," he said. "But how did he know when I was due back in Petrograd?"

Tuohy lifted the valise and fell into step alongside Alexinsky. "There is very little that happens that Kerensky doesn't know about," he said vaguely.

Alexinsky's eyes settled suspiciously on Tuohy. "You speak Russian with a slight accent?"

"I am half English," Tuohy explained. As Stalin had foreseen, this detail seemed to allay Alexinsky's suspicions; the English were known to be pro-Kerensky.

Outside, Tuohy led Alexinsky through a cluster of peasants brewing pots of tea on small open fires to the two-seater Pierce Arrow he had "borrowed" for the occasion. He deposited the leather suitcase in the luggage compartment and held the door open for Alexinsky, who was still clutching his briefcase under one arm.

"To be met by an automobile," laughed Alexinsky. "It is just like the old days."

"You are a very important individual," Tuohy told him. "My superiors are prepared to go to great lengths to see that no harm comes to you."

Tuohy took a roundabout route, driving through run-down neighborhoods and crossing out-of-the-way canals, going all the time in the general direction of the Vyborg section of the city. Alexinsky's eyes darted to the narrow, unfamiliar side streets. "Where are you taking me?" he inquired, making an effort to keep his voice natural.

"I'm sorry, I thought I told you," Tuohy said innocently. "The minister wants to see you immediately—something about bank accounts in your name. He instructed me to take the long way around to make sure you were not being followed."

Tuohy turned onto a narrow, badly paved side street off Chukova Street, then into an unpaved alleyway behind a row of abandoned stables. Darkness was settling over the city as he pulled the Pierce Arrow into a dilapidated stable with an open door. Tuohy cut the motor.

"And where is Kerensky?" Alexinsky asked nervously.

"He is waiting for you in the apartment upstairs." Tuohy pulled the stable door closed and bolted it from the inside. Then he walked around to Alexinsky's side of the automobile.

By now all traces of blood had drained from Alexinsky's face and his words came in a rush. "Look, I don't know you, but you have an honest face. Maybe we can strike a deal. I can make it worth your while—"

Tuohy only smiled. "Citizen Alexinsky, you are bothering yourself for nothing. Believe me, Kerensky is waiting for you upstairs. He considers you to be an important collaborator."

Tuohy opened the door, snapped his head in the direction of the staircase, and smiled again. "You are keeping the minister waiting."

Alexinsky glanced around uncertainly, then gingerly climbed out of the car and gazed up the dark stairs. At the top a partly open door seemed to confirm that he was expected. "You are absolutely sure he is there?" he asked Tuohy.

"You have my word for it."

Alexinsky put his weight on the first step, hesitated, then started slowly up the flight of stairs, which creaked under him. Tuohy helped himself to a cigarette, tapped it several times against the case, and stuck it into his mouth without lighting it. He drew his revolver from its wooden holster, sighted on Alexinsky's back, and squeezed the trigger. The shot sounded like the crack of a whip in the stable. Alexinsky's body hurtled through the partly open door onto a floor littered with empty beer bottles and old magazines. Taking the steps two at a time, Tuohy retrieved the briefcase, kicked Alexinsky over onto his back, and grasped his wrist to check for a pulse. When he felt one, he shook his head in irritation. Alexinsky's eyes twitched open. Tuohy, reaching out at arm's length, tried to wedge the barrel of his German pistol into Alexinsky's mouth. The wounded man pleaded with his eyes and gritted his teeth as if his refusal to open his mouth could save him.

"Beg for your life," Tuohy ordered.

Alexinsky made the mistake of saying "Please." As his mouth opened, Tuohy slipped the tip of the barrel deep into it. Alexinsky gagged—but Tuohy, relishing the moment, didn't pull the trigger.

"Comrade Alexinsky, there is very little that happens in Petrograd that *Stalin* doesn't know about," he whispered harshly.

Alexinsky's eyes glazed over in terror. Tuohy's fingertips tingled with power—and pleasure. Smiling faintly, he pulled the trigger.

Night, along with a thin, moist smog rolling in from the Baltic, had already engulfed the city when Tuohy, making his way on foot, reached the Anichkov Bridge, its tarnished bronze horses silhouetted against the last stray streaks of gray in the west. Tuohy paused in the middle of the bridge to make sure he was not being observed, then pried open the lock on the briefcase with a pocket knife and spilled the contents into the darkness below. He flung the briefcase in after the rest and headed by the most direct route he knew toward Arishka's flat.

"Americanitz, you are too rough with me," Arishka complained after Tuohy had pulled off her clothes and launched his assault. He positioned his body in an effort to get her to do something she had never done before, but she resisted. "I have heard of such a thing, but it does not appeal to me," she said in her forthright way. Tuohy persisted. Arishka gritted her teeth.

"For Christ's sake," Tuohy exclaimed, "it's not going to bite you."

Arishka made the mistake of saying "Please, Americanitz—"

Tuohy slipped it past her parted lips. Arishka gagged. Closing his eyes, oblivious to Arishka's panic, Tuohy relived the killing of Alexinsky until, smiling faintly, he once again treated himself to the pulling of the trigger.

At the stroke of midnight Tuohy joined the three-automobile caravan parked at the Moscow Gate at the end of Ligovsky Prospekt. Trotsky, struggling with a picnic hamper filled with sausages and wine, soon showed up along with several Bolshevik agitators, and the caravan set off for the front.

Trotsky, who had only recently returned to Petrograd—the British had removed him from the *Christianiafjord* and interred him at Halifax for a month before allowing him to continue on to Russia—curled up in the backseat, plugged his ears with wads of cotton, and sank into a deep sleep. Tuohy drove until he found himself dozing, then changed off with one of the agitators and slept fitfully in the passenger seat, his head banging against the window every time the automobile hit a pothole.

In the days that followed, Trotsky's caravan explored the moonscape of Russia at war. The evidence of battles and destruction was everywhere—and it was worse than Tuohy had imagined. Whole villages had been reduced to debris by enormous German cannon shells. The roads were clogged with refugees who, fearful of a new German onslaught, had loaded their possessions onto carts and headed east. Occasionally the caravan passed handfuls of Austrian prisoners being herded away from the front; once they even saw a German prisoner wearing a greatcoat and the distinctive spiked helmet.

Late one evening Trotsky's party bivouacked across the river from a hospital, and in the morning Tuohy wandered back over to flirt with an English nurse he had seen the night before. He arrived in time for the burial of a teenage soldier who had succumbed to shrapnel wounds. The body had been wrapped in a sheet and placed in a coffin. A priest, hoarse from officiating at funerals, uttered prayers over the coffin, which was swarming with flies. Eventually someone had the good sense to nail the lid shut. Tuohy, edging closer to the English nurse, thought he could hear the flies trapped inside buzzing to get out.

That afternoon they took lunch at a mobile field kitchen with its open air bread ovens lined up nearby, smoke streaming from their tin chimneys. Later, the three automobiles in the caravan were ferried across a river alongside a bridge that had been destroyed. They passed rows of barbed wire entanglements stretched in front of a freshly dug system of trenches; the trenches had been prepared as a fallback position in case the actual front line cracked. Behind a barn they found hundreds of rifles, half of them rusting and unusable, stacked against a wall; they had been salvaged from the battlefield and left for the raw recruits who arrived without weapons. The caravan skirted a troop of boy soldiers straining under the weight of their rifles and backpacks as they headed for the front to relieve a unit on the line.

Every time the caravan came across a unit, no matter what its size, no matter what the time of day, Trotsky would emerge from the backseat of his automobile, climb up on an ammunition box or a coffin, and with the light flashing from his pince-nez, lash out at the provisional government for its failure to take Russia out of the war. Propaganda, however, was not the principal reason for the trip. Trotsky had been sent out to sample the mood of the troops at the front. If it came to a showdown, would the rank and file soldiers support the handful of Bolsheviks who wanted to put an end to the war, or their officers who wanted to enforce military discipline and continue the war?

An answer of sorts came unexpectedly one night when Trotsky and his entourage were sharing a watery cabbage soup, cooked over an open fire, with soldiers behind the front line. The regiment had been ordered to return to the trenches facing the Germans. The regimental Soviet, dominated by Bolsheviks, protested the order. "We are finished spilling our blood," cried one of the young Bolsheviks, "so that the capitalists back in Moscow and Petrograd can fatten their bank accounts."

The regimental colonel, a gaunt officer with a chest full of medals, appeared soon afterward. "Men," he called, "the day the tsar declared war against Germany, he recited the oath that Alexander the First took at the time of Napoleon's invasion of our motherland in 1812." The colonel elevated his chin and began to recite. "I solemnly swear . . ."

In the shadows behind the campfires, a handful of soldiers stood up and joined their colonel in reciting the oath.

". . . that I will never make peace . . ."

Now there were several dozen soldiers on their feet, and the colonel's voice was lost in a chorus of voices.

". . . so long as one of the enemy is on the soil of . . ."

Suddenly the young Bolshevik who had spoken earlier stepped out of the shadows and plunged a bayonet into the stomach of the colonel. He pulled the bayonet free, and calmly walked away. Blood gushed from the colonel's tunic. He swayed on his feet and collapsed. Several junior officers who had been watching from the fringes sprinted for their horses and galloped off into the night.

The Bolshevik agitators from Petrograd tried to convince Trotsky that it would be wiser for them to leave immediately, and Tuohy wholeheartedly seconded the notion. But Trotsky was adamant: he wanted to observe at first hand how things turned out.

An hour later Tuohy heard the sound of automobile engines. Headlights stabbed out of the darkness on every side, and a dozen or so armored cars, enormous vehicles that looked like prehistoric monsters, closed in on the camps. "Soldiers," a voice cried through a bullhorn, "you have three minutes to stand parade with equipment and rifles. Anyone who doesn't obey this order will be shot."

"Now we shall see," Trotsky said calmly, "if they will fight for their rights or meekly give in."

For a moment it could have gone either way, and Tuohy loosened his pistol in its holster and prepared to pull Trotsky under one of their automobiles. Then several soldiers rose to their feet, kicked dirt onto their campfires, and fell in before the headlights of the armored cars. Others joined them until, finally, every soldier in the regiment was standing in line.

"Fix bayonets," the voice ordered through the bullhorn.

The soldiers drew their bayonets from their scabbards and snapped them onto their rifles.

"Present rifles," the voice ordered.

The rifles flew up in front of the soldiers. Four officers with drawn pistols started down the line of soldiers. One of them ran a finger over each bayonet as he passed. His finger came away from a bayonet sticky with blood. The officers pulled the soldier roughly from the line, relieved him of his rifle, and thrust him against the trunk of a tree. "Soldiers," shouted an officer, "this is the fate of rebels in your midst." And so saying, he extended his pistol at arm's length until it touched the nape of the neck of the soldier.

"Comrades," cried the soldier, "long live the revolution!"

A bullet tore through his neck.

"Sub-officers," shouted an officer, "take charge and move these men into the trenches. Execute."

In the eerie light coming from the armored cars, the soldiers hefted their rifles onto their shoulders and marched sullenly off into the night.

Absolute quiet settled over the fields. Trotsky, Tuohy, and several of the Bolshevik agitators went over to the body of the executed soldier. He was lying facedown at the foot of the tree. With a chill Tuohy saw that the soldier's long hair was tied into a knot at the nape of his neck.

"What regiment was that?" he asked one of the agitators.

"The Four forty-third Regiment of the One hundred tenth Division," the man answered. "Why?"

"Nothing."

He realized that the dead man was Arishka's husband.

The fat Uzbek who had traded the solid brass ear trumpet for the photograph of the naked princess kept it hidden in a drawer, referring to it on the occasions when his wife indicated, by a series of subtle gestures that had long since become a code between them, that she wanted to be made love to that night. Then one day the Uzbek was haggling with a Cossack who had come into possession of an envelope of cocaine. The Cossack hesitated about trading it for a saddle that had once belonged to a grand duke—his royal insignia was embossed on the leather—and ten English pounds sterling, so the Uzbek offered him the photograph of the naked woman to clinch the deal. "The man who sold it to me swore she is a genuine princess."

The Cossack ran the ball of his thumb over the body of the princess, then with a grunt of satisfaction tucked the ten-pound note and the photograph away in his orders ledger, hefted the saddle onto his shoulder, and departed.

8

White as the sheet that covered him, Zander sat propped up in a large bed. Heavy green curtains were drawn across the windows because daylight still bothered his eyes. Lili spoon-fed him chicken broth with the yolk of an egg mixed into it.

"Does your head still hurt?" When he didn't answer, she said softly, "Do you remember what happened?"

He remembered all right. "The colonel cut off my—"

"Oh, Alexander, you *don't* remember. He didn't—"

Zander created a wall so her words would not penetrate; if he allowed himself to hope, he would die of disappointment.

"You don't believe me?" Tears appeared in her voice. "See for yourself." She tore off the sheet.

Zander turned his head away and shut his eyes.

"If you won't look," Lili cried, "then feel." She took his limp penis in her hand as if she were lifting a wounded sparrow. With the tips of her fingers she kneaded the beak of the bird. "Now you can look, Alexander," she encouraged him quietly. "Turn your head. That's right. Open your eyes."

His skull throbbed; he thought he would be blinded by the pain. Light seeped into his brain. Images, washed by tears, came into focus.

What he saw confirmed what he could feel.

And then the image blurred again as Zander began to sob.

When he could bear to listen, Lili explained what had happened in the coal room. "You remember the young soldier on guard duty when we arrived—the one who said he was a Bolshevik? He and his comrades had been on bad terms with their officers for months. When one of his comrades spotted us being taken down to the

138

coal room, they held a meeting behind their barracks and voted to intervene. The first explosion you heard blew the door to the coal room off its hinges. The other explosions—the ones you thought were echoes—were gunfire; the soldiers shot the colonel and eight of the nine officers. They're holding the last one for us to take back to Petrograd when you're well enough to travel."

"How long have I been unconscious?"

"Today's the twelfth day. We brought a doctor out from Petrograd. He said you had a concussion, that after what had happened you might be afraid to wake up. He advised me not to move you until you were conscious, or dead."

"Where are we?"

Lili looked pleased with herself. "I commandeered a bedroom in the palace. You are sleeping in the bed that once belonged to Tsar Alexander the Second."

"If Leon could see me now." Zander had a sudden thought. "And Vasia? What of Vasia?"

"Vasia needed medical care badly. I sent him to Petrograd in the car that fetched the doctor."

"How was he?"

"Physically, he was all right. The blood clotted. A scab began to form. It tortured him to urinate, but he seemed to relish the pain." Lili picked up the bowl of broth. "That's enough talking for one day," she ordered. "Drink this. You need to regain your strength."

He woke up briefly in the middle of the night. His head still throbbed, though not as badly. The total absence of light made him feel as if he were adrift again in space. His pulse raced. His heart began to beat wildly. Then he realized he was not alone in the bed. Lili was asleep in his arms, one hand cupping, covering, protecting his lifeless penis. He tried to will an erection to confirm again that he was whole, but failed. He could feel Lili's moist, warm breath against his chest. He edged a palm flat against the cool skin of her back. So it is you, the flame of the candle, he thought. Then he realized that he had said it out loud. *"Chto?"* she muttered in a faint voice. She adjusted her position slightly, then sank back into a deep, peaceful sleep.

With each passing day Zander grew stronger. He slept less and spent more time propped up in bed. He became dizzy when he stood up, then the spells passed and he began to walk around the room for exercise. He thought about his job in Petrograd, and getting back to it, but when he raised the subject with Lili, she shook her head as if it were out of the question. "Give it time," she said.

Lili seldom let him out of her sight. Folded into the window seat, the sun bleaching her face, she told him a great many things about herself that she had never spoken of to anyone before. She had been raised by her maternal grandparents in the countryside because her father, who was considerably older than her mother, didn't appreciate having female children under his roof. "My grandmother was a delicate woman who always spoke French, smoked violet-scented cigarettes to keep what Mr. Pasteur called 'germs' at bay, and cut off any conversation she considered inappropriate by ringing a small silver bell that she kept handy for that purpose. Once, when I was thirteen, I continued describing a bodily function that was new to me after her bell had sounded, and my grandmother had me hauled off to an ice cold shower as punishment. My grandfather, on the other hand, was something of a radical—he entertained the notion that *some* women were equal to most men, and insisted that I be educated as if I were a boy. He hired a young Polish tutor and organized a school. There were nine of us in the class. I was the only girl." Lili laughed under her breath.

"The boys used to bait me all the time—they claimed I defended what I thought of as my territory before anyone had a chance to attack. I suppose it was true; I suppose, when you come down to it, I was pretty aggressive. The first person I ever made love to was the tutor. We were both virgins, so it didn't go too well. As a matter of fact, it went quite badly. I had shaved off my pubic hair because I thought the visible evidence of my sexuality shouldn't be hidden. He had never set eyes on female genitals before, and it frightened him. I still get that reaction occasionally."

"Why did you become a Socialist?" Zander asked another time.

"When I was eighteen I converted to Zoroastrianism, which is what the Uzbeks were before they became Muslims; I used to think that the world was a cosmic struggle between the spirit of good, personified by Zoroaster as Spenta Mainyu, and the spirit of evil, Angra Mainyu. Looking back now, I can see that it was my Zoroastrianism that made me ripe for Marx; he also sees the struggle in more or less black and white terms. There are the good guys. Then there are the bad guys."

"You're leaving out the economics."

"Oh, I never did understand the economics. What attracted me to Marx wasn't so much his concept that the state would wither away as his promise that under socialism the traditional bourgeoisie family would wither away. From my own experience, from everything I could see, the family seemed to me to be a kind of prison in which you served a life sentence. I wanted to be free, and Marx offered me a context in which I could pursue my freedom. When the Bolsheviks approached me about serving as a courier between Petrograd and Zurich, where Lenin was, I jumped at the opportunity. They gave me my chance to break away and I took it. I've been working for them in one capacity or another ever since. And I don't regret it."

As the weeks passed, Zander and Lili became more comfortable in each other's presence. Zander tried to read, and when his head began to ache he closed his eyes and dozed; his dreams, while still vaguely threatening, became calmer. When he opened his eyes again, he would see Lili watching him from her usual place on the window seat. They would exchange wordless smiles and he would drift off again to sleep.

Mealtimes Lili always managed to turn up with something special: a pitcher of fermented goat's milk, blinis with thick cream on them, some cheese made from ewe's milk, a piece of boiled chicken, once some piroshki with cabbage and meat in them, and even a bottle of greenish-colored wine from Georgia. The soldiers who had saved their lives were apparently scouring the neighborhood for delicacies for Zander; on one occasion they hinted to Lili that several of the dishes came straight from the table of Citizen Romanov.

And every night Lili took off her clothes and sponged herself in the flickering light of the candle and crawled into bed with Zander, crawled into his arms as if she fitted there, and covering his penis protectively with her hand, she would fall asleep. And every night he willed an erection, summoned it as if it were a spirit to be raised from the dead. And with each passing night he became more convinced that his manhood was forever broken.

"Not to worry—it will come," Lili assured him late one night, as if she had been monitoring his mounting sense of panic. She started to stroke his penis with the tips of her fingers, absently relishing the softness of the skin. "It will come, Alexander, I promise you."

"No!" The word was indistinguishable from a groan. "It is gone forever. I will never love a woman again."

Lili raised herself on an elbow and stared into the darkness; her emotions, under control for so long, had been stirred up. "You will love a woman again," she informed him as if it were a commandment. "You will love me . . . now."

In the darkness she bent her lips to his penis and slowly kissed it into life. She touched him in places he had been touched before—but never in quite that way; he felt as if he were being branded. Adrift in the pitch darkness of the room, he heard her murmur a line from one of Mayakovsky's poems; she invited Zander's "heart to the body's festival." Melting into the angles of her body until he was no longer sure where he left off and she began, he gratefully, greedily, accepted. He lost track of where he was in the bed, of where the bed was in the room, of where the room was in the universe. His only orientation was her; he clung to her as if she could keep him from going under. Her face, her breasts, her thighs, became raw from his three-week stubble. After a while Zander became aware that she was holding back; she resisted an orgasm as if it were a loss of control, a falling into, an aggression. "Come off," she ordered, a note of panic creeping into her voice. Her face contorted. "Come off," she begged several minutes later. "Who gives you the right to do this to me?" she whispered still later, but Zander never heard her.

And then, abandoning rhythm or decorum, she folded her knees against her chest and ceded.

Lili unwound cautiously; she feared that any sudden movement would send her spinning over the brim again. "Tell me frankly," she said, "do you think of me as a good lover?"

"To call a woman a good lover is to describe her ability to *take* pleasure from the act of love," Zander answered quietly. "In this sense you are a good lover."

Lili smiled at a thought. "Men have no idea what it is like to be penetrated," she said nervously. "Someday I will have to show you."

When they had slept for a while, Lili shook him awake and said, "Now it is your turn," and she made him hard and brought him in measured increments to the rim—and with a flick of her tongue dispatched him over its edge. "You, too, are a good lover," she called after him as he plummeted—there was both laughter and love in her voice—"but can you make a revolution?"

Spring hung in the air like laundry spread across a clothesline; like laundry it was stirred by occasional drafts of dry air and impregnated by faint garden fragrances. The rain, when it fell, felt warm to the touch, and those caught out in it seemed more aware of the sound it made when it hit the ground than its wetness. Sniffing at the spring from an open window, Zander thought about the revolution he had crossed an ocean and a continent to attend. "But can you make a revolution?" she had asked half jokingly—and half not. It was a pertinent question. He believed as strongly as ever in the existence of his moral center; in its ability to identify areas of absolute evil; in his obligation, before the ghost of his grandfather, before the memory of his brother, Abner, to set things straight where he could. But there was precious little place in this neat scheme of things for Lili; for love; for a sexual joining so intimate that the *intimacy* itself aroused the participants. Or so it seemed to him now, gazing out from the French windows of a tsar's bedroom, with Lili pressing her ear to his spinal column hoping to catch his heartbeat through his back.

As for Lili, she had always thought of that entity called "a couple" as a convenient hedge against loneliness, or growing old, or death. With Alexander in her life, she saw things in a different light. She had never before placed much value on her life; dying had always seemed a vaguely disruptive business, an inconvenience more than anything else. Now, when she thought about her death, or even worse, Alexander's, it appeared to her to be an awesome catastrophe; a terrible waste of possibilities; a pointless end to what had become, for her, an endless beginning.

And so they loved each other and lingered at Tsarkoe Selo. Lili summarily banned time from their lives. The only clock, she proclaimed as if it were a biblical commandment, was hunger—for each other, for food.

Yet the revolution, like the ticking of a clock in a bedroom, intruded on their consciousness.

As Zander regained his strength, he and Lili, in early June, took to wandering through the flat countryside surrounding the town. Lili always managed to come up with a picnic for these occasions—a wedge of crumbling goat cheese, a fistful of black bread, a scallion or two, a pinch of salt folded into a scrap of newspaper, some watery wine that would be set to cool at the edge of the river while she and Zander stripped and swam with all their force against the current. Once, she reached an underwater shelf ahead of him, and turning so that she was sitting on it facing him, she let him drift up between her legs to the magnified lips weaving in the current like some delicate pink sea anemone. Afterward they would dry themselves in the sun and nibble at their picnic and share the wine and fall asleep under a wild cherry tree that bore leaves but no fruit, and eventually make their way back toward town as the last pale pigments of the evening's sunset retreated in orderly fashion into the horizon. It was then that the young guardsman would pass on to them the rumors.

"Have you heard the latest, Miss Lili?"

"Listen to this . . ."

"Comrade Princess, would you believe it if I told you . . ."

The picture that emerged made it seem that the revolution was only a matter of time. In Petrograd, the famous Machine Gun Regiment, some ten thousand souls armed with a thousand water-cooled machine guns, had publicly declared for the Bolsheviks. The masses of workers were slowly falling under the spell of Trotsky's piercing logic, delivered almost nightly to an audience packed into the Cirque Moderne, a gloomy amphitheater lighted by five tiny gas spots hanging from wires.

There were other rumors: this or that regiment was said to be leaning in one or another direction; Kerensky was overheard boasting he finally had proof that Lenin was on the German payroll; there was the assassination, in a particularly grisly fashion, of the witness who was supposed to supply Kerensky with that proof. The young guardsmen, with no education of their own to draw on, invariably asked Lili and Zander their opinions. Could it be true that the sailors from the Kronstadt garrison, traditionally very radical, were threatening to provoke an armed insurrection? In a note asking about Zander's health, Tuohy also mentioned this rumor. Why was Kerensky making a whirlwind tour of the front, talking in his excited teenage voice about the need for victory over the Germans? Did it mean that yet another offensive was about to be launched? Did it sound reasonable, the story about the Bolsheviks being able to muster twenty thousand armed Red Guardsmen? Could anyone say with certainty that the only reason the Germans were delaying an attack to capture Petrograd was to see if Lenin would get his way about taking Russia out of the war?

Zander and Lili listened to the rumors and shrugged their shoulders and eventually retreated into the bedroom where a tsar had once slept. They drew the heavy curtains and touched a match to the wick of the candle and sponged each other in its dancing light, and then set about exploring possibilities that were assumed to be infinite. One night Lili gave Zander the lesson she had promised on what it was like to be penetrated. Another time she produced half a peach salvaged from that day's picnic next to the river, perfumed her vagina with it and then, as if it were the most natural thing in the world, alighted, like a butterfly, on the leaf of his lips.

When a visitor suddenly turned up, they scrambled into their clothes, curious to see who it might be. As a precaution, Zander fetched his German pistol, which had been returned to him by the guardsman, from its hiding place under a cushion on the sofa and stuck it into his waistband. "What is his name?" called Lili, struggling with the tiny pearl buttons of a high-necked blouse, but the young guardsman who brought the news admitted he hadn't bothered to ask.

Gasoline being next to impossible to come by, the visitor had arrived, rather dramatically it seemed, in an open carriage pulled by a troika of horses. The driver, according to the guardsman, had managed the team with extraordinary skill. Holding the mare in the middle to a rapid trot, letting the flankers canter with their heads flared outward, he had come flying into the courtyard at full tilt before reining in next to the guard's hut. Hearing the beat of the horses' hooves on the cobblestones and the tinkle of the silver bells strung like a necklace to each bridle, the four daughters of Tsar Nicholas had come rushing to their upstairs window. "Can we have a ride, then?" the princess Anastasia, the most impulsive of the four, had called down gaily, only to be shooed away from the window by the imperious arm of the tsarina, who, if she had guessed the identity of the troika driver, would surely have tried to kill him with her bare hands.

"Felix!" cried Lili when she set eyes on the visitor.
"Lichik!"
"Felix, come meet a comrade"—Lili, for once flustered, didn't know how to introduce Zander—"a com-

rade from Petrograd, and much more." She lifted her
chin and smiled warmly in Zander's direction. "Much
more, yes. His name is Alexander Til. He is my friend
and my lover and a brother to me, like you. Alexander,
meet my twin brother, Felix."

Zander realized that he was face-to-face with Felix
Yusupov, the princely slayer of Rasputin. But where
Lili was clearly a princess in a worker's guise, Felix was
more like a peasant masquerading as a prince. He had
coarse features that reminded Zander of a whore's rouged
face. His lips were fixed in a permanent pout, as if he
bore an unspoken grudge against the world. His gestures, darting forays into the air with long, feline fingers, conveyed nothing so much as feminine exasperation.

"Can we talk, Lilionochek?" Felix asked almost
plaintively.

"You can trust Alexander," Lili started to say, but
Zander was already heading for the door.

"He wants to speak to you alone. Such a thing is
normal—I am not offended."

"He is at least discreet, your latest," Felix said as the
bedroom door closed behind Zander.

"There is a strong possibility," Lili told him, settling
onto the sofa, "that my latest, as you so neatly phrase it,
will be my last."

Felix laughed out loud. "Since you do not have the
look of someone who is thinking of giving up men, I
assume you mean to say you have stumbled into a
serious love affair. Well, *tant mieux*," snapped Felix in
a way that made it clear he didn't believe a word she
said.

"How did you know where to find me?" Lili demanded. She was not particularly pleased to see her
brother; the ugly scenes he had made in Paris, and later
in the Steamboat, were still too fresh in her memory.

Felix sat down next to her, pulled off his boots, and
wiggled his toes. "My feet smell, but I rather like the
odor. Ah, Lissik, as far as the Bolsheviks are concerned,
I have a revolutionist's credentials: Felix Yusupov, the
man who shot Rasputin. Of course the reason I put a
bullet through the bastard was to save the tsar, or at

least the institution. Rasputin was giving royalty a bad name, not to mention a lot of bad advice on how to fight the war. When it comes to choosing between my class and the riffraff in the streets, I'll stand with my class, thank you. Every time." He sank back into the sofa and fixed his gaze on Lili. "How I found you is I asked in the right places." And he pantomimed talking on the telephone. "Yusupov here. Yes, *the* Yusupov. I wonder if you could tell me, et cetera, et cetera. Lissik, if you knew how I detest talking on the telephone."

Lili waited for him to explain what had prompted him to stray from the nocturnal pleasures of his estate near Petrograd.

"I came," he said, arching his plucked eyebrows into two inverted V's, "to talk you into leaving Russia with me before all hell breaks loose."

"Leave Russia!"

"Lisyok, we could set up shop in a divine Parisian *hôtel particulier*. On the right bank, it goes without saying. You could even bring the child along; I wouldn't mind. We could claim to be anything you wanted— husband and wife, or artist and model, or, or"—in his panic to get her to come, he was trying to be comic and convincing at the same time—"or even brother and sister, though, of course, no one would believe us for a minute—they'd see right through that, wouldn't they? And assume we were lovers." He moved closer to her, and she realized that his feet did smell. "You haven't forgotten that we were lovers, have you, Lissik?" he whispered. "It hasn't slipped your mind?"

For Lili, it had been just another frontier to cross, another way of expressing her contempt for the conventional. Fresh from an affair with a Russian poet, she had come across her brother in Paris. She knew him vaguely from her occasional visits to St. Petersburg. He had dared her to make love to him. She had slept with Felix the way she would have slept with anyone who asked her politely. "That was a lifetime ago," she said.

"Not for me it wasn't." He sank onto his knees and pressed his head to her thighs. "Lilionochek, Lilionochek, my own Lilionysh, don't you see it? I have come here to save you. If you don't want to leave Russia, we could hide out in my country estate. When the blood flows, they won't distinguish between a princess and an ex-princess. You are marked if you stay. Someday someone will stand you up against a wall because of who you were, as opposed to who you are." Felix lowered his voice to a harsh whisper. "You must collect the child and leave here. With me. Instantly."

"And what did you say?"

"I told him no."

"Just no?" She was avoiding his eye, Zander noticed.

"Why are you staring at me like this? What gives you the right to cross-examine me?"

"Just a simple no?" Zander repeated, unperturbed. "That was your answer?"

Lili looked up at him. "I said there was no question of my leaving you. Not now. Not ever. You are stuck with me, Alexander." She was suddenly insecure. "Assuming you want to be."

It had not been put as a question, but it screamed for an answer. "I want to be," Zander said simply.

"If you didn't, you would say so?"

Zander nodded.

"Yet something is bothering you."

Zander nodded again.

Lili thought for a moment she would have to draw it out of him, but then Zander reached over and laced his fingers through hers and told her.

"Two things . . . happened . . . this afternoon."

He said it with such gravity that her heart almost stopped beating.

"Two things?"

"You remember we heard that Kerensky was whipping up the troops at the front? Well, an enormous offensive has been launched. They say thirty-one divisions have been sent against the Austrians on the Galician front. The first reports speak of territory overrun, towns captured, prisoners taken."

"But how does this affect us, Alexander?"

Zander seemed impatient. "If Kerensky manages to

come away with a big military victory, it will strengthen
his hand and he will move against Lenin and the Bolsheviks. If the offensive ends in defeat, it will be the
moment for *us* to move against Kerensky and the provisional government."

"Us?"

The word dropped between them like a coin in a slot.

"We are Bolsheviks, and revolutionists," Zander said
softly.

"What was the second thing that happened?" she
asked.

"The second thing," Zander continued—she could
tell from his tone that there was no safety here—"is I
received a letter from Leon. You remember I told you
about him? My stepbrother? *My* twin."

"The one who is emigrating to Palestine to create a
Jewish state. That Leon?"

Zander nodded. "That Leon." He produced an envelope covered with a half-dozen overlapping cancellation
stamps, and slipped a letter from it. "I sent him a letter
when I got to Petrograd. He wrote to me in care of
Bolshevik headquarters at the mansion. They forwarded
the letter to the Steamboat. Tuohy sent it on here with
some Red Guards who arrived to bolster the local
contingent."

"And this twin brother of yours, this Leon, what does
he have to say for himself?"

Zander unfolded the letter and read:

Zander,

By the time you get this, I will be, God willing,
knocking on the gates of Palestine. I managed to talk
my lady friend into trading her pharmacy in the Bronx
for the questionable pleasures of the promised land.
So now, for better or for worse, as the *goys* in America put it, she is my missus and I am her mister and
we are off together to organize a homeland for the
Jews. She tells me I'm mad, and the truth is I'm not
sure she is wrong—though I am comforted by the
thought that anybody following a dream, from our

Moses right on down to you, Zander, must at some point experience serious doubts about his sanity. In any case, I am en route, and happy to be. If I have any regret, it is about our last conversation—you haven't forgotten the "stuffed" and the vodka glass that didn't break? Later, in my head, I went over and over it, especially the last words on the Brooklyn Bridge. I am afraid I let you go without making clear how much respect I have for you. It was this message that I meant to send you by waving from the end of the pier. I tried, over "stuffed," to convince you your way was wrong. You didn't give in. Now, looking back, looking ahead even, I don't know who is right and who is wrong; who is taking the hardest way, or the best way. More important, who is taking the way that will work. Not knowing, I want you to understand that I not only love you like a brother, but I honor the goddamned moral center that you inherited from Abner, may he rest in peace, and trust it to guide you—and I realize whether your way succeeds or fails doesn't say anything about whether you, Zander, succeed or fail. So: onward Jewish soldiers!

Zander couldn't restrain a melancholic smile. "There is a post-script."

Like everyone going to Palestine, I am shedding my Americanized Ashkenazi handle and taking a Hebrew one—Nachshon Ben Aminadav. In case you are interested, the original was a headstrong type who made a name for himself by being the first to charge into the Red Sea when Moses parted it for the children of Israel, presumably demonstrating to the others that the passage was safely open to Jewish traffic, and thus inspiring them to take the plunge also.

"It's a good letter," Lili said reluctantly. "Who is this Abner, and why does Leon say may he rest in peace?"

"Abner was my older brother," Zander said. "He must rest in peace because he died in the worst way a man can die."

Lili asked quietly, "How did he die?"

Zander turned to stare out the window. And he told her of that Saturday in March of the year 1911, the Saturday of the Triangle Shirtwaist fire: of the girls falling through the air like shot birds; of the terrible chivalry of his brother, Abner; of his father's plunge to his death down an elevator shaft with his sewing machine strapped to his back.

They were quiet a long while. Zander took several deep breaths and turned back to Lili. "It is very clear to me," he began tentatively, as if he were testing the ground ahead with a baton before each step, "that we must go back to our revolution."

"For our sakes, or for the sake of the revolution?"

"For both," Zander declared, suddenly on surer ground. "For us, because we have made a rendezvous, and we will each think less of ourselves, and each other, if we fail to keep it. What we have—together—is based on a very high opinion we hold of ourselves, and of each other. We must live up to the standards our love sets. Only then will this love be a great love and not an ordinary coupling. And then we must go back to the revolution because there can be no revolution without revolutionists."

She had believed it once, every word of it, everything between the words too; but there were other things to be put in evidence. She had taken revolution as her soulmate because she never imagined the existence of someone like Alexander. She was addicted to him; to his body, to his smell; to his licking of her wounds. . . . "When Helen was sailing back with Paris to Troy—" Lili stabbed a strand of hair behind her ear. She knew she had to get this just right. A great deal depended on it "—to Troy, and to the real world and to the responsibilities they would bear for having altered it—"

"Disrupted it," Zander corrected her, but he was instantly sorry he had interrupted.

"Altered, disrupted." She waved a hand to indicate it amounted to the same thing. "Anyhow, Helen tried to talk him, talk Paris, into turning aside, into settling on a little island in the Aegean, I think it was called Pelagos, to consecrating their lives to their couple in the belief that their union was extraordinary enough, had reached a degree of intimacy—you see what I'm driving at—that it took precedence over the affairs of nation states. Shit! I'm not saying this the way I want to."

Watching her struggle for words, Zander knew he had been right about her. She played with revolution the way a child plays with a new toy. Now something more stimulating had come along and she wanted to move on to it. Revolution was only a fashion, something you wore around your neck in public, like a fox fur or a hand-knit scarf.

"Paris didn't accept Helen's proposition," Zander said ardently. "I don't accept yours. I am going back."

In her panic, Lili grasped that her not wanting to go back had forced him into it. If she switched sides, the law of opposites would oblige him to stay. "If you want to go back, I want to go back too," she announced.

But Zander only smiled a very private smile and said, "Then it is settled. We will both go back. Together."

Which is how Lili discovered there was no law of opposites, and no way out.

The brawl in the Cave of the Wandering Dog began innocently enough. Several sappers from the Semionovsky Regiment of Life Guards, trying to impress the two whores they had picked up on the Nevsky, started taunting the Cossacks about the size of the horses they rode. One thing led to another. A bottle splintered against a wall. A table overturned. The two whores screamed. The others in the bar ducked for cover. Blows were exchanged. A knife flashed. One of the Cossacks fell across a chair, blood gushing from a severed artery.

Later his body was carried back to the barracks, and his worldly belongings were piled on the desk of the regimental colonel, who locked the office door and examined them in case there might be a stolen ring or some gold coins sewn into the folds of a cape. Which is how the colonel, a wilted man in his early fifties with a waxed mustache thick with grit, came across the photograph of the naked woman in the pages of the dead man's orders ledger.

On the back of the photograph someone who wrote only with great difficulty had spelled out the word "princess."

9

It was thanks to the Bolshevik contingent at Tsarkoe Selo that they managed to get back to Petrograd. The young soldiers were flattered to be asked for a miracle. Within hours they had come up with one: a working automobile, a French Renault, with enough gasoline in it to get them as far as Petrograd. The car's greatest fault turned out to be something of an advantage. The two rear doors could be opened only from the outside. Since they were going to take the officer-cadet who had survived the attack on the coal room back with them—for trial, and no one doubted for an instant, for eventual execution—they were able to deposit their prisoner, with his hands tied behind his back, in the rear seat and forget about him.

But for Zander it wasn't that simple.

They had covered about half the distance to the capital, when Zander, nervously glancing in the rearview mirror to see if anyone was trying to overtake them, spotted the face of the officer-cadet. He had long, fine blond hair and blond eyebrows. He stared out at the side of the road, biting his lower lip so hard that blood dribbled down his chin. In the dimness of the coal room Zander had never gotten a good look at his attackers. He's a baby, he realized now. He has never shaved in his life. He knows what fate awaits him in Petrograd; he's trying not to think about it—and failing. He's imagining the wooden stake against his backbone, the firing squad lined up. He's trying to decide whether to accept

or decline the blindfold. He notices the empty coffin off
to one side. . . .

"Don't think about it," Lili whispered, leaning closer
to Zander. Once again she had read his mind. Her hand
came to rest lightly on his thigh. "What they do to him
is not our affair."

The boy must have realized they were talking about
him, because he burst out, "It wasn't my idea, I swear
it to you. I thought he wanted to frighten you, no
more." The boy's lower lip trembled so hard he had
difficulty talking. "In the name of all—all that is holy—oh
God, please believe me."

"Stop your sniveling," Lili ordered. "You were man
enough to torture another man. Now be man enough to
take whatever you have coming to you."

With a shudder the boy brought himself under control. He shook his head to get a lock of blond hair out of
his eyes, and mustering his dignity, said in a voice that
clearly belonged to a child, "I ask you—I beg you—to
have the decency to shoot me. Now. If I am to die, I
would prefer to get it over with."

Zander remembered the stories about the teenage
soldiers at the front who were either spanked or shot
for disobeying orders, depending on the mood of their
officers. He swerved around a pothole and brought the
automobile to a wrenching, angry stop at the side of the
road.

"What are you doing?" Lili asked.

Zander opened the rear door and pulled the boy
roughly from the car.

The officer cadet said "thank you" in a weak voice,
and braced himself to receive the bullet he had begged
for. Only when Zander spun him around and began
untying the rope that bound his wrists did it dawn on
him that he was being set free.

"I thank you from the heart," the boy said. "I will
never forget what you do."

Without looking at him, Zander climbed back into
the driver's seat, and grinding the gears in his haste to
get away, sped off down the road. Behind, a cloud of
dust raised by the automobile's rear wheels almost ob-

scured the officer cadet, who could be seen plunging into the adjacent fields in case his former captors changed their minds.

"There's enough death in Russia," was all Zander offered to Lili by way of explanation, "without my adding to it."

"I love you," Lili announced, "because your memory isn't convenient."

At first she refused to let him in. "After what you did, you have one hell of a nerve showing up here," she said icily.

Tuohy kept his toe wedged in the door and regarded the half of Arishka's face he could see. "I got carried away," he said. It came across as an explanation, not as an apology, but with Tuohy an explanation had the same weight as an apology. "It won't happen again." Unless, he thought, you've acquired a taste for that sort of thing.

"It certainly won't," Arishka agreed with a bitter laugh.

"Look," Tuohy said, "lovers are impulsive people— they don't know what they're doing half the time."

"Real lovers," exclaimed Arishka, "don't oblige women to perform unnatural sex acts."

Tuohy had more important things to talk to her about. And he didn't have much time. "Arishka, open the door," he said. And he told her why he had come.

She took the news bravely. It didn't surprise her, she said, dry-eyed, with only a barely perceptible twitch in a cheek muscle betraying the deeper currents that flowed in her. She asked for details and Tuohy supplied them. She asked what had happened to the body and Tuohy told her; they had scooped out a shallow grave with their fingertips and buried him in it. He held out his hands, palms down to show her the dirt embedded under his fingernails. She took his hands in hers and inspected them, and—in a gesture that had nothing to do with Tuohy—brought one of his fingers to her mouth and tried to taste the dirt with the tip of her tongue.

"You really loved him," Tuohy said. Would anyone

try to taste the dirt under which he was buried? He wondered.

"He's dead now," Arishka said in a flat voice. "Tomorrow we will all be dead."

"Then live for today," Tuohy suggested, but she only shrugged her shoulders listlessly, as if to say that life, for the moment, was too heavy.

She offered to make him a meal—she had been issued some smoked bacon from the Bolshevik canteen, and had bought a cabbage and several duck eggs on the black market—but Tuohy said he was expected somewhere.

A woman, she thought. Seeing her thought written in her eyes, Tuohy said that he had been assigned to accompany Lenin to a cottage in the Finnish countryside. Lenin's nerves were frayed, Tuohy explained. He was suffering from exhaustion. He badly needed a rest.

"Will you come back?" she wanted to know, meaning to Petrograd.

"I'll be back," he promised, meaning to her. And for the first time in a long life of making promises to women, he meant what he said.

At the door Tuohy turned to her. "I think you should cry. It will do you good."

She smiled at this conception of how women should react to the death of a husband. But when the door closed behind him, Tuohy heard the hard, hollow sound of her forehead thudding against it.

The Cossack colonel framed the photograph of the naked princess to protect it, and hung it on the inside of his toilet door. Every Sunday, after attending mass at the barrack chapel, he would lock himself in the toilet and masturbate in front of the photograph. One Sunday the colonel invited the company chaplain back to his quarters for a tumbler of German schnapps before the midday meal. After his second schnapps the chaplain excused himself and went to the toilet. The colonel blushed as he remembered the framed photograph hanging on the back of the door. But when the chaplain returned, he made no comment on it, and thanking the colonel profusely for his hospitality, soon left. When the colonel locked himself in his toilet to masturbate, he discovered the frame still hanging on the back of the door, but the photograph had been removed.

He toyed with the idea of confronting the chaplain and accusing him of the theft. Since any accusation would lead to an investigation, he decided it would be prudent to let the matter drop.

Serafima, collecting dry laundry from the clothesline in the entranceway, spotted the automobile pulling up through the open front door and let out a shriek. Barefoot, wearing only a collarless shirt that fell to his knees, brandishing a rusty saber in two hands, Sergeant Kirpichnikov came flying down the steps to repel boarders. Alyosha Zhitkin, waving an enormous navy pistol, and Vasia Maslov, with a German rifle at the ready, appeared on the top of the landing. Melor, who had been pedaling the dentist's drill, poked his head and an Austrian bayonet out the office door.

"What's going on, woman?" Sergeant Kirpichnikov cried furiously.

"How many of them are there?" Alyosha Zhitkin called down, cocking his pistol.

Hippolyte Evremov, with his brass trumpet plugged to an ear, turned up at the door leading to the dining room. "Has it started, then, the revolution?" he shouted. Even though he could hear now, he kept his voice pitched high out of habit.

And then they appeared at the door, Lili first, followed by Zander so close behind her that it was instantly apparent to Appolinaria, who with Ronzha had rushed in alarm to the upstairs banister, that they were lovers, and intimate ones at that. "How can you be sure?" whispered Ronzha.

"If all they had done was make love," Appolinaria whispered back, "they would be touching each other to advertise the fact. But the nearness without the touching—it is a sign of great closeness." And she added, "Like us, heart of my soul."

In honor of the homecoming, everyone contributed to a feast. Alyosha concocted a bullion with some horsemeat bones, then removed the bones and added handfuls of diced turnips, carrots, and potatoes that he had been saving. Serafima whipped up blinis and served them with thick cream she had bought from a Finnish peasant in Petrograd. Vasia, a crooked half smile scarring his features, supplied two bottles of Polish vodka he had been given by the Red Cross when he left the hospital. Ronzha offered a third bottle bearing a Finnish label that everyone thought was counterfeit. When Hippolyte produced a tin of pickles, Ronzha, giddy from the vodka, rambled on about how Tolstoy had had a weakness for pickles; dozens of jars of them, grown and bottled at his country estate of Yasnaya Polyana, had been ranged along the shelves of his office in place of books.

After dinner Serafima, much to Melor's chagrin, hiked her skirt above her knees and belted out a bawdy Caucasian song about a girl cuckolding her husband at the seaside. Ronzha recited a new poem that began with the line, "Genghis Khan's banners, over which no bird would fly . . ." When he finished, Lili stood up abruptly. Thinking she was going to make a speech, Hippolyte tapped a knife against a glass.

"Friends," Lili announced, "I for one am exhausted." She turned to Zander, "Come to bed, my love."

Appolinaria's elbow shot out, catching Ronzha between the fourth and fifth rib. "What did I tell you?" she whispered triumphantly.

At the Kshesinskaya Mansion the next morning, Lili was welcomed back to her attic cubbyhole with open arms by the girl who had taken over the cipher chores in her absence. "Am I glad to see you," the girl exclaimed. "There's a deluge of messages from the Bolshevik agitators assigned to the Petrograd garrison. I can't keep up with the traffic."

One glance around the room made it evident why the girl couldn't keep up. Open books were piled on the table and chairs. A small mountain of crumpled papers had accumulated in the corners. A bottle of fingernail polish had fallen off the table, leaving a bright red stain on one leather-bound book and some of the messages.

Lili took a deep breath; like it or not, she was back in the revolution. "What we need," she instructed the girl, "is to put things into some kind of order. Let's start with the books. . . ."

Zander reported for duty in the basement room that had been set aside for the bodyguard pool. In his absence the contingent had grown considerably. Some forty men had been assigned to protect the leading Bolsheviks, all of whom devoted a good part of their waking hours to propaganda work among the masses of workers and soldiers.

Zander was greeted warmly by the bodyguards who knew him, and was stared at curiously by the others, who had heard about the American and his brush with death at Tsarkoe Selo.

That morning those not out on assignment were unpacking and degreasing Mosin-Nagant rifles that had been stored in an armory whose guardian had come over to the Bolsheviks.

The basement room had a small window high in the wall that looked out onto the court in front of the mansion. One of the bodyguards remarked that there was more traffic than usual that morning; motorcycles, some with sidecars, roared up every few minutes. "Something's cooking," another bodyguard, who bore scars on his face from industrial strikes in Tiflis, noted dryly.

During the course of the afternoon one after another of the Bolshevik bigwigs—Trotsky, Bukharin, Molotov, Zinoviev, Kamenev, Sverdlov—raced off to various corners of the capital. The basement room emptied as the bodyguards were dispatched to accompany them. At four Zander received a summons to the command center on the second floor. Stalin, reading through a file of deciphered messages, motioned with a snap of his head that he was to approach. "You took your sweet time about coming back," he said. He cut off Zander's explanation with an awkward wave of his crippled left arm. "The sailors are threatening to come in from Kronstadt and march on the Tauride Palace. The Machine Gun Regiment and the workers from the Putilov factory are ready to join them. They're all furious over the news from the front—the latest offensive has ended in another defeat. If the provisional government won't take Russia out of the war, they may try to install someone in power who will." Stalin handed Zander a sealed envelope. "You are supposed to be an imaginative scoundrel. Prove it. Find a motorcycle. Get this letter to Lenin before morning."

Zander scratched a quick note to Lili. "Off, maybe for several days, on assignment. No danger. I think of you. Z." He deposited it with Arishka on his way out. Flashing a note Stalin had scribbled on a scrap of paper—"The bearer is on an urgent mission for the Bolshevik Central Committee"—he commandeered a motorcycle in the courtyard and settled into the sidecar. The driver, an Uzbek named Chuvash, had been a motorcycle courier at the front and was accustomed to dodging the mortar shells the Germans lobbed at anything that moved. Whipping the machine first one way, then another, cutting across open fields to pass the occasional army lorry lumbering along on its wooden-rimmed wheels, he made his way toward Finland. Night fell, but Chuvash did not slacken his pace, though the single headlamp on the front fender, covered with caked mud, illuminated nothing.

It was after midnight when they crossed the Finnish frontier, and then roared into the little village of Neivola, nestled in the bend of a swiftly flowing river. Chuvash went off to sleep in a barn. Zander knocked on a half-dozen doors before someone opened an upstairs shutter and directed him to the dacha owned by Lenin's friend Bonch-Bruyevich; it was at the edge of the village, the peasant said irritably, the last house on the right if you followed the path that ran behind the barn across the way.

Zander meandered around in the pitch dark until he found the house and began to circle it in search of an unshuttered window on which he could knock. Suddenly he felt the barrel of a pistol pressed to the back of his head. "Move one muscle," a familiar voice whispered in Russian, "and I'll blow your head away."

"Atticus!"

"Zander? What are you doing in this ungodly place?"

Zander explained about the wild ride from Petrograd and the urgent letter for Lenin. "How is he?" Zander inquired. "In Petrograd they say he needs a good rest."

Tuohy snickered. "Between us, there's more to it than that."

"What do you mean?"

Tuohy drew Zander around to the back door of the small cottage. "The truth of the matter is he is very bizarre sometimes."

"Bizarre in what way?"

"You never know from one minute to the next how he's going to react. He seems . . . confused. And there's the business of the arsenic injections."

Zander remembered the hurried consultation between Krupskaya and the man he took to be a doctor in the doorway of Lenin's sister's apartment. So he *had* heard the words "arsenic" and "injection" after all.

"He's being treated for something serious," Tuohy said flatly.

Zander felt a chill down his spine; if Lenin were to collapse now, it would jeopardize the revolution. Nobody, not even Trotsky, could step into his shoes. "How serious?"

"I'm not a doctor—how would I know?"

Tuohy woke up Vladimir Bonch-Bruyevich, a heavyset, cheerful man with a black beard and steel-rimmed eyeglasses he wore even when he slept. A veteran revolutionist, he had lived for a time with Lenin and Krupskaya in exile in Geneva, and was now a leading Bolshevik propagandist. Bonch-Bruyevich turned up the wick on the kerosene lamp and read the letter Zander had brought. His mouth sagged open. "I'd better show this to him at once," was all he said.

Bonch-Bruyevich climbed the narrow wooden stairs to Lenin's room and knocked. Without waiting for a reply, he let himself in. A few moments later Zander and Tuohy heard Lenin thunder, "I must return immediately."

Zander said, "He sounds rational enough to me," but Tuohy only shook his head.

Tuohy brought an enormous seven-seat Paige around to the front of the dacha. Soon afterward Lenin, his shoulders hunched, his eyes vacant, came hurrying through the door. Barely glancing at Zander, he joined Bonch-Bruyevich in the backseat of the Paige, pulled out the Browning automatic he always carried in his pocket and placed it on his knees, his forefinger threaded through the trigger guard. Zander, in the front passenger seat, and Tuohy, driving, exchanged looks. There was some cryptic conversation in the back seat, with Bonch-Bruyevich doing most of the talking. Like a child impatient to arrive, Lenin would occasionally lean forward and tap Tuohy on the shoulder. "How much longer?" he would ask. As a cold, steel-gray dawn transformed the horizon, Lenin appeared to relax. He began to reminisce about his brother, and their childhood together in Simbirsk.

"We used to amuse ourselves playing war all the time," Lenin recalled, smiling tiredly. He tapped the Browning against a knee joint as if he were testing his reflexes. "Now we play at the real thing. If only Sasha could see me! In those days we would cut out soldiers from cardboard and color them with crayons. We made the generals taller than the others, as if height were the main requirement of leadership." Lenin snickered. "Sasha's army was always Italian, with Garibaldi at its head. Mine was American, with Grant leading. As for me, I was Abraham Lincoln."

The Paige passed a convoy of peasant wagons heading toward Petrograd loaded with cabbages, and crossed the frontier soon after; the soldiers on duty waved them on without bothering to look at their papers. "When we come to power," Lenin said, "we'll abolish all borders. People will be free to come and go as they like. Trotsky always talks about the United States of Europe. Why not?"

The Paige thundered across a covered wooden bridge that straddled a muddy river, and Lenin began to talk about what it had been like to be brought up on the banks of a river. He and his brother used to "take trips around the world"—they would row upriver, exploring various tributaries for the better part of a week, then hitch a ride back home on a passing steamboat. "Things heated up for me in 1901, and I decided I needed a nom de guerre in order to protect my family," Lenin recounted. "I would have used the Volga River, where I spent my childhood, but Plekhanov"—one of the great figures of Russian socialism—"had already adopted Volgin as his pen name. So I styled myself after the Lena River in Siberia."

Tuohy quipped, "So it is an accident we talk about Leninism instead of Volganism?"

Lenin was not amused. "There are no accidents in history, young man," he said. Suddenly his brow pleated like a curtain. Was he in pain, Zander wondered, or was he thinking about what lay ahead? "There are only leaders who correctly analyze the forces at work," Lenin mumbled, "and then exploit this knowledge."

Which was another way of saying, Zander thought, that a revolutionist is someone who gives history a push.

10

The old-timers playing dominoes on the quays, the peasant women rinsing laundry on the steps running down into the canals, had never seen an armada quite like it before. It appeared in the Neva at mid-morning, a flotilla of barges and tugboats and anything else that the sailors had been able to get their hands on. There were several dozen open sailboats, two eight-oar racing sculls, a smack with its fishing gear stowed, the mail cutter with the faded royal insignia still on its stack, a coal vessel with four fifths of its hull underwater and its deck crammed with sailors laughing wildly as each bow wave splashed across their feet. Even the famous four-masted training bark with its bare-breasted mermaid on the bowsprit had been commandeered.

Spilling into the streets around the quays, the sailors formed into ranks and started to march on the Kshesinskaya Mansion not far away. "Lenin! Lenin! We want Lenin!" chanted the sailors, many of whom carried rifles and cartridge belts slung over a shoulder. Their ranks were swelled by workers from the Vyborg district. Three quarters of a mile upriver, the soldiers of the Machine Gun Regiment, armed to the teeth and provoked by rumors that they were about to be shipped to the front to stem the latest German advance, poured across the Liteiny Bridge. From the Narva district, several thousand workers from the Putilov factory, carrying enormous red banners with gold-lettered slogans, marched up Sadovaya Prospekt. By noon the streets and gardens and alleys around the Bolshevik headquarters teemed with soldiers and sailors and workers. They climbed the walls and sat astride the branches of trees to get a better view.

"Lenin! Lenin! We want Lenin!" they chanted.

They were in no mood to be denied.

Inside the Kshesinskaya Mansion, on the second floor, Lenin paced back and forth before the French doors leading to the balcony. Ranged around the room were Trotsky, Stalin, Zinoviev, Kamenev, Bukharin, Molotov, Krupskaya, Inessa Armand, Lenin's two sisters, several Red Guard district leaders, along with a dozen rank and file Bolsheviks who had been in the building. Zander, next to the door, exchanged worried looks with Lili, across the room.

"Lenin! Lenin! We want Lenin!" the mob roared again.

His features as gray as ashes in a chimney, his shoulders hunched, a hand pressed to his forehead to appease a migraine, Lenin pushed aside the lace curtain and peered out the window.

"Do we agree to lead the revolution," he asked, "and risk everything we have built up now because the timing is premature? Or do we politely decline the invitation—thank you for asking, but we have a previous engagement—and wind up in the dustbin of history?"

Trotsky, leaning against a wall, polishing the lenses of his pince-nez with a wrinkled handkerchief, put the case for riding the crest of the wave. "There are at least fifty thousand of them out there," he said. "Many are armed. A word from you and they'll march on the Tauride Palace and arrest everyone in sight. If you turn up and proclaim a new government made up of Bolsheviks, there is a good chance you can get away with it."

"What are the forces guarding the Tauride Palace?" Stalin demanded from another wall.

Lenin seized on the question. "Yes . . . what are the forces guarding the Tauride Palace? Name the units that will definitely follow us if we take power. In whose hands are the armories? Where are the food supplies for Petrograd concentrated? In the event of a counter-revolution, has the security of the Neva drawbridges been provided for? Has the rear been prepared for retreat in the event of failure?"

A handful of gravel splattered against one window, and Lenin started. He's running out of time, Zander thought.

Lenin came up with a middle way. "If there is to be an uprising," he announced, his voice pitched a shade higher than Zander had ever heard it, "I consider it essential for the soldiers and sailors, for the workers in the streets, to have the impression that we are leading it. But if a coup d'état fails, it must appear that we had nothing to do with it."

"If a coup d'état fails," commented Trotsky from his place along the wall, "our enemies will place the blame on us *whether or not* we had anything to do with it."

Stalin chewed on the stem of an unlighted pipe; he had recently decided to cut down on cigarettes. "In my view," he said, "we win as long as we do not lose. And the provisional government loses as long as it does not win."

"Stalin is right," offered Kamenev, faint of heart whenever it came to action. "Our problem is not to win, but to survive. Because if we survive, we will eventually win."

If Lenin heard them, he gave no sign of it. "I will

advise the demonstrators to take their demands directly to the provisional government. If Kerensky loses his nerve, we will fill the vacuum. Stalin, you take some of the comrades with you into the street and accompany them. That way we can always claim we led them if it suits our purpose."

Trotsky said quietly, "But you won't lead them?"

Lenin exploded. "A revolution is constructed like a pocket watch. It's a series of different-sized wheels that are set in motion by *a conscious act*. The teeth of one wheel engage the teeth of a larger wheel and that one sets an even larger wheel turning." His hand swept back to take in the masses milling in the streets below. "There is no precision here. No predictability. We are not controlling events. Events are controlling us." In his agitation, Lenin's sentences began to emerge half-formed. "Prudence—we must be—it is easy to—who can say to me—well . . ." Around the room people fixed their gazes on the floor in embarrassment. "We must make the best of a bad thing," Lenin muttered. He sucked in air through his nostrils and exhaled, and the act of breathing deeply seemed to steady him. He produced a handkerchief from the inside breast pocket of his jacket and patted his forehead. Then he licked his lips. "Open the doors—I will speak to them now."

Zander looked at Lili, but she avoided his eyes.

On the balcony Lenin squinted out over the sea of faces and let the roar of the crowd lap against him. He swayed slightly, as if the roaring had had a physical impact on him, then steadied himself with one hand on the wrought-iron railing. He started talking before the cheering had subsided, and his first words were lost in the noise. ". . . if I limit myself to a few words, I have been ill." Lenin nervously adjusted the knot on his tie. "I greet you," Lenin began again in a strained voice.

"Can't hear, can't hear," several dozen sailors chanted from across the street.

"I greet you," Lenin repeated, this time his voice raised to a hoarse shout, "in the name of the workers of Petrograd. Your demands—for an end to the war, for bread, for land, for liberty—are just demands . . . just demands. The time has come for you to take matters up directly with the members of the provisional government. If they . . . if they do not give you satisfaction, you will know, yes, you will know what to do."

Those in the forefront of the crowd stirred uneasily. "But what *should* we do?" yelled one worker.

"Tell us what to do," called someone clinging precariously to a branch of a tree.

"Can't you see, comrades—he doesn't dare," cried a young machine gunner.

"We will dare!" roared a burly sailor from atop a parked automobile. "On to the Tauride Palace!"

The cry was taken up. "To the Tauride Palace! To the Tauride Palace!"

A navy bugler put a trumpet to his lips and sounded a shrill call. The sailors formed ranks, twenty deep, and started down the street toward the center of the city. The soldiers of the Machine Gun Regiment fell in, and behind them came the masses of workers with their red armbands and banners flying over their heads. Armored cars took up position at strategic intervals. With Lenin still watching uncertainly from the balcony, the long column of demonstrators snaked away from the Kshesinskaya Mansion.

Inside the Bolshevik headquarters, Stalin quickly organized a contingent to march with the protesters. Included in it were Zander, Lili, several Red Guard district leaders and their wives, and a stunning gypsylike sixteen-year-old girl named Nadezhda Alliluyeva, the daughter of a party stalwart, Sergei Alliluyev, who had once sheltered Stalin when he escaped from prison and who kept a room at his disposal now in Petrograd. Rumor had it that Stalin, who had lost his first wife to tuberculosis in 1907, was sweet on the young beauty, though this was the first time anyone had seen the two of them together in public. "Stay close," Stalin warned everyone, "in case there is trouble. Keep your pistols out of sight. All right. Let's go."

It was a gorgeous day for a parade. A brisk breeze swept in from the Gulf of Finland. Overhead, wisps of cloud trailed across the sky at right angles to the line of march. The Putilov workers began singing "The Marseillaise" and Lili laughed at the way they pronounced the words. The ladies put their arms around each other's waists, and falling into step behind their men, began singing "The Internationale."

Along the line of march, ranks swelled as thousands of workers joined the demonstration. "You were right about us coming back," Lili shouted excitedly to Zander, who was in front of her, his arms linked through the arms of his neighbors. "We are making history today."

They crossed the Troitsky Bridge and wound their way past the Champ de Mars, where the dead from the March revolution had been buried in a common grave. "Keep on your toes," Stalin called as they turned into Sadovy Street. Zander noticed him scanning the roofs and high windows; Stalin, the old street hand, was obviously expecting trouble.

And then it came. As the Machine Gunners reached the intersection of Sadovy and Apraksina, a bell atop the Church of the Assumption, two blocks away, started to toll. Almost instantly a long burst of machine-gun fire from the Apraksina Palace swept the marchers. Dozens of snipers began firing from the rooftops. Women screamed. Soldiers and sailors scattered in the street.

"Discipline ahead of everything," cried Stalin, drawing his pistol.

The chest of a Red Guard district leader next to Zander exploded in a burst of blood and flesh, and he pitched forward onto the cobblestones. The sailors up ahead began shooting wildly. An armored car, its siren wailing, raced up the street, spraying the upper windows with machine-gun fire and crushing wounded demonstrators under its tires.

It was Zander's nightmare come to life. He would be trampled to death by the rampaging sailors surging past him. He waded into them, his eyes closed, his mind reliving the struggle to claw his way up the narrow steps to the Triangle floor, only to be swept along by the screaming, panicky girls pushing downstairs. "Lili," he cried, standing his ground, breasting the wave. And then the sailors were past and he lunged toward her.

"To cover," cried Stalin. Zander grabbed Lili by the arm, along with the woman next to her, and began pulling them to the relative safety of a doorway. Behind them a girl stumbled and fell, and her head struck sharply against the curb. From the Neva end of Sadovy, an armored car, exhaust pouring from its tailpipe, careened toward them. Zander pushed Lili and the other woman into the doorway, then turned back and plucked the girl from the path of the armored car. As he carried her to the doorway, machine-gun bullets rained down around him, sending little splinters flying against his legs.

The young girl was unconscious, but there was no sign of a wound. Zander laid her on the ground next to where Lili crouched. He looked up to see Stalin's dark face peering past him at the girl—and only then did he realize that he had saved Stalin's lady friend, the young Nadezhda Alliluyeva. Stalin pressed his ear to the girl's chest. Her heart was beating. He looked up at Zander. "What you have done I will never forget even if I live to be a hundred," Stalin whispered fiercely. His good hand held his pistol to his heart. With a last worried glance at the unconscious girl, he turned back to the street and rushed toward the Apraksina Palace.

Within minutes of the first burst of machine-gun fire, evidence of the ambush littered the cobblestones: shoes, rifles, cartridge boxes, sailor caps, banners, broken glass, ribbons from a looted sewing shop. And there were the dead: dozens, perhaps hundreds of bodies sprawled in grotesque positions. Zander pulled his German pistol from its holster and started after Stalin.

"Alexander!" screamed Lili from the doorway; it seemed as if she had pressed her entire life into that one cry. But several grenades exploding farther along the street drowned her out as Zander raced off to join the combat.

The sailors who had charged into the Apraksina Palace discovered an entire family—including an old man in a wheelchair—huddled in a downstairs drawing room. Protesting that they had nothing to do with the attack on the marchers, they were dragged out the front door, lined up against a wall, and shot by an impromptu firing party. Other sailors worked their way up the marble staircase and began breaking into the rooms, killing everyone they came across. On the roof they cornered a wounded sniper, lifted him bodily, and flung him over the parapet.

Skirting the body of a dead horse, Zander looked up to see a sniper with a rifle at an oval attic window high above him. He kneeled, took aim, and squeezed off two quick shots. The sniper ducked back in. Several soldiers from the Machine Gun Regiment burst onto a balcony two floors below the attic. They carried the corpse of a man, which they pitched over the railing.

"Above you—a sniper," Zander yelled at the soldiers.

They waved and dashed back into the house. A few moments later a soldier stuck his head through and signaled cheerfully down to Zander. Soon after, the soldiers emerged from the front door with a prisoner in tow. He was an old man with white whiskers, wearing what Stalin had described as a "monkey suit," and it occurred to Zander that he was either a butler or a banker. A woman, probably his wife, dashed out the door after him and hurled herself at the Machine Gunners, who pushed her roughly away. They led the old man into the street and forced him to kneel.

"We must take prisoners," Zander cried. One of the Machine Gunners pressed his pistol to the back of the old man's head. As Zander looked away, he heard the sharp bark of the shot.

The firing began dying down and the marchers drifted back to the streets from the doorways and the buildings they had invaded. An army truck pulled slowly along Sadovy, and the living lifted the dead and piled them in the back of it. Medics from the Machine Gun Regiment bent over the wounded. Stalin planted himself in the middle of the street and raised his pistol over his head, and what was left of the Bolshevik contingent formed around him. Several shots rang out from a side street, followed by a long burst from a machine gun on an armored car. And then there was silence, and the angry curses of the sailors. Their rifles and machine guns at the ready, the marchers reformed their ranks and started again toward the Tauride Palace.

This time no one sang.

Zander, his pistol pointing toward the ground, his eyes scanning the roofs, threaded his fingers through Lili's. "Alexander, I thank you," she told him in a low voice.

"For what?" Zander asked, never taking his eyes from the rooftops as they moved down the street.

"I thank you for remaining alive."

The chaplain had a younger brother who worked for the provisional government in the propaganda subsection of the Ministry of Public Information. The younger brother, who chased every skirt he came across, went to great pains to convince the chaplain how pious he was. The chaplain, for his part, took a certain amount of sadistic pleasure in shocking his brother with demonstrations of his worldliness. Thus, looking for something to give his brother on the occasion of his forty-first birthday, the chaplain thought of the photograph he had swiped from the colonel's toilet wall.

The younger brother made a great show of being embarrassed by the photograph of the naked princess. "If this is your idea of a joke, it is not humorous," he said. "I will burn it." He cast the photograph aside and, casually changing the subject, told his brother what had happened that morning. The Bolshevik-led mobs had marched on the provisional government. Kerensky's nerves had not cracked. Troops loyal to the government had been rushed into the city. There had been a tense moment as the two sides faced each other. Then a rain had begun to fall. The mob had dispersed. Kerensky would profit from the situation to put an end to Lenin and the Bolsheviks once and for all.

When the chaplain had departed, the younger brother propped the photograph up against a lamp, poured himself a cognac, and sat back to sip his drink and study the body of the princess. It was, he had to admit, the most original gift he had ever received from his brother.

11

There was no post mortem; the Bolsheviks didn't have time for one. Stalin was the first to see the handwriting on the wall. "At most it will be a matter of hours," he warned.

Capitalizing on the passions aroused by the "July uprising," as he labeled it, Kerensky took over from Prince Lvov as premier, installed himself in the tsar's private suite in the Winter Palace, and proceeded to orchestrate his antibolshevik campaign. Writs were issued for the arrest of Lenin and other leading Bolsheviks on the charge of inciting to armed insurrection. The Cossacks, turned loose by the new premier, invaded the *Pravda* offices, smashed the printing presses, and put the Bolshevik's principal propaganda organ out of business. Lenin went into hiding in the apartment of Stalin's friend Sergei Alliluyev, had his telltale beard and mustache snipped off—Stalin himself wielded the scissors—and then was spirited out of the city to the Finnish countryside.

Zander and Lili went directly to the Steamboat to recover a hamper of clothing and Lili's old, arthritic, half-blind cat before going into hiding. They ran into Tuohy at the entrance. He was reading a note that the poet Ronzha and Appolinaria had tacked to the front door. They had run for it, Ronzha wrote, because, having lived in the house, they were afraid of being mistaken for Bolsheviks.

Inside, the Steamboat echoed with emptiness. Most of the cats had disappeared, and Lili immediately suspected that Melor had taken them as a food supply.

Tuohy's ear caught a scuffing noise overhead. "The house is not as empty as you think," he whispered, drawing his pistol and advancing up the stairs. Zander drew his own pistol and followed him.

Lili tried to hold Zander back. "Let them be," she said. "We will go into hiding without the hamper. It is not important." But when Zander pushed her hand away and continued up the stairs, she drew her nickel-plated "phallus," as she called her pistol, from the cloth bag she carried, slipped off her shoes, and went after him.

At the end of the corridor Tuohy pressed his ear to Lili's door. Zander cocked his pistol with his thumb. With a sharp blow from his foot Tuohy kicked open the door and plunged into the room. Lili and Zander crowded in behind him.

Otto Eppler looked from one to the other, his mouth open. He had carted all of Lili's books and letters to her bed, and was going through them. "I thought—that is, I assumed—what with everyone leaving—I thought you would not be back," he said lamely.

"You miscalculated," Tuohy said coldly.

"So it's you who stole Lenin's letter from my room," Lili said breathlessly. "You are the traitor in the Steamboat."

Eppler sat down heavily on the edge of the bed, as if he had come to the end of a long journey. "I . . . yes, I took the letter," he admitted.

"Who pays you?" Tuohy demanded.

Eppler was offended. "Nobody pays me."

"But you stole the letter and gave it to Kerensky?" Lili said.

"I arranged for it to fall into his hands, yes."

"But why, Otto? Whom do you work for?" Zander asked.

Lili, furious, cried, "In the name of what cause do you betray us?"

Eppler smiled tiredly. "In the name of common sense," he said. "In the name of pure Marxism. In the name of the millions of people who will suffer if this king of communism has his way, yes?" Eppler addressed himself to Zander. "I started to tell you one night when I had a bit too much to drink. You remember, yes? This Lenin of yours is taking communism down the wrong road. No good will come of it. No good at all. He is an elitist, yes? He creates elites. And he—yes?—he is the elite of the Central Committee. He is making footsteps, yes? After him others will follow in his path. The dictatorship of the proletariat will become the dictatorship of a single man."

"There is room within the party's ranks for divergences," Zander declared, "as long as we close ranks once the decisions are taken."

Eppler shrugged. "Close ranks. That's all I ever hear, yes? Close ranks. Communism, my young comrade, is not a sail cut from one kind of cloth, no matter how much Lenin would make it seem so."

"Lies!" cried Lili. "What he says are all lies."

"Ach, my dear lady," sighed Eppler, "you don't know your Spinoza. There are no such things as lies, he tells us in his *Ethics;* there are only crippled truths, yes?"

"He is a traitor," Tuohy told Zander, "and he must be dealt with as a traitor."

"Which of you will shoot me, then?" Eppler inquired with a sad smile.

Tuohy's pistol never wavered. "If there is one like him, there will be others. He is part of a conspiracy. We must turn him over to the comrades for questioning."

"The comrades," Zander reminded him, "are going underground."

"Then we must question him ourselves," Tuohy said. He advanced menacingly in Eppler's direction, and turned his pistol so that he was holding it by the barrel.

You're putting your eggs in the wrong basket, Leon had warned Zander. Russia will break your heart. Why did he hear Leon's voice now? Zander wondered.

Eppler said, "I will save you the trouble, my friend, of questioning—what a delicate way of putting it—an old German Communist who has a different vision from yours." And in one flowing motion he plucked a tiny capsule from his jacket pocket, popped it into his mouth, and bit down on it.

Tuohy lunged forward.

"Ach, would you . . . believe I never thought it would"—Eppler closed his eyes in pain—"actually end, yes?"

Zander sank to his knees next to Eppler. "What wouldn't end, Otto?"

Eppler exhaled very slowly, as if he had been punctured, and the word "life" was carried along on the last breath to leave his lungs.

Tuohy and Zander carried Eppler's body downstairs and lifted it into the barber's chair in the middle of his office. Zander straightened the dentist's tie, and folded his hands in his lap.

Tuohy said, "Don't lose sight of the fact that he was a traitor."

"He was an idealist," Zander contradicted him. "He saw things from another angle." He didn't follow the trend of thought further than that; perhaps he sensed that the terrain was treacherous.

Tuohy eyed Zander. "Ortona didn't teach you anything." Shaking his head in disgust, he went upstairs, collected his duffel, and disappeared without a word of good-bye.

Back in her room, Lili stuffed some clothes, along with a smooth-bored navy revolver and several handfuls of cartridges, into a small straw hamper. She took along her collection of solid silver teaspoons—they might come in handy for bartering—as well as her half-full bottle of Ideal perfume. As she was about to leave, she remembered the two sketches of her, souvenirs of Paris, one done by a young Spanish painter, the other by an artist who exaggerated her neck. She removed the one from its place on the wall, the other from a large hamper. At the door she paused for a last look around the room. She surveyed the wooden crates nailed shut, the slim French machine gun near the window, the silver samovar. Without a trace of regret she scooped up the old cat and her hamper, and leaving her door wide open, turned her back on the Steamboat.

It was Lili who had arranged, in the course of one quick telephone call, for them to go into hiding. When Zander asked where they were heading, Lili only screwed up her face and answered with what seemed to be a non sequitur. "Not to worry," she said, "I brought along some perfume." But she insisted on making a detour—though once again mysterious, she refused to discuss it.

The detour turned out to be a dilapidated nursery school attached to a church on the outskirts of the city. The nuns who ran it were English, and Lili had trouble making herself understood at the door. "I am—how you say?—wanting see my little girl?" Then an older nun, a heavy woman with a pockmarked face, spotted Lili and waved her in.

"You have come to take Ludmilla?" asked the nun in English, and when Lili didn't understand her she turned to Zander in frustration. "You don't by any chance speak English?" When she discovered he did, the nun breathed a sigh of relief and asked him to translate.

"No, I will not take her," Lili replied heatedly, "not now, not ever."

"Say to her that the little girl needs a mother," the nun instructed Zander, not bothering to hide her disapproval.

"A mother is what I cannot be," Lili replied. She appealed to Zander. "I can't even sing a child to sleep. When I try, they always put their hands over their ears. Ask her if I can see the child. It will only be for a moment."

The nun sighed as if the weight of the cross were on her shoulders. She led them down a corridor into a high-ceilinged playroom. Paint was peeling from the walls. Several panes in the windows were missing and covered with cardboard. Two dozen little girls, all of them wearing identical gray smocks, were playing with dolls or building blocks or drawing on large sheets of wrapping paper tacked to a wall. "She is over there," the nun said coldly.

Lili approached a little girl, who was coloring a picture she had made; it consisted of a microscopic fish swimming in an enormous ocean. Zander thought he recognized the little girl; the frightened eyes, the round face, the short curly hair were familiar. Then he remembered where he had seen her before—in a photograph pinned to a wall in Lili's attic cubbyhole.

"Here is the nice lady who visits you from time to time," announced the nun in halting Russian.

The little girl, who must have been about seven or eight, didn't look anything like Lili. Until she smiled. Then she was transformed magically into a spitting image: the same high cheekbones, the hint of flatness to her nose, the faint slant to her eyes, suggesting Tartar influence somewhere back in her bloodline. "Have you brought me anything?" the little girl asked innocently.

"It is not polite to ask for things," scolded the nun.

"There is no harm done," Lili said quickly. "As a matter of fact, I did." And on the spur of the moment she handed the old, arthritic cat to the little girl.

"What's wrong with its eye?" asked the little girl.

"She's blind in that eye," Lili explained.

"What do you say when someone gives you a gift?" coached the nun. She glanced at the cat as if she were appraising its culinary possibilities.

"I say thank you," the little girl said brightly.

"That's a very pretty picture you are coloring," Zander remarked. "Did you draw it?"

Ludmilla nodded shyly.

"What do you think of when you draw pictures?" Zander asked.

"Who is he?" Ludmilla asked Lili in a whisper.

"He is my friend. Now he is your friend too."

That seemed to make it all right. "When I do art," Ludmilla explained seriously to Zander, "I start with an idea. Then I draw a line around it."

"I see," Zander said.

Once outside, Lili didn't speak for several blocks. "I suppose," she finally managed, "I owe you an explanation."

"You owe me nothing," Zander said abruptly. A *sotnya* of Cossacks went by at a gallop, kicking up dust. When Zander glanced at Lili, her eyes were watery—whether from the dust or from emotion, he couldn't tell. He adopted a different tone. "You owe me nothing," he repeated in a gentler voice. "When you are ready, you will tell me. In any case, it will change nothing."

"I will tell you, Alexander—only not yet. I wanted you to see her. I wanted you to know where she was. If anything . . . anything should happen to me . . . I would take it as a favor—"

"You want me to look after her."

"I only want there to be someone in the world to whom she is special."

Zander accepted this with a nod. "Your daughter"—he discovered it was harder to pronounce these words than he thought—"your daughter will be special to me."

The chief of the propaganda subsection of the Ministry of Public Information studied the photograph of the naked princess through the magnifying glass. "I see what you mean," he muttered. "Her face is very Russian, but with a faint Oriental trace in the eyes—it should certainly appeal to a great many men. Of course we'll have to do something about the body—"

"That goes without saying," the younger brother of the chaplain agreed.

"Yes, indeed," said the chief of the propaganda subsection, loath to move the magnifying glass. Finally he managed to look up. "If this works out as I think, you will merit a letter of commendation. That will be all for the moment."

The younger brother of the chaplain let himself out of the office and closed the door soundlessly behind himself. Inside, the chief of the propaganda subsection bent back to the magnifying glass. He had never before had the occasion to observe at such close range the sex of a woman. "So that's what all the fuss is about," he said aloud.

"Well," Lili asked anxiously, "what do you think?"

"What I think," Zander said, delicately sniffing the air, glancing around with a distinct look of disgust on his face, "is that you're right. Nobody will find us here." And he tried to make a joke out of it. "Nobody would want to."

Lili screwed up her face too. "It is fucking terrible, isn't it?"

Zander deposited his belongings in a corner and sat down on the old mattress on the floor. "It's better than being at the tender mercies of some ardent antibolsheviks. I suppose you get used to the odor."

Lili pushed aside some jars filled with fetuses to make room for her hamper. She took the two drawings of herself from it and propped them on another shelf. Then she produced her bottle of Ideal perfume, and unbuttoning her shirt, sprinkled it liberally over her neck and breasts. "At least I can take your mind off the odor," she murmured, and settling onto the mattress next to Zander, she pulled his head toward her chest.

They had gone to ground, thanks to Lili's friendship with a doctor who secretly sympathized with the Bolsheviks, in one of the basement storage rooms of the six-story Institute of Science on Angliskyi Prospekt. "You'll be safe here," the doctor, a bald, middle-aged wisp of a man with a harelip, had assured them. He had given them one of the two keys that fit the door. "Lock it from the inside. The only person who comes down here is me. I'm the 'parts' custodian," he added with a leer.

Zander had understood what the doctor meant by "parts" the instant he stepped through the door. The walls of the storage room were lined with wooden shelves, and the shelves were filled with jars of anatomical parts preserved in formalin, a colorless liquid containing, as Zander's nose quickly detected, a high percentage of formaldehyde. There were livers, lungs, hearts, intestines, and brains. All were neatly labeled in a flowing script: LIVER—40-YEAR-OLD MALE, or BRAIN—18-YEAR-OLD FEMALE. One shelf held nothing but hearts, starting at one end with that of a twelve-week-old embryo, and winding up near the boarded-over transom with that of a ninety-five-year-old male. "At least we won't be lonely," Lili joked, and she assembled several jars that held the hearts, brains, lungs, and intestines of cats on the shelf nearest the mattress so she could have her favorite pets close by.

Zander and Lili quickly fell into a routine. They stripped and washed the first thing every morning at the single tap that ran into the deep laundry basin. The doctor with the harelip appeared at midmorning with books and newspapers and rumors, along with odds and ends he managed to swipe from the institute's commissary—half a cauliflower, a handful of cucumbers, some leftover bread. Lili and Zander took turns going out, always at the height of the morning, when the streets were full and they were least likely to be noticed. They scrounged for food in the black markets around the city; with luck they might come across a farmer willing to accept one of Lili's silver teaspoons in exchange for a side of cured ham or a sack of beets.

At the beginning, Zander thought that the environment, not to mention the odor, would dampen his appetite, sexual and otherwise. Curiously, just the opposite turned out to be true. Lili, stripped to the waist, overpowering the formaldehyde with generous doses of Ideal, took to holding provocative "conversations" with her "hearts" lined up on the shelves. To one heart, that of a twenty-five-year-old male, she talked about the effect shaving off her pubic hair had had on him. She reminded a twenty-nine-year-old male heart of what might have happened if he had been less of a gentleman. She berated a fifty-five-year-old male for abandoning her in Venice, and thanked a forty-four-year-old heart for teaching her the fine art of superimposing her fantasies over reality during the act of lovemaking. She plucked a twenty-seven-year-old female off a shelf and remembered her saying that only lovers can stand in the rain without getting wet.

It was an old habit of hers: teasing, testing new lovers with tales of the ones who had gone before. She glanced at Zander to see how he was reacting. A bemused smile played on his lips; he was taking it as . . . theater. Which only spurred her on. Lili hunted around until she found a twenty-six-year-old heart and described introducing him to the Chinese custom of warming your mouth with tea before caressing your lover. Lili watched Zander out of the corner of her eye as she removed a twenty-nine-year-old male heart from the shelf and pressed the jar to her bare breast. "You were my poet," she murmured, "my poet and my Paris."

Did she mean the city, Zander wondered, or the lover who wouldn't turn aside with Helen at the island of Pelagos?

"The city," Lili said, reading his mind.

"How can you know what I'm thinking?"

"The way you have penetrated my body, I have penetrated your head," she replied. And brushing her fingertips across the "hearts" behind her, she asked, "Are you jealous?"

"Of course I'm jealous," Zander answered.

"You regret that I had lovers before you? It is a matter all new lovers eventually confront, no? I order you to tell the truth."

"When I imagine you spreading your legs to other men—to other women too—my throat tightens. I have trouble breathing. But your *hearts*, as you call them—your hearts made you what you are. I prefer being jealous to having you different."

Lili slipped into his lap, into his arms. She unbuttoned his shirt and reached under it to stroke *his* heart. "I want to make love, my heart," she said softly.

Later, she whispered into his ear, "I am only just becoming accustomed to the miracle of an *us*." And as she never gave without taking away, she added, "Of all the hearts I have known, yours displeases me the least."

12

Arishka's note came directly to the point.

Atticus—I received your letter—the answer is no—to tell the truth I am not even sure I appreciate the offer—you are too violent for my tastes—we are revolutionists because there is no other way—we cry over every drop of blood shed—for you, shed blood only whets your appetites—all of them—I unfortunately speak from experience—as for lovemaking, I can be led but never pushed—your body is correct—your head needs work—also your spelling—comradely greetings—Arishka.

"Dear Arishka," Tuohy started a new letter. He looked up at Lake Razliv, the stub of his pencil poised over the sheet of paper he had torn from Lenin's notebook. A mosquito made the error of settling onto the back of Tuohy's wrist. He put the pencil between his teeth to free his palm and swatted it. Then he flicked the corpse off the back of his wrist with a fingernail and stared at the tiny stain of blood on his skin. He had to admit that blood did whet his appetites. But where was the harm? He shed blood on orders, and for a good cause. It wasn't as if he went out and killed the first person he came across. How could he explain the difference to Arishka? Better not to try. He could tell from her letter that she was waiting to be convinced. Her *no* was really *maybe*. Why else would she have told him his head needed work? Not to mention his spelling. "Believe me," he wrote.

I was happy to have a letter from you even if I wasn't happy with what it said. I am going crazy here with boredom. L. brought along gloves to keep the mosquitoes off his hands, a trick he learned when he was banished to Siberia. He squats all day in front of our shack writing. A dinghy comes across the lake once a day with food and letters and newspapers, and carries off L.'s letters to the comrades not in prison. L. is optimistic—he says the pendulum will swing. Whatever was bothering him in Petrograd has disappeared. He bathes twice a day and scrubs certain parts of his body with mud. But he seems alert and healthy. He even walks better. As for us, you and me, I propose we strike a bargain. I will work seriously on my head and my spelling. You, for your part, will take back your 'no' and send me a comradely 'maybe.' What do you say?

And he signed it, "Your comrade who would give anything to be in your arms, Atticus."

Eight days later, the dinghy from Razliv brought, among other things, a letter from Arishka. Tuohy tore it open. It bore one word: "Maybe."

The autumn rains began in earnest in mid-August. The drops were as large as any Tuohy remembered seeing, and they beat on the lake as if it were a drum. The nights grew bitter. Lenin took to sleeping with an overcoat on and a scarf wrapped around his head. The shack leaked; no sooner had Tuohy plugged one hole than another appeared. Then, one night, the thing they all feared happened. A hunter caught out in a downpour asked for shelter. Lenin shoved his books under the hay and pretended to be asleep. Tuohy also; his accent was not that of a typical Finnish peasant. Zinoviev muttered something about how the three of them had been hired to cut hay. The hunter studied them all with unblinking eyes, and never took his hands from the shotgun. When the rain let up he departed without a word. Not so much as a thank-you. Lenin decided it would be too risky for them to remain in the shed.

Tuohy sent word with the dinghy the next day. Meticulous plans were made. A comrade from Vyborg who was a member of an amateur theatrical group provided a blond wig for Lenin. Vasia Maslov rowed across the lake to take photographs of him in his wig for the false papers that would identify the Bolshevik leader as a worker at the Sestroretsk plant in Finland. Lenin's new identification card listed his name as Constantine Petrovich Ivanov. The choice of aliases struck him as an omen. "If I can preside over a workers' state as long as Constantine reigned over Rome, I shall die a happy man," he said.

On the night of August 21, guided by a local Bolshevik named Yemelyanov, Lenin headed for the frontier and Finland.

Tuohy made his way back to Petrograd. Arishka must have recognized his step on the stairs, even though—or perhaps because—he was taking them two at a time. She opened the door before he had a chance to knock. "Hello, Americanitz," she said shyly. And she took his

hands in hers and, in a gesture that had everything to
do with Tuohy, brought one of his fingers to her mouth
and kissed the tip of it.

They stood around the easel and studied the painting of
the Russian princess with a trace of Asia in her eyes.
Outside, behind the Tauride Palace, several youngsters
were torturing stray cats they had caught for that purpose, but the men in the room were too preoccupied to
pay attention to the almost human howls that rose from
the throats of the animals.

One after another the men around the easel nodded
approval. The minister was the last to agree; it was his
custom to let his subordinates commit themselves before he did. Finally he, too, nodded. "Have five thousand printed up as soon as possible," he ordered, and
he turned to the next order of business—the distribution of a forged letter purporting to come from the pen
of V. I. Lenin, thanking the German government for its
generous financial support in his drive to overthrow
the provisional government and take Russia out of the
war.

13

And so they watched for straws in the wind—and
waited: Lenin in the home of the Communist
police chief of Helsingfors; Stalin in the Alliluyev apartment in the Rozhdestvensky district of Petrograd;
Trotsky, who had surrendered in order to provoke a
show trial, in the Kresty Prison; Kerensky in the tsar's
private rooms at the Winter Palace; Commander-in-
Chief Kornilov at the general staff headquarters overlooking the Dnieper bluffs in Mogilev.

The first straw appeared toward the end of August.
Kornilov, visiting Moscow for a state conference, re-

ceived a tumultuous welcome from the crowds lining the route. Surrounded by his Tekinsky bodyguards, Kornilov went to offer up a prayer at the Shrine of the Virgin of Iversk, an act that escaped no one's attention, since it was part of a tsar's coronation ritual.

"Kornilov," raged Kerensky, pacing back and forth before the former tsar's Louis Quinze desk, "has a lion's heart and the brains of a sheep. He will ruin everything!"

"Kornilov," Lenin wrote the comrades in the capital, "is precisely what the doctor ordered to restore the Bolsheviks to good odor. As soon as the menace becomes obvious, we will offer ourselves as the guardians of the revolution."

Early in September, Kornilov ordered the Third Cavalry Corps and the Savage Division to move on Petrograd. Then he dispatched a crisply worded telegram demanding the immediate resignation of Kerensky and his entire cabinet, and the surrender of all civil and military authority to himself.

Kerensky rejected Kornilov's ultimatum, fired him as supreme commander, and sent a half-dozen regiments to block the approaches to Petrograd. But having taken all the appropriate precautions, he promptly lost his nerve. Worried about whether the workers in the city would actively oppose Kornilov if he got as far as the capital, Kerensky invited the Bolsheviks to participate in Petrograd's defense.

Hiding their smiles, the Bolsheviks immediately accepted. Trotsky walked out of prison on three-thousand-ruble bail. Twenty thousand rifles were handed out to factory workers—most of them to Bolsheviks or Bolshevik sympathizers. Bolshevik flying squads, their red flags whipping from their fenders, raced around the city alerting factories, mining bridges, and inspecting street barricades. Most important of all, the Bolsheviks' private militia, the Red Guard, was granted legal status and supplied with twenty-five thousand rifles and even some machine guns.

Kornilov's attempt to march on Petrograd fizzled. Bolshevik railway men tore up lengths of track to prevent the movement of troops. Bolshevik telegraph operators disrupted Kornilov's communications. The Third Cavalry Corps, bogged down between Pskov and Petrograd, abandoned the game, arrested its commanding officer—who quickly committed suicide—and placed itself under the orders of the Petrograd Soviet.

Kerensky dipped into the ex-tsar's supply of French champagne at the Winter Palace to celebrate the victory. He appointed himself supreme commander of the armies, and emerged from the Kornilov affair, on paper at least, with all the powers of a dictator. But the Bolsheviks, who celebrated with cheap vodka when they could find any, emerged *armed*.

The Bolsheviks were the heroes of the day. Bolshevik candidates by the thousands won elections to the small Soviets representing factories or military units. These Soviets began sending more and more Bolsheviks to represent them at the district Soviet level. Almost overnight the Bolsheviks found themselves with voting majorities in the crucial Petrograd and Moscow Soviets. Soon they dominated the Soviet's ruling presidium, and Trotsky resumed the post he had held in 1905—president of the Petrograd Soviet.

By the end of September, the pendulum had come full swing. Kornilov, his dark Kalmuk face drawn and bitter, was imprisoned in a monastery near Bikov. Kerensky was reduced to issuing proclamations *asking* the Bolshevik workers to return the arms that had been issued to them during the crisis. Lenin, smelling blood, moved to the Finnish border town of Vyborg to be within striking distance of Petrograd.

The army truck pulled up at a corner on Nevsky Prospekt. "Put one up on that wall," ordered a young officer.

An old soldier lugged over the can of paste and splashed some onto the bricks with a sticky brush. The young cadet with the short sword at his belt unrolled the poster and flattened it against the wall. "Is it straight?" he asked.

"What difference, straight or crooked?" groused the old soldier.

"It's straight," called the officer.

The artist from the propaganda subsection of the Ministry of Public Information had perfectly captured the Russian-ness of the model's face. There was even a faint Oriental slant to the eyes. He had draped the body with a togalike robe that fell from one shoulder, had painted the figure against an imperial blue background, and lettered in the slogan in bright red: THE WOMEN OF RUSSIA SAY *NO* TO BOLSHEVISM.

Ironing out the wrinkles with his palms, the cadet imagined he was running his hands over the woman's body; in his mind's eye he could feel her breasts beneath the toga.

"Get a move on," called the officer. "We have fifty more to do before the end of the day."

Like a fuse burning down, the days grew shorter. It turned dark in midafternoon, and stayed that way well into the next morning. The October sky, invariably choked with clouds, didn't help matters. A raw, damp fog rolled in off the Gulf of Finland. And if the weather wasn't depressing enough, there was a zeppelin scare; nobody could say for sure whether they had actually been sighted or were simply anticipated, but as a precaution the gaslights had been turned off in the streets.

But the Smolny Institute, at the bitter end of the tramway line some three miles east of the Winter Palace, blazed with light—people said it looked like an ocean liner from a distance. The Petrograd Soviet had been evicted from the Tauride Palace during the summer to make way for the Constituent Assembly, due to convene to replace the "provisional" government with a "permanent" government. The Soviet's representatives, scouting around for a suitable place to hang their hats, had quickly settled on Smolny, nestled in a U-bend of the Neva. The Smolny complex consisted of a former convent with graceful smoke-blue cupolas, and the adjoining barracklike institute, three stories high and two hundred yards long, built for the daughters of the nobility. Inside, the rooms had their original enamel plaques: LADIES' CLASSROOM NUMBER 4 or TEACHERS'

BUREAU. Over them had been tacked hand-lettered signs: FACTORY SHOP COMMITTEES, or CENTRAL ARMY COMMITTEE, or UNION OF SOCIALIST SOLDIERS.

As the Bolsheviks came to dominate the Petrograd Soviet, Smolny gradually became a Bolshevik stronghold. Security was strict; the Bolsheviks remembered only too well the sacking of the Kshesinskaya Mansion. Outside the main entrance, four rapid-fire machine guns, their canvas covers removed, their ammunition belts inserted, had been set up behind barricades of firewood. Several armored cars were parked conspicuously under the trees in the courtyard. Red Guards manned the roof armed with small, corrugated iron bombs filled with *grubit*, said to be more powerful than dynamite.

At any given hour a long queue of people waited impatiently at the entrance. Guards let them in four at a time and they were questioned inside the main door by Arishka and another woman, who demanded proof of their identities and details of their business in the building before they would issue passes.

"What about something to eat?" Tuohy whispered in Arishka's ear. "Zander's saving seats for us."

"I was sent by the comrades at the Obukhov factory," a tall, bearded worker was explaining to her. "We have thrown out the capitalist owner and set up a workers' committee to take his place. But we are not sure what to do next."

Arishka stamped a blue card and handed it to the man, who stood before her with his cap in his hand, shifting his weight from one foot to the other. "You want the Factory Shop Committee's room on the third floor," she told him. "Anya," she called to a girl with bobbed hair, "will you sit in for me while I take a break?"

On their way down to the refectory, Tuohy pushed Arishka into an alcove. "Not here, Americanitz," she breathed, but she made no effort to duck away. "I missed you this morning when I woke up," she told him. "Your place was still warm in the bed."

"I had to be in Vyborg by seven," Tuohy said, "and I was worried about getting a tram."

"How did it go?" Arishka asked.

"Trotsky was his usual brilliant self," Tuohy said. "It makes me nervous when he climbs onto a podium and talks to the workers while it's still dark. We could never prevent it if someone got it into his head to shoot him."

"Americanitz, I ask you to stop, please," Arishka pleaded as Tuohy pressed the beginning of an erection into her. "You embarrass me."

Tuohy backed off. "I enjoy embarrassing you," he laughed. "You look very pretty when your face turns red. For a Bolshevik, it's an appropriate color."

"You're an impossible man," she announced, and taking him by the hand, she pulled him toward the refectory staircase.

"We're over here," Zander called to them above the din.

Tuohy bought two meal tickets for four rubles, and he and Arishka took their places in the line. When they came to the serving section, a very fat woman with two gleaming silver teeth ladled *shchi*, cabbage soup, from an enormous cauldron into their tin bowls. Farther along they both helped themselves to thick slices of buttered black bread and wooden spoons from a basket, and shouldered their way through the crowd to the long table where Zander and Lili had saved two places for them.

"It's too noisy here to think," Arishka called, sliding onto the edge of the bench next to Lili. Across from her two Red Guards wolfed down their soup with an enthusiasm that came from not having eaten in several days.

"So what's new?" Tuohy asked.

"What's new," Zander called in English, "is Lenin's letter."

The comrades in Petrograd had received a plain-language letter from Lenin, who was on the Finnish side of the frontier, urging them to launch an armed uprising at once. It was only a matter of seizing the important buildings and bridges, Lenin argued, and Petrograd would be theirs. To which Stalin and the other members of the Bolshevik Central Committee, aghast, replied coldly, "The comrades have decided that future letters along this line must be enciphered."

Having to encipher his letters didn't seem to slow Lenin down. "The crisis is upon us," he wrote in one letter that Lili deciphered using Tolstoy's *Confession*. "It is criminal to delay."

"The chances of success are 100 to one in favor," he wrote in another letter enciphered using Dostoevsky's *The Gambler*.

"All of Europe is on the verge of revolution," he claimed in still another letter enciphered with Dostoevsky's *Notes from the Underground*, and he went on to threaten to resign from the Bolshevik Party and "agitate independently among the lower ranks" if the Central Committee did not see the light. The comrade who carried this letter sewn into the lining of her coat reported that Lenin was deep into Cluseret's *On Street Fighting* and Von Clausewitz's *On War*.

"I agree with him," Zander said. "In America they have a saying: Strike while the iron is hot."

Lili said, "If we wait for the Constituent Assembly, we can take power legally."

"Why mount a coup d'état when it is possible, with a little patience, to achieve the same thing without bloodshed?" ventured Arishka.

"I'm all for action," Tuohy asserted, running his hand along Arishka's thigh under the table.

"You are always for action, Americanitz," Arishka noted dryly.

After work, Tuohy took them all for a drink at Uncle Tom's Cabin (as the workers called it, though their pronunciation left those who understood English grinning), a *traktir*, or lower-class inn, across the street from the gates of Smolny. As Tuohy barreled through the crowd to claim a table, one of the Red Guards leaving it flipped a coin into a tea saucer for a tip. A young waiter with totally white hair materialized out of the smog. Pointing to a sign on a wall that read, JUST BECAUSE A MAN MUST MAKE HIS LIVING WAITING ON TABLES IS NO REASON TO INSULT HIM BY OFFERING A TIP, he held out the saucer to the tipper, who mumbled an apology and retrieved his coin.

"What I say," explained Tuohy as the waiter deftly deposited four steaming glasses of tea on the table, "is that the single most useful piece of information for a revolutionist is that people are incapable of making up their own minds. With all these different political parties, factions, and groups around, how can they be expected to pick?"

"Lenin always said it was not a matter of mustering a majority, only a question of which minority would have the nerve to accept power." This came from Arishka.

Lili noted Zander's expression. "Why are you so glum?" she demanded.

He shook his head. "Anyone can make a revolution. The big problem is judging when to make it. Too soon and you blow it. Too late and you no longer lead it."

"The thing that scares me about a Bolshevik coup," said Arishka, "is that it will result in civil war. And a civil war will destroy Russia."

"Maybe we have to destroy Russia," Tuohy said, "in order to save Russia."

"It would be a crime to destroy Russia," Arishka said flatly.

Zander blew on his tea. "I think it was Châteaubriand who said that crimes are not always punished in this world. But mistakes are. It would be a mistake not to make our move now, as Lenin says."

Several tables away, near the swinging door that led to the kitchen, four sailors crowded around a tiny table staring across the room at Lili. "It's her, I tell you," one of the sailors ventured.

"There is a resemblance," a sailor with eyeglasses admitted.

"I'd recognize the slut anywhere," the first sailor insisted.

"If it's not her, then it's her twin sister," another said.

"If it is her," said the youngest sailor, a boy in his teens, "she's got a hell of a nerve coming here."

"Just because she was stupid enough to come here is no reason she has to stay here," the first sailor said.

"Come on, mates," said the youngest sailor.

The four sailors waded through the crowd toward Lili.

"Company's coming," said Tuohy, perking up; the Irish in him smelled trouble.

"What can we do for you?" Zander asked politely.

"What you can do for us," the first sailor spoke up boldly, "is get that slut"—he looked down at Lili—"out of here. This is an honest workingman's hangout, and there's no place here for a lackey of the damned provisional government."

A hush settled over Uncle Tom's Cabin. Zander and Tuohy climbed to their feet. Zander removed his eyeglasses and tucked them into his jacket pocket. "You are making a very big mistake, comrade sailors," he said quietly.

Tuohy let his jacket slip open so that his holster was partly visible. "Why don't you all go back to your table," he said in a friendly tone, "before we take offense."

"You don't scare us," one of the sailors said belligerently. He grabbed an empty wine bottle from another table by the throat. The people nearest them scrambled out of the way.

"What is bothering you?" Zander asked the sailors.

"Don't pretend you haven't seen the government posters," the youngest sailor ventured. "It has her picture on it. 'The women of Russia say *no* to Bolshevism' is what the lettering says."

"My picture on a poster!" Lili exclaimed. "You must be out of your minds."

Zander said, "This lady has worked for some time for the Central Committee of the Bolshevik Party. She is known to Comrade Stalin personally. Her loyalty is beyond question. If there is a resemblance between her and a figure on a poster, it is a coincidence."

"There's no coincidence," the first sailor persisted. "It's her what's on the poster."

It was Arishka who saved the situation. "Comrade

sailors," she said, rising and planting herself between the sailors and her friends. "I have worked for the Bolshevik Party for four years now. There are people in this room who know me." She looked around for confirmation, and several men nodded.

"We can vouch for her," one mustached artillery man called. "Nobody gets into Smolny except if she lets him in."

"I know this woman to be a true and honest Bolshevik," Arishka continued. "Believe me, you are making an error if you think she has done anything to help the provisional government."

"Maybe the resemblance is a coincidence," the sailor with the eyeglasses told his comrades.

"If we did make a mistake," the first sailor said grudgingly, "when you see the poster you'll admit it wasn't our fault."

"Where can we find this famous poster?" Zander asked.

"They're all over," said the sailor with the eyeglasses. "There's one on Nevsky across the street from the great library."

"Why don't we take a look at it?" Zander said.

14

Arishka returned to her post at the entrance of Smolny. Zander, Tuohy, and Lili took the trolley back into the center of the city and walked over to Nevsky Prospekt. The poster across the street from the library had disappeared—Bolshevik squads went around Petrograd systematically defacing or destroying government posters—but they found another one intact farther down along Nevsky, not far from the Notre Dame of Kazan Cathedral. Tuohy used up all his lighter fluid so they could get a better look at it. Lili paled.

"It *is* me," she said in a whisper. "But how? Who would do such a thing?"

Zander glanced at the artist's signature, written in a tiny script on the lower right hand corner. "Do you know anyone named Tsipin?"

Lili shook her head. "I never met anyone by that name."

"You may not know Tsipin," Tuohy said grimly, "but Tsipin certainly knows you."

Tsipin vomited into the gutter in front of his building. "The moment you get your paws on some money, you blow it all at The Stray Dog," his girlfriend berated him in a whiny voice. "You didn't have to buy drinks for everyone and his brother who happened to be under the same roof. You might have thought about me for once. I could have had one of those Paris dresses the diplomat's maid was selling the other day." And she added whimsically, "I look fantastic in black lace."

Tsipin pushed past her up the stairs and through the front door. He climbed the rickety staircase that led to his studio in the back of the fourth floor. "I can't see a thing in this sewer of a hallway," his girlfriend called, feeling her way along behind him. At the door of the studio, Tsipin felt around in his pockets until he found the skeleton key. Then he struck a match so he could fit the key into the lock. Which was when he saw the two pistols pointing at his head.

"What—"

"Where are you, honey?" the girlfriend called from the third floor landing. "Say something so I can follow your voice."

The match sputtered out. The two pistols pressed into Tsipin's temple. "Talk to her," Tuohy whispered.

"I'm up here," Tsipin said in a sickly voice.

"You're not going to throw up again?" the girlfriend called. "If you do, it's you who's going to clean it up."

Panting from the effort, she arrived on the fourth

floor landing. "You could have bought me a pair of Italian shoes with the money you blew tonight," she whined into the dark, "instead of me having to stuff mine with newspaper to make them fit."

Tsipin struck another match. The girlfriend saw the two men with pistols, and swallowed. "Stay calm," Tuohy advised. "Think of your feet. If you scream, you'll never have to use them again."

"What do you want?" Tsipin asked once they were inside. The yellow light from the kerosene lamp made his complexion look waxen. "If you think you can hit me up for money, I spent it all tonight at The Stray Dog."

"That's true enough," the girlfriend said quickly.

"The money you spent tonight," Zander asked carefully, "is what you got for doing the government poster?"

Tsipin said, "Whose side are you on?"

"We are on the side of truth," Tuohy said pleasantly. "If you answer honestly, nothing happens to you. If you take us for fools and lie to us—" He drew his forefinger across his throat.

"The money you spent tonight," Zander repeated, "was for the poster?"

"The poster, yes," Tsipin nodded miserably. He tried desperately to clear his head so he could figure out which side they were on and tailor his answers accordingly. But he had drunk so much, he couldn't remember what the different sides were.

" 'The Women of Russia Say *No* to Bolshevism.' Whose idea was that?"

Tsipin managed to say, "*They* made up the slogan, not me. Personally, I'm not for or against anyone."

"You didn't support the overthrow of the tsar?" Tuohy asked in mock surprise.

Tsipin was confused. "The tsar was a tyrant who got his just deserts."

"Nicholas was God's anointed," Tuohy shot back, "who was betrayed by the Bolsheviks."

"I was not so much against the tsar," Tsipin squirmed, "as against that German wife of his."

"Who commissioned the poster?" Zander asked.

"The chief of the propaganda subsection of the Ministry of Public Information," Tsipin replied.

"And whom did you take for a model?" Zander asked. He barely breathed as he waited for the answer.

"I didn't use any model," Tsipin told him with pride.

"It's true, what he says, citizen-gentlemen," said the girlfriend.

"Who asked you?" Tuohy said.

"You made up the face you painted?" Zander asked.

"Not exactly," explained Tsipin. "I painted from a photograph that the chief of the propaganda subsection gave me."

"A photograph!" Zander and Tuohy exchanged looks.

"A photograph," Tsipin repeated weakly.

"You're lying," Zander said.

"Show it to them, for God's sake," the girlfriend begged the artist. "Then maybe they'll leave us in peace."

Tsipin produced the photograph of Lili. Tuohy caught a glimpse of it before Zander hastily buried it in his pocket.

"It's one of Vasia's photographs," Zander said.

"Vasia wouldn't sell this to someone from the provisional government," Tuohy said, puzzled.

"Why don't we ask the chief of the propaganda subsection of the Ministry of Public Information where *he* got the photograph?" suggested Zander.

The chief of the propaganda subsection, accosted in the street outside the ministry, at first denied having had anything to do with the poster. But when Zander confronted him with the artist's confession, he came up with the information that he had gotten the photograph from one of his staffers, whose name and address he agreed to supply when he was treated to a glimpse of Tuohy's German pistol nestled snugly in its wooden shoulder holster. The staffer acted, in turns, outraged and innocent, until he realized he could get off the hook by passing Zander and Tuohy on to his older brother, the chaplain, who had given him the photograph for his forty-first birthday. The chaplain was fresh from presiding over the burial of an officer who, acting on a dare, had ground up and swallowed a vodka shot glass at the height of a late-night orgy. "As a matter of fact," said the chaplain, "I removed the photograph from its frame behind the bathroom door of our regimental colonel." The regimental colonel, summoned to Smolny by a caller who claimed to represent the Executive Committee's Military Commission, pretended at first that he had never laid eyes on the photograph in question. It was only when he was advised of an urgent need for a regimental colonel with his qualifications at the front that he suddenly remembered the trooper who had been killed in a bar brawl. The trooper's friends were furious when they learned that their regimental colonel had swiped something from their friend's order book. "He got the photograph from the fat Uzbek what has the stand in the market behind the Kazan Cathedral," one of them told Zander. "It was part of a trade—a bit of cocaine for the saddle of a grand duke, ten English pounds sterling, and the naked princess," they remembered. The Uzbek played dumb until he understood that his interlocutors didn't give a damn about the cocaine. "*That* photograph," he wheezed. And he described the ancient man who traded it to him for the solid brass ear trumpet.

"Hippolyte!" Zander exclaimed.

"Why, the dirty old man," said Tuohy.

Hippolyte, who had moved back into his room at the Steamboat with a fifty-year-old woman he claimed was his niece, had a hard time making out what Zander was saying, even though he yelled directly into his ear trumpet. When he realized that Zander suspected him of *stealing* the photograph, however, he came clean. "Steal! A Bolshevik doesn't steal. Occasionally I liberate something from the exploiters."

"Then where did you get it, old man?"

"I bought it from that little chiseler Melor," Hippolyte said.

They were all waiting for the boy when he stepped through the front door carrying a cat's leg wrapped in newspaper—his mother, Serafima, Sergeant Kirpichnikov, Hippolyte, Hippolyte's "niece," Lili, Arishka, Tuohy, and Zander.

"Why are you all looking at me like that?" wailed the boy. "I tell you it's a rabbit's leg. I got it from a kid who got it from the basement of a rich capitalist who raises rabbits."

"And the photograph you sold me," old Hippolyte cried, shaking his brass ear trumpet in Melor's face. "Where did you get that from?"

"What photograph?" demanded the boy.

Sergeant Kirpichnikov unbuckled his belt and started to pull it from the loops on his army trousers.

"You gonna take the word of a deaf old man against me?" Melor gasped in panic.

"The photograph," the sergeant reminded him.

"I didn't mean no harm," Melor blurted out. "I swear I didn't. I found it accidentally by chance under Vasia's bed," he murmured. "Being as he likes boys better than girls, I figured he didn't really need it."

"You're a dirty little thief," shouted Hippolyte, "who sells stolen goods."

Sergeant Kirpichnikov said, "Even under socialism children need a good beating now and then."

"He's an only child," said Serafima. "What I mean is, he's only a child."

Zander took the sergeant's belt from him. "I'll take care of this," he announced. He led Melor out back and had him drop his knickers and bend over the low box that had been built by the Steamboat's original owner to hold garden tools.

Melor's screams of pure humiliation were audible for blocks around.

"It's you who deserves the beating," Zander told Lili when they were alone.

"If you feel so strongly about it," she retorted, "why don't you take your belt off and try?"

"If you hadn't posed for those photographs, Melor would never have gotten his hands on one and there would have been no poster."

"Listen to yourself! Someone steals a photograph, and it's my fault because it was a picture of me."

"If it were *just* a photograph of you, Melor wouldn't have bothered stealing it. It was a photograph of your cunt."

"My cunt is *my* cunt," Lili shot back in an exasperated tone that reminded Zander of Maud saying, "My underwear is *my* underwear," and he realized he had gone too far.

"I only meant—" he started to say.

"You only meant," she interrupted icily, "that now that we sleep together, you are the keeper of my cunt. With all your fine talk, you are like everyone else—possessive of the organ you are lucky enough to fuck."

"I thought the luck was mutual," Zander said with a nervous laugh.

"It was. It is," Lili said softly. "But I don't pretend to be the keeper of your cock because I suck on it now and then. Oh, Zander, what are we fighting about? Will you tell me?"

"We're fighting," he murmured, "because I was very frightened when I saw it was you on that poster. Some of our people might have gotten it into their heads that you were on the other side."

"It's a joke that I'm on the poster," Lili said. "Nobody takes these things seriously."

Zander, however, took it very seriously. When he explained what he had in mind, Sergeant Kirpichnikov, feeling partly responsible because he lived with Melor's mother, insisted on going along to lend a hand. "Be careful, Pasha," Serafima cried from an upstairs window as they set out for the printer's shop.

"Let the capitalists be careful," Sergeant Kirpichnikov called back gaily. He pulled up the collar of his army greatcoat against the raw fog and fell into step between Zander and Tuohy.

Except for an early morning patrol of bicycle troopers with their carbines slung over their shoulders, or an occasional hunched figure barely visible in the fog, the streets of Petrograd were deserted. The three men made their way on foot to a rundown neighborhood a long stone's throw off Nevsky Prospekt. A wrought-iron lamp hung over the door of an old building. A battered sculpture of a horse's head stood in a niche in the stable wall in the courtyard. An army ambulance packed with posters was pulling away from the loading door as they arrived.

"We are looking for Brikin," Zander told the worker at the loading door.

"Brikin don't usually get here until it's light out," the worker said sullenly. He wiped his hands on his ink-stained apron. "He's the owner, you see."

Zander had been counting on Brikin not being there. "We're from the propaganda subsection of the Ministry of Public Information," he explained. "We were sent over for the posters—the ones that say 'The Women of Russia say No to Bolshevism.'"

The workman burst out laughing as if Zander had told him a joke. "You've come for the 'No to Bolshevism' posters?"

"What is tickling you?" Sergeant Kirpichnikov demanded.

"What is tickling me, friend, is that if each of you carried as much as you could lift off the ground, there'd still be two or three thousand of them posters left."

Zander was prepared for the possibility that there were more than they could carry off. "Can we see them, at least?"

"It's no skin off my nose," said the workman slyly, "but if you're from the provisional government, then I'm from the moon."

"What makes you think we're not?" Sergeant Kirpichnikov asked sharply.

"Well, now, first off, there's the little red ribbon tucked into your lapel," the worker said. Sergeant Kirpichnikov's mouth fell open; sure enough, he had forgotten to remove the ribbon from his greatcoat.

"And this one with his walrus mustache," the work-man went on, indicating Tuohy with his chin, "I seen near that Trotsky fellow only yesterday morning."

"Enough of this horseshit," Tuohy said in English. He started to reach through his sheepskin *dushegreychka*, or soul warmer, for his pistol.

Zander restrained him. "Maybe it's true we're not from the provisional government," he told the work-man. "Will that change anything as far as you're concerned?"

"Far as I'm concerned, you can be from the moon," the workman laughed. "These days everyone's from the moon. Why should you be any different?"

"Where are the posters?" Sergeant Kirpichnikov asked.

"Soon as you tie my hands behind my back and point a gun at my head, I'll be glad to show you." He held out a length of cord. Tuohy shrugged and tied the workman's hands behind his back. Then he unholstered his pistol, cocked it, and pointed it at the man's head.

"Nobody said nothing about you having to cock it," the workman complained.

Zander nodded. Tuohy thumbed the hammer for-ward. "That's more civilized," said the workman. "Fol-low me." He led the way past two giant printing presses that were churning out leaflets with an ear-splitting rattle. "German rotary machines," the workman yelled over the noise of the presses. "Last word in printing. Uses curved stereotype cylinders, if that means any-thing to you. Print fifteen a minute from now to dooms-day long as you keep them inked and oiled."

Several workmen in ink-stained overalls watched the procession pass without a word. The storage room, a high-ceilinged brick hangar behind the main building, was filled with what looked like flat bales. "Each one of them has got a hundred posters," the workman said, indicating the bales.

"How many were printed altogether?" Zander asked.

"Press run was five thousand. Shipped a hundred a morning for three mornings. That leaves four thousand seven hundred. Shipped two hundred a morning for three mornings. That leaves four thousand one hundred. Shipped one thousand by train to Moscow day before yesterday. That makes three thousand one hundred left."

Zander turned to Tuohy. "I saw some cans of lubricating oil in the press room."

Moments later Tuohy and the sergeant were splashing oil over the bales.

"Best open some of these windows to let the smoke out and the air in," advised the workman.

"You sound as if you've done this sort of thing before," Pasha said. He flung one window open, then poked his elbow through the panes of the second when he found it was jammed.

"We been burned out four times," the workman said proudly. "Once by the left, once by the right, once by the Kronstadt sailors, and once by accident when a gas lamp exploded."

Sergeant Kirpichnikov struck a match and touched the flame to one of the bales. It caught with a whooshing sound. The flames skidded across the bales, turning the storage room into an inferno. The four men backed quickly out. Tuohy closed the door behind them.

At that moment three young military academy cadets appeared at the loading door; they had come for their morning supply of posters to paste up around the city. They spotted the worker with his hands tied behind his back, and Tuohy's pistol, and smoke seeping under the door of the storage room. One of them tugged an oversized revolver clear of its holster and pulled the trigger, but the pistol misfired. Tuohy snapped off a shot and the cadets ducked back out the door.

"This way," Zander called, sprinting for another exit.

Turning to follow him, Sergeant Kirpichnikov tripped over an electric cable and fell, his arms flailing wildly, into one of the German presses. The fingers of his left hand wedged in the rollers that pushed the paper through the cylinder. The sergeant screamed in agony. The workman with his hands tied behind his back kicked the electric plug free of its wall socket. The printing press wound down with a growl. Zander made a tourniquet from a scrap of cloth and tied it around the sergeant's forearm to stop the flow of blood. Sergeant Kirpichnikov passed out from the pain. Zander and Tuohy lifted Pasha and carried him through a door to the street. Tuohy flagged down the first automobile that passed and ordered the driver to take them to the Anglo-Russian Hospital on Nevsky. There the doctors took one look at the sergeant's mangled left hand and decided to amputate. As he was being wheeled into the operating room, Sergeant Kirpichnikov opened one eye and recognized Zander.

"Fucking Germans got me with one of their presses," he mumbled. Referring to the "Pasha" tattooed on the back of his fingers, he complained, "Now I'll have to tell everyone my name."

Zander broke the news to Serafima, who, contrary to what everyone expected, took it calmly. "With only one good hand," she said thoughtfully, "he'll need me to button his shirt for him, won't he, then?"

15

By early November, Petrograd was a sea of mud. At Smolny they laid planks *inside* because so much of it had been carried through the doors on boots. Only one thing could put an end to the mud: the first heavy snowfall. People longed for it almost as much as they longed for an end to the war. There was general agreement that the war might go on forever, but the first snow wasn't far off. Old-timers with rheumatism claimed they could feel its wetness in their joints, could smell its iciness in the tip of their nostrils. When it finally came, they said, smacking their lips in anticipation, it would smother the city in a quilt of soft white down. Petrograd would become calmer, quieter; the occasional crack of a rifle, as a sniper picked off a turtledove dumb enough to take the sawdust scattered on the pavement for breadcrumbs, would sound as inoffensive as a branch snapping under the weight of the snow. The droshky drivers, with their beards and brows frozen solid, would exchange their carriages for sleds, and the traces of runners would crisscross the city's streets. It was a healthy thing, the old-timers said, their eyebrows arched so no one would miss the double meaning, when people left evidence of where they had come from.

And if the first snow arrived soon enough, and turned out to be thick enough, they said, it might even dampen enthusiasm for the other thing unmistakably in the air: the *vystuplenie*, a coming out, or rising up, of the masses.

"What are *you* doing here?" Lili demanded when she opened the front door of the Steamboat and discovered her twin brother, Felix, delicately rinsing his fingertips in the entranceway fountain.

"My hands were . . . dirty," he answered in a hoarse voice. His lower jaw started to twitch and he caressed it with the palm of his hand until it stopped. "I needed to clean them. I needed to"—he looked up at her, his eyes half closed, his head cocked to one side—"talk to you."

"About what?" Lili asked absently. The last thing she wanted was another scene with Felix. She wondered if Zander would come home tonight. She had seen precious little of him in the last ten days. He was always on assignment. An endless number of messages had to be delivered as Trotsky spread his tentacles through the city. Heads had to be counted, arms had to be twisted, weapons had to be distributed, moods had to be gauged, promises had to be pried out of people who were all for you if you could convince them that victory was inevitable. Once Zander had even been sent out to test the thickness of the ice on the canals to see if Red Guard units could cross over without using the bridges, most of which were in government hands.

"Lissik, Lisyok, Lilionochek," Felix was pleading, wiping his fingers on his breeches as if he were sharpening them, "do you still warm your mouth with tea before you make love?"

"You've been drinking," Lili said coldly. She started toward the staircase, but Felix darted out to block her path.

"I saw the poster," he whined. "I saw the curve of your breasts under the toga." He reached out to feel her breast, but she shrank back.

"If you touch me," she informed him, "I'll scream for help."

"Scream, if it gives you pleasure." Felix cupped a hand around his mouth and yelled in a high-pitched voice, "Help, help." He tried to laugh, but it came out as a snarl. "So you see, my sister, my shadow, my Lissik, there is nobody here except a boy and an old man who is deaf." He lunged forward and pinned her wrists behind her. His face was inches from hers. He reeked of garlic. "I have come to save you," he announced. "Someday you will thank me. Yes, you will sink to your knees and search for ways to show your appreciation for what I am about to do."

"I don't need saving, Felix."

"There is going to be a revolution," he whispered fiercely. "Everyone is talking about it. Your Lenin snuck back from Finland. He convened a secret meeting of your Central Committee. At first they hesitated. But that Lenin of yours is a fast talker. Glib. A pitchman for elixirs at a country fair. *Tipyer ili nikagda*, he told them. *Now or never*. He brought them around. One by one. Everyone's talking about it. The Bolsheviks are going to try to take power. If they succeed, they will recognize you from the poster and string you up from a lamppost. If they fail, Kerensky's people will string you up with the surviving Bolsheviks. Don't you see it, Lissik, only I can save you."

Lili struggled in his grip, wrenched a hand free, and felt in her shoulder bag for the tiny pistol she always carried. Felix peered past her and nodded. A man stepped forward and pressed a large wad of cotton soaked in ether over her mouth and nose. Felix caught her free hand at the wrist and twisted it to get her to drop the pistol. Lili, her head swimming with dizziness, managed to squeeze the trigger. The crack of the weapon seemed to her to come from another room, another world even.

"Only trust me," Felix breathed into her face as she sagged into the arms of the man holding the cotton.

Zander, his face ashen, appeared suddenly at Tuohy's table in the canteen. Alyosha Zhitkin, the demolition expert, was right behind him. "I need your help, Atticus," Zander said quietly. Tuohy took one look at his expression and realized the matter was urgent. "See you around," he muttered to the comrades at the table, and he stalked off after Zander and Alyosha.

Heading out of Petrograd in the cab of a commandeered coal truck, Zander explained what had happened.

"How can you be sure she was taken by force?" Tuohy asked.

"Melor heard the shot," Zander said. "He worked up enough nerve to peek down from the landing. He saw Felix and another man dragging her off. He said she looked unconscious."

"Maybe the kid made the whole thing up," Tuohy suggested without conviction.

"We found her shoulder bag on the floor," Alyosha said. "Also a bullet hole in the floor. Also some cotton soaked in ether."

"But why would her own brother kidnap her?" Tuohy wanted to know.

"Serafima told me he's been pestering her for years," Alyosha explained. "She says he used to show up in the middle of the night, roaring drunk, in that troika of his. Woke the whole neighborhood. He'd bang on the door until she opened it. Then he'd scream at her, and when that didn't work, he would fall on his knees and plead with her."

"What did he want?" Tuohy asked.

"He was in love with her," Zander said. "He wanted her to move in with him."

Tuohy asked, "Where does he live?"

Alyosha said solemnly, "We're taking you there."

Local legend held that the small gem of a monastery overlooking the Dudergof Lakes, some fifteen miles southwest of Petrograd, was where the False Dmitri had been meticulously groomed as heir to the throne. After the mysterious death of Boris Godunov in 1605, the Boyars had whisked their pretender off to Moscow and crowned him tsar of all the Russias. But his reign didn't last long enough for Dmitri to learn his way around the Kremlin. Aroused as much by his Catholicism as his sins—the False Dmitri had a weakness for group sex—a mob stormed the holy of holies and murdered him, then burned his body, loaded his ashes into a cannon and shot them off toward Poland.

The night was alive with that peculiar whiteness of the northern latitudes that made material things appear one dimensional. Zander could see the silhouette of the monastery as he, Alyosha, Tuohy, and the four comrades they had brought with them in the back of the coal truck crossed the flat plain on foot; it looked like a painted backdrop on a silent film set.

Spread out in a skirmish line, they passed a stable full of horses, then an outbuilding that contained several rusty plows and an open Velie Bitwel Six. They ducked around a large open hangar. Inside, three magnificent horses, harnessed to the troika, pawed gently at the ground; Felix kept horses in harness day and night so he could race off into the plains whenever he wanted to let off steam. Crouching at the corner of the hangar, Zander, Alyosha, and Tuohy paused to get their bearings. To the right of the monastery they could make out the shadowy figures of men seated around several campfires. "Probably the deserters he's hired as his private army," whispered Alyosha.

"How many do you think there are?"

"Hard to say. A dozen. Two at the most."

The first floor of the monastery appeared shuttered and dark. Several second floor windows gaped open. From one of them came the tinny notes of a player piano and the vague sound of men laughing. Alyosha settled down inside the hangar to fix the fuses on his sticks of dynamite while Zander crouched at the corner staring at the building. He could feel his heart pumping. Breathing became painful.

A ground floor door banged open and a drunken

guardsman staggered from the monastery. He opened his fly and stood urinating into the night with his hands on his hips. "Ivan," he yelled at the top of his voice. The guardsman swayed. "Ivan, you prick, come out and hold my cock while I piss."

A figure appeared at a second floor window. "Get one of the whores to help you," a man's voice called down.

"Ivan, *darling*," cried the guardsman, pitching his voice high to imitate an irritated woman, "you never said no to me before. Have you found someone new then?" Laughing wildly, the guardsman returned to the monastery.

Alyosha crawled over to Zander and patted his satchel; his sticks of dynamite were ready to go. Zander glanced back toward the monastery. "Here's what we'll do," he said.

Ten minutes later the first stick of dynamite went off as Alyosha and two of the comrades from the back of the coal truck attacked the deserters around the camp-fires. There was a flurry of rifle fire, and two more explosions, then more rifle fire and yells as Alyosha stampeded the deserters toward the wood line. Tuohy lighted a fuse and arced a stick of dynamite up through a second floor window of the monastery, then raced after Zander, who was pounding up the wide stone staircase, his pistol drawn, two other comrades with rifles at the ready right behind him. Tuohy's dynamite failed to explode, but the sight of it coming through the window sent a half-dozen young Guard officers and three whores, in their corsets, scampering in panic from what had once been the monastery's beamed li-brary. One of the Guard officers, his shirt unbuttoned, his fly open, tugged an enormous sword from its scab-bard, leveled it at the attackers, sighted over it, and charged. A rifle shot rang out, then a second, and the Guard officer was flung back against a wall, blood spurt-ing from a gaping hole in his shoulder. The other offi-cers, dazed, intoxicated, unable to focus clearly, threw up their hands in surrender.

While the two comrades and Tuohy covered the pris-oners, Zander raced from room to room, kicking doors open and crying at the top of his voice, "Where are you, Felix? If you've hurt a hair on her head, I'll shoot your gut out. Do you hear me, Felix? One hair on her head and you're a dead man."

In what must have been Felix's bedroom, judging from the ornate bed in the middle and the half-dozen government posters of Lili tacked to the walls, he found an old man polishing the boots of the young officers. "Where is the prince?" Zander yelled, cocking his pistol and pointing it at the old man, but he never looked up from his polishing, and so Zander raced on. Kicking absently at the paraphernalia the Guard officers had left scattered around the rooms, Zander made his way back through the empty monastery to the landing. He found Tuohy standing over a kneeling Guard officer, his pistol cocked and pressed to the young man's skull.

"He's taken her to the Winter Palace," the Guard officer was saying. "I swear it on the head of my mother."

One of the whores huddled against the wall whimpered, "Your honors, he's telling the truth. They left this morning. Felix. Two of his Guard officer pals. The woman whose picture is on them posters."

Alyosha came running up the stairs, a pistol in one hand, a stick of dynamite in the other, a thin cigar dangling from his lips. "Did you find her?" he called.

"He's taken her to the Winter Palace," Tuohy replied.

Alyosha looked at Zander. "That's going to be a bit harder to capture than a monastery," he said.

16

The word spread quickly on the Smolny grapevine. That morning Trotsky had personally passed out pistols to his Central Committee comrades. Even the dullest Bolshevik understood what it meant. Preparations for the uprising were complete. All the military and Red Guard units were at their staging points, waiting only for the signal from Trotsky to march. Trotsky could be seen striding through the long vaulted corridors of Smolny, his face drawn, his collar filthy, his eyes practically closed from exhaustion. Thinking he might have gone blind, people scurried out of his way.

Arishka watched Trotsky disappear down a corridor.

"Have you heard from Zander?" she asked Tuohy.

"Not a word. He hasn't been back to the Steamboat in days. He's out there somewhere—looking for her."

Arishka nodded toward Trotsky's back. "Why doesn't he give the order to strike?"

"He is waiting for provocation," Tuohy explained. "When the coup is launched, it must appear to the masses to be an act of self-defense, a reaction against counterrevolution."

That afternoon Smolny was buzzing with excitement.

"Have you heard the latest?" Arishka blurted out. "Kerensky's made his move. If Trotsky wanted a provocation, Kerensky's handed it to him on a silver platter."

Kerensky had declared that a "state of insurrection" existed, had denounced Lenin as a criminal and had ordered the arrest of Trotsky and the other members of the Military Revolutionary Committee. Government units had occupied the telephone exchange, the post office, and the railway stations. Officer cadets were setting up command posts at the city's main intersections, halting automobiles and searching them for arms. Troops loyal to Kerensky were raising all the main bridges over the Neva.

Room Seventeen at Smolny, Trotsky's command post, was a madhouse. Military commanders argued in front of the enormous map of the city on the wall. Someone screamed into a telephone, "The bridges are to be lowered at all costs!" Trotsky stood next to a window dictating furiously to a secretary. "To all military units in the Petrograd garrison," he intoned, almost as if he could imbue the written word with his oral passion. "Order of the day number one. The Petrograd Soviet is in imminent danger! You are hereby instructed to prepare your regiment for action. Await further orders. All

procrastination and hesitation will be regarded as treason to the revolution." Trotsky waited for the secretary
to catch up to him. "You have that? Dispatch a copy by
motorcycle courier to every regiment immediately. *More
quiet, if you please!*" Trotsky strode over to the map,
wringing his hands in anticipation. "Send the Izmailovsky
Regiment to the Baltic railroad station. Have the
Volinskys and Pavlovskys move on the Troitsky and Liteiny
bridges. As for the Grenadiersky and Sampsoniyevsky
bridges . . ."

Trotsky's voice droned on.

Hollow-eyed, unshaven, Zander turned like a moth
around the Winter Palace. He wandered past the Jor-
dan entrance on the Neva embankment, from which
the tsars blessed the waters of the Neva every January;
past the Millionnaya entrance, guarded by several hundred girls from a women's battalion; past the commander's entrance, guarded by Cossacks and a detachment
from the Oranienbaum Military School. He gazed at
the palace's endless rows of windows and wondered
which one she was behind, and thought about her eyes;
it wasn't their largeness he remembered so much as
their intensity. She had a way of fixing him with her
gaze that left him with the impression she could see
into him. If she were to be killed now, just when all
their wildest hopes were about to come true . . .

The streets around the palace, both on the Winter
Canal side and the square side, teemed with Red Guards
and workers and sailors as the Bolsheviks moved into
position. There was a stench of garbage in the air; many
had been camping in the neighborhood for days. Zander came across several of his Kshesinskaya Mansion
comrades in his wanderings. They were dog tired, but
elated. The Tauride Palace had been occupied, they
said. Post offices, railroad stations, the telephone exchange, had fallen to the Bolsheviks without a shot.
Warehouses full of food were under Bolshevik control.
Everywhere government troops were melting away. Well
after midnight Zander noticed the cruiser *Aurora* dropping anchor in the middle of the Neva, her searchlights

probing the Nikolayevsky Bridge and the façade of the Winter Palace.

And still Zander turned around the silent building.

At dawn, in a narrow side street behind Palace Square crowded with Red Guards breaking open crates of rifles, he joined some children and sailors who stood in a semi-circle around a ventriloquist. He was a mutilated war veteran, bearded, lean, with one ear shot away and a leg missing below the knee. His right arm pinned a homemade crutch under his armpit. Over his left hand he had draped a tattered orange bathtub mat with dirty strands of curled wool straggling from its fringes—the kind of thing someone might find on a heap in the gutter after a mob had ransacked some capitalist's house. Which was, in fact, where the ventriloquist had come across it.

"No need to be respectful of him," the ventriloquist advised his audience, casting his beady eyes disdainfully at his dummy. "He's only an ordinary alley cat."

"Attention to what you say about me," warned the cat as the ventriloquist's Adam's apple bobbed.

"You think I was being disrespectful?" the ventriloquist asked the cat, his voice dripping with sarcasm.

The cat stood his ground. "It's the way you said 'alley' that rubbed me the wrong way." The fringes over the cat's eyes shook with indignation, and he scratched nervously at a flea.

The ventriloquist seemed to take a sadistic pleasure in teasing the cat. "The description was perfectly accurate. The truth of the matter is that you *are* an alley cat."

"Due to circumstances totally beyond my capacity to understand, no less control"—here the sailors snickered in sympathy with the cat—"I happen, for the moment, to spend a great deal of my time in alleys. That part is true. I don't deny it. But the fact that I've fallen on, eh, shall we say *difficult* times cannot obscure my nobility of spirit."

One of the sailors hooted scornfully. The cat gave him a dirty look and continued. "I come from a long line of pedigreed cats. I trace my roots back four thousand years to ancient Egypt."

"Ancient Egypt, you say?" The ventriloquist shook his head at this startling declaration.

"Ancient Egypt, exactly," the cat insisted, his head bobbing unhappily, tears forming where his eyes would have been if he had any. "We earned our ration in those days by keeping the rats out of the granaries. We were so important, the punishment for killing one of us, even by accident, was execution."

"People were executed for killing cats? You expect us to believe that?"

"Absolutely. Execution by asp bite, if you want to know all the dirty details. The convicted cat-killer was flung into a pit full of asps. What's more, the owner of the cat had to shave off his eyebrows in sign of mourning."

"If *we* were in ancient Egypt, and *you* died, *I'd* be expected to shave my eyebrows?"

"Both of them, exactly."

The sailors and the children, caught up in the dialogue, looked from one to the other as if they were following a tennis match.

"And what makes you think I'd mourn your death," inquired the ventriloquist with exaggerated politeness, "especially now, when cats are more valuable dead than alive?"

The cat jerked back its nose, offended. "More valuable dead?"

"Dead cats," the ventriloquist pointedly reminded the cat, "can be eaten."

"Eaten!" The cat appealed to the audience. "If he's going to talk like that, maybe he and I should go our separate ways."

The ventriloquist cocked his only ear as if he hadn't heard correctly. "You go one way, I go another?"

"Yes, exactly," declared the cat proudly, drawing himself up to his full height. "I'm perfectly capable of fending for myself. I don't need you."

The ventriloquist flashed a cruel smile. "Idiot! Without me you don't exist."

"Maybe it makes you feel like a whole man to think so."

"You little worm," the ventriloquist exploded. "Die!" And he flung the cat into the gutter.

The children and the sailors closed in to stare down gravely at the carcass. A child burst into tears. The ventriloquist prodded the body with the tip of his crutch. "Hey," he called, "I was only kidding. Get up."

The cat didn't show any sign of life.

"Cat killer, cat killer," chanted the children.

"Why don't we shave off *his* eyebrows?" suggested one sailor.

"The cat is only a bathmat," cried the ventriloquist.

But the sailors, nervous at the prospect of attacking the Winter Palace, were in no mood to confront reality. One of them produced a pair of scissors from a wooden box at his hip. Several others pinned the mutilated soldier to the side of the building. As the children cheered and Zander looked on, the sailor with the scissors stepped up and butchered the cat-killer's eyebrows.

And Zander, deaf to any pain but his own, went back to turning like a moth around the Winter Palace.

At Smolny, reports trickled in to Room Seventeen. Sailors from the *Aurora* had landed at dusk and lowered the Nikolayevsky Bridge. The Red Guards and soldiers waiting on Vasilevsky Island had swarmed across it to occupy the Mariinsky Palace. A Bolshevik checkpoint at the city limits had stopped a car heading for Finland with two men: a Swede named Nobel who had a factory in Petrograd, and a Finnish Army officer named Mannerheim.

Lenin, who had made his way on foot from his apartment to Smolny, took Trotsky aside to discuss what they would call officials of the government they would form in the morning.

"Anything but ministers," Lenin sighed. "That's such a vile word."

Trotsky suggested calling them People's Commissars.

"People's Commissars," Lenin repeated, nodding. "That might do, I think. What about the government as a whole?"

"It should be called a Soviet, of course," said Trotsky. "The Soviet of People's Commissars."

"That's splendid," Lenin said. "It smells of revolution."

Trotsky shook his head in wonder. "Whoever thought we'd live to see this day? The first Communist state on the face of the earth."

One of Trotsky's commanders came dashing over. "We just got confirmation by telephone," he exclaimed. "Kerensky's fled the Winter Palace. His Pierce Arrow was spotted heading down the Pulkovo Highway toward Pskov."

"What about the Winter Palace?" Lenin demanded. "Has it fallen yet?"

Trotsky avoided Lenin's eye. Everything in the city *except* the Winter Palace had fallen.

Lenin pressed his eyes shut to contain his rage, but it spilled over anyhow. "If we leave one point around which our enemies can rally, we can lose everything," he groaned. "I want the palace stormed *now*! I will personally consign to the firing squad the commanders who fail to carry out their assignments. Is that clear?"

Hundreds of Red Guards and sailors huddled in the doorways around Palace Square, waiting for the attack to begin.

"What time is it?" a young sailor asked.

A Red Guard struck a match and looked at his pocket watch. "It's almost ten."

"Could you talk louder please," a voice called.

"Hippolyte!" Zander cried. He fumbled around in the dark until he found the old man. "It's me, Alexander Til."

"I can't hear a word you say," shouted Hippolyte. "In all the excitement I lost my ear trumpet. You'll have to speak up if you want me to understand you."

At that instant a purple flare burst in the sky over the Winter Palace. It was the signal for the cruiser *Aurora*, anchored on the other side of the palace, to open fire. Its cannon boomed, and shrapnel rained down on the palace roof. The six six-inch field pieces in the Naryshkin Bastion of the Peter and Paul Fortress went into action.

A giant armored car lumbered across the square, parallel to the palace, firing its machine gun at the defenders. White sparks flew from the façade as the rounds chipped away at the walls. Windows shattered. "Has the fighting begun, then?" shouted Hippolyte. And leveling a rifle, he squeezed off a round in the general direction of the palace.

All along this side of the square, sailors and Red Guards opened fire. From behind firewood barricades, the defenders shot back. After a while there was a break in the shooting, as if both sides suddenly craved a moment of quiet. Across the square the main gates swung open with a squeal, and several hundred Cossacks of the Fourteenth Don Regiment rode out.

"Get ready for the counterattack, boys," called one of the sailors, fixing a bayonet onto his rifle.

But the Cossacks weren't counterattacking; they were abandoning the defense of the palace. Riding four abreast, they disappeared in the direction of Nevsky and their barracks. A throaty cheer echoed through the square, and the sailors and Red Guards resumed the attack. Several daring sailors dashed halfway across the square and flung grenades at the defenders. Stooped low, a group of Red Guards raced across to the commander's entrance. "They're setting dynamite," someone said. A moment later the Red Guards ducked into doorways as an explosion ripped through the night, blasting open the commander's entrance. From somewhere off to the right a trumpet shrilled. The sailors and Red Guards cheered and started forward. "Let's go," shouted a sailor. Hunched over, bayonets glinting at the tips of their rifles, the attackers trotted toward the firewood barricades. A fusillade of shots rang out from the palace. Several figures stumbled and fell facedown onto the cobblestones. The attackers jammed up uncertainly at the Alexander Column.

Suddenly old Hippolyte came tottering down the ranks. "Turn back, boys, or the Cossacks will shoot," he ranted. "It will end badly, I tell you. The Little Father will order them to shoot. There will be blood on the snow—"

Zander yelled, "This is not 1905, Hippolyte. We're going to win this time."

The old man didn't hear him. "The icons won't protect you," he cried. "Turn back before it's—"

From the palace gate a machine gun coughed. Hippolyte flung up his arms and pitched forward toward the palace. Zander raced over to where Hippolyte had fallen. "It's not 1905," he cried, cradling the old man's head in his arms. "You've got the year wrong."

"You'll have to"—Hippolyte coughed up some blood—"to speak louder if—"

His head snapped back and hung limply off to one side.

Zander laid Hippolyte gently back on the cobblestones and looked up. The sailors and Red Guards had dropped to a kneeling position in a ragged line and were firing and working their bolts feverishly. A whistle shrilled. They leapt up and ran toward the palace looming fifty yards ahead. Zander pulled his pistol from its holster and lunged after them.

The cadets defending the main entrance had disappeared by the time they got there. Cheering insanely, scrambling over the firewood barricades, the attackers pounded into the corridor and up the wide marble staircase. Zander saw Tuohy's head bobbing in the midst of a sea of sailors up ahead. Everywhere there were stacks of abandoned rifles, cracked crockery, broken furniture. The parquet floors were lined with rows of dirty mattresses. Heaps of cigarette butts, empty sardine tins, broken wine bottles, cluttered the corners. Some of the Red Guards began smashing open packing crates with their rifle butts. A worker darted past carrying a bronze clock. Another, with an ostrich feather stuck cockily in his cap, brandished a silver candlestick with an imperial monogram on it. Zander caught a glimpse of Serafima's boy, Melor, hurrying off with an armload of silk nightgowns.

"Comrades," cried one of the Red Guard captains, "don't touch anything. This is the property of the people."

Running heavily through the corridors, the sailors and Red Guards fanned out into the adjoining rooms.

Alyosha Zhitkin flew by, his satchel of dynamite bobbing on his hip.

"Did you see Lili or Felix?" Zander yelled.

"No sign of them," Alyosha called back. "There are hundreds of rooms—she could be in any one of them."

At an intersection of two corridors, Zander almost collided with a wall of Pavlovskys coming from the opposite direction. "The palace is ours!" one of them shouted. Somewhere nearby a grenade exploded, and then a second. Two cadets wearing visored caps that obscured their eyes and their fear trotted by carrying a comrade with blood spilling from a head wound.

Zander raced down a corridor and hurtled a barricade of furniture into the great White Hall, which had once served the Romanovs as a state dining room. He ran through the Tyemny Corridor, with its portraits of Russian generals staring down from the walls, then through the rotunda and the Arabian Hall into the Malachite Chamber with its columns, its fireplaces, its tables, its vases all worked from the green stone of the Ural Mountains.

Sailors and Red Guards jammed into the room, aiming their rifles and pistols at the ministers of the provisional government sitting around a large table. Several fingered crystal glasses in silver glass holders.

Zander spotted Tuohy across the room. "Any sign of Lili?" he shouted.

Tuohy shook his head.

A Bolshevik commander, Antonov-Ovseenko, in a pea jacket and broad-brimmed artist's hat, held up a hand for silence. "I am Representative of the Military Revolutionary Committee Antonov," he cried. "I announce that all the members of the provisional government are under arrest."

The sailors and Red Guards roared their approval. "Hur-rah!" rasped one of the sailors. The others took up the cheer. It spread to the hall outside, and down the corridors to the great rooms of the Romanov Palace until the whole structure seemed to tremble from the cry.

Zander plunged through the crowd back into the

Arabian Hall, then ducked through a door in a wain-
scoted wall and up a narrow staircase to another floor,
where he entered room after room, his pistol drawn,
hoping every time he opened a door that he would
discover Lili behind it. He passed sailors carrying off
leather trunks, and baby-faced government cadets trying
to get somebody to pay attention to them so they could
surrender. A hulking bearded worker lumbered past
with a wooden case full of wine bottles. Zander made
his way through a tiled room with a sunken tub. In the
small room next to it, he stumbled over two Red Guards
who were trying to unbolt the great porcelain stove
used for heating bath water.

Going down a corridor lined with hundreds of cavalry
sabers, Zander stopped at an open window. Four sailors
joined him. "Look," one of them said, leaning out and
pointing to the main entrance of the palace below them,
"they're carting the provisional government ministers
off to jail."

One of the sailors cupped his hands around his mouth
and called down, "Death to the government Ministers!"

Cries of "Hang the bastards!" and "String them up!"
drifted up from the square.

"Comrades," Zander said, "the proletariat isn't looking for vengeance." But even to his own ear his voice
lacked conviction, and it dawned on him that if Lili
were dead, vengeance was exactly what he would be
looking for.

"Shit," muttered another of the sailors, turning away
from the window in disgust, "they're taking all the fun
out of the revolution."

Zander made his way to the top floor of the Winter
Palace, where the servants were housed, and hunted
through a warren of small, low-ceilinged rooms. There
were no looters here because the things worth stealing
were on the lower floors. The walls, which were thin
partitions, were papered with grainy photographs of the
tsar and the royal family. Over every bed hung a metal
or wooden crucifix.

There was a commotion in a passageway. A woman
screamed, and the scream was cut off sharply. Zander

pushed through a crowd of Red Guards to a doorway. Inside the room were two teenage sailors, their rifles at their shoulders. Across from them, with his back to a window, stood Felix. He had his right arm around Lili's neck, pinning her in front of him as a shield. His left hand pressed a large-bore cavalry revolver to her temple.

Felix spotted Zander, and a thin, brittle, wild laugh seemed to tear itself from his throat. "Educate them," he shrieked. "Revolutions thrive on blood. It doesn't matter whose. Tell them to shoot and be done with it. And you can add two more bodies to the pyre."

"Put down your rifles, comrades," Zander instructed the sailors in a voice husky with fear.

The two teenagers exchanged looks. Their rifle barrels slipped down. Zander stared at Lili, then fixed his eyes on Felix. "If she dies, so must you," Zander said. He took a step in Felix's direction.

"Don't come any closer," Felix warned.

"Stay away," Lili said. "There is nothing to be done."

"What does he want?" Zander demanded. "What do you want, Felix?"

Another laugh escaped from Felix's throat. "It's these young gentlemen who *want* something. They're not even wearing gloves, and they want to put their hands on me. *On Felix Yusupov! A prince!* I want only to be left in peace. Kerensky will be back soon with the Cossacks. He will recapture the palace, the city, the country! Lenin will dangle from a convenient lamppost. Lili and I will go off to Paris."

Zander took another step in Felix's direction. "She doesn't love you," he said. "She loves me."

"You lie. Lissek, tell him he lies."

Lili hesitated. Zander nodded.

"He is telling the truth," Lili finally said.

Zander could feel Felix wavering, could see the center of his hate swinging toward him. In a moment, if he were lucky, the pistol would follow.

"Lies," Felix said weakly. "Lies!" he bellowed. And he raised the cavalry pistol from Lili's head and brought it around to bear on Zander.

Feeling the pistol lifted from her temple, Lili jerked

her head down and bit with all her force into the forearm pinning her to her twin brother. Felix screamed. Zander lunged forward, caught the wrist holding the gun, and pushed it into the air. A shot exploded in the room. Zander wedged his other hand into Felix's face. In an instant the two teenage sailors were alongside him, pushing Felix to the ground as Lili squirmed free from his grip.

"Lisyok, Lisyonysh, Lilionochek," Felix sobbed. "My sister, my shadow, my Lichik."

Felix was still ranting as they dragged him away, his feet scraping the ground, his voice floating back. "Lilionochek, Lissik, they are *touching* me!"

Zander kept his arm around Lili's trembling shoulder. "It is over," he told her.

"And the revolution?" she managed to ask.

Zander smiled. "That, too, is over. We've won. This is the beginning of the beginning."

Lenin couldn't restrain a grin of satisfaction. "So it is true. The Winter Palace has fallen."

"I was in the Malachite Room when they surrendered to Antonov-Ovseenko," Tuohy confirmed. "Here's the proof!" He produced from the pocket of his soul warmer a crystal glass in a silver glass holder that had been on the baize-covered table.

Kamenev splashed some vodka into the glass. "Let's drink to the victory of socialism," he suggested.

"Let's drink to the victory of the proletariat," Trotsky said.

"Let's drink to the victory of the vanguard of the proletariat, the Bolshevik Party, and its leader, Vladimir Ilich," Stalin said.

"Let's just drink," Lenin said.

Everyone laughed happily. One by one every person in the room raised the glass and took a sip. Stalin was the last in line. "To the success of our revolution!" he cried, and he threw back his head and drank off the last of the vodka. Then he removed the glass from its silver holder and threw it against the chimney.

The crystal bounced several times without breaking, then rolled back into the room.

The Bolsheviks stared at the unbroken glass in silence. "As the peasants say, there's more than one way to crack an egg," Stalin noted. Laughing roughly, he strode over and ground the crystal to bits under the heel of his boot.

Cigarette smoke filled the great ballroom of Smolny like a fog. Every few minutes someone would climb up on the podium and ask the comrades not to smoke. The nonsmokers took up the cry. "Don't smoke, comrades!" they called plaintively. But the smokers went on smoking.

Lenin made his way to the speaker's platform. The delegates to the Soviet, many of them carrying rifles fitted with bayonets—Kerensky's counterattack might come at any moment—roared their welcome.

"Len-in, Len-in," Tuohy chanted with the others. He lifted Arishka so she could get a better view.

Wearing shabby clothes and trousers that were too long for him, his chin bristling, his tiny eyes tearing because of the smoke, Lenin held his ground against the cheers. The ovation lasted several minutes.

Watching from a corner, his arm round Lili's waist, Zander thought how far Lenin had come in so short a time; only thirty-four weeks before, he had been living in poverty in Zurich. Now he ruled Russia.

Lenin waved a palm in front of his face to dispel the cigarette smoke. The mass of delegates took the gesture as a call for silence and quieted down. Lenin gripped the edge of the reading stand. He looked out over the heads of his audience. "We shall now proceed," he declared in a tense voice, "to construct the Socialist order."

Arishka tried to push Tuohy's head away. "No more, Americanitz. I ask you to stop."

But Tuohy was stronger than she was. After a time she said, "You are hurting me now."

"I could make love to you all night," Tuohy moaned as he reluctantly ceded to her.

"You have," Arishka said. "We must sleep for a while." She rolled over so that her back was to him and sighed. "Thank God we don't have revolutions every day. I don't think I could survive another one."

Ronzha finished tacking his winter coat over the tiny attic window and climbed down from the chair.

They could still hear the Red Guards firing their rifles into the air as they surged jubilantly through the narrow street under their window.

From the cot Appolinaria said, "The coat will keep light out, but what about sound?"

Ronzha shook his head in despair. "Nothing can keep sound out except deafness."

Appolinaria moved over on the narrow cot and Ronzha slipped under the quilt alongside her. "I love it when our bodies touch," she whispered. "Our souls too."

But Ronzha's mind was elsewhere. "The new order will certainly put an end to poetry," he said. "We must both of us prepare ourselves for the possibility that it will also put an end to poets."

"You are too pessimistic," Appolinaria said. "There are many among the Bolsheviks who are idealistic. Lili's friend Zander, for instance."

In the street below, several Red Guards worked their bolts and fired their rifles into the night. Ronzha closed his eyes tiredly. "The idealists will survive only slightly longer than the poets," he said.

They had planned a celebration at the Steamboat—blinis, melted butter, vodka served Russian-style in *kovshi*, drinking scoops—but with Hippolyte dead, nobody had the heart for it. At dawn Zander and Lili put on their overcoats and went for a long walk through the still city. Neither spoke; there seemed to be too much to say.

They strolled through the Winter Palace Square, past the sentries warming themselves at bonfires. Zander pointed out the spot where Hippolyte had fallen. Lili noticed some dried blood on the ground and touched her fingertips to it. "We must find a photograph of him and put a fancy frame around it," she said quietly.

From the far end of the square, a stallion pulling a carriage with only one wheel came careening past the palace. Some of the sentries lunged for their rifles, then laughed when they saw what it was. Lather covered the horse's flanks. Foam seeped from its mouth. Sparks leapt as its hooves, and the wheelless axle, struck the cobblestones.

"What a beautiful thing!" exalted Lili. "It is like our revolution, Alexander. Wild! Inarticulate! Unstoppable!"

Zander, struggling against a persuasive despair, watched the horse disappear out the other end of the square.

"What is it, Alexander?" Lili asked when she saw the expression on his face.

Zander said, "I have always detested the sound of horses' hooves." He winced with uncertainty; he wasn't sure if he was remembering . . . or anticipating.

BOOK 3

Just as the English have a special gift for humor, so do the Russians have one for cruelty. It is a peculiar, cold-blooded cruelty which tests the limits of human endurance. . . .

—Maxim Gorky, in his 1922 booklet, never published in the Soviet Union, *About the Russian Peasant*

Afterward, all of Petrograd went on a binge. Some sailors broke into the tsar's wine cellars. Trotsky ordered the Preobraznensky Regiment, one of the most disciplined in the capital's garrison, to guard the cellars. The entire regiment wound up drunk. The Pavlovskys took up positions around the palace. They got drunk. Bolsheviks from other regiments were trucked in. They got drunk. Red Guard commanders took over the job. They got drunk. Word spread. Crowds formed. Soldiers manning the armored cars sent to disperse them swayed suspiciously on their feet. The Soviet had the entrances to the cellars walled up. People pried the bricks from the windows and climbed in. Lenin ordered the cellars flooded. The fire brigades sent to carry out the order got drunk. A special commissar was endowed with emergency powers and dispatched to the scene. He wound up drunk.

Eventually the Bolsheviks succeeded in having the contents of the wine cellars pumped into the river. The Neva turned red with wine. Peasants selling cabbages on the quays took it as an omen. The Neva would run red again, they said, this time with blood.

1

En Route Ekaterinburg, 1918

The train crawled into the tunnel at Alataoust and ground to a stop halfway through it. Vasia Timofeyevich Maslov moaned, "Jesus, not again," and clutched his satchel full of cameras to his chest in the pitch black compartment. Zander, crammed onto the wooden bench next to Vasia, reached across in the darkness to touch Lili's knee and felt her fingertips run lightly over his knuckles to acknowledge the contact. With a series of jerks and the whine of metal resisting metal, the train lurched forward again. Minutes later it steamed out of the tunnel into the blinding, brittle sunlight and passed the enormous sign alongside the tracks marking the spot where Europe ended and Asia began.

"As-i-atika," said a peasant, sounding out the word on the sign syllable by syllable, and then the sense of what he had read penetrated and he leapt from his seat into the air and kicked the heels of his birch-bark shoes together.

Farther along the train others took up the cry as their compartments came abreast of the sign. "Asiatika! Asiatika!"

"I have never set foot in Asia," Zander told Lili. "The word sounds as magical as America did when I was a boy."

"I was raised in Asia," Lili said across the aisle. She fingered the cameo brooch, with the red stone in the center, pinned under the top button of her shirt and mouthed, "My love." Zander grinned in embarrassment and nodded quickly back at her.

"Where are your honors headed, then?" asked the peasant woman balancing a large bell jar full of leeches on her knees.

Vasia replied, "God willing, Ekaterinburg."

"Isn't Ekaterinburg where our new masters are keeping the *batyushka* Father?"

Zander's eyes met Lili's. "So they say," he told the woman, and to discourage more questions he turned away to look out the window at two shoeless peasant children and a goat sullenly studying the passing locomotive from a small rise.

At noon the train crossed a rusted steel trestle spanning a broad, rippling river. The peasant men stood up in the crowded compartments and solemnly tipped their caps to Mother Volga. Soon after, three short blasts of the engineer's whistle drifted back and the train, with a metallic screeching that dispatched shivers down spines, drew to a stop. One of the Red Guards trotted alongside the carriages shouting, "Wood time, everyone out."

The able-bodied men, Zander and Vasia among them, lined up in front of a cattle car for saws and axes and then slipped down the embankment and began attacking the birches beyond the rail line. The men cut the trees into meter-long lengths and stacked them on the flat-car behind the engine, while the women drifted through the shade of the birch forest hunting mushrooms. Then there was a twenty-minute wait while the engineer stoked the boiler with newly cut green logs. Lili kicked off her shoes and tied her skirt up at her knees and waded into a clear, shallow stream. On the bank Zander spread his map and tried to figure out where they were.

"What if the Whites take Ekaterinburg before we get there?" Lili called from the stream. "What if they execute the girls, and the Germans get insulted and attack?"

"What if? What if?" Zander called back, and he had a sudden vision of his father, pacing back and forth in frustration, saying, "What if the tsar was circumcised, or Jews didn't answer a question with a question?"

"That's no answer," Lili said from the stream.

Before Zander could be drawn into a discussion, three blasts sounded on the train's whistle. Zander scurried up the slope toward the carriages. Muttering playful obscenities, Lili followed, and the train started out again on its long, slow painful trek across the vast *barba*, the birch steppes that began on the outskirts of Moscow below the pistachio-green walls of the Zagorsk monasteries and stretched north and east to the end of everyone's imagination.

Trotsky had relieved Zander of his translating chores at the Commissariat of Foreign Affairs and had dispatched him, with Lili as his code clerk and Vasia as his official photographer, to Ekaterinburg and the Ipatiev Mansion in the center of town that served as a prison for the former tsar of Russia, Nicholas II, his wife, and their five children.

Arriving at Moscow's Yaroslavsky Station with priority travel vouchers in their wallets and Trotsky's handwritten instructions sewn into the lining of Zander's jacket, they had been caught up in the chaos of a Russia at civil war. There were no fixed schedules for trains, and they had had to camp on the quay along with hundreds of others. "We will never get there in time," Lili said anxiously after they had been there for sixteen hours; she had to shout to be heard over the droning voice on the platform loudspeaker reading, for the dozenth time that day, Mayakovsky's latest poem, "Order Number Two to the Army of the Arts."

> . . . Comrades,
> give us a new form of art—
> an art
> that will pull the republic out of the mud.

Zander spoke several times with the Bolshevik trainman who headed the committee that ran the station, but he only shrugged tiredly and said he couldn't produce a train even if the travel priority being held up before his eyes had been signed by God the Father and countersigned by the Holy Ghost.

Zander and Lili and Vasia eventually clawed their way onto a train and into a crowded compartment, where the windows were nailed closed and the smokers, Vasia among them, outnumbered the nonsmokers. In no time at all the air turned putrid, and things only improved after Lili, her lips visibly green, threatened to vomit on the next person to light up. Outside, stations flitted past, all of them mobbed with masses of coughing, spitting, cursing peasants carrying large gunnysacks and fighting to get on the train without bothering to find out where it was going. The peasants surged first one way and then another like algae in a tide. To Zander, watching from the window seat, his cheek pressed to the glass, it seemed as if the entire population of Russia were either in stations waiting for trains, or riding them.

Their train, pulled by a locomotive that looked like a relic from the previous century, was shunted onto sidings for hours at a time, and once for an entire day; the Bolsheviks who routed rail traffic that July later admitted they had simply forgotten about it. Sometimes trains passed filled with conscripts—city lawyers, factory owners, bankers—crammed into open cattle cars, being sent off to dig trenches. Once they spotted Trotsky's famous armored train, with its steel-plated boxcars and machine guns mounted on the roofs, speeding by. Several hours later, rounding a long curve that wound like a vine around the side of a mountain, they came to a smoldering village, and word quickly spread through the carriages that Trotsky's armored train had machine-gunned it to put down a peasant revolt. The lacelike wooden frames around the windows hung in tatters from the brightly colored *izbas,* and horses and cows and goats and several humans lay belly-up in the rutted paths. At twilight one day, Zander spotted a horse-requisitioning unit with its herd spread out under a gutted monastery on a rolling hill awash in baby sunflowers. And with the last intermittent rays of sunlight stabbing through a distant birch forest, they passed a sacked station with three figures hanging by their necks from beams. Each corpse had a notice pinned to the breast that read DEATH TO SPECULATORS. A nearsighted Red Guard in a belted leather jacket, who had expelled a peasant from the compartment the previous day and taken his place, squinted at the corpses through the streaked window, and repeated a Stalinism that had been making the rounds in Moscow: "So there is a bit of noise from the cells. Prison is not a resort!"

The latest Stalinism seemed to Zander a universe away from the idealism of Lenin's "We shall now proceed to construct the Socialist order!" In the exhilarating days after the Bolsheviks seized power, everything, anything, had seemed within the realm of possibility. Since no one had actually constructed socialism before, the comrades argued about how to go about it. Nobody, not even Lenin, dictated decisions. Everyone had an opinion and stated it. Factions formed, split, reformed as the debate—always open, often ferocious—raged. Votes were taken. Majorities ruled. On the question of brothels, for instance, the minority wanted to close them, but the eventual majority decided to collectivize them. There was general agreement that the sprawling cemeteries should be plowed up. (Signs were posted around Petrograd saying, IF YOU WANT YOUR DEAD, COME AND GET THEM, and people dragged rotting coffins through the street frantically searching for new burial places.) But there was a lively difference on what use the cemeteries should be put to. One faction proposed building enormous sports stadiums on the sites, another recommended constructing satellite cities, a third suggested recreating London's Kew Gardens on a larger, "Socialist" scale.

There was no lack of grandiose schemes. As Moscow and a string of other large cities fell to the revolutionists, someone proposed linking the Socialist outposts by enormous Zeppelins, each of which would be capable of transporting hundreds of passengers and thousands of tons of freight. The cemeteries, the Zeppelin faction proposed, could be transformed into sprawling ports for the lighter-than-air vessels. Stalin came up with the idea of putting demobilized soldiers to work building modern subway systems. Someone else seriously suggested constructing revolving iron-and-glass towers in the centers of the major cities. The structures, taller than the Eiffel Tower, would have huge open-air screens on which news films and Socialist slogans would be projected. The slogans would be composed, not by plodding propagandists, but by the country's poets who, following Mayakovsky's lead, would fulfill work quotas like any other proletarian. "Why should literature occupy its own corner?" declared Mayakovsky, who night after night roamed through raw, drafty factories bellowing out his poetry to puzzled workers. "Either it should appear in every newspaper, every day, on every page, or it is totally useless."

Faced with the prospect of building socialism from scratch, some comrades lost their nerve. An old Bolshevik named Teodorovich, upon learning he had been appointed Commissar of Food Supplies, suddenly remembered his asthma and headed for a Siberian spa; he had to be forcibly returned to his desk and the problems piling up on it.

Teodorovich had reason to panic. The food situation was desperate. The daily ration in Petrograd had been reduced to one hundred grams of bread, and an occasional herring head. Various comrades had different explanations for the shortages. Stalin saw sabotage at the root of the problem. Zinoviev came to the ingenious conclusion that there would be enough bread to go around if only the slices weren't so thick; he recommended something called "Soviet slices." Kamenev proposed digging up the main avenues of Petrograd and planting potatoes, but Lenin convinced a majority to vote against the idea on the theory that you don't give hungry people fish—you give them fishing rods.

Almost every issue aroused passions, touched nerves. Including that of the Party restaurant. Arguing that Communists with important responsibilities often lacked the energy to cope with them, a handful of comrades circulated a petition asking the authorities to set up a closed restaurant to provide nourishing meals for Party members only. In the time it took for the word to spread through Smolny, two factions formed. Tuohy, a member of the first faction, was all for the idea; if the vanguard of the proletariat didn't have the physical force to lead, he said as he passed around the petition, the working class would certainly fail to build a new society. Zander got wind of the plan from Lili, who had heard about it from Arishka, and promptly organized a petition *against* it. "You don't understand what the revolution is all about if you want to open a restaurant for Party people only," he protested, his eyes narrowing in indignation. "In the old days, the ruling classes used to say, 'The shortage shall be divided among the peasants.' We made this revolution"—in his mind's eye Zander could hear his brother Abner's voice, husky, ardent—"so that the shortages would be divided, as the surpluses eventually will be, equally among everyone."

"Alexander is quite right," Lili declared flatly.

"If they create a restaurant for Party people," Arishka said uncertainly, "it will be a temporary expedient—until the food situation is straightened out."

"We Communists are bearing the brunt of the fight," Tuohy insisted. "Our own restaurant is the least they can give us."

"We are creating precedents," Zander said. "If we give special privileges to Party people today, God knows what we will do tomorrow when things become plentiful."

"Sign here," Tuohy instructed Arishka. She refused to be ordered around. "The Bolsheviks have given the vote to women," Arishka observed coolly. "I am casting mine with Alexander." And she signed under Lili's name.

Eventually the two petitions wound up on Lenin's desk. He weighed both sides of the issue, and tipped the scales in favor of those calling for a special restaurant. "The working class cannot march in the vanguard of the revolution without its activists," he reasoned. "And the activists have to be cared for. It is my opinion that a closed restaurant should be organized."

It was—though Zander, nursing his moral center, steadfastly refused to set foot in the place.

Even after the Bolsheviks, five months in power, moved the capital to Moscow and installed themselves in the Kremlin, the business of the special restaurant left Zander visibly depressed. Lili, who was beginning to understand his moods, tried to reassure him. "You can't establish a new society overnight," she told him. "You have to give it time, my love."

Time, however, was the one thing the revolution didn't have. Lenin had been obliged to sign a humiliating peace treaty with the Germans, because without it there was nothing to prevent the Teutonic hordes from continuing their advance; the Russian armies, lured by the prospect of land distribution, had melted away. The first White Guards, under the command of Kornilov and Denikin, were taking to the field on the Don; their ranks swelled daily as an assortment of monarchists, former army officers, vengeful antisocialists, land owners and plain adventurists rallied to their standard. The

Cossacks of Orenburg were mustering around their Ataman, and would soon join the fray against the Bolsheviks. A crack Czech division, stranded inside Russia at the end of hostilities, had taken over much of the trans-Siberian railway and turned on the Bolsheviks. French, British, American, Canadian, and Italian units had landed at Murmansk; some saw the hand of the British Secretary of State for war, a rabid antibolshevik named Winston Churchill, behind the invasion. Advance elements of Japanese armies had come ashore in Vladivostok. In Moscow, Trotsky was frantically scraping together a ragtag army of Red Guards, sailors, and factory workers to stem the tide, but the prospects of success were not bright.

Before the Bolshevik Revolution, Lenin had resurrected the little-known Marxist notion of the withering away of the state; armies, police forces, bureaucracies, would begin to disappear the very day the Bolsheviks took power, Lenin had promised. But once he took power, Lenin appeared to see things in a different light. He still talked about the withering away of the state, but postponed the joyous event to some distant future "when no possibility of exploitation remains on earth." Armies were being fielded to defend the revolution from its external enemies. So it seemed only logical when, a month after the fall of the Winter Palace, the Bolsheviks took up the question of organizing a secret police to protect the revolution from its internal enemies. Trotsky was heard to quote Saint-Just—"Nobody governs innocently"—as he raised a finger in the affirmative. When he voted yes, Stalin muttered that to make an omelet you had to crack eggs. (Stalin's quip was greeted with nervous smiles; everyone understood that in Russian the word for "egg" also meant "testicle.") Lenin noted that when you cut down a tree, chips flew; it was clear where he stood. There were no dissenters. Which is how the All-Russian Extraordinary Commission for Combatting Counterrevolution and Sabotage came into existence. The commission instantly became known by its Russian initials "Ch.K." which was pronounced

"Cheka." The Politburo named Felix Edmundovich Dzerzhinsky, the gaunt-faced, fiery-eyed Polish Communist, as the Cheka's first chief. And Lenin himself provided Dzerzhinsky with his brief. "Remember: the good of the revolution," he remarked, his eyes wandering, his mind skipping ahead to the next item on the agenda, "is the highest law."

Dzerzhinsky needed only to be pointed in a certain direction and he marched. "We do not need justice," he lectured the first handful of Chekists, Tuohy among them, mustered in the organization's new headquarters, the Rossiya Insurance Building on Moscow's Lubyanka Square. "What we need is a battle to the death."

Tuohy paced back and forth beside the lead truck. "Can't you get them to load any faster?" he asked one of the men in the *prodotryad*, the food-requisitioning team.

The Chekist, a new recruit with a blond stubble on his chin and a needlelike Italian machine gun cradled delicately in his arms, called over to the factory workers who had come out with them from the capital. "How much longer, comrades?"

"Ten sacks, fifteen at most," one of the workers yelled back. "What do we do with the animals?"

"We take them," Tuohy told the recruit.

"We take them," the Chekist recruit called to the factory workers.

Tuohy studied the seven kulaks—the relatively well-off peasants who owned a cow or two and occasionally hired others to help them in the fields—leaning against the side of a barn. They were seemingly indifferent to what was going on around them, rolling thick cigarettes with their callused fingers, scraping wooden matches against the soles of their boots to light them. They had defied a Soviet edict requiring them to turn over most of their harvest to the state. Dzerzhinsky had dispatched Cheka teams into the countryside to enforce the edict. Tuohy now headed such a team—himself, three other young Chekists, a dozen factory workers mobilized for the occasion, two automobiles, two trucks. Their job was fairly routine. They pulled into a village, assembled all the males over the age of twelve, and convinced the poor peasants to denounce the "rich" ones. After that it was child's play to get the kulaks to reveal where they had hidden the harvest. A cocked pistol pressed against a son's temple usually loosened a father's tongue.

"We've got the grain," one of the factory workers said, hefting a burlap sack into the back of the truck. Several others dragged five lambs and two young pigs out of the barn on tethers and wrestled them into the truck. The last factory workers emerged from a house with a barrel of pickles, a crate of sausages, and a tub of butter.

From across the stream, not far from a shriveled oak, forty or fifty poor peasants silently watched the proceedings. At the barn the kulaks talked among themselves. They pushed one tall fellow toward Tuohy, but he lost his nerve and turned back to the group. They urged him forward again. He screwed up his face until his eyes practically disappeared in the folds of his skin. "Comrade Chekist," he called.

Tuohy's mustache twitched with pleasure. "You want to tell me where more grain is hidden?"

"Your honors have taken all the grain."

"Go ahead and ask him," grunted another kulak behind him.

The tall kulak gathered his courage and took another step in Tuohy's direction. "Your honors have also taken all the seed."

"We will feed the seed to Socialist birds in Moscow," Tuohy said. The three young Chekists guarding the kulaks snickered.

"Your honors, if there is no seed, there will be no crop next season. If there is no crop, there will be nothing for you to confiscate."

Behind Tuohy, the factory workers piled into the cabs of the trucks and into an automobile, started up the motors and edged out along the dirt track that ran parallel to the stream.

One of the young Chekists indicated the kulaks with a toss of his head. "What are we going to do with them?"

Tuohy glanced at the poor peasants watching from across the stream. "We are going to put them to work for our revolution."

An older kulak, hearing this, elevated his chin a notch. "We will not work for those who confiscate our grain. If you want our grain, you must buy it—and not with worthless paper money you print up like postage stamps."

The two trucks and the automobile disappeared around a curve. "You *will* serve our revolution," Tuohy said matter-of-factly, "as an example to others." He nodded to the three young Chekists. The one cradling the machine gun brought the muzzle around until it bore on the kulaks.

The tall kulak held up his hands the way a priest did when he blessed a crowd. "Your honors do not understand about seeds—" he started to say.

The young Chekist squeezed the trigger.

At the Church of All Mourners, across the Moscow River from the Kremlin, worshippers holding thin, flickering tapers swayed to the rhythm of the choral music. Icons shimmered on the marble pillars. Incense drifted up from silver censers wielded by shadowy priests in black robes. At midnight the long-bearded metropolitan in brocaded vestments shouldered his way past the leather-jacketed Cheka agents assembled to intimidate the worshippers and, mounting the altar, proclaimed in a high-pitched voice, "Christ is antibolshevik!" His words echoed through the vaulted domes of the cold church. Several Chekists near the door burst out laughing. Overhead, bells began to peal.

In the back of the church, behind a marble pillar, Appolinaria turned to Ronzha. Her cheeks were aflame, her eyes sparkling in the light of the candle she held. "My heart," she whispered, "my life, my love," and she reached up and bestowed on him the triple kiss of the Trinity, what Pushkin had called the "Resurrection kiss."

Later, walking back to the damp basement room they occupied in exchange for Ronzha working as the janitor of the building, Appolinaria asked, "Do you think we shall live to share another Resurrection kiss?"

"God knows," muttered Ronzha, who hadn't eaten anything in days.

"The Communists say there is no God," Appolinaria observed bitterly. "Maybe they are right after all."

"There has to be a God."

A note of hysteria crept into Appolinaria's voice. "How can you be sure?"

"If God does not exist," Ronzha shot back, quoting Dostoevsky's Ivan Karamazov, "all things are permitted."

During the Great War he had blown up bridges, pill boxes, barges, barracks—anything that the retreating Russians didn't want to fall into German hands. He had blown in doors, most recently during the storming of the Winter Palace. Once he had destroyed a dam, once he had diverted a river. But Alyosha Zhitkin, the demolition expert, had never done anything quite like this before. He rolled some cigar leaf into a twist of newspaper, lit it, and studied the church through a haze of smoke. The walls must be at least a meter thick. No architectural plans were available. He would have to go on instinct when he placed the sticks of dynamite. The workers who had been assigned to him were chipping holes in the bases of the pillars. The problem wasn't simply to destroy the church; that would have been just another day's work. No. The Minsk Bolsheviks had set up shop in the rectory building next door. They wanted the church to come down without damaging the rectory. Pity about the stained glass windows, Alyosha thought. He personally didn't harbor the slightest religious sentiment, but he respected art in all its forms. He glanced up and studied the cupola. From its center, an undernourished Christ presided over a pantheon of admiring disciples. When the pillars were felled, Alyosha calculated, the judgmental smile would be wiped from Christ's face and he and the disciples would come crashing down. The problem was the walls. Small charges buried in them every meter ought to knock out the underpinnings and bring them down too, he thought.

Alyosha worked through the night calculating the

sequence of the explosions and translating it into fuse lengths. In the morning the Red Guards cleared the area. Alyosha, a cigar dangling from his lips, personally cut the fuses to length and placed the charges in the prepared holes.

Word had spread through Minsk, and hundreds of old people had gathered at the barriers to see if the Bolsheviks could destroy a seven-hundred-year-old church in the time it took to pronounce the word "amen." Several black-robed priests standing in a group off to one side fingered jeweled crosses. Their lips moved in silent prayer.

When Alyosha judged everything was in place, he blew four blasts on his whistle. The three dozen workers crouching inside the church lit matches and cupped their hands around the flames. Alyosha blew again on his whistle. The workers touched the matches to the fuses and sprinted clear of the building.

The first of the charges, the ones planted in the pillars, went off two minutes later. They sounded muted, pulpy, almost like a beetle being squashed under a shoe. In slow motion the ceiling buckled inward. The cupola appeared to hang in the air for an instant, then dropped from sight. The charges planted in the walls began exploding. An enormous cloud of dust and debris mushroomed up, obscuring the church. For an anguishing moment Alyosha thought he could still make out the building through the haze. The old people would take it as a sign, would drop to their knees and fervently cross themselves. The priests would smirk triumphantly. The Bolsheviks would hold Alyosha accountable; the Cheka representative might even get it into his head that sabotage was involved.

As these thoughts flashed through Alyosha's head, the cloud thinned. The small church had been reduced to a mound of rubble.

The chairman of the local Soviet bounded over to congratulate Alyosha. "Ha! We shall now proceed," he cried, flailing his arms like a windmill as he consciously imitated Lenin, "to construct the Socialist order!"

2

A sprawling peasant market was in full swing in a dirt clearing next to the railroad station when the train, eighteen and a half days out of Moscow, pulled in to Ekaterinburg, a provincial mining capital of some seventy thousand souls on the Asian slope of the Ural Mountains. The sight of the relatively well-dressed townfolk milling around the carts, of the sturdy peasant women in outsized men's boots meticulously weighing on ancient balances carrots and onions and cabbages and calculating the prices on abacuses—all this transported Zander to the clutter of the "pig market" on Hester Street. He could see himself pushing through the crowd to the pushcart full of used spectacles, and rummaging through them until he found a pair that brought Engels's footnotes in his copy of *The Communist Manifesto* into focus. He realized he *missed* America, missed its easygoing disorder; missed its rough informality; missed most of all its potential for change. And he thought, almost against his will: If only the revolution had happened *there*.

Lili noticed the expression of his eyes. "Where are you?" she asked quietly.

Zander shrugged, as if he were shaking off the memory, or the question, or both, but Lili persisted. "Where are you?"

"I am in America," he told her with a touch of belligerence. He assumed she wouldn't understand. "I was daydreaming. I was wishing the Americans had revolted instead of the Russians."

Lili took it as a personal rejection. "I thought it was Russia you were nostalgic for. Make up your mind."

Vasia, who had overheard the exchange, muttered something about how this was the only revolution Zander had, so he might as well make the best of it.

"Vasia is right," Lili remarked. "Revolutions do not grow on trees. If we can make this one work, maybe it *will* happen there."

"Maybe," Zander said in a tone that indicated he was far from convinced.

Moving with his peculiar stiff gait, Vasia wandered over to the Bolshevik agitation-propaganda wagon at the edge of the marketplace and asked a young girl with a dirty red bandanna around her throat how to get to Voznesensky Avenue. The girl nodded in the general direction of the center of town as she tried to hand a copy of Lenin's latest tract to a peasant. He buried his hands stubbornly in his trouser pockets and allowed as how he could not read, and Lenin would be his last choice if he could.

Ekaterinburg had once boasted a public transportation system, but in the months after the revolution the horses had been eaten or requisitioned for the Red Cavalry, and the trolleys had been parked side by side in a public park and transformed into barracks for new Bolshevik recruits. So with Zander and Lili in the lead, and Vasia trailing after them snapping occasional photographs, the three made their way into town down the wide unpaved avenue along which the trolley had once run. They passed dozens of large mansions with elegant façades and glass visible in the windows that hadn't been boarded up. Twenty minutes later they turned right onto Voznesensky Avenue, and soon after spotted the Ipatiev house up ahead. Set back from the street, the two-story building with a white stucco front had belonged to Professor Nikolai Ipatiev until the local Bolsheviks turned it into "The House of Special Purpose," as they euphemistically termed it in their official reports. The "special purpose" they were referring to was the incarceration of Citizen Nikolai Romanov, his wife, their four teenage daughters, and their hemophiliac son, along with the family doctor and the last of their servants.

With the once-royal family installed, the Bolsheviks had built a wooden stockade near the façade, and a second beyond the courtyard so that from the street only the roof and several of the white-washed-over up-stairs windows were visible.

Vasia set up his tripod in the middle of the street and began adjusting his camera to take a photograph of the house. At the entrance of the outermost stockade, a guard lazily trailing a rifle behind him stepped into the street to see what was going on. A dozen children marching in rough formation came around the corner. They were carrying wooden sticks on their shoulders as if they were rifles, and leading another child whose hands were behind his back. The children pushed their "prisoner" against the stockade, and then formed a line facing him. "Take aim," one of the children cried, and they leveled their sticks at the condemned boy. "Fire!" the child in charge cried. The others mimicked the sound of rifle shots. The prisoner at the stockade crumpled in the dirt. The soldier watching from the gate laughed. Vasia redirected his camera and squeezed the plunger.

The child who had been "executed" jumped up and started brushing the dirt off his clothes. "Next time," he whined, "someone else has got to be the tsar."

Standing in the bright sun, Lili linked her arm through Zander's. "It is not hard to guess what the local people think is going to happen," she said.

"Let's hope we have not gotten here too late to influence the decision," Zander said.

Zander sensed the hostility as soon as he stepped across the threshold into Room Three of the Hotel America, diagonally across the street from the Ipatiev house. Producing the instructions he brought from Moscow only made matters worse.

"As a matter of fact, we have already made up our minds," said Alexander Beloborodov, a dour revolution-ist who seemed obsessed by the dark side of any situation that offered alternatives. In his early forties, Beloborodov was the chairman of the Ural Soviet, and as such the top Communist—as the Bolsheviks had taken to calling themselves—on the scene.

Commissar Yakov Yurovsky, the Cheka agent in charge

of the Ipatiev house and the royal family, tilted his chair back against a wall and fixed Zander with a suspicious stare. His mustache sagged limply in the damp air. "Nothing you can tell us will change the fact that the Czechs are tightening their hold on Ekaterinburg. When the wind is right, you can hear their cannon. They sound like distant farts." He smacked his lips at his own pleasantry. "Our boys are falling back. It is a matter of time before the Whites take the city."

There was a single knock on the door. Beloborodov called huskily, "Come." A Red Guard officer, unshaven, his uniform filthy, tramped into the room and handed him a note. Beloborodov frowned as he read it. "Permission granted," he told the officer, "on condition they blow the bridge before they pull back."

When the door closed behind the Red Guard officer, Beloborodov shook his head morosely. "I don't see that we have a choice," he told Zander. "The Hughes line is down, cut by Whites raiding our rear. Your lady code clerk can encipher messages from now to doomsday—there is no way any of us can communicate with Moscow. The instructions you brought are clear. Trotsky is saying what he would prefer, but he leaves it to us to make the final decision based on the local situation as we see it."

Yurovsky picked absently at an ear with a fingernail and examined it to see what he had come up with. He looked vaguely disappointed. "The tsar must die," he said flatly.

"You could try to evacuate him," Zander argued. "Trotsky considers a public trial desirable. The world must be allowed to see his crimes. Only then can the sentence of death be carried out without the foreign press portraying us as murderers."

Beloborodov shook his head again. "Whether the trial is held in Ekaterinburg, or in Moscow with Trotsky playing prosecutor, the world will call it murder. Better to put an end to the matter here than risk Nicky falling into the hands of the Whites and providing them with something to rally around. With Nicky dead, there can be no restoration."

"Nicky and the boy," Yurovsky corrected him.

"Nicky and the boy," Beloborodov agreed.

"You are going to execute the boy too?" Zander asked. "Even if the Whites recapture him, he is too sick to reign."

"He is not too sick to sign papers put in front of his nose," Beloborodov snapped in irritation. "It is pointless to argue with us. We have made up our minds."

Out in the street a horse whinnied tiredly. Beyond the door a waiter could be heard wheeling a cart full of dishes down the corridor. Zander nodded grimly. "What about the women?"

Yurovsky pulled out a silver pocket watch and glanced at it. "What about the women? This is not the moment for bourgeois sentimentality."

Zander suddenly felt exhausted. "Can I sit down?"

Beloborodov nodded toward a chair.

"Trotsky was formal about the women," Zander said. "Alexandra is a princess of the German House of Hesse. She is a cousin to the kaiser, a sister to Grand Duke Ludwig. The Germans have repeatedly expressed concern for her safety. There is a chance they will treat the execution of the tsar as an internal Russian affair. But there is no telling how they will react to the execution of a German princess. Or her daughters. If they want an excuse to scuttle the peace treaty and attack us, we will be handing it to them. Think carefully before you plunge us back into war with the Germans."

Beloborodov and Yurovsky studied the bowl of fruit on the table. Zander looked out the window at the Ipatiev house. Specks of sunlight sparkled off the tiles on the roof. Finally Beloborodov spoke up. "Even if the worst happens and she falls into White hands," he said carefully, "she could not serve their cause. She is a German princess. No Russian, White, or Red will rally to her."

Yurovsky's face screwed up in thought. His lower jaw worked as he chewed on the inside of a cheek. "There is a train leaving tomorrow morning loaded with gold bullion from the banks here," Yurovsky told Beloborodov. "I suppose we could send the women to Perm on it and take another look at the situation in a week or two."

Beloborodov turned to Zander. "We will give Trotsky half a loaf. We will evacuate the women—but not the men."

The lights in the first-floor dining room of the Hotel America had been turned up, and the tables had been arranged in a rough semi-circle. Beloborodov, Yurovsky, and several other Bolshevik commissars were seated behind the tables facing the ornate double-door through which the accused would enter. About twenty people, including Zander, Lili, and Vasia, looked on from chairs set along the wall. At precisely eight in the evening— the chimes of an English grandfather's clock in the lobby could be heard ringing the hour—the double-doors were thrown open and Nicholas Romanov, surrounded by four guards, made his way slowly into the room.

Nicholas had turned fifty at Ekaterinburg, but he appeared to be at least fifteen years older than that. His skin had the color and the texture of wax. His neatly trimmed beard was streaked with gray, his clear blue eyes were muddied by the dark pouches under them. He wore a soldier's khaki shirt with the Cross of St. George over the breast pocket and sweat stains under the armpits, khaki trousers and worn felt boots. Walking with an uncertain step, he approached his judges until he stood in the center of the semi-circle. Behind him, the guards closed the double-door and posted themselves with their backs to it.

Beloborodov cleared his throat. "Nicholas Romanov," he declared, "you have been summoned before the special military tribunal of the Ural Soviet to answer the charges against you, to wit: that you have been in secret contact with White officers plotting your escape from Soviet custody; that you are planning to renounce your abdication and attempt a restoration; that you—"

A soft, rattling sound came from the back of Nicholas's throat. "Your guards have been pilfering the last of our linen. Your sentries taunt my girls when they go to the lavatory. There are obscenities scrawled on the walls of the corridors through which they pass.

These and other abnormalities must be corrected . . . immediately."

The commissars behind the tables exchanged looks. Beloborodov intoned, "Nicholas Romanov, how do you plead?"

At the word "plead," the former tsar straightened his shoulders and elevated his chin. Then he sucked in air so rapidly the wind whistled through his front teeth. "So it has come to this," he whispered. "We are to be tried by judges who have already fixed the sentence."

From his place along the wall, Zander noticed the former tsar's legs trembling. Beloborodov must have noticed it, too, because he called, "A chair for the accused." Zander stood up and brought his own chair over to Nicholas Romanov. The former tsar of all the Russias looked down at the chair, but instead of sitting in it, he rested one hand on its wicker back for support and turned to the judges. "Pass your sentence and let us get on with this nasty business of settling scores. I will show you how tsars die."

The judges conferred in an undertone for several minutes. Beloborodov would have preferred to stretch out the charade but Yurovsky, his jaw working impatiently, wanted to cut corners. With a shrug, Beloborodov gave in. "Nicholas Romanov," he said, "the special military tribunal of the Ural Soviet finds you guilty of the charges brought against you and sentences you to the highest measure of punishment, said sentence to be carried out at dawn tomorrow, July 16, 1918. This court is adjourned."

Nicholas Romanov's mouth contorted. Watching from the sideline, it took Zander a moment to realize that the former tsar had greeted the sentence of death with a lopsided smile.

The sun was burning its way through a faint haze that shrouded the horizon. Dust stirred in the drifts of heat piling up against the side of the Ipatiev house. In the stillness, a distant sound—dry, menacing—reverberated through the courtyard; it might have been thunder, except the sky was cloudless. "The Czechs are getting nearer," Lili commented in an undertone.

Beloborodov emerged from the front door and strode up to Yurovsky, who was distributing Browning and Nagant pistols to the firing squad. "He is holding up better than the women," Beloborodov said. He nodded toward a barred window at ground level. "They are taking him down to the basement now. Let's get on with it—God knows how he will react when they bring the boy on down after him."

At that instant a muffled shout came from the basement room that had been chosen for the execution. Then a second, louder shout, and then a panic-pitched man's voice screamed, *"Nyet!"*

Yurovsky clicked the chamber of his pistol into place and led Beloborodov and the guards through the door into the house.

Inside the main entrance to the stockade that screened the Ipatiev house from Voznesensky Avenue, Zander kicked at a pebble, raising a small cloud of dust. Lili tucked her arm through his. "The decision about the boy is objectively correct. And Trotsky will be pleased when he hears we are getting the women out."

From the basement room a muffled, ragged volley of pistol shots rang out. A dozen birds nesting on the roof of the Ipatiev house beat their way into the sky. Zander's mouth tightened. Somewhere upstairs a woman shrieked. The shriek trailed off into sobs. A single shot sounded. And another. The sentries around the stockade who had been staring at the grilled basement window resumed their duties.

"We are builders," Lili whispered fiercely. "But before you can build, you must tear down."

"Woe to the revolution," Zander said, repeating Marat's dictum often quoted in Bolshevik circles, "that hasn't enough courage to behead the *ancien régime.*" He turned away with a particularly absorbed expression on his face.

Lili, watching him carefully, wasn't sure if he had managed to convince himself.

*   *   *

At midmorning, when the wind shifted, the rumble of the Czech artillery became explicit, and it seemed that all of Ekaterinburg headed for the railroad station in the hope of talking or bribing their way onto the last train out. In the avenues the dust kicked up by townspeople dragging enormous valises made it difficult to breathe. Where the peasant market had been two days before, there was now a swirl of men and women and children. The station itself was ringed by Red Guards who used the bayonets fixed to their rifles to keep the crowds back. The people in the front rank frantically waved passes that were long since out of date, offered gold coins or silver candlesticks or brass samovars to the soldiers. Behind, new waves piled up, pressed forward, shouted over the heads of those in front to demand what the holdup was.

"We will never get through this crowd," Lili called to Zander as they saw the mob ahead.

"We should have gotten Beloborodov to take us in his car," Vasia wailed. His eyes bulged in fear at the prospect of falling again into the hands of the Whites. "We should have started out last night instead of hanging around for the execution."

Zander said, "Let's not panic. They must be permitting those with passes through. Come on."

From Voznesensky Avenue came the wail of a hand-cranked siren. Three cars turned up the avenue toward the station, and Zander had to pull Lili out of their way. The first and third cars were open sedans, and the seats and running boards were crammed with Red Guards brandishing pistols. The middle car, a closed Renault sedan, had its windows painted over so that it was impossible to see who was inside.

"That must be the Romanov women heading for the train to Perm," Zander said. Grabbing Lili's hand, he darted forward in the wake of the convoy, and they were able to cover almost a hundred meters before the crowd closed in again. Shouldering their way through the mob, they finally managed to reach the ring of soldiers around the station.

"We have places on the train," Zander yelled at a

young officer, and he held up the three passes they had used on their eighteen-and-a-half-day trip from Moscow.

"As of midnight," the officer called back, "blue passes are no longer valid. Only red passes can enter the station."

"We are known to Beloborodov," Zander pleaded. "He didn't say anything about changing passes." But the officer, preoccupied with a woman trying to thrust a baby into his arms, was no longer paying attention.

Zander turned to Lili and Vasia. "Let's circle around and come at the station from the other side. With any luck we may find Beloborodov."

Pushing back through the crowd, they skirted the dirt clearing which the peasants used for their market, crossed the tracks, and came around on the freight side of the station—only to run into another line of Red Guards. Beyond them Zander could see the train sitting in the station. Smoke spiraled up from the long straight stack of the engine. Steam hissed from a nozzle near a wheel. Behind the engine was a flat car stacked with wood, and two freight cars with Red Guards manning machine guns at the sliding doors. The eight passenger cars were already mobbed with people who had somehow managed to get past the cordon of soldiers. Several passengers were tossing valises up onto the roof and climbing up after them. Near the middle of the train was a passenger car with its windows painted over. Beloborodov, wearing a khaki uniform and knee-length leather boots, stood next to the steps at one end of the wagon. "There he is," Zander cried, and he opened his mouth to yell to the head of the Ural Soviet, but his voice was drowned out by the shrill scream of the engineer's whistle. At the signal Beloborodov swung himself up the steps and disappeared inside the car. The train began to jerk forward. The people on the other side of the station howled in despair as they realized the last train out of Ekaterinburg was leaving without them. Even the Red Guards turned to watch it go; they were being left behind to fight a rear-guard action against the advancing Whites.

As the train picked up speed and disappeared around

a bend, a terrible silence settled over the station. Somewhere in the distance cannon thundered. People scanned the sky, hoping to spot storm clouds to which they could attribute the sound. But the only thing the sky was heavy with was heat.

Zander, Lili, and Vasia spent the next three days huddled in the Hotel America listening to the Czech cannon drawing closer and trying to work out a scheme to leave Ekaterinburg. The problem was transportation. All vehicles, whether horse-drawn or motorized, had been commandeered by the Red Guards left behind to defend the city. At one point Zander suggested they walk the two hundred miles to Perm, but they learned that checkpoints had been set up around the outskirts of Ekaterinburg; any able-bodied man without a red pass stamped by the local Cheka was liable to be taken for a deserter and shot on the spot. As for getting a red pass, they were only available in Room Three, the Cheka office—which had been padlocked since the last train with most of the Ekaterinburg Chekists aboard left for Perm.

When word reached the hotel that the first Czech scouts had set up a skirmish line in the eastern suburbs, Zander decided the moment had come to go into hiding. Carrying their belongings, along with a carton full of tins of food they had scavenged from the hotel pantry, they made their way down an alley behind the Hotel America. Hundreds of apartments and houses had been abandoned by Ekaterinburg residents fearful of being caught in a house-to-house street-to-street battle for the city. Not far from the hotel, where Voznesensky crossed Asiatika Avenue, Lili spotted a top-floor apartment with its windows shuttered over. They forced the lock on a back door and climbed what must have been the servants' staircase. Standing on Vasia's shoulders, Zander jimmied open the transom above the kitchen door of the apartment, dropped to the floor, and let the others in.

"This will do nicely," Zander said, surveying in the light filtering through a skylight the heavy furniture covered with sheets. Vasia returned from exploring the pantry and announced he had discovered a sack of oats, a shelf full of preserves, and several bottles of Bulgarian wine.

Peeking through the slats of a shutter, Lili studied the intersection below as the first Czech cavalry, armed with sabers slung across their backs, passed at a trot. When Lili turned back, all the blood seemed to have drained from her face. Zander read her thoughts. "They don't have the time, or the manpower, to search every apartment in Ekaterinburg," he reassured her. And himself.

That day passed, and the next, with scattered bursts of rifle fire, and the occasional rattle of a machine gun, echoing through the streets below. Once Lili, peering out between the slats, saw fifty or so Red Guard prisoners with ropes around their necks being herded along the avenue. Another time Vasia saw several open automobiles pass carrying Czech soldiers holding aloft pikes with human heads spiked on them. The sight depressed him so much he began spending most of his time curled up in the fetal position on a cot in a small room off the kitchen.

To make time pass, Zander told Lili stories about his childhood in America. He recalled the sizzling excitement of descending the Ellis Island ferry and setting foot for the first time on the soil of Manhattan; he had scraped up a palm full of dirt and brought it to his nose and filled his lungs with the odor of America. He described the buildings that disappeared into the sky; during his first few days in New York, his neck had ached from looking up all the time. He remembered staring with such intensity at the first Negro he had ever set eyes on that his father had been obliged to pluck at his sleeve and lecture him in Yiddish about the necessity for immigrants to be discreet. The more stories Zander told, the more that came to him: translating for his father into Yiddish the instructions printed on his portable Singer sewing machine; helping Abner ladle out soup in the People's Kitchen on Division Street; listening to Leon read aloud from a textbook on crop rotation in a singsong voice so his mother would think he was studying from a King James bible.

Late at night the stories would peter out. Then Zander and Lili would share half a bottle of wine and make love in one of the twin beds in the master bedroom. And the occasional hoofbeats that echoed up from the streets of Ekaterinburg only seemed to heighten the intensity with which they joined themselves to each other; passion had become an antidote for panic.

A week after their arrival they ran out of coal and began breaking up chairs to feed the cooking fire in the kitchen stove. They rationed themselves to one meal a day, a mash made by steaming oats in a pot, grinding the bloated grains, and then straining them through a sieve and adding water and wine. Zander calculated that at the rate they were going they had enough food to last a month and a half, by which time, hopefully, a Red counterattack would have retaken the city. There was absolutely no reason, he told Vasia one night when he complained bitterly of being cooped up, for any of them to risk going into the street for quite some time.

Which made Vasia's disappearance, when they discovered it the following morning, all the more difficult to understand.

3

"It is an old trick I picked up in Siberia," Sergeant Kirpichnikov explained. Kneeling down next to the teenage messenger who had removed his boot and stocking, he spit on the large needle threaded with coarse hemp. Pasha pointed the stump of his left hand at the enormous blister on the sole of the boy's foot. A handful of sharpshooters attached to the train gathered around. Tuohy and several other Chekists, their legs dangling from the edge of the freight car that held Trotsky's two automobiles, started singing a bawdy limerick to drown out—so Tuohy had mockingly announced—the patient's cries of pain.

"Is it going to hurt, then?" the young messenger asked Sergeant Kirpichnikov.

One of the new officers, fresh from Moscow judging by his bright red breeches, recited some lines from Gogol to tease the messenger. "If someone is going to die, he'll die anyway. If he's going to survive, he'll survive anyway."

"Get on with the operation, Pasha," Tuohy called down from the freight car. "A blister never killed anyone."

"You pass the needle and the coarse thread through the blister, so," Sergeant Kirpichnikov said. The young messenger grimaced and turned his head away. "Then you cut the thread, so." The sergeant pulled open the blade of his pocket knife with his front teeth and cut away the needle with his good right hand. "You got to be sure to leave some thread sticking out both sides of the blister. What happens is the thread absorbs all the pus." He patted the messenger on the back. "You can go back to your unit now. Tomorrow, if you are still alive, you can pull out the thread. It will be as if the blister never existed."

Trotsky's armored train had arrived at Sviyazhsk during a lull in the battle the night before. Ekaterinburg had fallen to the Czechs and the White Guards, and Kazan, the last important town on the eastern bank of the upper Volga, had been occupied soon after. By early August 1918, the military situation was critical. The front was crumbling; Red units were deserting or retreating at the first sign of a White probe. If the Czechs, regrouping around Kazan, succeeded in crossing the Volga, there would be nothing to stop them from sweeping across the open plain to Moscow. And that would mean the end of Lenin and the Bolshevik Revolution.

With no previous military experience, Trotsky, at forty-one, had been appointed Commissar of War. He had equipped a train with iron plating and layers of sandbags, installed gun turrets on the roofs of the box-cars, filled the wagons—by then so heavy the train required two engines—with a hundred or so crack sharp-shooters, a contingent of Chekists, ammunition, an assortment of rifles and machine guns and grenades, radio equipment, food, medical supplies, automobiles for scouting, a supply of gasoline, tobacco to hand out to the troops, even a printing press, and headed for the front. "My strategy," he announced, borrowing Wellington's comment on the eve of Waterloo, "is one against ten; my tactics, ten against one."

Along the route Trotsky was forced to dispatch "landing parties" to plug gaps in the line or put down local revolts, after which the train would work up steam and race off to the next trouble spot. At every junction or station, Trotsky assembled the raw Bolshevik recruits, mostly factory workers with civilian clothes still on their backs and the five-pointed red star sewn onto their shirts, and delivered his pep talk. Dressed in a belted leather jacket, breeches and boots, and a battered peaked cap, he portrayed the struggle as a crusade, and the recruits as "participants in a historic attempt to create a new society." To stiffen the Red Army's determination to fight, he issued a warning: "If any detachment retreats without orders, the first to be shot will be the commissar, the next the commander. Revolution," Trotsky added pointedly, "is a great devourer of men."

In the command car aboard his train parked at Sviyazhsk, Trotsky was poring over maps, trying to anticipate where the next White blow would fall when a messenger galloped up to the siding. Trotsky leaned out of a window to take his report: The Whites had ferried several bargeloads of troops across the Volga and landed them on the marshes north of Sviyazhsk. The Bolshevik troops facing them had abandoned their positions without firing a shot. The situation was desperate. If the Whites weren't pushed back immediately, they would consolidate their bridgehead on the west side of the Volga, and the road to Moscow would be open.

Trotsky ordered everyone on the train to arms, in-

cluding the cooks and the telegraphists. With the sharpshooters and the Chekists in the lead, and Trotsky
himself following along in one of his automobiles stocked
with boxes of grenades, the Reds rushed to plug the
breach.

By early afternoon Trotsky had moved his "landing
party" into position. With three blasts of the automobile's claxon, he signaled the attack.

Tuohy, crawling on his belly along a drainage ditch
parallel to the Volga, had difficulty keeping himself and
his rifle above water. He thought of Arishka curled up
in a nice dry bed in Moscow, and wished he were back
with her. He wondered if she was being faithful to him.
When her husband had been away at war, she had
allowed herself to be seduced by Tuohy. Why should
she act differently now that it was Tuohy who was off to
war? The thought of Arishka spreading her legs to another man depressed him enormously. If she has been
unfaithful, Tuohy decided, I will track down the man
and kill him. "Here lies Atticus Tuohy," he said aloud,
"who died a hero's death while his common-law wife
was raising the morale of the troops behind the lines."

There were bursts of rifle fire from the left as the
sharpshooters poured bullets into the White positions.
From a rise on the other side of a dirt path, the Whites
fired back. "Do you see any of the bastards?" the Chekist
crawling behind Tuohy whispered. A machine gun swept
the White position. The Chekist behind Tuohy rose to
one knee and fired blindly. Up ahead, three Whites
broke from the cover of a peasant's tool shed and raced
for the river and the barges drawn up on its bank.
Working the bolt of his Nagant, the Chekist behind
Tuohy picked off one of them, and then a second.
Leaping up and running in a crouch, Tuohy dashed for
the river's edge. He reached it as the third White
soldier, leaning on a long pole, shoved the raft off from
the shore. The two regarded each other for a moment.
Tuohy lifted his rifle to his shoulder, took deliberate
aim, and squeezed the trigger. The weapon misfired.
He worked the bolt and squeezed the trigger a second
time, with the same result. The click of the misfire

appeared to enter the soldier's body. He doubled over, then straightened and heaved on the pole again.

Behind, near the drainage ditch, several grenades exploded and Sergeant Kirpichnikov, yelling hoarsely, led the sharpshooters in a charge against the remaining Whites. Trotsky had ordered his men not to take prisoners. As the White Guards rose with their hands clawing the air, they were cut down.

At the Volga's edge, Tuohy pulled his heavy pistol from its holster and, holding it with both hands, sighted on the boy on the raft. He slowly squeezed the trigger. The pistol jerked up against his palms, blocking his view. When he lowered the pistol, the raft, spinning slowly upstream in a countercurrent, was empty.

That evening, in a clearing next to the armored train, Trotsky mustered the Bolshevik company that had broken and run at the sight of the Whites crossing the Volga on their barges. Trotsky himself presided over the drumhead court-martial. The company's commissar and commander were prodded forward at bayonet point until they stood in front of the kitchen table behind which Trotsky sat. "You are cowards and traitors to the cause of world revolution," Trotsky cried. "You know the penalty that awaits you. Do you have anything to tell me before I pass sentence?"

The commissar, an earnest, bearded young man in his middle twenties, managed a sad smile. "I have nothing to say in my defense. I was ready to die for the revolution when I quit law school for the army. I am still ready to die for the revolution."

The commander, a former tsarist officer in his forties, stepped toward the table. "I ordered them to stand and fight," he told Trotsky in a husky voice. "It was no fault of mine that they did not obey."

"Did you set the example?" Trotsky shot back. "Did *you* stand and fight?"

The former tsarist officer avoided Trotsky's eye. "I would have been alone. I would have been killed."

"Better to have been killed by them than by us," Trotsky sneered. He raised his voice. "I sentence the commissar and the commander to death by firing squad, sentence to be carried out immediately. As for the men in the company, I order one in ten to be shot, sentence to be carried out immediately." Trotsky waved a hand at the two hundred and sixty men lined up facing him. "Let our Chekists count out one in ten and carry out the verdict. Court adjourned."

Tuohy, the senior Chekist on the spot, strode across the clearing until he was face-to-face with the first soldier in the front rank, a veteran in his late fifties with a large scar where his right ear should have been. "You," Tuohy said. The man looked down and spat on the ground and stepped boldly forward. Tuohy counted down the rank, watching the relief flood onto the features of the men he passed, At the eleventh soldier, a boy of seventeen or eighteen, he said, "You."

The boy turned to his right and to his left for help, then looked back at Tuohy. "Why me?" he whined. "I only ran because the others ran. I don't want to die!"

"Stop sniveling and step out," Tuohy ordered.

Wiping his nose with the back of his hand, the boy limped forward, and Tuohy suddenly recognized him—it was the teenage messenger with Sergeant Kirpichnikov's thread through his blister.

In the hollow silence of the clearing, Tuohy continued down the ranks, counting out one in ten until twenty-six soldiers had been selected for execution. They and the commander and commissar were issued shovels and ordered to dig a trench at the edge of the woods bordering the clearing. When they finished, the shovels were collected and the condemned men were lined up, with their ankles bound, on the lip of the trench. The sharpshooters set up a machine gun facing them and fed the end of the belt into the breech with a metallic snap that resounded through the clearing. Some of the condemned men began to weep. The former tsarist officer traced the sign of the cross on his chest. The young company commissar straightened his shoulders and took a deep breath, his last.

"To a gangrenous wound," Trotsky told those within earshot, "a red-hot iron must be applied." And he nodded to the sharpshooters manning the machine gun.

*   *   *

As soon as he set about arming the revolution, Trotsky realized the new Red Army couldn't be led by soldiers' committees voting on whether to attack or retreat. To triumph over the Whites, his army desperately needed an officer corps. The only experienced officers available had served under the tsar. Eventually, Trotsky permitted some twenty thousand former tsarist officers to serve in the Red ranks, a fact that aroused a great deal of resentment, and no small amount of concern about where their loyalties would rest when the shooting started. Trotsky himself shared this concern, and took precautions. He had lists of the tsarist officers' wives and children compiled to discourage defections and treason. And he created a dual system of command, which had a Bolshevik commissar looking over the officer's shoulder at every level of the military structure. No order was valid unless it was signed by both, a stroke of genius that gave to the fledgling Red Army the military expertise to wage civil war, and the political expertise to defend the revolution.

Which is how Sergeant Kirpichnikov came to be detached from the armored train and assigned as commissar to the Twenty-Third Petrograd rifle battalion, dug in on the west bank of the Volga facing Kazan. "The trouble is, our men are not aggressive enough," Trotsky told the sergeant when he signed his commission. "They have become prisoners of the Bolshevik belief in the historic inevitability of our cause; they think all they have to do to win is survive."

Sergeant Kirpichnikov, who only vaguely grasped Trotsky's references to the dialectic and historical inevitability, understood from his tone that the commissar's job was to give the troops, and the officers who led them, a healthy kick in the ass. As soon as he arrived at the Reds' command post in a manor house behind the line, he goaded the battalion's battle-weary commander into action.

"You want me to send patrols *across* the river?" the commander asked incredulously.

"You are a prisoner of something or other," Sergeant

Kirpichnikov replied firmly. "You think all you have to do to win is sit on your ass. Sending men across the river will make the Whites think we are stronger than we really are, since it is not the kind of thing we would do if we were as weak as we are."

The officer followed his new commissar's advice—with startling results. The first raiding party brought back two prisoners, which raised Red morale, and a deserter who had a copy of a map showing the White positions on the east bank of the Volga. Trotsky studied the map and, concentrating his forces, applied his "ten against one" tactic. There followed a series of raids across the river that kept the Whites bloodied and off balance, and bought time for the Reds to bring up recruits from the cities.

As the Reds gained confidence, the pace of their probes across the river picked up. Sergeant Kirpichnikov invariably "chaperoned," as he laughingly put it, his commander on these nightly forays. Signs of battle fatigue appeared on the commander's face, but goaded by his commissar, he kept at it. After overrunning a White outpost at a mill one night, the sergeant suggested that they bring up reinforcements before dawn and hold the position for a day or two. "What do you say, Dmitri? Trotsky will be very pleased to have a foothold on this side of the Volga."

"You are a crazy man, Pasha," the commander replied, "but why not?"

Predictably, the Whites reacted violently to the presence of Reds on their bank of the river. At daybreak, the units of the Twenty-Third at the mill found themselves surrounded and outnumbered. They fought off attacks all that day, and the next. Neither the commander nor the commissar slept. Nerves frayed. The commander blamed Pasha for their predicament. Sergeant Kirpichnikov pointed out that on military matters he gave suggestions, the commander gave orders. Observing the commander's glazed eyes, the sergeant began to suspect he had pushed him too far.

That night they decided to break out. Using lumps of sugar set out on the floor to represent his own and the enemy's forces, the commander briefed his unit commanders. There would be a blocking force set up, he said, moving a lump of sugar into position, to protect the flank while the bulk of the Twenty-Third—here he maneuvered other lumps of sugar—would leapfrog their way along a gulch to the river. "Any questions?" he asked, pressing a hand to his cheek to suppress a twitch.

As they were leaving, the commander, his lids drooping from fatigue, noticed the half-witted peasant who lived at the mill retrieving the lumps of sugar. "A spy!" he cried. "He is taking the lumps to reconstruct our battle plan for the Whites."

"Dmitri, he was only collecting the sugar to eat it," Sergeant Kirpichnikov said.

"He must be shot," the commander insisted, "and the lumps of sugar must be eaten immediately."

The officers looked in bewilderment from their commander to their commissar. Sergeant Kirpichnikov caught the eye of a young officer wearing bright red breeches, and winked pointedly. "Take the peasant out and shoot him. Distribute the sugar to the men."

The peasant, whimpering unintelligibly, was dragged from the room. Moments later a shot rang out. Sergeant Kirpichnikov flashed what he thought of as his fatherly smile at his commander. It is not his fault, he thought. A man can take only so much. As soon as we get back to our lines, I will send him to the rear for a rest.

The sergeant and the commander stepped outside. The night was fragrant with the aroma of wild thyme, which grew along the rim of the gulch. Lying sprawled on the cobblestone walk leading to the mill was the body of the half-witted peasant. Blood seeped from an ugly head wound. The peasant was not yet dead, but soon would be. Several of the young officers stood around the body vigorously chewing on lumps of sugar. The young officer with the bright red breeches stepped up to Sergeant Kirpichnikov and fired off a smart salute. "I have carried out your orders, Comrade Commissar," he said.

Sergeant Kirpichnikov looked from the body of the

peasant to the others eating the sugar to the battle-
worn commander, and back to the officer who had
carried out the order. "But I winked," the sergeant
whispered.

"You what?" the officer asked in a puzzled voice.

"I winked an eye," Sergeant Kirpichnikov bellowed,
"so you would know I was not serious!"

"I took it for a nervous tic," the officer said weakly.

Around them the other officers swallowed the last of
the sugar. At their feet the peasant gasped, and lay still.

"Now the Whites will never know our plans," the
commander said with satisfaction. And he laughed wildly
into the fragrant night.

4

From behind a polished mahogany desk that had
been used, until recently, by a Bolshevik commissar, a gaunt colonel with a patch over one eye
surveyed the day's catch. "I want to congratulate you,"
he said without visible enthusiasm, fixing his good eye
on each man in turn, "for having had the sense to
abandon godless Bolshevism. The White cause wel-
comes you with open arms. You will understand, however, that before we can offer you unconditional amnesty,
we will require proof of your loyalty. In intellectual
circles, this is called reciprocity. Something for something, if you see what I am driving at."

A tall peasant in the middle of the line spoke up.
"We was told, your honor, we would be enlisted in the
White Army. Give me a rifle and I will prove you my
loyalty."

The colonel swallowed a yawn. This was his fourth
batch of defectors since the beginning of the week.
"There is no question of us giving you a rifle until we
can be sure in which direction you will point it."

"So what is it we have to do to show our loyalty?" another of the defectors, a factory worker, asked.

"Let your imaginations guide you," the colonel said pleasantly. "We want information about the Reds. We want details of their order of battle. We want to know what they intend to do next. Most of all, we want denunciations. The bigger the fish you denounce, the more likely we are to believe that you really have had a change of heart."

Vasia raised a finger to attract the colonel's attention. "What will happen to those of us who do not succeed in convincing you of our loyalty?" he asked in a voice so low the colonel had to strain to hear him.

The colonel's facial muscles worked hard to produce a tired smile. "We will shoot you," he explained.

They pumped up a tubful of water and sponged each other and then stood in front of an open window to let the warm night breeze dry their bodies. Somewhere on Voznesensky Avenue a dog howled at the half moon, but the sound only accentuated the absolute stillness of the evening. Instead of going to the bedroom, they piled up cushions on the floor near the open window and made love lingeringly, drowsily. It was as far removed from violence as lovemaking can get.

"There are so many ways to make love," Lili whispered into his ear.

"When we have tried them all," Zander whispered back, "we will invent new ways."

Afterward, they fell into a deep sleep where they were. Which was why, when the door was shattered off its hinges, neither Zander nor Lili had a pistol within arm's reach.

Armed men flooded into the apartment. Gas torches exploded into light. Shadows danced across the walls. Lili, clutching a sheet she had pulled from an armchair, was thrust roughly against a wall. She tried to shield her eyes with a forearm and called, "Alexander!" From the darkness beyond the torches she heard the sound of something heavy thudding into something soft, and a man grunting in pain. Underwear, a skirt, a shirt, stockings, a pair of shoes came flying out of the darkness and landed at her feet. With a semi-circle of men looking silently on, Lili dressed. An incredibly soothing voice ordered her to turn around and a hood was drawn over her head. Her wrists were bound tightly behind her back with a length of cord.

"My hands are numb," she complained as she was being led down the stairs.

"The rest of your body," the soothing voice replied, "will soon follow."

There was a short ride in an automobile, during which not a word was uttered by her captors. There was the sound of heavy doors opening and her own steps on a narrow, winding staircase, and endless corridors with doors opening in front of her and closing behind her with clicks that stabbed through her skull. Eventually the hood was pulled from her head and the cord was cut from her wrists and a door was opened and she was forced into a space so small that when they slammed the door behind her she could feel it pressing into her shoulder blades. She tried to raise her hands to massage her wrists, but there wasn't enough room to get them up. She realized she was in what amounted to a coffin standing on its end. "Let me out!" she yelled, and was instantly sorry she had given her captors the satisfaction of hearing her plead. If they had put her in here, she reasoned, it was not to let her out until she had been reduced to a whimpering supplicant who would tell them whatever they wanted to know before they executed her.

She took several deep breaths—the act of breathing deeply pushed her breasts against the front of her space—and willed her muscles to relax. Her feet felt heavy already, but there was no way to get her weight off them. Time went by, but she had no way of knowing how much. If I ever get out of here, she vowed, I will give up sex completely. She felt the urge to urinate, but fought it off for what seemed like hours. There were pinpricks of pain in the backs of her calves which spread gradually in every direction until she caught herself moaning out loud and realized she had been

moaning for some time. Her bladder was bursting, and
suddenly she couldn't hold it in any longer. The urine
trickled down her legs and filled her shoes and she
burst into tears of humiliation. She stopped sobbing
and decided to kill herself and tried to knock her head
against a wall, but it was so close that all she got for her
trouble was a splitting headache. An excruciating pain
stabbed through her legs and worked its way up her
back. She studied the pain, trying to figure out what
pain was until it became so intense she could no longer
think clearly. Gradually the numbness spread through
her body as the soothing voice on the steps had said it
would. And then she fainted.

When Lili came to, she was bound to a cot in a
prison hospital looking up into the oval face of a middle-
aged man with a waxed mustache that spiraled off into
corkscrews. He looked like a doctor making his rounds,
and she thought, I must tell him about my swollen feet
and how they ache when I try to change their position
in the bed. The man with the waxed mustache was
studying the contents of a dossier, humming to himself
as he turned the pages. Whatever his area of specializa-
tion, Lili thought, he is obviously very competent.

After a moment he glanced down at her. "Permit me,
dear lady, to introduce myself," he said softly—and Lili
instantly recognized the soothing voice she had first
heard as she was being led down the steps with the
hood over her head. "I am Investigator Solokov of the
Criminal Division of the Ural Directorate. As for you,
you are Lili Mikhailovna Yusupova, a Bolshevik and the
sister of the Felix Yusupov who killed Rasputin." Lili
started to mumble a denial, but the investigator cut her
off abruptly. "We have recovered your travel documents from the lining of your lover's suit jacket. We know
who you are. We know why you came to Ekaterinburg
—he to argue Trotsky's case for removing the tsar to
Moscow for a public trial, you to encipher and decipher
any messages he might have exchanged with Trotsky if
the Hughes line had not been down. On the strength of
these documents, you and your friend Til could have
been shot out of hand. You both have been kept alive in

order to respond to my questions. As soon as I am satisfied you have no further information to give me, you will both be executed."

A harsh laugh escaped from Lili's mouth. "Knowing that, neither of us will tell you anything."

"On the contrary, dear lady, you will reach the point where you will welcome your death. You and your friend Til will beg me to believe that you are holding nothing back so that I can reward you by ordering your execution." Solokov motioned to two orderlies in white knee-length medical coats. "Feed her, then take her back to her cell," he told them. "Give her a forty-eight-hour dose and let me know if she is ready for me."

With her feet scraping along behind her, Lili was dragged back up the narrow winding steel staircase and along the endless corridors and thrust again into the closetlike space with the door jamming into her shoulder blades.

"Oh, Alexander," Lili moaned, and the tears flowed down her cheeks into her mouth. She tasted the saltiness of her misery and somehow drew courage from the taste, and vowed she would never say a word to Investigator Solokov. The object, she instructed herself, was not to die quickly, thereby avoiding pain, but to die feeling she had triumphed over the man with the infinitely soothing voice. Perhaps, she decided, there is a fixed amount of pain in the world. It followed that the more pain she suffered, the less there would be available for Alexander. It seemed like a reasonable idea. And it allowed her, during the forty-eight hours in the box, to welcome the pain that flooded through her body, that occupied it like a conquering army, that consumed it until all her thoughts—her very vocabulary—seemed to narrow down to that one word: pain.

"Have you had enough?" one of the orderlies was asking. He had to prop her up when he opened the door because her swollen legs were incapable of supporting her weight. "Are you ready to talk with Investigator Solokov?"

Lili managed to shake her head, though it felt heavy on her body. The orderly laid her on the floor, sponged her face with cold water, and poured a ladleful of a souplike substance down her throat. He opened her shirt and pressed an ear to her chest and listened to her heartbeat. "You have already surpassed the average," he told her as he stuffed her back into the box for another forty-eight-hour dose. "But nobody has ever held out after three doses."

It had become a contest, Lili understood without putting it into so many words, between them and her sanity. If she could hold out long enough, the pain tightening like a vise around her body would push her over the edge into insanity. Investigator Solokov would get nothing from her except the babbling of an idiot. Already she had difficulty finishing sentences, organizing thoughts, concentrating on anything for longer than a fleeting moment.

In forty-eight hours there were millions of fleeting moments, each one more painful than the one that went before. She could feel herself approaching the precipice. Wetness dripped down the stumps that had once been her legs, but it never occurred to her that she had urinated. Oh, God, Alexander, where are you? In her imagination she reached out a hand to him. Come, let us leap together into insanity! She could feel the weight of his shadow on her. But then she lost his name; she could call him, but not by name.

"What is your name?" she screamed into the silence of her space.

The door opened again. The orderly, lowering her to the icy floor, reminded her. "Your friend's name is Alexander. He refuses to give in too," he whispered in her ear. "His suffering is indescribable. You can release him from his suffering by agreeing to tell Investigator Solokov what he wants to know. If you love your friend, let Investigator Solokov execute him."

"Yes," Lili muttered through her swollen lips. Her voice was unrecognizable. "I must kill Alexander before he suffers more pain. Take me to Investigator Solokov."

The room resonated with broken silence: hacking coughs, whimpering, sighs, sobs, whispered conversations that had the urgency of telegrams, the scraping of limbs over the stone floor as condemned prisoners, male and female alike, dragged themselves to urinate into the public bucket. Once, even, there was the unmistakable sound of lovemaking as a couple, on the night before their execution, joined their bruised bodies for the last time. In a far corner of the cell diagonally across from the thick wooden door, next to a stone pillar, Zander massaged Lili's calves to keep the muscle cramps at bay.

"Try not to think about it," he whispered.

Lili bit her lip. "It is coming back," she moaned.

"No, no." He massaged her calves more vigorously. "You are remembering the last one. Try to relax the muscles."

"Here it comes," Lili cried, and Zander could feel her muscles tightening under his fingertips. Lili flung her head back and gasped, "Oh, oh, oh, oh, oh," and then she howled in pain. The other prisoners, absorbed in their own misery, paid no attention.

Gradually Lili's breathing became more regular.

Zander, still massaging her legs, said, "Talk to me. It will take your mind off your cramps. Tell me what made you give in to Solokov."

"They told me you were suffering terribly. They told me the only thing that could save you from more suffering was if I cooperated. That way they would shoot you instead of torturing you." A sarcastic laugh rattled around the back of Lili's throat. "It seemed to make perfect sense then. What about you?"

"They let me catch a glimpse of you when they took you out of the box," Zander said harshly; the memory was not congenial. "They told me you refused to give in, that I had to give in so they could shoot you and end your suffering. I was confused. Ending your suffering seemed more important than holding back on Solokov."

Lili and Zander were confined, along with some sixty or seventy other prisoners, in a large holding room off the main cell block. The windows, high in the stone wall, had been bricked over, and the only ventilation came from the cracks in the panes of an overhead skylight that had been painted black. In the permanent twilight the prisoners sprawling around the crowded holding room existed as shadows, and it was only the sounds coming from them that made them human. Every day fifteen or so new shadows were thrust into the holding room. And every morning some of the shadows rose from their places along the walls and drifted toward the door, where a guard was reading out a list of names. A figure more shadowy than the others in his flowing priest's robes intoned a prayer for the dead as they filed out of the twilight world. "*Gospodi pomiloe, Gospodi pomiloe*—Lord have mercy, Lord have mercy," he chanted in a deep voice, and Zander, sitting with his back to the pillar, was reminded of the coronation scene from *Boris Godunov* with the choir chanting its despairing "Gospodi pomiloe." From the courtyard below came the muffled commands of an officer. Then a crisp volley of rifle fire—the snapping of dry twigs on a foggy day—reverberated through the holding room, through the skulls of the shadows waiting their turn.

"I lost your mother's cameo," Lili was saying. "They must have taken it when we were arrested."

"It is of no importance," Zander lied. He felt as if he had lost his last link with his mother.

After a while Lili moaned. "I always knew it *could* end like this." She reached out into the twilight and touched Zander's face with the ball of her thumb and felt the welts and the swelling. "But I never thought it would. We have not had enough time, Alexander."

Zander laughed under his breath. "No matter how much time we had, it would never have been enough."

"I am only sorry we are dying together. For selfish reasons I wanted you to survive me. Now there will be no one to look after my daughter."

"There must be a father somewhere."

There was an awkward silence. "She was conceived in Paris." Lili hesitated. "To tell the truth, I am not sure who the father is." She peered into the twilight, trying to make out Zander's features. "It could have been Ronzha. It could have been my brother, Felix." There was another long silence. Then Lili burst out,

"Do you hate me, Alexander, for having slept with my brother?"

Nearby, a shadow detached itself from the wall and shuffled across the floor toward the bucket. Zander turned back to Lili. "You are a revolutionist. A woman's path to revolution is not a man's. Women have to go through a period of sexual exploration to discover things about themselves that men take absolutely for granted. I have nothing to reproach you for, Lissik."

They talked on in undertones. Sleep might have been something that never existed. As the night progressed their voices grew desperate. Time, they both sensed, was seeping through their fingers. Soon there would be none left. "I love you, Alexander," Lili whispered fiercely. "I love your body and I love your head and I love the way you have of narrowing your eyes when you are annoyed, and I love how you cock your good ear when you cannot hear well, and I love your fucking moral center." She smiled faintly. "I cannot stand the idea of your dying."

"I love you too," Zander said simply. "All of you. Sometimes I have the feeling that I am you."

"You will see," Lili whispered, her lips brushing his good ear. "When the time comes, I will die like a man."

Zander shuddered. "I feel old. Old and tired. And without hope."

They were still deep in conversation the next morning when the guard stepped through the door and called out, "Lili Mikhailovna Yusupova, Alexander Yonkelevich Til."

At the stone pillar Zander's hand reached out and gripped Lili's wrist for a long moment. Then the two of them rose and, stepping carefully over the outstretched legs of the other prisoners, made their way to the door. They passed the priest murmuring "*Gospodi pomiloe, Gospodi pomiloe,*" and fell in between the guards lined up in the corridor outside the holding room.

Lili still had trouble with her swollen feet, so Zander kept an arm tightly around her waist as they moved through the endless corridors. Once again doors opened in front of them and closed behind them. From the cells lining the corridors, voices called out to them.

"Spit in their faces," one prisoner called.

"The revolution will triumph," yelled another.

"Hold open the door to hell—I won't be far behind you," a woman called with an hysterical cackle.

They descended the narrow winding steel staircase and ducking through a low door emerged into a courtyard. Zander looked around for the firing squad.

The officer of the guard read his thoughts. "Shooting is reserved for run-of-the-mill Bolshevists. Your deaths will be slower." He nodded toward a small truck parked nearby.

Lili hung back. Zander gazed into her eyes, and she looked away. "Come," he said.

"No."

"Come, please."

Lili shook her head.

The officer of the guard pushed her forward. Zander took her arm and drew her toward the truck. She struggled. "What are you doing? Let go of me!"

Hoods were drawn over their heads. Their wrists were tied behind their backs and they were pushed roughly into the back of the truck. Two guards climbed in after them and the truck set off toward the outskirts of Ekaterinburg. Zander, next to Lili on the bench, could feel her fear; her thigh and her shoulder were trembling.

Half an hour later the truck pulled up with a squealing of brakes. The rear doors opened and Zander and Lili were pulled out. Their hoods were removed. Zander glanced at Lili. She tossed her head to get a strand of hair out of her eye, and for a moment he thought she would be able to go through with it. But when one of the soldiers reached out for her arm, she shrank back and a cry that could have come only from a cornered animal escaped her lips.

They were in a field through which the railroad tracks ran on an elevated embankment. Ekaterinburg was on the other side of a wood; a distant church bell chimed the hour. A young officer with long, fine blond hair and

blond eyebrows stepped up and saluted the guard officer. "We will take over from here," he told him. The
guard officer and his men looked relieved. They climbed
back into the truck, the officer in front, the two guards
in the back, and drove off.

The young guard officer with the fine blond hair
stared at Zander, trying to catch his attention. Zander's
eyes opened slightly wider in recognition; he *knew* the
officer from somewhere.

"Let's get on with it," the officer instructed the four
soldiers waiting behind him. Lili sank limply to her
knees, whimpering. Two guards gripped her under the
armpits and lifted her to her feet and pulled her along
behind Zander.

"Help me, Alexander!" Lili cried.

Zander glanced back over his shoulder at Lili being
dragged along, her shoes scraping the ground. He looked
at the officer trailing a few paces behind. The young
officer seemed to nod to him—or was he imagining it?
His heart began to pound.

They climbed the embankment and crossed the rails.
Lili gasped in horror, and would have collapsed to the
ground but for the two soldiers supporting her. Zander
breathed in through his nostrils. He felt like throwing up.

In either direction as far as the eye could see, there
were decaying hands tied to the rails. They had been
amputated at the wrists by passing trains, and the condemned prisoners, blood gushing from the stumps, had
stumbled down the embankments away from the tracks
to bleed to death. There must have been a hundred
bodies scattered in the fields, all handless, all gray and
lifeless from loss of blood.

One of the guards forced Lili onto her stomach. With
his foot pressing into the small of her back, he cut the
cord binding her hands and stretched them over her
head so that her wrists were crossed on the rail, her
hands on one side, her body down the embankment on
the other. A cord was quickly passed around her wrists,
pinning them to the rail. All four guards then turned to
Zander. He offered no resistance as they pushed him
onto his stomach and bound his wrists to the rail.

His head was next to Lili's. He could make out the pinpricks of utter terror in the pupils of her eyes, but he didn't dare offer her hope.

Laughing among themselves, the four soldiers checked the cords once more, and then disappeared over the top of the embankment and down the other side. "Are their wrists bound well?" Zander heard the young officer ask. He could hear his boots scraping for a foothold on the other side of the embankment. Then the head of the officer appeared over the rail. "I will check to be sure," he said.

Next to Zander, Lili pressed her face into the dirt to stifle her sobs.

The young officer knelt down on one knee on a tie near Zander's head. "You recognize me, but you do not remember from where? You gave me my life once. You were taking me back from Tsarkoe Selo for execution. You stopped the car and untied my wrists and let me go in a field not very different from this one, except there were no bodies in it. Now I give you your lives in return." He produced a short ceremonial sword and sawed through the cord binding Zander's wrists. "The train is not due for another quarter hour. Wait a bit to be sure we have gone before you untie her and run for it. The area between here and Perm is crawling with Whites. If you are captured again, there is nothing I can do for you."

Zander managed, "Thank you for taking the risk."

The officer shrugged. "Your revolution is a disaster for Russia. Millions will die. I hope to God you lose." He stood up, brushed the dust from his knee with a gloved hand, and disappeared over the embankment.

Lili slowly turned to Zander. Her face was streaked with tears and dirt. She spat out dirt from her mouth and stared at him, stunned. Then a strained, crooked, ugly smile distorted her face. "What a gift life is," she said, and she started to sob quietly.

5

Z ander could see that Lili was dying mentally. The cells in her brain must be decaying under the strain, he told himself. Her mind tended to wander; it was often, judging from the expression on her face, blank. She was capable of concentrating for short bursts when he pushed her, but the only thing she seemed to expect was the worst. She could collapse in tears at the sight of blood from a mosquito bite she had scratched raw. And once she started sobbing, she would stumble along behind Zander for hours, blinded by tears, her body jerking spasmodically.

She had cracked like an old saucer. And he had become the caretaker of the pieces.

Now Lili lay curled up behind the hedges at the lip of a ravine that the peasants used as a garbage dump, twitching in her sleep. Zander crouched next to her, watching a fat, bearded priest drive a mule through rows of unharvested rye teeming with field mice, toward the village and the gutted church at its edge. In the distance a swarm of flies hovered over the priest's head, scattering when he swatted at them with the back of his hand, then regrouping instantly into something resembling a halo over a saint. The mule reared, frightened by the mice scurrying underfoot, and refused to advance. The priest cursed him to burn forever in a hell so hot it taxed an educated man's vocabulary to describe it. When the mule still didn't budge, the priest raised his robe and reared back and kicked him in the testicles. The mule bellowed in pain and crashed forward again through the rye toward the gutted church.

Moving across high pastures by the light of the moon, hiding by day, living on mushrooms and the roots of plants and what they found in the ruins of barns and houses, Zander and Lili made their way across the Ural Mountains toward Perm, a city some two hundred miles from Ekaterinburg. Armed bands of Whites, Reds, and even Greens—anarchist peasants who fought against both sides—roamed the countryside, killing the humans or the animals they came across. Hardly a night went by without their stumbling across bloated and decaying corpses. They had gone to ground one morning before first light, only to find, at sunup, that they were under a cliff against which several small bamboo cages had been suspended, each containing a prisoner who had been left to die of thirst and exposure. Hiding in a bog near a lake another time, they saw a band of Greens herd eight prisoners—it was impossible to say whether they were Whites or Reds—onto a long dock at the water's edge, tie boulders to their necks, and prod them off the deep end with the points of bayonets. "If we are in danger of being caught," Lili would say again and again, "you must cut my wrist with that rusty knife you found," and Zander, sharpening it on a flat stone, had to promise her he would do it. At first he would agree only to quiet her. But after he saw the corpse of a woman who had been gagged and raped and garrotted, he meant every word.

"We will never make it to Perm," Lili sighed one day as they scavenged for food through burned outbuildings of a once-flourishing farm. Around them everything had been demolished—poultry sheds, pigpens, milking stalls, horse stables. Several wild dogs, their rib cages visible in the moonlight, howled from the shadows of a stand of timber.

Except for one wing, the manor house of the farm, planted on a rise behind the outbuildings at the end of an alley of acacias, had been burned to the ground. Poking around that wing, Zander discovered a length of drapery and folded it into a mattress for Lili, who promptly curled up on it and fell into a fitful sleep. In the charred ruins of the main house Zander found a tin of halvah, a broken jar with some pickles still in it, and a metal box full of iodine crystals. Settling down in a corner near Lili, he added what he had found to his makeshift backpack, placed his rusty knife where he could get at it quickly and started to doze. The heat was oppressive. Two flies buzzing around his good ear woke him, but he brushed them away and, leaning against the wall, drifted off into a deep sleep.

The point of a saber tickling his throat jerked him back to consciousness. His eyes batted open. His body froze. Several dozen half-naked children of all sizes and ages had crowded silently into the wing of the manor house. Their bodies were covered with dirt and sores. The older ones—they couldn't have been more than twelve—had surrounded Lili and Zander, pinning them to the floor with outstretched cavalry sabers which were so heavy the children had to manipulate them with both hands.

"*Bezprezorni*," murmured Zander. "Don't move."

Before they left Moscow, they had heard about the *bezprezorni*, or homeless ones. There had been an article in *Pravda* describing the thousands of half-starved orphans roaming the countryside, hunting in packs, terrorizing villages, stealing or killing to survive, living by their own laws with the older children protecting the younger ones. There had even been a suggestion that some of the children, wild with hunger, had turned to cannibalism.

There was a shuffling of bare feet now as the children made way for their leader. He was dressed in a loincloth and wore a woman's fur cape flung over one shoulder. A hunting hawk, with a short leash attached to one claw and a hood over its head, clung to his raised wrist. The leader, who couldn't have been more than fourteen, surveyed the two prisoners with unblinking dove's eyes as he absently pulled a louse from his scalp and squashed it between his fingernails. Somewhere behind him a baby burst into tears. Another child began to sing to it in an undertone. The leader nodded at Zander's rusty knife. A young girl with burn scars over her chest promptly scooped it up and stuck it into her waistband. Two of the children dug into a canvas sack and produced a long chain, which they passed several times around Zander's arms and wrists before padlocking the ends together.

The leader looked down at Lili. "If you do not do as we say, we will cut up your friend and cook him." He glanced over the heads of the children nearest him and called, "Bring the babies."

Six young girls, naked except for tattered cotton underpants, their skin covered with layers of scabs, pushed through the crowd. Each carried an infant in her arms. "We found them yesterday," the leader mumbled, "in a village put to the sword by Whites. They will go to heaven if they do not get milk. Our girls have no breasts, but you do. Breastfeed our babies and we will spare you and your friend."

Controlling an urge to tremble, Lili glanced at Zander. She started to say, "I have no—" when she caught his almost imperceptible shake of the head. The *bezprezorni* obviously thought any woman with breasts had milk. Lili shivered. "Pass them to me one at a time," she said. She unbuttoned her shirt and took the first infant to her breast.

The baby fitted its tiny mouth over her nipple, but was too weak to suckle. Several of the *bezprezorni* squatted down around Lili to watch. One child who couldn't have been more than four years old began to cry. An older boy pulled a large gold pocket watch from a sack and pressed it against the child's ear.

"Tick-tick," the child giggled. "Tick-tick."

Lili passed the first baby back to its caretaker, and forced herself to accept a second. This one was covered with head sores oozing pus. It began to suck at her breast, and howled when the nipple failed to provide milk, but the infant continued sucking, and Lili's nipple became raw. Cringing, Lili thrust the baby off her chest. The children squatting around her sprang to their feet. Two of the older children leveled their cavalry sabers at Zander's throat.

Shuddering, Lili carefully drew the baby back to her chest and offered it the other breast.

By midafternoon each of the babies had had a turn at Lili's breasts. The leader dipped into a canvas sack and passed out sticks of smoked meat. Afterward, twenty of the *bezprezorni* formed a ring in the middle of the room and began to play *koshka-mishka*, cat and mouse. The object was for the "cat" inside the ring to break through and catch the "mouse," an emaciated eight-year-old girl who circulated outside the ring.

The game began playfully enough with the cat, a heavy twelve-year-old boy, rebounding off the locked arms of the children in the ring. Each attempt to break out evoked wild laughter from the *bezprezorni* watching from the sidelines. The laughter incensed the cat, who began hurling himself against the linked arms with more force. The harder he tried to break out, the more the others laughed, until finally the cat lowered its head, and grunting viciously, butted straight into the chest of one of the younger children in the ring. With a cry of pain the child fell back. The cat sprang through the gap onto the back of the mouse, grabbed her hair in both hands, and began pounding her head into the stone floor.

"For God's sake, stop him," Lili screamed from the corner of the room.

"But it is only a game," the *bezprezorni*'s leader, caressing the feathers of his falcon, called back.

The children squatting along the walls began clapping rhythmically. At each clap the cat pounded the mouse's head into the floor. Lili turned away and shut her eyes, but the tears flooded out anyway.

At sunset, the *bezprezorni* gathered up their belongings and babies and, filing out the door, disappeared into the night. True to their promise to Lili, they left behind the key to the padlock that bound Zander. They also left behind two babies that had gone to heaven during the day, and the body of the mouse sprawled in a pool of drying blood in the middle of the room.

Their faces blackened with mud, the raiding party set off two hours after sunset. All fourteen of them crowded into two fishing barks and poled their way across the river at a point several miles upstream from the White battery dug in on the headland commanding the Volga.

The guide, a young peasant who had been raised on the Asian bank of the river near Kazan, led the raiding party inland, away from the Volga, and skirting the edge of a field planted in cabbages, turned toward the promontory barely visible in the distance. Moving along a ditch used to circulate runoff from the river when it was high, the raiding party approached the campfire at the base of the promontory. Tuohy eased his head over the edge of the ditch and counted the silhouettes. He tapped the man next to him and held up two fingers. Then he motioned two of the Chekists forward. They drew knives from their belts and, crawling on their bellies, disappeared over the top of the ditch. Tuohy cocked his ear toward the campfire and strained to catch the sound. A faint breeze whistled through the underbrush. A frog croaked. There was a soft thud of feet running on the damp earth. Silhouettes darted in front of the campfire. Then everything was quiet.

"Let's go," Tuohy whispered, and he and the eleven men with him headed up the rise toward the White cannon dug in above them. As they drew closer Tuohy could hear someone washing tin plates in a bucket. Tuohy pointed a finger, dispatching a Chekist in the direction of the sound. The man who was doing the washing hummed to himself. Suddenly the humming ceased. Tuohy nodded toward the first of the two artillery pieces, its barrel elevated and visible against the night sky. He crawled forward with some of the Chekists until he reached the sandbag barrier, and slowly raised himself until he could peer over the top into the dugout.

There were seven men inside, four of them sound asleep, the other three propped up with their backs against ammunition crates playing cards by the light of an oil lamp. Tuohy sank back into the shadow of the sandbags and waited to give the other Chekists time to position themselves around the second dugout. He drew his knife from his belt. The men around him followed suit.

"Now!" he whispered, and he flung himself over the top and came down on the other side on one of the card players, burying his knife in the man's chest. Around him there were muted cries as men died before they had a chance to know what was killing them.

Tuohy stood up and peered in the direction of the second dugout. A Chekist trotted over and knelt on the rim of the sandbags. "It is ours," he whispered.

Two of the Chekists who knew something about artillery pieces set about spiking the guns so that they would blow up in the face of anybody who tried to fire them. Tuohy grabbed the lantern and walked over to the lip of the headland. He stared down at the Volga curving under his feet, then waved his gaslamp in a great arc. Below, on one of the four Bolshevik gunboats, someone signaled back.

The four boats, with Trotsky in command aboard the lead vessel, made their way around the curve under the promontory into the lagoonlike bay before the low, sprawling town of Kazan. The White flotilla—an oil barge, two river steamers fitted out with machine guns and cannon, a half-dozen gunboats—lay at anchor about two hundred yards dead ahead of Trotsky's makeshift armada.

The Reds fired star shells into the air behind the White vessels to outline them, then opened up with every gun they had. The oil barge exploded, spewing greenish flames into the sky. One of the riverboats caught fire and began to sink, stern first. From the headland Tuohy could see tiny figures leaping from the deck into the burning water. Behind a jetty on the shore, White machine guns and mortars fired back. One of the Red gunboats took a hit in the stern and turned in circles for a quarter of an hour until the crew managed to jury-rig a rudder. When Trotsky's flotilla steamed out of the lagoon half an hour later, all but one of the White vessels was sinking or sunk.

The victory left control of the river in Red hands, and opened the way for a frontal assault on the Whites entrenched in Kazan.

Perm, a city of sixty thousand on the European slope of the Urals, boasted a concert hall with a Venetian chandelier so massive nobody in his right mind would sit under it. There was a public park with a ten-horse manège imported from Paris. The local undertaker owned four motorized hearses of English manufacture, though three had been requisitioned by the local Chekists to transport prisoners. The church had a layer of gold leaf on its dome. Several of the taller buildings were equipped with elevators. And some of the principal streets had been paved, though only the ones paved in cobblestones were still intact; any wooden blocks had long since been pried up by people scavenging for firewood.

By late August 1918, the streets of Perm were teeming with refugees. There were so many that the soldiers manning the roadblocks at the city's perimeter had given up asking for identification papers, and simply waved everybody past who wasn't armed. Making their way through the outskirts, Zander and Lili felt as if they were being carried on a current. As the street narrowed, the crowd seemed to flow faster. "Hurry," a woman cried to her friends as she pushed past Zander, "or we will miss the fun." Ahead, a military parade ground with a low wooden fence around it blocked the street. Before the revolution, recruits for the tsar's war against Germany had worn away most of the grass practicing close-order drill. Now, drawn by the excitement, Zander pulled Lili up to a place against the fence. Across the parade ground, near a brick wall, six blackrobed priests had been tied to stakes. A firing squad of twenty young soldiers was marching into position facing the priests. The officer commanding the firing squad pulled his sword from its scabbard. One of the priests raised his voice. "God's curse on the head of anyone who shoots a priest—you will rot in hell!"

"Get ready," the officer ordered.

A murmur rose from the hundreds of people watching from the low wooden fence. The woman next to Zander said, "Yesterday they refused to shoot, but the boys were all local boys. So they went and brought in Uzbeks today."

Lili sagged against Zander. "I cannot take any more killing," she said dully.

Zander threw an arm over her shoulder and drew her

back into the crowd. Several people quickly squeezed into their places along the fence. Pulling Lili through the mob straining for a better view—one man had lifted his young son onto his shoulders—Zander could hear the bolts being thrown on the rifles.

"Take aim," the officer cried.

Lili jerked her hand out of Zander's and pressed both palms over her ears. Tears welled in her eyes. Zander held her head to his chest. She was trembling violently.

"Fire!" bellowed the officer.

The volley crackled over their heads. Lili cried out. Heads swiveled. "Is she against the extermination of the exploiters, then?" a worker asked suspiciously.

She is against killing, Zander wanted to say. She has seen too much of it. Russia has seen too much of it. But he knew it was not prudent to get into an argument; they had no papers, no identification of any kind on them. Pulling Lili along behind him, he turned his back on the worker and set out to find the Cheka office in Perm.

Lined up five abreast between police barriers, hundreds of refugees had gathered in front of the Cheka headquarters in the Excise Office Building on the corner of Pokrovskaya and Obvinskaya. A leather-jacketed Chekist with a holster on his hip stood on the top step holding a bullhorn to his lips and reading the latest edict. "By order of the Perm Soviet," he intoned, "anyone hoarding food will be shot on sight. By order of the Perm Soviet, anyone carrying firearms without a permit will be shot on sight. By order of—"

"What about the food coupons you promised for today?" a man shouted up at the Chekist.

"Food coupons," the Chekist shouted back, "are issued between nine and eleven in the morning."

"I have been here since dawn," a woman called. "There were so many ahead of me I couldn't get past the door."

"Come back tomorrow at nine," the Chekist instructed her. He glanced down at the paper in his hand. "By order of the Perm Soviet, anyone caught harboring an enemy of the people will be shot on sight. By order of the Perm Soviet—"

At the back of the crowd Zander listened to the edicts with mounting anger. He remembered the brutality of the Whites who had taken him and Lili prisoner. It occurred to him that factions warring with each other more often than not came to resemble each other. He had a sudden urge to share the thought with Lili; it seemed like an important insight. But one look at her contorted face convinced him that she was in no condition to discuss anything. "Come on." He pulled her away from the Excise Building. "There has to be a back entrance."

"I am reaching the end of my possibilities," Lili whispered.

"Your possibilities are infinite," Zander said, trying to force as much conviction as possible into his tone. But it wasn't something he himself believed.

Supporting Lili with an arm around her waist, Zander found the alley behind Pokrovskaya Street. A single sentry with a rusted rifle stood halfway down the alley, more interested in flirting with two teenage girls than in challenging Zander's right to be there. The back entrance of the Excise Office Building was guarded by a half-dozen Uzbeks who seemed to know only one word in Russian. "*Nyet, nyet,*" one of them cried when Zander tried to talk his way into the building, and he waved a large German pistol to show he meant what he said.

Behind them, at the entrance to the alley, a siren wailed, and two cars with Chekists on the running boards roared down the alley and pulled up in front of the building. The Chekists jumped from the running boards and pushing Zander and Lili roughly back, formed a cordon to the door. One of the undertaker's four English hearses drew up behind the two Cheka cars. Commissar Beloborodov, still wearing his army tunic and riding boots, emerged from the passenger seat. He looked up and down the alley, then went and rapped twice on the rear doors of the hearse. The doors opened and two Letts half-dragged a teenage girl out into the alley. She was bleeding from cuts on her face and chest. Her embroidered white blouse, with a tight-banded collar, was covered with blood and torn at one shoulder. The Letts pulled her into the Excise Office Building.

Lili put her mouth close to Zander's ear. "Did you recognize her?"

"Should I have?"

"That was the tsar's daughter Anastasia."

"Are you sure?"

Lili nodded.

Over the heads of the Chekists, Zander called out, "Comrade Beloborodov!"

Beloborodov turned and spotted Zander and lifted a hand in a casual wave. "Let them through," he ordered.

The commissar, guilty about having abandoned them in Ekaterinburg, quickly supplied them with money, identification papers, meal tickets, and travel authorizations on the next train west, which was due to leave in five or six days. Meanwhile he installed them in a room on the top floor of a lower-class hotel across the street from the Excise Office Building. Because they had come through the White lines with only the clothes on their backs, he had a trunk full of confiscated garments delivered to their room, with a note attached that said, "Beggars can still be choosers—take your pick. Compliments of Commissar B." The clothes had belonged to rich people and were of good quality, and Zander thought they would cheer Lili, but her lower lip quivered as she held a woman's dress in front of her, as if femininity belonged to another life that would never be hers again. "Cry if it will make you feel better," Zander suggested, but Lili shook her head violently—many of her gestures had become violent lately—and said in a high-strung voice, "If I start I will not be able to stop."

Lili agreed to change into a man's shirt and trousers—"because they are at least clean," she said—and they took a meal in the basement canteen of the Excise Office Building. As they were finishing, a Chekist came in, looked around, saw Lili, and passed her a note inviting her to mount to the second floor as soon as she finished eating.

"We have a woman prisoner and need a woman to watch after her while a doctor examines her wounds,"

Beloborodov explained when they arrived upstairs. "I thought your lady friend here might lend us a hand."

Zander started to say something about Lili being under a great strain, but Lili cut him off. "I will help if I can," she insisted to Beloborodov, and followed him through a guarded door into an inner office.

Anastasia was stretched out on a leather couch. One of her eyes was swollen shut from the beating she had been given. "The doctor is on his way up," Beloborodov said as he left Lili alone with the prisoner.

Lili knelt next to the couch and ran her fingers through Anastasia's matted brown hair, which had been cut short with shears. "Anastasia," she whispered. "It's Lili Mikhailovna. Don't you remember me? You visited my grandfather's estate one summer. We used to drive a cart, crouching, peasant-style, down the alleys between the lilac trees."

Anastasia's unswollen eye blinked open. "Lissik? Is it really you?"

Lili's lips quivered. She was afraid she would burst into tears again. "Who did this to you?"

"Oh, Lissik, I slipped away from the others—they are in a basement not far from here—Mother thinks the Bolsheviks will shoot us as they shot Father and poor Alexei. I flirted with a guard and fled when he slept and made it across the Kama River into the woods. I wandered around for days, but the Letts found me and beat me. Am I to die, Lissik? Are they going to shoot me?"

There were footsteps beyond another door that led to a corridor. Lili quickly backed away from the couch. A key turned in the lock. The door opened and a middle-aged man carrying a leather medical satchel entered. Sitting on the edge of the couch, he felt for Anastasia's pulse, then opened a large white handkerchief and spread it on the girl's chest and pressed his ear to her heart. Anastasia turned her head toward Lili, who motioned her with a finger on her lips to be quiet. The doctor examined the cuts and bruises around Anastasia's eyes and face and shoulders. He unbuttoned her blouse and examined the bruises on her breasts and ribs. "Does this hurt?" he asked, testing each rib with his fingertips. Anastasia shook her head no. "You will live, young lady," the doctor announced. He removed some iodine and cotton from his satchel and dabbed iodine on the open cuts and abrasions. Finally he stood up. "I am leaving a jar of Goulard water and some bromide salts," he told Lili. "Mix the two in a glass of lukewarm water and give her four teaspoons full every hour. It will relieve the pain and calm her."

He was about to leave when Anastasia sat up on the couch. "Thank you, Doctor," she said in a very formal voice, and she offered her right hand, palm down, the long delicate fingers for which the Romanov women were famous suspended languidly. Reluctantly the doctor took her hand in his and inclined his head. Anastasia told him with utter simplicity, "I am the Grand Duchess Anastasia, daughter of Nicholas the Second, Emperor of Russia."

The doctor dropped her hand and backed away as if his patient had a contagious disease. "I do not want to know who you are." He turned to Lili. "I did not hear a word she said. You are my witness. She has a fever. For all I know she is raving mad." The doctor snatched his satchel and, without another look at the girl on the couch, hurried from the room.

As the door closed behind him, Lili could hear the key turning in the lock again.

Beloborodov came in through the door that led to the inner office. He glanced at Anastasia, who had fallen back onto the couch in exhaustion. "Can you keep an eye on her until we decide what to do with her? I will get one of the wives of the Chekists to spell you."

When Beloborodov left, Lili went over to Anastasia, who was sobbing silently. "They are going to shoot me," she whispered. "I am not guilty of anything except being the daughter of the tsar."

"Maybe they are going to send you to Moscow and hand you over to the Germans in exchange for some of the Socialists in their prisons," Lili said hopefully.

Anastasia laughed bitterly. "You think they will exchange me with these bruises! You should see how they are treating Mother and my sisters. I tell you they have no intention of freeing us." Anastasia grabbed Lili's forearm. "Help me, Lissik. I am frightened to death."

Lili regarded Anastasia and recognized the terror in her eyes. She had the eerie feeling she was looking in a mirror. Controlling her own emotions with an effort, she leaned forward and began to whisper to Anastasia.

The wife of one of the commissars eventually showed up to relieve Lili. Back in their hotel room, she told Zander what Anastasia had said. He listened carefully, and finally announced, "I will speak to Beloborodov."

"Now," Lili insisted. There was an hysterical edge to her voice.

"It is late."

"Please. Now." And she added very quietly, "They are going to shoot her. I feel it in my bones."

Zander could see that Lili was reliving her own execution. "I will do what I can," he said quickly.

He had trouble finding Beloborodov—it took almost an hour to track him down—and when he finally confronted him, he had difficulty getting in a word. "Do not, I beg you, start in again about the German women," Beloborodov warned. His palm drifted around in front of his face as if he were waving away flies. "I have had it up to here with the German women. You would think there wasn't a civil war raging out there. You would think the Whites weren't closing in on Perm. You would think we didn't have to come up pretty damn fast with some solutions. And whatever you do, do *not* mention the name Trotsky to me. Trotsky is so busy playing the hero at Kazan, he does not have the time to reply to our requests for instructions. The hell with Trotsky. The hell with the German women." Beloborodov lowered his voice. "Comrade Til, you do not have the slightest conception of the weight I carry around on my shoulders."

Zander managed to say, "This is a matter of life and death—"

"These days everything is a matter of life and death," Beloborodov retorted. "Someone needs tooth powder and it is a matter of life and death."

"About the German women," Zander persisted.

Beloborodov waved his hand in disgust. "As far as I
am concerned, there are no German women. There are
Russian women, the wife and daughters of a Russian
criminal who has been executed for his crimes."

Zander could see he was only making matters worse.
He decided to try again when Beloborodov had calmed
down. He started toward the door just as two Chekists
burst through it into the office.

"She is gone!" one of them blurted out.

"Disappeared into thin air," cried the other Chekist.

Beloborodov sprang to his feet. "How is that possible? The door to the corridor was supposed to be kept
locked at all times if a guard was not physically there."

"It is the work of a traitor," the first Chekist ventured. "Someone must have stolen the key from its
hook in the front office and unlocked the door."

"Who was with the girl?" Beloborodov demanded.

"Dmitrov's wife, Tanya," replied the Chekist. "She
says she stepped out for five minutes to go to the toilet.
When she came back, the door was open and the girl
was gone."

"I will talk to this Tanya personally," Beloborodov
announced, and brushing past Zander, he strode out of
the room.

In the hours that followed, as squads of Letts spread
out through the town to search for the missing Anastasia, Beloborodov interrogated everyone who could have
had access to the key: the Chekists who worked in the
inner office, their secretaries, the messengers who had
been there that day, and the four women, Lili among
them, who had taken turns guarding Anastasia. His
investigation quickly bogged down. At least twenty people could have gotten their hands on the key and used
it to unlock the corridor door so that the girl could
escape.

Zander's stomach had knotted at the news of Anastasia's disappearance. If Lili were implicated, the Chekists
would not listen to explanations about how she had
been tortured and almost executed by the Whites. Racing back to their room, Zander had looked into her face

for some clue, but had found none; there was a vacant, far-off expression in her eyes, a limpness to her limbs.

He accompanied her to Cheka headquarters and stayed close to her as she waited with the others in the corridor for the summons to Beloborodov's inner sanctum. Across the corridor, one of the women who had spelled Lili smiled at her. Lili nodded back tiredly. "I tell you we have met before," the woman called across pleasantly. "I have a memory for faces. Yours is definitely familiar to me."

"Do you know her?" Zander asked quietly.

Lili shook her head. "I have never seen her before Perm."

"It will come to me," the woman remarked. She frowned as she stared at Lili.

Lili was eventually called into Beloborodov's office. She emerged ten minutes later. "He said I could go back to the hotel room for the time being," she told Zander. He took her arm and they headed for the stairs.

The woman who thought she knew Lili watched them go. She shook her head in frustration. Then she froze. Her eyes widened, her mouth gaped open. She *had* seen Lili before—on a poster, in Petrograd, before the revolution! She would never forget that face with the faint trace of Asia in the eyes. She even remembered the slogan printed across the poster. THE WOMEN OF RUSSIA SAY *NO* TO BOLSHEVISM.

"I must see Comrade Beloborodov right away," the woman told one of the guards at the door. "I know who opened the door for Anastasia."

Lili sat at the edge of the unmade bed twisting a piece of cloth in her fingers. She looked up at Zander with an ominous calmness that could almost have been mistaken for numbness.

"Where is she?" Zander whispered.

"Where is who?"

"You know who. Anastasia. If we're the ones who bring her back, we may be able to convince them you helped her because of what happened to you, that you were not responsible for your actions." He shook Lili by the shoulders. "For God's sake, Lissik, you have to tell me. Where is she?"

Behind them they could hear booted feet pounding up the wooden stairs of the hotel. Zander cocked his good ear for an instant, then turned back to Lili, a horrified expression in his eyes. He might have been watching his brother leap from the burning building.

"Why?" he pleaded.

Lili's eyes glazed over; they seemed to lose their ability to focus.

The pounding feet reached their floor. The muscles of her face twitched, and settled into a whimsical smile. "It is too late. It has been too late for me for a long time." She bit her lower lip. "Oh, Alexander, there are parts of you I have not been to yet!"

A half-dozen Chekists, with an agitated Beloborodov in the lead, exploded into the small room. "Lili Mikhailovna Yusupova," Beloborodov panted, "I arrest you"—he paused to catch his breath—"I arrest you in the name of the Ural Soviet for an act of high treason."

6

It was not a trial in the usual sense. No evidence was presented; none was needed. Commissar Beloborodov listed in a toneless voice the crimes that the defendant had admitted committing, after which he pronounced sentence. Zander became dizzy and bent his head down to his knees to keep from fainting. He barely heard the proceedings.

". . . Reverting to her class loyalties, did steal the key to the hall door from its hook on the wall . . . informed the accused Anastasia what she planned to do . . . the first moment she was alone, the same Anastasia tried the door, and finding it open . . . said Lili

Mikhailovna Yusupova, whose likeness appeared in a prominent antibolshevik poster in the days preceding the revolution . . ."

Lili, deathly pale, sat on a bench sandwiched between the two bearded Chekists. Her eyes examined the walls and the ceiling of the makeshift courtroom; she might have been drugged for all the emotion she showed when Beloborodov sentenced her "to the highest measure of punishment, such sentence to be carried out at the convenience of the Cheka authorities in Perm."

Zander cornered Beloborodov in the corridor outside the courtroom. "She is personally known to our top people in Moscow," he pleaded. The words started to gush out. "She once risked her life to carry messages and funds to Lenin in Switzerland. I ask you to let me cable Moscow . . . explain the situation . . . request leniency." Zander had to restrain himself from grabbing the commissar by the lapels and shaking him. "You have to consider what the Whites did to her in Ekaterinburg. Something inside her was broken."

Beloborodov shrugged impatiently, and gestured with a tired snap of his head toward the staircase. "If the Hughes line is functioning, you can try. I will give you twenty-four hours. After that, the matter will be in the hands of the comrades whose job it is to carry out sentences."

Beloborodov scribbled an authorization, and Zander ran with it clutched in his hand all the way to the railroad station. He controlled his trembling fingers in order to print out the message so the clerk could read it without difficulty. " 'Personal for Comrade Lenin,' " the Hughes clerk, whose spectacles had slipped down along his nose, repeated, and he mumbled his way through the rest of the message without showing the slightest interest in the contents. " 'She is the best of the best, the salt of the salt of the earth. If we kill off our revolutionists at every momentary lapse, who will be left to wage revolution? And in the end no one should be executed twice. Given past services and recent suffering leniency merited. I beg you to reply before twenty-four-hour deadline expires. Til.' " The clerk looked up at Zander. "This will go out on the line within the half hour," he promised.

"I will wait for a reply."

"You'd do better to go back into town and get some sleep," the clerk suggested. "Waiting will not make the answer get here faster. The incoming comes in bursts. The next batch is due at midnight, but they will never have time to answer by then. Another burst is due in at eight in the morning, and the one after that at four in the afternoon."

"I will wait," Zander insisted, and he settled onto a wooden bench in the baggage room behind the Hughes office and watched the large clock over the door tick off the last hours of Lili's life.

Huddled under a leaky poncho in a shallow trench outside of Kazan, Vasia Timofeyevich Maslov counted his blessings that he was still alive. He knew this state of grace might change at any moment. The Reds were tightening their vise around Kazan. Every day it seemed new units moved into positions facing them and provoked a skirmish.

Three days of constant rain had turned Vasia's trench into a bed of mud. The mud had one advantage—it absorbed the Red mortar explosions before they could do much damage; you had to be practically hit in the head by an incoming round to be killed by it. But every time Vasia moved, he could feel water squishing in the oversized boots that the Whites had issued to him after he deserted. Preoccupied with his lack of creature comforts, he thought less and less about Zander and Lili these days. He regretted having turned them in. But he had more or less convinced himself that their fate—they had certainly been shot out of hand—was inevitable. War was hell. Civil war was worse.

From across the field separating the White trenches from the Reds, a bugle sent some damp notes spiraling into the air. Vasia caught the hollow thud of the Red mortars dispatching the morning's ration toward the White lines. Crouching as he ran, a young White ensign in incredibly tight breeches made his way down the line. "Stand ready," the ensign ordered in an adolescent voice charged with excitement. "They will be coming over any time now."

The mortar fire intensified. Vasia threw a round into the chamber of his Nagant and raised himself to look over the rim of the trench. He heard the Reds yelling encouragement to each other in high-pitched voices. They came on in an uneven skirmish line, hunched over, trudging through the rain and the mud, their feet sinking in so far at each step that it was an effort to lift them out again.

On either side of Vasia, White soldiers braced their rifles on the soft edge of the trench and took aim. Vasia fired through the driving rain several times. The acrid smell of gunpowder stabbed up his nostrils, bringing tears to his eyes. A mortar round thudded into the ground in front of him and exploded, and a shower of mud rained down on his head, blinding him. He could hear the Red soldiers tramping toward him as he frantically tried to wipe the mud from his eyes. He jerked his shirttail out of his trousers and used it to wipe his eyes and looked up to see two burly Reds, the earflaps on their cloth caps arched out like wasp wings, bearing down on him. Vasia caught a glimpse of his comrades throwing up their hands in surrender. Instinctively he did the same.

The twenty-two White prisoners captured in the skirmish were marched across the swamplike fields in the pouring rain to the bank of the Volga and ferried across in small groups to the other side. There they were herded under lean-tos until the rain let up in late afternoon, then formed up into a column and marched, their hands clasped on the backs of their necks, down a muddy lane and across several fields to Trotsky's armored train parked at a siding. A group of Chekists, their leather jackets unbuttoned because of the heat, their wide belts sagging from the weight of the pistols on their hips, were waiting for them in front of a boxcar that had been converted into a field kitchen. A commissar tapping the business end of a riding crop against one palm stepped up in front of the prisoners. "Men," he called in a hoarse voice, "the tide is turning. This is your chance to throw in your lot with the winning side, to join the glorious struggle to create a better world. We accept every warm body that comes our way, no questions asked. The only ones we do not accept are Reds who went over to the Whites. Them we shoot."

Vasia kept his eyes fixed straight ahead. He had come into the line only ten days before, and didn't know well any of the men who had been taken prisoner with him. The chances of anyone on the Red side recognizing him were slim. He didn't care who won anymore. He longed only for the day the war would be over and he could return to his cameras. He would find a model like Lili, someone with white skin and long limbs and a way of looking through the lens to the world beyond. He would set up his tripod and study her upside-down image on the ground glass plate until—

"Zdravstvuyte, Vasia Timofeyevich."

Vasia, in the last row of the prisoners lined up before the commissar, turned his head and regarded the Chekist who had come up behind him. For an instant he looked like a blurred image on ground glass. Then he came into focus.

"Zdravstvuyte, Tuohy."

In his office in the Kremlin, under the yellowish cone of light cast by a desk lamp, Lenin attacked the batch of incoming cables piled in a wicker basket. He hadn't slept well in months, and he could feel another migraine coming on. He began to massage his temple with his thumb and forefinger. The first cable, from a peasant delegation in the town of Yefremov, requested Lenin's intervention to obtain for them a de-lousing station. The request had been denied by the local commissar, who was a city man born-and-bred and knew nothing about lice, so the peasants said. Lenin jotted a note on the corner of the cable: "See to this. Either the louse will defeat socialism or socialism will conquer the louse." The second cable, signed by twenty workers in a machine shop in Petrograd, complained that the Bolshevik in charge of their collectivized factory was running it into the ground. Lenin jotted: "Replace plant manager with someone nominated by the workers. Note that the proletariat is not insured against mistakes simply because he has carried out a revolution."

There was a thick pile of cables from women requesting their sons be freed of the obligation to serve in the Red Army in order to aid with the harvest. "Denied," Lenin noted. "Let the women farm while the men fight."

Last came a sheaf of cables from various people begging for clemency for a son or a husband who had been sentenced, for one transgression or another, to death. Lenin always kept these for last. He tried to judge each case on its merits, without letting sentimentality influence him. He took a deep breath and had started to read the first cable, when one of the telephones jingled on his desk. It was his secretary reminding him that the car was waiting to take him to the nationalized Mikhelson plant in the suburb of Serpukhovo, across the Moskva River. The cables would have to wait.

On that night of August 30 an unseasonal hoarfrost settled over Moscow. Temperatures dropped suddenly, and the few people abroad after dark felt chilled to the bone. Lenin's companion, Inessa Armand, wanted him to put on a pair of fur-lined galoshes, but he thought it would look ridiculous, in August, to go tramping around as if there were snow on the ground. Waiting his turn in the manager's office of the Mikhelson factory, he regretted he hadn't followed her advice. By the time he spoke, his toes were numb. The speech itself went well enough. "When the bourgeoisie rules," Lenin cried over the heads of the workers, "they give nothing to the toiling masses. Take America. A handful of millionaires insolently dominate, and the entire nation is in slavery. For us, there is one choice: victory or death!"

As Lenin made his way through the crowd toward the door, several workers tried to shake his hand. A dark-haired girl named Fanny Kaplan, in her late twenties, suddenly appeared directly in his path. "For me," she cried hysterically, "you are a traitor to the revolution." Then she whipped out a small revolver and fired three times at point-blank range.

Lenin was rushed by car to the Kremlin. With the help of his secretaries he managed to walk up to his third-floor apartment, where he collapsed on a chair in the vestibule. The first doctor to arrive reported that the Bolshevik leader's pulse was weak but steady. The doctor could feel with his fingertips the bullet lodged in Lenin's neck. The immediate problem was a hemorrhage into the left chest cavity that had pressed Lenin's heart to the right. With rest, with intensive care, the doctor said, there was a possibility the Bolshevik leader would pull through. For the moment there was nothing to do but wait and see.

The Hughes clerk shook Zander awake. "There is a long cable coming in from Moscow. It is being sent outside the regular burst, so it must be important. Maybe it is the one you are waiting for."

Zander followed the clerk into the wire room, where a clerk with earphones was copying off the message on a pad as it came over the line. Reading over the clerk's shoulder, Zander felt an incredible weakness flood into his limbs. He had to grab the edge of the table to steady himself. "To all Soviet authorities," the message read. "Lenin incapacitated by assassination attempt. Our answer to White terror will be Red terror. The rear of our armies must be cleared of White elements who conspire against the working class. Resort to mass executions. There must be no wavering, no indecision in the application of this order." The message bore the signature, "By unanimous decision of the Politburo."

Zander caught a ride into town in the automobile that brought the Politburo order to the Ural Soviet. The twenty-four hours was almost up and Beloborodov—who had not seen the Politburo message yet—was relieved when all Zander wanted from him was permission for a brief visit with Lili. He scribbled some words on a chit, and Zander raced off to the warehouse two blocks away that had been converted into a prison. He was accosted outside the front gate by a one-legged, one-armed man peddling something wrapped in small folded envelopes. "If you are visiting a condemned prisoner," the man wheezed, "the Chekists won't give a damn if you slip this to your friend." He added with a guttural laugh totally devoid of humor, "Makes their work that much easier."

Barely aware of what he was doing, Zander bought a packet.

Inside, Zander passed through several checkpoints and eventually found himself gazing through a small window covered with chicken wire. What light there was came from a single electric bulb, and it took his eyes a moment to become accustomed to it. Even then he had to strain to see more than a suggestion of a presence. In the instant before he could make her out, he imagined her—imagined her waxen complexion, imagined her occasional trembling when she lost control of her body, imagined her eyes, sunken and terrified, staring out trying to imagine him. Then the drawn gray face of a woman he barely recognized swam into focus.

Her eyes drifted closed for a long moment as she read in his expression that there would be no clemency. She was almost delirious with fear. She knew now that the thing she dreaded was coming true. "So I am to die," she said in a voice devoid of color or shading or hope.

Zander brought a hand up to his neck. He opened his mouth, but discovered he was physically incapable of speech. He had come to say good-bye, but he had lost language. He stared at her, etching into his memory the vision of her behind the wire mesh, her lips parted, her chipped front tooth gleaming with saliva.

"My daughter," Lili murmured. "You will look after her?"

Zander nodded miserably.

"Save Anastasia if you can."

Again he nodded, though if he could get his hands on Anastasia, he would surely turn her in in the hope of saving Lili.

Lili's jaw muscles twitched. She bit her lower lip, then released it. She wedged her fingertips through the wire mesh. "What will you do without me?" she asked in an almost inaudible voice.

Zander reached up and touched her fingertips with his own. He squeezed his lids shut to dam the flow of tears, but they spilled down his cheeks. For an endless moment he thought he was drowning.

"My poor darling," Lili moaned. She leaned forward and in a burst of concentration said, "We never dreamed there would be so much killing, but now that there is, it is even more important for the revolution to succeed. What a terrible waste if it doesn't."

He couldn't even bring himself to nod.

A guard opened the door behind Lili. "Your time is up, lady."

"My time is used up," Lili whispered. Her forehead fell forward against the mesh, and the chicken wire imprinted itself on her flesh. "How am I going to face this?"

Zander remembered the folded envelope in his pocket. Still incapable of uttering a word, he squeezed her fingertips to get her attention and pushed the envelope through the mesh to her. She folded it into her palm. A strand of hair drifted across one of her eyes. She made no move to remove it. "I know what this is. The other prisoners all dream of getting some."

"Come along, lady," the guard ordered from the door, "or I will have to make you come along."

Zander found a voice, though it was not his own. "Don't touch her!"

Lili heaved herself off her stool and stared down at Zander. Her lips were parted, as if she were about to say something. She turned abruptly and disappeared through the door, which was closed and bolted behind her.

Zander's eyes were still fixed on the door through which she had disappeared when they came to get him twenty minutes later.

The executions began, as executions do, at dawn, as if the start of day was somehow the appropriate time for the end of life. In Moscow, in the Kremlin, in a basement cell that had been used in the time of the tsars as an "oubliette" for unfaithful servants or unfaithful wives or collaborators whose collaboration was no longer required, Lenin's would-be assassin, Fanny Kaplan, was forced to kneel over the hole in a stand-up toilet as a large caliber bullet from a smooth-bored naval revolver was shot into the base of her skull.

On the bank of the Volga, near Kazan, thirty-four Red soldiers who had deserted to the Whites and then been recaptured were issued shovels and instructed to dig their own graves. Then the condemned men were ordered to kneel at the edge of the mass grave in such a way that their bodies would tumble into it. They did as they were told, as if they were co-conspirators in their own executions. Tuohy, who had volunteered for the job, moved down the line of kneeling men, "issuing bullets," he said, "one to a customer." After every six shots he fired, he would pass the empty parabellum to a Chekist following along behind him to reload. The Chekist handed the reloaded parabellum over with precision, slapping it into his palm as if it were a surgeon's scalpel, and Tuohy would turn back to the line of kneeling men and continue the executions.

Vasia Timofeyevich Maslov was the fourth man from the end. He listened to the hollow crack of the pistol shots drawing nearer, and smelled the aroma of the fresh earth waiting for his corpse.

After the thirtieth shot Tuohy handed the empty parabellum to the Chekist and accepted the loaded weapon. He turned to Vasia and thumbed back the hammer so that his victim could hear the working of the mechanism that would kill him. He branded the end of the barrel to the base of Vasia's skull—and waited. Several of the Chekists watching from the sidelines exchanged puzzled looks. Vasia tried desperately to think of someone he had loved. And still Tuohy waited. Vasia whimpered, "For God's sake, get it over with." And still he waited. Vasia, moaning in agony, remembered how much he hated Tuohy.

And Tuohy, reading his thoughts, squeezed the trigger.

In Perm, a half-dozen Chekists filed into the basement of the Berezin house on Obvinskaya Street. The windows had long since been boarded up, and the only light came from the flame dancing atop a tallow candle in drafts of air from the open door. The Empress Alexandra, the widow of Nicholas II, and her daughters Marie, Olga, and Tatiana were asleep on straw pallets on the floor. Sensing the presence of men, the tsarina sat up abruptly. When she saw the drawn pistols, she opened her mouth to scream. Then she remembered the sleeping girls and suppressed the scream. Tatiana, whose body was touching Alexandra's, felt her mother move and sat up too. The girl's eyes widened in terror. The tsarina brought a finger to her lips so that Tatiana would not awaken the other two girls. Then she crossed herself. Tatiana did the same with a violently trembling hand, then turned away and clamped her palms over her ears as the Chekists started shooting.

Two blocks away, Lili Mikhailovna Yusupova waited, with a hundred others, in a long, dark, moldy corridor on the top floor of the warehouse that the Chekists had turned into a prison. The executions had begun at dawn, but there had been so many prisoners to dispose of that they were still going on at noon. Glancing at their pocket watches, Cheka officials held a brief discussion and decided there would be no lunch break—for the executioners, or the condemned prisoners.

The prisoners, two abreast, their wrists tied behind their backs, shuffled forward toward the two freight elevators at the far end of the long corridor. In each elevator was a Chekist executioner with several pistols and a cardboard box of ammunition. Both executioners were addicted to cocaine. Their lids were half closed, their eyes red, their movements languid, as if everything were taking place underwater. The taller of the two was said to be a humanitarian, inasmuch as he dispatched his victims with a single shot to the nape of the neck. The other executioner was rumored to be a sadist who was taking revenge for a brother tortured to death by the Whites. Word had it that he sometimes fired past an ear before dispatching his victims; there was even the suggestion, passed on by guards, that this executioner occasionally shot female prisoners in their sexual organs, but this was discounted as scare talk.

The executions proceeded at the snail's pace imposed by the rhythm of the two elevators working in tandem. An executioner would pull a prisoner onto the open elevator. Arriving in the basement, he would push the prisoner against a makeshift mound of sandbags flecked with blood and shoot him. Then he would ride the empty elevator up as the second elevator with the other executioner and another prisoner came down. While the elevators were in motion, teams of Chekists would load the body of the last victim onto a wheelbarrow and cart it out to a truck backed up to a loading door.

Lili had consumed Zander's cocaine before leaving her cell, and almost immediately felt the effect; her body seemed to hover over reality, time seemed to slow down to where she thought she had a lifetime to live before her execution. The man next to her in the corridor was an old Jew who actually mumbled an introduction. Seeing the glassy look in her eyes, he turned away and began chanting prayers in Yiddish under his breath.

Lili loosened the line that moored her to the earth and let her thoughts drift. She saw her grandfather encouraging her to eat something, but she couldn't see what. She saw herself making love to someone in Paris, but she couldn't see whom. She caught a glimpse of herself bent over someone's sexual organ, coaxing it back to life, but she couldn't see if she succeeded. Other images flitted before her eyes like a film off its sprockets. She remembered hearing that you relived your entire existence in the last seconds of your life. But all she was getting were fragments, shards of an object broken into so many pieces there was no question of reconstructing it.

Lili opened her eyes and realized there were only eight prisoners ahead of her. Her heart began to pump blood more quickly. She tried again to slow time down, to stop it entirely. Imagine stepping up to the moment of your death and stopping time, she thought. You could squeeze the rest of a life into the moment that was left to you.

The open elevator glided up to the top floor and the executioner grabbed the shirtfront of the old Jew and pulled him, stumbling, forward. From the bowels of the building the crack of three pistol shots drifted up the elevator shaft. With the corner of her mind that was still lucid, Lili realized she had drawn the sadist. The elevator with the old Jew on it began to go down the shaft. Lili leaned forward and watched the bald spot on the top of his head disappear. She thought of leaping into the shaft, but with so much time left to her this seemed an insane thing to do. Another lifetime passed before the second elevator arrived level with the top floor. The Chekist, his sleeves rolled up to his elbows and beads of sweat glistening on his lower lip, reached for Lili's shirtfront. His thick fingers snaked toward her in slow motion; in slow motion they hooked themselves inside her shirt between two buttons, touching a breast, and drew her forward onto the elevator. With his fingers still wedged inside her shirt against her breast, his drowsy bloodred eyes stared into her heavy-lidded eyes.

From somewhere below came the delicate snap of a single pistol shot. Time had run out for the Jew, Lili thought. Now it is my turn. The elevator began to sink under her feet as the executioner and his condemned prisoner, both adrift on a cloud of cocaine, descended for their appointment, one trying to speed time up so he could finally have lunch, the other trying to make the moments left to her last forever.

Leon had warned him that Russia would break his heart, and it had. Gazing down at an old hairbrush Lili had used, at the strands of her dark hair tangled in the bristles, Zander was overwhelmed by the emptiness of her absence. She had been reduced, like his brother Abner, to a figment of his imagination.

The memory of her was all that was left to him. He could reconstruct her face, with the trace of Asia in the eyes. With a little effort he could even convince himself he could smell her body. But then his brain would remind him that she existed in his brain. And the images would fade as quickly as they had come. And he would be left gazing into a void so profound that the only appropriate sentiment was despair. His shoulders would sag under the weight of her nonexistence. He would bury his face in the dirty mattress and sob; for her, safely disappeared into death; for himself, stranded in this world without her.

A twilight that had an unearthly resemblance to soot was settling over Perm. Stretched out fully dressed on the cot in the top-floor hotel room under the attic, Zander let the soot settle over him. For an instant he was convinced it would smother him, and he sucked in air through his mouth to keep from fainting. From the attic over his head came a scuffling sound, as if some rats had darted in circles around each other—as if someone had stirred in his sleep. *Save Anastasia if you can*, she had told him, and he had wondered, even then, why Lili thought he would be in a position to save Anastasia. Again he heard the rats stirring overhead. He opened his eyes and studied the ceiling and saw for the first time the outline of a trapdoor above the dresser in the corner of the room.

Zander propped himself up on an elbow and listened with his good ear. For several minutes he didn't hear anything. Then came the creaking of a floorboard, as if a weight had shifted on it.

Cursing himself for an imbecile, Zander lit a candle and climbed onto the dresser, then stood up on it, crouching under the trapdoor. With a palm he eased it open and stuck his head and the candle through into the attic. The flame, caught in a draft, almost flickered out, then glowed back into life, revealing a young girl with enormous dark eyes staring at him from across the attic. She was bruised, cringing in a corner, trying to shrink back away from the light. She brought a hand to her mouth to stifle a cry, and Zander noticed her long graceful fingers. He whispered a name.

"Anastasia?"

"Where is Lili Mikhailovna?"

For a short, sharp moment Zander hated Anastasia

with an intensity that reached to the pit of his stomach. If she hadn't been here, Lili would still be alive. But the feeling passed. He understood more than ever the instinct that had pushed Lili to help the girl. It wasn't a matter of her siding with her class. It was simply that she had reached the point where she couldn't put up with suffering, her own or anyone else's. A glass of water spills over with only one drop too many.

"Please," Anastasia repeated. "Where is Lili Mikhailovna?"

"She has gone away. She told me to look after you."

Zander talked to her quietly for a time to gain her confidence, then helped her climb down out of the attic into the room. In the early hours of the morning they planned her escape. Using a fingernail scissor, he trimmed her hair very short, as if she had been treated for lice or ringworm. As the shape of her skull became visible, she looked almost boyish. Discarding her own clothes, she dressed in one of Lili's second-hand skirts and shirts. But there was still something about her that exuded royalty. "It is your hands that give you away," Zander decided. And he made her cut her nails very short, and wedge dirt under them by grating them against the soles of her shoes.

In the predawn darkness, he gave her what money he could spare, along with Lili's identification papers and travel authorization and meal voucher. Anastasia studied the documents, and looked slowly up into Zander's eyes. "So she is dead," she said in a voice that had lost its last lingering trace of music.

Zander didn't contradict her.

Long before first light they left the hotel, tiptoeing past the night clerk sleeping on a chair in the lobby, and headed through the dark, damp streets of Perm toward the railroad station. Two blocks from the station, soldiers at the first of several checkpoints were examining the papers of people heading for the train. Zander proposed to accompany Anastasia, but she insisted on going on alone. She walked away a few paces, then came back. "My memory is going. There are moments when I am not sure who I am. I will never speak of you to anyone, but I will pray for you even after I can no longer remember you. You never told me your name, and I do not ask you to tell me now. Whoever you are, I thank you." She was about to extend the back of her hand for him to kiss, but caught herself, flashed a sad half smile to acknowledge the mistake, and turned and headed for the checkpoint.

Watching from a distance, Zander saw a soldier with a lantern look at her papers and wave her on. Zander passed through the same checkpoint, and eventually found a place on the train heading for Moscow. He wondered if Anastasia was on the train.

He never saw her again.

7

The church on the outskirts of Petrograd had been razed to the ground, but the dilapidated nursery school that had been attached to it was still there, more dilapidated than before, if that were possible. The English nuns who ran it had died of starvation; they had given what little food they could get their hands on to the children. Some Russian nuns had taken their place.

"So you want to adopt a child," the Mother Superior, a brittle emaciated old woman, noted.

She peered at him through eyeglasses as thick as windowpanes, and still couldn't seem to see him clearly. She was sitting behind a plain kitchen table that served as a desk, and didn't look as if she had the strength to stand up. Zander had the impression that if anyone around her talked too loudly, she would crack.

"Not any child. A particular child. Her name is Ludmilla Yusupova. I was a friend . . . a very close friend of her mother's."

"The mother is dead?" the Mother Superior asked crisply.

"Dead. Yes. In the civil war."

The Mother Superior fingered an enormous black crucifix that hung from her frail neck. "For the first time in history the life expectancy of human beings is greater than a goldfish's—fifty years. But not in Russia. In Russia everyone dies young, or wishes they had." She nodded toward Zander's cane. "I see you have been wounded. Are you in pain?"

"Sometimes. But the doctors tell me it will bother me less as time goes on."

"Which side did you fight on?"

"Does it matter?"

The Mother Superior screwed up her wrinkled lips. "Of course it matters. It matters enormously. One side is for God, the other against."

"I fought for the Bolsheviks," Zander told her. He thought she had a right to know. "On the southern front. In Tsaritsin. On the Terek River. In Novocherkassk. In Rostov-on-Don. In Yuzovka. Along the Donets Basin. Toward the end I fought in the Crimea. I was wounded during the last days of the civil war."

"How?"

"I was in the artillery. A shell misfired, but with all the smoke we didn't notice. We rammed a second shell into the breech, into the shell that was still there. Both shells exploded. The two loaders were incinerated. I got off with shrapnel in my left leg."

"May God in his infinite wisdom forgive you for fighting on the wrong side," the Mother Superior said simply. "I am unable to. The Bolsheviks are scum. They have ruined Russia. It will never be the same."

"There has been a great deal of suffering," Zander agreed. "But we are trying to build a better society." He tried to sound optimistic. "Things will surely improve."

The Mother Superior produced a mournful smile. "We live in evil times. There are those who say God is dead, but of course this is not the case. He is only testing us."

"About the child."

"About the child." The Mother Superior sighed. "Not

many come around to adopt children these days. People have enough trouble feeding themselves."

An expression of relief spread across Zander's face. "Then you will not raise objections?"

"Objections! Good heavens, no. We turn away dozens of children every week. They crawl into basements and die of starvation. Now we will be able to take one of them in."

Twenty minutes later two nuns brought the little girl into the room. She was wearing a formless gray smock over a formless gray dress, and overshoes cut from an old carpet. She was carrying a paper bag which contained all of her worldly possessions—several pairs of worn underpants, a sweater unraveling at the wrists, a blouse, a cardboard crucifix, a homemade doll with string for hair.

Zander recognized her the instant she walked through the door. She had grown taller and thinned down since he had last seen her, and looked like Lili now even when she wasn't smiling. There were those unmistakable traces of Asia in her face: high cheekbones, a hint of flatness to her nose, the vaguest Tartar slant to her dark, brooding eyes. The resemblance made it difficult for Zander to speak.

"How old are you now?" he asked the girl after a moment.

Ludmilla looked at the Mother Superior, who nodded encouragement. "Almost eleven," the girl said shyly.

"Do you still paint pretty pictures?"

"The children have no paint, no paper," snapped the Mother Superior. She was reminding Zander he had fought on the wrong side.

"What do you do during the day?" Zander asked the girl.

"I pray," she said softly.

"Speak up. He won't bite you."

"I pray."

"Tell the nice gentleman what you pray for," the Mother Superior instructed her.

"I pray for Jesus to watch over me. I pray for peace, also for paint and paper."

With an effort Zander managed to kneel in front of her. "I was a good friend of your mother's." He studied the girl's face, and wondered if he was making a mistake; wondered if he could live under the same roof with a constant reminder of Lili. "She asked me to look after you. That is what I would like to do. If you are willing. Will you come away with me?"

"Of course she will go with you," said the Mother Superior.

"Will you?"

"If you like."

Zander used his cane to push himself up.

"Where will you live?" the Mother Superior asked.

"In Moscow. I share an apartment with four families. The authorities are organizing schools. Ludmilla will go to school with children her own age." He turned to the girl. "There will be paint and paper."

"Did Jesus supply them?"

"The state gives paint and paper to all children," Zander explained.

The Mother Superior frowned at Zander as if she were having second thoughts about his fitness to adopt an orphan. "If there is paint and paper," she told Ludmilla firmly, "Jesus is the one who is responsible. The state only *takes* things from little children."

Ludmilla clutched her paper bag more tightly. Zander reached down and took her hand in his. It felt cold and damp, and it struck him that the child would be frightened of leaving the only life she knew. "Do you like cats?" he asked on the spur of the moment.

"As pets or as food?" the girl asked with great seriousness.

"As pets."

Ludmilla smiled an infinitely sad, distant smile. "My mother brought me a cat the last time she came to see me. It was blind in one eye. The good Sisters cooked it as soon as she left. Because my mother brought it, I was given an especially large piece. They are soft and furry, cats are. I think I might like one for a pet, but we would have to keep it locked up so no one could cook it."

"Come," Zander said. "We will go to Moscow and look for a cat for you."

Moscow was caught up in its post-winter thaw. The paved streets were damp and slippery, the unpaved ones spongy underfoot. People tracked so much mud indoors that the Communist Party planned to organize vegetable gardens in entranceways, so the latest joke making the rounds claimed. Near the Kazan railroad station, peasants whipped the flanks of starving horses pulling wagonloads of freshly cut birch logs which would be bartered for thick window drapes that could be cut into shirts and skirts.

A Cheka automobile driven by a chauffeur moved slowly down Chkalov Street as the two passengers in the backseat scanned the housefronts looking for Number Forty-two. The car passed a line of stores whose names had been painted over and replaced with numbers, and drew up in front of a turn-of-the-century fortresslike apartment building. "This has to be it," Arishka said. "It's between forty and forty-four."

"I will be back when I am back," Tuohy instructed the driver. He leaned over his shoulder and jotted down the odometer reading on the back of an envelope so the driver would not be tempted to ferry around some private fares while waiting for him.

"Who is hurt if he makes something on the side?" Arishka whispered irritably as they got out of the car.

"It is a question of regulations," Tuohy told her. "The car belongs to the government. The gasoline belongs to the government. If he wants to drive a taxi, he should change jobs."

"Times are difficult, Americanitz."

"Let's not get into another argument," Tuohy said. He lifted one of the cartons out of the trunk compartment and handed it to Arishka, then took the other, larger, one himself and followed her under the portal and across the courtyard. A puddle with oil scum on the surface had formed in front of the rear door, and a plank had been thrown across it so the residents could go in and out without getting their feet wet. Tuohy and

Arishka started up the narrow wooden staircase. A child
with a runny nose almost hurtled into them, but they
flattened themselves against the wall to let him pass,
and continued on up to the fourth floor. Tuohy rapped
an elbow against the second door on the left of the
landing.

They could hear footsteps in the corridor beyond the
door. "A minute," a woman called. She threw the bolt
and opened the door a crack, then pulled it open when
she saw who it was.

"Serafima!" Arishka cried, and she leaned forward
and planted moist kisses on both her cheeks.

"What kept you?" Serafima demanded impatiently.
"You are the last ones here. Did you manage to find a
cake?"

"All they had at the Cheka commissary was cookies."
Arishka set her carton down and pulled a package from
it. She and Serafima arranged eleven cookies on a platter and embedded a wooden kitchen match in each.

"Please," Serafima pleaded with Tuohy outside the
door to Zander's room, "no fights with Ronzha."

"If he doesn't fight with me, I won't fight with him."
He touched the flame of his cigarette lighter to the tips
of the matches.

"Quick, before they burn up," Serafima said, and the
three of them pushed through the door singing "Happy
birthday to you, happy birthday to you, happy birthday dear Ludmilla, happy birthday to you." Zander,
Alyosha Zhitkin, Ronzha, Appolinaria, Sergeant Pasha
Kirpichnikov and Melor joined in, and everyone applauded vigorously at the end.

"Make a wish and blow them out," Zander told
Ludmilla.

"Without spitting on the cookies," Melor, now a husky
fifteen-year-old, cried excitedly.

Ludmilla gazed at the burning matches, seemingly
mesmerized.

"Can you say what flame is?" Ronzha asked.

Ludmilla thought an instant, then blew out the
matches. "Can you say where the flame went?" she
challenged Ronzha.

The adults greeted the answer with applause. "In effect," Ronzha conceded, "the question is well answered."

"Speech, speech," Melor shouted happily. He was a little jealous of all the attention Ludmilla was getting.

"I do not know what to say," Ludmilla said shyly.

"Say whatever comes into your head," Appolinaria suggested.

"I am very happy to be eleven. I hope I can someday be twelve."

"Of course you will be twelve," Serafima said quickly.

"You will live to be a hundred and twelve!" bellowed Sergeant Kirpichnikov.

Tuohy settled onto the bed next to Zander. "I brought two cartons for you—there's some bacon, some lard, a side of smoked ham, some tins of sardines, some cooking oil, a box or two of dried biscuits. There's even a couple of bottles of Georgian wine, and a tin of red ket caviar."

"I appreciate that, Atticus."

"Anytime."

In the middle of the room Ludmilla was trying on a woolen bonnet that Appolinaria had knitted using wool stripped from one of her old sweaters. Ronzha glanced at the two portraits of Lili that Zander had hung on the wall over his bed, and then back at the child, and shook his head. "The resemblance is uncanny," he told Appolinaria.

Serafima caught Melor staring at Appolinaria. She kicked at his foot and raised a warning eyebrow. He shrugged and looked away, but when Serafima began to talk to Ludmilla, Melor continued watching Appolinaria out of the corner of his eye.

Alyosha Zhitkin asked, "Can I give her my present now?" He went into the corridor and came back a few minutes later carrying a small cardboard box with holes punched in its sides. Everyone but Melor gathered around to watch Ludmilla open it. She gingerly pried up the cover, and her eyes widened. "Oh," she said. She dipped her hands into the carton and came out with a fluffy baby cat. She rubbed her nose in its fur. "Oooooh," she said.

"It is for you to give her a name," Alyosha told Ludmilla.

"I will call her . . . Lili," the girl decided.

Zander turned quickly away, and it was a moment before he felt sufficiently in control to turn back. He opened one of Tuohy's bottles of Georgian wine and passed around kitchen tumblers. Ronzha, who had become gaunt and partially bald, stood up and raised his glass. His eyes were red-rimmed; because of the lack of coal or firewood, the basement room in which he and Appolinaria lived was unheated, and neither had slept through the night in months. "I propose we drink to the residents of the old Steamboat who are missing from our little reunion," Ronzha said. "To Hippolyte Evgenevich, to Lili Mikhailovna, to Otto Eppler, to Vasia Timofeyevich. May they all rest in peace."

"I will drink to Lili and old Hippolyte," Tuohy called from across the room, "but I'll be damned if I will drink to the other two. They were traitors."

Zander said, "What makes you think Vasia was a traitor?"

"I saw his name on a list once," Tuohy said quickly. "He was taken prisoner fighting for the Whites at Kazan."

"You never mentioned that before," Zander said, puzzled. "What happened to him?"

Tuohy closed his eyes to indicate it was not the kind of thing you explained in front of an eleven-year-old girl.

"You're sure?" Zander asked in English.

"I didn't personally see it," Tuohy said. "But deserters who were recaptured were always shot."

Ronzha said, "Now that they are all safely dead, surely we can find it in our hearts to forgive and forget."

"On the contrary," Tuohy retorted hotly, "we must neither forgive nor forget. Their fate must serve as a lesson to others who would betray the revolution."

Serafima whined, "Americanitz, you promised. Not in front of Ludmilla."

Melor said, "I agree with Tuohy." He eyed Ronzha with scorn. "Once a class enemy, always a class enemy."

Appolinaria leaned toward Ronzha and whispered

something into his ear, but he shook her off. "They speak in clichés." He indicated Tuohy with a toss of his head. "Because he works for the Cheka is no reason for me not to say what I think."

Alyosha Zhitkin tried to change the subject. "Zander, you were in the Crimea when the last Whites were beaten back into the sea. Is it true that the Cossacks shot their horses at the water's edge before embarking for Constantinople?"

"They shot them, and we ate them."

Melor said, "As for me, I love the taste of horsemeat."

Arishka was whispering to Tuohy. "If he doesn't start in, I won't," Tuohy said. He turned to Zander. "Speaking of horsemeat, did you read about the gang we caught manufacturing sausages for the black market? *Pravda* said they were making the sausages out of horsemeat, but it wasn't true. They were really making them out of freshly dug up corpses."

Sergeant Kirpichnikov's eyes blinked open and he looked at Serafima. "Where did you get those sausages we had last week?"

Serafima covered her mouth with her fingers. "On a street corner. From a man with a valise."

"I think I am going to vomit," Melor announced.

Arishka held a partly knitted sweater in front of Ludmilla to check the size. "Can't we talk about something pleasant for a change?"

Alyosha Zhitkin turned to Tuohy. "What is the latest economic news?"

"That will not be pleasant either," Ronzha muttered under his breath.

"Now that the civil war is over and the interventionists have all left," Tuohy said, "the Party says that things are bound to look up."

"In fact," Ronzha said, "the economic situation is disastrous. Coal, iron, and steel production is a fraction of what it was before the Bolsheviks took power. Money has become worthless. In some factories workers are paid with what they produce—if they make shoes, they get shoes, and they must try and barter them for food. Only there is no food. The Bolshevik confiscation teams have taken almost everything from the peasants, including the seeds, and they are planting, when they bother to plant at all, just enough for themselves. Typhus and cholera are rampant. Factories are closing for lack of coal. Workers are fainting on the job from hunger. There aren't enough Chekists to slap them all back to consciousness. There are—what?—six hundred thousand or so Bolshevik Party members in Russia, but they are completely isolated from the general population. If free elections were held tomorrow—"

"A big *if*," sneered Appolinaria.

"—you Bolsheviks would be swept away. The only reason you are still in power is because you control the army, and the police." Ronzha's pent-up emotions flooded out like an angry river spilling over its banks. Zander looked away in embarrassment. "But you do not control the poets," Ronzha plunged on, his hands shaking, a hint of tears in his eyes, "even if you will not permit anyone to publish them."

"If you are not published," Tuohy said coldly, "it is because there is no place in the society we are constructing for negative thinking."

"What there is no place for in this society of yours is truth-telling," Ronzha said mockingly. "All truth-tellers are silenced."

"Mayakovsky's poetry is published in *Pravda*," Tuohy shot back. "Unlike some people who claim to be poets, he puts his poetry to work for the revolution."

"To make his poems simple enough for the masses," Ronzha declared, "Mayakovsky has stripped them of the images that gave them their power."

"He has stripped his poems of poetry," Appolinaria agreed. "There is nothing to hear in the silences between his words." And she added with a sly smile, "Any idiot knows that slogans are not the same thing as poetry."

"As for me," Melor announced brightly, "I like slogans more than I like poetry." And he quoted one. " 'I have seen the future and it works!' "

"Bread, land, peace—that's the ticket!" thundered Sergeant Kirpichnikov.

Ronzha waved a hand in disgust. "All your slogans cannot disguise the fact that you are terrorists."

Tuohy was on his feet now. "We didn't invent terror." He aimed his cigarette holder at Ronzha as if it were a loaded pistol. "We are only doing what Ivan the Terrible or Peter the Great or the Mongol hordes did in their day. We are fighting terror with terror."

"You have become addicted to terror," Ronzha retorted. "You need a daily dose to function. You will never break the habit."

For a long moment everyone could hear Tuohy and Ronzha breathing heavily like two boxers in their corners. Sergeant Kirpichnikov, in an unaccustomed burst of humor, cried, "I declare Atticus Tuohy the winner by a technical knockout." Even Ronzha had to smile. "Hell," continued the sergeant, "anyone who can talk about Ivan the Terrible or Peter the Great has to win."

Zander asked Tuohy, "What do you hear about Lenin's health these days?"

"The less said about that, the better," Tuohy answered in English.

"What did he say?" Melor asked.

"He said," Ronzha ventured, "that Comrade Lenin is suffering, as everyone in Moscow knows, from tertiary syphilis, which explains a great many things—the way he walks, for example, slapping his feet on the ground so he can be sure where they are from the sound they make, or the sudden mania he has for some person or program or some grandiose scheme, like electrification of all of Russia or world revolution."

Ronzha's outburst was greeted with stony silence; the adults in the room knew that it was dangerous to *hear* such things. Tuohy's walrus mustache bobbed nervously. "People have been arrested for saying less," he noted quietly.

Appolinaria covered her eyes with her hands. Ronzha seemed to be pleased with himself. "For once," he said, "I quite agree with our friend here. People *have* been arrested for saying *much* less."

Later, after Ronzha and Appolinaria had left, Zander

steered Tuohy into the communal kitchen. "Is it true what Ronzha said about Lenin?" he whispered.

"More or less."

"You won't file a report on Ronzha, Atticus, will you?"

"I don't have to. He already has a dossier as fat as your fist. He will talk himself into a grave one of these days."

"How long does Lenin have?"

"Two years, three if the arsenic injections can slow down the deterioration."

"Obviously Trotsky will step into his shoes," Zander said thoughtfully. "No one else has his magnetism, or his revolutionary credentials."

"In my shop," Tuohy said, "the smart money is on Stalin. He's quietly installing his own people at every level of the Party. Let's face it, Trotsky's an innocent next to Stalin. The Party *is* Stalin. I heard that old Koba has even ordered some professors to catalogue every word Lenin ever set down on paper. That way he'll be able to cite the gospel according to Lenin to justify anything."

Zander stared out of the window, which still had its double glazing from the winter with wads of cotton between the panes to absorb the humidity. He had received a postcard from Leon the week before; his stepbrother had gone to live on a kibbutz near Haifa, and described in a tiny handwriting that wedged words into every corner of the card the joys of living the life of a Jewish peasant. Zander wondered what Leon, observing events from the outside, thought of the Russian Revolution now. Were things about to look up, as the Party claimed? Or would the Bolsheviks be swept away in a free election, as Ronzha said? Below, in the courtyard, two old men in overcoats and scarfs were setting up a folding table in the corner touched by sunlight to play dominoes. Ludmilla's baby cat—Zander decided he would never call it Lili—was scraping around in the box of dirt they had put out for it on the floor under the sink.

The silence between them made Tuohy uncomfortable. He cleared his throat, but Zander continued to stare out of the window, his eyes narrowed, his thoughts far away.

Tuohy said, "So how are you making out these days?"

Zander turned back to the room. "Not badly. One of the tenants we share the apartment with works for the central lumber collective. He is paid in packages of kindling, and we get to cook on the embers when we have something to cook."

"And the leg?"

Zander rapped his thigh with his knuckles. "I'm stuck with the limp for life, but I figure I got off lightly." He shook his head as if he were trying to dislodge some unpleasant thoughts. "They say seven million died in the civil war. All that killing, Atticus, and what do we have to show for it?"

"The killing is history," Tuohy remarked.

"History," Zander murmured, "has a way of looking over your shoulder."

"You're beginning to sound like Ronzha. Without the terror we couldn't have won."

"Each side was trying to terrorize the other side," Zander said. "The result is that terror has become institutionalized. When someone disagrees with us, we don't try to persuade him, we terrorize him."

"You're growing soft, Zander. You're too tender-hearted to do what has to be done to bring about the new order."

Zander uttered a dry laugh. "What I'm growing is old, Atticus. I'm starting to wonder how much of myself I am expected to give away for the final victory of socialism. I'm starting to realize that I'm going to have to make a stand somewhere."

"When you make this stand," Tuohy replied carefully, "you and I might find ourselves on different sides of the fence."

Zander accepted this with a slow nod.

Tuohy pulled the Bulgarian cigarette from his holder and held it under the faucet to extinguish it. Then he flipped it into an open garbage pail. "Well," he said dejectedly, "nobody can accuse you of being an optimist."

Zander flashed an embarrassed smile that never quite made it as high as his eyes. "In Russia, an optimist is someone who doesn't know enough."

Tuohy snorted. "Here lies Atticus Tuohy," he intoned, "hacked to death by an intellectual armed with a sharp sentence."

He said it with a laugh. He didn't look very frightened.

BOOK 4

The people are silent.

—Alexander Pushkin's last stage direction in *Boris Godunov*

F
ive funerals:

His lips quivering, his eyes shut, his head bent, his worker's cap jammed down over his forehead, his knees pumping, the flats of his feet slapping clownlike against the damp cobblestones, Vladimir Lenin stumbled along like a blind man behind the funeral cortege. His wife, Krupskaya, kept a firm grip on his elbow, steadying him when he looked as if he might fall, steering him toward the niche in the Kremlin wall that had been prepared for the coffin.

Inessa Armand, Lenin's slim, graceful, golden-haired free spirit of a mistress—she had once written that even a fleeting passion was more poetic than the kisses of a vulgar married couple—had died of typhus in a mountain town in the northern Caucasus on September 24, 1920. Lenin had dispatched a special train to bring back the body of the only person outside his immediate family he addressed with the intimate "*ti.*" That Inessa had been Lenin's mistress was common knowledge in Party circles. Assembling for the funeral procession, several comrades had approached the Starik to offer condolences, but it was as if they were talking to a wall. The old man seemed shrunken. His hands trembled. When he finally opened his eyes and looked at someone he had worked with for twenty years, he didn't appear to recognize him.

Krupskaya's brow furrowed in preoccupation. She resented this public display of emotion, considered it tactless, even unbolshevik. It wasn't at all like Vladimir Ilich. Maybe he *was* getting old. Maybe the arteries of his brain were calcifying, as the doctors said. She glanced over her shoulder at the Politburo comrades trailing after them. All of them wore black armbands as a sign of mourning. Krupskaya noted Zinoviev and Kamenev exchanging comments in an undertone. Stalin joined the conversation, mumbled something. The other two nodded. She could imagine what they were talking about: that the Starik was not long for this world; that they had better start thinking seriously about the succession. If only she could make sure Lenin got his daily arsenical injections, some of which he missed because he couldn't fit them into his schedule, he might live longer than any of them expected. Or wanted.

At the Kremlin wall the cortege drew up in a semi-circle. Four young soldiers lifted the coffin and slid it into the niche. Behind them, a military band struck up a slow, funereal melody. Turning away from the niche, Lenin swayed visibly. Tears trickled down his cheeks. Krupskaya tightened her grip on his elbow and motioned for their car. Waiting for it to be brought around, Lenin began to mumble.

"What did you say?" Krupskaya asked.

The members of the Politburo stood around them, shifting their weights from foot to foot, studying the ground as if it held a secret.

"In Paris," Lenin said, "Inessa used to play Beethoven's 'Appassionata' on that awful piano with the missing middle A. Do you remember?"

Krupskaya gestured again for the automobile. What the devil was keeping it?

"It is a marvelous piece of music," Lenin rambled on. "I cannot think of any greater human achievement. I would like to listen to it every day. But I cannot listen to music so often. It gets on my nerves. It makes me want to say stupid things and pat the heads of people who, living in this vile hell, can create such beauty. Nowadays you must not pat anybody's head. They might bite off your hand. You have to beat them on the head." Lenin raised his voice. "Beat them without mercy, although it goes without saying we Bolsheviks are ideally opposed to the use of force." The Starik shook his head mournfully. "Better fewer, but better." His voice trailed off. "Better fewer . . ."

Moscow was caught in the grip of the most savage winter in memory, but Stalin, with one handrail of the bier resting on his padded right shoulder, didn't feel the cold. His cheeks were flushed with excitement, his eyes vivid, almost feverish. Things were going better than he dared hope. Trotsky, his archrival, hadn't even turned up for the funeral. Stalin had lied to him about when it would be held, and Trotsky, thinking he could never make it back in time, had stayed in Tiflis. Just as well, Stalin thought. As the peasants say, "I would sooner give an enema to a corpse than dine with a Yid."

Lenin had been ill much of 1922; had suffered a series of strokes that left him partially paralyzed and struggling to speak coherently. Confined to a wheelchair, he had been packed off to a government rest home in the village of Gorky. The few comrades allowed to see him had come back shaken. One of them recounted how he told Lenin that trolley car service was being expanded to the outlying proletarian sections of Moscow. *"Vot! Vot!"* cried the Starik, using the only word he was able to pronounce correctly. "That's it! That's it!"

On January 21, 1924, Lenin's temperature rose sharply. Convulsions followed. He lapsed into a coma, and died at 6:30 in the evening. His body was brought back to Moscow to lie in state in the Hall of Columns. For four icy days, hundreds of thousands of people filed silently, tearfully, past the open coffin. Today, the twenty-ninth, he was being buried with appropriate pomp in the temporary wooden mausoleum that had been erected in Red Square near the Kremlin wall. Eventually the body would be embalmed and displayed in a permanent marble mausoleum.

There were some members of the Old Guard who considered the Starik's deification unseemly; Lenin himself would never have tolerated it, they whispered. The poet Mayakovsky even published a poem criticizing the idea:

> I'm anxious lest
>   processions
>   and mausoleums,
>   the established
>   statue of worship
>   should
>   drown
>   in oily unction
> Lenin's simplicity.

Well, let them worry, Stalin thought. He, Koba, was more in touch with the common people than the coffeehouse Bolsheviks with their pince-nez wedged onto their Jewish noses. He knew what the superstitious masses out there needed was an icon to pray to. He would transform Lenin into this icon. He would feed the Russian hunger for the supernatural. When the time was ripe, he would even give them a resurrection: a new Communist tsar would rise from the ashes of the dead one.

First he would have to deal with the ugly little matter of Lenin's last testament, a letter the Starik had painstakingly dictated, a syllable at a time, days before his death. Krupskaya, the old goat, was already circulating copies to members of the Central Committee. "Stalin is too rude," the old man had written. "I propose removing him from his position and appointing someone more tolerant, more loyal, more polite and considerate to his comrades."

Stalin would silence Krupskaya by threatening to publish Lenin's early love letters to Inessa; some of them were explicit enough to make a whore blush. If that didn't turn the trick, he might have to appoint someone else to be Lenin's widow in her place! As for the testament, he would explain it away as the demented ravings of a man dying from the last stages of syphilis. The disease had eaten away at the Starik's mind as well as his body. It made him imagine enemies where none existed. Are we going to let his ravings divide the Party at this crucial moment, confuse the masses when what they need is a firm hand on the tiller? And whose hand would be firmer than that of the Party's tried and true general secretary, the foremost Leninist in the land?

He would present himself as the spiritual heir of the fallen leader. Where Stalin stood, that was Leninism! He would begin his speech to the Congress with an oath of allegiance. We swear to you, Comrade Lenin . . .

As for the few that resisted, he would force it down their throats.

Ronzha scrambled onto the base of the statue and pulled Appolinaria up after him so they could get a better view. Stretching off down Bolshaya Polyanka were masses of people—more than anyone remembered seeing in the streets since Moscovites turned out to greet Mary Pickford and Douglas Fairbanks at the railroad station four years before. Mayakovsky's coffin, resting on a raised platform on the back of an open flat-bed truck, came into view. Appolinaria was unable to restrain herself. "He was a propagandist, not a poet. I really don't see why we came."

Ronzha couldn't help smiling at the sight of the wreath on

the coffin. It was an enormous iron flywheel bristling with hammers, screws, and bolts. The inscription, in bold gold letters on a bright red ribbon, read: TO THE IRON POET—AN IRON WREATH.

"Perhaps I was too hard on him," Ronzha remarked. "I recognize as a colleague anyone who can put together one good poem, a couple of successful lines, even a word or two in the right order." As the truck pulled abreast, he removed his cap and bowed to the coffin, peasant style, from the waist.

The day before his death at the age of thirty-six, Vladimir Mayakovsky, the flamboyant poet who once invited the sun to have tea with him, had been heard to blurt out: "No! Everyone answers me no. Only no. Everywhere no." At ten in the morning, April 14, 1930, in his room in Lyubyansky Passage, he had taken a pistol from his desk and, holding it in his left hand, fired the single bullet in the chamber directly into his heart. A suicide note read:

> Life and I are quits,
>> and there's no point
> in counting over
>> mutual hurts,
>> harms,
>>> and slights.
> Best of luck to all of you!

Mayakovsky's open coffin was on display for three days at the Writers' Union, and half of Moscow—so it seemed—filed past to pay homage to the optimist who had taken the Bolshevik Revolution as the dawn of a new cultural era.

At the funeral, on April 17, the worker driving the coffin toward the crematorium obviously had no experience with corteges. He went too fast, leaving the tens of thousands of mourners straggling along behind.

Watching from the base of the statue, Ronzha put his own interpretation on this. "Mayakovsky was always impatient. It was his redeeming feature. He entered the revolution as if it were his own home—barging through the door, flinging open windows, spewing out his Whitman-like lines, never pausing for breath, never stopping to take stock. Well, maybe he knew something after all." After a moment Ronzha added, "When my time comes, I will certainly ride events also."

    *   *   *

Stalin was conspicuously absent from the small group that trailed after the ornate hearse, past the eroded tombstones in the cemetery behind the Novodevichy Monastery, past Gogol's grave, past Chekhov's, past the new headstone with "Mayakovsky" etched on it, to the freshly dug rectangular hole in the ground. There was no formal service, no eulogy. Businesslike civilians in blue suits and orange ties and belted blue raincoats lowered the coffin into the ground. The deceased's father, the Old Bolshevik Sergei Alliluyev, who had hidden Lenin in his apartment for several days in July 1917, picked up a fistful of dirt and tossed it onto the coffin. The others followed suit as they filed past. A man in a belted blue raincoat nodded at the gravediggers, and they began shoveling earth onto the coffin with a vengeance. They understood the sooner she was buried, the better.

The official version, published on a back page of *Pravda,* said that Stalin's second wife, Nadezhda Alliluyeva, had died of peritonitis, but everyone with connections in the superstructure knew the truth. The marriage between Stalin and Nadezhda, who was twenty-two years younger than he, had been stormy from the start. In the mid nineteen twenties, after one particularly vicious blowup, she had run off with the children to her parents in Leningrad. But Stalin, by then the undisputed *khozyain,* or master—Trotsky had been hounded out of the Party and the country, and the other Old Bolsheviks seemed to stumble over each other to stay in Stalin's good graces— obliged her to return. In the early thirties Nadezhda began studying synthetic fibers in Moscow's Industrial Academy. There she heard of the suffering caused by the first five-year plan, launched in 1929; about the great famine of 1931, the mere mention of which was considered a state crime; most of all, about her husband's policy of collectivization of agriculture. The Party had decided to liquidate the relatively well-off peasants known as kulaks and force all the others onto collective farms where, so the theory went, they would till the land with the efficiency of factory workers on an assembly line. The only trouble with the concept was that the peasants had killed their livestock, burned their crops, and destroyed their equipment rather than turn everything over to the collectives. In the confrontation that followed, something like seven million peasants died—with bullets in the neck, or through deportation to Siberia, or as the result of the famine brought on by Stalin's policies.

Nadezhda, the daughter of ardent revolutionists, raised the question of collectivization with her husband, but he cut her off with a remark about a woman's place being in bed. "I don't see what the peasants have to complain about," he told her another time. "Every one of them has the right to three square *arshin*s of land—enough to dig a grave!" And he slapped his thigh in pleasure.

When classes resumed in the fall of 1932, Nadezhda discovered that several of her friends were missing; it was whispered around that they had been arrested for talking to her about sensitive matters. Political realities, along with the deteriorating relationship with her husband, sent Nadezhda into a deep depression.

At a Kremlin banquet marking the fifteenth anniversary of the Bolshevik Revolution, Stalin called rudely to her from the head of the table, "Hey, you, have a drink!"

"Don't you dare 'hey' me!" Nadezhda retorted, and she stormed out of the party. That night, November 8, 1932, at Zubalovo, their family home twenty miles from the Kremlin, Nadezhda pressed a tiny Walther pistol to her head and pulled the trigger. She was thirty-one years old.

The housekeeper found her the next morning in a pool of blood. Someone finally worked up the courage to wake the *khozyain*, who slept in the small room with the telephone next to the dining room.

"Josef, Nadya is no longer with us!"

With her death, the last thread linking Josef Vissarionovich Dzhugashvili, universally known as Stalin, to the real world snapped. Family friends—most of them more attached to Nadezhda than to Stalin—gradually stopped coming around. There were no more boisterous after-lunch games of *gorodki* on the front lawn, with Stalin playfully squinting as he took aim at the bowling pins and exploding with pleasure when his eye turned out to be sharper than anybody else's. More and more moody, he retreated behind the walls of the Kremlin. There, surrounded by sycophants, he brooded about his enemies—and his *potential* enemies. He had always half-jokingly compared himself to Ivan the Terrible. Now, he noted, without a trace of humor in his voice, that Ivan had been shattered by the death of a young wife; that Ivan, convinced that she had been poisoned, had revenged himself on everyone around him in order to be sure the real culprit didn't escape unpunished.

Stalin, too, thought that his wife had been poisoned—poisoned against him! The guilty, once again, must not go unpunished.

It was about this time that Lady Astor, on a private visit to Moscow, asked Stalin in that offhand way the English upper classes had of baiting the devil, "When are you going to stop killing people?"

The interpreter froze. Stalin insisted the question be translated. And then, in the offhand way Bolsheviks had of telling the truth as if it were an outrageous falsehood, he replied, "When it is no longer necessary."

Stalin swept up to the Hall of Columns in one of his four bulletproof Packards—two had been sent ahead and one would follow behind, so that would-be assassins could never be sure which he was in—moments before they were scheduled to seal the coffin. Surrounded by security guards, he strode across the hall to the bier. The members of the Poliburo—whom Stalin privately referred to as "his kittens" —made way for him. Stepping up to the open coffin, Stalin gazed at the body. Then, apparently overcome by emotion, he leaned forward and kissed Sergei Kirov on the cheek. The gesture had distinctly Sicilian overtones.

At the Seventeenth Party Congress earlier in 1934, Kirov, the Communist boss of Leningrad, had emerged as the darling of the Party, an eventual successor to Stalin. The suggestion struck Stalin as unmitigated treason. To make matters worse, Kirov was a moderate on matters of policy and strategy, and easily the best orator the Party had had since Trotsky. Rumors circulated that some delegates already talked of pushing Stalin, who was fifty-five years old, out of his principal post, that of general secretary of the Party, and handing it to the young Leningrader, if not at this congress, then at the following one.

In the end, the delegates never worked up the nerve to confront Stalin, but they gave Kirov an ovation that left no one in doubt about his popularity.

Eleven months later Kirov was walking through the corridors of Smolny, Leningrad Party headquarters, when a man shot him in the back with a Nagant revolver. Learning of the murder, Stalin raced by special train from Moscow to personally unravel "the rich threads of treason" in the affair.

"*They* made me do it," a frustrated, alcoholic Party hack named Nikolayev replied when Stalin personally questioned him about the murder. "They gave me months of target practice. They told me that . . ."

His use of the word "they" provided Stalin with the excuse he needed to launch a purge that made Ivan the Terrible look like a prince of the church. Before the week was out, thirty-seven Leningrad "White Guards," including the unfortunate Nikolayev, had been sentenced to death for terrorist acts against officials of the Soviet regime. In Moscow another thirty-three victims joined them. Within a month, Zinoviev and Kamenev, two Old Bolsheviks who had participated in the October Revolution and later aided Stalin in his rise to power, had been sentenced to prison terms for encouraging terror. They would eventually be retried on more serious charges, and executed. Gradually the wave of arrests spread across the country; in Leningrad alone, some thirty thousand people were rounded up within a few months of Kirov's murder.

Each arrest would result in a confession, each confession would spiral into a new wave of arrests. Before it was over, Stalin would wipe out the Old Guard almost to the man. Hundreds of thousands would be shot. Millions would be packed off to Siberian camps. Only a handful would ever find their way back. The Great Purge, as it came to be known, would run its course only because the prisons could not hold more people. But by then, the boss must have calculated, the traitors who had poisoned Nadezhda against her husband would have fallen victim to this orgy of punishment.

As the cattle cars hauled the prisoners off toward "Asiatika" and points east, a four-line ditty made the rounds. It was not sung, only whispered.

> Hey, fresh tomatoes,
> Hey, want a cucumber?
> Stalin killed Kirov,
> Got him in the corridor.

1

Moscow, 1935

Bloated crystals of snow had been floating down like tiny parachutes for most of the day, blanketing the streets, forming graceful drifts at the sides of buildings, muting the whine of the pile driver spiking rusted steel stanchions into the foundations of the apartment building going up across from where the trolley stopped. Wearing the cap trimmed with "Stalin fur" (which was to say no fur at all) Ludmilla had given him on his forty-third birthday, Zander limped along in the gutter, where the snow had been packed down by government cars and pedestrians. They were lucky to live on Petrovka Street, one of the few blocks in Moscow that looked as if it could have been transplanted from Old St. Petersburg. The houses on both sides had sculptured entrances and large bay windows with lace curtains on them. Inside there were high ceilings on the *bel étage* and working fireplaces everywhere and doors that disappeared noiselessly into walls.

Ludmilla had been the one to find the apartment. "Zander, you won't believe this," she had cried breathlessly after racing back from her academy at lunch hour to make sure he got on to it right away, and she had described the two rooms that the parents of her best friend had just abandoned. The father, a professor of French at the university, had been questioned by the NKVD. Taking the event as a warning, he had decided to return to Frunze and accept a position as a guide in a local museum.

Zander and Ludmilla had lost their old apartment on Chkalov Street months before when the building was condemned to make way for a new hospital. They had farmed out their furniture with friends—the love seat with Tuohy and Arishka, the American rolltop desk with Sergeant Kirpichnikov and Serafima, the mirrored armoire with Ronzha and Appolinaria, the four kitchen chairs and the folding bridge table with Alyosha Zhitkin, the gilt-framed full-length mirror with Zander's some-time mistress, a motion picture actress named Misha—and lived like gypsies, a week with "folding bridge table"—they had taken to referring to people by the furniture they were guarding—two weeks with "mir-rored armoire," two days with "rolltop desk" because neither Zander nor Ludmilla could put up for long with Melor. Having stumbled on the Petrovka Street apart-ment, Zander had gone through the motions of filling out the appropriate forms in triplicate and submitting them to the appropriate clerk at the appropriate office, but he didn't think he had a hope in hell of getting it. Ludmilla—behind Zander's back—asked Tuohy to use his influence. One phone call from him and it was theirs.

Stamping his boots to get the snow off, Zander let himself in the front door with his latchkey, and exam-ined the open wooden box under the mail slot. As usual there were several books for the old Jew who lived on the ground floor. Religious Jews deposited the books on the doorstep as if they were abandoned orphans, or when they were thin enough, slipped them through the slot into the mailbox, knowing that the old Jew consid-ered any book with the name of God in it sacred and not to be destroyed. Zander once amused himself count-ing the stacks, and estimated that there were something like twelve thousand volumes stashed around the house—in the basement behind the coal bin, along one wall of the corridor leading to their door, along the corridor with the communal toilet at its far end, under the kitchen sink, in the closets, not to mention the old man's room, in which his narrow wooden bed seemed menaced by the piles of books towering above it on all sides. The neighbors who lived above them put up with the old man's idiosyncracy because, with so many books around, they were able to swipe as many as they wanted to light their cooking fires, or feed whole volumes into their tiled stoves when coal was impossible to come by.

Zander noticed several letters in the mailbox. He thumbed through them and pulled out one addressed to him. There was no stamp on it, meaning it had been personally delivered. The handwriting was slanted and bold, and Zander didn't recognize it. He held it up to the light bulb overhead and saw what appeared to be a sheaf of thin blue-lined paper. There was writing on it, but he couldn't make it out through the envelope.

"That you, Alexander?" Ludmilla was leaning over the second-floor banister. "Hurry on up. I have a million things to tell you. I see you didn't find vegetables." She closed the apartment door after him and helped him off with his overcoat. "I want you to be the first to know," she said, her eyes a sea of seriousness.

"Know what?"

"It's this way," she said, coming, as she always did, directly to the point. "I have fallen out of love again. I realize I said this one was different, and he was, I swear to you. But I found out he denounced the near-sighted drawing instructor who cracked that joke about the parrot—you remember, the one about the man losing his parrot and phoning up the NKVD to say it was missing and he didn't share any of its views. Anyway, I thought it was a lousy thing to do and I broke off with him, but I am going into mourning all the same for at least a week. I will probably be impossible to live with. I heard another joke today—"

"Lower your voice," Zander warned.

"The old man's half deaf. Even if he weren't he wouldn't know what I was talking about. The only things that interest him are Cossacks and pogroms and books with the name of God in them. I see you found some more downstairs. Here, give me one for the fire tonight."

Zander hung his hat on a hook in the hallway and followed Ludmilla into the room that doubled as a living room and his bedroom. Ludmilla's old, arthritic cat lay curled up in a wicker basket, sound asleep.

"About my joke," Ludmilla began to giggle. Zander smiled at the sight of her. When she was excited or happy, the traces of Lili on her face became explicit. Somehow he never tired of looking at her, no matter what her mood. It seemed only yesterday that he was hoisting her onto his shoulders to catch a glimpse over the heads of the crowd of the American movie stars Fairbanks and Pickford. How time slipped through your fingers. "It's this way," Ludmilla was saying. "One man tells another that an airplane carrying the entire Politburo crashed. The second man asks if anyone was saved. The first man replies, 'Russia.' " When Zander didn't react she said, "Don't you get it? The airplane carrying the Politburo crashed and *Russia* was saved!"

"I wish to God you wouldn't repeat stories like that. I wish you wouldn't even listen to them."

Ludmilla threw herself down on the rug next to the wicker basket and began to caress the cat, which didn't stir. "I am worried about you, Alexander. You used to enjoy a good laugh now and then."

"Times have changed."

"Nobody can accuse *you* of not loving Soviet power."

"These days it is not enough to love Soviet power. It has to love you."

Ludmilla said quietly, "What has changed, Alexander, is you. Do you know the lines from Akhmatova?" And flipping a stray strand of hair out of her eyes— Lili's gesture!—she recited:

> . . . faces fall apart,
> . . . fear looks out from people's eyes.

Seeing how grim he appeared, she abruptly changed the subject. "What's in the letter?" she asked, nodding at the envelope in his hand.

Zander tore it open and glanced at the signature on the bottom of the page. "It is from the mirrored armoire."

"Someday you are going to get into trouble for using code names," Ludmilla teased. "They are going to think you are a spy ring or something like that."

Zander read the note. "It's an invitation," he said. Ludmilla's eyes brightened; she adored Ronzha, and loved to listen to him recite his new poems. But Zander quickly dampened her enthusiasm. "You're not invited."

"What do you mean, I'm not invited?"

Zander shrugged. "Only the old crew from the Steamboat seems to have been invited. Appolinaria specifically says not to bring you."

Ludmilla's lips curled into a pout. "That's not very nice of her."

Zander was puzzled by the invitation. That Ronzha was going to recite a new poem seemed clear by Appolinaria's reference to "first readers." Since Tuohy, now an NKVD subdirector on Stalin's pet project, the construction of a showcase subway system under the streets of Moscow, would be there, Ronzha's new poem could not be subversive. The law of the land specified that anyone overhearing an anti-Soviet remark had to denounce the "enemy of the people" or face the same penalty as the person making the remark. What was more likely, Zander reasoned as he made his way to the end of the trolley line and walked the seven blocks to the prewar wooden apartment house that Ronzha and Appolinaria lived in, was that the poet finally had been talked into composing the obligatory "Ode to Stalin" that was required of writers if they hoped to publish anything else. Up to now Ronzha had resisted. He managed to scrounge a few rubles here and there translating French or Italian poems, or writing an occasional travel article for an editor willing to slip the piece past the censor. For the rest, he and Appolinaria begged or borrowed what they could from friends, confined themselves to one frugal meal a day, and waited for the apocalypse in the enclosed back porch that had been converted into a room, the holes in the planking stuffed with newspaper and an army blanket nailed over the door to keep the icy drafts out.

"For God's sake, come in quickly," Appolinaria cried, holding the blanket aside so Zander could duck under it into the room. She slammed the door behind him and let the blanket fall back over it. "So, that makes everyone," she announced to the others.

Zander dropped his coat on the pile on the floor in

the corner and went around shaking hands. "Atticus. How's the tunneling going? Alyosha. Pasha. Serafima. Melor, you're looking good."

"I am feeling good," Melor retorted defensively, as if there had been an implied criticism in the greeting.

Serafima made room for Zander next to her on the bed. "Something very special is going to take place," she whispered. "They have even organized a *dinner*."

Appolinaria, who had disappeared into the communal kitchen, pushed the door open with her foot and returned carrying a tray brimming with food. Ronzha followed holding two bottles of vodka and two bottles of Georgian wine by their throats. Everyone oohed and aahed. "Who has died?" demanded Melor.

Ronzha, wearing a frayed black velvet dinner jacket, black trousers, and a shiny ribbonlike black bow tie, nodded at Zander and announced with a determined smile, "Nobody has died . . . yet. This is a last supper." Zander thought he looked even more frail than the last time he had seen him. His hair had thinned and started to turn chalky. The skin hung loosely on the back of his hands as he poured the vodka.

Dressed in an ankle-length black velvet dress that may once have fit her and might again if she ate regularly, Appolinaria began offering around *zakuski*—small rectangles of black bread with pieces of Baltic herring and onion on them, miniature piroshki stuffed with vegetables, along with tiny sweet pickles. "There is not much," she apologized, "but nowadays enough is as good as a feast."

"The herring is out of this world," Serafima said, smacking her lips and eagerly reaching for more.

"Where did you find all this?" Alyosha Zhitkin asked, absently rolling a cigar leaf into a twist of newspaper.

"Everyone knows that, metaphysically speaking, Moscow lies downhill from the rest of the country," Ronzha answered. "Things have a natural tendency to flow to Moscow."

Tuohy's eyes narrowed imperceptibly. "I thought this was going to be a social occasion."

"It *is* a social occasion," Ronzha said. "I have composed an ode. To be precise, an ode to Stalin. Appolinaria has tried to dissuade me, but I have done it anyway. I thought it would be appropriate if those of you who with such high hopes greeted the revolution back in the Steamboat became my first readers."

"Reading it aloud will not be enough," Tuohy noted. "You will have to publish it."

The light in Appolinaria's eyes flared into flame. "I don't think anyone will be interested in publishing Ronzha's ode to Stalin. As sheer poetry, it is not that good."

Melor, who was wearing a double-breasted pinstripe suit jacket and a tie knotted tightly against the top button of his shirt, remarked, "If you was smart, you would have written it years ago."

"A poem," Ronzha replied carefully, "emerges only when it cannot stop itself from being born. This one had a long gestation."

"I suppose," Appolinaria said with a kind of ashen solemnity usually reserved for funeral pronouncements, "we might as well get it over with." She sat down on a wooden kitchen chair with a broken back, her body erect, her eyes focused on a horizon far beyond the walls of the small room.

Ronzha fitted a pair of glasses over the bridge of his nose and removed a sheet of paper from his breast pocket. Even with the eyeglasses he had to hold it at arm's length to make out the words. "Listen," he ordered, looking up for an instant at Appolinaria. He appeared to lose his nerve. She brought her eyes around and focused on him and encouraged him with a faint nod. He lowered his eyes to the page and began to read slowly and distinctly.

> We live, deaf to the land beneath us,
> Ten steps away no one hears our speeches.
>
> All we hear is the Kremlin mountaineer,
> The murderer and peasant-slayer.
>
> His fingers are fat as grubs
> And the words, final as lead weights, fall from his lips,

His cockroach whiskers leer
And his boot tops gleam.

Around him a rabble of thin-necked leaders—
fawning half-men for him to play with.

They whinny, purr, or whine
And he prates and points a finger,

One by one forging his laws, to be flung
Like horseshoes at the head, the eye or the groin.

And every killing is a treat
For the broad-chested Ossete.

Tuohy jumped to his feet as the poem ended. "I hope you know what you are doing," he snarled. He started to fling overcoats around, looking for his own in the pile on the floor.

Melor eyed Ronzha suspiciously. He understood something spectacular had occurred, but he wasn't quite sure what. Serafima spotted the doubt in his eyes. "Don't you see who he was talking about? 'Kremlin mountaineer . . . murderer and peasant-slayer!'"

Sergeant Kirpichnikov hissed, "For God's sake, don't go around repeating the damn poem. They will accuse you of *spreading* it."

Serafima appealed to Appolinaria. "How could you put us in jeopardy like that? After all we have been through together?"

Ronzha folded the sheet of paper into his breast pocket. Zander noticed his hands were trembling. "We have not put you in jeopardy," he told Serafima—though Zander had the uncanny sensation that the words were meant for him. "All you have to do is follow the letter of the law—denounce the poet for his heinous crime, the composition of a mediocre poem. Identify another enemy of the people lurking in the ranks of the intelligentsia. The authorities are experienced in such matters. They will investigate to see if the poem was lethal, if it imperiled the life of our Kremlin mountaineer."

It dawned on Melor what had happened. "I will denounce you!" he burst out. "Your poem about Comrade Stalin is blasphemy. What's more, you would not have dared to read it aloud if you were not protected by people in high places."

"That's quick thinking," Ronzha encouraged Melor. "Turn over the rocks of treason to look for the worms of conspiracy."

Alyosha Zhitkin stubbed out his cigar on a saucer and rose to his feet. "You have decided to commit suicide," he said evenly. "This was your way of doing it. All of us will have to denounce you to protect ourselves."

"All of you will have to make a choice," Ronzha agreed.

Zander was the last to leave. As the door closed behind Alyosha, he tried to stand up. He had been sitting so tensely, without the slightest motion, that the knee joint on his game leg had locked. He massaged it for a moment, and holding the headboard hoisted himself off the bed. Across the room Appolinaria collapsed in sobs. Ronzha put an arm around her and whispered into her ear. "It is over," Zander heard him say. "We have beat them all."

Zander slipped into his coat. He hesitated in front of the blanket covering the door. Ronzha looked up. Their eyes met. Zander said very formally, without a trace of irony, "It was thoughtful of you not to invite Ludmilla."

Ronzha nodded.

Zander studied the poet, studied his chiseled features, the fine lines fanning out from the corners of his eyes, his hawk's nose, his sunken eyes and the pinpoints of agony in them, the uncombed tufts of hair spilling off in all directions on his scalp. Curiously he looked perfectly sane.

Appolinaria wiped her eyes on her velvet sleeve. "Thank you for coming," she told Zander.

As Zander swept back the blanket with his arm,

Ronzha cried, "I had to make a stand or give myself away piece by piece. Surely you can understand that."

"You realize, of course, that he is stark raving mad."

"If he is mad, it's a divine madness." Zander pulled his collar up around his neck against the bitter cold. "There may be a hell for poets, but he won't burn in it."

After a moment Tuohy asked, "Am I walking too fast for you?"

"A bit."

Tuohy slowed down and concentrated on the sound of his feet compressing the frozen snow. He glanced over his shoulder to make sure his car was still following. It crawled along behind them, hugging the curb, at a discreet distance. He looked at Zander. "I want to make sure you're not going to do anything foolish."

Zander's shoulders jerked in a vague shrug.

"Look," Tuohy said. "You don't owe him a goddamn thing. He was a bastard for doing this to us. He deserves whatever he has coming to him, if only for that."

"Atticus, all he did was read a poem! It's not as if he threw a bomb at Stalin's car, or gave away state secrets—unless you consider calling Stalin a peasant-slayer a state secret."

Tuohy shook his head glumly. "I don't know why you're talking about this as if there's a choice to be made. Melor's going to denounce him for sure. Pasha will too; he's a straightforward man and knows an anti-Soviet remark when he hears one. Alyosha and Serafima will denounce him to protect themselves."

"And you will too?"

"Goddamn right I will." Tuohy expelled air from his lips in a frustrated burst. "If I didn't, they'd write on my tombstone, 'Here lies Atticus Tuohy, an asshole who didn't live to fight another day!'"

Zander turned on him. "Every time we give a piece of ourselves away, we say we do it so we can live and fight another day. It's a very convenient excuse. We live. But we somehow never get around to fighting another day. Jesus, Atticus, I've got as vigorous a sense of self-preservation as the next man. But I have to draw the line somewhere; at some point I have to defend what's left of myself."

"Drawing the line is a luxury you can't afford in Russia if you want to stay alive," Tuohy said softly.

"We didn't make a revolution in order to kill people for writing poems," Zander insisted.

Tuohy said stubbornly, "Bear in mind this revolution of ours is the only game in town."

"Some game! Look around you, Atticus. People vanish every day. Books disappear from shelves. Portraits disappear from walls, leaving behind patches where they hung for years. Photographs disappear from albums. Old letters disappear from drawers—we don't save them out of fear the writer might have rubbed Stalin the wrong way. Guest lists are destroyed as the last guest walks out the door." Zander threw his head back and took a deep breath and relished the icy sting in his throat and lungs. "Even if I wanted to, I don't see how I can denounce Ronzha. He may be Ludmilla's father."

Tuohy stopped in his tracks. "Lili told you that?"

Zander nodded. "She had an affair with him in Paris."

"So that's why she took them into the Steamboat. She was protecting her child's father." Tuohy thought about this for a moment. "It doesn't change anything as far as I can see." He looked at his wristwatch, and signaled for his driver. "I waited for you back there out of old time's sake," he said.

"I appreciate that, Atticus."

"Think about what I said."

The car pulled up and the driver came around to hold open the back door.

Tuohy tossed his eyes to indicate the driver. "Do you mind if we don't shake hands?"

"I understand."

"I'd take it as a favor if you wouldn't mention this conversation to anyone."

"Count on me."

"See you around," Tuohy said. Turning toward the automobile, he ducked into the backseat. The door slammed after him. A moment later the car pulled away from the curb and disappeared down the snow-covered street.

Zander didn't go directly home. He changed trolley cars at the top of Gorky Street and got off at the Byelorussian railway station to walk the two blocks to the new apartment buildings going up behind it. The last hundred yards were still unpaved, and he had to make his way like a tightrope walker along the planking over the sewage ditch. Inside the front door the night guardian lay slumped across his desk, an empty bottle of cheap wine and a dirty glass next to his head. Zander went past without making a sound, climbed to the third floor, and rang the bell next to the door at the end of the corridor. After a moment he could see light seeping under the door. Then he heard Masha approaching. "Who is it?" she called, and Zander caught the fear that thickened her voice; he could actually make out the sound of her sucking in her breath as she pressed an ear to the door and waited for a response. There was an intensity now to how people *listened*, Zander realized. Perfectly healthy Russians with twenty-twenty vision had developed the hearing ability of blind people. After midnight they could make out the faint screech of automobile brakes, night porters letting men in the front door, thick-soled shoes on the cement stairs, knuckles rapping against wood two floors below, whispered good-byes, soft sobbing from those left behind; in the morning they could hear silence where there should have been people yawning or farting or flushing a toilet after the first good pee of the day.

"It's me," Zander muttered, his lips pressed against the door.

Masha unhooked the chain and jerked open the door. "You might have phoned first," she berated him in a harsh whisper. "You almost gave me heart failure." She closed the door behind him quickly, furious with him— and at the same time relieved.

They had met two summers before when Masha, a fairly well-known movie actress, was filming in a studio in Alma Ata, and Zander, on vacation from his translating job at the Soviet news agency Tass, came down to subtitle an American film in order to pick up some extra cash. An article about her that Zander had read claimed she was so sure of herself she could sweet-talk birds down from the trees and get them to feed out of her palm. In the flesh she was a mixed bag of phobias. She had different signatures for different occasions, and for some unexplained reason made it a point never to eat noisy food. She vowed she would get through life without wearing eyeglasses or breastfeeding a baby, and had so far succeeded. At twenty-eight she was already afraid she was over the hill and wasted a good deal of energy fishing for compliments and then throwing them back in because they were too small. About her background she was incredibly vague; she never admitted to knowing anyone, including one man whom Zander later discovered was her father.

But her phobias disappeared like veils the instant a motion picture camera was directed at her. Her body tended to be clumsy in real life; on camera Masha didn't so much move as flow. Watching her in one film, Zander realized that she had the eyes of a frightened deer ready to bound off at the snap of a dry twig.

His turning up unannounced late at night had shaken her, and it took all of Zander's wiles to calm her down. "If you want to make love," she snapped, tightening the belt on her padded *khalat,* a Bukhara robe with long brightly colored silk sleeves, "it is out of the question. I am having my period."

"That's not why I came."

"You really gave me a scare." She stabbed a Russian cigarette between her lips and lit it with the tiniest cigarette lighter Zander had ever seen. "I have given up smoking American cigarettes," she explained from behind a cloud of smoke. "These days you cannot be too prudent. Why *did* you come?"

"I may be getting into hot water," Zander said carefully.

The blood seemed to drain from Masha's face. She sank into an easy chair, her deer's eyes straining to catch the sound of danger. "Did anybody see you enter the building?"

"The porter was out cold at his desk."

Masha took several nervous puffs of her cigarette. "I knew that business about Trotsky giving you the boat fare to return to Russia would catch up with you someday. They are going to make you out to be part of the Trotskyist ring conspiring against Stalin. You'll confess to incredible things. Oh, God, Zander, everyone who has had anything to do with you will be drawn into it. They will never believe we just liked to fuck."

"I figured out how to convince them," Zander said. "That's why I came."

Masha leaned forward. "How?"

"I want you to write a letter breaking off with me. Back-date it to when you left for location in Leningrad three months ago. I'll tell you what to say—something about you deciding I was not as ardent as I should be about communism or the leadership of Comrade Stalin. I'll put the letter in my desk. If I am arrested, they will be sure to find it. It will give you a role to play if they come around asking questions. For insurance, I'll write a letter to you that will pretend to be an answer to your letter. I'll say something about how I find your devotion to Stalin naive. If he is the genius you say he is, how come there is so little food available, that kind of thing. We will phrase it carefully so there won't be enough to merit a denunciation, just enough to get you off the hook."

"Wouldn't it be better if I said I didn't know you?"

"We have been seen together."

"You really believe the letters will work?"

"I think they will help you. Yes." Zander hesitated. "Masha, I need a favor in return."

Her eyes blinked at the snap of a twig.

"Do you still have that apartment in Alma Ata?"

Masha brought a hangnail to her teeth and began to gnaw at it.

"You once told me you wished you had a girl to take care of it, but you were afraid you would look like a capitalist if you employed someone full-time."

Masha said very quietly, "You have a phenomenal memory."

Zander said, "I think I know someone who would be perfect for the job. She needs to put some distance between herself and Moscow. Listen, Masha, I will protect you. And you protect her. You won't have to pay her, so you can't be accused of exploiting anyone. You can lend her the apartment, and not mention it to anybody. She will take care of it in return, and do some art research for a thesis on the side." Zander seemed to be talking to himself now. "Someone ought to be able to drop from view for several years like that. The research will take a long time. The longer, the better."

He thought of going off to work and leaving Ludmilla a note; that way she wouldn't worm more out of him than he wanted to tell her. But he eventually abandoned the idea. Better to confront her in person, he decided, and try to persuade her with the things left unsaid.

He hadn't slept a wink that night, but he didn't feel the slightest bit tired. He showered and shaved and changed into fresh clothes, and brewed up some ersatz coffee, and left her door ajar, hoping the aroma would awaken her earlier than usual. She wandered into his room, barefooted, folded into Zander's old bathrobe, threading her fingers through her neck-length hair to put some order into it. "In your opinion, Alexander, do ends justify means?" she asked sleepily, curling up in a chair, her feet tucked under her, her expression so utterly innocent she looked like a child asking someone to please explain to her why the sky was blue.

"It depends," he said evasively.

"On what?"

"It depends on what ends and what means you are talking about. To make sense, the question should be phrased differently. Does a particular end justify a particular means?"

Ludmilla let that sink in. She shook her head thoughtfully. "It doesn't work. In the real world you sometimes have to weigh a particular means without knowing for certain what end will flow from it. Which takes me back to the original question. Theoretically speaking, do ends in general justify their means?"

Zander shrugged impatiently. "Theoretically speaking, I suppose you would have to say that sometimes they do and sometimes they don't. Why are you asking?"

"It came up at the academy Komsomol meeting last night." Ludmilla burst into laughter. "Later, during the question and answer part, someone asked how come all the wreckers and spies being shot these days invariably got assigned to important posts before their wrecking and spying was discovered. The instructor hemmed and hawed for a few minutes. Then she said that the wreckers and spies hadn't been wrecking and spying, but doing their jobs as well as they could in order to worm their way into important posts so that they could wreck and spy. I had all I could do to keep from laughing out loud. The boy who asked the original question raised his hand again. 'If the people who had been shot for wrecking and spying haven't been doing any actual wrecking and spying, why were they shot?' he asked. This time the instructor turned purple. 'They had been shot,' she said, 'because the Party judged that they were *capable* of wrecking and spying, and being capable of wrecking and spying and actually wrecking and spying were the same thing.'" Ludmilla rubbed sand from the corners of her eyes. "They are completely insane, aren't they?" Without waiting for an answer, she asked, "How did it go at Ronzha's last night?" Here she tried without success to stifle a yawn. "Excuse me," she said.

"As a matter of fact, I want to talk to you about what happened at Ronzha's."

Something in his tone must have alerted her, because she came instantly awake. "I am all ears."

"It's this way," Zander began, preempting Ludmilla's favorite introductory phrase, and without going into specifics he told her that Ronzha had read aloud a poem that would certainly be considered anti-Soviet.

Ludmilla, uncoiling in her chair, demanded details. Zander refused to supply them. She got annoyed and accused him of treating her like a baby. "Believe me, I am telling you what you need to know," he insisted.

"Was Melor there?"

Zander nodded.

Ludmilla's eyes narrowed, accentuating their debt to the Orient. She was starting to put the pieces of the puzzle together. "The little jerk will probably denounce him."

"Melor will, and Atticus, and the others, too, to protect themselves."

"And you, Alexander? What will you do?"

"I will do what I should have done long ago. I will do what Ronzha intended me to do when he invited me to become the first reader of his poem—when he invited me to interpret his poem into existence. I will get back in touch with the place in all of us where the best of us resides, the place that knows right from wrong."

Ludmilla said vehemently, "I hate Ronzha for putting you in this position."

Zander pulled a chair over to hers and sat down. Their knees were almost touching. He spoke in a voice barely above a whisper. "Ronzha isn't doing anything to me. You must understand that. It's me who's doing this to me. Ronzha has reminded me of something I had forgotten—that there are choices to be made in this Soviet world of ours. But I make the choice. Ronzha's little poetry reading was a kind of poem in itself. He likes to say that a poem exists in the spaces between the words. The meaning of the evening existed in the space between Ronzha and his poem. He was demonstrating that Russia has become a country where everyone desperately wants to become an accomplice rather than a victim. Everyone except him. And now me. And maybe, if he makes his stand and I make mine, maybe something will change. Maybe others will make a stand, will refuse to play the game, refuse to become accomplices. Without accomplices there will be no Kremlin mountaineer, and no victims."

Tears sparkled in Ludmilla's eyes. She struggled to keep them out of her voice. "I cannot live without you, Alexander. Have you thought about that?"

He reached over and took both her hands in his. They were cold, clammy, the hands of someone experiencing death. "I have thought about little else the entire night," he told her. "A long time ago your mother understood she could either be an accomplice or a victim. She was terrified of dying, but she pushed herself to make the choice anyhow. I never was able to tell her how much I admired her. I saw her before her . . . execution, but I was physically unable to speak . . . I was the way you are now . . . I felt as if I were gagging on my emotions . . . I am following in her footsteps." The pitch of Zander's voice became more intense. "Russia has gone to earth, dug its head into the soil, become a root. My role is to feed this root with deeds. And I beg you to help me."

Ludmilla managed to say, "How can I help you?"

"You can help me by being the daughter of your mother. You can help me by going away so they cannot get at me through you."

"Go away! Go where?"

Zander told her about gilt-edged mirror's apartment in Alma Ata. Nobody would ask questions of a young woman minding an apartment and doing research on the art of Central Asia. If someone bothered to check out her last name, they would never connect it with an enemy of the people named Til back in Moscow. The two weren't related by blood. They were related by deeper things, of which the authorities knew nothing.

Ludmilla knelt down next to the wicker basket and stroked the old cat under her chin. She was rewarded with a purring that emerged from the back of the cat's throat. She looked up at Zander. "If you are making a stand, why can't I make one with you?"

"By going away you are making your stand. You are striking a blow against a revolution that has lost its way."

"And when must I go?"

"Today. This morning. Now!"

"What will happen to Ronzha?"

Zander only looked at her; the answer was evident. She buried her face in the cat's fur. When she spoke, her voice was muffled. "Lili is too old to travel. What will become of her if they arrest you?"

For the first time in fifteen years Zander called the cat by its name. "Lili will make her stand too."

Ludmilla burst out, "When I think I had another joke all ready for you this morning!"

"Tell it anyhow," Zander said softly.

Ludmilla smiled through her tears. She didn't trust herself to speak above a whisper. "I read in the youth newspaper that the minister of culture has ordered the formation of ten-man quartets. It's true, I swear it to you. Everything Soviet has to be bigger to be better. *Ten-man quartets!*"

Somehow neither of them could laugh.

When he pushed himself, Zander could be methodical. With Ludmilla gone—Zander had flagged down a taxi, loaded her two valises into the trunk, and sent her, pale but tearless, off to the railroad station—he set about destroying any traces of her that might help the NKVD track her down. He went through several photograph albums and envelopes full of snapshots, and burned every picture of Ludmilla, including those of her as a child. He destroyed all the letters and postcards he had written her over the years—they were bound with a yellow ribbon in a shoebox under her bed—and the few she had written to him. He burned her notebooks full of algebra and Marxist theory. He burned her report cards. He hid her books in the basement under a pile of books with the mention of God in them. He burned her English dictionary and her English grammar book. He burned the two copies of *Life* magazine she had gotten when she worked part-time as a tourist guide one summer. He burned her calendar with her notations in the margins—"Z's birthday" or "R's first reading." He even burned her collection of theater ticket stubs. While he was doing all this, he rehearsed what he would tell them. She had fallen in love with a boy. There had been a row. She had packed her things and gone off with him. No, he didn't have the vaguest idea who the boy was. No, he didn't know where they went. Let them try and pry another word on the subject out of him!

Zander left the hardest for last. He took a spoonful of rust-colored rat poison from a box in a shelf in the bathroom, mixed it into a ball of leftover rice and fish, and put it in the dish next to the old cat's wicker basket. The cat followed his every gesture unblinkingly. Zander felt the intensity of the cat's regard, and it crossed his mind that it understood what was happening. Well, it had had a long life, which was more than most people could expect these days.

At midmorning he caught the trolley downtown and headed for his office. For the past eight years Zander had worked for the Telegrafnoe Agenstvo Sovietskogo Soyuza, known as Tass, the Soviet news agency set up shortly after the revolution. Tass came in three versions: green Tass, which contained carefully screened news for public consumption; white Tass, which had more accurate foreign and domestic items, and was distributed daily to government ministries and various Party functionaries; and red Tass, printed on red paper and distributed daily to the top echelons of the government and the Party. Zander's work consisted of reading *The New York Times* and *The Times* of London, brought in daily by diplomatic pouch, and translating and summarizing the most important stories for inclusion in red Tass.

The five men and two women he shared a bleak, functional office with looked up when he arrived. Several made good-natured remarks about him keeping banker's hours, and Zander gathered from this that no one had yet come around asking pointed questions about him. It struck him, as he sat down at his desk and opened the most recent copy of *The Times* of London, that he had not yet burned his bridges. He could still scribble a one-line denunciation of the poet and slip it into the mailbox in the lobby. They would be annoyed with him for sending it by mail instead of phoning it in. But he would be off the hook. And where would be the harm? He would only be telling them what they already knew. Ronzha would never find out who had denounced him—and who hadn't. Ludmilla, beaming from ear to ear, would race back from Central Asia with some ridiculous item she had clipped from a newspaper: how the Soviet Health Commissar had declared the appendix to be a "bourgeois atavistic appendage" that every Communist should have out, or some such nonsense. He could almost hear Ludmilla's derisive laughter rippling through the room. With any luck the cat would have ignored the rice-and-fish ball in its dish and still be alive. And Zander, as Tuohy put it, could live to fight another day.

It all seemed so simple, so logical, that Zander's forehead began to throb with doubt. Was he making a fool of himself? It wasn't as if he could save Ronzha by not denouncing him. Ronzha was doomed; he had been doomed from the day the Bolsheviks seized power. If a sapling won't bend with the wind, it must break. People like Ronzha never gave communism a chance. An image of the poet leapt to mind. Zander remembered him staring at the broken mirror in The Stray Dog one night before the revolution and announcing, with smug pretentiousness, "If it brings only seven years of bad luck, we shall all be lucky." When you came right down to it, he really was an enemy of the people!

Happily for Zander, he had realized it in time. He would make his stand when it had a chance of changing something, when his personal sacrifice could be justified by its contribution to the cause of communism. Failing to denounce Ronzha was unadulterated sentimentality. How had Lenin put it? Sentimentality was no less a crime than cowardice.

Zander pulled a sheet of writing paper from his desk drawer. He had never composed a denunciation before. He studied the ceiling, considering the proper way to phrase it.

The colleague at the next desk, a matronly woman in her mid-thirties who lowered her head and peered over the top of gold-rimmed spectacles when she spoke to someone, plucked at Zander's elbow. "I think I may have found an item for tomorrow's red Tass," she said in a low voice. She held up an article she had cut out of one of the Berlin newspapers she regularly read. "Do you recognize her?"

Set into the article was a bad photograph of a gaunt young woman with a thin face and dark, haunting eyes. Zander could still hear the voice of the woman in the photograph telling him, "My sanity is slipping through my fingers like water . . . I will pray for you even after I can no longer remember you."

It was, without a doubt, Anastasia who stared out at him from the German newspaper.

"What an incredible story," the colleague from the next desk was saying. "The woman claims to be Anastasia, the daughter of former Tsar Nicholas, who died during the civil war. She says she escaped from Russia after her father was shot. She has been in and out of German insane asylums for years. Some say she is an impostor. But she speaks Russian, and seems to know intimate details about the life of the royal family— nicknames, things like that. It can't possibly be true, can it? It has to be some sort of capitalist plot to get their hands on the wealth the tsar kept in Swiss banks. Just the same, I suppose we should distribute the article. What do you think, Alexander? Alexander? You haven't heard a word I said."

Here was another poem, then: in the space between Zander's loss of nerve and the writing of the denunciation, Lili had contrived to send him a message from the past. Trying to save the life of Anastasia had also been a hopelessly sentimental gesture; the chances of her making it out alive had been one in a million. And yet here she was, in Germany, bearing witness by her existence— no matter that some people didn't believe her—that Lili's refusal to become an accomplice had been the right choice after all.

Zander crumpled the piece of paper on his desk. How effortless it was to join the accomplices of the world in order to save your own skin. He had had it right the first time; if he was hopelessly sentimental, at least it was sentimentality in the service of a noble cause.

When he arrived back at Petrovka Street that evening, Zander brought the Jew three Yiddish books that had been slipped through the mail slot during the day. The old man switched to his reading glasses and thumbed through them to the title pages. One had been printed in Warsaw two years before the turn of the century, the second in Krakow in 1883, the third in Prague in 1888. The last one had an inscription in Yiddish. "For Jonathan," it said in an elegant handwriting. "Remember: If trouble comes, use it." The inscription was signed, "From your father, Prague, the tenth of October 1888."

"If trouble comes!" the old Jew repeated, shaking his head, pulling at his beard. "Oy, they did not know what the word meant. *We* have trouble! But using it is not so evident." He reached up to deposit the books on a stack that already tottered precariously over his bed. "Those were the days," he muttered, "when people could add two and two and arrive at four. If, God willing, it should happen here," he said, "if people added two and two and got four, the whole place would come down around their ears. Pompeii would be nothing by comparison." The idea seemed to tickle him, and he flashed an impish grin that looked strangely out of place amid the eroded topography of his face.

In his room upstairs, Zander glanced at the cat; it was deathly still in its wicker basket. The ball of rice and fish had disappeared. He threw a towel over the cat's body, pulled a small cardboard valise from the closet, and began to fill it with things that would come in handy, assuming they let him keep them. He put in two pairs of woolen socks, some underwear, a spare shirt, a towel, a bar of soap, and a package of tooth powder and a toothbrush. There was no point in packing a razor; they took things like that away immediately so you could not kill yourself before they were ready to kill you. He glanced around the room. He was glad he had remembered to give Ludmilla the two small portraits of Lili done during her year in Paris. He slipped a shapshot of Lili, taken in front of the Kremlin wall, into his jacket pocket. He didn't think they let you keep anything that might remind you of the real world. But you never knew, so he took the photograph anyhow.

Zander realized he had not slept in thirty-six hours. He turned out the light and pulled off his high shoes and climbed into bed fully dressed. So many images competed for attention in his head that he felt dizzy. They would sort themselves out into one central thread, he knew, and the thread would uncoil, as he fell asleep, into a dream. But a corner of his brain would remain on alert, straining to catch the faintest screech of automobile brakes, the padding of thick-soled shoes on the worn carpet of the stairway, knuckles rapping against his door . . .

Ronzha had spent the morning dropping off batches of his poems and letters with friends for safekeeping. In the afternoon he took Appolinaria to visit the neighborhood library he had haunted in his youth. They kept their arms linked and spoke sparingly, and used the past tense, as if the only comfort available came from remembering. "I was thinking about the first time I worked up the courage to kiss you," Ronzha told her at one point. "You turned your head away and said, 'I do not live in my lips. He who kisses me misses me.' "

"I had no experience with the physical aspects of love," Appolinaria recalled. "You made me see things differently."

Wandering past the statue of Pushkin, Ronzha mused, "Morally speaking, it has been fairly easy to be a poet in Russia. The state—whether tsar or commissar—looms so large that it becomes the obvious enemy. It has always been us against them."

In the evening they returned to the closed-in porch and filled two cloth sacks with spare clothing and toilet articles. Appolinaria added a thin volume of Ronzha's early poetry, entitled *Visions*, knitting needles, and wool to her sack. Ronzha lingered a long time before selecting something from the makeshift shelves overflowing with books. He loved Gogol for being able to write a line like "Suddenly you could see far to the ends of the earth." He admired Pasternak and Tsvetayeva and Akhmatova; especially Akhmatova. His fingers caressed the spines of books he never expected to see again. "Dante, Marlowe, Milton, Defoe, Byron, Kipling had one thing in common—they were all spies!" He hesitated before a volume of Baudelaire, opened it at random, and read out several lines from a poem. "Baudelaire believed each poem cost him an orgasm," he said.

"That was never your problem," Appolinaria shot back.

Ronzha nodded in agreement. "And Marvell believed each orgasm cost him a day of his life." He smiled a meager smile. "Maybe that is why I am destined to die young."

Appolinaria averted her eyes; she didn't want him to see the tears in them.

Ronzha finally settled on the book he would take with him—a volume of Pushkin's poems. It was small enough to slip into his jacket pocket, and beautiful enough to take his breath away, and dense enough to give him food for thought for the lifetime that was left to him. It was Pushkin's reluctance to pronounce on high-sounding matters that drew Ronzha to his poetry now. "Contrary to appearances," he told Appolinaria, his fingers rifling the pages, "my main preoccupation has been with life, not literature." He added in an anguished voice, "But life must be lived in a way that is true to the poetic ideal. You do see that?"

Appolinaria sprang across the room and folded him in her arms. "You do not have to justify yourself to me."

His overcoat draped over his shoulders, Ronzha settled down next to his wife on the bed to wait. Appolinaria sat erect. Ronzha sat hunched over like a parenthesis, lost in thought. Very soon now, he knew, the messengers of death would be delivering an invitation with no hidden meanings lurking in the spaces between the words.

2

The tunneling shield had been pushing through fissured limestone as soft as sponge when it struck an underground river that morning. There had been no warning. One minute everything was going according to plan; the foreman on the shift had even telephoned back to say he expected to fill his quota. The next, jets of ice water knifed through the seams, flooding the section of the tunnel behind the shield and drowning thirty-seven of the forty-four men in the shaft. Engineers quickly put another compressor on the line, increasing the tunnel pressure to thirty pounds to the square inch, twice the norm, and the pumps began to gain on the water. But the seven survivors, along with the seventeen men thrown in to battle the flooding, developed stomach cramps as bubbles of nitrogen built up in their blood. The engineers called back for permission to pull them out, but the chief assistant in charge of the Moscow subway project, a burly forty-year-old Ukrainian miner named Nikita Khrushchev, refused. "This is the second incident in three days," he raged. "Every time the bastards get their feet wet they want us to hold their hands." Khrushchev leveled a stubby forefinger at Tuohy. "There are wreckers in the shaft masquerading as engineers. Get your ass down there and sort this out. I want the shield to advance one full meter on each shift. A centimeter less will be taken as sabotage!"

Tuohy was the senior NKVD man on the subway project. He had been assigned the job on the strength of his short stint at mining school and his experience working on the first New York City subway tunnel years before. In theory, he was supposed to be able to tour the tunnel head and tell at a glance who was dragging his feet. In practice, it was not what Tuohy knew about tunneling that counted; it was what he knew about people.

And what he knew about people was that they were hypnotized by the fear of having their names turn up on the list that passed across Stalin's desk every night, the one he glanced at while sucking on his pipe, very occasionally drawing a line through someone he wanted spared, then "sealed" with his initial in the upper right-hand corner.

At dawn the following day, everybody whose name was on the list was shot.

Before the death of Kirov, terror in Soviet Russia had been largely directed against real enemies: kulaks, Mensheviks, social revolutionists, landlords, capitalists—in short, people who would have toppled the regime if they had it in their power. Since Kirov's death, terror had become more random, striking veteran Bolsheviks, functionaries who owed their advancement to Trotsky, revolutionists who had known the boss back in his salad days, a great many of Stalin's in-laws, people who made the mistake of speaking up for other victims of the purge, and occasionally someone simply because the NKVD, as the Cheka was now called, needed to fill a quota. Once, a printer was arrested for making a typographical error while setting one of Stalin's speeches in *Pravda*.

The madness had a method. People who escaped the purge tortured themselves with imagined treasons and went back to work more ardent than before to hide their guilt.

Wearing a pair of fisherman's hip boots, Tuohy waded through knee-deep water to the wooden platform that served the engineers as a forward command post. One of the engineers, a bearded middle-aged man with a distinctly Jewish-sounding name, flattened out a damp plan on the worktable. "There is a crust of Jurassic clay right above the limestone," he shouted over the thumping of the compressors. "Our shield apparently tapped into an underground river, diverting it upward into this crust of clay." He pointed with a mud-stained finger to a cross-section drawing of the tunnel.

"The clay is swelling," shouted a second engineer. "If we don't keep the pressure up in the tunnel head, the clay will crush the outer casing. The shoring will snap like matchsticks."

"I don't see what the problem is," Tuohy called back impatiently. The naked electric bulbs strung overhead dimmed for a moment, and everyone raised their eyes to look at them. Then the bulbs came on again, and the eyes returned to the plan. "Increase the pressure even more if you have to," Tuohy ordered, "and keep it up until the tunnel head is clear of water and the men have reinforced the casing with cement."

"Cement takes twenty-four hours to set," called the Jewish engineer. His voice was hoarse from having to yell all day. "The men working in there will be dead by then."

Tuohy shouted, "Do you have an alternative to offer?"

The two engineers looked at each other, then down at the plan.

Tuohy yelled, "Comrade Khrushchev is furious about this setback. Assuming you can clear the tunnel head of water and shore up the casing with cement, how far will you have advanced this shift?"

"Maybe half a meter," the Jewish engineer yelled. "Maybe less."

"Then the next shift will have to produce a meter and a half for you to break even," Tuohy shouted.

"That is not possible under these conditions," yelled the Jewish engineer.

"You can advance a meter and a half if you take more risks."

"There are limits to what we can do," shouted the second engineer.

"Comrade Stalin has decided to show the world what Socialist labor and Socialist technology can accomplish," Tuohy shouted back. "Don't stand there and tell me there are limits to what you can do. If you can't fill the quota, we'll find engineers who can."

Tuohy happened to be inspecting the tunnel mouth the next morning when they started to bring out the workers who had been in the high-pressure section of the tunnel head. The first fourteen were carried out on planks, dead. It was apparent from their contorted limbs that they had not died painlessly. Eight more workers came out on stretchers, whimpering in agony, gasping to keep from suffocating. Only two men, their clothes mud- and vomit-stained, managed to walk out on their own.

Back at the NKVD field headquarters, down the hall from Khrushchev's office, Tuohy dictated his report. There had been wrecking, that much was evident. The water should never have been allowed in in the first place; once in, it should have been pumped out more expeditiously. If the wooden shoring had been adequate to cope with the swelling clay, the men would not have had to line the casing with cement. One of the two engineers on the shift was obviously trying to sabotage the subway project. He was probably taking orders from the German High Command. A writ was being issued for his immediate arrest. Tuohy expected his written confession on his desk within twenty-four hours.

A young NKVD recruit, recently transferred to Moscow from the Ukraine and eager to prove himself, asked Tuohy which of the two engineers was to be accused of wrecking.

"Either," Tuohy replied. "It doesn't matter. They are both guilty of something or other. The one we don't arrest will work that much harder to convince us of his innocence."

The recruit started toward the door to carry out the order. Tuohy called after him, "On second thought, arrest the Jew. Chances are he is the guiltier of the two."

Over the years Tuohy's face had grown fuller—as had his stomach. Now approaching his forty-fifth birthday, he had taken to parting his hair on the side instead of in the middle, and slicking it diagonally back to cover a thin spot. The red in his hair and the rust in his walrus

mustache had washed out, and appeared less flamboyant, though his nose was still atwitch for the female of
the species. He was having more than his share of
affairs; women seldom passed up an opportunity to
sleep with a Chekist. They would get his orgasm out of
the way and move on to more important matters. "It's
my sister's husband," one woman whispered in his ear.
"He was arrested a week ago Wednesday. They are
accusing him of sabotaging butter production by throwing nails in the butter while he was inspecting a factory.
You have my word for it, he is perfectly innocent. Not a
day went by without him speaking of Comrade Stalin in
the most reverent terms; he worshipped the ground he
walked on. There has obviously been a mistake."

On occasions like this—and there were many—Tuohy
would go through the motions of noting the man's name
on a slip of paper. But the only action he took was to
change mistresses; he certainly didn't want to run the
risk of being associated with relatives of someone who
threw nails in butter.

If Arishka knew about his philandering, she never
made an issue of it, a discretion that Tuohy appreci-
ated. Given the thickness of the walls of the new building they lived in, it would have been like broadcasting
their personal problems to the world.

The thickness of the walls notwithstanding, Tuohy
and Arishka fared extremely well by Soviet standards.
They had a sixty-five-square-meter apartment all to themselves, a car and a chauffeur at their disposal, access to
the Cheka commissary, and the right to vacation, free
of charge, in a Cheka rest home on the Black Sea for
three weeks a year. Eventually, if Tuohy rose high
enough in the ranks, he could expect to have the use of
a dacha in some birch forest near the Moscow River
outside the capital.

Returning home from the construction site, Tuohy
left his hip boots for the concierge to hose down and
dry out in the furnace room. The out of order sign was
up again on the elevator—since they had moved in, it
had been out of order more than it had been in order—so

he had to trudge up the five flights to the apartment, which did not help his mood any. He could hear the hum of Arishka's sewing machine when he let himself in the front door. It stopped abruptly and Arishka appeared at the bedroom door. She looked as grim as Tuohy ever remembeied seeing her.

"I have been calling all over for you," she said. "Where have you been hiding?"

"I was down at the tunnel head inspecting the damage from yesterday's flooding."

"Your assistant said you left the site at four. It's five to eight now."

Tuohy made a mental note to speak to his assistant. "I stopped by headquarters to pick up some new directives. Why the inquisition?"

Arishka lowered her voice. "Why don't you admit you were with one of your mistresses? It's all the same to me."

"If it's all the same to you, why bring it up?"

Arishka spun back into the room. "I ran into Serafima at the central post office this morning," she said over her shoulder. "We were both paying our telephone bills. She told me what happened at Ronzha's the other night. Now I understand why he didn't invite me—he wanted to protect me. He knew I would get into trouble for not denouncing him. Americanitz, how could you have done it?"

Tuohy loosened his tie and unbuttoned the collar button of his shirt; he decided he would know socialism had finally arrived in Russia when he found a laundry capable of doing collars without putting starch in them. "Don't waste your tears on Ronzha," he said. "He knew what he was doing."

Arishka turned on Tuohy. "I am not wasting my tears on Ronzha. I am wasting them on Alexander. I am wasting them on you and me. I went to Petrovka Street today. The apartment was empty. Some men in blue suits were throwing the last of the old Jew's books into a truck. They were bringing them out in a wheelbarrow— all those books with the name of God in them!"

Tuohy burst out, "You didn't ask anyone about Zander?"

"I'm not stupid. Anyway, I didn't have to."

Tuohy exhaled in relief. "Zander was picked up the night before last," he said. "They are still looking for Ludmilla."

Arishka said, "Can't you put in a good word for him? My God, Americanitz, he's your oldest friend. You know he is not an enemy of the people. What is happening in this country? He still limps around with shrapnel in his leg from the civil war!"

"Keep your voice down."

"I have kept my voice down for fifteen years!" Arishka retorted. "Everybody has kept their voices down for fifteen years. You would think the state was going to disintegrate if someone raised his voice."

She sighed and collapsed into an easy chair. Her anger had boiled over for once; now there was nothing left but a sediment of sadness. She looked up at Tuohy. "I am leaving you, Americanitz. I cannot take any more of this."

Over the years she had threatened to walk out on him a half-dozen times. On each occasion he had talked her out of it. But now Tuohy, too, felt as if the string had run out. They had long ago used up the reserves of affection that were left in them.

"Is there another man?" Tuohy asked. "Not that it would make a difference, but I'm curious."

Arishka shook her head quickly. No, she said, there was no other man in her life, there was only the emptiness of their relationship.

They were both civilized about the separation. Tuohy helped her pack her seventy-eight rpm record collection and generously let her take the Victrola, which was of German manufacture and could have brought a small fortune on the black market. He carried her packages and valises and the Victrola and the sewing machine down to a taxi and went around to the driver's side to give him ten rubles and instruct him to take her anywhere she wanted to go. As the taxi drove off, she averted her face so Tuohy would not be hurt by her lack of tears. The next morning he spread the story around that she had gone to Leningrad to take care of her sick mother; he didn't want people thinking she had been arrested.

At the office later that day one of Tuohy's assistants took him aside and handed him a yellow file folder. Inside were photographic copies of the identity card of a journalist named Lifshits, Arkadey Eremeyevich, age forty-seven, his Party card with the number Z345233, a permit to reside in Moscow, and a letter of introduction to the editor of *Komsomolskaya Pravda* from the editor of a local paper in Kiev. There was also a grainy photograph showing a gaunt man with a worried face who looked as if he might have been suffering from stomach cramps.

"You are sure it's him?" Tuohy asked.

The assistant nodded. "They have been meeting over lunch hour two or three times a week for months. Also I tracked down the taxi from the license number you gave me. He dropped her on Gorky, just after Mayakovsky Square. Comrade Lifshits shares an apartment with two other couples right around the corner from there."

"Why did it have to be a Jew?" Tuohy muttered. He studied the photograph of his competition.

"There is another thing," the assistant said. "The editor of the Kiev paper who signed the letter of recommendation has been executed for being part of a Trotskyist center trying to detach the Ukraine from the Soviet Union."

"Which makes Lifshits a member of a Trotskyist reserve center trying to detach the Ukraine from the Soviet Union."

Tuohy's assistant smiled.

Tuohy smiled back.

"Pick him up in the street," Tuohy ordered. "As far as anyone at his office or his apartment is concerned, he should simply disappear. Give him a choice. He can confess to being part of a Trotskyist reserve center carrying out orders to infiltrate our journals, or he can join the shock workers constructing socialism in the subway tunnel head. One or the other."

*   *   *

Arishka was already seated at the corner table in the private dining room when Tuohy arrived. She seemed on edge. "It was nice of you to come, Americanitz," she said as he slipped into the seat across from her.

"I wish you would stop calling me that in public. Did you order already?"

She shook her head. "You order for me."

Tuohy glanced at the menu, then signaled for the waiter. "Two number sevens to start. For a main course we will both take number thirty-seven."

"There is no number thirty-seven today," the waiter, an old man with a stubble on his chin and food stains on his wrinkled black dinner jacket, told Tuohy. He smiled, exposing two silver teeth.

"Forty-one then, but without the broccoli for me."

"There is no forty-one either, and no broccoli in any case."

Tuohy was tiring of the game. "What do you suggest?" he asked sarcastically.

"A hundred and three."

"A hundred and three, then. Two orders. And a bottle of Georgian wine."

"So how is the subway-building business going?" Arishka asked conversationally.

"Beautifully," Tuohy said with enthusiasm. "We are proving that Socialist labor can do anything the capitalists can do. And do it better. The first segment of the line will go into service before the summer. The stations are going to look like museums. They will make the subways in New York and London and Paris look like toilets by comparison."

The old waiter shuffled back with the wine, which he uncorked with difficulty and planted in the middle of the table. Tuohy filled Arishka's glass and his own.

"Here's to all the good years we had," Arishka said, raising her glass.

"To the good years," Tuohy agreed. He was wondering when she would get around to Lifshits.

Later, out in the street, Tuohy asked, "Can I drop you somewhere?"

"I would just as soon walk," Arishka said. She slipped her arm through Tuohy's. "Keep me company for a block or two. It will do you good to get some fresh air into your lungs."

For a while Arishka didn't say anything. Tuohy understood her well enough to know she was working up her courage. Finally she said, "Americanitz, I never asked you for a professional favor before . . ."

"Stop calling me Americanitz. If I can help you, I'll try."

Arishka nodded in a preoccupied way. "The family I live with, they have a friend, a journalist with *Komsomolskaya Pravda,* a member of the Party for fourteen years, an honest Bolshevik, the kind of man you would take to immediately. A straightforward man, not devious the way some people can be. A week ago tomorrow . . ."

She bit her lower lip. Tuohy said, "What happened a week ago tomorrow?"

"That's just it. Nobody knows what happened. He left his office at seven and was never seen again. We checked the hospitals. We reported him missing to the local militia. They couldn't find out anything. He seems to have disappeared from the face of the earth!"

"Did he have any girlfriends—someone he might have run off with?"

Arishka shook her head impatiently.

"Was there anything in his past? Any associations that might have compromised him?"

Arishka was silent for a moment. Then she said in a very small voice, "He was the protégé of an editor in Kiev who was shot as a Trotskyist." And she added vehemently, "This friend of ours, he spit on Trotsky! From the top of his head to the tip of his toes he was a Stalinist. When they printed one of Stalin's speeches in *Pravda,* he read every word of it. Sometimes he underlined entire sentences. The night before he disappeared he was reading Stalin's *History of the Communist Party* until two in the morning. It is still open on the night table next to his bed, if you don't believe me."

Tuohy refrained from asking her how she knew what

he was reading in bed at two in the morning. He took out a pen and a slip of paper. "Give me his name."

"Lifshits. Arkadey Eremeyevich Lifshits."

"I'll see what I can find out."

Arishka kissed him on the cheek. "I thank you, Amer—" She caught herself. "I thank you. I thank you from the heart."

The alarm was phoned back from the tunnel head at twelve-twenty. Khrushchev came storming in from his lunch break. "What's this about a fire in the shaft? Every time I turn my back some wrecker takes advantage!"

Details were sparse. Tuohy was sent to investigate. In a forward section of the shaft, the shift foreman and several engineers, their faces black with grime, explained the situation. A fire had broken out in the caisson. It had spread rapidly because of the compressed air, which was rich in oxygen. The shift foreman, acting on his own initiative, had reduced the air pressure. Because of this, at the shield end of the caisson, silt and a kind of brown ooze had poured into the shaft. Twelve men had died of smoke inhalation in the original fire. Three more had been buried alive in the silt. The survivors had fled the caisson in panic.

Tuohy could make out the survivors sitting sullenly on crates in a dim corner of the tunnel where electric lights had not been strung. Several of them were doubled over, coughing.

Tuohy issued his instructions. The shift foreman was to be arrested for lowering the air pressure without authorization; chances were he had started the fire himself in order to have an excuse to lower the pressure and bring on the silt. The only real question was who he was working for. The German High Command? The Japanese? The British Secret Service? A Trotskyist center? Tuohy expected a confession on his desk before the day was out.

As for the workers who had fled the caisson, they could return and redouble their efforts to meet the shift's quota of one full meter of forward motion, or face similar charges. The compressors were to be put back on the line immediately; the air pressure was to be raised to thirty pounds. Silicate of soda and calcium chloride were to be pumped through perforated pipes into the earth around the shield. The chemicals would congeal the silt, preventing more leakage. The workers could then bring out the silt that had accumulated in the caisson and get on with the job of tunneling.

One of Tuohy's men led the shift foreman away. The other man, the one who was eager to prove himself, went over and delivered a pep talk to the survivors. "For Comrade Stalin, for the cause of socialism, let's get back in there and show the world what the proletariat can do," he cried.

None of the survivors moved. "The caisson is full of smoke," one of them muttered. "It will take hours to pump it out. Anyone who goes in now won't stand a chance."

"If the smoke doesn't get us, the pressure will," another man grumbled.

Someone else said, "Raising the pressure probably caused the fire to start up again. The tunnel is a death trap."

Tuohy treated their refusal to return to work as a full-fledged mutiny. The survivors were shackled together in twos. Guarded by uniformed NKVD troops armed with tommy guns, they were marched out of the tunnel for interrogation and punishment.

Back in his headquarters Khrushchev raged at the delay and ordered a reserve shift into action.

Later Tuohy happened to see a list of the men who had died of smoke inhalation or been buried alive in the silt Among them was one Lifshits, Arkadey Eremeyevich.

That afternoon Tuohy phoned Arishka at her office. "Concerning that friend of yours—"

Tuohy thought he heard Arishka catch her breath on the other end of the line.

"You have learned something?"

"I couldn't find any trace of him," Tuohy said. He laughed lightly into the receiver. "He will probably turn up in a day or two with some story of having gone off on a secret assignment for *Komsomolskaya Pravda*."

Arishka was desperate enough to clutch at any straw. "You really think so?"

"I am sure of it."

"Here lies Atticus Tuohy," Tuohy told himself after he hung up the receiver, "who, on his death bed, was honestly able to say he had no enemies—he had killed them all!"

3

Zander had become a killer of time. He had learned to stretch the most inconsequential activity into a more or less agreeable half hour. Folding his blanket, turning back his straw pallet, sweeping his cell, washing out his toilet bucket, taking his "stroll"—four paces up, four paces back, repeated until his bad leg ached— could fill an entire morning. He would devote a pleasurable hour to hunting lice in his pubic hair and squashing them between his thumbnail and the wall. A fixed amount of time, usually the hour after lunch, was set aside for visiting the past; lying flat on his back on the pallet, he would close his eyes, conjure up a specific event, and reconstruct it down to the tiniest detail. He relived the pogrom during which Adler was doused with kerosene and set aflame by Cossacks; the passage through Ellis Island; the departure for Russia, with Leon waving from the end of the pier; and, again and again, making love with Lili. He had spent the previous afternoon and all of today studying an endless two-way stream of ants that stretched from the whited-over window high in the cell wall, across the stone floor and out under the heavy metal door with the Judas hole in it. The guards must have spotted Zander through the Judas hole on his hands and knees, because one of them came in with a Flit gun before the evening meal was distributed and exterminated the entire colony.

Zander reacted as if there had been a death in the family and went into a depression as deep as the one he experienced the day of his arrest. The disappearance of the ants suggested to him that his own disappearance could be achieved as effortlessly, that the people who performed the chore would think of it as a sanitary expedition.

Zander decided to discuss the matter with his neighbor, a military planner who had committed the crime of warning that in the likely event of a German attack, the Red Army might have to fall back before the technologically superior enemy and rely on its vast spaces to absorb the assault. "WHY HAVE YOU BEEN LOCKED UP?" Zander had tapped out on the wall the day he "met" the military planner. The prisoners used a simple code that divided the alphabet into twenty-five squares, five across, five down, and then tapped out the two-number group that corresponded to a particular letter.

"PREMATURE ANTIFASCISM," the answer had been tapped back. And his neighbor had added characteristically, "A TRANSGRESSION SECOND ONLY TO PREMATURE EJACULATION. HA HA HA."

Zander worked his "tapping" nail out of the toilet bucket and began: "ARE YOU THERE?"

"WHERE ELSE WOULD I BE? HA HA."

"MY CELL WAS INVADED BY ANTS BUT THEY KILLED THEM."

"I CAN SMELL THE FLIT GUN FROM HERE. THERE IS NO COMMUNITY MORE SOCIALIST THAN AN ANT COLONY. DENOUNCE ANT KILLERS FOR WRECKING THE ULTIMATE COLLECTIVE. GUARDS WERE PROBABLY TAKING ORDERS FROM GERMAN HIGH COMMAND WHICH WANTED TO DETACH ANT COLONY FROM SOVIET UNION. CERTAIN ANTS MIGHT HAVE SUFFERED SECESSIONIST TENDENCIES BUT COLONY AS A WHOLE WAS FERVENTLY STALINIST. DEATH OF ENTIRE COLONY WILL NEVERTHELESS SERVE AS LESSON TO OTHER ANTS WHO HARBOR

SECESSIONISTS IN MIDST. DEATH OF FLIT GUNNERS WILL SERVE AS LESSON TO OTHER GUARDS ON GERMAN PAYROLL. IN SHORT, EVERYONE INVOLVED WAS GUILTY OF SOMETHING. HA HA HA."

Zander tapped back, "HOW IS YOUR CONFESSION PROGRESSING?"

"WE ARE WORKING ON IT. EVERY TIME I STUMBLE OVER A DATE OR DETAIL THEY SHOW ME A PHOTOGRAPH OF MY THIRTEEN-YEAR-OLD SON AND REMIND ME THAT DEATH PENALTY IS APPLICABLE UNDER SOVIET LAW TO EVERYONE OVER TWELVE. I REDOUBLE MY EFFORTS. WHAT ABOUT YOU?"

"I KEEP TELLING THEM THE TRUTH."

"THE ONLY TRUTHS THEY WANT ARE THE ONES THEY CAN USE. HA."

Zander started to tap out an answer, but his neighbor interrupted him. "TRUSTY WAGON COMING AROUND. WHAT WINE DO YOU THINK THEY ARE SERVING TONIGHT? HA HA."

Zander pressed his good ear to the door. He could hear the trusty's wagon outside his cell. The "mail slot" in the bottom of the door opened, and a metal dish with a watery cabbage soup in it was pushed through. Curiously the slot didn't snap shut as it usually did. Zander bent his head until his ear was flat against the stone floor and looked through the slot. He could see two rubber-rimmed wheels of the wagon, and the thick-soled lace-up shoes of the man pushing it. The trusty appeared to stoop down. Then something was shoved through the slot, after which the door snapped shut.

Zander reached out and picked up—a book! Even holding it in his hands, it was hard for him to believe it. For a fleeting moment he wondered if the trusty had deposited the book in the slot because it contained the sacred name of God and he expected Zander to pass it on to the old Jew. Then he remembered where he was.

In the seven weeks and four days since his arrest, he had not laid eyes on a book. The only printed matter he had seen were the typed sheets summarizing his previous interrogation which he was required to sign at the beginning of every session. He opened the book to the title page and strained to read the print through his eyeglasses. The last diffusion of dirty light that filtered through the whited-over window during the day had disappeared. Zander glanced at the naked electric bulb dangling high overhead in the center of his cell. The filament seemed dimmer than usual, as if it worked on a rheostat and somebody had turned it down. Even standing directly under the bulb, he had trouble making out what was written on the title page. The letters swam before his eyes. He took off his spectacles and polished them carefully on his sleeve and hooked them on again, taking care to avoid irritating the scar behind his ear. He still couldn't force the writing into focus. Living in the constant dimness of his cell, his eyes had gotten weaker, there was no doubt about it. Zander dragged over the toilet bucket and set it on the floor upside down and stepped up on it to be nearer the bulb. With enormous effort he could make out some of the letters. "T-h-e v-e-n-t-u-r-e f T-u-n S-a-w . . ."

The Adventures of Tom Sawyer by Mark Twain! And the book—the ultimate time-killer—was in English! Zander's heart surged against his rib cage; he felt as if his chest would explode. He swayed dizzily on the toilet bucket, and had to spread his arms like a tightrope walker to steady himself. He turned to the first page and held the book at arm's length above his head so it could capture as much light from the bulb as possible. Zander's lips moved as he read. The print blurred. The voice inside his head trailed off. He raised his eyes and looked again at the light bulb. Was he imagining things? Or was it dimmer than before?

"THEY HAVE GIVEN ME A BOOK," Zander excitedly tapped out to his neighbor.

"BEWARE OF BOLSHEVIKS WITH GIFTS," the friend he had never seen answered. And he added: "EVEN WITHOUT. HA HA HA."

During one visit to the past, Zander relived his arrest. He had finally dozed off on his bed, when he heard what sounded like the faint grinding of gears outside the window. Was the driver acting under instructions when he ground his gears? If the operation went off too silently, wouldn't the other people living in the building or around it miss their nightly ration of fear? In the darkness—the luminous hands of the clock on the night table were poised at twenty-five past two—Zander leapt from the bed, and edging back the drapes, peered into the street. A limousine, dull black, four doors, with a thin trail of exhaust streaming from its tailpipe, had pulled up in front of the house. But nobody had gotten out of it. Zander thought he saw the lace curtains stir on a window across the street; up and down Petrovka, dozens of people, hundreds even, must have been studying the car.

At two-fifty, a municipal bread delivery truck drove slowly down Petrovka and pulled up behind the limousine. As if on signal, ten men wearing broad-brimmed fedoras poured from the limousine and the bread truck. The hollow echo of doors slamming rippled through the snow-dampened street. Downstairs, a gloved fist pounded on the front door. Zander could hear the old Jew cursing. "Goddamned Cossacks," he muttered in a rasping voice that had only exasperation in it. "Keep your pants on."

Zander sat down on the bed and began lacing up his high shoes. It was curious, he thought, how you could wait for your arrest with the unshakeable conviction that it was inevitable, and then be astonished when it happened. Of all the people living on Petrovka, why me? He started to tell himself that there must have been scores who were just as guilty. With a bitter smile he corrected himself: There *were* scores, and they were just as *innocent*.

Zander could hear feet pounding up the stairs. There was an instant of silence, then a single sharp rap on his door. He took a deep breath and walked over and threw the bolt and opened it.

"Alexander Til?"

Zander nodded. He wished he had prepared a little speech; a brilliant riposte that would reduce these servants of the state to shame. Even if he had prepared something, he wouldn't have been able to deliver it. His heart was beating wildly. He was very frightened.

"Under a warrant issued by the procurer general of the Moscow City Soviet," one of the NKVD men recited in an absolutely toneless voice, "you are hereby arrested."

"On what charges?" Zander managed to ask, but they brushed past him as if he didn't exist and fanned out into the small room. For the next hour Zander was completely ignored; he could have walked down the stairs and out the door and nobody would have noticed. Working in teams of two, the agents began searching the apartment. Every single book was rifled so that any loose papers in it would fall out. Erasers were pried from pencils. Ink was drained from wells. Candies were removed from wrappers. The dead cat was taken out of its bed and the wicker basket was searched. Drawers were turned upside down. The lining of jackets and of coats, the mattress were slit open. The pillow was torn apart and the feathers were spilled into a paper bag to be searched; several feathers escaped and floated around in the air. Floorboards were pried up. Wallpaper was peeled off. The overhead lighting fixture and the water bowl above the toilet were examined. One agent pulled on long rubber gloves and began sifting through the contents of the garbage pail. The pictures that remained in Zander's photograph album were peeled away from the page in search of secret writing. Anything that could be of use in the investigation—photographs, handwritten letters (including Masha's, breaking off their relationship), even a stack of unpaid bills—was thrown into a cardboard valise. When the agents looked as if they were almost ready to leave, Zander started to slip into an overcoat with the hem trailing down, but one of the NKVD men signaled to him with a finger as if he were a child. "Where you are going you will not need that," he said. He gestured for Zander to hold out his wrists and expertly snapped a pair of handcuffs on them.

Sandwiched between the agents, one of whom carried the suitcase full of photographs and letters, Zander limped down the stairs and out to the bread truck. For the second time in his life he felt the gravitational pull of the earth through the soles of his shoes. He didn't notice the cold, even though the temperature had dipped below freezing. The two rear doors were pulled open and Zander, with a helpful shove from one of the guards, climbed up onto a wooden bench inside. Four agents piled in after him. Two sat on either side of him, two across from him. The bread truck started up.

During the ride through the deserted streets of Moscow, the bread truck skidded, slewing sideways, its rear wheels striking a curb; even then nobody said a word. Twenty minutes later the truck pulled up. Zander could hear what sounded like enormous doors being eased open on their hinges. The truck started up again, then executed a U-turn and backed up in its tracks. More doors were thrown open. The truck continued backing up. Doors clanged closed after it. Finally the truck backed to a stop. The two NKVD men across from Zander opened the rear doors and climbed down. One of the men sitting next to Zander nodded toward the open doors. Zander jumped out, landing with his weight on his good foot. The agent carrying the cardboard valise took a firm grip on his forearm and guided him up some steps, through a door and down a long corridor to a bare, brilliantly lighted room. He pulled a small key from his overcoat pocket and unlocked the handcuffs. Zander rubbed his wrists.

"Strip," the man ordered. "Fold your clothing on the floor."

The room was unheated. Zander hesitated. "How long will I have to wait?"

"Strip," the man repeated in the same tone of voice. "Fold your clothing on the floor. Execute."

Zander removed his shoes and stockings and undressed, folding his clothing on the floor and standing on the pile to keep his feet from freezing.

After a while the door opened and two men dressed in white smocks came in. Both were very young. One had a pocket lamp. "Bend over, spread your cheeks," the man with the pocket lamp ordered.

They examined his body methodically, looked in every orifice where a poison pill or a razor blade could be hidden. A uniformed guard came in carrying a pair of what looked like gray pajamas. "You will wear your underwear, your undershirt, your stockings, your shoes with the laces removed, and these," he said, tossing the pajamas on the floor at Zander's feet.

The pajama bottoms had no string, so Zander had to grasp the waist with one hand to keep the pants from falling down. He shuffled after the guard, his feet flopping in his laceless high shoes, down a well-lighted corridor, then up a wide central staircase, past a checkpoint where another uniformed guard logged in everyone who passed in either direction, then down a long cell block to a holding cell at the very end.

The sickening metallic click as the heavy door closed behind him shook Zander to his core. He had steeled himself to face arrest; he had been determined, come what may, to confront his jailers with dignity. But standing in the middle of the cold, narrow cell, with a metal spoon in a greasy metal soup bowl and a toilet bucket for company, he felt overpowered by his isolation. He had come to Russia, as he had told the Jewish boy back on the corner of Essex and Hester in New York, ready to spill his blood for socialism. Now, clutching his pajama bottoms to keep them up, he knew beyond a doubt that he had made a terrible mistake. Old Hippolyte, Otto Eppler, Lili, Vasia—they were gone. Ronzha might be in the next cell, for all Zander knew. All that suffering, all that blood spilled, and for what?

Zander glanced bitterly at the walls of his cell. A thin film of mildew covered the stones. Maybe Ronzha really *was* in the next cell. Zander had an irresistible urge to talk to him, to tell him he understood what the poet had been trying to teach him by putting him to the test. He shuffled over to the corner and grabbed the metal spoon and began to tap out numbers on the wall. The old prison alphabet came to him easily; it might have been another foreign language that he was fluent in. A two, then a three for W. A three and a two for H. A four and a three for O. "WHO?"

For a long while there was no response. Just when Zander concluded the cell next to him must be empty, he heard a distant tapping. He pressed his good ear to the mildew and counted the taps. They spelled out "NICHOLAS SALMANOVICH RUBASHOV."

Zander couldn't restrain a snicker. It had an unnatural sound in the small cell. Rubashov was a famous Old Bolshevik whose picture had appeared in *Pravda* a hundred times. He had helped Stalin get where he was today. In his heyday, Rubashov had purged his share of revolutionists when it suited his purposes. "SERVES YOU RIGHT," Zander tapped back. "WHY HAVE YOU BEEN LOCKED UP?"

Zander could hear Rubashov starting to answer; he was probably using the metal edge of his pince-nez to tap on the wall. "POLITICAL DIVERGENCIES."

"BRAVO," Zander replied. "THE WOLVES DEVOUR EACH OTHER." And he turned back to his cell feeling as if he had survived a moment of insanity. Maybe there was something to hope for after all.

The thin-lipped interrogator, who had introduced himself back during the first session as Comrade Zhilov, opened the dossier and passed the typed-up summary of the previous session across to Zander. Zhilov uncapped a fountain pen and laid it on the desktop next to the sheets. Then he folded his hands behind his neck and leaned back in his chair and studied his prisoner with the patient eyes of someone who knew how things were going to end, but not when.

Zander leaned forward and picked up the sheets and tried to make out the typewriting. Finally he shook his head. "I can't sign these," he told Zhilov.

"Why not?"

Zander angled his good ear toward Zhilov to catch his questions. "I can't sign something I can't read."

"Your eyes have deteriorated," Zhilov noted. "What have you been doing to strain them?"

"As if you didn't know."

Zhilov took a magnifying lens from his drawer and handed it to Zander. Using the glass, he was able to work through the two typewritten pages and sign his name at the bottom of each sheet.

"We left off yesterday," Zhilov said, tucking the signed pages into the dossier and depositing the dossier in the top drawer, "with you about to explain your relationship with Trotsky in New York."

"I had no relationship with Trotsky in New York."

"According to deposition of Comrade Tuohy, on several occasions you traveled to the section of the city in which Trotsky lived to talk with him."

"There were not *several* trips. There was *one*."

"One. Several. It amounts to the same thing. You don't deny that you initiated the meeting?"

"It was natural for me to want to meet the famous Trotsky."

"What did you talk about?"

Zander massaged his forehead with his thumb and forefinger. He felt another of his splitting headaches coming on. Tomorrow he would really make an effort not to read anymore in his cell no matter what book they slipped through the slot. It was ruining his eyes. "Trotsky, as I remember, advised me to grow a beard." He felt his own seven-week beard with his fingertips. It was the first time he had grown one since New York. "Trotsky explained that I could disguise myself by simply shaving it off."

"You expect us to believe," Comrade Zhilov said sarcastically, "that all the world-renowned revolutionist Trotsky had to tell you was to grow a beard?"

"We couldn't very well have been plotting against Stalin because the Bolsheviks had not taken over Russia yet," Zander said with equal sarcasm.

"I must caution you again to confine yourself to answering my questions. If you please. The same Trotsky who according to you advised you to grow a beard later offered you money to book passage to Russia. He supplied you with a personal letter of introduction to Comrade Stalin in Petrograd. And he gave you the name and address of a man who could provide you with false papers so you could get out of the country. Did he select you for all this by lot?"

Zander remembered the scene in the basement office on St. Mark's Place. "Comrade Tuohy won the lottery."

"If Comrade Tuohy won the lottery, how come Trotsky supplied *you* with the means to return to Russia?"

"I suppose he was impressed with the fact that my grandfather had been a famous revolutionist."

"It had nothing to do with his wanting to plant people loyal to him in key places?"

"My loyalty," Zander said tiredly—they had covered this same ground the previous week—"has always been to the Party and the revolution. It has never been to a particular person."

The interrogator let a whistle of satisfaction escape through the space between his front teeth. "Now we are getting someplace. You admit that your loyalty has never been to a particular person. Which means it has never been to Comrade Stalin, even though Comrade Stalin epitomizes the Party. Which explains how you could allow yourself to hear an intellectual wrecker read a despicable attack on Comrade Stalin—an attack meant, without the shadow of a doubt, as a rallying cry, an anthem even, for anti-Soviet elements in our midst— without reporting it to the proper authorities."

"What I heard," Zander insisted, "was a poem composed by someone who had come to the end of his resources and wanted to force the system to kill him. Since when has listening to a poem been a violation of Soviet law?"

"Let me remind you once again," Comrade Zhilov said patiently, "that I pose the questions, and you answer them. Not the other way around. You seriously expect us to believe that at the time you heard the seditious poem, you were not in contact with the Trotskyist wrecking center operating in Moscow?"

"If there really is such a center, I certainly was not in touch with it."

"Let us move on," the interrogator said, "to your mission to Ekaterinburg during the civil war. Who was it who selected you for this assignment?"

Zander threaded his fingers through his scalp. His hand came away with a tuft of hair. The interrogator solicitously pushed an ashtray across the desk, and Zander deposited the hair in it. "My instructions, my travel voucher, were signed by Comrade Trotsky," Zander admitted.

"So once again we observe you carrying out the directives of Trotsky. And you would have us believe that this is mere coincidence."

"At the time Trotsky signed my instructions, he was Commissar of War. He issued orders to thousands of people and nobody considered them traitors because they obeyed him. They would have been taken for traitors and shot if they hadn't!"

"You were accompanied to Ekaterinburg by a female code clerk named Lili Mikhailovna, the twin sister of Prince Yusupov," the interrogator moved on smoothly. He took a photograph from under his blotter and held it up. Zander leaned forward and squinted. He realized it was his photograph of Lili, taken in front of the Kremlin wall before they left for Ekaterinburg. He reached out a hand for the photograph, but Comrade Zhilov slipped it under his blotter again. "You were on intimate terms with this woman. You do not deny this?"

Zander didn't say anything.

"This is the same Lili Mikhailovna who was shot as an enemy of the people for organizing the escape from Bolshevik control of an important prisoner?"

Again Zander remained silent. How could he explain seventeen years after the fact how Lili had suffered in the civil war; how their near execution had unnerved her; how she had rebelled against the killing and saved the first person she could?

"Do you want me to repeat the question?"

Zander shook his head. "Lili Mikhailovna was shot for helping someone else escape being shot. But I don't see the connection between something that happened seventeen years ago at the height of a vicious civil war, and the reading of a poem now."

"There is a connection between the two events," the interrogator insisted. "All that remains is for us, working together, to figure out what it is."

"HOW DID IT GO LAST NIGHT?" Zander's neighbor tapped out the next morning.

"SAME AS USUAL. I AM STILL NOT GIVING THEM THE TRUTHS THEY NEED. HOW ABOUT YOU?"

"I KEEP GETTING DETAILS OF MY SECRET MEETINGS WITH BRITISH SECRET SERVICE AGENTS WRONG. SO THEY PINCHED MY BALLS WITH PLIERS. I THANKED THEM PROFUSELY FOR THEIR HELP. PAIN IS A GREAT STIMULATOR OF MEMORY. HA HA HA HA."

4

They had confiscated his collected Pushkin the day of his arrest, but he remembered bits. "Stalin cannot be a genius," he mumbled. His lips were swollen from the beatings, two or three teeth were loose, talking was painful, but he needed to prod them on.

"How so?" inquired the interrogator with the bloodshot eyes and a complexion so sallow he looked as if he had been in jail longer than most of the prisoners. The other interrogator, the one with the calluses on his knuckles and a deranged fix to his gray eyes, was out of the room at the moment.

Ronzha gasped in pain. They had stripped him naked and wrapped him like an Egyptian mummy in wet canvas, and then covered him with warm blankets. As the canvas dried, it tightened around his body like a vise. At first it felt as if somebody were hugging him. Then it began to hurt. Eventually the pain would become excruciating, especially around his ribs, all of which were cracked or bruised. While he could still breathe, he would scream. Then he would pass out.

"How so?" the interrogator repeated. He bared two rows of decaying teeth in an encouraging smile.

The interrogator with the callused knuckles came back into the room buttoning his fly. Ronzha cited his source in his head; he was quoting from Pushkin's verse play *Mozart and Salieri*, from the episode in which Mozart, refusing to believe that Salieri wants to poison him, says, "Genius and crime are incompatible."

"Stalin cannot be a genius," Ronzha said slowly, "because genius and crime are incompatible."

"What does he say now?" Callused Knuckles asked.

"In his decadent intellectual way, he is accusing the leading light of international communism, Comrade Stalin, of being a criminal."

Callused Knuckles brought up a burp of displeasure from the back of his throat, and gave Ronzha a playful open-handed slap across the face. The poet's head snapped back into the stone wall. The crack reverberated through his skull. Flashes of light danced on the surface of his eyes, and for an instant he thought the room had exploded. The pain was intense . . . overpowered the thinking process . . . no longer originating thoughts . . . not enough air . . . everything gone blank . . . pain receding . . . he would have to emigrate . . . poets had become internal émigrés . . . they wandered off into the labyrinth of literature, where Soviet power couldn't follow . . . Pushkin would be waiting for him somewhere in there . . . Pushkin would protect him . . .

They brought him around with a bucket of ice water to the face. For a long moment Ronzha was convinced he was dead. Gradually it dawned on him he was only wet. He figured out where he was. And eventually, who he was.

Because the days followed one another, they had come to resemble one another. He had trouble remembering the sequence in which events took place. Had he been tortured before he was arrested, or after? At what point had they brought him back to consciousness with a bucket of water in the face, before or after he passed out? Had he somehow managed to recite his poem on Stalin before he wrote it? He was embarrassed to ask. They would think him a fool, or worse; a crazy man. He himself knew he wasn't crazy. He had only lost touch with the sense of sequence; it was like someone without depth perception looking at a landscape.

Bloodshot Eyes assumed the role of male nurse and helped Ronzha on with his clothes. It was a long, drawn-out affair. Stepping into his pajama bottoms a leg at a time, pulling them up, doing up the buttons of the pajama top, were matters that required major concentration on both their parts. Where Callused Knuckles inflicted pain, Bloodshot Eyes went out of his way to avoid it. Ronzha had given the matter some thought. In the end he decided that Callused Knuckles and Bloodshot Eyes must have started out their careers on some middle ground, and gravitated away from each other so that they would complement each other; they had become, in a manner of speaking, lovers who functioned efficiently because they came at a problem from opposite ends of the spectrum.

Bloodshot Eyes eased Ronzha onto a wooden chair, fitted his eyeglasses to his head, and handed him the typed confession. As Ronzha read it, Bloodshot Eyes uncapped a fountain pen and fitted the cover onto the back end. "You only got to sign your name and your troubles are over," he told Ronzha in an almost caressing voice. "There will be a trial at which you can confirm your confession. Then off you go to Central Asia for a fiver at the most. After all, it was only a poem."

Ronzha knew Bloodshot Eyes was lying through his decaying teeth. They had badly damaged his body. It would never do to trot him out for a public confession. Once he signed, he would be taken down to the basement, where the walls were so thick they dampened the sound of pistol shots to the nape of the neck. More than once Ronzha had been tempted to give in to them, tempted to put an end to his exile from the labyrinth of literature. But he always caught himself at the last moment. A poet did not live in the present. He lived in time. He was responsible to the poets who went before him and to the ones who would come after him. To him it was as if all poets in time came from the same bone

and the same marrow and the same seed. Above all, he
must not betray them by signing a false confession.
Even this poetryless era must have its portion of poetry: someone who cannot be lured into the Socialist
mold; who does not bend before the Kremlin mountaineer and the half men who flock around him. His only
hope of release, he knew, was to push his tormentors to
kill him by accident.

Ronzha held out his hand for the fountain pen. Bloodshot Eyes slapped it into his palm. Ronzha flattened the
confession on the desk and leaned painfully over it and
scratched a signature at the bottom of the page.

Callused Knuckles and Bloodshot Eyes exchanged
triumphant looks. Callused Knuckles snatched the sheet
of paper off the desk. "He signed 'Franz Kafka.' "

"Who is this guy Franz Kafka?" Bloodshot Eyes demanded in annoyance.

"Maybe he is a co-conspirator," Callused Knuckles
suggested with a snarl.

"You are trying my patience," Bloodshot Eyes said.
"I ask you again: who is Franz Kafka?"

Ronzha started to cough up a laugh. Callused Knuckles approached the chair and punched the poet in the
stomach, cutting off his breath and the laugh with it.
Ronzha doubled over.

"We want to know who this Franz Kafka is," Callused
Knuckles told him.

Bloodshot Eyes wagged a finger like an irritated school-
teacher. "What is Kafka's connection with the anti-
Soviet Trotskyist movement?" When Ronzha didn't reply,
he shrugged at Callused Knuckles, who slapped the
poet hard across the face.

More blows followed. Ronzha started going under
again. He experienced the blows without undue dis-
comfort; he was anesthetized against pain. The questions fell like drops into his ear.

Hamlet's father had died from drops in the ear. With
any luck he would too.

"Tell us who Franz Kafka is."

"A highly placed Bolshevik who wrote the anti-Stalin
poem you read?"

"Kafka is definitely a foreign-sounding name."

"Is this Kafka character your contact with the German High Command?"

"A German Jew who reports directly to Hitler?"

Before he lost consciousness completely, Ronzha heard Bloodshot Eyes say to Callused Knuckles, "We got to find out who this Franz Kafka is or we will be in a lot of trouble."

When he came to, he was stretched out on his straw pallet in the common cell. Madame Zubina was bending over him, her face a mask of concern, wiping away the dried blood with a piece of silk she had torn from her slip and dampened with saliva. She kept a rough army blanket draped like a shawl over her thin summer dress with daffodils printed on the fabric. She had been picked off the street the previous August, and then somehow overlooked. She had never been accused of any crime, never been summoned for questioning—and, aside from the blanket they gave her the day she was logged in, never been issued with winter clothing when the season changed. It was as if she had ceased to exist. "Be simple," Madame Zubina, who must have been in her late sixties, chided the poet now. She had a way of talking that sounded like a pigeon cooing. "Sign whatever it is they want you to sign."

Ronzha tried to work his lips, but they were too swollen to move. He thought of Appolinaria. Tears welled in his eyes. Be simple, Madame Zubina advised. He recalled a character named Nezhdanov—in Turgenev's *Virgin Soil*—explaining his imminent suicide by saying, "I could not simplify myself."

"Me too," Ronzha managed to mutter like a ventriloquist, speaking without moving his lips.

"You too, what?" Madame Zubina asked. She brought a finger up to her lips. "Never mind. Save your strength. Don't talk. Listen."

Ronzha listened for the silences. There was a continuous buzzing in his ear where Callused Knuckles had punched him harder than usual. He tried to will the buzzing away, to turn it off as if it were static on a wireless set, but it wouldn't disappear. He needed silence desperately. He needed to hear the poetry in the silences between the words, but the silences were slipping away, and the poetry with them. Soon they would both be beyond his reach.

The saving grace of the common cell was that it had a relatively rich cultural life. At midday the guard opened the door and tossed in a pile of toilet paper—pages torn from confiscated books—and the prisoners quickly gathered in the middle of the cell to compare notes. With any luck they would find four or five consecutive pages from the same book, and organize a "reading" after lunch. At midafternoon the inmates assembled for the daily lecture, which was held in Ronzha's corner so he could attend. Two weeks before there had been a brilliant talk on plankton by a famous marine biologist. The previous day an expert on fossils, a former curator of the Moscow Natural History Museum, had presented evidence to support his conclusion that the earth had experienced a periodic cataclysm, which wiped out whole species, every twenty-six million years.

"Maybe *that* explains what is happening in Russia!" a well-known Jewish radio comedian cried excitedly. "The twenty-six million years you're talking about, they must be up this year. Stalin is only doing nature's work. This time the species to be wiped out is obviously the human race."

The night of the lecture the radio comedian had been called out for interrogation. "Keep my pallet warm," he had stage-whispered as he headed for the door. "I am going to warn the authorities about this twenty-six-million-year business." He had let his jowls droop in mock despair. "It's just my luck to be born when a cataclysm is due."

When Ronzha woke the next morning, the comedian's pallet was still empty. He never returned to the cell.

Two nights later the interrogators got around to Ronzha again. "God bless you," Madame Zubina whispered as she helped the poet to his feet.

"Since all things are permitted, I no longer believe

God exists," Ronzha told her in his ventriloquist's voice. "But God bless you too."

Threading his way a step at a time around the pallets, the poet headed for the door of the cell. Madame Zubina caught up with him. "I lost my son to the terror," she whispered urgently. "I beg you to let me adopt you."

"No," the poet said.

"But why?"

Ronzha said, "I don't want you to lose a second son." He reached for her hand and touched his swollen lips to the back of it.

In the interrogation room Callused Knuckles was pulling on a pair of skin-colored surgeon's gloves. "Bruised hands?" Ronzha asked solicitously.

Callused Knuckles glared at him menacingly.

"He is only trying to provoke you," Bloodshot Eyes warned his colleague.

Callused Knuckles went back to pulling on his gloves.

Bloodshot Eyes waved Ronzha toward the wooden chair in the middle of the room. The poet, who was wearing a long-sleeved prison jacket over his shirt, shivered involuntarily. The night before, Madame Zubina had pressed her lips to his forehead as if he were a small child and had announced that he was running a fever, but Bloodshot Eyes took the shivering for a sign of fear. He pulled up his chair so that he was facing Ronzha. "Look," he began, "what if we worked out a compromise? Yegor here, and me, we got to come out of this with something to show for our troubles or they will accuse us of lack of vigilance, of covering up a conspiracy even."

Ronzha shivered again, and Bloodshot Eyes thought he was getting somewhere. "What if we was to drop the charge about you being in actual touch with the Trotskyist center? What if we was to settle for you admitting that reading out that poem was your way of trying to contact other people who thought like you? In other words, it was the first stage of a conspiracy. You did not actually plot with anyone. You was only reaching out to find others to plot with, maybe hoping, let's say hoping, if there was enough of you, to offer your services to the Trotskyist center. Since no actual sabotage was committed, you would get off with a slap on the wrists. What do you say to that?"

Ronzha's ventriloquist voice rasped out. "Can I ask you a question?"

"Ask. Ask."

"I heard that Lenin's body in the mausoleum has been replaced by a wax dummy because the embalming fluids couldn't stop the syphilis from decaying his corpse. I would like to know if this is so."

Bloodshot Eyes stood up and scraped his chair away to give his colleague room to work in. Callused Knuckles strolled over to Ronzha and measured him the way a tailor might size up a client for a suit. Then he swung. The blow landed on the poet's nose, shattering the bone, the cartilage, with a sickening crunch. Ronzha's head snapped back. The chair he was sitting on went over. The poet's head struck the stone floor. He coughed up blood.

Callused Knuckles righted the chair, and holding Ronzha at arm's length to avoid getting spattered with blood, set him back down on it.

"You hit him too hard," Bloodshot Eyes said worriedly. "His eyes are not focusing."

"I hit him like I always hit him," Callused Knuckles protested.

"Can you hear me?" Bloodshot Eyes called to Ronzha. He waved a hand in front of the poet's face.

Through a haze of pain the poet could make out a voice, but it seemed to come from the other side of a river. Had he finally crossed the Styx? If so, only a little bit of the journey remained. It was time, he told himself, to begin thinking about last words. His thoughts turned to Pushkin. He had fallen under the bullet fired by D'Anthes. In the dark library of the little house on the Moika Canal, he had screamed in pain for one full day and half of the next. Moments before he died, Pushkin had opened his eyes. "Good-bye my friends . . . life is over!"

Ronzha wanted to do better than that.

Suddenly the poet was desperately afraid he would not finish the voyage. He needed more help. Although it was extremely painful, he tried to move his lips. "Identification of morality . . . with a single leader, whether Hitler or Stalin, is a reversion . . . a reversion to infant . . . infantile . . . infantilism," he said.

He closed his eyes and waited for the blow. It landed above his right eye. Ronzha sensed himself spilling over backward. The buzzing in his ear grew to a roar; he was standing on the far bank of the Styx, directly under a waterfall. He felt his heart abruptly stop beating. He forced Gogol's line through his dead lips.

"Suddenly you *could* see far to the ends of the earth."

5

The two men who turned up at the theater were so well-dressed that Masha took them for producers. They folded their overcoats neatly over the backs of seats in the twelfth row of the empty auditorium and settled down to watch the rehearsal.

"You are coming on too strong, Masha," the director called up from the front row. He was an intense young man who wore special eyeglasses with tinted lenses even indoors. "You have to keep in mind you only just met him."

"I thought the object was to let him know I was interested," Masha replied. She stood facing the director with her hands on her hips, watching the two producers out of the corner of her eye. It wasn't her imagination; they both seemed to be paying a great deal of attention to her.

"You can let him know you are interested, but in an *expensive* way, as opposed to a *cheap* way, if you see what I mean. The trick is to project the new Soviet woman's confidence in herself without losing her basic sense of modesty. Take it again from where Evgeny asks you if his application for Party membership has been processed."

Masha slipped on the prop eyeglasses and turned to face the actor who played Evgeny.

"I am sorry to bother you," he began.

"You are not bothering me," Masha replied briskly. She tried to make her voice sound more businesslike than before. "That's what I am here for."

"I was wondering," Evgeny went on, appropriately hesitant, "if my application to join the Party has been processed yet."

"What's your name?" Masha asked with the slightest intonation of annoyance.

"Kotin. Evgeny Sergeyevich Kotin."

Masha allowed her eyes to widen a notch. "The aviator? The one who landed alongside the icebreaker trapped in the Arctic?"

Evgeny smiled modestly.

"I thought you looked familiar! I saw your photograph in *Pravda*." Masha let a note of sexual excitement creep into her voice. "The one of Comrade Stalin pinning the medal on you." Here she dipped into her husky register; if the two producers had a motion picture role in mind for her, they couldn't help but be impressed. "Tell me something. What is he *really* like?"

Evgeny thought a moment before answering. "He looks you right in the eye. His handshake is firm, honest, straightforward—the handshake of a working-man. He asked me questions about my airplane—about its navigational equipment, about the special runners I used to land on the ice cap, about the performance of high octane fuel in low temperatures—that showed he was an expert on the technical aspects of aviation. I will tell you something I haven't told anyone before—I slept more soundly after I met Comrade Stalin. Our country's fate is in good hands."

"That's better," the director called up. "That's much better."

Later, the two producers, their overcoats draped over

their arms, came around to Masha's dressing room. The door was open, but they knocked anyhow. "Please come in," Masha called. She tried to project that she was interested, but in an *expensive* way.

One of the men hung back at the door. The other, smiling politely, approached and held up a card for her to see. Masha assumed he was identifying himself as a member of the All-Soviet Producers' Union. Then she caught a glimpse of the letters NKVD. Her first coherent thought was to thank God she was sitting down. Her second was that she had to convince them she was innocent. "I swear to you on a stack of Bibles," she blurted out. "I don't believe in God myself," she stammered hurriedly. "The business about Bibles was only an expression. But I swear to you it was a joke. I can see now, in the cold light of day, that it may have been in bad taste."

The man who had shown her his card asked, "What was a joke?"

"The little ditty I sang at the party last night. I'd been drinking quite a lot—"

"What little ditty?"

Masha took a deep breath. They obviously knew all about it, or they wouldn't be here. They were testing her. The best tactic was to tell them everything and convince them of her honesty. What a little fool she was. She'd been drinking, but she hadn't been drunk. She'd been showing off for the screenwriter who asked her if she had ever played the role of a singer. By way of an answer, she had draped herself Marlene Dietrich-like across a piano, one arm thrown back to thrust her breasts into the silk of her blouse, and belted out a two-liner known as "The Moscow Blues."

> The NKVD has run out of glue,
> I haven't had any mail for weeks.

Everyone had thought it was quite funny at the time. Now it seemed to have lost all its humor.

The man who had posted himself at the door advanced into the dressing room. "She thinks we came because of the song she sang last night," he told his colleague.

"That is not the reason," the first NKVD man assured her. "That is not it at all."

"We can take a joke as well as the next person," the man nearest the door assured her.

Masha sank back into her chair. "Why are you here?"

"We understand you were intimate with a man who worked until recently for Tass. His name is Alexander Til."

Masha treated them to her most innocent smile. "Alexander and I broke up months ago!"

"You did know him though?"

She nodded feebly.

"I am afraid we are going to have to invite you to come back with us. We want to ask you some questions about him."

"Am I being arrested?"

"Let us say you are being detained," the man nearest the door replied. "If you answer honestly, if you clear up any misunderstanding, you will be on your way home in no time."

At their office the two NKVD men hung their coats and Masha's on wooden hangers on the back of their door, then began to ply her with endless cups of coffee and endless questions. Where exactly had she met Til? What did he talk about? Who were his friends? What was the relationship between him and his step-daughter? Who had been close enough to the step-daughter to hide her? At one point the NKVD man who kept refilling Masha's cup with coffee asked if Til was "normal."

"Normal in what way?"

"Normal sexually."

Masha averted her eyes to project the new Soviet woman's basic sense of modesty. "Yes," she said in an almost inaudible voice.

Throughout the afternoon she stuck to the cover story she and Zander had worked out. "I wrote him the letter because I didn't want to face the pain of breaking off with him in person," she told them. Again, she let her voice slip into its husky register; she knew that most men found it irresistible. "I was attracted to him, I admit it, because I thought he was an honest revolutionist, a real Party man. When I discovered he was not as ardent as I thought, I put an end to our relationship."

One of the NKVD men reached into a file folder, pulled out a piece of paper, and held it up for her to see. "Is this the letter you are referring to?"

"That's it," Masha cried excitedly. She allowed little flutters of vulnerability into her voice. "That's my letter. I would recognize it anywhere. Now that I think of it, he even wrote me an answer."

The NKVD man produced that letter too. "We took the liberty of searching your apartment before we came to the theater."

It was getting dark outside. One of the NKVD men stood up and switched on the overhead light. Then he did something that sent a chill down Masha's spine. He switched from the polite second person plural "*vui*" to the more intimate "*ti*," which, in the context of an interrogation, sounded, as it was meant to, insulting and menacing.

"You are not being very helpful," he complained in a thin voice.

"I think the best thing is for you to spend the night here," the other said; he also used "*ti*." "Sleep on it. Maybe tomorrow you will do better."

Spending the night at the NKVD holding center meant following its regulations concerning detainees. Two uniformed NKVD soldiers escorted Masha to a dressing room with long, low wooden benches and metal hooks on the walls for clothing.

"Undress," one of them ordered.

The two soldiers stood there leering at her with silly grins on their broad peasant faces. "What are you waiting for?" the other asked.

"I am waiting for you to behave like gentlemen and leave."

"If you will not undress yourself, we will undress you," the soldier with the widest grin warned her.

"You wouldn't dare," Masha said, backing away from them. Both soldiers started toward her. "All right, all right," she cried, holding up a palm. Furious at being humiliated this way, she spun around and began removing her clothing.

"Into the shower room with you," one of the uniformed guards ordered.

With one hand covering her breasts and the other over her pubic hair, she padded barefoot between the guards through an archway into a large, cold, white-tiled room with a dozen shower nozzles protruding from the walls on either side. One of the soldiers tossed her a bar of dark brown soap that smelled of tar. To catch it, Masha had to expose her breasts and pubic hair. The two soldiers laughed happily. Tears streamed down Masha's face. "Stop babbling," one of the guards ordered, nodding toward the nearest showerhead.

Masha tried the left-hand faucet. Nothing came out of the nozzle.

"There is only cold," the other guard said, and they both laughed at the expression on her face. "Cold is good for the nipples," the guard added. "Makes them stand to attention."

Back in the dressing room, Masha found a bearded man in a white medical coat waiting for her. A saliva-soaked cigarette dangled from his chapped lips. He wore a tight-fitting transparent glove on his right hand and held a battery-powered army field lamp in his left. "Turn around and grab your ankles without bending your knees," he ordered in a bored voice.

Masha understood instantly what he had in mind. She backed up until she was flat against the icy wall. "Never," she said in a furious whisper. "I will die first."

The medical attendant signaled with his hand for the two soldiers to help him. They closed in on Masha from either side. "Please," she whimpered as they reached out and gripped her wrists. In an instant she was folded over like a napkin. The attendant kicked her legs apart, and dropping to one knee, roughly inserted a finger into her anus, and then two fingers into her vagina. Masha gagged on a scream, and threw up on the floor beneath her head.

"She's clean," the attendant said.

Later, the two soldiers handed her a dark cotton dress that reeked of disinfectant, a pair of slippers with no backs, and an old army blanket that smelled of vomit. They took a meticulous inventory of her clothing— "One lace brassiere, pink; one pair of cotton underpants, pink, with hand-sewn initials on the seam"—and insisted she sign it. They turned her pocketbook upside down, spilling the contents onto the floor, and listed on a form everything that was in it. Then they led her, shuffling along between them in the slippers without backs and the dress that smelled of disinfectant, down a corridor to a minuscule room with a toilet bucket in it, and nothing else. The toilet bucket was full. "Sleep well," one of the guards called with a laugh as he swung the door shut after her.

"For the love of God, come back," Masha screamed at the closed door, and she pounded it with the flat of her hand until her wrist ached. Wrapping herself in the foul-smelling army blanket, she sank onto the floor in a corner of the pitch-dark room and cried her heart out.

She tried to sleep, but the smell of the toilet bucket and the blanket, and the thoughts racing through her head, kept her alert. In the middle of the night a heavy door clanged shut not far from her. After a while she heard the distinct sound of someone tapping on the wall of her cell, but she had no idea what it meant, and she didn't tap back.

In the morning the same two uniformed guards returned her clothing, insisted she check to make sure everything was accounted for, and had her sign a receipt. She was allowed to dress in private, and led through the corridors back to the room where the two NKVD men were waiting for her. One of them politely held out a seat for her. The other brought over a steaming cup of coffee and a fresh bun.

"Sugar?" he asked.

"Two."

"Excuse my fingers." He dropped two lumps into her cup. She stirred the coffee with a small spoon, and when it was cooler began sipping it. The NKVD men didn't rush her. When she had finished, one of them relieved her of the cup and saucer.

"Thank you," she said.

"It was only a cup of coffee," the NKVD man said with a pleasant smile.

The other NKVD man, sitting behind the desk, cleared his throat. "Have you"—he again addressed her with "*vui*'—"thought of anything else during the night you might want to tell us about Alexander Til?"

"Actually," Masha answered, trying without success to keep her voice from sounding cheap, "I have."

From the window over the kitchen's pitted sink, Ludmilla could make out the mountain range that dominated the city of Alma Ata. Snow covered the peaks twelve months of the year. The peasant who sold her the koumiss, fermented mare's milk, claimed you could see China from the highest peak of the highest mountain. Ludmilla remembered a line of Gogol's that Ronzha loved to recite: "Suddenly you could see far to the ends of the earth." If only she could *go* to the ends of the earth! It probably wouldn't make any difference. There would be people there waiting to denounce you, and police waiting to arrest you. In this little game of life, she decided, there were no winners, only players.

She opened the small door of the cooking stove and threw in half a shovelful of coal, then added a pinch of salt to the soup of herring heads simmering on top of the stove. It occurred to her, not for the first time, that one of the most depressing things in life was to cook for yourself. After the soup she would eat the herrings, which she had marinated in sweet vinegar, along with a kind of kasha made of unground rye. It was all very unappetizing.

Ludmilla had been in Alma Ata, in Masha's apartment, for sixty-six days, which worked out to nine and a half weeks, which worked out to a week more than two months. Pressed, she could even say how many hours. And hardly a single one of them went by without her having an imaginary conversation with Alexander. "It's this way," she would begin, and in her mind's eye she could see him angling his head so that his good ear was cocked at her. "If all our top people who make the plans work for the Germans the way Stalin says, why does Hitler need thousands of spies to find out what our plans are?" And she could imagine Alexander's brow furrowing, and him saying, "I hope to God you don't ask other people this kind of question." And her complaining, "But you didn't answer me!" And him shaking his head and saying, "The answer is self-evident."

Ludmilla was straining out the herring heads from the soup when she heard a rush of footsteps on the stairs. Her first thought was that it was Vanka, the teenage son of the couple on the second floor, running up to tell her to turn on the radio to such and such a frequency, that they were playing something of Prokofiev's or Stravinsky's. Then she heard a heavy fist hammering on the door and she knew it wasn't Vanka; he always knocked with his knuckles, three light raps, then three more.

"It's this way," she said out loud, trying to control the fear that surged up through her body to her throat and tightened around it so that it suddenly became difficult to breathe. "There is no reason for me to be alarmed. All that has happened is that Russia is a lottery and my number has come up."

Whoever was at the door pounded again. Walking with a determined step, Ludmilla went to open it.

Like the other boxes before it, Arishka had devoted hours to the packing of this one. She had weighed it several times to make sure it didn't go over the allowed limit by so much as a feather. She had checked off each item on the mimeographed list as she put it inside: one woolen shirt, two pairs of woolen socks, a pair of shoes, one undershirt, one toothbrush, five bars of soap, a

pound of sausages, a pound of cheese, a loaf of bread
not to exceed half a pound, a pound of apples. She
knew Arkadey didn't smoke, but she had added three
ounces of tobacco and a supply of matches and cigarette
paper on the theory that he could use it for bartering
with other prisoners.

Now, clutching the box to her breast, she waited
with hundreds of other women outside Butyrskaya Prison
off Novoslobodskaya Street in north-central Moscow.
There was an icy wind that morning, and the women
had all pulled kerchiefs over their heads. The array of
colors and textures stood in sharp contrast to the gray-
ness of the day and the grimness of the occasion. They
stood patiently, wordlessly, in the line that snaked alongside the brick battlement and under an archway, then
diagonally across a cement courtyard to a green door
with a small sign over it that read, INQUIRIES BUREAU.

Most of the women kept their heads bent under their
kerchiefs and their eyes fixed on the feet of the person
in front. Occasionally, though, Arishka's eyes met those
of another woman, and there would occur a flicker of
recognition that passes between absolute strangers who
share the same pain.

Arishka had been queuing for almost two hours, when
she noticed a woman up ahead staring back at her.
Arishka nodded faintly. The woman gave up her place
in line to join Arishka.

"For God's sake, don't ever tell Pasha that you have
seen me here," Serafima Fedorovna whispered.

"Of course I won't," Arishka whispered back. She
nodded toward the box in Serafima's hands. "Who is
that for?"

Serafima answered in an even lower whisper, "Zander. He has been in for over two months now. All
because of a poem. It was anti-Soviet and all that, but
what I think is that the writer should be punished, not
the listener. I mean, you can always keep people from
writing, but how can you keep them from listening
when you don't know what you will hear until you have
heard it? When I tell this to Pasha, he gets furious with

me. He says women should keep their noses out of things that don't concern them." Serafima glanced at Arishka's box. "Who are you queuing for?"

"A friend." Arishka smiled sadly. "He disappeared a month ago. I am hoping against hope it is all a mistake." She began to sob very quietly. "The worst part is nobody will say where he is. So I have been going from prison to prison and leaving a box with his name on it at each one. I do a different prison every time I can get a day off. I've done Lefortovo and Lubyanka already."

"Can't your ex help?" Serafima, always practical, asked.

"He tried, but he hasn't been able to find out anything."

"Well, with any luck, he may be in Butyrskaya," Serafima said hopefully. "Maybe he and Zander are cellmates."

By midafternoon both Arishka and Serafima had advanced inside the inquiries bureau. Two women stood behind the counter weighing each package on a butcher's scale suspended by a chain from the ceiling, then meticulously noting in an enormous ledger the name of the sender and the addressee. Both women wrote the way people do who have only recently learned how to. The nibs of their pens scratched painfully across the page, then lifted off and hovered as the women examined what they had written for errors.

One of the women weighed Serafima's package, and made the appropriate notations in the ledger. The other woman took Arishka's package, and checked the name on it against a typewritten list. "We got no Lifshits, Arkadey Eremeyevich, here," she told Arishka, sliding the package across the counter.

Arishka pushed it back again. "Could you take it anyhow, just in case?"

The woman shook her head angrily and pushed it back to Arishka. "We accept packages only for prisoners on the master list." She looked past Arishka and called, "Next."

Arishka didn't move. "Please," she insisted. "They accepted my package at Lefortovo and Lubyanka and they didn't have his name there either."

"It is out of the question," the woman said stubbornly.

In her desperation Arishka began to raise her voice. "I am going down on my knees. I am begging you, one woman to another. How will it hurt you to take my package?"

The other woman behind the counter reached for a telephone.

"Come away," Serafima pleaded. She linked her arm through Arishka's and started to pull her toward the door.

"Get her out of here before I call the guard," the woman with her hand on the telephone ordered. She fingered the telephone the way a policeman might have caressed the butt of his pistol.

"Think of it as good news," Serafima tried to tell Arishka as they walked back across the courtyard. "It means he is not here."

Arishka's voice emerged in a barely stifled scream. "Oh, Arkadey, where are you?"

Scores of women on the line, hearing the cry of pain, raised their eyes without raising their heads.

"Be strong," someone called as Serafima pulled Arishka past.

"Have faith."

"Don't bear children!"

Leaning over the railing of the last balcony in the Bolshoi—the seats were so high up the regulars referred to the section as "paradise" —Alyosha Zhitkin watched the members of the orchestra file onto the stage. There was a stir when Stalin appeared in the royal box. Several hundred people in the orchestra section turned and started applauding, but Stalin cut off the ovation with a pleasant wave of his hand.

Below, on the stage, the first violinist stood with his back to the audience and offered the orchestra a middle "A." The violinists closest to him picked it up. Then the cellos. Then the base fiddles. In a moment the middle A, inflated like a balloon, was ricocheting around the orchestra. What would happen, Alyosha asked himself, if the first violinist were off key? Would somebody stand up and tell him? Or would the entire orchestra tune to the wrong note? Would a first violinist who gave the wrong note be considered a musical wrecker?

There was a smattering of applause as the conductor pushed the soloist up to the piano in a wicker wheelchair. The house lights dimmed. The audience settled down. Stalin, obscured in the shadows in the back of the royal box, relighted his pipe. Onstage, the pianist warmed his hands between his paralyzed thighs for a long moment, then slowly lifted them until his fingers were poised over the keyboard. Alyosha wondered if the stories about the pianist were true. It was rumored that he had been arrested after his wife's brother canvassed delegates at the Seventeenth Party Congress about the possibility of kicking Stalin upstairs and turning over his post of Secretary General of the Party to Kirov; had been crippled by NKVD interrogators trying to beat a confession out of him; had only been saved when Stalin casually asked for one of his recordings.

After the concert Alyosha squeezed into a crowded trolley heading out to the ring road, and walked the last half mile to his home.

The nights were still sharp, but the cutting edge of winter had been blunted. Any day now the first buds would appear on the trees that had not been cut down for firewood, and if Moscow was not hit by a last frost, they would eventually blossom. Turning the final corner, Alyosha was annoyed to notice a light on in his third-floor room; the price of electricity being what it was, he always made it a point to turn everything off when he left. He paused inside the lobby to roll a cigar and light it on the embers of the one in his mouth. Then, his mind a total blank, he climbed the steps to the third floor and let himself into his room.

Neither of the men waiting for him stood when he entered. One of them held up a card and when Alyosha, frowning, had taken in its contents, he nodded toward a chair. Alyosha said, "Do you mind if I hang up my overcoat first?"

"Drape it over the back of a chair," an NKVD man with a puffy red face ordered. "You may need it again before the night is over."

Alyosha turned his back on the two men and deliberately took his time hanging up the overcoat in the closet. When he finally sat down, it was on a chair that he pulled over, and not the one the NKVD men had prepared for him.

The second agent was younger than the first, and his short stubby hands reminded Alyosha of a line from Ronzha's poem: "His fingers are as fat as grubs." With his fat fingers the agent pulled a brown government envelope from his breast pocket, carefully removed two typewritten sheets of paper from it, and reached across to offer them to Alyosha.

"You want me to read these?"

"We want you to sign them. If you feel you must read them before you sign them, we will not raise objections."

Alyosha studied the two pages carefully. Then he looked up. "Not a single word is true. Not one."

The younger NKVD man said, "We would not have asked you to sign if it were not true."

Alyosha shook his head. The cigar danced on his lower lip. "I never saw him meet with"—here Alyosha named a prominent member of the Politburo who had recently been executed as a German spy—"in the back of a coffeeshop."

The red-faced agent said, "You cannot be certain your friend Til did not meet him."

Alyosha's shoulders heaved in frustration. "How the hell could I be certain he did *not* meet with someone?"

"Then he could have met with him?"

"He could have. But I did not see him do it."

The red-faced agent tried a new tack. "You did your duty when the anti-Soviet poem was read. Til did not. Why don't you draw the correct conclusion from his behavior?"

"I denounced the poet because his poem was anti-Soviet. If I knew Til had committed an anti-Soviet act, I would denounce him too. But I won't invent things. All this"—Alyosha slapped the two typewritten sheets with the back of his hand—"is bullshit. I never saw him speaking to this man. And he never tried to draw me into a conspiracy. He never said any of the things you say he said. Not to me."

The younger of the NKVD men popped out of his chair and walked over to look out of the window. The red-faced agent took several noisy breaths through his nostrils. "You have a clean record," he said carefully. "Nobody's accusing you of anything. But your Party is asking you to sign a piece of paper that the Party needs. Russia is surrounded by enemies. We must make examples to discourage traitors before they have a chance to betray the country and the Party."

The younger agent went over to the wall switch and flicked the overhead light off and on several times. Then he returned to the window and cupped his hands around his face and peered out into the night. From the street came the distant cough of several automobile engines starting up.

"We have ways of making people sign things we want them to sign," the red-faced agent told Alyosha.

Alyosha stood up. "All right. Let's go."

The two NKVD men exchanged looks. The younger one walked over to Alyosha, casually slapped the cigar out of his mouth, spun him around, and shoved him roughly against the wall. Then he kicked his feet apart and body-searched him. "He is clean," he told his colleague.

He pulled Alyosha's overcoat from the closet and checked it too, and tossed it to him. Then he produced a pair of handcuffs and clicked them open and held them out.

Alyosha seemed to lose heart. "Can I see those papers again?" he asked.

The younger agent snorted and started to reach into his breast pocket for the government envelope. "You are saving everybody a lot of—" Before he could finish the sentence, Alyosha stepped forward and hit him with all his strength in the stomach, and then pushed him back into the second NKVD agent, who clutched at the back of a chair to keep from falling. Alyosha bolted from the room down the stairs to the lobby and ducked through the door that led down a long, unlighted corridor to the alleyway behind the building. He could hear the two NKVD men bellowing inside the building as he pulled open the outside door and trotted off into the night.

He didn't really see he had much choice. Signing his name to a total fabrication was out of the question. And he was not about to let himself be arrested. Which narrowed his options down to the brewery. In a long-forgotten past it had been a gem of a church, built to honor some empress or other, its high central dome decorated with the most benevolent Jesus Alyosha had ever laid eyes on. Immediately after the revolution the icons had been tossed onto a bonfire in the cloistered patio behind the church, and the building had been converted into a brewery; instead of incense, it smelled now from hops and yeast.

The night watchman was surprised to see Alyosha arrive so early. "I thought you wasn't going to blow her until the day after tomorrow?"

"They have pushed up the schedule," Alyosha told him. "The cranes are going to be available early, so they can start clearing and laying foundations that much sooner."

"Well, seeing as how it is you," the watchman said, and he pulled open the door of the wooden stockade that had been thrown up around the church.

Alyosha sent the old man home and padlocked the stockade door on the inside. Standing directly under the benevolent Jesus, he rolled himself a cigar, lit it, and began uncoiling lengths of electric wire from the reel and laying them out on the floor. The fine art of bringing down churches had changed from the days when he planted sticks of dynamite and cut fuses so they would explode in the right sequence. Now the dynamite came in compact rectangular cartridges. Each of the packages had two terminals. You taped the packages to the bases of the supporting pillars and wired them up to a central console fitted with a battery and a sequential timing device. You could fire the charges all at once, or in a fixed sequence, and build in a delay so the person who threw the switch had time to light up a cigar and meander out of the church and around the corner before the first explosion.

It took Alyosha the better part of two hours to connect the explosive packages to the central console, and another half hour to double-check the terminals. He fixed the sequential settings so that the charges would all go off at the same instant, and set the delay knob at zero. He was rolling the last of his Bulgarian tobacco into a twist of newspaper when he heard the squeal of a bullhorn outside in the street, somewhere beyond the wooden barrier.

"Zhitkin," shouted a voice Alyosha thought he recognized. "You have one minute to come out with your hands over your head."

Alyosha touched the end of his new cigar to what was left of the old one between his lips. He flicked the butt away and played the smoke around in his mouth for a delicious moment.

"You have thirty seconds," warned the voice of the bullhorn.

Alyosha exhaled and peered up through the smoke at the benevolent Jesus, his arms spread as if he were floating down; behind him, the dome billowed like a parachute breaking his fall. Jesus's mouth, Alyosha observed, appeared to be stretched into a faint commiserating smile. It was curious he had never noticed the expression before. Jesus smiled down from such a great height, he looked as if he might be in paradise.

From outside the church came the sound of sledgehammers knocking the rusted hinges off the wooden door of the stockade. An instant later the door was shouldered open and a mass of uniformed NKVD troops, rifles at the ready, surged toward the church. Behind them came the two NKVD agents from the night before. Both held pistols.

"You should have signed when you had the chance,"

the red-faced NKVD man called across the church. Several of the soldiers kneeled and took aim at Alyosha.

Squatting next to the console, Alyosha treated himself to a last drag on his cigar as he closed the contact that would bring the only paradise he would ever know crashing down to earth.

6

Zander had gone two full weeks without an interrogation; without setting foot out of his cell; without hearing the sound of a human voice; without human contact except for his chats with the prisoner in the next cell.

"HOW ARE YOUR EYES?" the neighbor tapped on the wall one morning.

"WORSE. I GET PINPRICKS OF PAIN IN THE PUPIL. WHAT'S NEW AT YOUR TRIAL?"

The neighbor tapped back: "MY FAMILY WAS THERE. EVERYONE LOOKS SO NORMAL. EVEN ME. HA. PROSECUTOR VISHINSKY ASKED IF I HAD BEEN TORMENTED BY MY INTERROGATORS. I SAID IT WAS ME WHO HAD TORMENTED THEM FOR TWO AND A HALF MONTHS BY REFUSING TO CONFESS." There was a pause. "AT LEAST MY SON WILL KNOW I HELD OUT FOR A WHILE."

Zander tried to cheer up his neighbor. "IF THE TRIAL GOES WELL, THE SENTENCES MAY BE LENIENT."

"I HAVE NO ILLUSIONS. THE PRISONS ARE OVERCROWDED, THE CEMETERIES ARE ONLY HALF FULL. HA HA HA."

Although he wouldn't have given his jailers the satisfaction of admitting it, Zander desperately missed his nightly interrogation. It provided a form to the day, gave him something to look forward to. Keeping his wits about him as he fenced with his interrogator had come to seem like useful exercise, the mental equivalent of the long walks he forced himself to take in his cell every morning. Without the nightly sessions, the days, the hours, dragged; no amount of ingenuity could kill all time.

Physically, Zander was deteriorating rapidly. His hair fell out in great clumps. A thin fuzz began growing on the bald spots of his scalp. His eyes were worse than ever; he suffered from constant headaches, and occasional bouts of dizziness that developed into nausea and, once, vomiting. They still slipped books through the slot, and his neighbor repeatedly warned him that they obviously wanted to ruin his eyesight. Zander resisted for long stretches, but time hung around his neck like a leaden medallion, and so he eventually gave in and climbed onto his upside-down toilet bucket, and holding the book up at arm's length, struggled to make out in the dim light of a half-electrified filament the blurred words that still danced across the page.

One morning Zander woke with a particularly painful headache. The trusty wheeling the cart collected the metal breakfast dish through the slot and moved on down the corridor, and Zander, with an entire day stretching endlessly before him, started to pace between the walls of his cell, counting off the steps, determined no matter how much his bad leg ached to do a full four kilometers before lunch, determined also to get through the day without straining his eyes reading the book that the trusty had slipped through the slot that morning. He was brought up sharply by the unmistakable sound of a bolt being thrown on his door. The second bolt was thrown. A young, fresh-faced guard Zander had never seen before beckoned to him from the threshold of the cell.

A pang of panic stabbed Zander's heart and he involuntarily gasped. Interrogations took place at night. Executions took place in the morning. Had they gotten tired of the game and decided to end it?

Zander studied the guard's face for a clue, but found none. At the end of the long corridor Zander, shuffling along in his laceless high shoes, clutching at his pajama bottoms, was steered to the left, and he felt a sudden weight on his chest, a tightening of arteries, a pumping of blood; for interrogations, he had always been taken to the right. They came to a door with a glass window in it. A guard on the other side opened it, and locked it after them, and noted their passage in his log. They descended a metal staircase that reminded Zander of the one in P.S. 160 on Suffolk and Rivington in Manhattan; he could almost hear Leon calling, "Let's get our asses out of here, Zander—they're taking out kids' tonsils through their throats!"

Two flights down, the guard led Zander through a door and then through a maze of well-lit corridors to another door with a wooden bench outside it. He motioned for Zander to sit, and took up a position with his back against the wall facing him. Gradually Zander's heartbeat returned to normal. It didn't look as if they were going to shoot him after all. At least not this morning.

Several minutes later a trusty dressed in an inmate's gray pajama trousers and shirt, and wearing a wrinkled smock that had once been white, came hurrying down the corridor from the opposite direction. Seeing the prisoner on the bench, the trusty did something that struck Zander as nothing short of miraculous: he talked directly to him. What he said was even more amazing.

"I am sorry to have kept you waiting. If you will step into my office—"

Zander looked at the guard, who nodded permission. He followed the trusty into the room, careful to leave the door ajar behind him. Glancing around, he realized he was in a medical office of some sort. The floors, the walls, were spotless. The trusty motioned him into a chair with a high, straight back, and opening a large cabinet, began laying out what looked like optical instruments on a table. "I am going to check your eyes," he explained. "You can have confidence in me. I was trained in Berlin before the Great War, and practiced in Moscow until . . . well, let us say I practiced in Moscow for many years."

The doctor had a difficult time folding Zander's lids back with his thumb. Every time he tried, Zander's head jerked away; he was remembering the alcoholic German doctor turning back the lid of his mother's eye with a buttonhook and announcing that he had discovered traces of trachoma. By sheer persistence the doctor finally managed to examine Zander's eyes. "Do you suffer from headaches?" he asked at one point. "Dizziness? Intermittent pain in the retina? Hmmm. Doesn't surprise me. Your eyes show definite signs of vitamin deficiency. When was the last time you had your vision checked?"

Zander said he had gotten new eyeglasses about three years before.

"Your eyes have deteriorated a great deal since then," the doctor noted. He fitted Zander's glasses over his eyes and hung an eye chart on the opposite wall. "Cover one eye and read the middle line," he ordered.

Zander leaned forward and tried to force the line into focus. "I can't."

The doctor dropped two lenses into a binocularlike contraption and fitted that over Zander's head in place of his eyeglasses. "Try the middle line now."

"It is better," Zander said, "but still blurred."

The doctor replaced the lenses with two others. Zander's mouth fell open in discovery, and he called out the letters excitedly. "R-S-P-F-I!"

"When do I get new eyeglasses?" Zander asked as he was about to leave the office.

The doctor said, "I am only permitted to prescribe. It is the job of others to supply you with the actual glasses." Squeezing Zander's elbow, he whispered urgently, "My name is Evpraksein. Konstantin Evpraksein. Repeat it."

"Konstantin Evpraksein."

"If you get out of here, I have a wife, an old mother, two daughters." Evpraksein whispered an address and made Zander repeat it. "Embrace them for me. Nothing more. Only say I am alive. Only say I think of them."

"If I get out, I will do it."

"WHERE WERE YOU THIS MORNING?" Zander's neighbor tapped on the wall of the cell that afternoon.

"I WAS TAKEN FOR AN EYE EXAMINATION."

"HA HA HA. VERY HUMOROUS. NO KIDDING, WHERE WERE YOU? YOU HAD ME WORRIED."

"AN EYE EXAMINATION, REALLY. HOW DID THE MORNING IN COURT GO?"

"I WAS SPLENDID. I ADMITTED MEETING JAPANESE AGENTS IN STOCKHOLM EVEN THOUGH I HAVE NEVER BEEN THERE IN MY LIFE. I DESCRIBED THE RESTAURANT DOWN TO THE COLOR OF THE TABLECLOTH. MY INTERROGATOR BEAMED WITH PRIDE. PROSECUTOR VISHINSKY ASKED ME HOW I COULD BRING MYSELF TO BETRAY MY COUNTRY. I REPLIED THAT THANKS TO THE INSPIRED LEADERSHIP OF STALIN WE HAD A NEW RUSSIA, BUT DID NOT UNFORTUNATELY YET HAVE NEW RUSSIANS. HA HA."

Zander tapped, "YOU SHOULD RESIST TEMPTATION TO WISECRACK IN COURT. IT WILL ONLY GET YOU IN TROUBLE."

"WHAT AM I IN NOW? HA HA HA HA HA HA HA HA HA HA."

The maniacal laughter of his neighbor was still ringing in Zander's ear when the interrogation sessions resumed that night. Walking through the door into the room where the questioning took place, he was astonished to see Melor gazing up at him from the other side of the interrogator's desk.

"Melor! What are you doing here?" Then it dawned on Zander. "Serafima said you were doing something important, but she never said what. Now I see why she was so vague."

"Sit down," Melor instructed Zander with a curt wave of his hand. He was dressed in a thick blue suit with narrow lapels, and wore an orange tie. He had let a stubble sprout on his chin, and reeked of cologne.

Zander wondered if he kept a bottle in a drawer and freshened up between prisoners. He wondered if it helped. Set neatly on a corner of the desk were a knife and fork and spoon wrapped in a piece of linen; like all interrogators, Melor took his meals at the prison commissary because it was free, but he apparently didn't think the silverware there was clean.

"What happened to my old interrogator?" Zander asked.

"Comrade Zhilov," Melor informed him with smug satisfaction, "has been arrested for being part of an anti-Soviet Trotskyist conspiracy. His failure to get your confession gave him away."

"That puts you in a difficult position," Zander said. He was already relishing the give and take of the interrogation. Time passed without his noticing it. "If I continue to deny any connection with the famous Trotskyist Center," he added with an innocent grin, "they are likely to conclude that you are part of the conspiracy too."

Melor smiled back, though there was no trace of innocence on his pudgy face. "On the contrary, the arrest of my predecessor puts *you* in the difficult position. We both of us understand that for my own security, I cannot fail."

Zander sneered. "What are you going to do, beat a confession out of me?"

Melor scraped back his chair and pulled a thick dossier from a bottom drawer. "We are not brutes," he asserted, opening the dossier on the desk. "We are psychologists. We search like priests for the psychological levers that will get you to confess to crimes you have committed, or are capable of committing."

"You are sick," Zander told him. "You and others like you are sending tens of thousands of innocent people to their deaths."

Once again Melor smiled. He appeared to be very sure of himself. "You talk to me of tens of thousands. Every year since history began millions have been killed by imperialist wars and epidemics and famines. They were also innocent, but nobody lost sleep over the injustice done them. We Stalinists proposed to reorder the world, to eliminate wars and epidemics and famines. If we must liquidate a parasitic peasantry in the process, so be it. We are not women." He leveled a finger at Zander. "You should have remained in New York. Revolution is not for people with weak nerves."

"Or scruples."

Melor snickered. "The individual is nothing. The Party is everything. Ends justify means. This is unshakable."

Zander sat back in his chair. "When you were a kid I once asked you what you wanted to be when you grew up. I remember you answering 'I want to be taken seriously.' At least you are taking yourself seriously."

"I also have my memories from the Steamboat," Melor shot back. "You were very full of yourself then, too, the idealist who came home to fight the good fight. But when we were busy storming the Winter Palace, you were racing through the halls like some dog in heat looking for its mate. I will admit it to you. I volunteered for the job of interrogating you not only because the case is important; not only because your name is Til and people will pay attention to your fate. I volunteered because there are scores that need settling. I hold no grudge against you for the beating you gave me with Pasha's belt. You caught me fair and square. But I bear a grudge against you for not denouncing Ronzha. Even today there are people who whisper that that filth, that scum, is a hero, a great poet. I know better. He was never fit to spit on my shoes. That is why I need your confession. To expose Ronzha. But I leap ahead of myself. For the moment, let us take things in logical order." Melor pulled three typewritten pages from the dossier and handed them across the desk to Zander. "Read these," he ordered.

"I can't. My sight has deteriorated."

"I almost forgot about the eyeglasses." Melor pulled an eyeglass case from a drawer, removed a new pair of round steel-rimmed glasses, and held them out. "See if these are better than the ones you have on."

Zander hesitated. He could hear the prisoner in the

cell next to him warning, "Beware of Bolsheviks with gifts."

"Take them," Melor insisted. "They will not bite you."

Zander removed his old glasses and hooked the new ones over his ears. And in one instant the world came into focus. The effect was magical. Even his headache seemed to recede. He picked up the pages and glanced at the signature on the third page. Then he went back and began to read from the top of the first page. He wondered how Tuohy could have brought himself to sign such a pack of lies.

Melor remarked, "You can see the evidence against you is conclusive."

Zander said, "Of course none of this is true. I have never met"—he named the member of the Politburo recently executed for being part of a Trotskyist conspiracy. "I have been to the restaurant in question, but years ago, to celebrate Atticus's marriage to Arishka. You were there too. The business about Ronzha is crazy. As for me trying to entice Atticus into a plot to assassinate Stalin, it is his word against mine. And I deny it."

"You do not deny you used the code name 'mirrored armoire' to refer to the deceased traitor Ronzha?"

Zander looked away and breathed quietly for a while. He removed the eyeglasses and brought his thumb and third finger to massage his closed lids. "So Ronzha is dead." He opened his eyes and looked at Melor. "It doesn't surprise me. Reading his poem was a form of suicide."

"You do not deny you used the code name 'folding bridge table' to refer to the deceased wrecker Alyosha Zhitkin?"

"Is Alyosha also dead, then?"

"Faced with arrest for anti-Soviet activities, he committed suicide, which proves he was guilty. You do not deny you used the code name 'full-length mirror' to refer to your mistress, the actress known by her professional name, Masha?"

"I can explain these code names," Zander said in

exasperation. "When we lost our apartment in Chkalov Street, we had to leave our furniture with friends. As a joke, Ludmilla and I began calling everyone by the furniture they were guarding for us. Jesus, we even referred to your mother and Pasha as 'American rolltop desk'!"

"I have already filed the appropriate papers," Melor said evenly. "Sergeant Kirpichnikov will be questioned about the significance of 'American rolltop desk.' "

"Pasha is your stepfather!"

"If my right arm were guilty of anti-Soviet activity," Melor replied—again he flashed the smile that did not have at its source humor—"I would cut it off."

"I suppose you would."

Melor held out his hand, palm up. "The eyeglasses, if you please."

"I can't keep them?"

"When you sign your confession. Not before."

"HOW WAS COURT YESTERDAY?" Zander tapped out on the wall when he was brought back to his cell from the session with Melor.

"HA HA HA HA HA HA HA HA HA HA HA HA HA HA HA HA."

"ARE YOU ALL RIGHT?"

"HA HA HA HA HA HA HA HA HA HA HA HA HA HA HA HA HA."

Melor handed the eyeglasses across the desk. Zander put them on and through the haze of his headache began reading Sergeant Kirpichnikov's confession. "This is a lie," he mumbled tiredly. "This too." And again, "This too. How could I have attended a secret strategy session of the Trotskyist Center in Petrograd when I was in Alma Ata translating a film that month?"

"It is always possible that the sergeant's memory lapsed, that he got the date wrong. Nobody is perfect."

"I deny the whole thing," Zander said in a low voice. He raised a hand to his forehead and tried to massage the throb of pain away, but it persisted.

"The eyeglasses, if you please," Melor said, holding out his hand.

* * *

"TODAY," Zander's neighbor tapped. "THEY WENT TOO FAR."

"EXPLAIN."

"I ADMIT BEING A SPY. I ADMIT BEING A SABOTEUR. I ADMIT BEING AN AGENT OF INTERNATIONAL CAPITAL SCHEMING TO BRING ABOUT DOWNFALL OF WORLD'S FIRST WORKER'S PARADISE. BUT VISHINSKY EXAGGERATES WHEN HE PUBLICLY ACCUSES ME OF PLOTTING ON BEHALF OF HITLER AND GERMANY. I AM, AFTER ALL, A JEW."

Zander tapped back, "ON THE CONTRARY, YOU SHOULD ADMIT IT. CHARGE IS SO PREPOSTEROUS IT WILL UNDERMINE CREDIBILITY OF YOUR CONFESSION."

There was a long pause. Then: "I HADN'T THOUGHT OF THAT."

"Before the deranged criminal Ronzha died," Melor told Zander one night, "he identified a co-conspirator. Unfortunately the two men handling the interrogation were Trotskyist agents infiltrated into the NKVD in order to wreck the investigation and cover up the real criminals. When it appeared that the poet would cooperate, they beat him to death. Even then he tried to identify the man who acted as the liaison between him and the Trotskyist Center. The two interrogators insisted he said the person's name was Kafka, but this was a transparent lie. Under questioning they have admitted that the go-between identified by the criminal Ronzha with his dying breath was someone named Til." Melor pushed a single sheet of paper across the desk, along with the eyeglass case. "See for yourself."

Zander didn't doubt for an instant that the confession of the two interrogators named him, but he slipped on the glasses anyway in order to have a few precious moments during which everything would be in focus.

"I DID AS YOU SUGGESTED. I ADMITTED RE-

PORTING DIRECTLY TO HITLER. I EVEN DE-
SCRIBED HIS MUSTACHE."

"WHAT WAS THE REACTION?"

"MY SON CRIED OUT THAT I WAS SCUM OF
THE EARTH."

"I AM SORRY IF I GAVE YOU BAD ADVICE."

"NOT YOUR FAULT. I SEE NOW THERE IS
NOTHING I CAN SAY THEY WON'T BELIEVE.
HA. TOMORROW I AM GOING TO CLAIM TO BE
VIRGIN BORN. ON SECOND THOUGHT, MAYBE
I SHOULDN'T. I DON'T WANT TO GET MY OLD
MOTHER IN TROUBLE. HA HA HA HA HA HA."

Zander began to notice the first faint signs of impa-
tience in his interrogator. He wondered if Melor had
been given a deadline to secure the required confession.

"You will not have to rack your brain to figure out
what to confess to," Melor assured him one night. "I
will help you with the details." He slipped several
typewritten sheets across the desk, along with the eyeglass case.

Zander put on the glasses and lingered over the
pages, reading through them carefully, even rereading
them when Melor let him.

"So you got to Appolinaria too," he said when he
came to the signature at the bottom of the confession.
"It would have been like her to sign just so she could
join Ronzha."

"She is filth, like him," Melor burst out. "They both
revolt me." He calmed himself with an effort. "I have a
second confession to show you tonight." He pushed
another paper across the desk.

Zander read through it. "The usual inventions . . .
more lies. Who is it who wrote it?"

He skipped to the end. The confession had been
signed by Masha. Zander looked up. He hoped his eyes
were inscrutable. He hoped Masha had kept her part of
the bargain. He hoped to God they hadn't gotten their
hands on Ludmilla.

"VISHINSKY ASKED FOR THE DEATH PENALTY

FOR ALL THE ACCUSED. THE AUDIENCE, IN-
CLUDING MY SON, TOOK UP THE CRY: DEATH
TO THE TROTSKYIST TRAITORS! I KICK MYSELF
FOR BRINGING THE BOY UP BADLY."

"IT IS NOT EASY TO RAISE CHILDREN IN
RUSSIA."

"IT SHOULD NOT BE TOO DIFFICULT. WE
LIVE IN A COUNTRY WHERE IT IS HARD TO GO
WRONG. ALMOST EVERYTHING IS PROHIBITED,
AND WHATEVER ISN'T PROHIBITED IS OBLIGA-
TORY. HA HA."

Twenty minutes later Zander's neighbor resumed the
conversation. "HA HA HA HA."

Zander was sure now that Melor was working against a
deadline. The sessions lasted longer every day; it was
dawn by the time he got back to his cell. Melor went
over the evidence again and again, as if he were hammering nails into a coffin. There was Zander's associa-
tion with Trotsky. There was an affidavit, signed by
someone who said he had been present in Ekaterinburg
at the trial of Nicholas II, accusing Til of having betrayed
his sympathies when he stepped forward and gave his
own chair to the accused monarch. There was the matter of Lili's execution. There was Zander's failure to
denounce the traitor Ronzha when he tried to rally
anti-Stalinists with his subversive poem. There were
the confessions. Granted a detail or two may have been
contradictory, but they all pointed to the same conclusion: that Zander and Ronzha had been members of a
Trotskyist Center; that Ronzha's poem had been part of
a scheme to identify like-minded people and recruit
them into the ranks of the Trotskyist conspiracy.

Zander tried to defend himself with logic. "If I had
really been a member of a Trotskyist Center, I would
have rushed to denounce Ronzha as soon as I realized
the others had."

Melor brushed this explanation aside with the palm
of his hand. "Why do you protect him?" he asked with a
passion Zander had not yet seen during this phase of

the interrogation. "I can tell you he was a pervert, a decadent member of the old intelligentsia."

Very early on Melor had figured out that the only crime in life was getting caught. He had sold several of the princess's cats on the black market, and had used the money to buy sausages, and Serafima had gushed over how smart he was when he said he had found them in a garbage pail behind a rich Jew's house. He would have gotten away with stealing the nude photograph of Lili, too, if stupid old Hippolyte had not gone and traded it for an ear trumpet. Melor had even come away from the storming of the Winter Palace with a sack full of loot and nobody the wiser, and had been treated as a hero since because he had been in the building at the right moment in history.

Melor had loved the Steamboat with a passion. He had explored every corner of it, from the crawl space under the back porch to the secret corners where bats hung from their heels in the attic. It was one of the great charms of the Steamboat that at night its timbers creaked like those of a ship under way. Melor attributed the sounds to ghosts.

One night he had nipped at Pasha's hidden bottle of vodka. Feeling more adventuresome than usual, he had posted himself at the peephole in the wall of the downstairs bathroom. Crouched in the narrow space under the stairs next to the mops and brooms, a blanket draped over his shoulders, he waited for someone to appear in his limited field of vision. Suddenly he heard the creaking of timbers. A ghost was descending the stairs over his head. He pressed an eye to the peephole. The door of the bathroom opened, the electric light against the far wall clicked on. He could hear someone feeding wood into the stove that heated the water. Whoever was there must have been undressing. And then Appolinaria stepped into view. She was naked and carrying a small wooden bucket of heated water, which she spilled into the copper tub, then turned back to fill it a second time from the large basin on top of the stove.

Appolinaria moved like a ballerina, planting her toes first and then sliding down on her heels with each step. Her hair, which she always wore in braids twisted elaborately around her head, hung loose; Melor noted with awe that it reached almost to her waist. His breath came in soundless pants.

Having filled the tub with several buckets of warm water, Appolinaria turned to look at herself in the mirror, which hung from a nail on the wall over the peephole. Melor's heart began pounding in his chest with such intensity he thought it would give him away; Sergeant Kirpichnikov would hear Appolinaria's frightened cries and pull him from the closet and beat the daylights out of him with his army belt. But he wouldn't utter a sound; for now he knew what Appolinaria looked like naked.

Appolinaria backed up and frowned at her reflection in the mirror, then turned and stepped into the copper tub. She knelt and began sponging her neck and flat breasts. Melor reached through the buttons of his nightshirt and fingered his erection.

Overhead, another ghost could be heard descending the stairs. Then someone rapped softly on the bathroom door. Appolinaria must have expected it, because she leaped for the door, threw the latch, and jumped back into the tub. In a moment Ronzha, naked, bony, all angles where Appolinaria was curves, spilled another bucket of hot water into the tub and climbed in. She turned her back to him. He gathered her hair in one hand and began sponging her with the other. Then he leaned close to her and pressed his lips to the nape of her neck. His right hand slipped over her shoulder and began caressing her tiny, almost invisible nipples with the wet sponge.

In the closet, behind the peephole, Melor pushed his erection into the wall in delicious pain, then swayed back on the balls of his feet and breathed deeply through his open mouth so as not to make any noise. He leaned forward and looked again through the peephole. He could see the two of them talking earnestly to each other. Apparently they were arguing about something. With his eye to the hole, Melor could not hear what they were saying through the thick wooden wall. When he put his ear to the hole, he could make out what they were saying—but he could not see Appolinaria's breasts. So he began to alternate, ten seconds for his eye, ten for his ear.

"—before it is too late," she pleaded in an undertone.

"It is out of the question," Ronzha replied tensely. "I could never write poetry outside of Russia."

"If the Bolsheviks take over, they will get around to killing their poets eventually."

"What an honor to live in a country where they take their poets seriously enough to kill—"

Melor put his eye to the peephole. They continued to talk, soundlessly, one of her hands resting lightly on his bony shoulder, one of his cupping her breast. Melor listened again.

"—Moscow at least," she urged.

"Let's see what happens first."

"Perhaps Kerensky will sweep them away. Then we can live in peace."

"If Kerensky wins, we must protect her the way she protected us all these—"

Melor peered through the hole. She was leaning against him now, her arms around his neck, her lips kissing his ear, or talking into it, he wasn't sure. Melor listened again.

"—you and her in Paris?"

"Less than nothing." He was annoyed. "We were lovers for a moment. Then the moment passed."

Melor put his eye to the hole and watched the two figures in the tiny copper tub. Ronzha turned his head. He seemed to be looking directly into Melor's eye. Frightened, Melor pulled back from the wall abruptly. His head bumped into the handle of a mop, pushing it against the stairs with an audible thud. Melor froze. He could hear a door open inside the bathroom. An instant later Ronzha, wrapped in a large bath towel, yanked open the closet door. He looked at the peephole and then stared furiously down at Melor. Gradually the lines around his eyes relaxed. "Go to your room," he finally told Melor.

"Aren't you going to tell Pasha?" the boy whispered.

Ronzha shook his head.

"Aren't you going to beat me?"

Again Ronzha shook his head. "Every boy at one time or another does what you did. Don't do it again."

When Melor thought about the incident afterward, he understood it had been a turning point in his life. He had always wondered what the upper classes did to each other that prompted Sergeant Kirpichnikov to describe them as decadent. Now he thought he knew. The discovery was mingled with a feeling of intense humiliation. Ronzha had caught him in the act of catching them in the act, but he hadn't taken the boy seriously enough to punish him. It was this aspect of the incident that troubled Melor the most.

To be taken seriously became his obsession.

Zander heard a metal door clang shut nearby. It meant his neighbor had returned to his cell. Sentences were to have been passed that afternoon, but he was afraid to ask; he was afraid he knew.

Zander had to say something. "THEY WILL BE TAKING ME FOR INTERROGATION IN A FEW MINUTES."

"IN CASE YOU ARE CURIOUS, THEY GAVE ME AN HM."

"HM" stood for "highest measure of punishment." His neighbor had been sentenced to death.

"I AM TERRIBLY SORRY," Zander tapped. "WHEN?"

"FIRST LIGHT. YOU WILL PROBABLY BE IN CONFERENCE. HA. I SUPPOSE THIS IS OUR LAST CONVERSATION."

"GO OUT IN STYLE IF YOU CAN."

"STYLE SUDDENLY DOESN'T SEEM IMPORTANT TO ME. I PLAN TO SHOUT 'LONG LIVE STALIN' AS THEY SHOOT ON THE OFF CHANCE IT CAN HELP MY FAMILY." The neighbor paused. Then: "I HEAR THEM COMING FOR YOU. GOOD-

BYE FOREVER. LET'S TAP TO EACH OTHER IN
THE NEXT WORLD. HA. A LAST WORD OF AD-
VICE FROM A PREMATURE ANTIFASCIST. WHAT-
EVER YOU DO"—Zander's escort was throwing the
bolts on his door now, and his neighbor began tapping
furiously—"DON'T DO IT PREMATURELY. HA HA
HA HA HA HA HA HA HA HA HA."

"You look preoccupied," Melor noticed as Zander took
his seat.
"I am in mourning."
"Anyone I know?"
Zander attempted to bring Melor into focus. Without
success. There was a throbbing under each lid that
wouldn't go away. "I am in mourning for Russia."
"Very dramatic," Melor said sarcastically. "Suppose
we start from the beginning." He opened the bulging
dossier on his desk and pulled out a sheet marked
"Chronology." "You were first singled out by the criminal Trotsky in New York in 1917 . . ." His voice droned
on. Zander's mind wandered. He imagined his neighbor pacing his cell waiting for the first hint of first light.
". . . Returned to Russia on the same ship as the criminal Trotsky . . ." His thoughts went back to Ekaterinburg,
and he wondered how Lili had spent her last night on
earth. ". . . Acting on direct orders from the criminal
Trotsky, you traveled to Ekaterinburg. . . ." Zander
remembered the train sweeping out of the tunnel and
the enormous sign ASIATIKA coming into view and everyone applauding and cheering; at the time they had
felt as if they were conquering a new continent.
". . . Betrayed her Party by helping an important
prisoner . . ."
Melor stopped reading to offer interpretations that
Zander would deny, then went back to his text. Pain
stabbed through Zander's forehead. He tried to close
his eyes, but that seemed only to hurt more. The night
wore on. Papers were passed across the table, along
with the magic eyeglasses. "Lies," Zander said tiredly.
"All lies."
And then suddenly Melor glanced at his wristwatch

and stood up and turned out the overhead light and the desk lamp and threw open the steel shutters on the only window in the room to reveal the first gray streaks in a sky still thick with night.

From the courtyard six floors below came the distant tread of men marching across cement. Melor, at the window, listened. Zander, in his chair, also. A metal door opened. An officer barked an unintelligible command. A hysterical voice shouted, "Long live—" The cry was cut off by a volley fired with such synchronization it sounded like one shot. Melor closed the metal shutters and the window, and turned on the lamps.

"Who do you think he was wishing long life to?" Melor asked, settling back into his desk chair. He shrugged. "Trotsky probably. Where were we?"

Zander wanted to scream that the executed man had been wishing long life to Stalin, but the idea seemed ridiculous; Melor would never believe him. Zander felt as if he were losing touch with reality. Not only his eyes but his mind had trouble focusing.

"Read this," Melor instructed, pushing still another sheet of paper at Zander, along with the eyeglasses.

Zander fitted the glasses over his eyes and saw immediately that it was not another confession. It was a court verdict. Someone was being sentenced to twenty-five years at hard labor. He looked around for the accused's name. And found it.

Masha had broken her side of the bargain. They had tracked down Ludmilla.

"She was arrested in an apartment in Alma Ata," Melor was saying. "She will be an old woman when she gets out. Assuming she is still alive to get out."

"Has this been imposed?"

"The trial is scheduled for tomorrow. There is still time for mitigating circumstances to affect the outcome."

He reached over and retrieved Ludmilla's sentence, and passed another paper to Zander. "I, Alexander Til, freely confess to having committed the following crimes," it began. "First, that I was a member of an anti-Soviet Trotskyist Center whose aim was to bring about the

assassination of General Secretary Stalin, and the downfall of the Socialist order . . ."

"You are an intelligent man," Melor said softly from
across the desk. His eyebrows arched together in concentration. "What difference will it make if you confess
to accusations that are not precise? In your heart you
know you have thought traitor's thoughts, posed traitor's questions. You will be relieved of a great burden
when you confess to these accusations because you are
guilty of something."

"What will happen to Ludmilla?"

"We will throw her back into the pond. We are only
interested in big fish."

Zander rubbed the fuzz on the top of his scalp with a
palm. "What will happen to me?"

Once again Melor arranged his features in his very
peculiar smile. "Punishment," he said with obvious
conviction—Zander realized that only an idiot would
have questioned Melor's sincerity—"is redeeming. People who commit crimes need to be punished. The absence of appropriate punishment can be humiliating."

Melor uncapped a fountain pen and deposited it on
the desk in front of Zander. "Of course, you can keep
the eyeglasses once you sign," he reminded him.

Zander reached for the pen to give the last of himself
away.

There was some discussion of holding a public trial. The
name Til was known in revolutionist circles; the trial of
his grandson would attract attention. His fate would
serve as an example to others. In the end people in
high places abandoned the idea. They were not convinced they could count on him to cooperate—to repeat
his confession in a public forum. The decision was taken
to publish his confession and dispose of him in private
proceedings.

The trial lasted four minutes. Even then it was running long. The three men in uniform sitting behind the
table passed around the confession, then put their heads
together and talked in undertones. Standing with his

wrists handcuffed in front of him, Zander looked up at the large wooden propellerlike fan slowly stirring the air over his head.

"I don't see that we have a choice," one of the judges was heard to say.

"All in favor?" another asked.

Three yellow pencils were held aloft, eraser ends up. The judge in the middle regarded Zander for the first time. "Acting in accordance with the appropriate resolutions of the Central Committee and the appropriate articles of the Penal Code, most specifically the law of 1 December, 1934, the NKVD special tribunal hereby sentences you to the highest measure of punishment."

The guards behind Zander reached for his elbows, but he shrugged them off. If he was able to, he wanted to go out in style.

Stalin glanced at the filigree hands of the clock on the mantel. It was not quite eleven-thirty. The English ambassador was due at midnight. He was one of those old-school diplomats who would turn up in Savile Row pinstripes with an outrageously discreet gold chain across his vest attached, no doubt, to a Patek Philippe repeater. There would be several minutes of small talk, during which the ambassador would casually indicate he came from an old family. As if everyone didn't come from old families! Even he, Soso Vissarionovich Dzhugashvili, came from an old family, though his father had been nothing more than a shoemaker from Gori who met his maker in a drunken brawl. What made an old family old was that some of its members along the line kept records. Old family, my ass, he thought.

Stalin's secretary knocked on the door and stuck his head into the room. A dispatch had come in from the Soviet ambassador in Berlin. "Urgent for Stalin. March 7, 1936. Chancellor Hitler has informed Reichstag he is scrapping clauses of Versailles *diktat* which provide for a demilitarized region on German side of Franco-German frontier. German troops reportedly occupying the major cities of the Rhine zone." Stalin sucked impatiently on his cigarette. Had the French moved? he asked his secretary. No. They had canceled leaves and put their frontier forces on alert. But they had neither mobilized nor marched.

Stalin sensed that Herr Hitler was smarter than anyone gave him credit for. He understood psychology. He had a feeling for the essential weaknesses of the capitalist countries. He was employing what the peasants call "salami" tactics; he was going for what he wanted a piece at a time. The Rhine zone was the first bite. If he got away with that, and Stalin thought it likely, Hitler would cast around for another tasty morsel—the Sudentenland, say, or a slice of Poland. Inevitably his appetite would carry him to the Soviet frontier. And then there would be war. The Western democracies, and especially the Englishman Churchill, would sit back and relish the spectacle of the Soviet Union and Germany clawing at each other's throats. They might even help the side that was losing in order to prolong the bloodletting. All this fine talk of forming an alliance to keep Hitler in check! France, barricaded behind its Maginot Line, England barricaded behind its Channel, America barricaded behind its impenetrable naiveté—none of them would lift a finger to help Russia. The peasants had a saying: Nobody groans when another man's tooth aches.

Stalin still had time to strengthen the Soviet Union before Hitler turned east. All those who, at the first setback, might rise up against him must be liquidated. The ranks of the Party must be purged, purified. The army must be cleansed because it wasn't yet Stalin's army, it was still Trotsky's army. When Hitler struck, there must be no plotters left in the country. Not one. Then Russia could face the Germans the way Alexander Nevsky had faced the Teutonic knights—all pulling together. The peasants say a team of horses is as strong as the weakest among them; and they have been known to kill the one that lags to raise the average.

Stalin, too, would kill the ones that lag to raise the national average.

Stalin knew Russia was not only full of laggers, but outright enemies of the people; hundreds of letters

arrived at the Kremlin every day cursing Stalin, cursing
his mother for bearing him, cursing his father for supplying the seed, cursing the ground he walked on,
threatening his life, predicting he would burn in everlasting hell when it was over. Well, he, Stalin, would
bury the haters and the laggers; he would bury them
and dance on their graves to pack down the earth on
their decaying corpses.

Stalin's secretary hesitated at the door. "Would the
Secretary General care to seal the list before or after
the visit of the English ambassador?"

"I will get it out of the way before," Stalin said. The
secretary handed him a portfolio with several typewritten pages in it. Stalin carried it to the glass-topped
desk, put on his eyeglasses, switched on the lamp. He
remembered another peasant saying: The darkest place
in a room is under a lamp. Well, he liked dark places.
They made him feel comfortable.

He opened the portfolio and began going down the
list. He recognized many of the names. Tonight, for
instance, the second name on the list rang a bell. Wasn't
he the regional Party second secretary who had been
rude to him at a dinner in 1926? And this name. He
was someone Stalin remembered from his Tiflis days, a
local Party organizer, very full of himself even then, a
lady's man who spent half his time recruiting females
into the Party's ranks and the other half seducing them.
Well, he would get what was coming to him.

Stalin's eye continued down the left-hand column,
then up the middle column, then down the right-hand
column. It was boring work, but he made it a point to
read every name before he signed his initial on the
upper right-hand corner of the last page. He recognized
someone else as a Kirov man who had spoken against
him in the cloakrooms during the Seventeenth Party
Congress, and then taken the floor to praise him to the
skies in public. Another name on the top of the second
page seemed familiar. There had been two brothers,
one named Konstantin, the other, younger, named either Pavel or Petr; both had worked in Trotsky's secre-
tariat in the early 1920s. Only Konstantin was on the

list tonight. He must make a note to ask what had become of the other brother. If Konstantin was a traitor, the other was certainly guilty too. Even if he wasn't, he might join the anti-Stalinists to revenge his brother.

Halfway down the last column of the last page, Stalin recognized another name, Alexander Til. He looked up, looked out from the darkness of the desk lamp. It was Til who, with bullets raining down around them, had pulled Nadezhda out of the path of an armored car when the Bolshevik procession had been ambushed during the July days before the revolution. Stalin had feared she was dead until he put an ear to her chest and heard her heart beat. He remembered glancing up at this Til fellow and saying, "What you have done, I will never forget even if I live to be a hundred."

Others had later poisoned Nadezhda, had turned her against her lawful husband, had driven her to her death, but Til had risked his life to save her. So be it. Stalin took a fountain pen that wrote in red ink and drew a neat line through Til's name. Then he scribbled in the margin: "A patriot—how did his name wind up here? Review entire case."

Stalin finished the list, sealed each page with his initial, and handed the portfolio back to his secretary. He could hear voices in the outer office. That would be the English ambassador come to talk about Hitler's move in the Rhine zone and collective security. Stalin stubbed out his cigarette and put the ashtray in a drawer of his desk, and then packed a pipe and lit it; he knew that smoking a pipe made a man look thoughtful, patient. He buttoned the top button of his tunic and stood up. He was glad he had worn the boots with the built-in lifts. He made it a point to look visitors in the eye, and detested when he had to look up to them to do this.

There was a knock on the door. Sucking on his pipe, sending a cloud of fragrant smoke billowing into the air, he called out pleasantly, "Come."

7

Five additional funerals (without corpses):

Appolinaria stood hunched over the skillet on the one-burner gas cooker, stirring diced onion and dried mushrooms into the leftover rice and talking to the pan. Her long hair, sheared off in prison because of ringworm, was growing back the color of pewter. "What do you think?" she asked the pan, and stopped stirring to catch the reply. She heard one and it made her laugh. "I had forgotten about Tolstoy's wife. They say she copied off *War and Peace* by hand seven times, but that was child's play compared to what I am doing. Sonya only *copied War and Peace*, my heart. She didn't *memorize* it. You see the difference? I have stored your work in my skull. Three hundred and thirty-two complete poems, not counting variations, version one, version two, that sort of thing. And then there are the scraps: the poems you started and never completed, the ones you completed and never started. Alexander is coming after lunch for the ceremony. If you decide to talk to him, be polite. He denounced you, but only after you were dead."

"Are you sure you want to go through with this?" was the first thing Zander said when he arrived. He was still breathless from the stairs. He posed the question before saying hello, how are you.

"You do not look well," Appolinaria noted. She pulled up a chair for him.

"It's my prison tan. They say it takes a year to get rid of."

"I am going through with it," Appolinaria announced. "Ronzha is not against the idea. He thinks, as I do, we must consecrate his death with a ceremony. Since they did not give me his body to bury, I must improvise." Appolinaria offered a sad smile. "I have reasoned it out this way. I have been going insane since my release from prison. I rack my brain but I can't figure out why they let me go. Maybe it was a mistake. And maybe I will decide to kill myself. If his poems exist only in my brain, and nowhere else, it will give me a reason to stay alive. To stay sane, even."

There was, Zander had to admit, a kind of mad logic to her scheme. So as soon as he gathered his strength, they pulled the trunk out from under the bed and Zander, perched on the kitchen chair, handed down the cardboard boxes from the top of the closet. Appolinaria had spent weeks collecting the papers from the trusted friends around Moscow Ronzha had left them with. Now she opened the trunk and the boxes and piled the papers—sheafs from lined notebooks, embossed letter-writing paper stolen from Parisian hotels, napkins, theater tickets, calling cards, all with Ronzha's poems scratched across them in his fine, slanting handwriting— on the floor in front of the porcelain stove with its pipe dipping toward the wall and into and up the chimney. Zander crumpled some of the papers and dropped them in the stove. Kneeling next to it, he opened a small grille in the bottom and lit a kitchen match. He looked up at Appolinaria to see if she had changed her mind. She was biting her lip and sobbing and nodding. "For God's sake, light it, light it!"

Zander touched the match to the bunched paper. Flames leapt into view. Appolinaria settled onto the floor next to him and together they began feeding Ronzha's artistic production over the past twenty-two years into the fire. The room grew warm. Zander removed his suit jacket. Appolinaria opened a window. The piles of paper on the floor shrank. Zander read the first line of one poem before burning it. Appolinaria closed her eyes and tilted her head back and recited the rest of the poem, even noting the place where Ronzha had been unable to decide between two verbs.

It was midafternoon when Zander burned the last

sheaf—it was a blank page torn from an English guide-book of Switzerland and labeled: "Personal Notes"; across it Ronzha had written "The only Paradise is Paradise Lost—Proust."

When the stove had cooled, Zander opened a grille and using his cupped hands scooped the ashes into a wide-mouthed earthenware urn that had been washed out but still smelled of pickles. Appolinaria sealed the urn with a wax cap. "His poems are wheeling through my brain like galaxies," she said. "I feel dizzy."

Zander slipped back into his suit jacket and helped Appolinaria into a cotton overcoat. He tucked the urn under an arm and together they left the apartment. They walked four blocks to the trolley station, rode it to the end of the line, and hiked into the countryside past the prefabricated apartment houses springing up in furrowed fields. Zander, with his limp, set the pace; Appolinaria slowed down to stay abreast. It was Sunday and there was no traffic on the road. They walked without talking to each other. When they could no longer see any sign of civilization, they turned down a rutted road into a forest of white birches. The forest ended abruptly in a steep slide down to the Moscow River. "This is as good a place as we are likely to find," Appolinaria said.

Zander handed the urn to her. Uncapping it, she pulled out a handful of ashes. "Ashes to ashes, dust to dust, or whatever," she muttered. Her eyes glistened. She looked up at the brilliant white clouds being lashed across the sky by high winds unfelt on earth. "Dearest Ronzha," she cried, "if you are watching us from a corner table of some celestial Stray Dog, kindly take this as an act of love." With that she began casting the ashes into the air, handful after handful, until the urn was empty and the view of the river below was masked by the soot drifting down toward it.

"Now he is dead," Appolinaria calmly announced when the last of the ashes had been discharged into the air. "Now I can begin mourning him properly."

In a gloomy hallway several days later, Zander had

difficulty finding the right door. He could see the whitish glow of the nameplates, but he couldn't read them even with his new eyeglasses. He was about to abandon the search and come back in the morning, when a door opened and a woman set out a lidded garbage pail. She was startled to see someone in the hallway.

"I am looking for the Evpraksein apartment," Zander told her.

She squinted at him and decided it was none of her business. "One flight up, second door on the right." She closed the door before Zander had a chance to thank her.

He found the door and knocked softly on it. After a moment he knocked again. He could hear a faint scuffing inside. He knocked a third time. The door opened the length of the safety chain. The eye of an old woman peered out. It was very alert.

"You do not know me," Zander said quietly, "but I have a message for you from Konstantin Evpraksein. You must be his mother."

The woman snickered. "I am his wife, not his mother."

"Excuse me. I thought . . . what I mean is . . ."

"I own a mirror. I know what I look like," the woman snapped. "It is a natural mistake." She shut the door and unhooked the chain and opened it wide. Zander entered a large room filled with furniture. There were four beds and two tables and eight wicker chairs and two easy chairs and several side tables and a sofa with a high curved back and two dressers and an armoire. Every surface was covered with lamps and bookends and candlesticks and samovars and tortoise picture frames without photographs and ashtrays and a collection of glass paperweights with rural scenes in them. It was, Zander realized, as if the contents of an entire house had been stuffed into this space.

The door closed behind Zander and he found himself facing four women. Two were in their twenties, but it was possible to guess their ages only from the way they dressed. From their faces, from their posture, they might have been twice that. The other two women looked as if they were in their seventies. The one wrapped in a shawl was. She was Evpraksein's mother. The other woman, the one who had answered the door, must have been roughly as old as her husband, but then Russia aged people prematurely these days.

"My name," Zander began, "is Alexander Til. I was, until recently, in prison—"

"You were in prison," Evpraksein's wife interrupted carefully, "and they let you out?"

"It happens occasionally." Zander was swept by a wave of guilt at being alive; even he couldn't explain why it had worked out as it did. "While I was inside, I was taken for an eye examination. The doctor was an inmate—he fitted me with these." Zander fingered his thick eyeglasses. "The door was open and there was a guard outside, but the doctor managed to whisper his name and address before I left. He said he had a wife, a mother, two daughters. He charged me, if I ever got out, to send his love to them."

"How long ago did this take place?" the wife asked.

"I have a bad leg. Do you mind if I sit down?" The older of the two daughters brought a chair. Zander sank gratefully into it. The four women hovered over him. He looked from one to the other. "This happened four months ago. I have been out of prison two months. I apologize for not coming sooner, but I have not been well."

"What did Father say?" the older daughter asked as if Zander had not already delivered the message.

"He said to send you his love. Only that. There was no time to tell me more."

The other daughter said in a tight voice, "He is a traitor, a wrecker. We have no wish for his love."

The wife of Evpraksein said, "We have reason to believe he is dead."

Zander said, "How do you know that?"

"We sent him packages as often as the regulations permitted. Two weeks ago the last one we sent came back to us. They had stamped the word 'deceased' across the front of the package in large letters."

"Maybe there has been a mistake," Zander said.

Evpraksein's mother shook her head. "I feel it in my

bones, there is no mistake. Our Konstantin is certainly dead."

"For us," hissed the younger daughter, "he has been dead since they took him. Do you know what it has done to our lives to have a father who betrayed his country?"

Evprakseïn's wife reached for Zander's hand and squeezed it, and nodded her thanks. "We were about to light a candle," she told him.

"A memorial candle," added the mother.

"Just a candle," insisted the younger daughter. "It has no special significance."

"Stay with us for a moment, if you like," the wife said.

"I am . . . I am honored to participate with you in the lighting of a memorial candle for Dr. Evprakseïn," Zander said.

The wife released Zander's hand and took a simple candle from a dresser drawer and lit it with a kitchen match and, tilting it, let some of the wax spill into a saucer. She planted the candle in the spilled wax, steadied it, and stood back. The younger of the two daughters let a burst of air flutter through her lips and stalked off to fog up the window with her breath. Evprakseïn's wife and mother and oldest daughter, and Zander, gathered around the candle to silently contemplate the mystical flickering of the memorial flame.

"I blame myself," Sergeant Kirpichnikov said, shaking his heavy head, tapping the stump of his left hand on the kitchen table. "I ought to have beaten him more than I did."

"I should have put my foot down the day he came home wearing that leather jacket and said he was working for the people Atticus Tuohy worked for," Serafima said. She used the edge of her shawl to dab tears away from the corners of her eyes. "He was basically a good boy, Pasha. He always remembered my birthday."

"He remembered your birthday," Sergeant Kirpichnikov muttered, "because I reminded him."

"He let himself be reminded," Serafima said impatiently. "That showed he cared."

Sergeant Kirpichnikov got up and went over to the stove and stirred the soup with a large wooden spoon. He looked across to Zander and cleared his throat. "There is something I have been meaning to say to you."

Zander thought he knew what was coming. "You don't owe me any explanations," he told Pasha. "Everyone knows you had to do what you did."

"Say it to him anyhow," Serafima instructed Pasha.

Again the sergeant cleared his throat. "I am not much given to speeches, or excuses, but I hold it necessary to tell you I am not proud of what I did. If you decided never to talk to me again, I would give you the right of the matter. It is only that Melor called me in and showed me all the evidence against you, showed me the business of the American rolltop desk being your code for me, and said we could save ourselves by coming clean, it was our only choice."

"I understand," Zander said. "I bear you no grudge."

But the sergeant had to finish. "So when he put the paper before me, to tell you the godawful truth, I never even read the damn thing. I asked him where I signed, and he showed me, and I signed." Pasha breathed in deeply through his enormous nostrils. "And that is how it was. And I am ashamed to tell you this, but I had to get it off my chest."

Zander nodded. Everyone was silent for a while. Pasha sat down again at the kitchen table. "At least eat something," Serafima told the two men.

"I am not hungry," said the sergeant. He pushed his bowl away.

"Maybe later," Zander said. He turned to Pasha. "How did you find out about Melor?"

Serafima began crying again. The sergeant filled Zander's glass, and his own, and both men downed some vodka. "He always came for dinner on Wednesdays," the sergeant began.

"Wednesdays, always," Serafima agreed. "He brought packages from the commissary. Lard. Bacon. Butter sometimes. Sweets sometimes." And she burst out, "I tell you he cared more than he let on."

"When he didn't show up Wednesday, she got worried," Pasha continued. "I thought he might have been off with a girl, but Serafima made me go around to his place anyway. He had a small apartment, but he had it all to himself. I knew something was wrong as soon as I turned the corner. There were two cars and a truck, and some men in blue suits and orange ties were carrying down boxes and piling them in the back of the truck. They weren't taking furniture. And they didn't look like moving men to me."

"When he came home and told me," Serafima picked up the story, "I thought I would have a heart attack. We waited all day Thursday for word. You can imagine the state I was in. By Friday morning it was either find out what had happened to him or kill myself."

"I was against her going," the sergeant said.

"A mother," Serafima burst out, "is not like a girlfriend or a wife even, though I have nothing against wives. A mother is a mother, and if she feels her son is in trouble, she will walk through burning oil, through walls, you see what I mean?"

Zander nodded sympathetically.

Serafima pushed herself to her feet and circled the table and settled back into her chair. Zander tried to imagine her charging up to the front door of Butyrskaya Prison and demanding to see her son. "You will have to go through appropriate channels," the guard would have said, but Serafima, who had put on weight over the years, who had in fact become quite fat, would have shouldered her way past the poor man into the courtyard. Zander could imagine her scanning the dozens upon dozens of windows and shouting, "Melor, it's me, it's your mother, Serafima. Come out this instant!"

"I never made it to the front door," Serafima said in a whisper; she felt if she talked any louder the dishes would come crashing down from the cabinet, the overhead fixture would fall out of the ceiling. "The place was jammed with mothers, there must have been half a hundred of us, all squeezed up on the curb so the traffic could pass, milling around the closed door, some sob-bing, some angry, all ready to walk through burning oil for sons who had disappeared. I suppose," Serafima added after a moment, "if there is an afterlife, the entrance to hell will look like that."

"It was me," Sergeant Kirpichnikov continued, "who saw his name in the newspaper. I do not usually read these things, but with Melor missing and all . . . you must have seen it—the announcement on the inside page of *Pravda* about the arrest of the head of the police. Only the week before they ran a photograph of him standing next to Comrade Stalin, and the caption identified him as Stalin's right arm. Turns out the right arm was a German spy! And down in the story they listed twenty-six lower-level functionaries who had been tried and convicted and . . . and . . . you know what I'm getting at . . . and Melor's name—"

"My little Marx-Engels-Lenin-Organizers-of-Revolution an agent of imperialism!" Serafima cried. "Can you believe such a thing? With a name like that? An agent of imperialism! My Melor!"

Sergeant Kirpichnikov reached into the pocket of his tunic and took out an article torn from the pages of *Pravda*. Melor's name was underlined in pencil.

"I always dreamed of seeing his name in print," Serafima said, "but God knows I didn't want to see it in print like that."

Sergeant Kirpichnikov offered the article to Zander. He read it and passed it to Serafima. She pressed it to her bosom. "I gave birth to him and bathed him and clothed him and loved him for thirty-one years. And this is all I have to show for it—his name in an article in *Pravda*. How, I ask you, can such a thing have hap-pened? How? I ask you."

"Control yourself," Sergeant Kirpichnikov pleaded. He had closed the door of the room, but he was still afraid the people they shared the apartment with would overhear them.

Serafima nodded miserably. "How?" she whispered. "How? I want to know how."

*   *   *

Arishka clutched the twelve red roses wrapped in
newspaper to her breast. Ludmilla walked on one side
with a wrist hooked through her arm. Zander, limping
along on the other side, was about to slow down, but
decided the exercise would do him good. They headed
across the small park sandwiched between the wide
boulevard and the Kremlin wall toward the tomb of the
unknown soldier.

"There is a terrible difference between someone who
has died, and someone who has disappeared," Arishka
was saying. "When someone is dead, the survivors at
least know where they stand. When someone has only
disappeared, you are left in a limbo—you slide back
and forth between despair and hope, and there is no
middle ground, no place you can plant your feet and
begin to reconstruct your life."

"You don't need to explain," Ludmilla assured her.
"You are doing the right thing."

"You really think so?"

"Absolutely."

"Even the hypnotist?"

"Even the hypnotist. Someone in your position has to
try everything."

Arishka breathed a sigh of relief. "It means a great
deal to me to hear you say that. Some of my friends
thought going to a hypnotist was ridiculous. I don't see
why. These days people use hypnosis to help them stop
smoking, or stick to a diet. So why not use it to convince yourself someone is dead?"

"Did it change anything?" Zander asked. "Did you
come away feeling any different about your friend?"

"I have to admit it really helped me. Overnight I
stopped hoping. I became convinced in my heart of
hearts that there was only one explanation for his disappearance. I continue to dream about him, but in my
dreams he is always dead. Even when he talks to me,
he is dead. There is no doubt in my mind that I will
never see him again."

"At least you know where you stand," Ludmilla said,
squeezing Arishka's elbow. "That's more than most can
say."

"Kindly keep your voices down," Zander cautioned. "There will be people at the tomb, and we don't want anyone overhearing this kind of conversation."

"You do see, don't you, that you can't live with doubt?" Arishka said. "You can't function. One day last winter I left the office without putting on my galoshes. I didn't realize it until I found myself waiting in knee-deep snowdrifts, waiting for the trolley, but by that time it was quicker to go home than back to the office." Arishka lowered her voice so only Ludmilla could make out what she was saying. "Even my period was affected. My whole life I have been as regular as the moon. After Arkadey disappeared"—Arishka quickly corrected herself—"after his *death,* I would go five weeks, six, once even seven. If I had been sharing a bed with a man and that happened, I would have been lining up for another abortion."

"Pay attention, now," Zander warned. They were approaching the tomb. It was directly under the Kremlin wall, and covered with bouquets and wreaths. An eternal flame burned at its foot, and two soldiers in smart uniforms with rifles at parade rest stood motionless on either side of the flame. Several civilians in blue suits and orange ties hovered off to one side, watching the crowd file past.

"Whose idea was it for you to put flowers on the tomb?" Ludmilla whispered.

They joined the queue, about twenty people, and advanced step by step toward the roped-off area.

"The hypnotist suggested it. I did three sessions with him altogether, and he didn't give them away, let me tell you. At the last session he put me into a trance and suggested that Arkadey *was* the unknown soldier; that he was buried here in the tomb. When I woke up, he told me what he had done and I said, why not? He *might* be buried here. It was possible. I mean, whoever is buried here is unknown, so why couldn't it be Arkadey?"

The people in line ahead of them moved on, and Arishka stepped up to the cord and stared solemnly at the flame and the tomb. Then she reached over the cord and gently added her bouquet of roses to the flowers and wreaths piled around the base of the stone.

Walking back through the park, Arishka was morbidly silent. Zander glanced at Ludmilla behind Arishka's back. Ludmilla shrugged. Arishka pulled a lace handkerchief from her purse and blew her nose into it. She began sniffling. Tears welled in her eyes and brimmed over onto her cheeks. Her body shook with silent sobs.

"Are you all right?" Ludmilla asked worriedly.

Arishka moaned. "We had so little time together. It took me months to work up my nerve and tell Atticus I was leaving. It was torture—loving Arkadey and sleeping with Atticus. Then just when we were starting our life together, I lost him."

Ludmilla said, "At least you know now that he's dead."

Arishka stifled her sobs in her handkerchief. "What if it isn't Arkadey in the tomb? What if it is someone else, and he is still alive?"

Sergeant Kirpichnikov was in bed with a cold, but he insisted on Serafima going anyway. So Zander wound up escorting what the ladies teasingly called "his harem" to the film. The theater was crowded and they had to take seats down in front in order to stay together. The house lights dimmed. Quick shots of Red Army tanks fording a river and Soviet athletes clearing hurdles and a glistening submarine breaking to the surface through a layer of Arctic ice introduced the newsreel. The first item concerned the recent trial of the census takers. There was a sequence showing them in the courtroom, their shaved heads bowed in guilt; they obviously were unable or unwilling to look directly at the camera. "The glorious Soviet intelligence service," explained a passionate voice-over, "has smashed a viper's brood of traitors in the Institute of Soviet Statistics."

Zander had read about the affair in *Pravda*. The chief census taker, someone named O. A. Kvitkin, along with most of his statisticians and demographers, had been shot for "wrecking the census." They had counted noses and come up short. The Soviet Union, according to

Stalin, should have had a population of 180.7 million. The census takers could find only 164 million souls. Which left a shortfall of 16.7 million. The counting, said the *Pravda* article, had been done by "foreign agents whose sinister purpose was to discredit the Communist Party and its Great Helmsman, J. Stalin."

"How could sixteen point seven million people be missing?" Ludmilla had demanded after Zander had read the article to her.

"Appolinaria has lost Ronzha," Zander had replied. "Arishka has lost her friend Arkadey Lifshits. Serafima has lost Melor. You came very close to losing me. Millions died when they forced the peasants onto the collectives. Millions more have disappeared in the purges."

Ludmilla had stared out the window for a long while. "My God!" she had exclaimed suddenly. "Sixteen point seven million! My imagination can deal with dead people only when they are individually wrapped."

On the screen the newsreel flickered and cut to what the voice-over described as "the work of the builders, as opposed to the wreckers." There followed a long sequence showing the opening of a segment of the Moscow subway. A train with bunting across the front of the first car was pulling into a brightly lit station. The doors opened. Stalin himself, smiling, waving modestly to the crowd of people applauding him, stepped onto the platform. He looked around at the marble columns and nodded in approval.

The stations, the voice-over explained as the camera followed Stalin's gaze across the vaulted ceilings and coffered recesses, were veritable people's palaces, with mosaics and frescoes and enameled bas-reliefs and stained glass murals. It demonstrated, he went on, what Socialist labor could achieve when it rolled up its sleeves and got down to work.

There was a shot of a burly man, identified as N. Khrushchev, stepping up to Stalin to receive the Order of Lenin for directing the work of the "volunteers" who dug the tunnels. Arishka, sitting on one side of Zander, said quietly, "Say what you want, it is a great achievement. I can't wait to ride in one of those cute little trains."

"Shhh," a man sitting behind Arishka whispered.

The camera cut to another award ceremony. Fifteen men in suits and ties stood lined up on the platform in front of a mosaic depicting Russian knights in armor charging Swedish invaders. Stalin moved down the line, pinning a medal on each man's lapel and shaking his hand.

The subdirectors of the subway project, the voice-over explained, get a personal word of thanks from Comrade Stalin for their dedication to his vision of creating the most modern subway system in the world, far and away outclassing the subways in such cities as New York, Paris, or London.

Ludmilla, on the other side of Zander, plucked at his sleeve. "Isn't that Uncle Atticus?"

The seventh man in line was at least a head taller than everyone around him. His forefinger dabbed nervously at his large walrus mustache as Stalin stepped up to pin the medal on him.

"That's Atticus, all right," Zander whispered.

The task of digging through the shifting spongelike soil under Moscow had been dangerous work, the voice-over droned. Despite incredible safety precautions, workers had been injured. Some had even given their lives so that socialism, in the form of a metropolitan subway system, might be advanced. The tunnels, the announcer's voice suggested dramatically, had become their tombs; the subway had become their monument.

Zander barely saw the film that followed. The sight of Tuohy being decorated by Stalin had come as quite a shock. He had not forgotten the denunciation that Atticus had signed, the lies he had invented, the enthusiasm with which he seemed to have trotted them out and marched them across the page. There had been no evidence of hesitation, no quibbling; Tuohy had personally seen Zander talking to so and so, had personally heard him say such and such. It had screamed for an explanation, an apology. But in the five months since his release from prison, there had been no word from

Atticus. He had taken his failure to get in touch as an expression of guilt—until he spotted his broad face and smug smile in the newsreel. It was the smile of someone who had been devoured by the system.

Lying awake in his bed that night, Zander felt as if he had returned from a funeral. He understood that the subway tunnels beneath Moscow's streets were really a common grave. Other things besides the bodies of workers trapped in mud slides and cave-ins were buried down there: the last trace of his friendship with Atticus Tuohy, the man who had come with him from America, for one; the lingering hope that the revolution he had helped make might yet transform Russia into the promised land. "We never dreamed there would be so much killing," Lili had said, "but now that there is, it is even more important for the revolution to succeed." Zander had hung on her words when he mourned her; had hung on them after his arrest; had clung to them when he was driven to sign a false confession to save Ludmilla.

It was not a hope a reasonable man could hang on to any longer. And so he let go of it; he released it into the air and watched it rise like a helium-filled balloon until it was a speck of dust in the sky. And then it vanished entirely. And Zander, gazing up at the shadows cast by a streetlamp onto the ceiling, went into mourning: for Russia; for himself; for the pure waste of it all.

BOOK 5

Le despotisme russe non seulement
compte les idées, les sentiments pour
rien, mais il refait les faits, il lutte contre
l'évidence, et triomphe dans la lutte; car
l'évidence n'a pas d'avocat chez nous.
—Custine, *Lettres de Russie, 1839*

My future is in my past.
—Epigraph, in English, that precedes Part II
of Akhmatova's "Poem Without a Hero"

The peasants were on to something, he decided, when they claimed time had wings. It was twenty years to the day since his wife had died, poisoned by scoundrels and wreckers and, he now knew, Zionists trying to destroy what he had painstakingly constructed. He had marked the anniversary with a visit to her tomb at the Novodeviche Cemetery; he had stared for a moment at the hauntingly familiar marble bust with the inscription, "To Nadezhda Alliluyeva from a member of the Communist Party, J. Stalin." Back at Blizhny, Stalin's housekeeper, Valechka, brought him a glass of warm milk with two lumps of sugar on the saucer. He sweetened the milk and settled tiredly into his favorite easy chair under the enormous photograph of Nadezhda. Valechka added a log to the fire and worked the bellows to stir up the flames, then turned on the radio. "Music's what the doctor ordered," she insisted when he halfheartedly waved her away from the radio.

"Don't mention the word 'doctor' to me," Stalin muttered in irritation. "They're all a bunch of cosmopolites and Zionists." But he let her have her way when he heard the announcer say that Yudina would be playing something or other.

He listened to the music and sipped the warm milk and looked at the photograph of Nadezhda and let his thoughts drift back to their early years together. He had been rough with her, it was true, but then he had been rough with everyone. What was it that the German bitch of a tsarina had written to Nicholas before the revolution? "Russia loves to feel the whip—it's their nature."

The music came to an end. On the spur of the moment

Stalin reached for the phone. "Get me the commissar in charge of the radio committee," he ordered the operator.

A few minutes later the commissar was on the line.

"Comrade," Stalin said. "I heard Yudina play something on the radio just now. Can you tell me what it was?"

The commissar checked his program notes. "It was Mozart's Piano Concerto Number Twenty-three," he informed Stalin.

"Ah. Mozart. Of course. Send me over a copy of the record in the morning."

The commissar appeared to hesitate.

"Is there a problem?" Stalin asked curtly.

"Not at all," the commissar replied quickly. "I will have the record in your hands first thing tomorrow."

In his office at the radio building the commissar hung up the receiver. "That was Stalin himself," he grimly told his assistant. "He heard Yudina play Mozart's Twenty-third on the radio, and wants a copy of the record."

"Oh my God," moaned the assistant. She collapsed into a chair. "The performance was live. There is no record!"

The commissar convened a meeting of department heads to deal with the crisis. "I am open to ideas," he told them.

Someone suggested they all kill themselves, but nobody laughed. The comrade in charge of programming thought they should give Stalin a recording of Yudina playing something else, or someone else playing Mozart's Twenty-third Piano Concerto, and admit that the concert had been live. The commissar kneaded his knuckles until they were raw. "Comrade Stalin personally telephones and asks for a record and you expect me to tell him there isn't one. This is out of the realm of possibility."

"He's going to find out eventually," moaned the woman in charge of daytime news broadcasts.

The commissar's eyes narrowed. "He's not going to find out. We're going to make a record of Yudina playing Mozart's Piano Concerto Number Twenty-three!"

That night the commissar convoked Yudina, assembled the orchestra in the radio studio and began cutting a master record. The first conductor's hand shook too much to lead the orchestra. A second was roused out of bed and whisked to the studio, but he also was too nervous to conduct. A third conductor was summoned, but not told whom the recording was for. He got through the score.

At six in the morning technicians working from the master cut a single record. It was slipped into a single jacket that had been designed and printed during the night.

At dawn the commissar drove out to Blizhny and handed the record to a bodyguard, who gave it to Valechka, who deposited it on the dining table next to Stalin's plate.

When Stalin showed up for breakfast at noon, he was surprised to find the record there. He had forgotten he'd asked for it.

1

Moscow, 1952

The last thing in the world Nachshon Ben Aminadav wanted was a reception. "It's traditional," the minister assured him with a stoic toss of his shoulders. "This is a depressing post. We do a pour for newcomers so they won't feel as if they've landed on the moon." The minister scribbled something on a pad and pushed it across the desk. "For your cover, for your mission," he had written, "it is better to go through the diplomatic motions and let everyone, including our own people, think you really are the Counselor for Trade Affairs."

Nachshon peeled the sheet of paper off the pad, along with the one under it, and burned them both in an ashtray. Fixing his features in a reluctant smile, he followed the minister down to the ground-floor dining room. The nine Israeli diplomats and their wives were milling around a long table loaded with *zakuski*. They were uncommonly cheerful; they had been drinking for a while. Someone slipped a glass of vodka into Nachshon's hand. The minister cleared his throat. "Meet Nachshon Ben Aminadav, our new Counselor for Trade Affairs."

"Welcome to Moscow," said the Counselor for Cultural Affairs.

"Welcome, welcome," echoed the others.

"*L'chayim*," the minister said, raising his glass. "To life." He avoided Nachshon's eye.

"*L'chayim*," Nachshon repeated with a grim smile. He nodded thoughtfully and tossed down his dose of vodka.

"Give us your impressions of Moscow," someone called.

"He only arrived this afternoon," the minister said protectively.

"The first thing you notice," Nachshon said, "are the lines. Everywhere you look, lines."

"Most of the time," a diplomat with white hair said, "they don't even know what they're queuing for. They see a line and they join it, figuring they're bound to need whatever's being sold."

"Russia," one of the wives called in a high-pitched voice, "may be a worker's paradise but it's not yet a shopper's paradise."

Everyone laughed at this.

The Counselor for Cultural Affairs peered at Nachshon over his bifocals. "So where did you say you were coming from exactly?"

"I didn't say. But it's Tel Aviv that I'm coming from."

Someone started to tilt a vodka bottle, but Nachshon covered his glass with his hand.

"Is this your first overseas posting?" an attaché asked. Nachshon nodded in a way that could have been taken for a yes or a no.

"You must have enemies in high places," a code clerk said. "To get Moscow, I mean."

Again everyone laughed.

"Do you have a specialty?" an undersecretary asked curiously.

"I am more of a generalist than a specialist," Nachshon answered vaguely.

"That's enough quizzing for one day," the minister announced. "Our new colleague has been traveling for seventy-two hours. He needs to freshen up, to sleep."

After the reception the station chief, who was listed on the manifest as an undersecretary, led Nachshon up to the holy of holies, a room within a room that the code clerks used for enciphering and deciphering. He began spinning the dial on one of the safes. "This can wait until tomorrow if you are tired," he offered.

"Yesterday," Nachshon told him, "was already too late."

The station chief, whose name was Mordechai Shapiro, pulled open the safe door and took out a file folder. He and Nachshon sat down at the long kitchen table the code clerks worked on.

"Can we talk in here?" Nachshon asked.

Shapiro nodded. "This is the one place in the building where we can talk." He untied the ribbon and opened the folder.

"My God, there's not much in there," Nachshon said. "What have you been doing for two years?"

"Look," Shapiro shot back, "hold on to your criticism until you've been here a week and can see for yourself what the situation is."

"What the situation is is desperate," Nachshon retorted.

Shapiro screwed up his face. "We've managed to identify the commissar in charge of minority resettlement—"

Nachshon waved a hand in disgust. "Get rid of one commissar, another will take his place. What do you have on the man himself?"

Shapiro pulled a sheet of paper from the dossier. "This stuff is like panning for gold," he said. "We act drunk and laugh too much and pick up a nugget or two at a diplomatic reception. We have a Jewish woman who gives massages to the mistress of someone on the Politburo. We get odds and ends from her. We have a Jewish girl who sleeps with one of the guards at the dacha. She's our best source."

Nachshon grunted. He was not impressed.

Shapiro exhaled. "Most of the time he leaves the Kremlin through the Borovitsky Gate. They use four identical black Zil 101s. Armored, probably. They weave in and out, they pass one another. Even if you know

which car he's in when he leaves the Kremlin, you
don't know where he is by the time he hits the Arbat.
The convoy travels at high speed. All the traffic lights on
the Arbat, and farther up on Bolshaya Dorogomilovskaya
and the Mozhaisk Highway, are switched to green for
them. There are militiamen and police cars at every
intersection. Personally, I don't consider it possible to
get anywhere near him en route."

"Afterward what happens?"

"Afterward the convoy turns left off the Mozhaisk
Highway beyond the last block of apartment houses.
Onto a government road forbidden to civilian traffic. I
talked to a Yugoslav who has been up it a couple of
times. The road is intestinal—it twists sharply as it
climbs through a forest of black pines and white birches.
There are militiamen stationed along it at intervals.
There are two barriers. There's a high wooden door in a
fence. There's a long avenue that ends at the dacha.
Door to door, from the Kremlin to the dacha, is twelve
miles. That's roughly an eight-minute drive."

Shapiro spread out a map and traced the route with
the eraser end of a pencil. "The dacha's called Blizhny.
The place is called Volynskoye, near Kuntsevo, southwest of Moscow. Here."

Nachshon closed his eyes and rubbed his lids with
the tips of his fingers. Then he opened them and studied the map for a long time. Then he shook his head.
"What do you have on the dacha?"

Shapiro sighed; what he had on the dacha showed
only how airtight the security arrangements were. "The
outside perimeter is patrolled by two-man detachments
and dogs. Inside it's an armed camp. There's a hexago-
nal guard building near the main building with hundreds of crack troops on duty at any given time. There
are searchlights all over the park. There are land mines.
There are trip wires. There are dogs."

"People do get in to see him occasionally," Nachshon
said sarcastically.

Shapiro ignored Nachshon's tone. He had to make
allowances for someone who had been sent to Russia to
do the impossible. "Even the Politburo members are

searched," he explained patiently. "They have to hand their briefcases over to the duty officer. A Von Stauffenberg would never get through this security ring."

Shapiro pulled a pack of American cigarettes from his jacket pocket and offered one to Nachshon.

"Would you mind not smoking?" Nachshon said. "Smoke irritates my eyes. What's the inside look like? Where does he sleep?"

"There's a big room where he holds court. We know there's a fireplace; the old man loves fires. We know there's a large photograph of his dead wife. We know there's a record player. We don't know much else. There's a corridor on the first floor that leads to bedrooms. Some say there are four. Some say six. They're apparently identical—no windows, armor-plated doors, one set of keys which he keeps in his jacket pocket. When he goes to bed he goes into the corridor and closes the door so nobody can see which room he's chosen to sleep in that night." Shapiro added with a frustrated laugh. "You'd think the bastard was afraid someone was going to try to assassinate him."

"You'd think," Nachshon agreed. He was silent for a long while; Shapiro thought he might have dozed off. After a while Nachshon scratched the side of his nose. Then he shook his head, which was almost bald. "There has to be a way to get somebody inside—a maid, a waiter, a plumber. Someone."

Shapiro snorted. "People who set foot in the place are screened. Someone with a drop of Jewish blood in his veins or a circumcised cock would never get past the barriers on the government road."

Nachshon was having trouble keeping his eyes open. He got up and circled the table and stood with his back against a wall to ease the pain in his spine. He still had the hulking look of a linesman who played American football before padding was used. He was built close to the ground; his late wife used to joke that he had a low center of gravity, also a high threshold of pain. When he planted his feet he looked unmovable. When he lowered his head and started forward he looked unstoppable. Now, standing with his back to the wall, he felt suddenly used. It wasn't the traveling that was catching up with him; it was the urgency of the problem he had come to solve. His thoughts drifted to Zander. He would have given his right arm to know if he was still alive. He remembered as if it had happened yesterday the time they had dined on "stuffed" and he had tried to talk him out of going back to Russia. "For me, Palestine is not the promised land, but Russia could be," Zander had told him all those years ago.

Nachshon had corresponded with him more or less regularly until the mid thirties. With the first of the great public trials under way, Nachshon had stopped writing on the theory that it would be safer for Zander if he didn't correspond with someone abroad. When Zander's letters ceased, Nachshon had hoped it was for the same reason. But deep down he doubted it. Knowing Zander, knowing his moral convictions, Nachshon considered it extremely unlikely that he had survived the purges.

"If you want my opinion," Shapiro was saying, "you're dreaming if you think there's a way to get to him." He returned the dossier to the safe and closed the door and spun the combination, and checked the handle to make sure it was locked.

"I am dreaming," Nachshon admitted. He smiled tiredly, a faraway look in his eyes. "But then, Herzl once said that all human activity begins in dreams."

From the window Zander could see Ludmilla hurrying through the snow toward the building. Minutes later he heard her burst through the front door of the communal apartment. It slammed behind her with such force that the framed photographs of her husband and children rattled against the walls. She pounded down the corridor in her furlined galoshes and threw open the door of the living room. "Oh, God, Alexander, I humbly apologize. I really do," she cried. Her nose was beet red from the icy air outside. Tinsels of frost clung to the fringes of hair visible beneath her knitted bonnet. "I won't blame you if you don't baby-sit again for a month. I would have been back on time if I hadn't stopped to queue. They were selling a treasure, Alexander—leather gloves from Czechoslovakia! I bought a pair for everyone except Azalia because they didn't have sizes that small. You are a seven, aren't you? That's what I have written in my notebook. 'Alexander's hand—size seven.' Here, try them on. Were the children bloodsuckers?"

Zander undid the newspaper and pulled out the pair marked with a "7" and started to fit his right hand into one of the gloves. "Vanka finished his homework and went downstairs to play with a friend. Aza got another nosebleed—she's lying on your bed with toilet paper stuffed in her nostrils."

"Personally, I think they come from the altitude—living on the ninth floor like this, the air has to be thinner. Leonid laughs when I talk altitude, but what does he know—he's only a doctor. Do the gloves fit?"

"They're perfect. I haven't seen leather like this in years. How much do I owe you?"

Ludmilla threw her coat over the back of a chair and began to unsnap her galoshes. "It's a birthday present," she insisted. "Happy fifty-nine."

"I am fifty-eight until the twenty-second of the month. Don't rush me," Zander said moodily.

"Did you manage to get any work done while I was gone?"

"I translated four or five pages. But there's no hurry. Anytime I hand it in is all right. It's dull academic material. They pay by the page. And badly. Well, at least it gives me something to do."

Ludmilla sighed one of her drawn-out musical sighs that never failed to impress Zander as *philosophical*. It occurred to him that people in Russia left a great deal unsaid these days, and what was unsaid often came out in the form of a sigh. "I think," Ludmilla said, "it's a crime against humanity when someone like you can't find a regular job."

"If I didn't have the word 'Israelite' on my internal passport, I'd stand a better chance. No one in his right mind is hiring Jews anymore."

"Ha! That reminds me of a story," Ludmilla said. "Have you heard the one about the Jew and *Pravda*?

It's this way: The Jew reads an article that says the Soviet Union is not only going to catch up to America but will surpass it. 'When we surpass America,' the Jew tells his wife, 'we will get off and live there!' "

Zander didn't crack a smile. "I hope to God you don't tell stories like that in front of the children. One of them might repeat it and then where would you be?"

Ludmilla rolled her eyes. "I may be slightly crazy, but I'm not insane!"

Zander lowered his voice. "These are bad times for Jews."

Ludmilla tossed her shoulders in irritation. "I'm not Jewish," she snapped without thinking what she was saying.

"Your stepfather is Jewish," Zander said harshly. "Your husband is Jewish. Your children are half Jewish."

Ludmilla saw he was hurt. "I didn't mean that," she said quickly. She pulled on a pair of slippers and stretched out on the daybed that her eleven-year-old son, Vanka, slept in at night. Her good spirits had evaporated. Zander noticed for the first time fine lines fanning out from the corners of her eyes, and wrinkles on her forehead. She had put on weight, too, and had begun to look her age, which was forty-two. She was obviously more worried than she admitted. "When the war ended," she was rambling on, "I thought it would be different. Leonid came home alive, which was a blessing I had dreamed of but never expected. And we had proved beyond a doubt that we loved our country, that we were loyal to it, that we weren't wreckers and foreign agents. And now Stalin's starting all over again. He's setting the clock back to the nineteen thirties. Leonid has actually packed a small overnight bag and keeps it hidden under the bed. He doesn't know I know, but I know. Leonid's a doctor, not a political person. Why would anyone suspect him?"

Zander felt his flesh creep. She was right, of course; it was starting all over again. The arrest of several prominent Yiddish writers the previous week had really shaken him. According to *Pravda*, they were "Zionist agents of American imperialism." A Jewish literary critic

Zander vaguely knew had been fired from his journal. A Jewish writer friend of his who had published seven novels couldn't find anyone willing to publish his eighth. Rumors were circulating about the Jewish doctors attached to the Kremlin medical service; they were being investigated because of alleged ties to international Zionist organizations. More ominous still was the letter signed by several prominent Jews, including a chess champion, a composer, and a popular writer, asking Comrade Stalin to permit the Jews to redeem the great harm they had done Russia with hard labor in some remote region of the motherland. To Zander, it looked as if Stalin was planning to finish what Hitler started.

It was dark out and the temperature had dipped to minus twenty-seven by the time Zander started home. Ludmilla had wanted him to spend the night—Vanka could double up with his sister and Zander could sleep on the daybed in the living room—but he knew Zsuzsa would worry herself sick if he didn't turn up for dinner; she had lost her father and two uncles and her older brother in the purges. So he pulled on his new gloves and turned up his collar and accepted Ludmilla's offer of a second woolen scarf and with a last wave up to her from the sidewalk headed for the trolley station.

The streets were crowded with people hurrying home from work, and once again Zander noticed how, more than seven years after the end of the Great Patriotic War, almost every man managed to wear some scrap of uniform—a khaki scarf, a khaki greatcoat, army boots, sniper's mittens with a special opening for the trigger finger, an aviator's sheepskin jacket with its lambswool collar. It wasn't, Zander understood, so much because people lacked winter clothing; it was more a question of everyone being fiercely proud to have been part of the military machine that crushed Hitlerism. Zander himself was wearing one of the brown woolen shirts under his jacket that had been issued to him the day he reported for duty. Except for a stint digging tank traps as the Wehrmacht approached the outskirts of Moscow, he had spent the war in an office translating into Russian American field manuals that came with Lend Lease equipment. Still, he felt as if he, too, had made a contribution to the triumph of the Soviet Union, and he wore his old army shirts as a badge of pride.

Arriving at the trolley station, Zander discovered that the overhead power line was down. An emergency unit had blocked the street with its truck and was putting up ladders to repair the line. When Zander politely asked the foreman how long it would be before the trolley returned to service, he muttered, "We're working as fast as we can," by which Zander understood that it could be hours. He started toward the nearest metro station, which was a good fifteen minutes away on foot. He was halfway down the block when he noticed a communal taxi coming toward him. On the spur of the moment—he seldom took taxis because of the cost—he stepped into the gutter and waved his cane at the cab. The driver pulled up and leaned across the passenger's seat and Zander shouted an address. The driver reached out and opened the door. "Be quick," he called, "so we don't lose our heat."

Zander slid into the seat and hurriedly pulled the door closed. As the taxi started forward he turned to nod politely at the two people already in the backseat.

"Zander!" the woman cried. When he stared at her in puzzlement she said, "Don't you recognize me under all this fur? It's me, Masha. And this is my husband, Andrei. Sweet pea, you remember me telling you about the American who came back with Lenin to make the revolution in Russia? Here he is in the flesh. Alexander Til."

Zander had seen Masha in several films during the war and several more since, and remembered reading somewhere that she had married a director who had made a name for himself doing "tractor" stories, which was another way of describing films that glorified collective farms. "You absolutely must come up for a drink," Masha said. "I won't take no for an answer."

"I would take it as a favor if you accepted," her husband said. He had an open, decent face, but the bloated, blurred look around the eyes of someone who drank too much. "I would like to talk to you about

Ronzha," he added. Andrei tilted his head and squinted at Zander, watching him closely to see how he reacted to the mention of the poet's name. Ronzha was not someone who was talked about openly. People lucky enough to own a volume of his early poetry disguised it in a dust jacket from another book. "You see," Andrei said with a wink, "Masha *has* told me about you."

Zander was tempted, but Andrei's reference to Ronzha made him uneasy. "My wife is expecting me," he said. "She'll be worried if I don't get back soon."

"So you're married," Masha said. "Who is the lucky woman?"

"Her name is Zsuzsa. She's half Yugoslav. I met her during the war," Zander said. "We got married right after it, as soon as we could find a place to live."

Masha asked Zander what kind of work he did these days. Zander replied vaguely that he was between jobs.

"What exactly do you do?" Andrei asked.

"Anything."

Andrei studied Zander again and nodded slowly. He reached into his breast pocket and pulled out a small white card, which he offered to Zander. "If you like, come by my office tomorrow," he said. "Anytime after nine. I might have something for you."

When Zander got home and told Zsuzsa what had happened in the taxi she turned the calling card in her fingers, as if looking at it from another angle might reveal more about the man whose name was printed on it. "Very fancy," she said skeptically, running a fingertip over the letters. " 'A. S. Bagdanov. Chairman, Motion Picture Collective.' What do you make of it?"

Zander shrugged. "I don't like being permanently unemployed. I have to take the chance."

Zsuzsa went back to stirring onions in the frying pan. Her mother, an old woman who had been widowed in the thirties and still dressed in black, stuck her head in the door of the communal kitchen. "Smells good, Zsuzsa," she called. "I see Alexander finally got back. I'm not rushing you, but when do you think I'll be able to start cooking my cabbage soup?"

"Give me another quarter hour and the kitchen will

be all yours," Zsuzsa told the old woman. As soon as her mother had gone, Zsuzsa shook her head. "I don't like the business of him mentioning Ronzha's name in front of a taxi driver. Everyone knows they are all informers. Your chairman of the Motion Picture Collective is either an idiot or a *provocateur*, if you ask me."

"The driver didn't look as if he would know who Pushkin was," Zander said. "Anyway, Ronzha was a nickname. There are not many of us left who called him by that name."

Zsuzsa was not convinced. She chewed on the inside of her cheek for a moment. "I don't like it," she said finally. She glanced up from her onions. "Don't forget that Masha denounced you once."

Zander, sitting in a kitchen chair, seemed to hunch down into it. "And I denounced Ronzha," he said softly.

"One thing has nothing to do with the other," Zsuzsa said in exasperation. "Ronzha was dead when you denounced him. You were very much alive when that motion picture actress denounced you."

"She didn't have a choice," Zander insisted.

Zander's coming home late had frayed Zsuzsa's nerves. "I must have missed the whole point of Ronzha reading his Stalin poem to a roomful of people," she blurted out. She kept her voice under tight control so her mother and the other couple living at the end of the corridor wouldn't hear her. "I somehow got the impression from you he did it to demonstrate that even in the worst of times a choice is precisely what people did have."

Zander threw an arm over her shoulder. "I'll be careful."

"Have it your way." Zsuzsa turned back to her onions.

At nine the next morning Zander was scanning the listings in the lobby of a relatively new building opposite the central post office on Gorky Street. He found Motion Picture Collective and rode an elevator up to the seventh floor. Elevators always managed to remind him of Atticus Tuohy and "tunneling up." He hadn't set eyes on Tuohy since the war—he had bumped into him at a metro station which was being used as a bomb shelter during air raids. Atticus had pretended to be delighted to see Zander again and they had talked of getting together and exchanged addresses. But when Zander tried to look him up soon after, he found a pile of rubble where the apartment building had been, and he learned from the block warden that the building had been bombed out *before* Tuohy had given him the address.

At the Motion Picture Collective, Andrei Bagdanov ushered him into his office. "I am delighted you came," he said immediately, and he looked as if he meant it. Waving Zander to a couch in the corner, he settled into a leather chair facing him. He produced a bottle of Polish slivowitz from a shelf under an end table, poured out two brimming glasses, and passed one to Zander. They clanked glasses and drank.

"Masha told me about the favor you did her—" Andrei began.

Zander interrupted. "I never did Masha any favor."

"She doesn't see it that way," Andrei said. "Neither do I. She felt sick to her stomach when she denounced you. She still loses sleep over turning in the girl. You could have denounced her back but you didn't. Frankly, I'd like to do something to make it up to you."

Zander said, "I have no experience with making films."

"Masha told me you used to do subtitles for American pictures during your vacations."

Zander nodded cautiously.

Andrei poured out two more measures of slivowitz. "The Motion Picture Collective over which I preside," he began to explain, "is really a distribution agency. We have hundreds of films and we deal directly with the movie theaters. We have a sideline too. During the last great Wehrmacht offensive against the allies, what the Americans call the Battle of the Bulge, the Germans overran some American army bases and captured a packet of Hollywood films. They were taken back to Berlin and made available to high German officials who were nostalgic for the Gish sisters or Garbo or Charlie Chaplin. At the end of the war our boys liberated the films along with Berlin, but we didn't return them to the Americans—we keep them in basement vaults in this building."

Andrei picked up his tumbler and downed the contents in one swallow and set it down on the tabletop so sharply Zander thought the glass would crack.

Zander said, "You want me to subtitle these films. Is that it?"

"Not exactly," Andrei said. "There are a hundred forty-seven of them in all. Subtitling would be too expensive for our budget. We get requests for these films from some of our senior Party people who are interested in seeing how decadent America is. You still speak fluent American? From time to time I could give you work doing a running translation of a film as it's being shown. I could pay you, say, a hundred rubles for a night's work."

Zander watched Andrei pour out another glass of slivowitz for himself. He had a grudging admiration for anyone who could drink alcohol this early in the day; like the sigh, it was another way of expressing the inexpressible. "There's something I ought to tell you," he said. Andrei looked up. Zander hesitated. Then: "I don't want you to get into trouble because of me."

Andrei waved a hand. "You're a Jew. Masha already told me. So what? If you agree to take on the work, it comes more or less under a freelance directive, which means I pay you out of a special fund and don't have to file a formal notification of employment."

Zander sipped his own glass of slivowitz. "A hundred rubles for a few hours work is hard to resist."

"The films are shown in private apartments," Andrei said. "The projectionist is usually fed in the kitchen afterward. You probably will be too. And the food tends to be first rate."

"When would you want me to start?"

"Tonight if you like. We're sending over a film called *King Kong* to show to one of the members of the Politburo. Fay Wray is fantastic in it. What I mean is, fantastically decadent." With a wink Andrei lifted his glass again. "So: Let's drink. To decadence, in all its forms."

"To decadence," Zander agreed. And he, too, scalded his throat with slivowitz.

"This your first time out, is it?" the projectionist, who had introduced himself as Grinka, whispered. He was a young man with unruly hair and a multi-colored hand-knit tie, the knot of which bobbed comically against his Adam's apple as he spoke. He deftly threaded the tip of the film through the projector up into the empty reel and snapped the lid shut. The equipment had been set up at one end of a long, rectangular dining room. The thick oak table had been pushed against a wall and folding chairs had been lined up in two rows. A portable screen had been suspended from a hook on the far wall. "The important thing," Grinka continued, "is not to be nervous. Take a tip from me—you treat a member of the Politburo as if he were an ordinary factory comrade, and he'll love you for life. They appreciate a good show of equality."

At nine-fifteen Nikita Khrushchev, laughing boisterously, led his wife, Nina, and several couples into the room. Some of the men held cognac glasses. Khrushchev carried the bottle by the throat. "Are you ready for us, Grinka?" he demanded. He shook hands with the projectionist, asked him how his family was, chatted for a moment about the weather. Spotting Zander, he said, "So it's you who's translating for us tonight."

"Yes, comrade."

Khrushchev's bald, fat head bobbed up and down in an emphatic nod as he offered a fat hand for Zander to shake. "Khrushchev," he said, introducing himself.

"Til."

"You speak American?"

"Fluently."

"Well, I've managed to muddle through on nothing but Russian," Khrushchev said with a satisfied chuckle. "I won't know if you are translating what the actors say or making it up as you go along. As long as it sounds good." Laughing good-naturedly, Khrushchev shooed his guests to their places. "Ladies up front," he called.

"Men behind. Smoke if it gives you pleasure. Don't if it doesn't. Somebody get those lights."

In the darkness Grinka started the projector. The titles appeared. Cigar smoke filtered up through the waving beams of light. Watching from the back of the room, Zander remembered how he and Abner once released a jar full of moths in a motion picture theater on the Lower East Side; the moths, attracted by the beams of light from the projector, had cast enormous shadows on the screen that scared the female pianist supplying background music. He wondered what had become of his other brother. What he wouldn't give to see him once more—to see if Palestine had become Leon's promised land.

The opening scene flashed on the screen. Fay Wray uttered her first lines. Zander translated.

"Don't be afraid to speak up, comrade translator," Khrushchev ordered.

When Grinka changed reels, Zander observed Khrushchev and his guests. The men had the easy, sure style of people accustomed to privilege; they sucked noisily on fat cigars and gulped cognac. Khrushchev splashed more cognac into any glass that looked half empty, and held court with a series of vaguely scatological one-liners that kept the men laughing loudly. The women, in a group off to one side, were more restrained. None of them smoked or drank. They spoke, when they spoke at all, in undertones, and nodded in emphatic agreement whenever Nina Khrushchev made a remark. When one of the women laughed out loud, she instantly brought a hand to her lips to stifle the sound.

"It happens to be true that our trees are smaller than American trees," Khrushchev was saying. "Our long winters stunt them. Go push out roots when the ground is frozen! But try to cut down a Russian tree that has grown slowly. The wood is dense. It'll break the teeth on your saw. As to American trees, you can cut them down with a dull kitchen knife. As I see it," he plunged on, everyone hanging on his words, "this sums up the basic difference between your average Russian and your average American."

Grinka snapped the cover of the projector shut. Khrushchev motioned for the man nearest the lights to switch them off. The film came on again. The African tribesmen had tied Fay Wray on a platform and were watching from the top of their stockade as Kong, roaring, emerged from the dense rain forest to claim the sacrifice. "It's always the same," Khrushchev wisecracked from his seat. "Nowadays the *chernozhopy*"—the Russian word had the same sense as "niggers" —wear fine clothes, but underneath they're all cannibals."

This drew appreciative snickers from several of the guests.

When the film was over, Grinka and Zander were invited by a maid into the kitchen, where they found two plates heaped with chicken livers and potatoes, along with half a bottle of Georgian red wine. Khrushchev ambled in to fetch another bottle of cognac, and Zander noticed the shelf brimming with liquor bottles when he opened the closet door. "I liked the way you translated," Khrushchev remarked to Zander. "What did you say your name was again?"

"Til. Alexander Til."

Khrushchev registered this with a curt nod of his bald head.

Zsuzsa was waiting up for Zander when he got back to the apartment. "How did it go?" she asked anxiously.

"Khrushchev himself complimented me on my translation."

"He didn't ask you how you came to speak American?"

"He only said he had muddled through with his Russian."

"Muddled through is one way of putting it," Zsuzsa sneered. "He sent a lot of people to their graves with his Russian." She rose on her toes and buried her face in Zander's neck and said, "You are too dear to me, that is the heart of the problem. Those people live in a viper's nest. If you look at one of them cross-eyed, they will come for you in the night."

"You're blowing it up out of proportion," Zander reassured her. "It is only a job."

"I worry about you," Zsuzsa whispered into his neck.

She pulled back and smiled up at him, and Zander was struck again by the peculiarity of her smile—it always made her look uncomfortably close to tears. He took the expression as further evidence of the human condition in Soviet Russia: how close laughter and tears really were; how at times the emotion balanced on a razor's edge and could go either way.

Zsuzsa seemed to Zander to have been worrying about him from the moment he set eyes on her. He had drifted out of the cloud of a coma to see the pained expression draped across her face like a flag. It was a vision he would never forget. "Can you hear my voice?" she had asked, pronouncing each word distinctly, smiling down at him as if she might burst into sobs if he failed to answer.

He had nodded feebly and uttered the word "yes" only, so he thought at the time, to prevent her from crying. At the sound of his voice the smile had installed itself more firmly, the edges of her mouth fanning out, her eyes relaxing. She had taken his hand in both of hers—the backs of her hands, like her face, were swarming with freckles—and leaning forward until she hovered directly over him, she had spoken soothingly. "You will have a thousand questions. When you are stronger, I will answer them all. For the moment you must take my word for it that you are not seriously wounded. You had a concussion, caused by the explosion of a bomb or an artillery shell. Aside from that there wasn't a mark on you. With rest, with time, you will be as good as new."

She tried to pull her hands free, but Zander kept a grip on her wrist. "Did the Germans take Moscow?" he wanted to know.

Zsuzsa produced the pained smile of hers again. "They came close enough to see the spires. But the tank traps people like you dug stopped them."

Zander had been mustered, along with thousands of others involved in what the Party considered "nonessential" war work, on Gorky Street. They had been issued pickaxes and shovels from the backs of army trucks and marched through the deserted streets of the city to the outskirts to begin constructing a last line of defense against the Panzer divisions closing in on the capital. During the day they could hear the hollow thud of artillery shells bursting in the west; at night they could see flashes lighting up the horizon. On the third day the overcast skies cleared and the German Stukas, diving out of a ceramic sun, came at them in waves. Burrowing into the corner of the deepest tank trap, pressing his nostrils into the fragrant earth until it was difficult to breathe, Zander could hear the explosions of the Stukas' bombs along the trench line. He thought he heard what could only have been a bomb plowing into the spongy ground—it had been raining for days—and remembered listening to the absolute stillness as he waited for it to explode.

The silence was the last thing he had heard. "According to the dossier that came with you," Zsuzsa told him several days later, "you were as close to an exploding bomb as anyone has gotten and still lived. The shock waves traveling through the ground are what caused your concussion. You were covered with dirt and they had to dig you out. At first they thought you were dead, but some bright comrade had the sense to check for pulses in the bodies waiting to be buried. He found one in you. And here you are today."

Zander had been evacuated from Moscow to a peasant village called Yundola on the Asian slope of the Urals, not far, curiously, from Ekaterinberg, which was now called Sverdlovsk. There was no electricity in the village, but the streets were wired with loudspeakers from which martial music or war news blared constantly. The closed hangar that served as a village center for Party meetings and propaganda lectures and weddings and funerals had been fitted out with cots and converted into a sanitarium for convalescent soldiers. There were twenty-seven of them, some with missing limbs, some blind, two with total amnesia, all under the care of Zsuzsa and an old man who claimed to have been a male nurse in the First World War. In the beginning Zander had taken Zsuzsa for a doctor. He was surprised to discover, the first time they went for a stroll together, that she was only a *feldsher*, a semi-qualified medical attendant. She had completed a year of medical school when the war broke out. When the first wave of casualties swamped the Soviet Union's hospitals, anyone with the slightest medical background was pressed into service. Zsuzsa was given a military medical manual that described which wounds were treatable and which were so grave that the wounded had no hope of surviving. Through trial and error she became, in the space of six short months at a field hospital, a qualified surgeon. She knew nothing about rheumatism and asthma and precious little about hernias and hemorrhoids or the common cold, but she was pretty much of an expert at removing limbs or digging shrapnel out of any part of the anatomy. A great many of her operations had been performed, because of a lack of anesthesia, with orderlies pinning the wounded man to the operating table. "I can still hear their screams," she confided to Zander one day. "That was the most difficult part for me—inflicting unbearable pain in order to save their lives. But I gritted my teeth and forced myself to do it. God, it was a nightmare. Was I relieved when they assigned me to Yundola."

During what had become their regular afternoon walk, they had climbed the slope that began beyond the last woodshed and ended in a high meadow a few hundred meters above the village. From there it was possible to see the valley that split the hills on the other side and the snow-capped Ural Mountains that were higher than the lowest clouds. That particular afternoon they had been talking about war again. Zsusza watched the currents of air undulating through the high grass of the meadow. Her eyes blinked rapidly. A pained smile spread across her face—and then the smile ceded to the pain and she burst into tears. Zander put an arm awkwardly over her shoulder and pulled her against his chest and felt her body trembling against his. After a while she became calmer. "I am truly sorry about that," she told him, panting slightly, wiping tears away with the back of her hands. "I don't usually lose control of myself."

"There was no harm done," Zander said. "People need to cry occasionally."

"All this space, all this quiet, makes it hard to believe there is a war raging beyond those mountains," she said. "It's hard to believe *feldshers* are cutting bullets out of young boys being held down by orderlies." She flung herself onto the ground and opened another button of her shirt and spread wide her collar to get some sun on her chest and neck. "When the war is over I am going to go back to medical school and learn about all the things I missed—runny noses and warts and measles and chicken pox. I plan to specialize in ingrown toenails."

Settling down next to her on the ground, Zander suddenly found himself staring at the rise and fall of her breasts under her khaki shirt and the triangle of skin she had bared to the sun. It struck him that she was sensual without being aware of it—as sensual as snow is, or the rippling flow of a shallow brook. He was overpowered by the urge to feel her coolness, to taste her wetness. Without premeditation he reached out and undid the next button of her shirt. Her eyes flicked open. Her tongue moistened her upper lip. Her fingertips came to rest so lightly on his knuckles he wasn't sure if she were restraining him or encouraging him.

"Why do you hesitate?" she asked huskily.

"I didn't know if you would appreciate my . . . gesture."

She smiled her smile that could go either way and gently guided his fingers down to the next button. Her shirt parted like a curtain opening on the first act of a new play. Zander undid the other buttons. Leaning over Zsuzsa, he gratefully buried his face in the swell of a freckled breast.

2

Tuohy strolled over to the sideboard for a bottle of mineral water. "Keep talking," he instructed the department head who was reporting on the transportation situation. He filled his glass and carried it back to his place at the head of the conference table.

"We calculate we will require," said the aide, a stoop-shouldered bureaucrat with the pasty complexion of someone who had worked indoors for thirty years, "a minimum of three hundred railway wagons a day for a period of ten days to deal with the situation in Moscow. Mustering this kind of rolling stock will pose no insurmountable problems—we will simply cancel all civilian traffic during that period. With three hundred wagons, we're talking forty-five thousand people a day, or four hundred fifty thousand in the ten days that the operation lasts."

"Would you use several railway stations or a single station?" Tuohy asked.

"From the point of view of efficiency, of localizing the potential disturbances, we think it would be advisable to use a single station. We would propose a fifteen-wagon train every hour for twenty hours a day, with a four-hour interval to clean the station and the toilets."

Tuohy sipped his mineral water thoughtfully, then picked up a pencil and resumed his doodling. "How would we get them to come to the railway station?" he asked the man sitting directly across from him. He was the MGB (as the NKVD was now called) expert on the "Jewish problem."

"There can be no question of rounding them up," the expert replied. "What with two and a half million Jews nationwide, and four to five hundred thousand of them in Moscow alone, we don't have that kind of manpower available. What we do have is lists. We would do a

470

mailing. Summon them to appear at such and such a station at such and such an hour. Specify how much baggage they were permitted to bring with them. Most important, specify the eventual sanction for those who fail to comply. My guess is we would get ninety-eight percent of them to walk in under their own steam. Then it would be a problem of logistics—there could be no question of the trains running late, for instance, and the deportees piling up."

"If I commit my department to three hundred wagons a day, that is precisely what we will deliver," the pasty-faced bureaucrat said stiffly.

"Correct me if I'm wrong," an intense young MGB aide who worked for Tuohy interjected, "but I'm under the impression that the actual trip to Birobidzhan near the Chinese frontier will take five days."

The railroad man nodded. "Five full days," he agreed.

"Which means we would have to position stocks of food along the route to feed the Jews," the young MGB aide noted.

"Not necessarily," Tuohy said. "We could require them to show up with a five-day supply of food in their baggage. That way we would be responsible only for drinking water. That's what we did when we deported the Crimea Tartars to Siberia."

"What about foreign journalists?" an MGB department head asked. "They are bound to find out about the deportation before it is a fait accompli. The publicity could be embarrassing for us. The capitalist press, which always paints our actions in the worst possible light, is likely to say we are picking up where Hitler left off."

"We could cordon off the entire area around the station," the young MGB aide suggested. "No foreigner would be permitted past our barriers."

An older man who had been silently following the conversation lifted a forefinger. Tuohy nodded respectfully at him. "The foreign press will pose no problem," the older man, who directed the department that dealt with nondiplomatic foreigners in Moscow, said flatly. "We will divert their attention—organize something for them outside of the capital they won't want to miss. A birthday party for Comrade Stalin in Georgia, for example. Or a tour of the Leningrad naval facility."

"The American press will be the most dangerous to us," the railroad man said. "Everyone knows it is owned and staffed by Jews or their hangers-on."

"It is for this reason," the older department head said tiredly, "that their stories will be discredited."

"The Jewish press," Tuohy added, "didn't kick and scream at the German final solution—stories about the extermination of eight hundred thousand Polish Jews were printed on the back pages. And in any case, we are not exterminating the Jews—we are simply creating a Jewish autonomous republic and inviting them to move to it. There is a difference."

One of Tuohy's young, bright people, a rising star in the Commissariat of Minority Resettlement, which Tuohy headed, caught his boss's eye. "Nobody has spoken about the absolute necessity for laying a solid psychological groundwork for the deportation," he said.

"Psychology," the old MGB man said sneeringly, "is a capitalist discipline that blames problems on infant sexuality rather than on the economic factors cited by Marx as the root cause of society's ills."

Tuohy sensed it was the moment to assert himself. His older colleague had been passed over for the job of Commissar of Minority Resettlement and seemed to hold it personally against him. "With all respect to my colleague's years of experience and obvious expertise," he said lazily, still doodling on his pad, "psychological considerations must be dealt with." He looked up from his doodling. "There are two central problems as I see it. First, we must suppress any instinct on the part of the Jews to resist resettlement; let us not forget that when they were pushed to the wall they rose up against the Germans in the Warsaw ghetto and managed to hold out against them longer than Poland held out at the start of the war. Secondly, we must suppress any instinct on the part of the non-Jewish community to see the Jews as victims and sympathize with them, thereby undermining the authority of the Party and the state. I agree with my young comrade on the importance of preparing the psychological terrain carefully. There is already a general tendency on the part of Greater Russians to see Jews as an alien element in our society. We must exploit this tendency. It would be helpful, for instance, if we could uncover a Jewish plot against the Communist state, or Stalin himself; if we could demonstrate that Jews are agents of our enemies. Confessions, it goes without saying, would be desirable. Deportations, when they came, would then be seen as a normal punishment for proven transgressions. There would even be a case to be made—I leave it to the comrades dealing with the propaganda aspects of the plan to develop this theme—that unlike Hitler, we have bent over backward to be lenient. Our solution to the Jewish problem will be seen to be a humanitarian one."

The conference droned on. Tuohy's thoughts drifted. He wasn't worried about missing anything; the conversation was being recorded by a stenographer and he would have to go over her notes later in any case. He considered himself eminently qualified for the important MGB post of Commissar of Minority Resettlement. He had cut his teeth on resettlement problems during and immediately after the war. He had had a hand in the deportation to Siberia of the predominantly Moslem mountaineers of the Northern Caucasus, many of whom had been openly sympathetic to the German invaders; in the space of a few days tens of thousands of Chechens, Ingushi, Karachais, and Balkars had been herded onto railway boxcars and sent east. The Buddhist Kalmuks and Volga Germans had eventually followed in their footsteps. There had been some talk, as Soviet troops raised the hammer and sickle over the ruins of Berlin, of deporting the entire population of the Ukraine—a great many Ukrainians had greeted the Germans as liberators—but the project had been abandoned because there were so many of them.

Tuohy had been a sector supervisor in the first deportations. When things in his zone had gone off without a hitch he had been promoted to an area supervisor, and then to second in command for the Kalmuk deportation. So it was only natural that they turned to him when the idea was first put forward to deport the Jews to the other end of the country. At the moment the project was in the contingency stage, but Tuohy had a strong hunch that Stalin would go through with it if the plans were carefully drawn and looked sensible. The old man, Tuohy knew, had a lifelong antipathy toward Jews; many of the rivals he had annihilated over the years—including Trotsky in Mexico in 1940, via a Bolshevik agent who buried an ice ax in his skull—had been of Jewish origin. Hadn't he said on more than one occasion that Russia's two and a half million Jews were a vast reservoir for spies, dissenters, and troublemakers? Hadn't he ordered, the previous summer, the execution of the twenty-five Yiddish writers and intellectuals who had been in prison for years? The spontaneous demonstration that greeted the arrival in Moscow of the Israeli Foreign Minister, Golda Meir, in 1948, had only confirmed Stalin's suspicion of the existence of a vast Zionist plot against him and the Communist state. No, Tuohy didn't for a moment doubt the old man was as serious about the Jews as he had been in the early thirties about the kulaks; the Jews, in a manner of speaking, *were* latter-day kulaks, a collective enemy that needed to be mercilessly rooted out.

And there was no telling how high in the superstructure someone might climb if he managed to take care of this little gardening chore for the boss. Tuohy smiled to himself as another epitaph came to him: Here lies Atticus Tuohy, who came from the earth and returned to the earth—and in between gardened!

The housekeeper bustled about the room, drawing curtains to keep out the light of the electric streetlamps, fluffing the pillows on the single easy chair she had pulled around to face the portable screen, arranging a footstool, positioning the side table with the telephone. Grinka snapped the cover closed on the projector. He tested to make sure the machine was properly threaded, then nodded to the housekeeper. "We are ready whenever he is," he told her.

Looking as if his thoughts were a world away, Vyacheslav Mikhailovich Molotov strode stiffly into the room and sat down in the easy chair. The housekeeper turned off the lights and took up a position with her back to a wall, her hands folded over her large breasts. Grinka started the projector. The titles flashed on the screen. That night the film was *The Jazz Singer*, starring Al Jolson.

"Focus, if you please," Molotov ordered.

Grinka twisted the lens to adjust the focus. "Is that better, comrade?"

Molotov, toying with the pince-nez dangling from a black cord around his neck, didn't bother to answer.

Standing directly behind Molotov, Zander began translating the dialogue as the actors on the screen spoke their lines. From time to time he glanced at the back of the head of the man in the easy chair. His hair was slicked down and neatly parted. He looked more like an aging professor than the second most powerful man in the Soviet Union. According to a recent article in *Pravda*, twelve cities and towns and villages had been named after him. His name had also been given to one of the highest peaks in the Pamir Mountains, to a cape in the Arctic Ocean, to a district of Moscow, to a warship and a merchant ship and to the country's largest automobile plant. Yet, as almost everyone knew, his wife was lingering in a prison camp in Kazakhstan and there was obviously nothing he could do about it.

Rumor had it that the question of arresting Polina Molotova had turned up on the Politburo's agenda; that when it came to a vote, Molotov had daringly abstained. His wife, who was the godmother of the Soviet perfume industry, had committed the crime of being Jewish, and Molotov had been unable to muster the courage—or the audacity—to vote *no*.

Two thirds of the way through *The Jazz Singer* the telephone sounded in the darkness. Grinka instantly switched off the projector. The housekeeper's arm shot out and the flame-shaped electric bulbs in the elaborate overhead chandelier came alive. Molotov twisted a quarter turn in his chair and picked up the receiver.

"Speaking," he said. He listened for a moment.

"Good evening to you, Josef Vissarionovich," he said.

"The most recent report indicates the situation is the same as it was yesterday. The front is stable. Neither the Koreans nor the Americans show any signs of launching an offensive. The armistice talks are stalled—it is my view that they will remain that way until Eisenhower replaces Truman in the White House. Then we may see some movement."

Molotov listened for a long while. His brow furrowed. "That's the first time I heard that. I will get a cable off to our people in Washington tomorrow to see if they have any information about Eisenhower being partly Jewish."

"No, no, you didn't interrupt anything important. The Motion Picture Collective sent over a film for the evening."

"American?"

"*The Jazz Singer*, starring someone named Jolson. I don't remember his first name."

"To tell you the truth, it never occurred to me that he was Jewish. Personally, I didn't even like his singing. Now I understand why. It is well known that only Negroes can correctly perform jazz."

"I look forward to it."

Molotov dropped the receiver onto its cradle. His eyes narrowed, his lips pursed. The housekeeper reached for the wall switch. Molotov stood up abruptly. "There is no need to project the end," he announced. "The film is a waste of time."

Still looking as if his thoughts were a world away, he left the room.

It had been Ludmilla's idea to combine the celebration of Zander's fifty-ninth birthday with a trip to Leningrad. Vanka, who was going on twelve, and Aza, who was eight and a half, hadn't been there in two years. And it would give them all an excuse to visit Arishka and Appolinaria and Serafima and Sergeant Kirpichnikov again. The four of them shared a three-room flat in one of the modern prefabricated apartment buildings that had spread like fungus across the suburbs.

"Living inside one of these monstrosities," Arishka was saying with a playful twinkle in her eyes, "is not nearly as bad as it is made out to be. It is true the elevators never seem to work—the woman who lives above us spent all of yesterday morning stranded between the fourth and fifth floors yelling for help—but walking stairs happens to be good for the hips. And after a while you don't hear the toilets flushing or the next-door neighbors arguing in that controlled voice that people use in communal apartments when they're angry."

"If the walls are so thin," Zander said, "maybe we should avoid this kind of conversation."

"I can see you haven't changed," Arishka said.

"Zander's right," Zsuzsa said. "These days you can't be too prudent."

"Granddad Zander always gets nervous when someone says something anti-Soviet," Aza explained brightly.

"Just because someone criticizes something doesn't mean he is anti-Soviet," Arishka told the child.

Vanka, who was sprawled on the floor thumbing through back issues of *Soviet Life*, said without looking up, "We tell anti-Soviet stories at school all the time. I don't see what Zander is so nervous about."

"Zander," Zsuzsa explained impatiently, "has seen the inside of prisons. He has good reason to be nervous."

The boy's eyes widened and he looked up at Zander. "You've been in prison? How come nobody ever told me? What for?"

"It's a long story," Zander said. "I'll tell you some other time."

"It's a short story," Appolinaria said. "I'll tell you now if you like."

Ludmilla asked Serafima, "Have you heard the one about the man who said he was born in St. Petersburg, educated in Petrograd and married in Leningrad. When he was asked where he wanted to live he said, 'St. Petersburg.'"

Serafima didn't laugh. "I'm not sure I get it."

Ludmilla sighed. "Maybe I'm not telling it well."

Ludmilla's husband, Leonid, pushed Sergeant Kirpichnikov into the room in his new wheelchair. Pasha was

wearing a khaki tunic with his old Medal of St. George
pinned to the breast. Spittle drooled from the sagging
corner of his mouth. Serafima came over and dabbed it
away with her handkerchief and adjusted the blanket
over his legs. Zander planted himself directly in front of
the wheelchair and said in a gentle voice, "Hello, Pasha. It's good to see you again."

The sergeant stared at Zander without uttering a
sound. There was a faint, lopsided smile on his lips and
a vacant stare in his eyes. He tapped the armrest of the
wheelchair rhythmically with the stump of his arm. Aza
peered around Zander's legs at the stump, pulled a
face, and went back to sit with her mother.

"The only person he recognizes," Serafima whispered
to Zander, "is me, and then only sometimes. The best
is if we get on with the party."

Arishka said with false enthusiasm, "So how does it
feel to be almost sixty, dear Zander?"

"It feels the same as when you're *almost* fifty, or
almost forty. You worry about crossing thresholds."

"The way I look at it," Appolinaria said, "growing old
has its good side—it'll be over that much sooner."

"What will be over that much sooner?" Aza asked. As
usual, the adults around her were talking in riddles.

Ludmilla said, "We brought the children all this way—
the least we could do is keep the conversation pleasant
for a change." Rolling her eyes in annoyance, she headed
for the kitchen.

"That's the trouble with this country," Appolinaria
commented. "Outside the apartment the Party censors
what we talk about. Inside, we censor ourselves. There
are no real conversations anymore."

Leonid said, "Ludmilla's only worried about the children hearing things they shouldn't hear."

"What *were* you in prison for?" Vanka asked Zander.

"He went to prison," Appolinaria announced firmly,
"for refusing to denounce someone."

Sergeant Kirpichnikov perked up. "Marx-Engels-
Lenin-Organizers of Revolution told me to sign on the
dotted line," he growled in a hoarse voice, "so I signed.
Where was the harm?"

The children, who had never heard the sergeant utter a word until that moment, stared at him in awe. "Don't be frightened," Serafima told them quietly. "Sometimes he remembers a piece of the past and out it comes."

"I'm not at all frightened," Aza said in a frightened voice.

Ludmilla appeared at the swinging door of the kitchen carrying a homemade cake ablaze with thick candles. She set it on the Formica table before Zander. He counted the candles. "Why are there only fourteen?" he asked.

"It's symbolic," Leonid said.

"In Russia," Appolinaria put in, "everything is always symbolic."

"Fourteen was all we could find," Ludmilla explained in exasperation.

"Blow them out, blow them out," chanted the two children.

Zander filled his lungs and blew. He got all except one before he ran out of breath.

"Not blowing out all the candles in one breath is symbolic too," Appolinaria remarked dryly.

"It means you're growing old," Arishka said.

Zander took another breath and blew out the remaining candle. Everyone applauded. Zsuzsa came over and kissed him lightly on the lips.

"The least you could do is give us a speech," Leonid insisted.

Zander pushed on his cane and rose to his feet. "The great advantage of family gatherings," he said, glancing around, smiling thoughtfully, nodding faintly, "is it permits you to count your blessings. I thank you all from the heart for *being*."

"Being *what*?" Aza asked in frustration. Another riddle!

Vanka puffed out his cheeks and punctured them with his forefingers, producing a perfect imitation of an explosion.

"Don't do that!" Serafima screamed—but it was too late.

Across the room Sergeant Kirpichnikov's eyes filled with terror. He puffed out his cheeks and began mimicking the sound of hand grenades going off one after the other. The explosions were unevenly spaced and very realistic.

"Dear God in heaven," Appolinaria moaned. "When will the war end?"

The summer of 1941 had been the worst in memory for mosquitoes. There were those who seriously believed that German bombers passing overhead had seeded the Ukraine with billions of larvae to harass the Red Army. The situation was especially desperate near a body of stagnant water. Some of the mosquitoes were so large, city boys mistook them for praying mantises. The mosquitoes didn't appear to know fear or prudence. They would alight on a forearm or the back of a hand with incredible audacity. Soldiers took to smearing their exposed skin with urine, but the only thing this seemed to keep away was other humans.

Sergeant Kirpichnikov was absently scratching an enormous mosquito welt that was already raw and bleeding as he bent over the radio set. For a moment all he and the others could hear was static. The soldier turning the crank that powered the radio slapped the back of his neck, then inspected the stain of blood on his palm. "Got the bastard," he muttered.

"Don't stop cranking," the sergeant ordered in annoyance.

On the radio a voice gradually separated itself from the static. The eight men gathered around the set leaned closer.

"My brothers, my sisters, I turn to you, my friends."

The speaker could be heard breathing heavily as if he were very agitated. He paused to sip some water. Then he went on. "Our country is in serious danger."

He was drowned out by another burst of static.

"He's accused us of being a lot of things over the years but never his brothers and sisters," a wiry, battle-weary machine gunner said bitterly.

"All it takes is some Nazi tanks heading for Moscow

and suddenly we are his friends. What bullshit," a cook said.

It was not surprising that Stalin's speech evoked resentment. The Great Helmsman, the tried and trusted disciple of Lenin, the wise leader who could be seen in the newsreels sucking thoughtfully on the stem of his Dunhill as he listened to the reports of his military commanders, had not been heard from since the Germans launched their attack across the Soviet frontier ten days before; he had disappeared as surely as a shadow does when the sun darts behind a rain cloud. There were rumors he had suffered a nervous breakdown when he learned that the "invincible" Red Army had melted away before the Panzers plunging toward the heartland. Now, as the static faded, the voice of Stalin could be heard again, summoning his brothers, his sisters, his friends to a holy war against the *Nemtsi*, the tongueless ones, the Germans.

"I say to hell with him," said a private who had an arm in a filthy makeshift sling. "For years he's been boasting the Germans would break themselves against our frontier. And here we are cut off behind their lines inside our borders."

"If you ask me," said a soldier who looked as if he wasn't a day over seventeen, "we ought to be figuring out how to surrender."

"Surrender!" another soldier with an artillery insignia on his sleeve piped up. "Haven't you heard about concentration camps?"

"That's probably a lot of propaganda bullshit like everything else we've been told," the seventeen-year-old said.

A city boy who had spent a year at Moscow University slapped at a mosquito buzzing around his ear. "I agree," he said. "You have to take these horror stories about Germans with a grain of salt. After all, they're the people of Goethe and Schiller and Beethoven and Bach."

A Moscow journalist who had been trapped behind German lines with the unit he was covering snickered. He was a nearsighted man with beady eyes and round steel-rimmed eyeglasses.

"Why do you snicker?" Sergeant Kirpichnikov demanded. "If you know something, spit it out."

"You have forgotten what the people of Pushkin and Turgenev and Tchaikovsky and Tolstoy have been doing to the peasants and the Party for the last ten years," he said. "In any case, for me there is no question of surrendering. I happen to be Jewish."

"I don't know what we're arguing about," the sergeant said. "Stalin may have gone to extremes, I grant you. But he's not the enemy. Hitler is the enemy. The Germans are the enemy. They have invaded the Motherland. It is not for us to talk of surrendering. We must fight them until they are dead, or we are."

The artillery man pounded the table with his fist. "The sergeant's got it right. We must take our radio and our weapons and go deeper into the woods and form a partisan unit and harass the invaders."

"A partisan unit," cried Sergeant Kirpichnikov. "That's the ticket."

Someone broke out the last half-bottle of vodka left to them and passed glasses around. The sergeant raised his aloft. "Death to the mosquitoes and the *Nemtsi!*" he cried.

Everyone laughed. "Death to the mosquitoes and the *Nemtsi,*" they repeated in chorus.

In the early days of the war soldiers cut off by the lightning blitzkrieg advance of the German armies organized their partisan units along democratic lines. They elected their commanders and approved his tactics with voice votes. Sergeant Kirpichnikov, at fifty-three, was the oldest man present and the highest ranking one. On top of that, he had seen combat in World War I—he still wore his Cross of St. George on his breast—and the civil war, which made him the most experienced too. His name was proposed by the artillery man and seconded by the cook and the Moscow journalist. The vote was unanimous. Which is how the sergeant came to command the partisan unit that took his name, the Kirpichnikov Red Star Partisan Brigade.

Operating from a series of base camps hidden in isolated parts of the countryside, constantly on the move to avoid betrayal by collaborators, the Kirpichnikov Brigade—its ranks swollen by other Red Army stragglers—began staging hit-and-run attacks on the German rear.

In Moscow good news was in short supply, so the commentators recounted the exploits of the courageous partisans operating behind German lines. Partly because it had a working radio and was able to communicate with Moscow, partly because one of its members was a journalist who knew how to dramatize events, attention soon focused on the Kirpichnikov Red Star Partisan Brigade. Hardly a week went by without news of another of its exploits reaching Moscow. A German storage dump had gone up in flames. A convoy carrying ammunition toward the front had been ambushed and fourteen of the eighteen trucks had been destroyed. A bridge over the Pripet had been blown up, a railway tunnel had been blocked, a Waffen SS Lieutenant Colonel had been taken prisoner and executed by firing squad in retaliation for the hanging of two of Kirpichnikov's wounded partisans left behind after a raid.

The partisan war was fought at night, since the poorly armed partisans couldn't risk daylight confrontations with the Wehrmacht. Neither side bothered with prisoners. As the partisans became more daring, the Germans started taking hostages from villages and towns in the area, and executing ten of them for every German killed. By the second winter of the war the peasants tended to see the partisans as the source of all their troubles and turned against them. There were more and more instances of collaborators leading German punitive expeditions along the almost invisible trails that led to the partisan camps. Partisan casualties mounted. Food supplies dried up. Starvation was a real possibility; the partisans had already started eating the dogs that hung around their camp.

Toward the end of December 1942, the sergeant's brigade, whittled down to thirty-seven men and eight women and two children, got wind of a cache of sweet potatoes that the peasants from a nearby village were supposed to have hidden under the floorboards of their former Party headquarters. There was a heated discussion about whether the Germans were baiting a trap. Finally the sergeant proposed that those who felt the risk was worth taking set out with him to bring back the sweet potatoes.

Under an unusually heavy snowfall that muted all sound, the sergeant led twelve men and two women— one of whom was breastfeeding an infant inside her dogskin overcoat—out of the forest and along a frozen stream toward the village in question. Surveying the village from a rise through captured Zeiss binoculars, Sergeant Kirpichnikov announced that nothing looked out of place. Smoke spiraled up from chimneys. Several men could be seen fishing through holes they had cut in the ice covering a pond. He could even make out two children building a snowman in front of the village hall.

Walking in two files, the partisans entered the village along its only street and drew up in the courtyard before the former Party headquarters. The sergeant strode forward to knock on the door with the stump of his hand. A whistle shrilled. All the shutters on the houses facing the courtyard were flung open. At each window was a German soldier kneeling behind a machine gun. The German officer who had responded to the knock pressed the tip of his Luger into the sergeant's stomach. "Resistance is futile," he said in excellent Russian. "One gesture and my men will slaughter you."

The area commander was delighted to discover that the famous Kirpichnikov himself had fallen into his hands. He decided that the partisans would be executed, but in a way that would provide a memorable example for others tempted to follow in their footsteps. The day after their capture, Sergeant Kirpichnikov, along with the twelve men and two women—the infant still at the breast of one of them—were marched under heavy guard through the village out into a field. Their wrists were attached to fence posts behind their backs with lengths of wire. The German soldiers stood around smoking and stamping their feet to keep warm as two ordnance experts tinkered with a box full of grenades, dipping the firing pins into a pail of water and then holding them in the air until there was a thin coating of ice on them. The firing pins were then reinserted and the grenades activated. As long as there was ice on the pins they would not explode. The Germans went down the line inserting a grenade under the shirt of each partisan; the woman who had the infant at her chest found the grenade nestled between her breasts and the baby. Then the Germans piled into a truck and roared off.

Exhaling into the cold air, Sergeant Kirpichnikov called out, "Above all, dignity." Down the line of prisoners the baby at the breast of its mother could be heard whimpering. Several of the men struggled to free their wrists. One of them, the Jewish journalist, spat curses at the sky. Another cried. Another sagged forward in a dead faint. The woman who had the infant inside her dogskin coat stared at the sergeant in horror. "Do something!" she screamed.

Gradually the heat given off by the body melted the coating of ice on the firing pins, and the grenades began exploding. The first one went off at the far end of the line, killing the Jewish journalist. Everyone strained to look. Seeing the bright blood and pieces of flesh and clothing on the snow, they turned away.

The worst part was not knowing at what instant the explosion would come. One of the women began babbling incoherently until the grenade exploded against her chest. Two more grenades went off simultaneously, one to the sergeant's left, one to his right. Then three more in quick succession. "Dear Lord Jesus," the woman with the baby screamed—and her grenade went off. The sergeant sucked in his stomach and held his breath and heard the pulse pounding in his ear. There were two more explosions, and another, and then three more so closely spaced that the new explosion cut into the echo of the preceding one. Sergeant Kirpichnikov forced himself to look around. There were no people tied to fence posts, only splashes of color and fragments of clothing at the base of each. And still his grenade didn't explode. His lips twitched, his facial muscles sagged. Spittle ran down the side of his face. And still there was no explosion. He thought about the grenade pressing like a tumor into his stomach; he could feel the silky iciness of the metal, the roughness of its roundness. And still there was no explosion. He realized his eyes were open but he couldn't make out anything but the light. He tried to force himself to focus but his brain was no longer in touch with the muscles that did that work. He tried to scream but was unable to produce more than a gurgling that sounded like bubbles breaking the surface of a pond.

And still there was no explosion.

Two members of the Kirpichnikov Red Star Partisan Brigade who had had second thoughts about the sweet potatoes and had followed the others came across the sergeant that night. One of them gingerly extracted the German grenade from inside his shirt and flung it into a snowbank. And still there was no explosion. "Faulty firing pin," the other partisan commented.

Gripping the sergeant under his armpits, they dragged him into the woods toward the base camp. When they stopped to rest, the sergeant sagged against a tree. Spittle ran from the corner of his mouth. His eyes failed to focus. He puffed out his cheeks and began mimicking the sound of hand grenades going off.

The explosions were unevenly spaced and very realistic.

Appolinaria drew the curtain that separated her half of the room from Arishka's. She had already recited in her head her morning ration of twenty-five of Ronzha's poems—she would, as usual, do another twenty-five in the evening before she went to sleep. That way she recited each poem at least once a week. She slid the larger of the two cardboard valises out from under the bed and snapped open the lid. Before she touched anything, she pulled on the rubber kitchen gloves she kept hidden under the mattress; she didn't know much about the business of fingerprints, but she didn't want to take the risk of leaving any. She selected a sheet of ordinary writing paper from the middle of the package, and an ordinary envelope from another pile. She flattened the paper on the small table she used for letter writing and picked up her fountain pen. It was a delicious moment and she savored it. Of course it wasn't true that you couldn't say what you thought in Russia. You could say anything as long as you didn't leave fingerprints and printed it out so there could be no question of tracing the handwriting.

JOSEF, she began, painstakingly printing out each letter in capitals.

She looked up, squinting thoughtfully. She had been writing to him regularly once a week for the past four years. Her instinct told her he was reading her letters personally; they were too intimate for an underling to risk keeping them from him. At times she could almost feel the bond between them, the tyrant who ruled over a people he was essentially afraid of and the woman who had the knack of seeing into the most veiled reaches of his evil heart. Smiling viciously, she went back to her printing.

YOU WILL BE SEVENTY-THREE YEARS OLD NEXT WEEK, ACCORDING TO MY CALCULATIONS, WHICH MAKES YOU ROUGHLY TEN YEARS OLDER THAN ME. (I SAY *ROUGHLY* BECAUSE I DON'T WANT YOU TO GO AND ARREST EVERY PERSON IN THE COUNTRY BORN IN 1889 IN ORDER TO CATCH ME; WE BOTH KNOW YOU ARE CAPABLE OF IT.) I CAN IMAGINE THE FEAR WITH WHICH YOU LIVE—IT MUST SURELY CLOUD YOUR EVERY WAKING THOUGHT, YOUR NIGHTMARES TOO. IT IS NOT SIMPLY THE FEAR OF PERMANENT DISAPPEARANCE INTO THE MAW OF DEATH WHICH EVERYONE SHARES, THOUGH IN RUSSIA THOSE OF US WHO ARRIVE AT OLD AGE HAVE THE ADVANTAGE, THANKS TO YOU, OF HAVING LIVED WITH THIS FEAR OUR ENTIRE LIVES AND THUS ARE MORE OR LESS USED TO IT. NO, IN YOUR CASE, JOSEF DZHUGASHVILI, YOU WILL BE OBSESSED WITH THE FEAR THAT YOU WILL BE STRUCK DOWN—BUT WON'T DIE! YOU WILL REMEMBER LENIN AFTER HIS STROKE BEING PUSHED FROM ROOM TO ROOM IN A ROLLING CHAIR, STRUGGLING TO PRODUCE DISTINGUISH-

ABLE SPEECH AND WITH SUPERHUMAN EFFORT
MANAGING AN OCCASIONAL *"VOT, VOT."*

Appolinaria looked up again. A grim smile of anticipation disfigured her thin lips. ADMIT IT, JOSEF, she
printed carefully.

YOU HAVE BEEN TURNING AROUND THE IDEA
LIKE A VULTURE CIRCLING A DEAD HYENA. LET
US TOGETHER IMAGINE WHAT IT WOULD BE
LIKE. THE ROLLING CHAIR WILL HAVE TO BE
IMPORTED, SINCE THE SINGLE MODEL PRO-
DUCED HERE UNDER YOUR LATEST FIVE-YEAR
PLAN IS EXTREMELY UNCOMFORTABLE: I MY-
SELF AM NOT CRIPPLED, BUT I HAVE HAD OC-
CASION TO SEE A NEW ONE AT CLOSE QUARTERS
AND I KNOW WHAT I'M TALKING ABOUT. YOURS
WILL COME FROM, SAY, ITALY, AND HAVE IN-
FLATABLE WHEELS AND A SUSPENSION SYSTEM
AND SOFT FOAM UNDER YOUR BOTTOM, AND
AN AXLE THAT TURNS WITHOUT SQUEAKING.
IN MY MIND'S EYE I CAN SEE NIKITA PUSHING
THE ROLLING CHAIR, ALL THE WHILE TELLING
YOU WHAT THEY HAVE DECIDED. THEY WILL
PROBABLY FORM A TRIUMVIRATE IN THE FIRST
STAGE OF THE SUCCESSION TO SPREAD THE
RESPONSIBILITY FOR THE TRANSITION AROUND.
THERE WILL BE TALK OF DETHRONING THE
GREAT HELMSMAN AND DENOUNCING YOUR
EXCESSES—THE PURGES, THE DEPORTATION OF
ENTIRE CLASSES OF PEOPLES. YOU WILL TRY
TO FORM SENTENCES, EVEN PHRASES, TO AR-
GUE WITH THEM: YOU WILL EVENTUALLY CON-
SIDER IT A TRIUMPH TO UTTER A RECOGNIZABLE
"VOT." JUST WHEN THE CONVERSATION BE-
COMES INTERESTING, THE VISIT OF YOUR HEIRS
WILL HAVE TO BE CUT SHORT—YOU SEE, JO-
SEF, YOU WILL HAVE LOST CONTROL OF YOUR
BOWELS, AND IT WILL BECOME IMMEDIATELY
EVIDENT TO EVERYONE IN THE ROOM THAT A

MALE NURSE SHOULD BE SUMMONED TO MAKE
YOU PRESENTABLE.

CONSIDER ANOTHER ASPECT. SOMEONE
WHOM YOU HAVE NEVER LAID EYES ON BE-
FORE WILL SHAVE YOU EVERY MORNING WITH
A STRAIGHT-EDGED RAZOR. HE WILL LATHER
YOUR FACE AND NECK, AND SHARPEN THE
STRAIGHT EDGE AGAINST A STROP, AND TILT-
ING UP YOUR CHIN BRING THE BLADE TO YOUR
NECK, AND YOU WILL ASK YOURSELF—FOR
YOU WILL BE INCAPABLE OF ASKING SOMEONE
ELSE!—IF HE HAS LOST A BROTHER OR A WIFE
OR A FATHER TO THE CAMPS; IF HE HASN'T A
SCORE TO SETTLE.

ALL POWER WILL SEEP FROM YOUR GRASP
ONCE YOU ARE NO LONGER ABLE TO SPEAK.
THOSE AROUND YOU WILL REALIZE THAT YOU
ARE INCAPABLE OF ORDERING AN ARREST. YOU
WILL SUFFER SLIGHTS, INDIGNITIES. PEOPLE
WILL BEGIN TO TALK OPENLY IN FRONT OF YOU
ABOUT YOUR CONDITION AND ITS IRREVERSIBIL-
ITY. YOU WILL UNDERSTAND FROM THEIR TONE
THAT THEY HAVE NO REGRETS. YOU WILL HEAR
THEM LAUGH A LAUGH THAT IS BROUGHT UP
FROM THE BACK OF THE THROAT—THAT HAS
NO MIRTH, THAT IS FULL OF BILE. YOU KNOW
OF COURSE THAT THEY DETEST YOU: YOU KNOW
THE MORE THEY EXPRESS ADMIRATION AND
LOVE, THE MORE THEY ARE COVERING UP THEIR
TRUE FEELINGS. NOW YOU ONLY GUESS AT IT.
BUT LISTENING TO THEIR VOICES FROM YOUR
ROLLING CHAIR, YOU WILL HAVE NO DOUBT IN
YOUR MIND. YOU WILL WONDER WHY YOU
SPARED THEM. YOU WILL PRAY EARNESTLY,
USING PHRASES AND FORMULAS YOU LEARNED
AS A YOUNG MAN IN THE SEMINARY, FOR A PAR-
TIAL RECOVERY ONLY TO ORGANIZE THE DISAP-
PEARANCE OF THOSE WHO FLOCK AROUND YOU.
YOU WILL GROW AFRAID TO EAT THE FOOD
PUT IN FRONT OF YOU, TO DRINK THE TEA
TILTED UP TO YOUR LIPS. YOU WILL WILT ON

THE STALK OF YOUR BODY, JOSEF. YOU WILL
FEAR OBLIVION, AND LONG FOR IT. YOU WILL
RAISE A TREMBLING FINGER AND POINT AT THE
SKY TO INDICATE TO THOSE AROUND YOU THAT
YOU PREFER TO DIE.

I'M RIGHT, AREN'T I? I KNOW YOU AS YOU
KNOW YOURSELF: BETTER EVEN.

SO HAPPY BIRTHDAY TO YOU, JOSEF DEAR.
MAY YOU LIVE TO BE A HUNDRED IN THAT
ROLLING CHAIR OF YOURS. I WISH IT TO YOU
WITH ALL MY HEART.

SLEEP WELL IF YOU CAN, JOSEF.

Appolinaria, drained from the writing of the letter,
printed her signature.

MOTHER RUSSIA.

She folded the paper and slipped it inside the envelope and used a damp sponge to seal it and paste on the
postage stamp. She wasn't sure if they could trace saliva. She addressed the envelope to "JOSEF STALIN, THE
KREMLIN, MOSCOW."

Tomorrow, wearing her winter mittens to keep fingerprints off the envelope, she would casually drop it
into some out of the way mailbox and begin thinking
about what she would write in her next letter.

3

Dressed simply in his pale, pressed generalissimo's
tunic with the top button casually open, his khaki
military trousers a shade darker than the tunic tucked
into soft boots, Stalin presided over the late dinner
from his usual place, the first seat to the left of the head
of the table. As always, he picked at his food and

watched the others gorge themselves; he had long ago discovered that you could learn a great deal about people by watching them eat. Stalin had given up cigarettes for good early in December, which made him more irritable than usual. To make matters worse, another of those diabolical letters had arrived that morning; he made a mental note to talk to Beria about it after the film. Something had to be done even if it meant arresting everyone in Russia who was *roughly* sixty-three! He counted out ten drops of iodine from an eye dropper, added some Borzhom water to the glass, and grimacing, drank it off in one long swallow. To get the taste of iodine out of his mouth he nibbled on some *dzhondzholi*, a sour plant from Georgia, and followed it with a sip of Georgian wine. As soon as his glass was empty, Valechka appeared at his elbow to fill it. He motioned for her to lean closer. "Vasily's drinking too much," he told her, referring to his son at the far end of the table.

Valechka nodded. Moments later, she reached over Vasily's shoulder when she thought he wasn't looking and snatched away the bottle of vodka in front of him. Vasily turned back from talking to Khrushchev and grabbed her wrist. "Since when do you edit my drinking habits?" he demanded.

"It's me who edits your drinking habits," Stalin called from his end of the table. "You may be the chief of aviation of the Moscow Military District, but I am still the commander in chief." If he had been less irritable, Stalin might have left it at that. But he added, "They tell me your hands shake so much you can't pilot an airplane anymore."

Vasily kicked back his chair and rose shakily to his feet. He stared belligerently at his father, batting his bloodshot eyes, collecting his thoughts. The others around the table studied their dinner plates in embarrassment. Vasily swayed back dangerously, then swayed forward again. "I may not be able to fly but I can remember," he retorted. Then he belched.

Khrushchev tried to tug Vasily back down into his

chair, but Stalin's son shook him off. "I remember, you see, and I drink to forget."

"And what is it you would like to forget?" Stalin challenged. "Your dachas or your racing kennels or your shady dealings with the hoodlums you hang around with?"

"Do you really want me to tell you in front of everyone?"

"I have no secrets from my associates."

Vasily gripped the edge of the table to steady himself. "I remember my brother Yakov, who was captured by the Germans and then executed when you refused to exchange him for some lousy Nazi general."

"Yakov," Stalin said darkly, "should never have let himself be taken alive."

"I also remember his wife, Julia, who was arrested when Yakov was captured and accused of betraying him, though God knows how she could have managed it from her Moscow apartment. Of course the fact that she was Jewish had nothing to do with her arrest."

"You've said enough!" Stalin burst out. "You're drunk." He waved to Valechka to get his son out of sight.

She tried to take Vasily's elbow, but he jerked away. "I'm going under my own steam," he announced. He reached across the table and grabbed a bottle of *pertsvoka* with its peppers floating inside and, laughing drunkenly, weaved his way toward the door.

Stalin leaned toward Beria, the MGB chief, sitting at his right, and spoke to him in Georgian. "Make sure he doesn't get behind the wheel of a car in that condition," he ordered.

Beria's clouded, bulging eyes came alive behind his pince-nez. He bolted from his seat and trotted after Vasily.

Malenkov shook his fat head in commiseration. "Our young people have forgotten what it was like to make a revolution."

Khrushchev, not to be outdone by Malenkov, said, "He should never have said what he did."

Stalin folded his hands on his chest and leaning back, studied his kittens through lidded eyes. It was true, of course, what the letter writer had said—the day he couldn't speak up, they would spit on him. He ought to do something about them, ought to replace them with younger men who weren't so full of themselves. Khrushchev was still running off at the mouth, his "g's" exploding in a guttural Ukrainian roll; how the man loved the sound of his own voice. "Vasily put his father in an awkward position," Khrushchev told the others. "And in Stalin's own dacha!"

"The peasants have a saying," Stalin said. "Nothing is awkward except putting your pants on over your head. As far as this being Stalin's dacha, Stalin doesn't have a dacha. The state has a dacha which it puts at the disposal of Comrade Stalin."

"That's what I meant," Khrushchev said lamely.

"I notice," Stalin told Khrushchev, "you have new boots on tonight. I happen to know a thing or two about boots. Let me have a closer look at them."

Khrushchev paled. "They're not that special," he said defensively.

"Toss one over."

Khrushchev reluctantly pulled off one of his boots and passed it to Malenkov, who passed it to Voroshilov, who handed it on to Zhdanov, who gave it to Stalin. Stalin turned it around in his hands, rubbed the leather between his fingers, peered into it to read the lettering stamped there. "Made in Italy," he said slowly. He looked up in mock surprise. "These are Italian boots! What's the matter with Russian shoes? Aren't they good enough for you?"

Malenkov, Khrushchev's arch rival in the Politburo, barely contained a smile of satisfaction. Khrushchev, for his part, turned red in the neck. "They were a present from my wife," he said in a whiny voice. "I couldn't refuse them without insulting her."

Stalin started the boot on its way back to Khrushchev. "Come on," he called, heaving himself out of his chair. He had tired of his little game. How he ached to stick one of the cardboard stems of a "Kazbek" *papirossy* in his mouth and fill his lungs with smoke. "It's time for a film or two."

With Stalin leading the way, the group passed through the long passage that connected Stalin's private quarters to the main house, and filed into the room that had been converted into a theater. Khrushchev noticed Zander standing next to the projector. Anxious to get back into the boss's good graces, he told Stalin, "I see you took my tip about the translator."

Molotov told Khrushchev, "I'm the one who recommended him."

Stalin's eyes blinked slowly, cunningly, like a dove's; how he loved to watch his kittens scramble for his favor. It was one of the few pleasures left to him in his old age. He nodded absently at Til, then stopped to take a closer look at him. "What did you say your name was?"

"Til. Alexander Til. I worked as a bodyguard in the Kshesinskaya Mansion before the revolution."

Stalin rapped his knuckles against the side of the projector in pleasure. "*Vot, vot.* It's true now and then a detail slips my mind, but people I never forget." He squinted at Zander more intently with his yellow eyes. "But weren't you arrested before the war? I seem to remember seeing your name on a list."

Stalin glanced at Khrushchev and Molotov to see what effect this would have on them. Judging from their expressions, both were bitterly regretting they had recommended Til's services to Stalin.

Zander said carefully, "I was arrested, but then I was released."

Stalin smacked his lips noisily. "If you were released, you were obviously innocent. Our security services are infallible. What's the film tonight?"

"It's called *The Public Enemy*, with James Cagney and Jean Harlow."

Stalin clapped his hands together once. "I like that Cagney fellow. I saw him in a picture called *Angels with Dirty Faces*. Ha! He reminds me of Beria sometimes. They both have the short man's habit of breasting events as if they were waves—they thrust out their chests—have you noticed it?—and tilt their heads and concentrate on surviving because they think victory goes to the last one around." Stalin dispatched a brief laugh in Beria's direction. Beria had no choice but to take it as a pleasantry and join in. Stalin turned back to Zander. "Who can say they're not right? To the survivor belongs the spoils." He headed for his seat. "Well," he added, waving the back of his hand at the projectionist, "let's get on with it."

Before the overhead lights went out, Malenkov, who was sitting on Stalin's right, leaned across and said something in an undertone that made the boss laugh through his nose. In the darkness, as *The Public Enemy* flashed on the screen, Zander could still hear the sound of an old man wheezing away in pleasure.

Pleading heavy schedules the next day, most of the kittens left Blizhny after the first film. Malenkov and Khrushchev hung around for *The Blue Dahlia*, and then called for their limousines. Only Beria stayed on for *Ninotchka*. He had seen the film several times already, but he had recurrent sexual fantasies about Greta Garbo and didn't mind seeing it again. When the last reel was over, the lights came on and Valechka handed Stalin his glass of warm milk with two lumps of sugar on the saucer. He and Beria strolled back through the passageway to the private wing of the building. "You know I got another one of those damned letters," Stalin told Beria in Georgian. "I recognize the printing—it's her again."

Beria looked miserable. "Not a word of it is true. Not one. If I outlive you, I will declare your birthday a national holiday. An international holiday even."

Stalin regarded Beria with his beady eyes. "You won't outlive me"—here Beria turned a shade of gray— "because I plan to live forever." He wheezed with satisfaction when he saw Beria's face. "What I want to know is who is writing these devil's letters?"

Beria wiped a damp palm with a handkerchief. "From the internal evidence, we are convinced the writer is a woman. Beyond that . . ."

"What about fingerprints?"

"This one was like all the others. Whoever writes

them probably wears gloves. The letter has your secretary's prints on it. The envelope has your secretary's
prints and another set belonging to the central post
office worker who sorts mail addressed to you, and two
or three other sets of prints which we couldn't identify—
though I'm sure they don't belong to the letter writer,
since the unidentifiable prints on the envelopes are
always different."

"The paper?"

"Common letter-writing paper, the same as the previous letters—available in eighty-two stores in Leningrad alone. Also, she may not be buying it. She may be
stealing it from an office."

Stalin's face screwed up. "What about the saliva tests?"

Beria shook his head. "My scientific people don't
think she licks the envelopes or the stamps—they think
it is tap water applied with a sponge or a damp cloth."

Stalin dropped both lumps of sugar into his milk and
stirred it with a long spoon. He gave Beria one of those
lidded looks that often made people think he knew
the answer to the question he was about to ask. "How
many women between sixty and sixty-five are there in
Leningrad?"

Beria wasn't sure he had heard correctly. "How many
women altogether in Leningrad? Between sixty and
sixty-five?" He nodded slowly as it dawned on him what
Stalin was driving at. "I suppose," he said, "there are
not all that many."

"How many of them lost someone in the thirties—
someone very close? It would have had to be a close
relative."

Beria was beginning to appreciate, once again, the
peasant cunning of his boss. "A woman between sixty
and sixty-five who lives in Leningrad and lost a husband
or a father or a child."

"One more thing," Stalin said. He took a long swig of
milk and wiped his lips on the back of his sleeve.
"Someone who lives in the same apartment as the writer
of the letter is confined to a wheelchair. It is of recent
Russian manufacture—and has been bought sometime
within the last few months."

Beria brought a hand up to his forehead. "Of course," he cried with unrestrained awe. "The wheelchair will lead us to the letter writer!"

The New Year's Eve party at the minister's apartment was in full swing. Several of the wives kept ferrying in from the kitchen plates of chicken Kiev and boiled potatoes. The cultural attaché uncorked the wine. The minister himself went around refilling glasses. Someone put an Israeli record on the phonograph. Several of the younger secretaries and assistants peeled back the rug and, linking arms, began circling in a hora. The others gathered around, clapping to the rhythm of the music. When the record finished, the man who ran the visa section—it was one of the standing jokes in the legation that he spent his days breathing on his rubber stamps to make sure the rubber wouldn't go dry from disuse—pulled out a pocket watch and announced that it was five minutes to midnight. The Israelis of Russian origin handed out scraps of paper. "It's traditional," one of them explained. "You write a wish and then you burn the paper and on the stroke of midnight you eat the ashes. That way the wish comes true."

"Three minutes," the visa man called.

Nachshon Ben Aminadav scribbled a few words on his piece of paper, dropped it on a saucer, and lighted the corner with a match.

"Two minutes."

When the paper had been reduced to ashes Nachshon pushed them into a small pile in the center of the saucer. The last time he had burned a wish and eaten the ashes he had been sharing a bedroom with Zander and Abner in the apartment on *ulitza* on the Lower East Side of Manhattan.

"One minute."

It had been Zander, with his love for things Russian, who had resurrected the tradition. Abner, who prided himself on being modern, had laughed it off as a superstition and refused to take part. Nachshon's mother and Zander's father had looked on uncertainly; ashes, his mother had said, couldn't be good for the stomach.

He and Zander had been left to uphold the tradition. "Now!"

Nachshon raised the saucer to his mouth and lapped up the ashes on his tongue. Then he took a quick sip of wine and swallowed. Around the room everyone applauded.

"Happy 1953," the station chief, Mordechai Shapiro, growled the next morning. He was fighting a pervasive hangover. They were meeting in the room within a room to go over the most recent reports. "What did you wish for last night?"

Nachshon smiled pleasantly. "The death of Stalin."

Shapiro pulled a file folder from a shelf in the safe and brought it over to the table. "What's new," he told Nachshon, "is this from the Jewish girl who sleeps with one of the guards out at Blizhny. I'm only showing it to you because you said you wanted to see everything no matter how inconsequential it seemed."

Nachshon nodded.

"Stalin sees movies almost every night, you know that. Sometimes they're Russian films, and they only need the services of a projectionist who comes in an unmarked police car and carries in the reels. The projectionist is Russian, a Party member, and an employee of the security apparatus. As far as I can see, there's nothing for us there. Sometimes Stalin watches American or English films—probably stuff captured from the Germans during the war. For this they bring in someone who speaks English and can give a running translation. There have been a half-dozen English translators in the past two years. Apparently Stalin is never satisfied. The other night they brought in somebody new. Our source's boyfriend body-searched him in the guard room, that's how he knew about it."

"Description?"

"Sixtyish. Thin. Medium height. Almost bald. Hard of hearing in one ear. Walks with a limp, uses a cane."

Nachshon caught his breath. "Is there a name attached to the description?"

Shapiro nodded. "A family name. Til, with one or two l's. Our source couldn't ask about the spelling."

"Til! You're sure of the name?"

Shapiro looked over the top of his eyeglasses at Nachshon. "That's what my source remembers the guard saying. Does the name mean anything to you?"

When he slept at all, he slept fitfully. He would come instantly awake in a cold sweat at all hours, cocking his good ear to catch the wheezinglike whistling that seemed to originate in the bowels of the building. He brooded over his food and left most of it uneaten. He spent hours in front of the double-glazed window staring at the giant new snowplows clearing off the latest accumulation. Other than the single article on the front page of *Pravda* that he had clipped and read and reread and folded away in his breast pocket, he refused to have anything to do with newspapers and ignored questions.

"Grandpa, is it true what *Pravda* says about Detroit, America?" Vanka asked when Zander was visiting their apartment one afternoon. And running his finger under the words so he wouldn't lose his place, he read, "In the streets from morning until night crowds of people with emaciated faces roam about. Unemployed, more unemployed, everywhere unemployed."

"Leave Grandpa alone," Ludmilla instructed her son. She was very edgy these days, short-tempered, preoccupied. She recognized the distant look in Zander's eyes; she suspected they were thinking about the same thing.

"What's 'emaciated' mean?" the boy asked.

"It's what you look like when you haven't had enough to eat," Ludmilla snapped. "Out you go."

At first Zsuzsa took Zander's remoteness as a personal rejection. "Is it something I've done?" she whispered. "Something I've said? Only tell me. Clear the air." When he didn't answer, she exploded, "Getting information out of you is harder than pulling teeth."

Serafima, who was staying with them while she was trying to convince the appropriate bureaucracy to increase Sergeant Kirpichnikov's disability pension, pressed a motherly palm to Zander's brow and announced he had a fever. Secretly relieved by the prospect that the

problem was physical, Zsuzsa begged Zander to see a
doctor. There was one living on the ground floor who
made private visits if you paid cash, she said.

Zander only shook his head and withdrew further
into himself. Memories lapped against him and then
receded, passing under a fresh memory rippling in.
Like Dostoevsky's *Bobik*, he thought that he could
make out the voices of the dead calling to each other in
the cemetery.

"If you are one of those Bolshevik Yids, already circumcised," a voice snarled, "I will cut the whole thing
off."

"Once you have made the revolution, you must every
morning, without fail, stand quietly for a moment and
remember *why* you made it."

Zander recognized still another voice, that of an old
man: "What I breathe for, what I fart for, is to live long
enough to see the Socialist revolution sweep across
Europe as Vladimir Ilich promised me it would."

And inevitably there was the voice that made his
heart stop beating while it lasted. "Promise me," it
begged, "you will not blame the revolution."

He relived Lili's execution, which he had never wit-
nessed but only imagined over and over again until it
was engraved on his skull. It struck Zander that the
older one grew, the easier it became to deal with his
own suffering, and the harder it became to cope with
that of other people. What had happened to him seemed,
with hindsight, commonplace; what happened to others
was tragedy.

Seeing Stalin after all those years had started the
memories wheeling through his head. "You think you
have stumbled into a madhouse," Stalin had said the
day Zander handed over his letter of introduction to the
boss on his arrival in St. Petersburg. Stalin, Zander
remembered, had spit the husk of a dried sunflower
seed onto the floor. "Admit it, you think so." Maybe
Stalin had been on to something; maybe Russia was a
madhouse and the effort to superimpose a Socialist
order on it had been doomed from the start.

In photographs and posters and newsreels, which

were always shot from the best angles and then re-
touched, Stalin came across as a sturdy peasant, his
eyes squinting wisely, a modest grandfatherly smile
playing on his kindly face. But in person he was an old,
bitter, frightened man—and a sick one at that. His hair
had turned white and thinned so much that his scalp
was clearly visible. His body was dwarfish, ungainly,
with a large paunch. His skin was full of dark blotches.
His breathing was shallow; he actually panted when he
became excited, a sure sign that he suffered from hy-
pertension. Once, while the projectionist was changing
reels, Zander had heard Khrushchev crack a joke about
Ivan the Terrible. Stalin had leaned forward excitedly,
his stunted arm chopping the air for emphasis, and
greedily sucking oxygen in shallow gasps had said, "God
got in Ivan's way. I am not similarly handicapped."
Later, carrying his glass of warm milk, he had headed
back to his private quarters after the last reel of the last
film with the uncertain step of someone who had to
deal with the possibility of tripping over his own feet.
"The peasants have a saying," he had been telling Beria
as he passed Zander. "People cling to the stones that
crush them."

Maybe that was the explanation Zander had been
unconsciously searching for all these years—why the
great Bolshevik revolutionists, one after the other, had
publicly admitted being guilty of crimes they hadn't
committed; why generals and admirals, armed to the
teeth and surrounded by loyal troops, had marched
docilely before firing squads; why millions of ordinary
people had gone to their deaths crying—here Zander
remembered with a pang his neighbor in prison in the
thirties—"Long live Stalin!"

Standing at the window, watching a dirty dusk descend on the snow-covered streets and roofs of Moscow
at three in the afternoon, Zander pulled from his pocket
the article he had torn out of *Pravda*. It was dated
January 13, 1953. The headline read: "MISERABLE
SPIES AND ASSASSINS MASQUERADING AS PRO-
FESSORS OF MEDICINE." Underneath, the Tass
communiqué said: "Some time ago the organs of State

Security discovered a terrorist group of doctors whose aim was to shorten the lives of leading figures in the Soviet Union by means of harmful treatment." According to the article, two members of the Politburo had been done to death by the doctors, all of whom were attached to the Kremlin medical service. Nine doctors were listed; six of the names were clearly Jewish. Halfway through the story Zander spotted the ominous words *i drugiye*—"and others."

It was only a matter of time before more names would be added to the list. And Ludmilla's husband, Leonid, was a cardiologist attached to the Kremlin medical service.

"I am worried sick," Ludmilla admitted to Zander the day the article appeared. "When I say good-bye to him in the morning I'm not sure I'll ever set eyes on him again. Oh, Zander, you know about things like this. Maybe he should take an appointment with the security service and tell them directly that he is not involved. Do you think that would help?" She shook her head in annoyance. "It's a crazy idea, I know it. The thing is, they're innocent. Leonid knows all of them—they're doctors, not spies or murderers. It's insane to think they work for some international Zionist conspiracy." Ludmilla went to the door and opened it a crack to make sure the children were not within earshot, then joined Zander at the window. "He is mentally ill, isn't he, Zander?"

He shook his head yes, very slowly, very carefully.

He had come to no conclusions, made no decisions. But when his turn came to use the communal bathroom the next morning, he studied his face in the mirror over the pitted sink and decided not to shave. He wasn't sure why he wanted to grow a beard, but the prospect of having one made him feel as if he had taken a step in an inevitable direction. Almost immediately the memories stopped rippling in; the voices from the grave grew weaker and disappeared.

Zsuzsa noticed the difference instantly. "Welcome back to the world," she said with undisguised relief. She reached up to caress the stubble on his chin with the palm of her hand. "I see you are growing a mask."

"All of us wear masks," Zander told her tiredly. "I am only going to wear a different one."

Because he specialized in Jewish affairs, the problem ended up on his desk. "His name is Kermit something or other," the Politburo secretary was shouting over the static on the other end of the telephone line. "He is a New York congressman with a large constituency of Isaacs and Abrahams, you see what I mean? Which I suppose explains why he is asking to see this Feldstein fellow."

"You don't have to shout," Tuohy shouted into the phone.

"Speak up," the Politburo secretary shouted back. "The line is bad. I can barely hear you."

Details were brought over by messenger that afternoon. The congressman, who was leading an American congressional delegation on an official visit, had filed two requests with the Russian embassy in Washington. The embassy advised that the congressman in question was an influential member of the House of Representatives, and suggested that his requests should be granted if it were at all possible. Stalin agreed; he wanted the Americans to come away with a good impression.

The first request concerned the Yiddish poet Yitzhak Feldstein; the congressman wanted to see him so that he could put to rest once and for all recurrent rumors circulating in Jewish circles in New York that the poet was languishing in jail, or even dead. The second request was more personal. As a child he had been acquainted with a revolutionist named Alexander Til, who later returned to Russia to take part in the Bolshevik Revolution. The congressman wanted to know if Til was still alive, and if so, could a meeting be arranged.

Tuohy knew exactly where to put his hands on Til. The dossier of everyone of Jewish origin who worked in any capacity for leading organs or important members of the Party passed across his desk. He had been somewhat surprised to see that his old friend had wound up translating American films for high officials and, eventually, for Stalin himself. Tuohy had scribbled an endorsement—"Til is an Old Bolshevik with no known ties to Jewish religious groups, Israel or the international Zionist conspiracy"—and had sent the file on its way.

Feldstein, of course, was another matter. "Is he still alive?" Tuohy asked the deputy from the Fourth Bureau who dealt with prisons and camps. "If so, is he presentable?"

The deputy phoned back within the half hour. Feldstein was both alive and presentable. He was being held in solitary confinement in Lubyanka, Block B, while he was groomed for a show trial; Feldstein, moreover, was considered to be a Category A "Zek," in as much as he had two living parents, a wife, and two children whose welfare depended on his being cooperative.

Tuohy decided to kill two birds with one stone—he would organize a luncheon for the visiting American at which both Til and Feldstein would be present. With Til to occupy him and old times to catch up on, the congressman would pay less attention to the Yiddish poet. Tuohy accordingly ordered for Feldstein to be lodged in a small suburban hotel that the security services ran; he was to be well fed and allowed to take the sun on the hotel's top-floor enclosed solarium.

As for Til, Tuohy would issue the invitation personally.

4

JOSEF, the meticulously printed letter began.

YOU ARE BACK AT YOUR OLD STAND, AREN'T YOU? NAMES ENDING IN *ITZ* OR *SKI* OR *SHTAM* ARE ITCHING YOU, SO YOU ARE STARTING TO SCRATCH. OH, IT'S NOT A CASE OF MY SEEING HANDWRITING ON THE WALL. (IN

RUSSIA, GRAFFITI IS AGAINST THE LAW.) IT IS MORE A MATTER OF READING BETWEEN THE LINES, SOMETHING ALL OF US QUITE NATURALLY BECOME EXPERT AT. I NOTICED, TO GIVE YOU A FOR INSTANCE, A REVIEW OF A MOTION PICTURE IN *PRAVDA* THAT SOMEHOW MANAGED TO AVOID MENTIONING THE NAME OF THE PRINCIPAL ACTOR, WHO HAPPENED TO BE JEWISH. THE SAME EDITION OF *PRAVDA* BOASTED THAT IT WAS A RUSSIAN WHO CREATED THE PERIODIC TABLE, BUT CLEVERLY AVOIDED SAYING IT WAS A JEW NAMED MENDELEYEV. THERE'S A NEW BOOK OUT ON THE GREAT PATRIOTIC WAR THAT DOCUMENTS ALL OF THE GERMAN ATROCITIES EXCEPT THOSE COMMITTED AGAINST JEWS. AND SO ON. AND SO FORTH. SO YOU SEE, JOSEF, IT IS REALLY CHILD'S PLAY TO FIGURE OUT WHAT YOUR TWISTED HEAD IS ON TO THESE DAYS.

WHAT YOU ARE ON TO, OF COURSE, IS JEWS.

BELIEVE ME, I HAVE GIVEN IT A GREAT DEAL OF THOUGHT. AND I THINK I UNDERSTAND WHY. YOU HAPPEN TO BE ONE OF THOSE RARE INDIVIDUALS, JOSEF, WHO DEFINES HIMSELF BY HIS ENEMIES. YOUR WHOLE CAREER HAS REVOLVED AROUND ENEMIES: CAPITALISTS, LANDOWNERS, THE TSAR, TROTSKY, ZINOVIEV, KAMENEV, BUKHARIN, KULAKS, GERMANS ARE A FEW WHICH LEAP TO MIND. AND NOW, IN YOUR DEMENTED DOTAGE, YOU ARE CASTING AROUND FOR A NEW ENEMY TO OCCUPY YOU, TO FULFILL YOU, TO DEFINE YOU. AND IT'S THE JEWS YOU'VE SETTLED ON.

KEEP IT UP, JOSEF, AND YOU WILL RUN OUT OF PEOPLE TO DESIGNATE AS ENEMIES. KEEP IT UP AND YOU WILL BE ALL ALONE IN THIS VAST COUNTRY. WITH EFFORT YOU WILL CLIMB THE STAIRS TO THE TOP OF LENIN'S TOMB AND GAZE OUT OVER RED SQUARE ON MAY DAY, BUT IT WILL BE *EMPTY*. YOU WILL WANDER UP GORKY STREET AND INTO THE LOBBY OF ONE OF THOSE GROTESQUE GOTHIC MONSTROSITIES YOU CAUSED TO BE CONSTRUCTED. BUT YOU WILL FIND ONLY SILENCE INSIDE THE REVOLVING DOOR. EVERYONE WILL HAVE BEEN PURGED, INCLUDING THE PURGERS. AND THEN, AND ONLY THEN, WILL YOU CONFRONT THE LAST, THE SLYEST, THE LONELIEST ENEMY OF THEM ALL.

IN A MIRROR.
SLEEP WELL IF YOU CAN, JOSEF.
MOTHER RUSSIA.

Watching from the back of the room as he waited for the reel to be changed—that night they were projecting Erich von Stroheim's decline and fall of a San Francisco dentist in *Greed*—Zander thought Stalin looked particularly on edge. They were only on their second film of the night, but Stalin had the haggard, drawn, sly appearance of someone who was beyond tiredness, beyond sleep even. Was he afraid of closing his eyes? He wheezed more than he usually did, cutting off his kittens with an impatient wave of his good hand or an imperious grunt. "I don't agree at all," he snapped when Molotov quipped that the greediest person he had ever come across was Winston Churchill. "Churchill would slip the odd kopeika out of your pocket, but only to keep up his pickpocketing skills. Roosevelt, on the other hand, always went after the big gold coins." Stalin wheezed in satisfaction.

"Churchill once told me to my face that we Russians were the ones who were greedy," he plunged on. "It was at Potsdam, right after the war. He said it jokingly, but I could see he meant it. He was annoyed because we were removing rolling stock and factories from Germany and carting them off back home by way of reparations. I looked the old goat right in the eye and told him Russia had fought the war for the spoils. He sucked on one of those fat cigars of his—God, what I'd give for one puff on a cigarette!—and said the English had fought for honor and glory. So you know what I told him? I told him everyone fights for what he doesn't have. That's what I told the old fart."

There were peals of laughter from the kittens, but Stalin hardly seemed to notice their reactions. He glanced over his shoulder and saw the reel was ready and barked, "Lights." Beria called out in the darkness, "Til, what's the name of the actress who plays the dentist's wife?"

"Zasu Pitts," Zander replied hoarsely. He peeled off the cellophane from one of the sucking candies Zsuzsa always slipped into his pocket and put it into his mouth.

"Well, Pitts has got a great pair of tits," Beria said after a moment.

As the film started, Stalin muttered something that didn't make any sense to Zander, though it obviously did to Beria, judging from the way his head bobbed in the semi-darkness of the theater. "The last letter narrows it even more—she must be a Jew," Stalin said.

"A Jew, of course," Beria agreed enthusiastically. "She gives herself away."

There was some heavy drinking after the second movie. Stalin challenged the kittens to guess how many degrees below zero it was outside, the idea being that everyone had to drink a brimming glass of vodka for each degree he missed by. Beria rolled his eyes around playfully and announced it was minus twelve, and smirked with such pleasure when Stalin told him it was only minus seven that the boss accused him of missing on purpose so he could have more to drink. "As God's my witness—" Beria began, his bloodshot eyes bulging innocently, his hands gesturing, like a child's, palms up, but Stalin signaled for the third film, *Saboteur*, directed by Alfred Hitchcock. Zander sucked on a candy to ease the hoarseness and started translating the dialogue.

It was six in the morning by the time one of the dacha Packards ferried the projectionist and Zander back along the private government highway to Moscow. Shadows of pines and birches flitted past in the icy predawn morning as the automobile wound its way down to the suburbs and turned sharply onto the Mozhaisk Highway. Out of the corner of an eye Zander saw the headlights of a taxi parked on a side street snap on. The taxi turned onto the highway behind them. He scratched at his beard, as if it were the newness of what Zsuzsa called his "mask" that was making him feel suddenly uneasy. He looked back through the rear window. The taxi was the only other automobile in sight.

The projectionist, who had dozed off with his head against the window, stirred, "What's bothering you, comrade?"

"I think we're being followed."

The projectionist snickered. "Watching that spy picture tonight planted ideas in your brain."

When the Packard turned onto the Arabat, the taxi kept going and disappeared, and Zander realized that the projectionist had been right; his imagination had been working overtime. The driver dropped the projectionist across from the chess club on the inner ring and Zander at the next metro stop the car came to; he was embarrassed about being chauffeured around in one of Stalin's Packards and didn't want any of his early-rising neighbors to see him coming back in one.

Waiting on the platform for his train, Zander again felt the back of his neck crawl. He turned abruptly and saw a middle-aged man farther down the platform avert his eyes. When Zander boarded his train the middle-aged man stepped into the next car. But when Zander got off seven stations later, the man in the next car remained on the train.

"You look preoccupied," Zsuzsa noted as they took breakfast on a small table in front of the double-glazed windows of their bedroom. "Anything you want to talk about?"

Zander remembered the curious snatch of conversation between Stalin and Beria. "The last letter narrows it even more—she must be a Jew." He summoned the image of the taxi trailing behind them on the Mozhaisk highway, and then another of the man who averted his eyes on the metro platform.

"It's nothing," he said as convincingly as he could. He stood up and parted with his fingertips the thick curtain that Zsuzsa had spent so much money on they actually had a fight about it. The street below, glistening with packed snow, was deserted. But in a window across the way Zander thought he caught the slight movement of a curtain. Was someone else imagining he was being followed?

"Something is the matter," Zsuzsa said in a voice thick with worry. She, too, was imagining, Zander realized. What she was always imagining was his death.

*   *   *

Tuohy slammed the sheaf of papers down on his desk. "You've had them for four weeks and this is all you have to show for it! And you call yourselves interrogators?"

The seven men seated around the conference table kept their eyes lowered. The totally bald interrogator sitting on Tuohy's left reached for a glass of mineral water, then thought better of it. "We are working under certain restraints," he started to explain. "The process of extracting credible confessions is obligatorily slower under these conditions."

"What restraints are we talking about?" Tuohy demanded sharply.

The bald interrogator hunched his shoulders lightly. His head appeared to retract into his body like a turtle's. "It was specified that the accused doctors were being prepared for public trial," he told Tuohy. "This precluded physical methods of interrogation, since there could be no question of leaving visible marks on their bodies."

"I don't believe what I'm hearing," Tuohy whispered sarcastically. "You couldn't beat them up or stub out your cigarettes on their faces, so you were unable to get confessions? You are back in the Middle Ages. All of you." He tapped the sheaf of papers with the palm of his hand. "These doctors have wives, don't they? They have sons and daughters and brothers and sisters who live in comfortable apartments and draw rations from the Kremlin food center and attend Moscow University, but they could as easily be on the next train to Siberia. What's the matter with you people? Use your imaginations! If you want someone to admit in open court to being in the pay of international Zionism, of using his position in the Kremlin medical service to mess up an operation and kill a patient, you have to *convince* him that his interests are best served by confessing. If you lead him carefully, he will wind up begging you for an opportunity to make a clean breast of things."

The telephone on the table next to Tuohy rang. Tuohy snatched the receiver off the hook. "I thought I told you—" He listened for a moment. "Ask him to stay on the line. I'll be with him in a minute." He dropped the receiver back on the hook. "Look," he told the interrogators, "this shouldn't be very complicated. These doctors led privileged lives. When they traveled abroad to medical conventions, they held secret meetings with American intelligence agents and representatives of international Zionism. When they diagnosed illnesses of important personalities, they purposefully made errors. When they performed operations and the patients died, it was premeditated medical murder. I'll be surprised if you can't find some nurses who saw the doctors leave malignant tumors where they were and sew their patients back up again." Tuohy dismissed the interrogators with a curt nod. "If you can't come up with the material we need, we will have to look into the possibility that you are the ones who are tainted by Zionist sympathies."

As the door closed behind the last interrogator, Tuohy snatched up the telephone. "Put him on," he snapped. Then he spoke in an entirely different voice. "Zander, it's Atticus. Atticus Tuohy." He paused. "It has been a long time," he agreed. "I'm sorry to keep you waiting but I had some people in my office. So, what's this I hear about you translating motion pictures for the boss himself?"

Zander must have said something humorous because Tuohy chuckled appreciatively. "Listen, Zander, the reason I called is to invite you to a lunch I'm organizing a week from tomorrow. An American congressman named Kermit something-or-other will be in town. He's sent word through the embassy that he knew you when he was a kid and would like to see you again."

Tuohy listened for a moment. "Of course! Maud's boy, Kermit. She was the one who lived in Brooklyn Heights, wasn't she? Well, old Kermit has come a long way. So what do you say?"

"Of course this is an official invitation," Tuohy said after a moment. "I'll personally be present at the meeting, so there'll be no question of anyone misconstruing it."

"Good. I'll look for you. A week from tomorrow. Noon. At the Metropole."

JOSEF,

BELIEVE ME, I SEE YOUR PROBLEM, EVEN IF I DON'T SYMPATHIZE WITH IT. YOU WANTED THE BEST ARTISTS IN THE COUNTRY TO PUT THE FINAL TOUCH ON YOUR IMAGE. IT WAS SOMETHING THE PROPAGANDISTS COULDN'T PROVIDE— ANOINTMENT BY GENUINE TALENT. THE HACKS, OF COURSE, DELUGED YOU WITH OPERAS AND ODES, BUT THE TINY PART OF YOU THAT IS PEASANT-SAVANT (AS OPPOSED TO THE GREATER PART, WHICH IS PEASANT-BRUTE) UNDERSTOOD THAT BECAUSE THESE THINGS WERE ORDERED UP, THEY WEREN'T WORTH THE PAPER THEY WERE WRITTEN ON. SOMEWHERE ALONG THE WAY IT MUST HAVE DAWNED ON YOU: THE ONES WHO AGREED TO BEND THEIR ART TO YOUR SERVICE WERE THIRD RATE: THEY DIDN'T HAVE MUCH ART TO BEND. THE REAL ARTISTS, THE ONES WHOSE CREATIONS WERE LIKELY TO STAND UP AS ART AND THEREFORE OUTLIVE THE SUBJECT AND THE ARTIST, COULDN'T BE THREATENED OR BOUGHT OR MANIPULATED.

THAT WAS THE PROBLEM, WASN'T IT, JOSEF?

YOU WANTED TO BE IMMORTALIZED WHILE YOU WERE STILL MORTAL, BUT YOU COULDN'T FIND ANYONE WILLING TO DO IT. IN A SENSE, YOU WERE SIMPLY CONTINUING A LONG TRADITION OF ANTAGONISM BETWEEN THOSE WHO WIELD POWER AND THOSE WHO WIELD THE PEN. WHY WAS YESENIN CONSIDERED COUNTERREVOLUTIONARY? EXPLAIN IF YOU CAN, WHY MAYAKOVSKY, DESPITE HIS EAGER ACCEPTANCE OF THE POSSIBILITIES OF REVOLUTION, WAS A POLITICAL HOOLIGAN? EXPLAIN, ALSO, IN WHAT SENSE THE IMMORTAL POETRY OF AKHMATOVA WAS ANTI-SOVIET? ACCOUNT FOR THE FACT THAT THE FIRST PRINTING OF TSVETAYEVA WAS LABELED A GROSS POLITICAL ERROR? WHY IS BULGAKOV NOT PUBLISHED HERE? WHEN WILL MANDELSTAM AND VOLOSHIN AND RONZHA AND GUMILEV BE GIVEN BACK TO US? WHY

ARE CHAGALL AND STRAVINSKY AND NABOKOV LIVING IN EXILE, THE PROPERTY OF OTHER CULTURES?

AH, JOSEF, IN YOUR OLD AGE YOU MUST SUSPECT THAT YOU HAVE GAINED A KIND OF IMMORTALITY. MAYBE IT IS NOT EXACTLY WHAT YOU BARGAINED FOR, BUT IT IS IMMORTALITY NEVERTHELESS. YOU WILL GO DOWN IN HISTORY AS THE KREMLIN MOUNTAINEER, THE MURDERER AND PEASANT-SLAYER. THE HALF MEN AROUND YOU SLOBBER OVER YOUR SHADOW. THEY COMMENT ON HOW IT STRETCHES GRACEFULLY ALONG THE GROUND, HOW IT PUTS EVERYTHING INTO PERSPECTIVE. BUT THEY ONLY WAIT FOR YOUR SUN TO SET TO GIVE YOU YOUR REAL IMMORTALITY. STATUES OF YOU WILL BE PULLED DOWN FROM THEIR PEDESTALS. PHOTOGRAPHS OF YOU WILL DISAPPEAR FROM WALLS. MENTION OF YOU WILL BE DELETED FROM HISTORY BOOKS. CITIES AND TOWNS AND HAMLETS CALLED AFTER YOU WILL REVERT TO THEIR ORIGINAL NAMES. YOUR CORPSE WILL BE DEEMED UNFIT TO LIE ALONGSIDE LENIN IN THE MAUSOLEUM YOU CAUSED TO BE CONSTRUCTED IN RED SQUARE.

YOU WILL BE REMEMBERED, JOSEF. OH, HOW YOU WILL BE REMEMBERED! BUT NOT THE WAY YOU THINK.

SLEEP WELL IF YOU CAN, JOSEF.

MOTHER RUSSIA.

Beria's problem was that he had drunk so much vodka at dinner, he couldn't focus with two eyes open. His solution was to keep one of them closed. "I swear it to you on the head of my mother," he whined. "I swear it on the grave of my father." The ring of fat around his stomach vibrated like jelly. He pulled an enormous handkerchief from his hip pocket and toweled the sweat off the palms of his hands. "Statues of you will cover the land. Every public building will be required to have one. More towns and cities—an entire republic, why not?—will be named after you. The country even: The Union of Stalinist Socialist Republics! And I will personally deal with the editor who touches your name in a history book."

Stalin didn't seem impressed. "She is a witch, this woman. I have the impression she sees into the future. She tells me things no one around me would dare to say." He turned abruptly on Beria. "Where are you in your investigation?"

Here Beria felt on safer ground. "I have not been sitting on my hands. Two thousand two hundred and four of the latest model wheelchairs from the Red Sunset Wheelchair and Crutch factory in Kiev have been distributed through outlets in Leningrad in the past six months. I have teams of agents combing records. There are six thousand eight hundred and twenty-three women aged sixty to sixty-five living in communal apartments or old age homes where one or more of the wheelchairs are in use. If we make allowances for the women who are certifiably insane or deaf or dumb, we are looking at about six thousand arrests. My people tell me they can wind this whole business up in forty-eight hours."

Stalin's head bobbed up and down. Beria, disconcerted by the gesture, added weakly, "With any luck you will have gotten your last letter from Mother Russia."

Stalin's head continued to bob; watching with one eye, Beria imagined he saw a buoy riding on a ground swell. "It seems to me," Stalin said slowly, articulating each syllable, "we ought to narrow the list even further."

"Narrow the list even further?" Beria repeated. He wondered if only one of his ears was functioning. "Why bother?"

But Stalin was off on a tangent of his own. "Did you notice anything in the last letter—anything that seemed familiar?"

Suddenly Beria was having difficulty focusing with a single eye. He closed that one too.

Stalin reached across to the thick pile of letters on the table and plucked one off the top. He fitted his eyeglasses onto his nose and tilted his head back so he could peer through the lower half of his bifocals. He started to read. " 'You will go down in history as the Kremlin mountaineer, the murderer and peasant-slayer. The half men around you . . .' " His head arched forward and he regarded Beria through the top half of his glasses. "Kremlin mountaineer, murderer and peasant-slayer, half men—these phrases are somehow familiar to me."

Beria opened both eyes and studied the two Stalins before him. "How, familiar?"

"It seems to me there was a seditious poem back in the thirties that used these expressions. You have specialists, you have records—see if you can't find out who wrote the original."

"What time," Zsuzsa asked anxiously at the door, "do you think you'll be home?"

"Ludmilla said the concert ends at ten-thirty. If the trolleys are running in all this snow, they'll be home by eleven. I should be back by midnight."

"For God's sake," Zsuzsa said, "if you see you're going to be late, phone me." She tightened the scarf around his neck and handed him his cane. "Promise?"

"I promise."

"Now that you've promised," Zsuzsa said, "I'll worry twice as much if you don't call."

Zander trudged through the snow to the trolley station on the corner and looked down the street to see if one was coming.

An old woman with a moth-eaten fox fur twined around her thin neck came up behind him. "Do you see a miracle?" she asked.

"Nothing in sight," Zander told her. "We may have quite a wait."

The old woman did a little dance in the snow. "Agitate your feet, young man. I read somewhere you can get frostbite when the temperature falls below minus twenty." She saw the smile on Zander's face. "Take it as a joke if it tickles you. It's your feet that will freeze, not mine."

A government Zil came slowly down the street hugging the curb and pulled up in front of the old woman and Zander. "Another one of those government drivers moonlighting as taxis," sneered the old woman. "In my day they would have been put up against a wall. We might as well tell him where we're headed." She stepped forward and pressed her face to the passenger window and shouted, "I am going to Number Twenty-four Enthusiast's Avenue, comrade chauffeur."

The driver, barely visible in the darkness of the car, shook his head no. Zander looked again to see if a trolley was in sight, then called out the address of Ludmilla's apartment building. Anything was better than getting frostbite waiting for a trolley.

The driver reached across and opened the door on the passenger's side of the car. The old woman croaked, "Some people have all the luck." Zander slid in and closed the door. The front wheels spun on the snow. The car started forward. The driver, a young man with thick round glasses and a prominent nose, glanced at Zander's cane.

"War wound?"

Zander nodded. "The civil war. Shouldn't we settle the price before we start?"

The driver shrugged philosophically. "I'm not greedy. You can pay me whatever you think the ride is worth."

"That's a good technique," Zander remarked. "I'll bet most of the people you pick up pay you more than you would have asked."

The driver shrugged again. "Some pay more, some pay less. It averages out. And I don't have to demean myself by haggling."

The Zil passed two more people waiting at another trolley station—one of them actually stepped into the street and waved a bill—but the driver never even slowed down. "You have something against ruble notes?" Zander asked, amused at the obvious independence of the driver.

"They weren't going where I was going," the young man said after a moment.

"How could you know that? You never gave them a chance to say where they were going."

The young man glanced again at Zander and smiled a

crooked smile. "Nobody in Moscow is going where I'm going."

The way the driver had phrased it was curious enough to make Zander pay attention to the route they were taking. The avenues, the buildings, were not familiar. The car began twisting and turning through a labyrinth of narrow back streets between the inner and the outer rings north of the Kremlin. Zander was suddenly alarmed. "What the hell are you doing?" he demanded.

"I am making sure," the driver replied in a voice so utterly casual it was instantly evident he was a professional, "that you are not being followed."

Zander remembered the headlights on the Mozhaisk Highway. "Why would anyone want to follow me?" he demanded.

Instead of answering, the driver flashed another of his crooked smiles.

Zander tried to sort out his thoughts. "Where are you taking me?" he asked after a while.

"To dinner."

"With whom?"

"The people I work for said if I told you the menu, you'd know the whom."

"The menu?"

"You're having *stuffed* for dinner."

For a moment Zander wondered if he had heard correctly.

The driver laughed under his breath. "I was told you would be pleasantly surprised."

The Zil pulled up at a deserted corner. "Halfway down the block is an alley. And halfway down the alley, on your left, you will find an unlocked door. It's a prerevolutionary building and the door used to be the servants' entrance in the days before everyone was a servant of the state. Climb three flights. My employer says you will smell the cooking. Knock on the door the odor comes from." The driver nodded encouragement. "Good luck to you."

Zander started down the street. He turned to see if the automobile was waiting, but it had disappeared. They must have been pretty sure he would keep the appointment, he thought. If Zsuzsa were with him, she would tug in panic on his arm and pull him back the way he had come. "How do you know they're not baiting a trap to test you?" she would ask, her voice breaking in panic as possibilities transformed themselves into probabilities.

Still Zander trudged on through the snow. He saw the mouth of the alley, so narrow it could have been taken for a crawl space between buildings. Inside, it was pitch dark.

Zander hesitated.

There was only one person in the world who would have invited him to a dinner of "stuffed."

He looked around. There wasn't a soul in sight. He studied the windows across the street. Shutters were closed, curtains were drawn. With an audible sigh— what was he getting himself into?—he plunged through the opening between the buildings into the darkness of the alley. He had to run the tip of his cane along the wall like a blind man and feel for the door. He found the knob and tried it. It was unlocked as the driver had said it would be. Unlike most Moscow doors, this one didn't squeal; someone had gone to the trouble of oiling the hinges. Recently.

Zander began climbing the stairs, which were lighted every two flights by a low wattage bulb hung high enough overhead so nobody could swipe it. On the second landing he caught a whiff of cooking. He climbed slowly to the third floor. The odor was more pronounced. He studied the door from which it seemed to come. There was no mark of any kind on it. He poked at it twice with the tip of his cane. He could hear someone moving in the corridor beyond the door. They were the footsteps of a heavy man. And then the door was pulled wide open and Leon surged across the threshold and there were tears streaming down his cheeks as he wrapped his arms around his stepbrother, his "twin," and then they were pounding each other on the back and nodding because the moment was beyond words.

"Come in, come in," Leon finally managed to whisper, and he drew Zander into the apartment and closed

the door behind him and threw two enormous bolts to
lock it. Gripping Zander under the elbow, Leon led
him down the corridor into a small dining room with
a small round table set with a half-dozen dishes full
of "stuffed." Zander sank gratefully into a chair.
Leon sat down facing him. "It was yesterday we ate
'stuffed' together in that Rumanian restaurant," he said
huskily.

"To me," Zander replied, "it was a thousand years
ago. What are you doing in Moscow, Leon? You're
supposed to be in Palestine."

Leon filled two shot glasses with vodka. He pushed
one carefully across the table to Zander. "Palestine," he
said teasingly, "we now refer to as Israel." He raised his
glass. "*L'chayim.* To life."

"To life and to you, Leon. In my wildest dreams I
never thought I would set eyes on you again."

They both sipped their vodka. Questions seemed to
close in on them from every direction. Answers tugged
at other questions. Leon's mother had passed away in
New York. Leon's wife who had abandoned her pharmacy in the Bronx to follow him to the promised land
had died of swamp fever while they were clearing land
for a kibbutz near the Sea of Galilee. One of their three
sons had been killed in the 1948 War of Independence.
There were grandchildren, but Zander didn't remember how many. There was talk of a second marriage that
ended in divorce when the woman couldn't stand life
on a kibbutz. There was mention of some vague assignments that took Leon to East European and South
American countries.

"This Ludmilla you keep talking about," Leon said at
one point, "must be the daughter you wrote me about
in the early twenties."

"She is like a daughter," Zander said, and he told
Leon in half sentences things he had never dared write
him: about his love affair with Lili; about how she had
saved Anastasia; about Lili's death.

"So," Leon said thoughtfully, "I remember telling
you that revolutions don't change things, they only

rearrange them. Your revolution seems to have rearranged them for the worse."

They picked at the food, eyeing each other across the table, smiling happily, nodding but not talking. Eventually Zander asked, "How did you find me?"

Leon raised his eyebrows. "Excuse me if I don't answer you. What you don't need to know I won't tell you."

"Whose apartment are we in?"

Leon shook his head; that was something else Zander didn't have to know.

"Do I need to know what you are doing in Moscow, Leon?"

"I was wondering when you'd get around to that one. Officially, I'm the Counselor for Trade Affairs at the Israeli legation."

"And unofficially?"

Leon grunted. "Unofficially, I'm here to save the Russian Jews from another holocaust."

Instinctively Zander looked around. Leon understood the gesture. "Here it is safe to talk," he assured him.

"How are you going to save the Jews?"

"I'm going to arrange for the death of Malechamovitz. That's the Yiddish name for the Angel of Death."

"What's the Russian name?" Zander felt a knob of dull pain rising in his chest; he knew the answer.

"Josef Vissarionovich Dzhugashvili, better known by his Bolshevik nom de guerre, Stalin."

"You are a crazy man," Zander breathed in a barely audible voice.

"What I am is a religious man," Leon shot back.

"Back on *ulitza* I don't remember you talking much about God."

Leon pushed away his plate and leaned over the table. "I believe in the God of history," he said. His voice was barely more than a whisper, but there was no mistaking the intensity of his words or his commitment to the convictions behind them. "I believe in the Jewish people and their destiny. I believe most of all in the State of Israel as the embodiment—and the guarantee—of that destiny. If Israel is to survive in a sea of Arabs, it must have immigrants. American Jews will never come in great numbers for obvious reasons. That leaves Russian Jews. One day this phony communism of yours will explode and the Jews will be able to leave. For this to happen they must still be alive. Keeping them alive is what I'm doing here." Leon exhaled, snorted, then smiled in embarrassment. "So I've put my cards on the table sooner than I thought I would."

Zander stared at his plate. "I believe in history too, Leon. What is a Socialist if he isn't someone rooted in history? But you wrap up your history in a neat package. For me it's more difficult." He raised his eyes uncertainly.

Looking at them, Leon suddenly remembered the Yiddish actress who had once described Zander's eyes as "bruised." He realized that his twin had been hurt, and badly. "Go on with your history," Leon encouraged him.

Zander said, "It is not easy for me. In Russia we don't have conversations like this anymore."

"That's maybe one of the problems. Try."

Zander shook his head in frustration. "I go over it in my head again and again and I can't find the beginning."

"The beginning of what?"

"The beginning of where it went wrong. We started out with such high hopes, Leon. We were going to liberate the workers and create a society where people could live freely. You don't know what it was like right after the revolution. Scrubwomen and secretaries used to sit in on meetings of ministries. Anybody could give an opinion or disagree with someone else's. Everything was possible. The sky was the limit."

Leon poured out more vodka. "It was a brave idea that went wrong," he said. "They'll be arguing for centuries whether it was the idea that was flawed, or the people who imposed it. My own view, for what it's worth, is a little of both. You had a lot of enthusiasm, a lot of idealism, nobody can take that away from you. But to remain democratic a party, a government, must go back to the masses periodically for its mandate. Lenin avoided this—"

"He had to. We were surrounded by enemies. We were attacked from all sides."

Leon shrugged. "You want to find the beginning of where it went wrong. To preserve the revolution from its enemies, Lenin improvised. When the improvisations worked, the Bolsheviks institutionalized the improvisations; they abandoned the dream for the improvisations. Trotsky used Red Terror to beat the Whites. Here you are, thirty-five years later, still using Red Terror."

"It's true what you say—the Party doesn't care what it presides over as long as the Party presides," Zander said. "Opposition to the Party line is indistinguishable from treason toward the working class and the state. And traitors are generally shot in this worker's paradise of ours."

Zander was silent for a long while. Then he said, "Do you remember the vodka glass I threw against the wall of the restaurant?"

"I remember it didn't break."

"You were right after all, Leon. I came to the wrong revolution."

Leon said very quietly, "Maybe you came to the right one."

Zander stared at him across the table. Leon said, "Did it ever occur to you that you were *put* here by my God of history? Do you really think it is an accident that you survived the civil war, the purges, the Second War? That you wound up translating captured American films for the Great Helmsman?"

Zander was stunned. "How do you know what I do?"

"I know what you do and where you do it and who is there when you do it. Zander, my God of history has reunited us for a reason. I need your help."

"It is out of the question."

Zander scraped back his chair, but Leon said in a sharp voice, "At least hear me out."

"No!" Zander heaved himself to his feet. "What you are suggesting is not possible. Even if I were willing to take the risk, I have a family to think of."

"We'll get them out. All of them. We'll get you out too."

Zander turned his bad ear toward Leon to cut off the conversation. "I am not a murderer. And who is to say what comes after Stalin won't be worse? Kill Stalin and you may have to deal with Beria."

Leon also rose to his feet. "Believe me," he said, "nothing can be worse than Stalin. Here he is planning to exterminate the Jews and you talk about what might come after him. It's like trying to decide whether Hitler was the ultimate reflection of German rationality or German irrationality. What does it matter? Who cares? The thing to do is to stop him. And then intellectualize about it afterward."

"I'm sorry to disappoint you, Leon. But I'm not your man."

Leon was becoming desperate. "I don't ask you to make a decision now. I ask you only to think about it."

Zander started toward the corridor. Leon caught up with him at the door of the dining room and gripped his elbow. "For old time's sake you can do me one favor. Memorize this telephone number. That way if you change your mind you can contact me. Only that, Zander. Put the number in your head. You're not committing yourself to dial it."

Zander considered the matter for a moment, then walked over to the telephone. The laminated card on it read B-141-21. He repeated it to himself several times.

At the servants' door Leon gripped Zander's hand. "Either way, it was one of the great joys of my life to see you again."

"For me too," Zander said with emotion.

"Tell me the number."

"B-one forty-one, twenty-one."

"If you do call, use a public pay phone. An old woman will answer. Tell her only that you enjoyed her 'stuffed' so much you want to have another meal like it."

"I won't call, Leon."

"You'll be making a tragic mistake if you don't."

"We aren't twins—we don't think alike."

Leon recognized this echo from their conversation on the Brooklyn Bridge. "I didn't believe you the last time you said that. And I don't believe you now."

* * *

Zsuzsa sprang at Zander as he came through the front door. "Where in God's name have you been?" she exploded. For once she didn't care if the people they shared the apartment with heard them or not. "Do you know what time it is? It's a quarter to two, that's what time it is. Ludmilla is frantic—when you didn't turn up, she was sure something terrible had happened to you. She hasn't stopped telephoning—"

Zander brought a palm up against his forehead. "I forgot completely about baby-sitting!"

"Oh, Zander, how could you do this? Ludmilla sent Leonid over to give me a sedative, but it didn't help. I imagined you lying in a snowbank. I imagined you with a mistress. I imagined you being carted off to prison." Zsuzsa was weeping now. "I imagined everything I could imagine to imagine."

Zander wrapped his arms around her and pulled her head against his chest. "Calm down. I'm here now. I can explain everything."

The telephone on the little table in the hallway began ringing. "That's Ludmilla again," Zsuzsa whispered. "Where did you disappear to tonight?"

"I came across an old friend. We started talking and lost track of time. That's all there is to it."

"Who was this old friend you came across?"

The phone was still ringing. Zander shook his head slightly. "It was someone from another world."

5

Yitzhak Feldstein had the look of someone with no illusions about time being on his side. Bitter laughter brimmed from his sunken eyes. A dead cigarette with a soggy filter dangled from his bloodless lips. "Yitzhak Feldstein, Alexander Til," Tuohy said by way of introduction. The Yiddish poet assumed that because Zander was there, he was one of them. He raised his head and nodded indifferently and lowered it again.

Tuohy had been waiting in the lobby of the Metropole. Zander hadn't set eyes on him since the time they ran into each other in a bomb shelter. Seeing him again after so long, Zander was struck by how he had gone to seed; his body had become soft, pudgy even, though there was still something very hard in the lines of his face. "The years race by," Tuohy was saying as he led Zander upstairs to a private dining room on the second floor, "and we pant along after them to keep up. I don't know about you, but I get heartburn when I think we're in 1953 already." At the door Tuohy had grabbed Zander's elbow. "You remember a Yiddish poet named Feldstein? Your man Kermit asked to meet him, too, so I invited him to lunch. I hope you don't mind."

Zander knew that Feldstein had been raked over the coals for his Zionist leanings in a rambling *Pravda* article the previous summer, after which the poet had dropped from sight. Everyone had assumed the worst. Now he was relieved to hear that Feldstein had not been arrested. Maybe it was a straw in the wind. Maybe Leon was exaggerating the threat to the Jews after all.

"I heard you read a poem of Emily Dickinson's at The Stray Dog before the revolution," Zander told Feldstein as he settled into a chair directly across the table from him.

Feldstein perked up. " 'If I can stop one heart from breaking,' " he recited in Yiddish, " 'I shall not live in vain.' "

"That's the one," Zander said.

"It has to be—it's the only Dickinson poem I ever knew. You speak Yiddish?"

"I spoke Yiddish before I spoke Russian."

In the shadow of their sockets the poet's eyes fluttered nervously. "I remember The Stray Dog. That was the night Ronzha got into a fight with someone over the role of the artist in a period of violent transition."

"I was there too," Tuohy remarked. "It was Ehrenburg he argued with."

"No. It was Meyerhold," Zander said.

"He's right," Feldstein said. "It was Meyerhold. I can still hear Ronzha's voice in my brain. 'We shall see who compromises his integrity when the managers of the economy begin to manage art.'"

"The managers of the economy," Tuohy said sternly, "take the view that artists should serve the masses by heightening their Socialist consciousness, and not simply entertain."

"I agree, of course," Feldstein said with a smirk. "It was Meyerhold, not Ronzha, who was correct."

A waiter wearing an impeccable white dinner jacket with a plastic carnation in the buttonhole wheeled over a wagon loaded with *zakuski* and began to set plates out on the table. Another waiter, this one in a black dinner jacket, uncorked two bottles of excellent Bulgarian red wine. He poured some into a wineglass and held it up to the light to check for sediment. Then he started filling the glasses. Feldstein stared at the food and seemed to be trying to discreetly breathe it in through his nostrils. Tuohy glanced at his wristwatch. A young man appeared at the door of the room. "He's on his way up," he whispered. A moment later he opened the door wide and the American congressman strode through. He caught sight of Zander. Smiling broadly, he walked directly up to him and held out his left hand. Zander got to his feet and they shook hands, Zander using his right hand, Kermit his left. "Well, you haven't changed all that much," Kermit said enthusiastically. "But I have."

"You haven't changed much either," Zander said, though all he really recognized was Kermit's crippled right arm.

Kermit turned to look down at the Yiddish poet. "And you must be Yitzhak Feldstein." He offered his left hand across the table. "I consider it a privilege to meet you."

Half-rising out of his chair, Feldstein shook his hand briefly. "Pleased, I'm sure, Mister," he said in awkward, accented English, and settled back into his seat.

Tuohy was on his feet introducing himself. "My name

is Atticus Tuohy. I'm an old friend of Zander's—we came from New York to join the revolution together."

"Any friend of Zander's . . ." the congressman said with a crisp smile.

Tuohy gestured toward the empty seat. The congressman sat down. Feldstein took this as a signal that he could start eating and began plucking *zakuski* from the plates and popping them into his mouth.

"How is your mother?" Zander asked.

Kermit said, "She died two years ago next month."

"I'm sorry to hear that," Zander said. "Maud was a spirited lady. How did she die?"

"She came home late one night and was mugged on her doorstep. You knew Mother. Her reaction was perfectly in character. She resisted. The muggers pushed her down the stairs. Her skull was fractured. She lapsed into a coma and never came out of it."

"America," Tuohy said, "is a violent country."

Zander glanced at Tuohy to see if he meant this ironically, but Tuohy kept a perfectly straight face.

Kermit turned to Feldstein. "I must tell you that I asked to meet you in order to put to rest rumors circulating in the Jewish community in my district that you had been arrested."

The Yiddish poet smiled sourly. "You can see for yourself that I am free like a bird is free. . . ." He spooned a generous portion of Baltic herring covered with thick cream onto his plate, then helped himself to some marinated green peppers.

Kermit said, "Is there any truth to the suggestion that the Soviet government is cracking down on Jewish writers? You can speak freely, I'm sure, in the presence of Zander and his friend here."

Feldstein talked with his mouth full. "No truth whatsoever, Mister. I personally never seen no case of persecution. We are as free as we have always been to write what we want."

"My Jewish colleagues in New York tell me you haven't published anything in years. If you are free to write what you want, how come?"

Tuohy followed the conversation closely, looking from

Feldstein to the American congressman as they spoke.

Feldstein shrugged. His eyes settled on a dish of pickled onions in front of Zander. "If I don't publish," he told Kermit, stretching across the table for the onions, "it is because the quality of my recent work has not been what it should be."

Feldstein looked up suddenly and spotted the horror in Zander's eyes as he caught a glimpse of the poet's bare wrist jutting from his sleeve. On the wrist was the unmistakable ring of rawness that comes from wearing manacles for long periods. Feldstein snapped at Zander in Yiddish, *"Ich hob ein michpocheh, die kinderlach—sayer leiben hangt in vos ich mach."*

Feldstein dished onions onto his plate as he calmly continued the conversation with Kermit. "So you see, Mr. American Congressman, unlike America, decisions here are taken on artistic merit and not the artist's racial roots or political views. Tell my Jewish friends in New York to stop straining their skulls about me and start worrying about the Negroes getting lynched in their own backyard."

After lunch Zander walked Kermit to the door of the dining room. "What was it he said to you in Yiddish back there?" Kermit asked in an undertone.

Zander, still in a state of shock, tried to keep his tone even. "I only caught part of it—I think he was telling me he hadn't eaten pickled onions since his wedding day."

"He looks . . . pale, don't you think?"

"It's winter here, Kermit. Nobody goes out in the sun very much."

"Well, frankly, I'm relieved to hear that the rumors in New York are just anti-Soviet propaganda."

They shook hands. "It was a pleasure to see you after all these years," Kermit said. "My mother often wondered what had become of you—the young, idealistic revolutionary who went to Russia to fight the good fight. I wish she were alive so I could tell her."

Back at the table Tuohy coughed twice into his fist. Feldstein reluctantly stood up. "Thanks for the lunch," he told Tuohy. "Anytime you need me to meet another American congressman, I can always arrange my schedule."

"I'll remember that," Tuohy said coldly.

Feldstein started toward the door. "So I guess I'll be going," he said in a strained voice. He seemed to be waiting for someone to contradict him.

Zander reached for his cane hanging on the back of his chair. "I'll walk you down to the lobby," he told Feldstein.

Tuohy stirred. "I would have organized transportation," he remarked to Feldstein in a lazy drawl, "but I thought you said you were meeting a friend."

Feldstein slipped a cigarette between his lips but didn't light it. "I am meeting a friend," he told Zander. "He must be waiting for me down in the lobby by now."

"Maybe I know him," Zander said in desperation. He didn't want the conversation to end. He knew that when it did, Yitzhak Feldstein would no longer be free as a bird.

Feldstein looked at Zander. Their eyes met. "You don't know my friend. If you knew him you wouldn't like him. He's an unpleasant Yiddish poet who goes by the name of Malechamovitz."

"I've heard of him," Zander murmured.

Feldstein cocked his head quizzically. Once again bitter laughter brimmed from his eyes. "I thought you might have." And he turned on his heel and left for his rendezvous with the Angel of Death.

Tuohy signaled with a finger and an assistant turned up the volume on the tape recorder. Feldstein could be heard speaking in English. "If I don't publish," he was saying, "it is because the quality of my recent work has not been what it should be."

"Here comes the Yiddish," Tuohy whispered. He and the Yiddish translator leaned toward the loudspeaker. Feldstein's voice croaked, *"Ich hob ein michpocheh, die kinderlach—sayer leiben hangt in vos ich mach."*

The Yiddish translator looked at Tuohy. "He says, 'I have a family, children—their lives hang on what I do.'"

Tuohy had already listened to the segment of the

tape on which Zander explained to the American congressman, "He was telling me he hadn't eaten pickled onions since his wedding day." Zander is one of us, Tuohy thought. He can be counted on. But the Yiddish poet is another story. He had tried to tip off Zander in Yiddish so that he could pass word on to the congressman and, through him, the Jews in New York. "The slimy bastard," Tuohy said out loud. "Nobody double-crosses me and gets away with it."

When Zander arrived to baby-sit for the evening, two days after his lunch at the Metropole, Leonid was uncommonly curt. He nodded and shook hands without so much as a word and left the room. Ludmilla drew Zander into a corner. "You have to make allowances," she said. "He's very tense. The police came to his office this morning and confiscated all of his medical records. Oh, Zander, what's going to happen to us?" She pulled out an article she had torn from a back page of *Pravda*. "The noose is tightening," she said tearfully. "Have you seen this?"

"I don't read the newspaper anymore," Zander said. He took the article and held it up to the light.

Under the headline, "DEATH OF A TRAITOR," the story described the arrest and suicide of a Yiddish poet, Yitzhak Feldstein. He had been charged with being a Zionist agent, the article said. Confronted with irrefutable evidence of his treason, he had twisted his pajama bottoms into a cord and hanged himself in his cell.

Looking away from the article, looking past Ludmilla out the window, Zander found the world incredibly calm, almost as if he were in the eye of a storm. " 'If I can stop one heart from breaking,' " he recited, " 'I shall not live in vain.' "

Ludmilla was puzzled. "What does that have to do with Yitzhak Feldstein?"

Zander said, "It's his legacy to me."

Zander slipped the coin into the slot of the pay telephone and dialed the number. The old woman on the other end let the phone ring forever before she picked it up. "B, one forty-one, twenty-one?" she said, raising her voice slightly to indicate she was posing a question.

Zander took a deep breath. And then a second. He wasn't sure he would speak until he heard his own voice. "I had a dinner of *stuffed* at your apartment about a week ago. It was exceptionally good. I was wondering if we could organize another meal like it."

The old woman giggled. "So you enjoyed my cooking. It doesn't surprise me. When were you thinking of coming?"

"Tonight."

"Too soon," the old woman shot back. "I need time to shop. I need time to cook. I need time to think. Today is Wednesday. The soonest I can make it for is Saturday. Are you free Saturday?"

"I think so."

"Let's say Saturday then. The car that picked you up last time will pick you up at the same place at eight-thirty sharp."

"Eight-thirty," Zander repeated.

"Can I offer you some advice? You don't mind? Here it is. Don't eat between now and then. That way you will work up an appetite."

The old woman giggled again.

It came as a revelation to Zander that there really were spies in the Soviet Union. Since the thirties, hundreds of thousands had been accused of spying, and admitted it, and been executed for it, but Zander had assumed the charges were trumped up. Now, slowly, he came into contact with a group of people who were doing precisely what Soviet propaganda said its enemies did: they were plotting to kill Stalin. There was the philosophic young man with the prominent nose who drove the Zil and who announced, the second time he had Zander as a passenger, that his ambition in life, assuming he survived long enough, was to breed irises. There was Madame Nilovna, who lived in the apartment where the meetings between Leon and Zander took place; she always seemed to be giggling at one thing or another. There was Shapiro, a nearsighted middle-aged man from the Israeli legation who took down on paper every word Zander uttered and then pored over the record of the conversation as if it were a poem to be explicated. There was a silver-haired man who sat in on two sessions without saying a word, and without being introduced. There were the voices of others Zander never set eyes on. They came from the kitchen, these voices. One was masculine and spoke in Hebrew. The other sounded like that of a young woman. "Only Jews care about the death of Jews," Zander once heard her say when the old woman came through the swinging door with a pot of thyme infusion. "For others it is an intellectual exercise."

And the center of this web of spies was Leon. "Describe the part where they search you," he instructed Zander one night. Leon nodded at Shapiro, who nodded back to indicate he was ready.

"We've been over that," Zander said tiredly; being a spy so far was boring.

Leon said patiently, "We want to go over it again. If you please."

"I am picked up in front of the office of the Motion Picture Collective," Zander began, "along with the projectionist and the reels of the films he will be showing that night. We are driven out along a government road closed to civilian traffic to Blizhny. There are two checkpoints, but the guards only look at our faces and wave us past. The limousine goes through a high wooden door and pulls up in front of the guard building."

"The one that's shaped like a hexagon?" asked Leon.

Zander nodded. "We are taken inside. A guard passes a hand-held metal detector over us."

"He checks everything," Shapiro read from the notes of a previous session. "Assholes, armpits, pubic hair."

"Then I'm patted down by one of the guards. He checks inside my cuffs and works his way up. He feels my balls. He removes anything he finds in my pockets. He winds up threading his fingers through my hair even though there isn't much of it left."

Shapiro looked up at Leon. "He never said what they did with the contents of his pockets."

"You skipped that last time," Leon agreed. "What we want to know is what they do with the things they take from your pockets."

"They're spread out on a table. An officer picks up whatever catches his eye and turns it around in his fingers. Then I'm told to put the things back in my pockets."

"What kinds of things do you have?" Leon wanted to know.

"A handkerchief. Loose change. A leather key wallet with keys inside. My wallet with my internal passport and some bills and my veteran's card."

"What else?" Leon prompted.

"A ball-point pen. A small metal disc which lets you figure out what day of the week any date in this century falls on."

"You're not forgetting anything? Think hard, Zander."

"I usually have some sucking candies wrapped in cellophane. Zsuzsa slips them into my jacket pocket. My voice tends to go hoarse when I translate for long stretches. I suck on the candies to lubricate my throat."

"Good," Leon said, though for the life of him Zander couldn't figure out why he seemed so pleased.

At eleven they took a break. Madame Nilovna brought in a steaming pot of nettle tea, which she gigglingly described as being excellent for loose bowels and bleeding gums. Zander jokingly noted he wasn't suffering from either. "Yet," said Madame Nilovna.

"She's not what you'd call an optimist," Leon commented.

After the nettle tea break, Zander described his lunch at the Metropole with Feldstein and Tuohy two weeks before.

Leon asked, "Atticus Tuohy?"

Zander nodded carefully. "Atticus Tuohy," he confirmed.

Leon and Shapiro exchanged sharp looks. Shapiro said, "Do you know what your old friend Atticus Tuohy does for a living these days? He is the commissar in charge of minority resettlement. He is the one who is organizing the details of Stalin's holocaust."

Zander was badly shaken. "Atticus is dealing with

Jewish affairs?" When Leon nodded, Zander closed his eyes for a long moment. "That means he's the one who decided the fate of Yitzhak Feldstein."

Shapiro said, "And hundreds of others—if not thousands."

"I suggest," Leon remarked, "that we get back to work."

"What we'd like," Leon told Zander at another point, "is everything you can tell us about Stalin himself. No detail is too inconsequential. Start with the moment you set eyes on him. Where does he come from? Who is usually with him? How close physically do you actually get to him? That sort of thing."

Shapiro honed the point of a pencil on a sharpener in the form of a miniature tractor and bent over his pad.

"Dinner ends late," Zander began. "Anytime between eleven and one or even two in the morning. Beria is always there. Khrushchev, Molotov, Malenkov, Kaganovich, Bulganin are there sometimes. Once his son Vasily was there—though he left before the film started. Valechka, Stalin's housekeeper, told the projectionist he had been kicked out for drinking too much. Stalin and his guests come to the projection room through a long, tunnellike corridor that connects Stalin's private quarters to the other part of the dacha. Stalin always nods hello when he enters. He passes about two arm's lengths from me down the aisle and takes his place in the front row. At intermission he stands up to stretch his legs. Sometimes he wanders over and sits down next to someone else until the second film is ready to roll. Once or twice he leaves through a side door—I assume he was going to the toilet because several others occasionally disappear and reappear through the same door."

Shapiro looked up. "What if you have to go to the toilet?"

"The projectionist and I go back to the guardhouse entrance. There's a toilet right off it which the guards use."

"Go on," Leon said encouragingly. "You're doing fine."

"There's not much more to tell. Valechka seems to know the running time of the films we show. She always turns up as the last reel is ending and switches on the overhead lights. She has a glass of warm milk on a saucer which she hands to Stalin as he heads back through the corridor to his private quarters. Sometimes he goes back alone. Sometimes Beria accompanies him. The projectionist packs up his reels, and I help him carry them to the car that's waiting to take us back into the city."

Shapiro drew a double line under the words "warm milk" on his pad and held it up so Leon could see it. Leon nodded. "Zander, tell us more about the warm milk Valechka brings in."

"The glass always has a spoon in it."

Shapiro said, "My mother used to put a spoon in a glass before she poured in anything hot. It's to keep the glass from breaking."

"It's to stir in the sugar," Zander said.

"What sugar?" inquired Leon.

"There are some lumps of sugar on the saucer. Stalin obviously likes to sweeten his milk."

"How many lumps? With or without paper? What kind of sugar?"

"Two lumps, I think. Yes. Two. Ordinary cubes of brown sugar. Without paper. The kind you buy in boxes in the grocery store. When they have sugar."

No matter how much Zander told him, Leon always wanted more details. Which door did Valechka use when she came into the room? The side door that led to the kitchen, Zander said. Where did she stand as she waited for the film to end? Against the wall, next to the table on which the reels were stacked, right behind the projectionist. Did she hold the glass of milk or put it down on the table? She put it down, Zander remembered, to walk over to the light panel, which was against the back wall on the other side of the room. When the reel ended she switched on the lights, returned to get the milk, and handed it to Stalin as he passed on his way back to his private quarters.

The next session took place four days later because

Zander had been summoned the other nights to translate films, twice at Stalin's dacha, once at Malenkov's Moscow apartment, once at a private screening room in the Kremlin at a party presided over by Beria.

Leon surprised Zander by suggesting that the time had come to talk about getting him and his family out of Russia. "What we must find out," he said, "is who will be leaving with you."

"How will we be getting out?"

"I will tell you the how after you tell me the who."

Zander raised the delicate subject with Zsuzsa the next morning. Acting on instructions Leon had given him, he took her into the bathroom, locked the door, and turned on the shower.

"You think there are microphones?" Zsuzsa asked in alarm.

"It's only a precaution," Zander said. "I want to talk to you about something important." And he began to explain in general terms that the old friend he had come across the night he never turned up at Ludmilla's to baby-sit was his stepbrother Leon from New York, who was now an Israeli diplomat. Leon had connections, Zander said. He was offering to get them all out of the country.

"Leave Russia! Where would we go?"

"To Israel. We would start new lives there."

Zsuzsa sat down hard on the side of the bathtub. For a long while she didn't utter a word. Her eyes darted from side to side as if they were giving chase to fleeting thoughts. Eventually she looked up at Zander. "How dangerous is it?"

"He says they have gotten several dozen people out of the country in the last few years without anyone being caught."

"And you are prepared to go?"

"With you. Yes."

"I couldn't leave my mother."

"We will take her with us."

"What about Ludmilla? What about Leonid and the children?"

"Everyone will go."

"What about Arishka and Serafima and Appolinaria?"

"I don't think Serafima will leave Pasha. And I don't think Arishka will leave Serafima. But I am hoping Appolinaria will go with us, if only to get Ronzha's poems out of the country."

"My God! So it has come to this," Zsuzsa moaned. A grim smile spread across her lips. "If you are ready to take the risk, I will take it with you."

"There is no question of you going without us," Ludmilla said when Zander broached the subject—in her bathroom, with the shower running full blast. Ludmilla turned to her husband. "Isn't that right, Leonid?"

"What if we are caught?" he asked worriedly. "What will become of the children?"

"What will become of them if we stay?" Ludmilla shot back. And she provided the answer to her own question. "They will become like everyone else in this intellectual hothouse—radish Communists."

Zander didn't understand. "What are radish Communists?"

Ludmilla flashed one of her wicked smiles. "Radish Communists are red on the outside and white on the inside."

Leonid shook his head. "How can you joke at a time like this?"

Ludmilla, suddenly serious, said, "I am not making a joke. I don't want my children to have to spend their lives acting like hypocrites to stay alive. I don't want you to keep a packed satchel under your bed. I don't want to wait for them to come for you in the night." Her voice quivered with intensity. "I want to be able to talk to you about important things without going into the bathroom and turning on the shower. I love you dearly, Leonid. I love our children. I want us all to be free."

Leonid turned to Zander. "So the matter is settled. If you can make the arrangements, we will all emigrate."

Checking to make sure his name was not on a call list for a Saturday night film, Zander caught an express train to Leningrad early the following morning. "Why in heaven's name didn't you phone to say you were coming?" Arishka said. "We would have organized a meal."

"Blinis and cream," Serafima chimed in, "with Polish vodka." She studied Zander's beard as she spoke. "I think I like it."

"I want to talk to you," Zander explained. His expression was so serious the two women expected the worst and were relieved to hear—by then they were in the bathroom and the shower was running—that nobody had been arrested. "What with the business of those Kremlin doctors and most of them being Jewish, we've been worried sick about Leonid," Arishka admitted.

"Why did you come?" Serafima asked.

"We have all decided to leave—me, Zsuzsa, Zsuzsa's mother, Ludmilla and Leonid and the children."

"Leave?" Serafima repeated as if she didn't understand the word.

"Leave Russia," Zander said.

"Legally or illegally?" Arishka asked. Her eyes narrowed until she appeared to be squinting at Zander.

"Illegally. I know some people who can get us out. They have done it before and succeeded. I came to Leningrad to ask you if you would go with us."

Serafima shook her head sadly. "I have never said this out loud before, but our revolution has been betrayed. Go if you can, dear, dear Zander. As for me, I could never bring myself to leave my sergeant."

"Go, go, by all means go," Arishka whispered fiercely, "but I could never abandon Serafima. Perhaps Appolinaria will want to go with you. There are Ronzha's poems to think of."

Serafima burst into tears. Arishka put an arm around her shoulder and hugged her. "I am crying," Serafima said between sobs, "because we will never see each other again if he leaves."

"Maybe Stalin will die," Arishka said hopefully. "Maybe things will change. Maybe the frontier will open and we will all meet once a year in Helsinki."

"Maybe not," Serafima said gloomily. And she started sobbing again.

Afterward, Serafima whipped up some scrambled eggs and onions and the three of them sat around the kitchen waiting for Appolinaria, who had gone out to mail a letter. "What's taking her so long?" Zander asked. "There's a letter box on the corner."

Arishka looked at Serafima. "I suppose we can tell him now that he's leaving the country." She darted to the sink and turned on a faucet full blast. "I'm a fast learner," she said with a shy smile. "What Appolinaria's writing are anonymous letters to Stalin himself in the Kremlin. She takes the trolley so she can mail them from letter boxes in different parts of the city."

Zander groaned. "And you let her do this?"

"There's no chance of her getting caught," Serafima said calmly. "She wears gloves when she writes them so as not to leave fingerprints. That's how come we know about it—Arishka saw her writing a letter with gloves on one night, and it all came out."

"If it makes her feel better," Arishka put in, "I don't see where the harm is."

Appolinaria returned as they were finishing lunch, her cheeks pink from the cold, a satisfied look on her face. "Zander, what are you doing in Leningrad?" she asked as she leaned forward to plant a kiss on his cheek.

"What's this about you sending letters to the Kremlin?" Zander asked in a whisper.

Serafima motioned for Arishka to turn on the tap again. "We told him about what you were doing," she whispered. "I hope you don't mind."

Appolinaria did something she hadn't done in twenty years—she blushed. "I write him once a week," she said in a low voice, "and tell him how much he is detested. With any luck he reads them himself and gets hot under the collar. Maybe he will even have a heart attack."

"With any luck they're going to find out who is doing the writing," Zander whispered. "You've got to stop doing that."

"You're being a worrywart," Appolinaria insisted. "I

take precautions—there's no way under the sun they can trace the love letters back to me. Now stop talking about it and tell me why you've come to Leningrad."

"He's emigrating," Arishka told Appolinaria. "He is offering to take you with him."

"What about you and Serafima?"

"There's no question of me leaving Pasha," Serafima said.

"There's no question of me leaving Serafima," Arishka said.

"Well, there's no question of me leaving either of you," Appolinaria said. She looked around whimsically. "I could never live anywhere else. Russia was where Ronzha had his roots. And somewhere his body is mingling with its soil."

"We thought you might want to leave to get the poems out," Arishka said.

"Getting the poems out is a splendid idea," Appolinaria said. "But they can travel without me." She turned to Zander. "What do you think? Will you take Ronzha's poems out and have them published in the West?"

"Of course I will," Zander said instantly.

"In that case," Appolinaria said, "we have our work cut out for us."

It was two in the afternoon when they began. Zander seated himself at a table with a pile of paper and several ball-point pens and started to write in a tiny script as Appolinaria, pacing back and forth behind him, dictated. "I'll start with one you may remember," she said. "Ronzha recited this to his first readers in The Stray Dog one night before the revolution." And angling her head and half-closing her eyes, she brought up from memory the poem that ended:

> Fragments of red wine
> and sunny May weather—
> and, breaking a thin biscuit,
> the whiteness of the slenderest fingers.

Serafima ferried in pots of warm tea to help Zander remain awake. Appolinaria seemed to rise above bodily needs. For the next fourteen hours she floated back and forth across the room summoning the poems as if they were old friends. She felt faintly sorry, she admitted at one point, to be parting with them, but relieved in the end to share them with the world. It was almost four in the morning when she stopped pacing and stood directly behind Zander to read over his shoulder. "One more and we've done it," she said in a voice grown almost inaudible with hoarseness.

"Listen," she whispered, employing the expression that Ronzha had always used before he read. And with her lips almost touching Zander's good ear so that only he could hear her, she recited the poem—"All we hear is the Kremlin mountaineer,/The murderer and peasant-slayer"—that had cost her husband his life.

"That's everything," she said huskily. "I am emptied." And she turned away and covered her eyes with a forearm.

> JOSEF, (the letter began)
> WE HAVE MORE IN COMMON THAN YOU THINK, YOU ASTRIDE YOUR EVEREST OF CORPSES, ME HIDING LIKE A SPIDER IN MY HOLE IN THE WALL. WE BOTH HAVE DINED ON HUMAN FLESH! WITH ME IT WAS TO KEEP MY BODY ALIVE, BECAUSE WITHOUT MY BODY MY MEMORY WOULD HAVE CEASED TO EXIST, AND I WOULD HAVE LOST THE POEMS THAT SWIM AROUND MY HEAD LIKE MINNOWS IN A POND.
> HERE, IN CASE YOU ARE INTERESTED, IS HOW I CAME TO EAT HUMAN FLESH: IT HAPPENED IN LENINGRAD DURING THE GREAT PATRIOTIC WAR. (YOU REMEMBER THE GREAT PATRIOTIC WAR, DON'T YOU, JOSEF? THAT WAS WHEN SIMPLE PEASANTS WROTE OUT THE NINETY-FIRST PSALM AND SEWED IT INTO THE LINING OF THEIR CLOTHES AND RACED OFF TO DIE FOR STALIN. THAT WAS WHEN EVERYONE IN THE COUNTRY BREATHED A SIGH OF RELIEF — FINALLY THE ENEMY COULD BE OPENLY IDENTIFIED AND WAR COULD BE OPENLY WAGED.)

FOR A THOUSAND DAYS THE GERMANS LAY SIEGE TO OUR CITY. NOTHING CAME IN OR OUT, NOT A TRAIN, NOT A TRUCK, NOT A PEASANT CART. IN THE WINTER WE SUFFERED FROM TYPHUS, IN THE SUMMER FROM DYSENTERY. THERE WAS NEVER A DAY, NEVER AN HOUR WHEN GERMAN ARTILLERY SHELLS OR BOMBS WEREN'T EXPLODING, WHEN DELAYED ACTION MINES WEREN'T GOING OFF. ENDLESS FILES OF BEARDLESS BOYS IN GRAY CAPS, WITH WINTER LONGCOATS ROLLED AND STRAPPED TO THEIR BACKS, PICKED THEIR WAY THROUGH THE RUBBLE HEADING FOR THE TRENCHES IN THE SUBURBS. LOOTERS WERE SHOT ON STREET CORNERS. THE LITTLE BREAD THAT WAS DISTRIBUTED WAS TWO-THIRDS SAWDUST. OH, JOSEF, WE KNEW IN OUR HEART OF HEARTS THAT THE GERMANS WEREN'T GOING TO WIN, BECAUSE THEIR ULTIMATE GOAL WASN'T TO WIN THE THING BUT TO FIGHT IT: IF THEY HAD WANTED TO WIN THE WAR, THEY WOULDN'T HAVE SYSTEMATICALLY DESTROYED THE MANPOWER AND THE BRAINPOWER THAT COULD HAVE BEEN MOBILIZED, WITH A SNAP OF THE FINGERS, TO LIBERATE MOTHER RUSSIA FROM YOU, JOSEF. FROM YOU. BUT THAT'S ANOTHER STORY. (OR IS IT?)

IN ANY CASE, THE SITUATION IN LENINGRAD WAS DESPERATE. THE HARDEST TIME WAS THE WINTER OF 41–42. THEY SAY NOW THAT THREE HUNDRED THOUSAND DIED OF HUNGER DURING THOSE NIGHTMARISH MONTHS. I MYSELF WAS LIVING IN THE BASEMENT OF AN APARTMENT BUILDING THAT HAD TAKEN A DIRECT HIT. THERE WAS A TUNNELLIKE ENTRANCE THROUGH THE RUBBLE WITH A BLANKET STRETCHED ACROSS IT TO KEEP OUT THE COLD IN WINTER, THE FLIES IN SUMMER. WITH ME WERE TWO WOMEN, S. AND A. BEING FAT, S. SUFFERED FROM HUNGER THE MOST, BUT SHE HAD MORE PROTEIN STORED IN HER BODY TO FEED OFF,

AND THUS MORE STAMINA. IT WAS SHE WHO
SCOUTED FOR SOMETHING TO EAT WHEN WE
WERE TOO WEAK TO MOVE. FOR NINE DAYS
SHE HAD COME BACK EMPTY-HANDED, AND WE
THOUGHT THE END WAS WITHIN ARM'S REACH.
ON THE TENTH DAY S. DRAGGED HERSELF
DOWN THE TUNNEL AND OUT INTO THE STREET
TO TRY ONE LAST TIME. A DEAD PIGEON,
THE DECAYED CARCASS OF A CAT, A MAGGOT-
INFESTED RAT WOULD HAVE BEEN CONSIDERED
A FEAST.

S. RETURNED AT THE END OF THE DAY CAR-
RYING SOMETHING LONG WRAPPED IN OLD
NEWSPAPER. SHE PLACED IT GINGERLY ON A
TABLE AND WE GATHERED AROUND, A. AND I,
AND WATCHED HER PEEL AWAY THE PAPER,
AND THEN SOME DIRTY BANDAGES, TO REVEAL
(AS I WRITE THIS A LUMP OF NAUSEA MOUNTS
TO MY THROAT!) A HUMAN LEG. SHE HAD RE-
TRIEVED IT FROM A GARBAGE PAIL BEHIND A
HOSPITAL. IT HAD BEEN AMPUTATED BETWEEN
THE KNEE JOINT AND THE HIP AND HAD FRO-
ZEN SOLID IN THE COLD. WE HAVE ONLY TO
DEFROST IT BIT BY BIT, S. SAID, AND EAT IT. IF
WE PROCEEDED SPARINGLY, IT WOULD KEEP
US ALIVE THROUGH THE WINTER. WITH SPRING
THERE WOULD BE AIRLIFTS, AND BREAD.

WITH AN AX WE HAD, S. HACKED OFF A PIECE
OF THE THIGH AND PRESSED IT BETWEEN HER
OWN THIGHS TO DEFROST IT. WE SHARPENED
ONE OF OUR KITCHEN KNIVES ON A BARBER'S
STROP AND A. MADE SOME NEAT INCISIONS ON
THE SKIN, PEELING OFF SMALL SQUARES AND
THEN THE THREE OF US SAT THERE GNAWING
WITH OUR BICUSPIDS ON THE FLESH OF ONE
OF THE TWENTY MILLION OF OUR BROTHERS
OR SISTERS WHO (ASSUMING THE AMPUTATION
WAS FATAL) DIED IN THE WAR WE FOUGHT FOR
YOU, JOSEF.

SO HOW DID I FEEL EATING HUMAN FLESH?
I FELT (TO TELL THE GODAWFUL TRUTH) I WAS

ENGAGED IN A RELIGIOUS RITE, NOT UNLIKE
THE EUCHARIST. I REMEMBER BREAKING A
THIN BISCUIT OF FLESH BETWEEN MY TEETH
AND THINKING OF YOU, JOSEF. YOU WHO SPENT
YEARS IN A SEMINARY, YOU WOULD HAVE CON-
SECRATED WITH FRAGMENTS OF RED WINE AND
A THIN BISCUIT THE HOLY COMMUNION HUN-
DREDS OF TIMES. YOU WERE WITH US, JOSEF,
LIKE AN UNHOLY GHOST, DURING THE RITUAL.

AND YOU, JOSEF—HOW DO *YOU* FEEL, ATOP
YOUR EVEREST OF CORPSES, NIBBLING ON THE
FLESH OF YOUR SERVANTS? ARE WE TALKING
PROTEIN WHEN YOU BRING THE THIN BISCUIT
OF FLESH TO YOUR BICUSPIDS? WHAT EXACTLY
ARE YOU NOURISHING BY THE NEVER-ENDING
DEVOURING OF YOUR PEOPLE? DID YOUR YEARS
IN THE SEMINARY GIVE YOU THE TASTE FOR
WINE AND BISCUITS? FOR THE RITUAL CELE-
BRATION OF DEATH? FOR THE HOLY COMMU-
NION OF COMMUNISM?

ARE YOU, JOSEF DEAR, STARK RAVING MAD?

THAT IS THE ONLY EXPLANATION THAT STRIKES
ME AS HAVING A SHRED OF SANITY.

SLEEP WELL IF YOU CAN, JOSEF.

The letter, like the ones before it, was signed: MOTHER
RUSSIA.

"Are you there, Josef Vissarionovich? Can you hear
me?"

Beria was clearly excited. Words spilled out. " 'Kremlin mountaineer' and 'murderer and peasant-slayer' are
from a poem by the poet Ronzha, who died during
interrogation in the nineteen thirties. He is survived by
a widow named Appolinaria, who shares a flat in Leningrad with a woman whose first name begins with A, and
another whose first name begins with S. The one whose
name begins with S is fat. S has a common law husband
who is confined to a Red Sunset wheelchair purchased
five months ago."

Stalin brought up a "hrmph" of satisfaction from the

back of his throat, but it seemed only to spur Beria on. "I tell you, the pieces fit. The puzzle is solved. The game is over. The three women, Ronzha's widow, S., and A., were in Leningrad together during the Great War. Also the expression 'fragments of red wine' in the last letter comes from another poem by the late Ronzha. The woman Appolinaria must have memorized everything he wrote. That's what she means when she says she would have lost the poems swimming in her head like minnows if she had lost her memory."

Beria gasped for air as if he had surfaced from a prolonged dive.

Stalin was silent for a moment. Then: "I knew there was one somewhere out there."

"One what?"

"One traitor. One wrecker. One who wanted me to die."

"She won't be out there long," Beria swore. "We will dispatch people tonight and erase her. Her friends also. It will be as if they never existed."

Stalin perked up; one of his eyelids twitched. "I don't want her hurt. She is a seer. She sees into the future as well as into the past. And she is not afraid to say exactly what she thinks. Bring her to me—I will talk to her. I will install her in an apartment in the Kremlin and consult regularly with her."

Beria pushed away the woman who was fiddling with the buttons of his fly and cupped his hand around the speaker. "You want me to bring her to the Kremlin? Alive?"

"Of course alive," Stalin wheezed again. "How else can I speak to her?"

Beria hung up the phone. The second woman in his office drifted around behind him and began stabbing at the inside of his ear with the tip of her tongue. Beria hardly noticed. "He wants her alive," he murmured. "The world is going crazy."

6

Leon was edgy. Earlier that week Jewish extremists had bombed the Soviet legation in Tel Aviv. Three days later Moscow used the bombing as an excuse to break diplomatic relations with Israel and order the Israeli diplomats out of the country. He and Shapiro would be leaving with the minister that night.

"Our Russian-Jewish friends will carry the ball," Leon reassured Zander, who was very disturbed by the prospect of Leon's sudden departure. "I promise you they'll do everything under the sun to get you and your family out."

Zander laughed through his nose. "That's easy for you to say. You're leaving on a diplomatic passport." He held up his hands. "I'm sorry—I didn't mean that. I guess I'm nervous."

Leon nodded. "Nothing is easy for me to say. I only control myself more than most." He grunted in the general direction of Shapiro, who discreetly gathered up his notes and slipped out of the room. "Listen, Zander, I hate going, but there's not much more I could do for you even if I were here. A last word of advice—when the time comes to act, don't fall into the trap of thinking too much." Leon looked hard at Zander, who nodded. "Let's move on," Leon said. "When are Ludmilla and Leonid and the children starting south?"

"They take the train to Sochi tomorrow."

"They have memorized the information you gave them?"

Zander indicated they had. "They will install themselves at the rest home and go through the motions of vacationing until they hear from their aunt Nilovna—she will say something about the weather in Moscow being unbearable. Then they telephone the number you gave me. Wearing only the clothes on their back, they will rendezvous with your man. He will smuggle them onto an Italian freighter offloading in the bay." In an anguished voice Zander asked, "You are sure this is going to work? I'll kill myself if I learn when I get to Piraeus that they've been taken prisoner."

"Nothing is one hundred percent sure," Leon said. "But the Sochi route is the nearest thing to it. The freighter has a special soundproof room built into one of its holds. The port authorities could suspect there was a family being smuggled out and, short of putting the ship into drydock and tearing it apart, still not find them."

Zander seemed reassured. "Zsuzsa and her mother are taking the train to Leningrad tonight. They will go directly to the address you provided."

"Once again," Leon said, "the escape route is as close to perfect as we can make it. They'll be stretched out on mattresses in a false compartment over the rear wheels of a Swedish truck. The truck comes in filled with Swedish products and returns loaded to the brim with Russian products. The frontier guards would have to unload the entire truck to get to the secret compartment. Once your wife and mother-in-law are in Finland, they'll join the driver in the cab. We have false passports for them and they'll simply drive across into Sweden, rest a day or so depending on the old woman's condition, and start out by train for the south of Italy and the ship to Israel. Our people will be accompanying them the whole way."

"Which leaves me," Zander noted.

Leon smiled faintly. "Which leaves you. You will be brought back to Moscow by the limousine that took you out to the dacha. If you have managed to make the switch, and only if you have managed to make the switch, you will ring up Madame Nilovna."

"I work into the conversation the phrase from de Tocqueville. 'In revolution, as in a novel, the most difficult part to invent is the end.' "

"Our car will pick you up at the usual corner twenty minutes after you make the phone call. You'll go out in the trunk of a Greek diplomat shipping his belongings home after a tour of duty. The truck will be Greek, the driver a Greek Jew traveling under diplomatic passport. The crates and trunks in the truck will be sealed with diplomatic seals, which the frontier guards have no right to break. It will be a long trip for you, Zander—at least forty hours, maybe as much as forty-eight. You won't be taken out of the trunk until you reach our warehouse in Piraeus."

"What if the frontier guards have dogs that sniff out people?"

"We've thought of that. The trunk has a thin lead lining. When you pass through control points, the driver will signal you by tapping on the trunk with a pole. You'll close off the air vent. There is enough air inside the trunk to keep you breathing for several hours."

"It will be hot inside, won't it?"

"Very. You get in wearing only your undershorts. You'll have a supply of bottled water, also bags to pee into or vomit into."

Later, at the door, Leon handed Zander the candy box wrapped in gift paper. "I'm giving you this only because you insisted."

"If something goes wrong, I want to have a way out. I don't want to end up in one of those interrogation cells. Is there a silencer with it?"

"I'm not sure what that's going to change, but there's a silencer. Two clips with seven bullets each. You'll return it to our people who take you out of the trunk in Piraeus. From that point on you'll be traveling as an American tourist. I don't want the Greeks to pick you up for carrying a pistol."

Leon flung an arm over Zander's shoulder and accompanied him to the servant's door of the apartment. "The next time we meet," he said quietly, "it will be, God willing, in Israel. And the world will be a safer place for Jews." Leon shifted his weight from one foot to the other. "You don't hold it against me that I have used you?"

Zander looked at his shoes and up at Leon. He was remembering, once again, that last meeting on the Brooklyn Bridge. "I take it as a sign of affection."

Leon recognized the phrase and laughed under his breath. "I told you then, I tell you now: God bless you, Zander. I love you dearly."

"I love you too, Leon. See you in the holy land."

"In the holy land. God willing."

Appolinaria had noticed the difference immediately. No sooner had she emptied her head of the poems than she started losing them. At first it was only a word here and there that eluded her. Then a phrase or two. Then complete sentences. Now there were whole chunks of poems that she couldn't recall no matter how hard she concentrated.

In a sense what had happened was only natural. She had been the living repository of the poems since the day she and Zander burned the originals, sixteen years before. Once they existed again on paper, the hemisphere of her brain that bore the burden of preserving Ronzha's three hundred or so poems began relaxing. Maybe, just maybe, this was how things were meant to be, she thought. She had borne the burden and had passed it on and it was time for her to rest, even if the act of resting seemed uncomfortably close to the act of dying.

From somewhere outside the double-window came the sound of an automobile door slamming. Who would be coming home at this hour at the end of February? And in an automobile? Appolinaria slid off her cot and slipped her stocking feet into the heelless felt slippers next to the bed and shuffled over to the window. She parted the Venetian blinds with two fingers. Below there wasn't one automobile but a dozen, along with two wagons with barred windows. Scores of men in winter coats and fedoras were taking up positions on either side of the street. Appolinaria angled her head so she could see the corner. A police bus had pulled diagonally across it to block the street to traffic, and files of uniformed militiamen with rifles at the ready had formed a line.

Obviously the authorities had discovered the whereabouts of a major state criminal and were closing in on him. A group of men detached themselves from the mass of plainclothes detectives milling beneath her window and headed directly for the entrance of her building. Several of them appeared to have pistols in their hands. Appolinaria thought of waking Arishka, asleep on the other side of the blanket that divided the room in two, but decided against it. The poor dear worked hard and needed every minute of sleep she could get. Instead, Appolinaria shuffled across the room to the door and opened it a crack. From the gut of the building she could hear men pounding up the staircase. The footfalls grew louder.

Suddenly she knew the identity of the state criminal.

With the poems safely out of her head and down on paper, there was no reason for her to procrastinate. She locked the door of her room and removed the key and slipped it into her bathrobe pocket. She shuffled back to the bed on her side of the blanket and felt around on the shelf over it for the basin she sometimes used to soak her feet in when they were swollen. She found it in the darkness and brought it down to her lap. The razor blade would be in it. She had put it there the day she wrote Stalin his first love letter. She rolled back the sleeves of her bathrobe, baring her wrist. She could see the whiteness of the skin in the darkness. She felt for a vein with two fingers, and found it, and in a quick slashing motion severed it with the razor. She experienced a stinging sensation, then a flowing warmness. She severed the vein on her other wrist and held both hands over the basin on her lap so as not to make a great mess for Serafima and Arishka to clean up.

A fist hammered on the front door of the apartment. She heard Serafima crying, "Hold on to your water. I'm coming."

An army tramped into the living room. Someone beat on the bedroom door. Arishka cried out in alarm. A moment later she was at the door. "I can't find the key," she called through it. "Wait until I put on the light."

Arishka switched on the overhead bulb and came around the edge of the blanket and saw Appolinaria holding her two bleeding wrists over the basin, and gasped.

"It's the letters I wrote," Appolinaria whispered weakly. "For the love of God, help me die."

"Do you have the key?" a voice called.

"I'm looking for it," Arishka said very quietly. Then she screamed, "I'm looking for it!" She bent over Appolinaria and kissed her forehead.

"She's stalling," a voice said.

"Stand back," someone else yelled.

Axes began to splinter the wood. In her bed, Appolinaria swayed with dizziness. Arishka put an arm around her shoulder to steady her. Appolinaria rested her wrists in the oozing contents of the basin and leaned back against the pillows and tried to recall some lines from one of Ronzha's poems that had escaped her earlier. "The whole room is invaded . . ." That was it. "The whole room is invaded."

Somewhere so far away it might have been in a different life a door burst off its hinges. Appolinaria's lips silently mouthed the lines that came to the dying hemisphere of her brain.

> Fragments of red wine
> and sunny May weather—
> and, breaking a thin biscuit,
> the whiteness . . .

Two nights running, Zander had failed to pull off the switch. On Thursday night he had translated part of *The Great Ziegfeld*, and had caught the faint sound of Stalin humming along with "A Pretty Girl Is Like a Melody." The film had been stopped and one called *Brother Orchid* shown in its place after Khrushchev suggested, during an intermission, that Ziegfeld was a Jewish-sounding name. On Friday Zander had translated *Ninotchka* with Greta Garbo and Melvyn Douglas, and a second film, *Dead Reckoning*, with Humphrey Bogart and Lizabeth Scott. On both nights he might have gotten away with it. Acting on Leon's instructions, he had been taking in a cube or two of sugar wrapped in paper, along with his sucking candies, for the past week. "It's to give me strength for the third film," he had joked when the guard officer who turned out his pockets noticed the sugar on the table. On Thursday Zander had started carrying the lump of sugar that Leon had given him at their last meeting. As the film was about to end, Valechka had placed the warm milk on the table behind the projectionist and had moved to the other side of the room to be ready to turn on the lights. Zander had taken a step back. The projectionist, a shadow on the other side of his machine, had been absorbed in the last scene of the film. The music had soared. Zander had glanced at the warm milk—its whiteness seemed to glow in the dark—and at the saucer with the two cubes of sugar in it. He had fingered the sugar in his pocket, peeling away the paper. It would have been child's play for him to snatch one of the cubes and replace it with Leon's cube.

Ludmilla was in Sochi with her family waiting for the phone call from Aunt Nilovna. Zsuzsa and her mother were with Leon's man in Leningrad. Everything was in place. Including Zander, standing within reach of the glass of milk Stalin would drink before disappearing for the night into one of his six bedrooms and double-locking its armored door from the inside.

And yet he had failed to act. It was true, of course, what Leon had said about thinking too much. What he was thinking of was the incredible responsibility someone takes on himself when he changes the course of history. It was one thing to join tens of thousands of others in the making of a revolution. But to act on your own—to commit murder—was another order of things. What if Stalin didn't die and used the *real* attempt on his life as an excuse to crack down even harder on the Jews? What if the regime that came after Stalin was worse? His heirs might trip over each other to prove how Stalinist they were. In his mind's eye Zander could see innocent men and women and children being dragged from their apartments all over the Soviet Union by Stalin loyalists who worshipped the ground the Great Helmsman walked on.

On Saturday, the last day of February, Zander haunted the empty rooms of his apartment, his brain a whirl of conflicting thoughts. He summoned his voices—Lili's, or that of the man who forged his passport back in New York, or his brother Abner's—but the messages from the past were confused. He pulled the candy box from under the bed and undid the gift wrapping and considered using the pistol on himself, but that was no answer either; the fact that he had gotten his hands on a pistol would arouse suspicion. His family, his friends, would be interrogated. The plot against Stalin might unravel. Zionists would be blamed. The Jews, once again, would be made to suffer. The pogrom Zander had been trying to head off would be launched with even more enthusiasm.

At midmorning Zander was summoned to the hall phone by one of his neighbors. It was the Motion Picture Collective. He was to stand by that night. The car would pick him up at the usual hour. They would start showing films sometime after midnight.

Zander hung up the receiver. The phone sounded again, as if the act of severing the connection had activated the bell. He let it ring a second time and picked it up.

"I want to talk, please, to a person named Til," a woman's voice said.

"This is Til speaking."

"Alexander Til?"

"I am Alexander Til."

The woman on the other end cleared her throat nervously. Her words seemed muted; it dawned on Zander that she must have been holding a handkerchief over the speaker. "I am calling from Leningrad. You don't know me, but I was a friend of a friend."

Zander started to mention a name, but the woman cut him off. "Maybe it is better if we don't get specific. The woman who was a friend of yours spent a lot of her time pushing someone around in a wheelchair, if you get the picture."

"I understand," Zander said. "Is she ill?"

He could hear coins being pushed into a slot. "I guess you could say that. She once left me your name and phone number and said if anything ever happened to her or the people she lived with, I was to do her a favor and tell you about it. I liked her a lot, you see, so I am doing the favor. They were all arrested last night. I saw the whole thing from my window. Dozens and dozens of militia went into the building; there were so many you would think they were arresting Adolf Hitler. The man in the wheelchair was pushed out first. He was blabbering about something, but they went and shoved him into a wagon and slammed the door and you couldn't hear his voice no more. The fat woman who was my friend came out next. She was handcuffed to another woman. They were both crying hysterically." More coins were pushed into the slot on the other end of the line. "Are you still there? Someone was brought out on a stretcher. The head was covered with a blanket, so whoever it was must have been dead. My block captain told me this morning the dead woman had cut her wrists—she had been caught writing threatening letters to someone in the superstructure. That's all I know. I have to go now. Do you think you can do something to help them?"

Zander had difficulty breathing; difficulty speaking. "I think so," he managed to say.

"Then for God's sake do it," the woman blurted out.

The line clicked dead in Zander's ear. He continued to hold the phone, hoping it would come to life again. Finally he dropped it back onto the cradle. His legs had become limp and he had to make an effort to keep from sinking to the floor. Lines of poetry came to him from out of an ether of pain:

> We live, deaf to the land beneath us,
> Ten steps away no one hears our speeches . . .

That night Stalin's stag dinner dragged on later than usual and the film didn't get underway until a quarter past one in the morning. The first movie was Alexander Dovshenko's prewar epic *Aerograd,* about the construction of an army aviation post in the wilds of Siberia. Zander, with no translating chores, was kept on tap in the guardroom off the main entrance. There were magazines stacked on a side table and coffee warming on an electric heater, but he didn't bother with either; he sat alone in the room on a straight-backed wooden chair, thinking furiously: of Appolinaria and Arishka and Serafima and Pasha, of Zsuzsa and her mother, of Ludmilla and Leonid and the children, of Feldstein and Tuohy, of Leon, of Lili. The time had finally come to make amends—to put an end to the fraud he had been part of.

A guard with a broad peasant face poked his head in the room and told Zander that Stalin had decided to run a second film. Malenkov and Bulganin wanted a Russian picture, Khrushchev and Beria an American one. Stalin had taken a look at the mimeographed program notes that came with the reels and decided on the American film.

"Til's here," Khrushchev said as soon as he entered the projection room. "Will someone hit those lights."

Stalin said, "I want to take a leak." He ambled toward the side door and disappeared. Watching him go, more lines drifted through Zander's head:

> All we hear is the Kremlin mountaineer,
> The murderer and peasant-slayer . . .

Khrushchev chatted in an undertone with Beria. Malenkov pulled some papers from his breast pocket and began reading them. Bulganin closed his eyes and dozed. When Stalin returned, ten minutes later, Malenkov tapped one of the papers he was reading. "Eisenhower is putting out feelers about you coming to Washington for a summit conference."

"Think of the American films we could get to see over there," Beria said.

Stalin, wearing a pressed generalissimo's tunic and military striped trousers tucked into spit-shined boots, lowered himself into his seat. "The great Prince Vladimir was once visited by a cardinal who arrived from Rome in a gilded palanquin carried by servants. You know the story? The cardinal invited the Prince to visit

Rome. Vladimir told him, 'Bring Rome here.' If Eisenhower wants to see me, bring Washington here!"

> His fingers are fat as grubs
> And the words, final as lead weights, fall
> from his lips . . .

There was a gust of laughter from Stalin's cronies. Wheezing with pleasure, Stalin waved a hand tiredly at Valechka, who darted for the light switch.

In the darkness the titles of Harold Lloyd's *Safety Last* flashed on the screen. Zander began translating the story of the hard-up clerk who, in order to impress his girlfriend, offers to climb a skyscraper. Beria and Khrushchev were soon roaring with laughter. Bulganin could be heard snoring away in his seat. Every now and then Stalin wheezed in amusement.

> His cockroach whiskers leer
> And his boot tips gleam . . .

Toward the end, with Lloyd dangling precariously from the minute hand of a gigantic clock twenty stories above the street, even Bulganin was paying attention. Valechka, who had left the room at the start of the film, slipped back through the door. Zander could see she was carrying the saucer and the glass of milk. He fingered the lump of sugar in his pocket, removing the paper from it. "The End" appeared on the screen. Valechka put the milk on the table and went to turn on the lights. Zander reached back and switched lumps of sugar and dropped the one from the saucer into his pocket just as the overhead lights illuminated the room.

Stalin was already on his feet. "Anyway, why would I want to talk to Eisenhower?" Zander heard him tell Malenkov. Stalin laughed slyly. "The peasants have a saying. When a wolf attacks, you don't try to tame it. You kill it." He started up the aisle. Nodding vaguely at the projectionist and Zander, he picked up his glass of milk and disappeared through the door down the tunnellike corridor leading to his private quarters.

* * *

For Zander it came under the heading of unfinished business. He had gotten back to his apartment at five-thirty in the morning and immediately used the hall phone to call Madame Nilovna. "I've gotten home," he told her. "I called so you would not worry about me. I was reading de Tocqueville on the train and came across a sentence I thought you would like. 'In revolution, as in a novel, the most difficult part to invent is the end.' "

Madame Nilovna let the air out of her lungs in a long "Ahhhhh." It took a moment or two for her to regain her composure. "It was thoughtful of you to pass it on to me. I shall copy it into my Commonplace Book as soon as I hang up. I shall read it to all my friends before the morning is out."

Going through the motions that seemed to him to be almost predestined, Zander shaved off his beard. For the second time in his life he had the curious sensation of staring at his own face in a mirror and barely recognizing it; once again the beard had done its work. He collected the cardboard folder containing all the poems Appolinaria had dictated to him, the gift-wrapped box of candy, and the two small paintings of Lili done during her days in Paris—one, he now guessed, was by Picasso, the other by Modigliani—and let himself out of the apartment as silently as he could.

The government Zil driven by the young man who dreamed of raising irises was waiting for him on the corner. "Where are we going?" Zander asked as he slid into the rear seat.

"I have been instructed to take you to a warehouse in the northern suburbs of the city," the driver replied over his shoulder. He glanced at Zander in the rearview mirror. "Is it true, then?" he whispered with great emotion.

"Is what true?"

But the driver only smiled a crooked smile.

As the car swung onto the inner ring, Zander leaned forward. "I have to make a quick stop," he said, and he gave the driver an address.

"The people I work for said nothing about a detour."

"It will only be a minute or two. I want to drop off a box of candy."

"I don't know."

"Believe me," Zander said, "it is essential or I wouldn't ask you."

The driver pulled up on a side street around the corner from the address Zander had given him. "Only a minute or two," he reminded Zander anxiously. "People are waiting. The truck must be on its way by sunup."

The apartment building was one of a series built after the war for second-level party and government people. Tuohy's flat was on the fifth floor. Zander used the staircase instead of the elevator, found the door with the brass plate engraved with "A. Tuohy," and rang the bell. He pressed it a second time, and a third. Stifling a yawn, Tuohy called through the door, "Who the hell is it at this ungodly hour?"

"It's me."

Tuohy must have recognized Zander's voice, because he swung open the door without another word. He was wearing a long terry-cloth bathrobe with his initials on the breast pocket, a winter scarf wrapped around his neck, and thick woolen socks on his feet. He cocked his head inquisitively at Zander. "To what do I owe the honor?"

"I'm in trouble," Zander told him.

"If you are in real trouble," Tuohy said, "I may have to arrest you myself." He shrugged. "I suppose you might as well come in." He kicked the door closed behind Zander and led him through an enormous living room crammed with Danish modern into a paneled den. Tuohy turned off an elaborate modern overhead chandelier and switched on some quieter table lamps and bent to put a record on the Magnavox built into the wall-to-wall shelves across one entire side of the room. "I've forgotten what you like," Tuohy said. "Classic or modern?"

"You never knew what I liked," Zander told him.

The sound of American jazz filled the room.

"I'm sorry," Tuohy said. "What did you say just then?"

"Nothing important."

Tuohy sank into a soft leather swivel chair and spun around to face Zander, who was studying the contents of the room as if he were making an inventory. He took in the mahogany desk with a glass top, the open liquor cabinet filled with bottles, and the shelf above it crammed with crystal glasses of all sizes and shapes. He took in the Magnavox and the collection of several hundred phonograph records and the two polished brass horses on end tables on either side of a leather couch. He took in the leather of the couch, which was pale brown and soft. He took in the Persian carpet under his feet. He took in the grained wooden humidor, and the enormous glass ashtray next to it in the form of a swan; it was being used as a paperweight to hold down a pile of file folders.

Tuohy said, "I've done all right for myself."

Zander said, "Property is theft."

Tuohy's head snapped back and forth in annoyance. "You haven't changed much in thirty-five years."

Zander set the candy box down on a table and began unwrapping the paper that covered it. "I translated an American film for Stalin at Blizhny a few hours ago. In the darkness I slipped a lump of sugar onto the saucer next to the glass of warm milk he takes back with him to his bedroom. The sugar was poisoned."

Tuohy's expression didn't alter, but his facial muscles froze. His ambiguous half smile might have been cast in bronze. He turned his head carefully and glanced at his desk, judging the distance between himself and the drawer in which he kept his loaded pistol. He decided he was nearer to it than Zander and was about to lunge for it, when he noticed the object Zander had removed from the box of candy.

"The bulbous lump at the end of the barrel is a silencer," Zander noted.

"I'm not stupid," Tuohy remarked. "If Stalin has really been poisoned, all hell will break loose."

"We used a poison that makes it look as if the victim has had a stroke."

"If it looks like a stroke, why are you in trouble?"

"I'm in trouble because I committed myself to a revolution that turned out to be totally corrupt—the revolution was corrupt, the system it created was corrupt, the people who led it were corrupt. Russia never stood a chance."

"You're full of shit," Tuohy burst out. "The Soviet state has real achievements to its credit—we wiped out illiteracy, we wiped out famine, we built an industrial base from nothing. We've come a long way—"

Zander whispered bitterly, "We dreamed a bigger dream, Atticus."

Tuohy swiveled impatiently to his left and then back again. "Revolutions aren't made by dreamers. They're made by people who crack skulls. I suppose we couldn't avoid having a dreamer or two in our ranks. We collected them the way you collect lint in your trouser cuffs. From time to time we turned out our cuffs and brushed them clean and got on with the job." He threw back his head and narrowed his eyes and gazed at Zander. "Of course I don't believe a word you said about the lump of sugar. Stalin is the most well-guarded person on the face of the earth. What you describe is impossible."

"Whether you believe me or not isn't important. Stalin is either dead or dying at this moment."

Tuohy stirred in his swivel chair. Gripping the pistol with both hands, Zander brought it up until it was pointing directly at him.

"What do you think you're going to do with that?" Tuohy drawled sarcastically.

"I am going to shoot the man who killed Yitzhak Feldstein."

A bitter laugh made its way to the surface from the depth of Tuohy's body. "Here lies Atticus Tuohy," he intoned. "Death is a debt one owes to nature. I've paid!"

"You've spent your life cracking skulls," Zander said. He took a step forward. "Tens of millions of skulls have been cracked by you and people like you. And what does Russia have to show for it? We forgot *why* we made the revolution, Atticus. We gave too much of ourselves away making it and then protecting it. Ronzha had it right. You can't give anything of yourself away because once you start, there is no logical reason to stop. And one day you wake up and there's nothing left. Of yourself. Of the revolution. Of the dream."

Tuohy sneered. "You couldn't shoot Ortona back in New York. What makes you think you have the guts to pull the trigger now?"

Zander took still another step in Tuohy's direction. "That's what the revolution has done to me," he said softly. "It has made me capable of looking a man in the eye and taking his life."

"Are you sure?"

Zander considered the question. "No," he said finally. "I'm not sure. I only think so."

And then he shot Tuohy in the heart.

Outside in the street again, Zander was climbing into the Zil when he heard a sound that made his skin crawl. He rolled down a window and let the cold air bathe the dampness on his face. From around a corner an old horse appeared. It had blinders on its head and ribs bulging out of its hide. It trudged along leaning into its traces, straining under the weight of a wagon piled high with cabbages from a collective farm. The horse stumbled over a pothole. Cursing, the peasant riding on the wagon lashed out with his whip, searing the flanks of the animal. Jerking its head back against the bit in its mouth, the old horse struggled on down the street. The sound of the hooves receded.

In the automobile Zander winced with certainty; this time he knew he was remembering.

A Russian translation of *The Prince* lay on the night table next to the bed. Yudina's recording of Mozart's Piano Concerto Number Twenty-three was playing softly on the Victrola; every time the record reached the end and rejected, someone started it again. A half-dozen doctors bent over the patient, straining to catch any word he might utter. Khrushchev, Molotov, Bulganin, Malenkov, Beria wandered in and out of the room from time to time to see how things were going.

Things were going badly.

There had been no sign of life from Stalin's private quarters all day Sunday. By Sunday night the guards were frantic. Members of the Politburo were summoned. They held a quick conference and gave the security people permission to break into the bedrooms. It was a tedious job. Guards worked through Sunday night and into the early hours of Monday morning with acetylene torches, etching their way through the armored doors. The first of the six bedrooms they broke into was empty. The second also. And the third. In the fourth bedroom they found Stalin, fully clothed, lying face down on a rug. Gingerly they turned him over. He was still breathing, but barely. His eyes were rolled back. His lips were black and covered with foam.

Doctors were rushed out from Moscow. After a quick examination they announced that Stalin had suffered a stroke. He had lost his powers of speech. His right side was completely paralyzed. He kept slipping in and out of a coma. He breathed with difficulty, sucking in air in shallow gasps. Oxygen was brought. Cardiograms were taken. Camphor, caffeine, strophanthin, glucose, penicillin were administered. The only time Stalin showed any sign of life was when an old nurse applied leeches to the back of his neck. *"Vot! Vot!"* he cried feebly. "That's it! That's it!"

By Thursday his condition had deteriorated. He seemed to be gasping more and taking in less air. His contorted face was turning black; people who visited for the first time didn't recognize him. It was as if he were being slowly garroted to death. His daughter, Svetlana, sat at his bedside stroking and kissing his good hand. Just before ten in the evening Stalin's eyes blinked open. He tugged his hand out of Svetlana's grip and raised a trembling finger to point at something above his head. Everyone in the room looked up.

When they looked back, Stalin was dead.

Valechka fell to her knees next to the bed and began wailing like a peasant. Khrushchev, with tears streaming down his cheeks, led Svetlana from the room. Beria darted for the front door of the dacha. "My car!" he shrieked at the top of his lungs. "Bring around my car!"

Zander was subjected to a long—and because Leon wasn't there, a relatively unpleasant—debriefing in a Greek safe house. The Israelis were nothing if not discreet. They noted in passing that one of the bullets was missing from a clip Zander had returned with the pistol; they noted, too, the news that the Commissar for Minority Resettlement had been found shot to death in his Moscow apartment.

"Do you have any comment to make on this?" one of the Israelis asked politely.

Zander shook his head.

"Let's go over again the moment when you made the switch. Are you absolutely sure that the lump of sugar we gave you ended up on the saucer?"

"I'm positive."

"The whole thing happened very rapidly—it could have fallen to the floor."

"No. It was on the saucer."

Time dragged. Zander grew moody and his moods turned into a depression. There were hours when his companions in the safe house had trouble getting a word out of him. The uncertainty—had Stalin taken the poison? Did the Russian leaders realize that the Great Helmsman had been assassinated? Was Zander being hunted?—left everyone's nerves frayed. "You asked me that already," Zander snapped at one point. "I categorically refuse to be grilled like a schoolchild."

It wasn't until Wednesday morning, March 4, that Soviet radio programs were interrupted to inform Russians that Stalin had suffered a stroke. In the safe house in Piraeus, the Israelis with Zander breathed a sigh of relief. "So the sugar was on the saucer after all," one of them said.

An Israeli doctor among them analyzed the medical

bulletins that came out of Moscow—the authorities spoke
of a cerebral hemorrhage, of paralysis of the right side,
of loss of speech, of serious cardiac and respiratory
complications. "The man is dying," the doctor concluded. "It is a matter of hours." On Friday, the sixth,
the Kremlin announced Stalin's death: "The heart of
Josef Vissarionovich Stalin, Lenin's comrade-in-arms,
wise leader and educator of the Communist Party and
the Soviet people, has stopped beating." In the safe
house the half-dozen Israelis gathered around the short-
wave radio broke out a bottle of slivowitz. The Israelis
to a man rose to their feet and raised their glasses to
Zander. Several of the toughest-looking among them
had tears in their eyes. "So the bastard has met his
maker," one of the younger Israelis muttered. "May
Yahweh damn his soul to the lowest and hottest level of
Dante's hell."

Within a week of Stalin's death it was evident that
the Soviet Union was entering the post-Stalin era. There
were unmistakable straws in the wind. *Pravda* for the
first time in memory referred to the "Soviet Constitution," and not the "Stalin Constitution." Someone quoting from one of Stalin's books failed to describe it as
"inspired." The new edition of Olzhegov's *Dictionary of
the Russian Language* went to press with no definition
for the word "Stalinist"; the previous edition had devoted four lines to the subject. More to the point,
articles attacking Jews and Zionists disappeared from
the Soviet press. Then the Kremlin doctors were released and it was announced that the accusations against
them were without foundation. "I think," the Israeli in
charge of the safe house told Zander, "you can go home
now."

Home, of course, was Israel. One morning before
dawn Zander was driven to a small airport outside
Athens, where a private plane was waiting to take him
to the promised land. On arriving in Lod Airport he
was whisked to an office in one of the hangars. Leon
stepped out of a knot of Israelis and embraced Zander,
Russian-style, on the lips. A short man with white hair,
wearing black trousers and an open-necked white sport

shirt, came forward. "We will keep this brief," he said gravely. "There can be no medals, no public recognition for what you have done. Only a handful of us know about it, and we have sworn before the God of our fathers never to reveal the secret. But I want to be sure you know—I speak to you from the depths of my being— that you have done a great thing. God put you in the right place at the right moment, but *you* acted. And you acted as only a deeply moral man could act. I give you the undying gratitude of a people returned from the brink of annihilation."

The man with the white hair never offered to shake hands with Zander. Having finished his little speech, he took a step backward and bowed deeply from the waist, the way a Russian peasant might bow to an icon of the Holy Father. Behind him the other Israelis followed suit. Then they turned and filed silently out of the room.

"Well, it's not everyone who is met at the door of Israel by the prime minister," Leon noted. When he saw the look of surprise on Zander's face, he said, "I thought you would recognize him—that was David Ben-Gurion. And here comes the rest of the reception committee."

Another door burst open and Zander's entire family, with Vanka and Aza in the lead, thundered into the room. Aza leapt into Zander's arms and planted a wet kiss on his lips. "Now that Zander's here," she announced brightly, "we get to go to Jerusalem."

"I don't like it here," Vanka whispered in Zander's ear. "They don't speak Russian."

"What took you so long, my love?" Zsuzsa asked, embracing Zander in turn. She flashed a pained smile that was a hairbreadth away from tears. "Your brother, Leon, assured us that you were safely out of the country, but we were worried all the same."

"He was giving us a helping hand in Greece," Leon said quietly.

"Imagine," Zsuzsa's old mother exclaimed, "someone emigrating at my age! To tell you the truth, all this adventure makes me feel like a young girl again."

"You've heard the news," Ludmilla said when she hugged Zander. "The old goat kicked the bucket. Good riddance if you ask me. I have a good Israeli joke for you. It's this way . . ."

After lunch Leon led Zander up the narrow steel walkway around the top of the control tower for a breath of fresh air. "The Mediterranean is beyond the rise over there," he said, pointing. Leon tilted his large head and observed Zander. "You haven't been very talkative since you arrived. You know that all of Israel is rejoicing in the death of Stalin."

"From what I heard in Greece, all of Russia is in tears," Zander said. "Do you really think his death will change anything?"

"There are tears in Russia," Leon agreed, "but they are what the Romans called *lacrimae rerum*—tears of events. Things will change. First Stalin's generation, which aided and abetted his crimes, must grow old and die. The next generation will be half Stalinist, their children a quarter Stalinist." And Leon repeated firmly, "Things will change. The Russians are a great people and deserve better."

Zander turned to stare out in the direction of the sea. "It's been a long journey," he said, more to himself than to Leon. "My feet are heavy. My heart also."

From beyond a rise to the north of the airport came the faint sound of a carillon. Leon noticed Zander angling his good ear in the direction of the bells. "Do you remember the bells we heard on the Brooklyn Bridge?" Leon asked.

Zander laughed under his breath. "Was I innocent. I thought they were ringing for me. I thought Russia was summoning me."

"It was," Leon asserted with passion.

Zander strolled around to the other side of the walkway and looked out over the promised land. He felt a blast of hot air on his cheek.

Leon came up alongside him. "The Arabs call it a *khamsin*," he said quietly. "It's a wind that blows in occasionally from the desert. An old Bedouin once told me that it originates in the furnace of the earth—that it blows to remind us of what might have been."

A vague smile touched Zander's lips. *"Khamsin,"* he repeated. He listened again for the musical peal of the carillon, but all he heard whistling past his good ear was the desert wind.

Author's Note

Russia has been a flame to the moth in me since I first went there in 1964, driving in from Finland and leaving by way of Brest Litovsk. Over the years there were more trips to the Soviet Union and East Europe, each of them, to use the title phrase of Lesley Blanch's lovely book about Russia (Collins, 1968), "a journey into the mind's eye." When I abandoned journalism and started writing novels in 1970, it seemed like the most natural thing in the world to set my stories in Russia, and write about Russians. Looking back now, I can see that in six of my seven published novels (the exception is *Sweet Reason*) I was turning around the ideas and stories and characters of *The Revolutionist*. In 1981, encouraged by my friend and literary agent, Ed Victor, I devised the rough plan for this book and began the formal research. Reading into the subject took roughly two years, the writing, three. For those who are interested, I would like to list the books that I found particularly helpful:

The Russian Revolution by Leon Trotsky (Simon & Schuster, 1932)

The Russian Revolution by Alan Moorehead (Harper & Brothers, 1958)

The October Revolution by Roy Medvedev (Columbia University Press, 1979)

Ten Days That Shook the World by John Reed (Penguin Books, 1966)

To the Finland Station by Edmund Wilson (Farrar, Straus & Giroux, 1972)

The Life of Lenin by Louis Fischer (Harper & Row, 1964)

Stalin by Adam B. Ulam (The Viking Press, 1973)

Three Who Made a Revolution by Bertram D. Wolfe (Dell Publishing Co., 1948)

Studies in Revolution by E. H. Carr (The Macmillan Company, 1950)

Russia in Transition by Isaac Deutscher (Hamish Hamilton, 1957)

Ironies of History by Isaac Deutscher (Oxford University Press, 1966)

The File on the Tsar by Anthony Summers and Tom Mangold (Harper & Row 1976)

I Love by Ann and Samuel Charters (Farrar, Straus & Giroux, 1979)

The Great Terror by Robert Conquest (The Macmillan Company, 1968)

Labyrinths of Iron by Benson Bobrick (Newsweek Books, 1981)

Russia at War by Alexander Werth (E. P. Dutton & Co., 1964)

Conversations with Stalin by Milovan Djilas (Harcourt Brace & World, 1962)

The Time of Stalin by Anton Antonov-Ovseyenko (Harper & Row, 1981)

The Death of Stalin by Georges Bortoli (Praeger Publishers, 1975)

Twenty Letters to a Friend by Svetlana Alliluyeva (Harper & Row, 1967)

Finally, two of the most moving books to come out of Russia in this century, written by one of the most astonishing Russians of any century:

Hope Against Hope by Nadezhda Mandelstam (Collins and Harvill, 1971)

Hope Abandoned by Nadezhda Mandelstam (Atheneum, 1974)

My principal preoccupation in *The Revolutionist* has been to show how someone as decent as Zander could have been attracted to the Bolsheviks at the start, and repelled by them in the end; to suggest, in other words, where the greatest political experiment of the twentieth century went very wrong. Spurred on by Robespierre's rule of thumb about history being fiction, I have taken a novelist's liberties with the subject matter, and I think I owe it to a reader who has come this far with me to point out the major ones.

Rumors about Lenin suffering from syphilis have circulated for decades but were never to my knowledge substantiated. I myself tried (unsuccessfully) to track down a French doctor in Paris who, according to an old White Russian general I spoke to, once treated Lenin for this disease. Still, I have made my Lenin suffer from syphilis, which in its tertiary phase affects the mind and actions of a victim, because it seemed to me to clarify several things that were otherwise tricky to explain: his mercurial moods (refusing to budge in July 1917, and then single-mindedly spurring everyone to revolution three months later, when the plum would have fallen to them anyhow at the Constituent Assembly); his grandiose schemes (world revolution, electrification of Russia, etc.); the relative ease with which Stalin managed to play down Lenin's last testament with its explicit criticisms of Stalin.

Another liberty: Again, there have been rumors, but no hard evidence, that Stalin did not die a natural death. In fact, his last days are shrouded in Kremlin secrecy and no one has yet been able to say with absolute certainty how he died. Given the number of people around him who feared for their lives and had a great deal to gain from his death, murder cannot be ruled out.

My greatest liberty, one I took with emotion, was to ascribe Osip Mandelstam's poetry to my poet, Ronzha. Ronzha, in some respects but by no means all, was inspired by Mandelstam, whose poetry and life have been an inspiration to everyone interested in things Russian. Through my character Ronzha, I have tried to show what I thought Mandelstam was up to when he composed his Stalin poem and then read it aloud to a room full of people. I only hope that I have done the poetry, and the poet, justice.

R.L.
Paris

The following is a preview of
Robert Littell's bold new thriller

THE ONCE
AND
FUTURE SPY

coming in hardcover in spring 1990

The Beineke Library,
Yale University . . .

Shivering, the Weeder rose to his feet. He felt an icy hand caress his spine. He would race off to the nearest police station, he would tell the sergeant on duty—what? That a mugger had tried to incinerate him the night before because he knew that an agency of the United States Government was planning to explode a primitive atomic device in Tehran on the Ides of March? Because he had set out in his bumbling way to stop what he considered an atrocity without bringing the world down on the Company's head? Nobody would believe him. Even worse, someone might—and he would be fitted into a straitjacket and shipped back to the Company in question by the local police who preferred not to get involved in matters of national security.

Whatever he decided to do, he would be a fool for hanging around Yale. They had been waiting for him once, they would be waiting for him again. He tried desperately to remember some of the things he had learned at the Farm about avoiding surveillance. All he could come up with was the story of the OSS agent who had thrown the Gestapo bloodhounds off the scent by urinating on his tracks. He couldn't see that urinating on his tracks would have the slightest effect on the people who were after him. It occurred to him that the best thing would be to abandon his clothing at the motel, abandon his almost-classic car. He would rent an automobile in New Haven and disappear into New England. Even if they discovered he had rented a car, they would have no way of knowing in what direction he had headed. If he could manage to stay out of their clutches until the Ides of March . . .

From somewhere below him in the glass core of the Beinecke Library came the thud of a heavy fire door being slammed closed. The sound seemed to skate along the glass walls of the building within a building, to resound through the stacks. At the back of the glass tower another fire door slammed shut. And a third. The Weeder edged between two stacks and peered down through the glass wall at the main lobby, sandwiched between the inner glass tower and the outer shell of the building, two stories below him. A rail-thin woman wearing a scalp-hugging feathered hat with a black veil masking half her face (was he imagining it or did she look familiar too?) was standing at the main desk, looking up. She spotted the Weeder and wagged a finger at him, as if he had disobeyed a biblical injunction and was being mildly chastised for it. A burly man the Weeder instantly recognized as the fire breather from the faculty parking lot the night before appeared at the other end of the lobby. He was holding an enormous pistol, fitted with a silencer, at present arms. He saw the woman with the veil pointing and followed her finger until he spotted the Weeder. The burly man formed his left forefinger and thumb into a pistol and sighted over it at the Weeder. He mouthed the words, "Bang, bang! You're dead!"

And then the Weeder saw the Admiral, hunched over like a parenthesis, his mane of chalk-colored hair flying off excitedly in all directions. The Admiral backed up to get a better view of the Weeder, studied him with his bulging eyes for a moment, then turned toward the large red fire box of the wall. He broke the glass with a small hammer hanging next to it, pulled open the door and pushed down the large brass lever to the position labeled "Danger—Exhaust."

From the dozen or so grilles installed in the walls of the inner glass tower came an ominous hissing.

The Weeder had worked in the library his junior and senior years and understood instantly what the sound meant. The Beinecke housed some of the rarest books and manuscripts in the world. In the event of fire there was a system to seal off the glass core where the books were stored by closing hermetic fire doors and then pumping out the air. No air, no fire. There was supposed to be an alarm to warn the people working in the stacks that they had thirty seconds to clear out.

A pulse throbbed in one of Weeder's ears as he raced for the narrow metal staircase that corkscrewed up to the top floor of the core. Plunging up the steps, already short of breath, he became aware of the gravitational drag of the earth pulling at him through the soles of his shoes. With each step, lifting his feet took more effort. His vision started to blur. A rasp stuck like a bone in the back of his throat. His lungs burned. Gasping for air, he clutched the railing and hauled himself up hand over hand. He reached the top floor and sagged against a whitewashed brick wall and lashed out wildly with his palm, searching for the small glass box that had been installed during his senior year. The throbbing in his ears grew into a roar, drowning out the hissing, and the space around him began to go dark, as if the light were being sucked out of the glass tower along with the air. Suddenly the tips of his fingers struck something smooth. He willed his fingers into a fist and plunged it into the glass, groped through the shards for the mask, fumbled in what had become a nightmare to fit it over his face as his knees ceded to gravity and he sank in the general direction of the center of the earth.

Four

Wanamaker kept a tight rein on his emotions, grunting into the telephone every now and then to indicate he was receiving the Admiral loud and clear and not appreciating a word he said. Had he misjudged the Admiral after all? he wondered. Walking back a cat was a cerebral activity perfectly suited to Toothacher's manifold talents; acting on the conclusions may simply not have been his cup of tea. Wanamaker shrugged a shoulder. When he came right down to it, what choice did he have?

"On paper," the Admiral was saying, "the plan looked perfect. Maybe that was the problem . . . the perfect is the enemy of the good. Our jackass of all trades removed the fuse to the alarm system so it wouldn't go off when we closed the fire doors. The air, according to the printed notice on the fire box, was extracted from the inner glass tower in thirty seconds. Are you still there, Wanamaker?"

Wanamaker grunted.

"We waited eleven minutes before pumping the air back in. Eleven minutes should have been enough to suffocate him three times over. Houdini could only hold his breath for four minutes."

Wanamaker, bored with the details of the game when he already knew the final score, grunted again.

"Our jackass and your man Friday went in and searched the stacks from top to bottom. You can imagine our stupefaction when they couldn't find our friend." The Admiral must have sensed that he was losing his audience. "Aren't you curious how he got out?"

Wanamaker grunted. The Admiral decided to interpret this as an expression of interest. "They didn't find our friend, but they did find a glass box built into the side of a wall on the top floor which said, 'Oxygen mask for emergency use only. Break glass with hammer to get mask.' Or words to that effect. The glass, of course, was broken, the oxygen mask missing. Nearby there was a metal ladder spiraling up through the roof of the glass tower to a submarinelike escape hatch. The escape hatch led through a crawl space to the roof of the library. On the back wall of the library building was a fire escape, with the bottom length of ladder lowered to the ground. Are you getting the picure?"

Another grunt crept stealthily over the telephone line, followed closely by a question: "You still think he'll assume it was a coincidence?"

For a moment the Admiral didn't respond. Then, very quietly, he said, "You ought to know that our friend saw me."

"You let him get a look at you!"

The Admiral could hear the note of astonishment in Wanamaker's voice, could picture him rolling his ungroomed head from side to side in frustration, could imagine the flurry of dandruff flakes, dislodged, drifting past the rumpled shoulders of his unpressed sport jacket into an open container of low-fat cottage cheese. Toothacher screwed up his face in disgust. In his view what was killing the Company was too much HYP—too much Harvard, Yale, Princeton. When he caught up with the Weeder there would be one less.

"He was looking down from the stacks," the Admiral continued. "He saw me depress the handle that set the pumps to work sucking out the air."

"Good God! If he saw you, he recognized you. We both took your course at the Farm." Wanamaker must have been lighting a fresh Schimmelpenninck from the soggy stump of an old one glued to his lower lip, because he didn't say anything for a while. Then: "He'll go to the police."

"What would he tell them?" the Admiral asked. "That the Company he works for is trying to kill him? The detectives would commit him for psychiatric observation. If they believed him the whole story would come out—Stufftingle, the Ides of March, the Company eavesdropping through ordinary garden-variety telephones. Think of the headlines in *The New York Times*. Think of the scandal. Congress would castrate the Company. No, no, fortunately for us our friend has a reputation as a patriot. My guess is he'll run for his life. We should be able to catch up with him in a matter of days. Ha! He'll still be a patriot, but with any luck he'll be a dead patriot!"

Five

The Weeder tried the number from a downtown Boston booth, got the recorded message again. "You've reached Snow," a husky voice, vaguely self-conscious, vaguely irritated, snapped. "I don't take calls or return them except on Sundays. And then not always. Don't bother leaving a message."

He left one anyway. "It's me again. Silas Sibley. This is the fourth time I've called in three days. I've come a long way to see you. I'll call back later in the day. Can you do me a favor and turn your machine off and answer your phone? It's important. To me at least."

To kill time he drove over to Charlestown and climbed Breed's Hill and roamed around the battlefield for several hours. Listening to the wind whistling past his ear, the Weeder felt the pull of history and slipped over the line into an incarnation. The whistle of fifes was carried to him on the wind—the lobster lines, decimated in two previous assaults, were forming up for the third attack. He could see the hundred or so militiamen behind the rail fence on the flank of Breed's Hill fitting new flints in their muskets so the guns wouldn't misfire. Cocking his head, he thought he heard the moans of the British wounded crawling away from the rebels. He caught the distant sound of shouted commands. It was the British general Howe ordering his men to remove their heavy backpacks so they could advance more rapidly. The Weeder saw Howe taking up position at the head of the light infantry and grenadiers heading for the rail fence. Colonel Knowlton, in command of the militiamen at the rail fence, yelled for his men to hold their fire. Howe shouted an order. The front rank knelt, the lobster line aimed and dispatched a volley at the rebels. Most of the shots flew high; the lobsters, the Weeder knew, tended to overshoot because they used too much powder for the weight of lead in their cartridges.

Howe drew his saber. The Red Coats leveled their bayonets and broke into a trot. When the lobster line reached the stakes that the rebels had hammered into the ground forty yards from the rail fence, the militiamen fired. The Weeder could see the young officers around Howe crumpling to the ground. The lobster line itself cracked like an eggshell. Howe could be heard bellowing urgent commands. The Red Coats closed ranks and continued on. The Weeder could see Colonel Knowlton waving an arm wildly; could see the militiamen, out of powder, lacking bayonets, scurrying away. The Red Coats fired a last volley at the fleeing rebels. Smoke obscured the rail fence, then slowly drifted away. The Weeder spotted Howe staring back across the fields at the hundreds of Red Coats sprawled in the grotesque positions that dead men assume. Howe's face was a mask of shock, of dismay. The thin throaty cheers of the surviving lobsters reached the Weeder.

And then, as if a needle had been plucked from a phonograph record, the cheering stopped and the Weeder found himself listening again to the wind whistling past his ear. The sound lured him back against his will into the present. His face corkscrewed into a sheepish grin as he realized what had happened; running for his life across a colonial landscape, he had taken momentary refuge in history.

It wasn't the first time that history had provided this service, had given him a place to go when he didn't like where he was.

His lifelong obsession with Nate had been part escape, of course. But there had been more to it than that. Much more. The Weeder had always attributed his fascination for Nate to an emotion he presumed he shared with his illustrious ancestor, namely an abiding commitment to a delicate tangle of lovers and relatives and friends; to an extended family which, when you pushed it out far enough, constituted the entity known as "country." In a deep sense Nate and the Weeder subscribed to the same social contract: with all its faults there was something here, some ideal, albeit unachieved, worth fighting for.

Running, and running scared, looking over his shoulder to make sure the Admiral wasn't one jump behind him, the

Weeder felt closer to Nate than he ever had before. Nate too had been running scared, had been looking over a shoulder, had (the Weeder supposed) failed to see whatever it was that finally caught up with him in time to avoid it; had gone to meet his fate fortified, as far as the Weeder could figure out, only by a cranky patriotism, a vision that derived its power from a knowledge of how things were and how they could be. Nate, in short, had had high hopes. The Weeder, following Nate's star, shared them.

The sun was hovering over the rooftops of Charlestown when the Weeder squeezed into a telephone booth, fed some coins into the slots and dialed the Concord number again. It rang four times. A female voice came on the line.

"Yes."

"It's Silas Sibley. We spoke on the phone three weeks ago. You said I could come up and talk to you about a project I'm working on."

"Didn't you get my letter?"

"Your letter? No. I left New York last week. I was doing some research in New Haven."

"I wrote you that I'd changed my mind." The voice on the other end of the line hesitated. "Can I ask you a question?"

The Weeder said, "Please."

The voice changed pitch slightly. It was interested instead of defensive. "What sign were you born under?"

"I'm a Capricorn."

"What's your ascendant?"

"To tell you the truth I don't know what you're talking about."

"What's your birth date?"

"I was born the same day as Elvis Presley, January eighth."

The response seemed to alter the chemistry of the conversation. "Ah," said the voice on the other end of the line. Then, reluctantly: "Come if you must." She gave him directions. Did he know the road that ran past the North Bridge? Seven and a half miles after the bridge he was to turn right. There was a mailbox. Painted bright red. The road was unpaved. Eventually it forked. He was to stay left. The road ended at a house. The voice on the phone suggested a time. The Weeder eagerly agreed. He started to mumble his thanks but the line went dead.

Back in his car, the Weeder's thoughts drifted to the Admiral. He would have discovered the scorched Volkswagen parked on a side street near Yale by now. He would have guessed that the Weeder had switched to a rented car and started asking around. He might have gotten a description of the Hertz car the Weeder was driving; might have asked the state police, on a pretext, to look out for it. Searching his memory, the Weeder recalled a lecture at the Farm about avoiding surveillance. "Change cars, change trains, change buses, change hotels," a one-time station chief had advised. "Change clothing, change routines, change habits, change anything you can possibly change."

"How about wives?" the Weeder, always ready with a quip, had asked innocently.

The class had laughed. The instructor had said, "If you can change wives it wouldn't hurt, but it's probably easier to change cars."

With three hours to while away before the rendezvous, the Weeder decided to cover his tracks. He drove through rush-hour traffic to Logan Airport and abandoned his Hertz Toyota in the long-term parking area. He hopped an airport shuttle to the terminal, waited in line for a taxi and asked the driver to take him to an Avis office in downtown Boston. The taxi driver studied his passenger in the rearview mirror. "You can get a bus over to the Avis place here at the airport," he said.

The Weeder shook his head. "I'm superstitious about renting cars at airports."

Muttering something about different folks having different strokes, the driver swung his car into traffic.

At the Avis counter the Weeder made a point of asking directions to Cape Cod, and even had the agent trace the route on a map for him. Then he headed out the Massachusetts Turnpike toward Concord. He got to the post office just as it was closing and retrieved the pawn ticket he had put in an envelope and addressed to himself care of general delivery, Concord. He stopped for a hamburger and chips at a diner, lingered over two cups of coffee to make time pass, finally started toward the house where the woman who called herself Snow lived.

He turned off the main road at the red mailbox and bounced along the unpaved road full of potholes, his headlights playing on snowbanks from a storm the previous week, on fallen trees, on what was left of an old fence. Around a curve the headlights picked out the weathered planks of one-story house set in a clearing. Light from several candles flickered in a window. The Weeder killed his headlights and walked up to the door.

It opened before he could knock. A woman wearing corduroy jeans and a loose-fitting flannel shirt stood in the doorway. She held a candle in a holder with a reflector that directed the light onto the Weeder. Her own face was lost in shadows.

"I'm Silas Sibley," the Weeder announced.

"You don't look like a Capricorn," the woman observed.

"What do Capricorns look like?"

"Generally speaking they don't look frightened. They're more open, more seductive. You really didn't get my letter?"

He shook his head. "I must have left New York before it arrived."

The woman said, "What's done is done. You might as well come on in. My friends call me Snow. If you become one you can too. Until then you can call me Matilda."

The Weeder closed the door behind him, stamped his feet on the mat, threw his overcoat across the back of a wooden chair and installed himself in front of a fire crackling in the chimney that formed the center of the house. He held his hands toward the flames and rubbed his fingers together.

The woman named Snow set her candle down on a small table. She glanced in annoyance at the Weeder's overcoat, decided she didn't like where he had thrown it and hung it from a peg on the back of the door next to a mackinaw. Watching her, the Weeder thought: What she cares about she is fanatic about.

Snow appeared with a glass and offered it to the Weeder. "Prune cider," she announced. "Homemade, it goes without saying. When's the last time you saw prune cider in a supermarket? Drink it—it's good for the digestion, ingrown toenails, warts."

The Weeder took his first good look at Snow. She had incredibly pale skin and dark straight hair cut short and parted in the middle, with wisps curling off negligently from her sideburns. There was a pencil-line scar over her right brow. Her fingers, curled around the glass she offered him, were long and thin, her nails bitten to the quick. She seemed more tangible, more down-to-earth, than he had imagined she would be the two times he had spoken to her on the phone. It came as a relief to him that he wouldn't have to invent her.

Taking the prune cider from her, the Weeder looked around the cabin, or what he could see of it in the flickering light of the chimney and half a dozen candles. It seemed to be an echo of her: spare where she was gaunt, solid, no-nonsense furniture to match her solid, no-nonsense clothes. An assortment of cameras and lenses and tripods were heaped on a long scrubbed oak table in a corner. A high, narrow-framed black-and-white photograph of a nude hung on one wall. The woman in the photo, seen through a partly open door, masked her face with her fingers and peered through them at the camera. Her eyes conveyed shyness or sadness—or all of the above. The photograph was illuminated by a candle set on the floor. In the photo the nude was illuminated by a candle set on the floor at her bare feet.

The house smelled of freshly baked cookies, which the Weeder spotted cooling in a tray on a window ledge above a woodburning stove. It also smelled of camphor.

"The camphor," Snow said, reading his mind, "comes from the mackinaw over there. I found it yesterday in a trunk filled with camphor balls." Walking with a limp so slight it seemed more like a hesitation, she crossed the room and sat down in a rocking chair. She rocked back and forth, toying with a gold wedding band as she sized up her invited, then uninvited, then reinvited guest. The Weeder seemed mesmerized by the photograph of the nude. "You are wondering whether the woman in the photograph is me, but you are too conventional to ask," Snow guessed. "The answer is yes. Kundera has a character somewhere who talks about a girl's face lighted by the nudity of her body. That's the effect I was trying for." She twisted in the chair to look at the photograph, studied it for a moment. "In the end clothes are a form of mask," she observed, thinking out loud. Turning back to the Weeder, she waved a hand toward his clothes. His trousers were rumpled, his sport jacket frayed at the sleeves, his shoes scuffed. There was a suggestion of irony in her voice as she asked, "Is this how you normally go calling?"

The Weeder grinned sheepishly. "Thoreau, who came from this neck of the woods, said you should distrust any enterprise that required new clothes."

Snow flashed a strained smile that the Weeder immediately recognized; it was the smile people used when they wanted to keep from crying. He had seen it on his mother's face at the funeral of his father; had seen it in the mirror the day he came home from work to find his wife had taken his son and left for good.

"What is it you want from me?" Snow asked.

"What I want," the Weeder told her, "is polite intercourse."

"That's a strange way of putting it."

"Why did you change your mind about seeing me after I phoned from New York?"

"I figured I had enough to worry about without adding your problems to my list."

The Weeder remembered the nails bitten to the quick, the strained smile thrown up like a barrier against tears. He realized that she had been ambushed—though by what he couldn't say. "What do you worry about?" he asked her now.

"I worry about urethane in the wine, about acid in the rain, about parasites in the sushi, about radon in the potato cellar under the house. I worry about too much ozone in the air damaging my lungs. I worry about the earth overheating. I worry about a new Ice Age. Only yesterday I read that our galaxy is heading for a collision with the Andromeda galaxy."

"That won't happen for billions of years," the Weeder said. "The sun will have burnt out by then."

Snow nibbled absently at a cuticle. "I worry about that too. Just because the sun sets at night is no guarantee it will rise in the morning." She leaned back tiredly in her rocking chair. The Weeder, remembering Nate, thought: People who are afraid are more interesting than those who aren't. Snow must have been reading his thoughts because she snapped, "I don't worry to be interesting. I worry because I'm lucid."

"Lucidity," the Weeder remarked, "is the enemy of passion. You're always aware of yourself being aware of yourself."

Snow regarded the Weeder as if she were seeing him for the first time. After a moment she said, "Aside from polite intercourse, what do you really want from me?"

"Snowden's your married name, isn't it, Matilda? Your maiden name was Davis. Your father was one of the Acton Davises, a direct descendant of Isaac Davis, who was killed leading the Acton Company against the British at the North Bridge in Concord in 1775."

The Weeder put his glass down on the edge of the chimney and settled into a high-backed wooden chair facing Snow. "Isaac Davis was married to a second cousin he met on Long Island. Her name was Molly. In those days a girl's father picked her husband for her—it had to do with uniting families and farms, not love. When Isaac fell in love with Molly he asked her father for her hand in marriage, and was flatly refused. So Molly got herself pregnant by Isaac to force her father's hand—he could risk a scandal or let them marry and hush things up. A great many girls did this in those days. It was the only way they could have a say in whom they married. Her father gave his consent and the young couple married and moved to Acton. The baby died a few days after it was born and the death was recorded in the Acton town ledger. Isaac was killed at the North Bridge. Molly was given her widow's third, which consisted of a slave named John Jack, who was valued at a hundred and twenty pounds sterling, a horse and a cart, and some cash—and sent packing by her husband's family, who had enough mouths to feed. She returned to Long Island and wound up keeping house for a great-aunt living on a small farm in the village of Flatbush. Her child, your ancestor, was born on that farm."

"I don't see where all this is leading," Snow said. "I don't see what you want of me."

"I'm coming to that. Molly's maiden name was Fitzgerald. She detested the British with a passion. There wasn't anything she wouldn't do to get at them. She became an ardent, outspoken patriot, championing the rebel cause at town meetings, which—if you read the minutes of the meetings—rubbed some of the town elders the wrong way, since women in the colonies weren't supposed to meddle in politics. Isaac, on the other hand, seems to have been very proud of her. When the British threatened to march on Concord, Molly organized the women into groups that made cartridges and rolled bandages. After she was widowed and exiled to Long Island, she wrote an acquaintance of her late husband attached to the Commander-in-Chief's staff offering her services to the rebel cause. Two days ago I discovered an unpublished letter from this acquaintance, whose name was A. Hamilton, indicating he took her up on the offer. A spy sent out behind the British lines made his way across Long Island to Molly Davis's farmhouse in Flatbush. She helped him scout the British positions in Brooklyn."

The Weeder, drained, settled back in his chair.

Snow rocked forward in hers. "And then what happened?"

"That's just it. I don't know. The trail ends with Molly Davis. A week later the spy was caught by the British and hanged at an artillery park in Manhattan on what's now the corner of Third Avenue and 63rd Street. What happened during the missing week is a mystery."

"How can I help you solve it?"

"There's a hint in a letter Hamilton wrote to the spy's brother that Molly Davis kept a diary. The answers to my mystery must be in its pages." The Weeder studied Snow's face. "The answer to your mystery too."

Snow didn't understand. "What mystery is *my* mystery?"

"The baby conceived out of wedlock by Molly and Isaac died soon after birth. Isaac was killed at Concord in April, 1775. Molly's baby—the great-grandfather of your great-grandfather—was born in Flatbush in 1777. Which means Isaac Davis wasn't his father."

"I've always heard that Molly was pregnant when Isaac was killed, that whoever recorded the birth made a mistake when he copied off the date in the ledger."

"Maybe."

"What does 'Maybe' mean?"

"It means maybe. And it implies 'Maybe not.' "

Snow let the rocking chair glide back again. "My grandfather sometimes went on for hours about the Revolution and Isaac and Molly. He could talk a streak once he started. To me it was all spilt milk, though I admit I used to wonder what she was like."

"She was strong-willed," the Weeder said. "You could see that from the way she got herself pregnant so she could marry the man she loved. She was supposed to have been a great beauty. At least that's what Isaac Davis said, but he may have been prejudiced. I came across two references to her in diaries written by other Acton women. That's how I know about her. Even in the puritanical colonial times girls tended to pretty themselves up to attract men. But Molly seems to have toned herself down. Her hands were rough and blistered from working on the farm; she is said to have worked the fields like a man. Her hair, for practical reasons, was cropped short. She favored loose-fitting clothes . . ." The Weeder's voice trailed off as he realized he could have been describing the woman sitting across from him in the rocking chair. "I'm guessing," he continued carefully, "but behind her bold gaze must have lurked a shyness, a sadness. She'd been ambushed by grief. She'd lost a baby at birth, a husband. That kind of thing leaves its mark on the eyes."

The Weeder's story, his ardor in recounting it, seemed to weigh on Snow. "If you've come to me for the diary, I don't have it," she said. She noticed the disappointment in his face and added, "Maybe you'll have better luck at the local historical museum—they have a collection of Revolutionary diaries."

"I've been in touch with the museum. I've been in touch with the library. You're my last hope. Are you sure there isn't an old trunk somewhere? That's where you find this kind of document."

Snow shook her head.

"I suppose your grandfather must be dead?"

"Long dead and long buried." A thought occurred to her. "He used to show me photographs in an album."

The Weeder said, "Photographs won't help me—"

"I remember," Snow said, "that he kept the album in an old wooden sailor's chest with an enormous padlock on the outside. I always suspected there were other things in the trunk beside the photo album."

"Where is the chest now?"

Snow thought a moment. "I suppose everything Granddad had went to his wife, who was younger than he was. When she died she was living with my grandfather's sister, Esther, who's my great-aunt. Esther's still alive. She sold the house and moved to Boston a few years ago."

"Will you give me her address?"

"It won't help you any. Esther's become a recluse. Since she lost all her hair she won't let anyone she doesn't know come calling."

The Weeder asked in a low voice, "Will she see me if you're with me?"

"She might."

He smiled at her. "How about it, Matilda? Will you help me solve our mystery?"

Snow ran the ball of her thumb across the scar over her eyebrow. "I'll make you a deal," she said suddenly. "I don't drive anymore and I need a ride into Boston tomorrow. You drive me in and hang around while I do a couple of errands, and I'll take you over to meet my great-aunt Esther."

(Now read the complete book, on sale the week of April 1, 1990 wherever Bantam Books are sold.)

ROBERT LITTELL is a former *Newsweek* journalist and the author of seven previous novels. His works include the critically acclaimed *The Sisters, The Defection of A.J. Lewinter, The October Circle, The Debriefing, The Amateur,* which was made into a feature film, and the upcoming *The Once and Future Spy.* Mr. Littell makes his home in France.